Dance of Wings

JAMIE A. WATERS

Cover Art: Deranged Doctor Design
Editor: Sam Everard
Proofreader: Tracy Dickey

ISBN: 978-1-949524-31-4 (Hardback Edition)
ISBN: 978-1-949524-30-7 (Paperback Edition)
ISBN: 978-1-949524-29-1 (eBook Edition)

Library of Congress Control Number: 2022917735
First Edition *June 2025

THE DRAGON PORTAL SERIES

*For Adriane, the little sister of my childhood.
You've shown me what resilience looks like—with grace, courage,
and heart. You are a reminder that even in the darkest of times,
light can shine through.*

CHAPTER 1

"You should turn me into a dragon!"

Sabine arched her eyebrow at the tiny pixie peering up at her with wide, hopeful eyes. Blossom's purple and yellow hair was arranged in some sort of design that reminded Sabine of flower petals. Ever since she'd received a magical boost in the underworld, Blossom had begun matching her hair with her dress and using a splash of glamour to make them as colorful as possible. She'd be a tiny rainbow terror in dragon form, creating havoc and leaving a trail of glittering pixie dust in her wake.

"I'm not turning you into a dragon," Sabine said, turning back to stare across the horizon as a low thrum of fatigue plagued her. They'd need to land soon. She could feel Malek's weariness through their bond growing with each passing hour.

Pressing her hand against one of his sharp claws that gripped their carrier, she sent a fortifying wave of magic over him. The rush of love that swept over her in return was as intimate as a caress. She lowered her head and smiled, marveling at how even a touch of a dragon's power could make her heart soar.

Blossom's wings twitched, her lips turning downward in a thoughtful pout. Sabine could almost see the wheels turning in the pixie's head. The novelty of flying in a dragon's clutches had worn off after the first day. Now Blossom was simply bored and looking for a new source of entertainment.

"If I were a dragon, I could challenge Malek to a race," Blossom said wistfully. "Think how fast we'll make it to the Sky Cities!"

Sabine made a noncommittal noise, peering over the edge of the makeshift carrier she'd created using branches from a silver tree. The ground rushed below them at an almost dizzying speed. The thought of going even faster had her stomach lurching in queasiness. Although, part of that could be Malek's movements. No one said a dragon's flight was smooth.

"We're going fast enough," Sabine said, shaking her head. Pixies might have wings, but the fae were never meant to soar the skies like birds.

"Give it up, bug. Sabine needs to conserve her strength," Bane said, leaning back and closing his eyes. The demon had taken to resting while they were in the air and guarding them at night so she and Malek could sleep.

Blossom landed on one of the carrier's silver branches and glared at Bane. "You're just jealous you don't have wings."

Bane opened his amber eyes and glared at Blossom. "If I tear yours off, I'll have a pair, won't I?"

Blossom squeaked and dove onto Sabine's shoulder. "I knew it! You *are* jealous! Everyone wants wings!"

Rika wrinkled her nose. "Been there, done that. I think I'll pass on the experience."

Sabine's mouth twitched in a grin as she glanced over at the dark-haired teenager flipping through a book she'd found in their bag. Several weeks earlier, an accidental transformation turned Rika into a part-butterfly humanoid. Magic didn't act quite right around human seers, and Rika was growing into her powers with remarkable alacrity.

"Sabine," Malek's voice slipped into her thoughts. The mind-touch speech ability was still new, but it was growing stronger every day.

She immediately pressed her hand against his claw to reinforce their connection and asked silently, *"What is it?"*

"We're approaching Imenel, the city that acts as a gateway to the Sky Cities. We'll stop there overnight and leave word for Levin and Esme before traveling to my clan's home."

Sabine turned to stare in the direction they were flying. All she could see was a blanket of trees below them. It was a welcome sight compared to the vast expanse of barren land they'd seen during their travels. Centuries had passed without the touch of the fae in many parts of the world.

She suppressed her instinctive desire to reach out to the land and focused on Malek instead.

"How long until we arrive?"

"I recognize some of the landmarks. The city and coast will be visible in another twenty minutes. I'll land a distance away so we can enter on foot. It's been several years since my last visit. I'd like to get a feel for things before we announce our arrival."

"Don't push yourself too much, Malek. Another few hours won't make much difference. I can feel your fatigue."

A gentle caress of Malek's heated power trailed over her skin. *"I'll feel better once you're safe within the Sky Cities. The Wild Hunt and your family can't touch you there."*

Sabine sighed, unable to argue the point. Her enemies wanted her dead, and there were scarce few places in the world where she'd be out of their reach. If someone had suggested a few short months ago she'd be safe hiding amongst her once-feared enemies, she never would have believed them.

She pulled away and turned to her companions. "Malek says we'll be landing soon. We may be able to stay in an actual inn tonight."

"Finally." Rika closed the book and placed it inside the traveler's pack. The magical bags had been a gift from Faerie and miniaturized the contents to make traveling easier. "The thought of a real bed and a bath that's not a lake or river sounds fantastic. And food. Delicious food that's something other than travel rations or burned rabbit."

Bane snorted. "Tired of traveling already, little seer?"

Rika grinned. "I got spoiled living in the dwarven city."

Blossom rubbed her hands together. "Speaking of food, I bet they have some yummy new flowers down there. Lots of fae used to live in this area before the dragons claimed it. Only the bravest pixies still venture here. The ones who returned had all sorts of stories about what they'd found."

Sabine smiled at the pixie. "I'm curious about the plants and flowers myself."

Bane stood and leaned against the railing beside Sabine. He lifted his face to the wind and inhaled deeply. "I smell salt in the air. We're approaching the coast."

Sabine took a deep breath but couldn't detect anything. Bane's senses were sharper than hers. "Do you know much about Imenel?"

"It's similar to Akros," Bane said, referring to the mostly human city where she'd hidden from the fae for over ten years. "Many of the residents are human and closely allied with the dragon clans. The dragons and their hoarding tendencies have made it a fairly profitable port."

Rika attached the traveler's pack to her belt and stood. "Have you been there before, Bane?"

Bane didn't reply right away. "Not in many years and never openly."

Rika started to ask a question, but Sabine shook her head in warning. The teenager pressed her lips together and nodded in understanding. Bane was often reluctant in sharing details about his past, and any such discussions needed to be handled delicately.

Leaning against Bane, Sabine asked quietly, "Do we need to hide your identity?"

"That won't be necessary," Bane said, running a hand over her hair to siphon off a trace of her magic. "There is no one among the living who would dream of betraying me."

Sabine nodded. Bane had been an extremely successful assassin for years. With his ability to sense and even manipulate someone's life force, he had a natural affinity for such work.

Blossom landed on Sabine's shoulder and asked, "Do you think Esme will be there?"

Sabine smiled. "I hope so. Malek said they'd planned to meet us in Imenel. Levin and Esme had a bit of a head start since they left Razadon weeks before we did, but we've traveled a more direct route. If they're not there yet, we'll leave a message letting them know to meet us in the Sky Cities."

Bane straightened and stared across the horizon, his clawed hand tightening around the makeshift railing. Sabine looked up at him and then in the direction he was staring. There was nothing but endless blue sky and clouds ahead of them.

"What is it, Bane?"

"I'm not sure yet. Something's not right."

Sabine frowned. Trusting Bane's instincts had saved their lives more than once. She'd be a fool to discount him now. She reached for him, supplementing his power with her own. His midnight skin glowed with an eerie blue light, his horns shifting to pale silver as he tapped into the full force of his magic.

Bane's eyes narrowed. "Six life forces traveling this way and moving in formation. They're moving fast."

Blossom hopped up on the railing. "Life forces? Like a bear? They know all the good honey spots."

"Not unless bears suddenly have wings. Let the dragon know we're about to have company."

Sabine pressed her hand against Malek's claw and spoke over their mental connection. *"Bane senses six life forces flying in our direction. Any idea whether they're friend or foe?"*

"A wyvern squadron shouldn't be patrolling this far from the Sky Cities unless something's wrong," Malek said. *"If Bane senses them already, they'll be within sight in moments. Can you hide yourself from view until we determine their intent?"*

Sabine quickly tapped into her magic, causing her skin markings to glow with a silver and gold light. Flinging her power outward, she used their shared bond to attach the illusion against Malek's dragon scales. It wouldn't stand against touch, but the glamour would shield the carrier and its occupants from view. Anyone who looked upon them from outside the carrier would see nothing but an obsidian-colored dragon soaring the skies.

Sabine pinned the other end of the illusion in place. It pierced her skin, and she inhaled sharply at the sacrifice the magic demanded. All magic had a cost, and she would accept this one gladly if it kept her companions safe.

"It's done," she said to Malek.

"Then hold on tight," Malek said wryly. *"You're about to discover how dragons greet one another. I'm afraid this dance may not be as pleasurable as the private one I had planned for you."*

Sabine sent a pulse of her power outward to grow additional handholds in the branches of the silver tree. "Malek says our flight's about to get a little bumpy. Hold on."

Rika quickly looped her arms through the handholds and gripped the branch tightly. "Seeing as how the nearest exit is plummeting to our death, I'll stay inside."

Sabine arched her brow when Blossom landed on her shoulder. The pixie grabbed Sabine's hair tightly, holding on to her makeshift reins.

"Really, Blossom? What happened to all your talk about having wings?"

The pixie grinned. "Safety first."

Bane tensed beside her, his eyes flashing silver as he readied himself. Sabine turned back to the horizon, watching as six dark shadows eclipsed her view of the pristine blue sky. They were huge creatures similar in appearance to Malek, but lacking his monumental size and grace.

"Wyverns," Bane muttered in disgust. "They're the roaches of the dragon world. A pity they weren't all exterminated millennia ago."

Sabine didn't respond, captivated by the unfamiliar sight. The wyvern's wingspans were nearly half the size of Malek's, and instead of four legs, they only had two. Their coloring was different too. Malek's scales were the color of polished obsidian, each one glittering with what appeared to be stardust. They shifted and changed in the light, camouflaging him against the night sky. These other creatures, however, possessed the deep jewel tones of precious gems rarely seen outside the dwarven mines.

Without warning, Malek banked sharply. Sabine staggered, holding on tightly to the handholds while Bane and Rika did the same. The wyverns matched his movements, still on a path to intercept them.

Blossom yanked hard on Sabine's hair and shouted, "Wheeeee! Do it again, Malek!"

Sabine winced. Despite her small size, the pixie had a powerful grip. "I'm rather attached to my hair, Blossom."

Blossom managed a sheepish grin. "Oops. Sorry, Sabine. I got caught up in the moment."

A sharp blast of Malek's dragonfire trumpeted outward toward the approaching figures. Malek's voice filled her head, the language strange yet eerily familiar as he called out to his brethren. Something about the cadence of his words reminded her of the ancient language of the gods, but she couldn't make out the meaning.

The creatures didn't alter their course or speed. They were still on a direct path toward them. Sabine frowned, sensing Malek's unease increasing through their bond.

"What's happening?" she asked.

"They're not responding, nor are they deviating from fighting formation. Hold on tight. We need to evade them."

Before she could call out a warning to her friends, Malek dove downward, narrowly avoiding a wyvern's sharpened claws. Rika screamed, the sound slicing through Sabine's thoughts and fracturing her hold on the illusion shielding them from view. A wyvern broke out of formation and dove toward them, his glowing serpentine eyes focused on the carrier in Malek's grip.

"Sabine, get down!" Bane yelled, covering her body with his as the wyvern's jaws came within touching distance. Malek struck their attacker with the sharpened edge of his tail, but the wyvern merely renewed his efforts. Sabine lifted her hand and blasted the creature away from them with a strong expulsion of magic.

"The glamour won't hold!" Sabine shouted, realizing in dismay that Rika's seer abilities were interfering with the illusion. The other wyverns had realized Malek was carrying passengers and were now focused on them. These weren't simple beasts, but intelligent creatures working together to attack their chosen quarry.

One of them slammed into Malek's side, sending the

carrier's occupants sprawling across the floor. Rika crashed into Sabine with enough force to steal her breath. Malek banked sharply again and dove downward. Sabine's silvery hair whipped away from her face as the ground rushed up to meet them.

Letting out a panicked cry, she and Rika slid across the floor of the carrier. Bane caught Sabine's wrist and yanked her upright. She looped her arm through the handholds again and reached for Rika just as Malek pulled up, narrowly avoiding a blast of dragonfire from one of the creatures. It was impossible to fight and hold on at the same time.

"Hot! Hot! Hot!" Blossom screamed, yanking on Sabine's hair again.

A few of the leaves on the carrier caught fire. With a pained cry, Rika jerked away from the flames. Sabine shot out her hand, using her magic to wrap vines around Rika's waist. She did the same to herself and Bane before calling upon the merfolk's power to summon water from the air.

"Hold on!" she shouted, dousing the fire and weaving a protective barrier around the carrier to better withstand the heat. It wasn't as powerful as Malek's shield, but it was better than nothing.

"You're too vulnerable up here," Bane snarled, his silvered eyes focused on the wyverns surrounding them. "We need to get you into the forest."

"We go together or not at all," Sabine said.

Blossom tugged on her hair again. "I like the forest idea! Let's do that! Lots more places to hide."

Another blast of dragonfire shot in their direction. Malek banked sharply to avoid it, the carrier swinging wildly in his grip. Two of the wyverns broke free from the formation, trying to flank him. Malek dove downward again, the ground rushing to meet them before he zigzagged over the treetops.

Malek was flying defensively, with the wyverns still in pursuit. They continued to harry him, using their superior numbers to force him closer to the ground. Two of them focused their attacks on the carrier, the heat from their dragonfire nearly scorching despite Sabine's efforts. Perspiration coated her skin from the relentless heat.

"If they ground him, we're all dead," Bane shouted. "I've seen these tactics before. He can't fight them off while he's carrying us, and you're cut off from the land. Tell him to drop you. It's our only chance. I'll buy you some time to get to safety."

Bane was right. She and Bane had some immunity to dragonfire, but Rika and Blossom didn't. Malek was using too much of his magic, trying to insulate them from the worst of it. He was already weary from the long flight.

Reaching for Bane, she infused him with a powerful burst of magic. "Do what you need to do. Fight well, my protector."

He nodded and sliced his sharpened claws through the vines to free himself. Climbing on the edge of the carrier railing, he waited until the right moment and leaped into the air.

Sabine inhaled sharply as he dove downward, landing hard on one of the dark blue wyverns. The wyvern reared back, pulling out of formation as he tried to unseat his passenger. Bane was using a combination of claws and horns to penetrate the wyvern's thick scales as he climbed up the creature's back.

"Hold on tight," Sabine yelled to Rika, who was staring at Bane with a mixture of shock and admiration. Rika whipped her head toward Sabine and nodded, her knuckles turning white from how hard she was gripping the handholds.

Sabine scanned the forest below them. *"Malek, drop the carrier!"*

She felt him immediately reject the demand. *"I won't allow any harm to come to you, Sabine. You're mine to protect."*

"Of all the highhanded dragon instincts," Sabine muttered in frustration. Sending a sharp wave of reassuring power through their bond, she urged, *"Don't be foolish, Malek. Give me to the forest, so I can fight by your side."*

Malek turned sharply again, causing Sabine to stagger. Rika squeezed her eyes shut, her face bright red and dripping with moisture. One more brush with dragonfire might be her last.

Panicked, Sabine shouted, *"Malek! There's no time to explain. Trust me!"*

"Your word you'll do whatever's necessary to protect yourself."

"You have it. Now focus on taking care of my dragon."

"Always," Malek promised. *"I'll take you as low as I can and try to draw them off."*

"Watch for Bane," she warned before turning to Rika. "He's going to drop us. Hold on!"

Malek dove downward, the forest floor rushing to meet them again. Sabine inhaled sharply as they brushed the edge of the forested canopy before pulling up from the dive. Malek released them and Rika screamed again as the carrier spun out of control. Blossom shrieked in Sabine's ear, yanking hard on her hair.

Sending out a wide blanket of magic, Sabine reached for the awareness of the trees below them. They met her willingly, embracing her power and unfurling their branches to greet the carrier forged from the bough of a silver tree.

The carrier landed in the branches with a jolt. The trees pulled them downward, closing the canopy around them and temporarily shielding them from view. It would only take one burst of dragonfire to burn through the tree cover. They needed to get to the ground immediately.

While the carrier lowered to the forest floor, Sabine said,

"We need to move as soon as we touch down. Is everyone all right?"

Rika winced and rubbed her ribs. The vines had held her in place when they'd fallen, but it hadn't been gentle. Her arm was beginning to blister from where she'd been burned. "Mostly burns and bruises. I'll live."

"My wing's broken, Sabine!" Blossom cried. "I can't fly!"

Sabine sent a trace of magic over Blossom. The pixie glowed with a golden hue, her special brand of magic knitting the fragile wing back together. Unfortunately, she couldn't do the same for Rika.

Movement above them caught Sabine's attention. Two of the wyverns had broken away from the group and were attempting to locate the carrier through the dense trees. They hadn't yet seen where Sabine and Rika were hiding, but it was only a matter of time before they were discovered. She didn't see the one Bane had been fighting, but she could sense the demon. At least he was still alive.

"Stay close and keep quiet," Sabine whispered, climbing out of the carrier and stepping onto the leaf-covered ground. Rika nodded and quickly cut through the restraining vines holding her in place.

"The trees are screaming, Sabine," Blossom whispered as she landed on Sabine's shoulder. "The wyverns are burning them. They still remember the Dragon War and think this is the end." She sniffed and wiped her eyes. "I don't want the forest to die."

Sabine froze. If the forest retained enough awareness to converse with a pixie, there was another ally they could call upon. "Blossom, I need you to take Rika to the forest guardians on my behalf. They can hide her from the wyverns and heal her arm."

Blossom's eyes widened. "But Rika's human! They'll demand—"

Sabine held up her hand. "There's no time for negotiations. If they wish me to aid them in protecting what's left of their forest, they will honor my request. We'll settle any debts once the battle is won."

Blossom's mouth clamped shut, and she nodded. "Come on, Rika. We have to hurry!"

"Be careful, Sabine," Rika said, before running after the small, glowing pixie.

A sharp pain lanced through Sabine, but it wasn't her wound.

"Malek," Sabine whispered, pressing her hand against her side. She reached out across the bonds she shared with both Malek and Bane. They were wounded but still fighting. She sent a wave of fortifying magic to them before turning to face the fire burning through the trees.

This was her place of power, and she'd defend the land for as long as she had breath.

It was time to kill some wyverns or die in the attempt.

CHAPTER 2

$\mathcal{S}$abine slid one of her daggers from its sheath. Pressing the point of the blade into her skin, Sabine allowed a drop of blood to fall upon the forest floor. A pregnant hush filled the air. She crouched and pressed her hand against the ground, reaching for the essence of the land.

Closing her eyes, she whispered in the language of her birth, *"Nexulum."*

The wind blew softly, trailing its light and feathery touch through Sabine's silver hair. She took a deep breath and exhaled slowly, allowing the magic of the forest to embrace her. Each of the marks of power on her arms and legs flared with an otherworldly luminescence.

The sound of the trees screaming in agony filled her thoughts, urging her to act. Their pain was as sharp as a blade dancing upon her psyche, but she forced herself to breathe through it. She acknowledged their sacrifice and used it to further enhance the land's magic, weaving it together with her own. Their deaths would add to her strength, and she would see vengeance enacted against those who caused their destruction.

When she opened her eyes, her vision and other senses had sharpened. She had merged her power with that of the land, and in exchange, it offered her a gift of clarity and focus. The dark greens and browns of the forest were richer and more vibrant. She could sense each individual life essence contained within the forest's boundaries. The forest animals cried out in alarm and fear as they raced deeper into the woods, with Rika and Blossom right behind them.

A cracking noise overhead caught her attention, and she leaped out of the way as a burning tree came crashing down. She jerked her head upward, her gaze trapped by the glowing golden eyes of the two wyverns hunting her.

Sabine inhaled sharply, the acrid scent of scorched wood and ash nearly choking her. This close, she could make out the individual details of each wyvern. One reminded her of flames with a deep red color that glowed like embers, except for the tips of his black wings. The other was topaz-colored with a jagged slash of red across his scaled face that made him appear like a creature pulled from one of her childhood nightmares.

Summoning her magic, she flung it outward in a shocking blast toward the two wyverns. The one she'd dubbed Flame narrowly avoided it, but her power slammed into Slash and sent him flying backward. The nearby trees cracked and splintered from the impact, crashing to the ground.

Sabine lifted her hands, directing her magic toward the largest still-standing tree near the fallen wyvern. Its branches stretched and stabbed, piercing his leathery wings and pinning him to the ground. He roared in pain and fury, unleashing his dragonfire to destroy his makeshift restraints.

His friend, Flame, narrowed serpentine eyes on Sabine. Flapping his wings, his chest expanded as he readied his attack. Sabine dove to the side, narrowly avoiding a burst of dragonfire that singed the ends of her hair. Malek might have given her some resistance to dragonfire, but she wasn't invincible. It could still kill her.

She turned and ran, trying to lead the wyverns away from the direction Rika and Blossom had headed. She needed to buy them time to get to safety. Leaping over fallen trees and rocks, she raced through the forest as one who had been born to it. Branches moved out of her way, anticipating her movements before she could make them.

Sabine flung condensed power toward her assailants as she fled. The wyverns overhead roared their frustration, burning the trees in their pursuit. Her magic was making them hesitate, deepening the divide between them. If she could find some cover, she could launch an attack.

A sharp pull on her magic caused her to stagger. She fell, the rocks scraping into her palms. The wyvern's dragonfire licked at the ground near her feet. Her blood boiled, and she cried out from the searing heat.

A furious roar overhead shook the ground beneath her. Sabine scrambled to her feet and forced herself to keep running.

Malek. It had to be him. If he was pulling on her magic, he was in serious trouble. Another roar caused the trees to tremble.

The terrifying scream of a wyvern filled the air. She stumbled again, falling on the mossy ground. Breathing heavily, she pushed herself back up. The trees were burning around her at an alarming rate. None of them could keep this up much longer.

The sounds of battle overhead were deafening. Malek was almost directly above her, fighting multiple wyverns. He was both fierce and merciless, using his sharpened tail and talons to subdue his opponents. He moved through the air with the precision of a surgical knife, slicing his assailants when they tried to press their advantage.

Sabine caught sight of Slash and Flame among the remaining wyverns. They were still trying to locate her, but Malek was blocking their pursuit. He was expending too much magic trying to protect her, and she didn't know how Bane was faring except he was still alive. A wyvern broke away and dove toward her, but Malek's powerful jaws latched around the wyvern's throat, driving him away from her.

The marks on her wrist warmed. Sabine glanced down at the pulsing golden glow, understanding instinctively what the renegade goddess offered. Each mark represented the power gifted to the original races entrusted with safeguarding Aeslion. Combining the magic of the artifacts would give them the advantage they needed, but such knowledge would indebt her even more to Lachlina.

One of the wyvern's talons pierced Malek's midsection, and Sabine pressed her hand against her side from the pain that lanced through their bond.

Sabine narrowed her eyes, her magic building within her. She withdrew her knife and pricked her finger.

So be it.

"So it shall be, daughter," a voice whispered on the wind. *"Embrace your power, and glimpse your destiny."*

Magic swirled around Sabine with the building force of a hurricane. Focusing on the marks the goddess had etched into her skin, Sabine traced the first symbol with her blood.

It was the image of a chalice, the artifact entrusted to the fae. As the power rushed through her, she felt the nearby trees turn their attention toward her as the wind whipped around her. The branches rustled and shook, reaching for her like a child calling to their mother. The power was as familiar to her as breathing, and she embraced it willingly.

"You *must become the chalice—the vessel to hold all other magic*," Lachlina said, her voice slipping into Sabine's thoughts. *"Allow the power to fill you, and shape it as you will."*

Understanding dawned, and Sabine traced the next mark —a priceless pearl that was the symbol of the merfolk's power. As it pulsed in time with her heartbeat, rain fell, first slowly and then with greater force. It pelted the ground, soaking through her clothes and plastering her hair and clothing against her skin. Lightning struck the ground near her, filling the air with the sharp and metallic scent of ozone.

She gathered the magic and sent it outward, directing the storm to extinguish the greatest threat. The smoky scent of charred wood filled her nose as the rain doused the burning trees. She extended her arms and lifted her head to the sky, feeling the power in the rain coating her skin. The storm that surrounded her was nearly as volatile as the one raging within her.

The third mark was that of a hammer, a sign of the dwarves. As she traced the mark, the power surged within her and the ground trembled beneath her feet. The unbridled fury and power of the land rumbled its rage, demanding justice for the harm these interlopers had caused. She reached for the damp earth, using her will to shape the wet mud into a giant, lifeless golem.

As she traced the fourth and most recent symbol of a curved blade upon her skin, Sabine gasped as the power of life and death surrounded her. The glamour that had been shielding her true appearance fell away, causing her skin to shine brilliantly, like a beacon in the storm.

"*Animore*," she shouted, bringing awareness to the creature she'd crafted with the dwarven power. Like a puppeteer pulling its strings, she directed the golem to defend the land. As it hurtled fallen trees and boulders skyward, the wyverns were forced to dart out of its path, giving Malek an advantage.

This power had never been Lachlina's to wield, yet Sabine had come to know it intimately. As she continued to breathe life into the creature, Sabine felt the icy chill of death take hold. Her blood began to freeze, causing her fingers to tremble and teeth to chatter. This power had never been designed to be contained, but rather to act as a bridge between life and death. If she didn't release it, death would consume her.

With a strangled cry, she directed the magic toward the nearest wyvern. A streak of lightning shot from her fingers, straight into Flame's chest. The wyvern staggered in midair and then plummeted toward the earth. He crashed into the nearby trees, bringing them down with his substantial weight.

Sabine waited for the imbalance of the wyvern's death to hit her, but nothing came. The realization rocked Sabine to her core. Instead of feeling off-center, she felt strangely energized as though this foreign magic had fulfilled some purpose that balanced a different sort of scale. This magic was seductive, and it would be too easy to lose herself to its thrall.

Sabine inhaled sharply, catching sight of Bane still fighting on top of a wyvern. He was using his poisoned claws and horns to slice the creature into ribbons. With an agonized bellow, the wyvern began to fall. Bane leaped free just in time, narrowly landing on Malek's back. The injured wyvern landed on the ground with a resounding thud that echoed through the forest. His blood spilled on the forest floor, and the land's strength surged within her as the forest embraced his power.

The wyvern reared his head, his serpentine eyes filled with intelligence and loathing as he glared at Sabine. He opened his mouth as though to send more dragonfire in her direction.

Without thinking, Sabine lifted her hands to block his attack. The goddess quickly took hold of her, using the death magic at Sabine's command. A flash of gray and silver lightning ripped out of her, slamming into the wyvern. He staggered back, his eyes becoming unfocused as small crystals of ice formed on his scales. A moment later, he collapsed in a heap.

Sabine gasped, her vision swimming. She could dimly hear Lachlina's laughter echoing in her thoughts. The forest floor quaked beneath her, lightning striking nearby. Another tree fell, its loss sending a shockwave through Sabine's entire body. She shook her head, trying to distance herself from Lachlina's influence.

Bane grabbed one of the spikes on Malek's back and crouched, his skin glowing with a bluish gleam as he tapped into his magic. He pushed off again and landed on another wyvern, digging his claws into the creature's back.

A second wyvern dove toward Sabine. She gathered her power, stopping abruptly as Malek's powerful jaws closed around the creature's throat. His claws tore into its belly. The wyvern flailed and let out a screech, trying to escape his ironclad grip. They plummeted downward, Malek using his more substantial weight to subdue it. Sabine could dimly hear him calling out to her, but he was too far away to make out the words.

One of the fallen wyverns struggled to rise, but Sabine unleashed more of the death magic toward him. Her skin flared with a golden light as she embraced the power and sent the wyvern into the Beyond. The ground continued to rumble under her feet, the wind and pelting rain making it difficult to see the battle above her. Relying on her bonds with Malek and Bane to keep her aim true, she urged the golem to lift another giant fallen tree and send it speeding through the air toward one of their attackers.

The goddess marks on her wrist glowed gold again, heating to an almost burning frenzy. Sabine shouted a wordless cry, unleashing the power in an explosive blast.

It slammed into Slash with a wild ferocity, tearing through one of his wings. Malek dispatched the wyvern he was fighting and went after Slash, who was in a freefall and heading directly for her.

Malek knocked the wyvern aside, landing protectively in front of Sabine. She struggled to pull back on her magic, refusing to give into the goddess's increasing demands for more control. If her death magic accidentally touched Malek, it would catch him in its grip.

The goddess's fury raged within her. She cried out as the power continued to build, demanding to be used. None of these winged invaders belonged in Aeslion, including Malek. They needed to be eradicated, or the land would never be safe.

"*Separare*," she screamed, trying to separate her thoughts from Lachlina. She'd destroy herself before allowing any harm to come to the man she loved.

"Release the power!" Malek shouted, his form shimmering as he returned to human form.

She shook her head, trying to push it back. Lachlina was too powerful. The deaths of these wyverns had strengthened the goddess's resolve. She had to separate her thoughts from Lachlina first.

"Sabine, it's over," Malek said, walking toward her. "You must release the power. This isn't you."

"Don't touch me," she warned, doubling over at the sharp pain whipping through her. The ground continued to tremble. Lightning struck a nearby tree, causing it to splinter down the center. She cried out as pain lanced through her arms, her skin glowing gold as Lachlina's hold deepened.

Malek ignored her and grabbed her arms, yanking her close. He winced as some of the power transferred to him, but Sabine battled it back. He met her gaze with his clear blue eyes, the intensity in them gripping her as intently as the magic coursing through her.

"You can do this, Sabine," he urged. "Push Lachlina back. We're safe. Think of Rika and Blossom. You're the one putting them in danger now."

Sabine took a shaky breath, focusing on Malek as she fought to separate herself from Lachlina's will. It hurt. Oh, gods. The pain was excruciating. It was worse than the hours she'd spent with the Elders marking her skin. It was more intense than the death of her magic when the Wild Hunt had pursued her. It was almost as though her soul was being sundered from her body.

"Focus on me," Malek demanded, his tone brooking no argument. "I will not lose you to some self-centered bitch of a goddess."

Sabine continued to hold Malek's intense blue gaze, determined not to let Lachlina win. She wouldn't lose him either. Curling her fingers into his shirt, Sabine yanked him down and kissed him. Her magic wrapped around him, allowing the storm within her to change directions. If there was one thing Lachlina could never understand, it was the fierce and undeniable love she felt for this dragon.

Desire and passion flooded through her, and he swept in, understanding instinctively what she needed. His heated magic wrapped around her, and he lifted her into his arms. She wrapped her legs around his waist, their tongues mating together as he consumed her mouth. Her power danced over his skin, and he groaned. His hardness pressed against her core, and she nipped at his lower lip. She ran her hands under his shirt, needing to touch him.

Dimly, she was aware that Lachlina had fled from her thoughts. The ground had stopped shaking, and the wind died away. The golem had returned to the earth, leaving a crumbled husk of dried mud behind. The storm that had raged mere moments before eased away and the sun began shining once again.

Yet none of it assuaged the passion-filled tempest Malek's touch evoked.

Gods. She wanted him.

"Before you two start tearing off clothing, you might be interested to know that one of the giant flying lizards got away."

Sabine broke their kiss and turned her head toward Bane. His eyes still had a silvered glow from the recent battle. Blood covered him, with a deep gash on his head that was bleeding freely. He held his arm at an awkward angle, but he was alive.

"Your timing is impeccable, as always," Malek said dryly.

Bane snorted.

Sabine pulled away from Malek and rushed over to the demon. Pressing her hand against Bane's midsection, she used the contact to send a powerful wave of magic over him. He wrapped his arm around her, holding her close as his injuries knit back together.

"You're all right?" she asked, watching as Bane's eyes reverted to their normal amber.

He gave her a curt nod and squeezed her waist. "I'm fine, little one. But this attack doesn't bode well for our intended visit to the Sky Cities."

Malek's jaw hardened as he stared at the bodies littering

the forest floor. "I didn't recognize this group. They refused to respond to my inquiries, nor were there any markings that might identify their allegiance."

"That's unusual?" Sabine asked, wincing as Bane inspected her scraped hands and began healing them. At least Malek's wounds usually disappeared when he shifted back to human form. She could still sense his exhaustion, but more than anything, he was incensed by this attack.

"It should not have happened," Malek said, lifting his gaze to study the sky. "I'm less concerned about not recognizing them. There are too many to know them all by sight, but they damn well should have answered my demands."

"Any idea why they didn't respond to you?" Sabine asked.

"All wyverns are oathbound to follow the commands of a greater dragon, unless prior orders countermand such directives. It happens, but it's rare."

"I don't understand."

"We're divided into clans, each with its own agenda and purpose," Malek explained. "The wyverns are beholden to all greater dragons, regardless of their sworn clan affiliation. The only exception is if there's a blood bond, similar to your relationship with your beastman protector. If a greater dragon enters such an arrangement with a wyvern, it often extends to the wyvern's entire family. They become part of that greater dragon's clan and fall under their protection."

Sabine tilted her head, considering him. "Then the only reason these wyverns wouldn't have responded to you was if they or a family member were blood-bound to another greater dragon?"

"Yes, and it would need to be a clan powerful enough to risk raising their hand against mine. There are few who might fall into that category, but I've been gone a long time. It's possible the political situation has changed more than I expected."

Bane snorted. "One lizard is the same as the next."

Malek gave him a dry look. "Just as all demons are the same?"

Sabine ignored their argument and studied the surrounding destruction. Without her aid, it would take centuries for the forest to fully recover. She was feeling ill-used from Lachlina's influence, but she couldn't stand by and allow the forest to wither and die.

Bane reached out and touched her temple, his eyes flaring silver briefly. Another sharp stab of pain lanced through her as he healed her wound. She winced and absently touched her face, unaware she'd even been bleeding. Malek's expression darkened.

He stalked toward her, his gaze furious and promising retribution. Yet his touch was gentle as he tilted her head to inspect the area Bane had healed. He gave Bane a nod before bending down and lightly kissing her temple.

In a low voice, he murmured, "Never again, Sabine. For every injury you suffer, I'll see it returned to them tenfold."

"You shouldn't make such promises to a fae," she said, pressing her fingers against his lips. He kissed her fingertips and captured her hands, running his thumbs across her healed palms.

Holding her gaze, he lifted her hands and placed a kiss against each of her palms. "I'm making that promise to *you*, Sabine. You're mine to protect."

Bane tensed, his eyes gravitating toward the sky. "We have another wyvern incoming."

Malek straightened as an emerald green wyvern with gold-dusted wings flew into sight. His shoulders relaxed as he said, "It's all right. It's Levin. He might have some answers about the wyvern who escaped."

Sabine's eyes widened. On top of the stunning wyvern sat a red-headed witch Sabine knew well. "Esme's with him!"

Levin landed on the ground in front of them, tucking his wings behind him. Esme waved from her seat on his back and called out, "Think you guys could have left a few trees standing? We felt the aftershocks all the way in Imenel's port."

CHAPTER 3

$\mathcal{E}$smelle climbed off Levin's back and landed lightly on the ground. The moment she touched the earth, her face paled and she collapsed.

Levin's wyvern shape disappeared in a flash of light. He reappeared a second later as a dark-haired human man. He crouched beside Esmelle and pulled her into his arms. "Esme! What is it? Are you injured?"

Unable to respond, Esmelle simply shook her head and squeezed her eyes shut. Her entire body trembled uncontrollably, her teeth chattering from untold agony. Vines burst upward from the ground, snaking around Esmelle's ankles and wrists. Levin began ripping them away from her, but twice as many sprouted up in retaliation for his attack.

"Cesare!" Sabine shouted, accompanying her order with a sharp lash of power. The vines fell away, slithering back into the ground like a child being reprimanded.

Sabine kneeled in front of the part-dryad witch. Clasping Esmelle's hands, Sabine wrapped a tendril of questing power around her friend, searching for any signs of nefarious magic or influence.

Sabine muttered a curse, not tearing her gaze away from Esmelle. The magic within this forest had a stronger pull than anything Esmelle had previously encountered. She didn't have enough training to resist the forest's call. Sabine hadn't even considered warning her, a fact that she was now kicking herself for not anticipating.

"It's wild magic," Sabine said, weaving together a reassuring blanket of power to encompass Esme. It wouldn't alleviate the pain, but it would hopefully insulate her from the worst of its effects and keep the forest from fracturing her psyche. The only person with the ability to rise above this sort of magic was Esme herself.

"Wild magic?" Malek asked. "Is that similar to the power possessed by the Wild Hunt and the mark we share?"

"Yes. This was once a Silver Forest, where the trees stood as sentient guardians. When the Dragon War destroyed them, the soil absorbed the magic and infused it into new growth. Without the fae nearby to direct the power, it's become wild and unharnessed."

"What can we do to help her?" Levin asked.

"Focus, Esmelle of Norwood," Sabine demanded, infusing her voice with power. "You can rise above this. Trust in your inner strength and innate gifts."

With angry tears streaming down her cheeks, Esmelle lifted her head and declared, "The forest's soul is broken, and the land weeps from its loss. Can't you feel it?"

"I do," Sabine admitted. "But you must not let it rule you."

The vines broke through the ground again, trying to reach Esmelle. Sabine narrowed her eyes and slapped her palm against the earth in warning. A subtle shiver ran through the soil, and even the wind stilled. The vines curled into themselves, retreating to the safety of the earth's embrace.

"Why are the plants doing that?" Levin asked.

"Esme is a kindred spirit," Sabine explained, squeezing Esmelle's hands gently to help focus the witch's attention back on her. "The forest is crying out, and Esme's magic is responding to its call."

Esmelle took a shaky breath and shook her head. "Oh, gods. This is beyond me. I can't heal it, can I?"

"No," Sabine said softly. "Let it pass through you. You can survive this. Don't fight the current—ride it."

Esmelle's voice trembled as she exhaled. "I'm trying, but it's dragging me under."

"What's causing this?" Levin asked, looking around the forest. "If this place is hurting Esme, I can fly her out of here."

"She cannot be moved while the magic holds her captive, or you risk destroying her mind," Sabine said, weaving another barrier to help buffer the forest's song of lament. "She must navigate this on her own."

"Levin," Malek said quietly. "Sabine obviously knows what's going on. Let her concentrate."

Levin's anxiety was only compounding Esmelle's pain. Sabine's fae blood recognized the suffering could be used as a magical offering, one powerful enough to restore the land. The marks on her wrist warmed as Lachlina's desires once again aligned with her own.

She sought to ward against it, trying to ignore Lachlina's whispers to use the magic she'd absorbed through the artifacts. With a mere thought, she could help Esmelle and heal the land. It would be such an elegant and simple solution.

No.

Taking a deep breath, Sabine pushed aside the seductive thought. If she interfered, Esmelle would never learn how to navigate such magic. If this had happened when Sabine wasn't around, Esmelle would have been lost forever. It was imperative Esmelle embrace her gifts if she had any hope of surviving them.

The marks on Sabine's wrist burned as Lachlina's impatience grew. Sabine scrambled to quickly reinforce her mental barriers. She would not be a pawn to the renegade goddess, at least not more than she already was.

"Sabine?" Malek asked quietly. "What's wrong? Is it Lachlina again?"

Sabine nodded, trying to clamp down on Lachlina's influence. The goddess was growing stronger, her promises more enticing. That, combined with the residual magic in this ancient forest and her concern over Esmelle, was almost too much to withstand.

A loud cracking noise filled the air. Sabine lifted her head, watching as a burned tree fell downward. It slammed into a healthy tree, toppling it to the ground. Sabine winced as the forest's wail became even more frenzied. Esmelle cried out.

The vines poked free of the ground, and Sabine glared at them. They quickly retreated.

"This isn't working," Levin said, turning to Sabine with a plea in his eyes. "I've seen how powerful you are, Sabine. If you could create a forest in the middle of Akros, you can heal this one and stop Esme from suffering."

"She is trying to teach the witch," Bane said, gesturing at Esmelle. "You do neither one any favors with your endless chatter."

Levin's voice rose. "If there's a price, I'll pay it. Anything to end this."

"No," Esme gasped. "You don't speak for me."

Sabine stood and narrowed her eyes on Levin. The goddess rose swiftly, her magic coursing through Sabine's body. The forest's lament roared within her, demanding justice.

Sabine flung her hand in Esme's direction and said, "Your kind caused her suffering, wyvern. And now you cause her more by fracturing her focus. I owe your kind *nothing*. If you insist on bartering with me, it will be at the expense of your life."

"Sabine, no," Esme managed on a gasp.

"Levin, back off," Malek said, taking a step toward Sabine and reaching for her. "This isn't you, Sabine. Look at yourself."

Sabine glanced down. Her skin glowed a brilliant gold, nearly blinding in its intensity. If any humans had been around, they would have immediately become fae-struck. She would have doomed them to the mindless worship her kind could cause, even to the point they would forgo all interest in survival. It was a wonder Esmelle wasn't affected.

Sabine closed her eyes and tried to reinforce her mental barriers. She had to push back Lachlina's influence, or she'd end up killing Levin. His magic was too similar to the wyverns that had nearly destroyed the forest. The smell of charred wood and smoke still choked her senses.

Malek took her hands in his, causing a gentle warmth to trail over her skin. His voice slipped into her thoughts like a thief. *"Tell me what you need."*

She glanced down at Esme who was still trembling. *"You have to get Levin away from here. Lachlina views him as a threat. She tolerates you, but she'll destroy him without a second thought. I can't protect him and help Esme. Lachlina's too close to the surface."*

"Take a walk, Levin," Malek ordered. "Now."

Taking a deep breath, Sabine looked into Malek's eyes that held all the mystery of a twilight sky. If her emotions were the catalyst needed to break Lachlina's hold, then focusing on Malek was the best choice. Lachlina's hatred for dragons was legendary. The goddess could never understand the depth of Sabine's feelings for Malek, or the hidden strength she'd found in his love.

"Sabine," Malek murmured, his eyes softening. *"When you look at me like that, there isn't anything I wouldn't do for you."*

Something eased inside her, and the marks on her wrist cooled. Lachlina's influence slowly began to wane, but Sabine could still feel her lurking beneath the surface.

"I'm not leaving her," Levin said, crouching beside Esmelle. "You're all standing around debating while she's breaking. Someone has to care."

Malek's hand shot out and wrapped around Levin's throat. With a strength that could never be confused with a human, he tossed Levin backward into a nearby tree. Esmelle cried out as it splintered from the force. Sabine muttered a curse and tightened the protective barrier around Esmelle.

"You're out of line, Levin," Malek growled, narrowing his eyes on the wyvern. "Control yourself, or I'll do it for you. You don't understand what's happening here."

Levin roared and tackled Malek. They rolled on the ground, fighting with a viciousness that reminded Sabine of her time at the Unseelie court. The demons would often battle one another when they were seeking patronage from a powerful fae family. Sabine glared at the two men in irritation.

"Perhaps demons and dragonkind have more in common than I expected," Bane said, eyeing the battle between Malek and Levin with approval. "The technique isn't bad, but your dragon fights with sheathed claws."

The vines tried to break free from their earthen prison again to embrace Esmelle. Sabine stamped her foot. The leaves flattened, like children caught misbehaving. If the forest's magic had its way, it would consume Esmelle completely. She needed to stop this battle so she could concentrate on her friend, not the pointless dominance games between dragons and wyverns.

Malek was making an obvious effort not to harm Levin,

but he wasn't gentle by any means. When one well-timed blow to Malek's nose drew blood, it was enough to fracture Lachlina's lingering hold. Sabine refused to allow any further harm to Malek, especially in her defense. She shoved Lachlina out of her thoughts and took a step toward the two fighting men.

Flinging out her hand toward some of the still standing trees, Sabine called upon them with her power. With a creak and a groan, the trunk bent down and imprisoned Levin within its branches.

"If you attempt to break free and damage these trees, you'll only hurt Esme more," Sabine warned.

"Hmm," Bane murmured, crossing his arms over his chest. "He would make a suitable sacrifice to restore the forest. That is, if your trees don't mind a bit of indigestion."

Sabine gave him a dry look. "I'll keep it in mind."

"Don't hurt him," Esmelle managed on a gasp, drawing Sabine's attention back to her. "It's the mating instinct. Levin warned me he would be overly protective right now."

"You stupid lizard," Bane said with a snarl, eyeing Levin with distaste. "Sabine is the only thing keeping your witch from being eaten by the forest. She's trying to teach her, not harm her. It's a wonder how dragonkind in the mating frenzy survive their stupidity."

Malek wiped the blood from his nose. "It's something we've wondered about as well." Lifting his gaze to regard Levin, he added, "Think, brother. None of us intend Esme any harm. *You know this.*"

Levin's shoulder sagged, and he took a ragged breath. "It's difficult to think clearly when she's suffering."

Malek walked over to Levin and spoke quietly to the wyvern.

Sabine kneeled in front of Esmelle again. She took her hands and wound another insulating blanket of power around her. "Ignore everything except for me and what you're feeling. Harmonize your power with the forest's song. Guide your magic with mine."

Esmelle added her magic to Sabine's weaving, her efforts more confident and requiring less correction. The vines swayed gently, almost as though they were watching Esmelle's magic take shape.

Sabine squeezed Esmelle's hands and said, "Allow me to act as the bridge between you and the land. I cannot take your pain, but you *can* give it to me."

"No," Esme whispered, shaking her head stubbornly. "Their sacrifice needs to be honored. These trees and plants were innocent. Their lives were stolen. I'll do my part to honor them and their sacrifice."

"A dryad's place has never been to accept the pain of such a loss," Sabine said gently. "Theirs is to protect and serve the forest. They are the guardians for those unable to defend themselves. Do not take on more than you were meant to."

Esmelle took a shaky breath and nodded. She closed her eyes, and Sabine watched as Esmelle's body glowed with a faint bluish-green light. The magic cascaded over her and flowed down her arms and into Sabine.

Sabine accepted Esmelle's pain as her due, using it to reinforce the protective barrier around her friend. While Esmelle was a powerful magic user in her own right, she'd never had an opportunity to fully explore the other aspects of her dryad abilities. Sabine had tried to instruct her over the years, but their powers were vastly different. It was the equivalent of trying to teach Blossom how to perform major magic like the fae.

The forest's anguish resonated through every fiber of Sabine's being. Once again, she heard the echoed cries of animals that had tried to flee, desperate to escape the wrath of the flames. She felt the loss of every majestic oak, each delicate fern, and hundreds of gentle blossoms.

Sabine lowered her head, her hair falling in a silvery curtain over her face. The taste of ash was bitter on her tongue, but she accepted their sacrifice as her due. Her skin markings glowed brightly as the magic settled within her.

She clamped down on the discomfort, knowing she'd need to find an outlet before it became uncontrollable. As a fae, she could wield a great deal of power, but it needed to be used or would bubble over like a boiling cauldron. If that happened, she wasn't sure any of them would survive it.

Esmelle managed a weak smile. "It's manageable now. I still feel the pain, but I can handle it. This wasn't exactly what I was envisioning as far as reunions went."

Sabine squeezed Esmelle's hands one last time before releasing her. "No, but I'm glad to see you just the same." She hesitated, looking down at the seemingly innocuous vines at Esmelle's feet. They'd crept closer again while Esmelle had been sharing magic with her.

"I think it would be best if you accompanied me when I retrieve Rika and Blossom," Sabine suggested. "The forest will be out of sorts until we put it to rights."

When Esmelle nodded, Sabine stood and glanced down at herself. Her dress was wet, torn, and stained with dirt and soot, but at least most of her magic was suppressed. She couldn't do anything about the faint glow until she purged some of her excess magic. As it was, she was as jittery as a pixie who had sipped nectar from a purple-speckled cavena plant.

Even with Sabine's magic this close to the surface, Rika's seer abilities should give her some immunity from becoming fae-struck. At least, Sabine hoped. The longer Rika and Blossom remained in the care of the forest guardians, the riskier it would be to them. The guardians wouldn't harm Blossom, but they viewed humans differently.

With a brief brush of her power, Sabine released Levin from his makeshift prison. He rushed over to Esmelle. She leaned into him, resting her head against his chest and murmuring something too softly for Sabine to hear.

Sabine watched them for a moment, struck by the tenderness and care Levin was displaying toward her friend. Malek often looked at her the same way, as though she were the most important thing in the world. Sabine absently touched the goddess marks on her wrist, wondering if Lachlina would ever understand Malek and Levin weren't their enemies.

Malek approached Sabine and searched her expression. "Are you all right?"

Sabine nodded and leaned against him. He wrapped his arms around her, accompanying his touch with a heated brush of his magic.

Bane approached the newly sprouted vines and studied them. They were pretending to act like normal plants again, but Sabine knew their attention was focused on her and Esmelle. This entire forest possessed more awareness than any she'd seen outside of Faerie. It was surprising given their proximity to the Sky Cities.

"I need to speak with the forest guardians," Sabine said, watching as Bane poked at the vines with his claws. "Given what happened here, it would be best if you, Bane, and Levin remained here while Esme and I visit their grove."

Sharp thorns burst out of the vines. Bane leaned back and considered them.

She sighed. "I would suggest not provoking the foliage while we're gone. It's already agitated."

New leaves sprouted and unfurled, revealing tiny dark blue flowers that began to bloom. As far as apologies for bad behavior went, the flowers were a nice touch. She noticed it decided to keep its thorns. Sassy little plant.

Esme lifted her head and asked, "Rika and Blossom are with the forest guardians?"

Sabine nodded. "It was the safest place for them."

Bane harrumphed and abandoned the vines. "A queen does not chase after her subjects. It would be more expedient to command the forest guardians' attendance and be done with it."

Sabine arched her brow. "After we've destroyed their forest? A queen's responsibility is to protect her people. I won't cause further insult by forcing them to attend to me."

Malek frowned. "The wyvern who escaped could return with reinforcements at any time. Are you sure going alone is a good idea?"

Sabine hesitated. "It's not ideal, but it's necessary. We've harmed them, Malek. You saw how the damage affected Esme. What they're experiencing is far worse. The two of us can move through their grove unchallenged. If I can make amends, I must go."

Malek cupped her face and kissed her softly. "Then we'll hold here until you return."

"I don't think it's a good idea," Levin said, taking a step closer to Esme. "I've never seen you hurting like that before. What happens if Sabine's not able to pull you out next time?"

Esme arched her brow. "Are you suggesting we can't take care of ourselves?"

Levin winced and rubbed the back of his neck. "I just meant if I need to take you away from here quickly, I need to be close at hand."

"I won't be caught off-guard again," Esmelle said firmly. "Sabine and I have handled ourselves well enough in the past. If she believes we'll be safe, I trust her judgment." She jabbed Levin in the chest with her finger. "You should too. I told you before that Sabine's been teaching me. She would *never* hurt me."

Bane shrugged. "As long as there's one tree left standing in this forest, Sabine and Esme are far safer in the forest guardians' grove than anywhere. Our presence will only make their negotiations more… challenging."

"How so?" Malek asked Bane. "I can understand their misgivings about a dragon in their presence, but you're allied with the Unseelie fae."

Bane grunted and didn't deign to respond. Instead, he walked over to one of the dead wyverns and began inspecting its scales.

Sabine shook her head. "Bane's dealt with the forest guardians in the past. They typically avoid men, unless they're interested in creating new progeny. It's unlikely they would consider any of you suitable candidates."

Esme walked over to Sabine and asked, "How do we do this?"

Sabine took Esme's hand and pressed the other one against the trunk of a nearby oak tree. She sent a pulse of power into the wood and murmured, *"Avelare."*

The bark shifted somehow, becoming almost translucent. Its image shimmered, forming a gossamer green veil over the surface of the trunk.

Esme stared at the portal in shock. "You created a doorway to the in-between."

Sabine shook her head. "No. I merely summoned it. This doorway has existed for millennia, but it's a carefully guarded secret."

Malek stepped forward, his brow creased in concern. "This doorway has been here undisturbed for this long? We're less than a day from the Sky Cities. My people have traveled through this forest and never noticed it."

"It's not stationary and very well hidden," Sabine

explained. "The forest guardians act as anchors in the sacred grove, allowing those with the necessary magic to move between connected forests. Even among my people, the ability to summon this sort of doorway is rare. It only responds to those with an affinity for the forest's song."

Esme lifted her hand, hovering her fingertips in front of the greenish glow. It brightened as though sensing Esme's presence. "There's a resonance with my magic. It feels… welcoming. Is that what you're talking about?"

Sabine nodded. "Yes, but remember this is wild magic. What may appear welcoming on the surface often possesses hidden depths. You should be safe when we meet the forest guardians, but keep to the practices as though you were dealing with the fae."

Esme darted a glance at Bane and teased, "These guardians can't be any more challenging than dealing with a pair of demon brothers for ten years. Let's go get Rika and Blossom."

Bane scowled at her.

Sabine grinned, but her humor faded almost immediately. "Hold tight to my hand and your sense of self. You may feel one with the forest, but you are not *of* it. Don't lose yourself to the magic when we cross the threshold."

Esme's brow furrowed, but she nodded. Without waiting a moment longer, Sabine stepped through the portal and into the sacred grove.

CHAPTER 4

Malek and Levin stared at the tree, which now appeared to be nothing more than an ordinary oak. Malek flexed his fingers, trying to suppress the nearly overwhelming urge to go after Sabine.

She wasn't acting like herself. Lachlina's thoughts were blending with Sabine's more frequently, and it was taking her longer to come back to herself.

He hadn't missed the way she tossed and turned at night, or the quiet moments between them that carried an unspoken weight. She was worried, and Malek was at a loss on how to help her.

"Watching that tree won't make them reappear any faster," Bane said, turning away from them. "They'll be gone for at least an hour. Perhaps two, if the dryads prove to be more stubborn than usual."

Malek watched as Bane headed toward one of the fallen wyverns. The demon's nonchalance was surprisingly reassuring. If Bane suspected Sabine might be in danger, he never would have allowed her to enter the sacred grove without him.

"I don't like this," Levin muttered, still staring at the oak tree. "If Sabine was right, our magic won't allow us to reopen the doorway to follow them."

"I can still sense Sabine," Malek admitted. Their connection was tenuous, but it was growing stronger every day. He felt her pulse within his thoughts, a shining light hidden behind a veil.

The thought made him pause. The few times they'd traveled through the in-between together had been... odd. The place was familiar somehow, calling to him on a deeper level. He shook his head. Some innate part of him knew he could navigate the darkness, especially with Sabine as his lodestone.

Levin blew out a breath. "At least you have that much of a connection with Sabine. That sort of bonding is almost unheard of among non-dragonkin."

"We have to trust in their abilities," Malek said, scanning the nearby trees. If this forest was truly sentient, he wouldn't divulge any of Sabine's secrets where they could be used against her. But Levin was right; he'd never heard of another dragon bonding so deeply with a fae. Something about Sabine's magic was different.

Malek turned to his friend and asked, "Do you honestly believe Bane would have allowed Sabine to go if this was dangerous?"

"No," Levin grudgingly admitted and scrubbed his face with his hands. "How the hell have you been dealing with this? I know how capable Esme is, but every instinct is screaming for me to take her to the Sky Cities where she'll be safe."

Bane snorted and looked at them over his shoulder. "The witch would wear your skin as a cloak before allowing anyone to cart her off."

"He has a point," Malek agreed with a wry smile. "Sabine would likely do the same, or worse, to me."

Bane shot him a wicked grin and crouched beside the wyvern. "Worse, much worse. But it hasn't stopped you from attempting to take her to your den since almost the first moment you met her. I'm still hoping to watch that battle."

"I haven't heard you objecting overly much lately. Could it be that you finally agree Sabine will be safe from her enemies once she's in the Sky Cities?"

"Perhaps from the fae and the Wild Hunt," Bane said with a shrug and ran his dagger across the glittering scales of the red wyvern. "I'm more interested in whether you intend to let her depart the Sky Cities. That's going to be the deciding factor in whether you're the greater threat."

Malek arched his brow. "Is that a bit of respect I hear?"

Bane scowled. "What are you going on about now?"

"Obviously, I'm as fearsome as the Wild Hunt," Malek said with a grin. "It's about time you demons started respecting dragon might."

Bane snorted. "For now, you're simply more useful than a block of coal. Let's see if your so-called 'dragon might' can roll this wyvern. I want to check something."

Levin chuckled and walked over to the wyvern Bane was inspecting. "Might as well. It'll give us a chance to get a better look at its markings."

They took up position on one side. On Bane's signal, all three of them strained, pushing the large creature on his side to expose his belly.

"Interesting," Bane said, running his claws over the scales. Despite the attack, Malek couldn't help the pang of regret at the loss. The wyverns' survival rate wasn't as abysmal as the greater dragons, but their numbers were becoming fewer every year. They couldn't risk further infighting, or they'd never survive.

Malek backed up and studied the reddish wyvern. The tip of each individual scale was dark at the edge, giving it the appearance of having been dipped in black paint. It was a striking and memorable design.

Malek frowned. "Some of these markings are familiar, but I don't recognize him. He's younger than I first thought."

Levin frowned and walked around the body. He inspected the snout and rubbed one of the brow ridges. "Far too young to be running patrols. His markings would have likely changed over the next few decades. Did you identify yourself before they attacked?"

Malek nodded. "Even if I hadn't, my coloring is distinctive. Unless something drastic changed in the past several years, my father is still leading our clan."

"Fair point," Levin acknowledged, checking the wyvern's teeth. "Would you look at that? They're way too small. I'd cut off my tail if he managed to hit the century mark."

Malek muttered a curse. He'd known the wyverns were inexperienced, but this one was younger than he'd thought. What the hell had their clan been thinking?

Levin eyed the wyvern with a mixture of anger and grief. "I'll check the others, but I suspect it'll be more of the same. None of them should have been out here without an experienced flight commander. And they never should have challenged a greater dragon. That's sheer suicide without a skilled and experienced wyvern squadron."

"They moved as a unit but didn't fight as one," Bane said, wedging his knife under a scale. It looked like the demon was trying to pry off one of the wyvern's jeweled underbelly scales.

"What the hell do you think you're doing?" Malek demanded.

"If an enemy falls on the battlefield, will you abandon his weapons for some bizarre sense of morality? Or will you collect them and learn what you can so you might continue the fight?"

"Even if you remove a scale, it won't possess any magic. Those must be gifted."

"You're thinking too small, lizard," Bane said, withdrawing a second dagger and using it to pry the scale loose.

Malek shook his head and turned back to Levin. "Bane's right about their tactics. I held back initially because of their inexperience. At least until they targeted Sabine."

"And in doing so, you have revealed your weakness to your enemies," Bane said, walking over to another of the dead wyverns.

Malek frowned, not liking the sound of that. If they knew how vulnerable he was because of Sabine, they would target her. He'd brought her here to keep her safe, not to thrust her into more danger.

"There are only three or four clans in a position to challenge yours," Levin said quietly. "If this was a move to take out the heir to the Obsidian Clan, they'll try again. Your father could also be in danger."

"My father wouldn't have held back as long as I did, and neither one of us are easy targets." Malek crossed his arms over his chest, regarding the dead with distaste. Even if they managed to eliminate both him and his father, there was also his mother and sister who could lead their clan.

"It's more likely this attack was related to our mission," Malek admitted. "Unfortunately, that gives us another problem to consider."

Levin arched his brow. "There's something worse than an assassination attempt?"

"A *successful* one," Bane said, peeling off a scale and holding it up to the sunlight. It glittered brilliantly, like a priceless gem with a trace of the inner fire each dragonkin possessed. Bane tucked the purloined scale into a pouch at his waist. "I believe the dragon is suggesting someone learned of our plans. These attackers either knew or suspected our intended route and when we would arrive. Whatever method you were using for communication has likely become compromised."

Levin muttered a curse. "The merchants. Since we separated in Razadon, we've been relying more heavily on them to smuggle messages through our network. Someone in our house must be working against us. They were the only ones who knew our method of communication and what the coded messages meant."

Malek nodded and rubbed his chin in thought. It had to be someone in their inner circle. Not even the council knew the details of his mission to seek out the fae. Before he left, they'd been divided on their stance regarding the Dragon Portal and the fae who guarded it. Some wanted to force the fae into revealing its location and take control of it, while others wanted to destroy the fae outright to prevent this from happening in the future.

Given the volatile nature of the debate, Malek and Levin had decided it would be best to keep their mission as quiet as possible. But why send young wyverns to attack them? Were they hoping to incite the other clans to violence for these senseless deaths?

He turned back to Levin and asked, "Did you already send word to your family about our arrival?"

Levin shook his head. "No. We only arrived in port earlier today. The minute we felt the aftershocks from the battle, Esme knew it was Sabine. I heard your call a few minutes later."

"Don't alert them yet. It might be wise to maintain a low profile while we're in Imenel."

"What are you thinking?" Levin asked.

"Many of Imenel's residents work in the Sky Cities. If they've heard any gossip, they'll speak more freely if they believe we're also human. We'll need some disguises, especially since we only have one warding medallion between us."

Levin held up his hand to stop Malek from handing it over. "It doesn't hide you as well as the one you lost, but it's better than nothing. A greater dragon will draw more attention than a wyvern. I've probably already been recognized. Perhaps the witch who crafted them can be persuaded to create another."

Malek hesitated and then nodded. Dealing with Idola was tricky. The witch wasn't beholden to any dragons. Malek had never been sure where her loyalty lay.

"We'll speak with her before we head to Imenel. Either way, we'll need to keep our distance when we're in the city. If you make some discreet inquiries around the docks, I'll see what I can learn in the trading district. Around this time tomorrow, I'll take Sabine up to the city by way of the crystal lifts. That will give us a day to learn what we can."

"It would be wise to retrace your steps," Bane said, glancing over at Levin. "Who did you speak with when you arrived? How many knew your ship by sight? Was your crew native to the city?"

Levin frowned. "We lost a number of people during the merfolk attack. The newcomers were mostly picked up after we left Razadon. Sailors can be a rough lot, but no one stood out as being suspect. Most of them went on leave right after they received their wages." He was quiet for a moment, rubbing his chin in thought. "The last storm hit us pretty hard. I met with the dockmaster to arrange for repairs and have what was left of our cargo unloaded. Esme and I had barely made it to the market square before she sensed

Sabine. I don't want to suspect him, but Kipp was the only one we had contact with."

Malek shook his head at the thought of the dockmaster being involved in the attack. "Kipp would cut off his arm before conspiring against us. Whoever discovered your arrival in Imenel likely had sentries watching the harbor for the ship. They may have been the ones to send word to the wyverns about our approach."

"That makes the most sense," Levin agreed, but he didn't appear pleased by that fact.

Bane began prying off a second scale. "You've forgotten the wyvern who escaped. He will report back to his masters all he learned during the attack."

"There's nothing to be done about that until we return to the Sky Cities," Malek said, before turning back to Levin. "Did you recognize him?"

Levin shook his head. "He might possibly be related to the Copper or Gold Clan. Without getting a closer look, I can't be certain. I was too far away to make out any details."

Bane placed the second scale in his bag. He gestured deeper in the forest where another wyvern had fallen. "Another demonstration of your 'dragon might' is in order. Unless, of course, you're unable to rise to such a challenge."

"You're not going to tell me what you want the scales for, are you?"

Bane smirked and didn't reply.

Malek crossed his arms over his chest and waited.

Bane chuckled. "They are not for me, lizard. If Sabine shares their purpose with you, that will be her decision."

Malek nodded. He started to follow the demon, but Levin stopped him.

"What about Esme and Sabine? If the doorway isn't stationary, will they be able to locate us if we move away from this tree?"

"I believe the small lizard is even more pathetic than you," Bane muttered in annoyance.

Malek bit back a grin. Over the last few weeks, Malek had noticed a marked difference in the way Bane treated him. Their trials together and Malek's obvious loyalty toward Sabine had softened Bane's distrust. While Bane still wasn't overly friendly, his sharp tongue no longer had the same bite. Unfortunately, Levin hadn't yet proved himself to the distrustful demon.

"You seem very confident they aren't in danger," Levin said, his gaze suspicious. "What do you know about these forest guardians that we don't?"

"More things than you can count, worm," Bane said.

Malek gestured in the direction of the fallen wyvern. "It would be faster to just tell him what you know, so we can focus on getting your task done."

Bane let out an aggrieved sigh. "As I said before, Sabine will not remain in their sacred grove for long. While the dryads do not dare harm her outright, they will be eager for her to leave their haven as quickly as possible. As long as we remain in this forest and within their influence, Sabine will be able to locate us."

Malek studied Bane carefully. "Why will they be in a hurry to have her leave?"

Bane's eyes went half-mast and a cruel smile crossed his face. "Because with a flick of her wrist, Sabine can destroy their sacred grove and wipe out all dryads from Aeslion. They, however, cannot outright cause her harm. Her blood fuels their existence, for they were the children of Theoria, Sabine's namesake. Did you not wonder why a part-dryad witch was chosen to teach Sabine how to hide among the humans?"

Malek stared at him. "That's why you conscripted Esme's help all those years ago? Because of her dryad heritage?"

"Indeed," Bane said, his amber eyes briefly flickering to silver. "By her very nature, she cannot harm Sabine. And betraying Sabine would be a mistake that none would survive."

CHAPTER 5

Sabine exited the portal and landed lightly on the moss-covered ground. Ancient trees towered above them, their bark pulsing with glowing silver and gold veins that reached to the sky. The dark green foliage overhead created a dense canopy that cast the forest into eternal twilight. Glowbugs danced over the mossy ground, offering a hint of illumination while Sabine's eyes adjusted to the darker setting.

The trickle of a dancing river nearby filled the air with its song, accompanied by the faint rustle of the wind as it teased the branches of the trees with its playful touch. Sabine inhaled deeply, breathing in the rich scent of wild mint and other herbs. They sweetened the air with an intoxicating perfume that reminded her of the forests in Faerie. Closing her eyes, she allowed the magic of this place to envelop her in its embrace. It reminded her of home.

Esme released her hand. Sabine opened her eyes, watching as Esme took several steps deeper into the forested area. The wind stopped abruptly. Even the trees seemed to take notice of their presence, their branches turning in

Sabine and Esmelle's direction. Instead of a welcome, the forest seemed wary of their arrival. Sabine's skin pebbled, and she resisted the urge to rub her arms to rid herself of the uncomfortable sensation.

"I've never felt anything like this," Esme whispered, staring up at the trees. "This forest. I feel it like a second heartbeat, almost as though it's part of me."

"It is," Sabine admitted, holding out her hand to better read the land. The forest guardians were close, but she had the impression the forest's attention was concentrated elsewhere.

Curious, she sent her awareness outward, trying to get a better sense of what she was feeling. Her skin began to shimmer with a golden glow as the power within her began to build. She faltered and pulled back on her magic. The luminescence dimmed, but it didn't fade completely. She stared down at her hands, realizing in shock that the golden color had nearly fully eclipsed the silver. This hadn't been Lachlina's doing. The goddess was silent within her.

Her thoughts drifted to the mirrored image of herself she'd seen in the Hall of the Gods. The hellhound, Azran, had told her the golden glow was a reflection of what she was becoming. She just didn't know what that meant.

"Sabine?"

Sabine lifted her head to meet Esme's worried gaze. She managed a smile and shook her head to indicate they'd talk later. They appeared to be alone, but this forest possessed an awareness just like the ones near Faerie.

"This place is part of your heritage," Sabine said. "Once upon a time, we would have seen places such as this throughout all of Aeslion. This is but an echo of the magic that once spanned the world."

Esmelle glanced over at her. "You're talking about the time before the portal? Before the dragons came?"

Sabine nodded and began heading in the direction she sensed the guardians. "Yes. It wasn't only the dragons and their kin who helped destroy our forests. Many of the gods didn't consider the destruction and death they caused as anything more than collateral damage."

Esme made a noncommittal noise. "Knowing them as I do, I can't imagine Levin or Malek destroying a place like this. Although, Levin was quick to threaten the destruction of the forest. They don't see it the way we do, do they?"

Sabine sent out a faint tendril of questing power as they walked, not wanting to alarm her friend yet. The guardians were working some form of major magic, but she couldn't detect their intent from this distance. It was strange they hadn't sent someone to escort them to the glade. Blossom should have sensed their arrival and come to find her, too.

"No, they don't," Sabine said with a sigh. "Dragons can't sense the aura of power that surrounds every living thing. To them, it's simply trees, dirt, and water."

When Sabine had been forced into hiding among the humans, she'd been unsure whether it was possible for a fae to endure living in a colorless city made of dead wood and stone. She'd suffered every day, surrounded by the bones of ancient forests the humans had used to build their cities. It wasn't until she'd formed a bond with Malek that he'd realized the pain it caused her and the scope of what he was lacking.

Through her, he'd begun to develop an affinity for the magic in their world, just as she was gaining some benefits from his nature. But if they'd never met, Sabine suspected he would have set fire to the forest as easily as the other wyverns. It was one more reminder of their differences.

"Will you tell me about this place?" Esme asked, glancing over at her. "It doesn't feel like any forest I've been in. It feels… untouched."

"It *is* untouched, at least by human hands," Sabine said, ducking under a low-hanging branch. "Few can enter this place, except by a forest guardian's leave. You're an exception, but only because of your dryad blood. As beautiful as it is, the grove's origin story is not a happy one. The tale is often told to fae children, both as a warning and as a reminder of our purpose."

Esme brushed back her red curls. "Most of the Faerie tales you've told me aren't happy ones. Will you share it with me?"

Sabine hesitated and then nodded. "Yes, but this lore can never be shared with outsiders. I'll have to bind your words to prevent them from passing your lips."

"I figured as much. Levin understands there are things I'm unable to tell him, especially where you're concerned." She straightened her shoulders. "If I have any hope of understanding my dryad side, I need to learn everything you're willing to teach me."

"All right," Sabine agreed. "There are many variations of this story, but the basic premise is the same. This is the version taught to me by my mother."

The wind blew softly, setting the tone for the story. A hush filled the forest as though even the trees listened. Magic gathered around Sabine, infusing her voice with power as she recited the tale.

"Once upon a time, Aeslion was covered with ancient forests, lush mountains, and crystal-clear lakes. Animals that no longer exist moved throughout the land and oceans, unhindered by mankind. Magic was everywhere—in the air we breathed and surrounding every living thing. The gods walked this world then, confident in their power and place in the universe. It was a time of peace, bounty, and harmony. There were no wars to speak of... until the dragons came."

The wind rustled the leaves in the trees overhead, almost

as though they knew what was coming. Esme shivered and rubbed her arms.

"The dragons descended upon Aeslion, burning and destroying everything in their path. The merfolk attempted to extinguish the flames, but the water dragons forced them into the deepest recesses of the sea."

A light rain began to fall, the dampness clinging to Sabine's skin. The forest darkened, and a chill filled the air. Several leaves began to fall, drifting to the ground. Esme stopped and caught one in her outstretched hand before allowing the land to reclaim it.

"Our storms weren't enough to squelch the fires," Sabine said, staring up at the canopy of trees as they walked. "The aderyan, the winged race and messengers to the gods, were the first to fall to the dragons' wrath. Once they no longer protected our skies, the dragons turned their attention to our forests. My people fought alongside the demons and dwarves, our cries echoing throughout the land as we were struck down. And as each fae died, the world began to die with it."

"Gods," Esme murmured, pressing her hand against her stomach. "To hear you talk about it, I can almost see it."

"It was a time of profound suffering," Sabine said quietly. "Fathers lost sons, mothers lost daughters, and the fires continued to burn across the land."

Sabine swallowed, her heart hurting at the devastating loss. She may not have been alive to see it, but the Elders who had lived it had been marked. Her mother had spoken of the dragons with such fury that even the forests outside Faerie had trembled from her rage.

"When the war threatened the very existence of this world, Theoria went to her father. Although she was descended from gods, Theoria was a child of Aeslion. She was the first of the fae and a demigoddess in her own right, but her powers were tied to the land. She knew the loss of the forests would mean her certain death."

"Theoria. As in Sabin'theoria?"

"She was my great-great-grandmother," Sabine admitted. "Vestior, Ruler of the Underworld and Keeper of the Balance, controlled the doorways to the in-between. He had immeasurable power, yet despite Theoria's pleas, he refused to evict the dragons from this world. Instead, he gifted his only daughter with this forest, so she might seek refuge from the dragons' assault. She evaded the dragons, but remaining here was never part of her plan."

"Wait," Esmelle interrupted. "The ruler of the underworld created this *forest*?"

Sabine nodded. "The gods all had many names, and the underworld wasn't always what it is now. After his daughter's death, Vestior became known as Harbinger of Nightmares. In his anger and grief, every living creature was thrust into horrific dreams, forced to repeatedly relive the pain of Theoria's death. Many were driven mad and claimed by the Wild Hunt, while others sought to fade from this world in a desperate attempt to escape the nightmares he unleashed."

"If he was that powerful, why didn't he stop the dragons when Theoria asked?" Esme asked. "Wouldn't that have made more sense than allowing them free rein to destroy everything?"

Sabine hesitated, absently rubbing the marks on her wrist. After meeting the Huntsman, she'd begun to realize there was much more to these old stories than she'd realized.

"I'm not sure," Sabine said with a frown. "This story, as it was told to me, was passed from mother to daughter. If Vestior shared his reasons with anyone, his words have been lost to the ages."

Esme stumbled over a rock, but it quickly disappeared

into the earth. Several other nearby rocks sank beneath the soil, making their path less hazardous.

"Okay, that's kind of cool," Esme said, pressing her hand against a nearby tree she'd grabbed to catch her fall. The leaves on the tree shook slightly, almost like a dog wagging its tail enthusiastically. Esme stared up at it in surprise and then tentatively ran her hand over the bark.

Sabine stopped walking and sent out another searching pulse, trying to locate the forest guardians. They still hadn't moved. The strange power she sensed seemed to encompass an area far larger than she'd originally thought. Whatever the guardians were doing didn't feel like any normal dryad magic she'd encountered before.

Sabine frowned, growing increasingly worried about Blossom and Rika. Too many things weren't adding up. They'd been walking for a considerable amount of time. Normally, magic was quick to obey her unspoken commands. Yet, for some reason, the doorway had dropped them off a great distance from the heart of the grove. At least the forest was still responding to them, as evidenced by the disappearing rocks.

Esme released the tree and turned back to Sabine. "You mentioned Theoria never planned to stay here. Why not?"

"Ah," Sabine murmured, weaving her power into her voice as she continued the story. "After the aderyan fell, the dragons turned their attention to the fae. Knowing her children's lives were at stake, Theoria made the ultimate sacrifice. As her lifeblood spilled on the forest floor, she threaded the roots of the trees through reality to create a bridge for the fae to pass. She summoned the fae from the farthest reaches of the world and transported them back to Faerie, where they were strongest. With her dying breath, Theoria breathed life into the forest guardians to act as anchors, so this place might exist in perpetuity. She died, so the fae might live and one day have a chance to reclaim Aeslion."

At Sabine's words, the wind picked up and turned colder. Brushing her hand against a nearby tree, Sabine sent a reassuring touch of power through the woods. The breeze softened, warming slightly from Sabine's touch.

Esmelle swallowed. "She died to bring life to this grove?"

"Yes. Without her sacrifice, I'm not sure any of my people would have survived. We've been able to maintain Faerie's borders and safeguard our forests, but little else. We don't have the numbers to venture beyond our borders to heal the rest of Aeslion."

A single white flower bloomed in front of them, a symbol of hope and rebirth. Its petals were impossibly fragile, yet the rich fragrance that filled the air was nearly intoxicating. Sabine bent and cupped the flower, breathing deeply of its magic. With a smile, she returned a trace of her power to the land in exchange for its offering.

She straightened and continued walking. "Dryads act as sentinels or gatekeepers, protecting the forests from invaders and allowing the fae and their allies to move throughout the world, unseen by the dragons. In return, the sacred grove shelters and nourishes them. Each fae who passes offers a gift of power to help sustain them. As long as the dryads remain to anchor this grove, Theoria's magic lives on."

"That's why you call them forest guardians," Esme murmured. "They guard the doorways to the forests and alert the fae when the land needs their touch."

Sabine nodded. "Yes. The relationship between us is symbiotic. As the number of my people have declined, so have the number of dryads. The forests have suffered as a result."

The marks on Sabine's wrist burned with renewed vigor. Sabine clamped her hand over her wrist and reached out with her senses. The strange magic was building even more rapidly now. They were getting closer to its source, but it wouldn't take long before it reached a tipping point.

"Come on. We need to find Blossom and Rika quickly. Something's wrong."

Sabine hoped Rika's seer abilities would offer some resistance to this strange magic. Blossom was attuned to the natural elements of the forest, but Rika didn't have any such protection. The minute she sensed Sabine's magic, Blossom should have sought her out. The fact she hadn't meant something was seriously wrong.

Esme blew out a breath. "Where? This is ridiculous. We've been walking forever. How do we find these blasted forest guardians?"

At Esme's words, some of the nearby glowbugs lifted away from the moss to illuminate a winding pathway in front of them.

Sabine gestured toward it and said, "That way."

"Clever," Esme said, arching her brow. "New trick?"

"I wasn't the one asking for a path to show us the way to their glade," Sabine said with a teasing smile and hastened her step. "I was simply following the forest's call."

"Wait, what?" Esmelle asked, scrambling to keep up with her.

"Magic will be quick to obey your commands here, even when those wishes are unspoken. This is part of your birthright, as are the consequences of using your innate gifts."

Esme arched her brow. "So I need to be careful, even with my thoughts?"

Sabine gave her a curt nod. "Just like Faerie will often anticipate my wishes, you'll find this place responding to you. But don't rely upon it or be ambivalent with your intentions. Wild magic frequently acts in ways we don't understand, especially when it believes it holds a claim over you. Embrace the magic, but do not let it rule you."

"Embrace the magic," Esme murmured, her expression turning thoughtful. The forest brightened and flowers sprung from the moss, their emerald leaves unfurling as though stretching from a long slumber. They grew rapidly, their blooms exploding in a riot of color. The deep red hues of their petals reminded Sabine of Esme's hair when the dawn light danced upon it.

Esme grinned. "I could get used to this."

Sabine stopped abruptly and whirled around to face her friend. "All magic has a cost. You're part of this place, even if you've spent your life outside of it. The more you use this magic to create, the more entwined you'll become. Tread carefully, Esme. What happens over the next few minutes may shape the rest of your life."

"No pressure, right?" Esme blew out a breath and flexed her fingers. "All right. Point taken. Let's find these forest guardians, so we can get back to the boys."

CHAPTER 6

Sabine continued leading the way, following both the path of the glowbugs and the building power she sensed deeper in the forest. A strange metallic tang in the air reminded her of the corrupted magic she'd experienced back in Razadon.

As they passed another tree, Sabine brushed her hand against the bark. The corruption hadn't permeated its core yet. Whatever was affecting this place was recent enough that the forest guardians had been able to resist its influence. But the recent attack on their forest must have weakened them. It was only a matter of time before the corruption spread. That might explain the building magic, especially if they were taking steps to purge the infection.

The tree line ended abruptly, revealing a large clearing. A thin greenish barrier sprung from the earth, barring their way forward. It reached upward, curving in a dome to encompass the entire glade. The air was dense here, almost like syrup steeped in power. Whatever magic was contained within the pulsing barricade called to her, beckoning her forward. Sabine took a step closer, trying to see what lay beyond the hazy surface.

In the center of the glade stood an ancient oak, larger than any Sabine had seen outside of Faerie. Standing in a circle around it were a dozen dryads, their hands clasped together as they swayed back and forth. Vines encircled their wrists and traveled up their arms, connecting them with the land.

Esmelle stopped in front of the barricade. "What is that? Some kind of ward?"

"Don't try to cross it," Sabine warned. All her instincts were screaming that one misstep could prove disastrous.

She crouched and pressed her fingers into the dirt, trying to sense the depth of the barrier. It was almost as though the ground had been severed where it had entered. Whatever this ward was, it was likely designed to contain and amplify the power from the magical working. If she could sense it from out here, the potency of what lay within had to be extraordinary. The backlash from simply shattering the ward could have dire consequences.

Blossom appeared almost in front of them, but on the other side of the barrier. The tiny pixie's wings were tinged with red, and judging by her panicked expression, they'd barely arrived in time. Blossom pointed to the area behind her and shouted something.

Sabine shook her head and said, "We can't hear you. Tell the guardians to lower the ward."

"I don't see Rika," Esmelle said, trying to peer through the barrier. "It's hard to see much of anything through this thing."

Blossom scrunched up her face in confusion, shedding glittering pixie dust wildly. If the pixie became any more upset, she might burn herself out before Sabine could reach her.

Sabine frowned and shouted, "Calm down, Blossom. Are you okay? Where's Rika?"

Blossom's eyes widened and nodded hastily. Her image shimmered briefly before becoming a tiny tree with wings. Sabine blinked at the strange floating apparition.

"An oak?" Esmelle asked, taking a step closer. "Did you know Blossom could turn into a tree?"

Sabine shook her head. "I think it's a new ability."

Blossom's image flickered again, and she became a flying, miniature version of Rika. A second later, she was back to normal. She cycled through the same illusions twice more before reverting to her normal appearance. Such an expenditure of magic would have once rendered the pixie unconscious. Ever since Blossom had received a magical boost in the underworld, her capacity for glamour seemed to have increased.

Pounding her tiny fists against the barrier, Blossom shouted something else. Sabine wasn't much of a lip-reader, but it looked an awful lot like Blossom was saying, "They're turning Rika into a tree!"

Sabine froze. They wouldn't dare do such a thing.

Esmelle darted a glance at Sabine. "Tell me I misunderstood."

Sabine shook her head and stepped closer to the barrier. This was going to be dangerous, but she had to know for sure. She lifted her hands and pressed them against the barrier, infusing her magic into it. The image cleared slightly, allowing her to better see what lay beyond the ward.

Rika was standing beside the ancient oak in the center of the dryad ring. Some sort of vined magical tether was tied around her waist, connecting her to the oak. A strange silver glow surrounded her and brightened with every rhythmic motion of the dryads. And with each pulse, Rika's image faded a bit more. She collapsed onto the ground, tears streaming down her face.

Rika clawed at the connection around her waist, trying to rip it away. She shouted something, but no words came out. She was too far gone from this reality. The merging had already begun. That's what Blossom had been trying to tell them.

Esmelle whipped her head in Sabine's direction. "I thought only fae faded like that. What the hell are they doing to her?"

A blinding fury swept through Sabine. The ripples of her anger sent shockwaves through the grove, and the ground beneath her feet trembled. The greenish color of the barrier shifted, taking on a golden hue as her emotions bled into it. The wind stilled. The glowbugs retreated. The surrounding plants began to wither. Leaves drifted from the trees, curling and shriveling as they touched the ground. Blossom dove under a fallen leaf, her red-tipped wings poking out and quivering.

"Sabine, stop! You're changing the forest," Esmelle shouted.

Sabine yanked her hands away from the barrier, clamping down on her emotions. Just like in Faerie, the sacred grove was responding to her whims. If she lost control, she would endanger Esmelle, Blossom, and Rika. At least the disruption had slowed the progression of the ritual and bought them a few more minutes.

Lachlina's thoughts hovered at the edge of her mind, threatening to seep into hers. The marks on her wrist burned with a scorching heat. The goddess wanted to crush this barrier and destroy everyone who threatened the sanctity of this place, regardless of the consequences. Calling upon her reserves of strength, Sabine tried to reinforce her mental barriers to keep the goddess at bay.

"You're glowing again," Esmelle said softly. "It's not like you to lose control. What's happening?"

"It's Lachlina," Sabine said. "For now, let's just say these so-called guardians have manipulated Theoria's gift for their own ends. They're trying to turn Rika into one of them."

"What are you talking about? Dryads are born, not made."

"Not always," Sabine said, pressing her hand against the ground and sending a reassuring wave of power throughout the land. The trees unfurled with new growth, and the green of the leaves deepened until a threading of silver veins once again appeared.

Blossom crawled out from underneath the leaf where she'd been hiding. The pixie brushed small flecks of dirt off her pink dress and looked over her shoulder to inspect her wings for damage. She gave Sabine a thumb's up sign and flew into the air.

With a relieved sigh, Sabine straightened. "When there's a remarkable need, the land can transform a sympathetic human into a guardian through a ritual. If they're successful, Rika will become part of the root system anchoring this grove to Aeslion. I can't allow that to happen. She'll be tied to *every* sentient forest remaining throughout the world."

Esmelle's brow furrowed. "To what end?"

"Should any tree or plant in any of their forests be harmed, I'll have a duty to defend them unto death. If Blossom told them Rika was under my protection, they may be looking to capitalize on that oath."

Esmelle bristled. "Okay, not only is that wrong, but Rika's a seer. Magic doesn't affect her like a typical human."

"Normally, you'd be right. They must have found a loophole."

"Can't we just blast the stupid thing apart?" Esmelle asked, glaring at the barrier.

Blossom waved her hands to get Sabine's attention. Her

image shimmered brightly. The pixie reformed a moment later as a tiny hooded skeletal figure wielding a staff.

Sabine stared in shock. "The Huntsman?"

Blossom changed her illusion back to herself. She staggered in midair and plummeted toward the ground, narrowly stopping the impact before she crashed. She spun around and landed belly first on the ground, her wings twitching before going completely still. She crossed her eyes and stuck her tongue out of the side of her mouth. A second later she made a face and spit out dirt, scrubbing at her tongue with a vengeance. With a look of annoyance, she flung herself back on the ground, resuming her dramatic death scene.

"Has she gone mad?" Esmelle asked, staring at the pixie. "Is the nectar more potent here or something?"

Blossom opened one eye to find them still watching her. She gestured to the barrier again before snatching up a nearby piece of clover. The pixie rolled over onto her back, holding the clover over her chest as a burial bouquet. She huffed and nodded toward the barrier expectantly.

"She's trying to warn us against bringing down the barrier," Sabine said with a frown. What Blossom was suggesting was beyond far-fetched, but it had the ring of truth. "I think she's trying to tell us this is another doorway, not a ward designed to keep us out."

"What? You got all that from Blossom's weird dance?"

Sabine nodded. "Blossom can't cross the threshold because it's forbidden, not because of any lack on her part."

"I'm still not following."

Sabine studied the shimmering barrier more carefully. If this was truly a doorway, she'd never seen one so large. The amount of power needed to sustain it was staggering. "The Huntsman made Blossom swear not to manipulate any doorways for one lunar cycle. I'm forbidden from doing the same."

Esmelle frowned. "But we came through a doorway to get here. So did Blossom."

"It was an established crossroads doorway," Sabine explained. "The guardians anchor the forest doorways around the world, allowing access to the grove from any location under their control. They always take some of our magic in exchange for passage."

Sabine paused, considering the implications. The dryads didn't possess enough power to do this on their own. If they had primarily used Sabine's excess magic to move part of the grove, she would be feeling far weaker. Something else was powering it. Something forbidden.

"You've thought of something else, haven't you?"

"This is speculation on my part," Sabine said. "Rika's mortal, and her resistance to magic makes her unsuitable for their purposes. By moving her farther betwixt, to a place between life and death, they've stripped her defenses and opened her up to the magic of the universe. Only a great source of power could have moved part of this grove."

"They didn't get all this magic from either one of us," Esmelle said, her expression turning thoughtful. "What are you thinking?"

Sabine relaxed her eyes, staring into the barrier. A hazy and hooded figure loomed at the edge of her vision. As soon as she tried to focus on it, the image wavered and disappeared. A cold chill rushed through her, stealing her breath.

The Huntsman was observing them, and he was furious. Whatever these dryads had done to move the grove had invoked his wrath, as well as Lachlina's fury.

After Sabine had met with him in the underworld, he'd told her the Wild Hunt would not pass beyond the boundaries controlled by the Sky Cities. They couldn't take a chance the dragons would learn his identity. In truth, he was the god Vestior, one of the Tuatha Dé who had stood by his brethren while they waged war upon the dragons. Vestior, in his Huntsman guise, wouldn't have appeared now unless the situation was dire.

Sabine turned to Esmelle and spoke quietly and urgently. "I need your oath, Esme. Swear to me, by blood and magic, that anything you learn, see, hear, or experience while we remain outside of our reality must remain a closely guarded secret."

"You know I would never betray you."

Sabine grabbed her hand and said, "I cannot protect you unless you swear to me. There are things at play that are beyond my ability to ward against. For the sake of our friendship, I need your sworn oath."

Esmelle shivered as though a cold wind settled over her shoulders, but she nodded. "I, Esmelle of Northwood, swear by blood and magic that anything I learn, see, hear, or experience while we remain outside of our reality, or within this grove, shall remain a closely guarded secret."

Wild magic swirled around them, acknowledging Esmelle's spoken words. Sabine blew out the breath she'd been holding. For good or ill, it was done. At least Esmelle now had a chance to survive what was to come.

"When I traveled to the underworld, I visited the Well of Dreams and drank of its power," Sabine explained. "The dryads must have discovered that connection and are somehow pulling magic directly from the Well. It's the only thing left in our world that has enough power to break apart reality. Unfortunately, its magic is dwindling. The sooner the Well is exhausted, the sooner our world will die."

"You're serious?"

Sabine nodded.

Esmelle narrowed her eyes. "Oh, hell no. I don't care what

excuses they have. They're supposed to be guarding the forests, not endangering the rest of the world. We need to get Rika out of there and stop them."

Sabine gathered her power, the glow of her skin cutting through the surrounding shadows. "On that, we're in agreement. They made a serious mistake by moving her to a place between life and death. No matter what restrictions have been placed upon me regarding doorways, it's my *duty* to restore the balance."

"What can I do to help?"

Sabine's magic faltered at Esmelle's words. Despite her heritage, Esmelle was still mortal. "You need to leave before I attempt this."

Esmelle stared at her in surprise. "What?"

"Return the same way we came," Sabine said. "The doorway back to the forest should open for you. If you warn Malek and Bane, they may be able to stop me before I go too far." She touched the marks on her wrist, trying to shake off the foreboding sensation. "If I tap into my full strength without a buffer, I may not be able to recall myself."

"You're talking about using those marks, aren't you?" Esmelle asked, gesturing to Sabine's wrist.

"Not intentionally, but when my interests align with Lachlina's wishes, the boundaries between us blur. It's dangerous, but I can't utilize my full strength without drawing upon her power."

"No," Esmelle said, her tone firm and unyielding. "I may have been a mess back in that forest when you were trying to talk me down, but I'm not blind. I know something's going on with those marks. I'm not willing to give the goddess any more opportunities. We'll do this ourselves."

Sabine hesitated. She'd seen this stubborn glint in her friend's eyes countless times back in Akros. When the street children had needed help, Esmelle had been a fierce protector and advocate on their behalf. Now that Rika was in trouble, Sabine knew nothing less than physically removing Esmelle from the grove would stop her from trying to help.

"This will be incredibly dangerous, especially for you. Even if I help shield your mind, you'll be standing against the combined strength of twelve dryads with centuries of experience. If you waver in your resolve, even for a moment, you'll lose control of the magic. This grove may not survive if that happens. Neither will you."

Esmelle frowned at the barrier. "Nothing like a little pressure, right?"

Sabine took a step closer and said, "If you have any doubts, I'll do this on my own. I'm not willing to lose one friend in an effort to save another."

"And I'm not willing to lose you to an angry goddess," Esmelle said, crossing her arms over her chest. "Now stop stalling. Tell me what I need to do."

"Very well." Sabine nodded at Esmelle's fierce determination. "Take off your shoes. You'll be stronger if you connect with the land. Until the dryads recover from the interruption of their ritual, you'll be the only thing standing in defense of this grove. It needs to feel your touch. The contact should also help to keep you grounded."

Esmelle quickly kicked off her shoes. Sabine reached over and traced a protective rune on Esmelle's forehead, infusing her magic into the symbol. In the language of Faerie, she murmured the words for resolve and focus. The rune glowed briefly before fading from view, but the enchantment would linger for some time. She prayed to whatever gods might still be listening that it would be enough.

Esmelle reached up to touch her forehead. "Any other last-minute advice?"

"The timing will be critical," Sabine said, unsheathing her blade. "Just focus on directing my power into the barrier. As soon as you feel the barrier weakening, you *must* break contact with it. If I shatter the bindings while you're touching it, you'll be caught in the magic."

"Gods," Esmelle muttered, glancing at Sabine's knife in annoyance. "We're doing the cutting and rhyming thing, aren't we?"

Sabine smiled. "All magic requires a sacrifice, and rhyming helps focus your intent."

"Yeah, but just once I'd like to help you perform major magic without having to open a vein or pull a rhyme out of thin air. Did I ever tell you I ran away from the orphanage before I finished school? They made me recite awful rhymes too." Esmelle straightened her shoulders. "Fine. I'll wing it. Let's do this."

Sabine pressed the tip of the blade against her finger. She pierced her skin, watching as her offering welled to the surface. Three drops of blood fell to the ground.

The air stilled, creating an uneasy silence in the glade. Sabine passed Esmelle the knife and watched her repeat the gesture. The moss under their feet began to shift. Small tendrils of vines emerged from the ground, gently weaving around Sabine and Esmelle's legs.

Sabine sheathed the blade and took Esmelle's outstretched hand. Threading her voice with power, Sabine called out, "By blood and by magic, we align our purposes into one. By will and by might, we return that which must be undone."

The wind began to blow, softly at first and then building with power. Sabine's silvery hair whipped away from her face. An eerie howl filled the air, and a strange green glow filled the forest.

Esmelle pressed her hand against the barrier and shouted into the wind, "Our powers and wills are merged, bound with friendship and love. I am the vessel, directing the power at hand." She paused, her nose wrinkling. "We stand as guardians, in protection of the land."

Sabine winced at the terrible rhyme. It wasn't the worst she'd ever heard, but it was close. She reminded herself it wasn't so much the words as it was the intention. Without Esmelle being able to invoke the ancient language of the fae, this was the best they could do under the circumstances.

The trees above them shook, the branches trembling at the raw power filling the air. Sabine reached for the magic contained in the depths of the soil that gave the trees and flowers life. Infusing it with the Huntsman's death magic, she took a deep breath and allowed the pressure within her to build. Her skin began to glow, softly at first, and then building with intensity. The power of life and death clashed within her, threatening to overflow.

"*Valithen,*" Sabine shouted, sending a tidal wave of power through Esmelle and directly into the barrier.

Esmelle screamed, arching her back as magic ripped through her. The ground rumbled. Deep spidery chasms erupted from the earth, creating a starburst pattern around the barrier. Sabine could feel the dryads turning their attention to Esmelle.

"Keep going!" Esmelle shouted, tears streaming down her face. "I've got this. You can't let them have Rika!"

Trusting Esmelle at her word, Sabine took a deep breath and called upon even more power at her command. She pulled on her ties to both Malek and Bane, using their magic to strengthen her focus. She combined the strength of her bloodline with the ancient power that had first formed this grove, sending all of it toward Esmelle. The greenish barrier began to thin, its surface bubbling and wrinkling. She took everything she had and sent it outward in a blinding blast.

"Now, Sabine!" Esmelle screamed, yanking her hands away as though they burned. "Hurry!"

CHAPTER 7

Malek paced back and forth, his gaze drifting between the tree where Sabine had disappeared and upwards to search for approaching adversaries. So far, the skies remained clear but that could change at a moment's notice. He shook his head at the waste of life that still littered the ground. He'd planned on purging the bodies with dragonfire, but Bane had stopped him.

The demon claimed Sabine would need their sacrifice to negotiate with the forest guardians. Malek wasn't sure what that meant, and Bane was being characteristically tightlipped about providing an explanation. There were countless facets of Sabine's magic that remained a mystery. He had to trust she knew what she was doing.

A tremendous surge of power flooded through Malek, nearly bringing him to his knees. It was even stronger than the last wave a short time ago. His thoughts filled with Sabine, until he could almost feel her beside him. His vision blurred for a moment, and he could have sworn he smelled the faintest trace of night-blooming flowers that always surrounded her.

An overwhelming sense of urgency and determination filled him as Sabine's emotions spilled across their bond. Her power slammed into him and merged with his own before being yanked away, directed elsewhere. He staggered at the sudden loss, reaching for a nearby tree to steady himself.

Something was wrong. She never would have resorted to using such power twice in a short time and risking Lachlina taking control again unless the need was dire.

"What is it?" Levin demanded, taking a step toward him.

"Sabine's in trouble," he said, pushing away from the tree and racing toward the place where she'd disappeared. He had to get to her before it was too late.

Bane grabbed his wrist before he made contact with the tree. "You cannot force your way into the sacred grove. That way lies madness. I feel her pull as well, but you must resist. Sabine will survive whatever obstacles she's facing there, but it's unlikely she'll survive your loss. She needs you and your magic, dragon. You must not do this."

Malek yanked his hand away from the demon. "You've been to the grove before. How did you enter?"

"I have not," Bane bit out, the admission obviously something he wasn't inclined to share. "I have met with and summoned dryads to various forests, but their grove has been off-limits to all but the sidhe since the portal was sealed. Theoria's sacrifice enabled the grove's protections, and none may enter except by invitation."

Sabine pulled again on his magic, even harder this time. Bane's eyes and horns turned a brilliant silver. A fierce snarl ripped from the demon's throat, his claws extended. The magic left both of them abruptly. They staggered from the sudden loss.

"She's using too much power," Bane said in a low growl, leaving clawed score marks against the tree. He clenched his hands and pounded against the bark.

"Knock it off," Levin snapped. "We can't damage the forest!"

Bane whirled toward Levin, fury blazing in his silver gaze. "Make demands of me again, lizard, and I'll shove your tail down your throat."

Malek could relate to his frustration. The urge to go to Sabine was clouding his thoughts and instincts. Everything within him warned he had to reach her or risk losing her forever. With every pull of power, he felt pieces of her being stripped away. He had to stop her before she went too far. If she lost consciousness again, she'd be vulnerable to all sorts of potential dangers.

"I retract my earlier statement, dragon. Sabine would not draw power from us, unless there was a dire need. I still say the dryads won't harm her, but I cannot imagine what would cause her to deplete our remaining strength so soon after an attack. Sabine is neither careless, nor a fool. If you have a way of breaking the barriers to the grove, I will not stop you."

"I'm not worried about the damn dryads," Malek bit out and slapped his hands against the tree. "It's that bitch of a goddess that has me concerned."

He opened the bond he shared with Sabine completely, allowing his thoughts and mind to merge with hers. He let out a shout as pain and agony lanced through him. The tree glimmered green and red and the leaves began to curl from smoke.

"Malek, no!" Levin shouted.

Malek ignored Levin, dimly aware Bane was pulling Levin away. Instead, he pushed forward, determined to break through the boundary he could sense at the edge of his thoughts.

Dragonfire exploded from his fingertips as Malek tore a rift through reality. In a blinding burst of light, he shed his human skin and burst through the jagged doorway he'd created. Darkness surrounded him, but he ignored it and focused on his destination: Sabine.

"Hold!"

The mental command pummeled against him with enough force that each of Malek's scales reverberated from the force of the shout. He whipped his head in the direction of the voice, prepared to strike. A hooded figure appeared in the darkness, his skeletal hand wrapped around an unusual staff Malek recognized. Malek huffed, smoky tendrils curling upward in the air as he unfurled his wings. Lightning raged around the two of them, threatening to strike.

"Huntsman," Malek said, focusing on the golden light surrounding the figure. It was similar to the glow of Sabine's skin since she'd begun absorbing the artifacts. When he peered between the shadows and golden light, Malek caught a hint of something else beneath the surface. It was almost as though a type of glamour surrounded the Huntsman.

The ground solidified beneath his feet, but Malek somehow knew it was an illusion. They had to be in the in-between. That strange oddness permeated the air, making it unnecessary to breathe. Even his body felt peculiar, out of sync somehow. It was almost as though something fundamental was missing within him. The urgency to find Sabine was still there, but it had lessened somehow. She was close. He wasn't sure how he knew that, but he could feel her like a second heartbeat.

The two regarded each other for a long time before the Huntsman spoke again. *"She is unharmed."*

Disconcerted with the ease the Huntsman used mind-touch to communicate, Malek said, *"I will see for myself."*

"Then See," the Huntsman said, striking the staff on the makeshift ground with a peal of thunder. A shimmering green glow erupted from behind the Huntsman. He stepped

aside to allow Malek a hazy view of what appeared to be some sort of clearing. A large tree stood in the center of the image while a dozen women surrounded it.

Rika was laying on the ground beneath the tree. Her image was out of focus, as though she wasn't quite there. Malek hadn't thought Rika had been harmed during the attack, but if something had happened, that might explain why Sabine was pulling such vast amounts of power. He searched the image for any sign of the woman he loved.

A rush of relief went through him at the sight of Sabine standing a short distance away. She was whole and unharmed. Her features were still hers, a sign Lachlina hadn't taken her over. But she was too pale, exhaustion etched across her delicate features.

Sabine's skin glowed with that brilliant golden hue as though she were performing some sort of major magic. It pulsed against the soft green that surrounded Esmelle. Somehow, the two of them were connected and performing a magical working together.

Malek took a step toward the grove, but lightning struck the ground in front of him. The Huntsman held up a skeletal hand and warned, *"There is a cost to entering."*

Malek narrowed his eyes. *"You dare try to keep her from me?"*

"None may enter the Heartwood without paying a price. Yours will be dear, and likely far more than you are willing to pay." The Huntsman rested both of his hands on top of his walking staff, his glowing red eyes focused solely on Malek. *"Should you force entry into the grove, that way will be forever sealed to you and your kind. Moreover, it will wither and die, for your kind cannot abide a place of creation."*

Malek studied the Huntsman, weighing the veracity of his words. *"If Sabine is in danger, I* will *enter the grove. No matter the cost."*

The Huntsman didn't respond right away. Instead, he looked beyond the greenish glow and in Sabine's direction. *"Like the rest of your kind, there are few places I am forbidden to travel. The Heartwood is one of them. Theoria chose this location as her final sacrifice, knowing that none could stop her. She could have chosen a different life, one beyond the boundaries of the mortal realm. But she chose death over losing her ties to Aeslion."*

He turned back to regard Malek with piercing red eyes. *"Sabine was offered a similar choice, and like Theoria, she chose to remain bound to the land. If you force entry into the Heartwood, you will sunder its last anchors to Aeslion. Or do you seek to unmake Sabine's choice for her, dragon?"*

Malek's gaze sharpened on the Huntsman. Sabine had told him what transpired when she'd nearly died back in Razadon. The Huntsman had offered her a place at his side and in the in-between, rather than risking certain death. She'd refused his offer, trusting in Malek to save her. It had been the first time she'd fully opened her heart to him, sharing the depth of her feelings and binding them together irrevocably.

He didn't know anything about these anchors or the consequences the Huntsman claimed, but he would do nothing to endanger Sabine. If there was a chance she'd be trapped in the grove or possibly killed, he would wait—no matter how difficult the thought might be.

"Sabine's choices are her own. She wished to live and remain by my side. I will stop at nothing to ensure that future with her. However, she is not fully in control of her actions. Lachlina's influence grows stronger." He paused, considering the Huntsman. *"Will you guarantee Sabine's safety from Lachlina?"*

A storm rumbled overhead. The Huntsman was quiet for so long that Malek wasn't sure he would answer. Malek exhaled, emitting another stream of smoke. The longer he waited, the more his sense of urgency grew. It was imperative they find a way to break the chains binding Lachlina to Sabine. Malek had hoped the Huntsman might provide some answers. Barring that, he intended to seek a resolution among his people. They might not be as strong as they once were, but dragon magic was no small thing.

"The bond between them is one that even I cannot break. It may only be severed by mutual agreement and without malice, or else the balance will fracture."

Malek growled low in his throat. *"Then you leave me with little choice, Huntsman. Each time Sabine draws upon Lachlina's power, she falls deeper into her thrall. I will not allow that to happen, even if I must enter the grove to save her from herself."*

"Then you doom your own kind, dragon, as well as the woman you claim to love."

"You speak in riddles," Malek snapped. *"Explain. And make it quick."*

"You must seek answers from your own kind, dragon. The Elders among you know well the consequences of violating the protections of the grove. It is their shared fate you gamble with if you force entry."

Malek blew out a breath, sending more tendrils of smoke outward. He'd never heard of the grove before now, nor had Levin. He doubted the Huntsman was all that concerned over the fate of his people. But his interest and fixation on Sabine was worrisome. Even among his people, the Wild Hunt was spoken of with no small measure of respect. Every time Malek seemed to turn around, the Huntsman was nearby, his attention singularly focused on Sabine.

Malek eyed the Huntsman suspiciously. *"What is your interest in her? Who is Sabine to you?"*

Lightning struck the ground in rapid succession. The Huntsman turned away from Sabine and once again focused his glowing red gaze on Malek. The look would have chilled a human to the bone. Fortunately, he wasn't human.

"She is presently in no danger. That is all you need to know. Once her business is concluded, she will be returned to the forest. I suggest you do the same. The longer you remain in this realm, the weaker the anchors become."

The Huntsman's form began to mist, becoming less corporeal somehow.

Malek snarled, steam rising once again. Dragon smoke encircled the Huntsman, clinging to his robe and preventing him from fully disappearing. *"I will have your oath that you will safeguard Sabine from all danger while she is in the grove, or I will wait here until she departs. I will not trust her safety to anyone who refuses to make such an oath."* He narrowed his eyes, letting the full force of his magic swirl around him like a maelstrom. *"And should any harm befall her, then your precious anchors be damned. It won't only be the grove that pays the price."*

The Huntsman regarded him with a weighted gaze. *"Very well, dragon. You may remain and observe. It will be interesting to discover which of your loyalties will win out in the end."*

With a wave of his skeletal hand, the Huntsman shrugged off Malek's smoke as easily as a cape. He disappeared from view, but Malek could still sense him somewhere nearby. He ignored the sensation and focused again on the hazy image of the woman he loved. Bane had said she'd come to no harm from the forest guardians and the Huntsman claimed the same thing. He trusted in her and her abilities, but if she needed him, he intended to be at her side.

No matter the cost.

CHAPTER 8

Sabine brought her hands together with a thunderous clap. Lightning shot down from the sky, striking the barrier and shattering it. Magic exploded in all directions, flinging the dryads backward and knocking them to the ground. Only she and Esme remained standing, protected by the ties to the land in their reality. They were both shaky, buzzing with exhilaration from channeling so much power. A few months ago, Sabine never would have been able to perform such a feat.

Blossom surfed the air current on an oak leaf that had shaken loose with the blast. She hopped off the leaf and landed lightly on Sabine's shoulder. "Perfect strike, Sabine! Way to go, Esme! Dryad bowling for the win!"

Esmelle wobbled. Sabine wrapped her arm around Esme's waist before she could fall. "Are you all right?"

Esme gave out a breathless laugh. "I'll live. But next time, you can direct the power. I'm a little too human to survive doing that very often. And for the sake of all the gods and their kin, no more rhyming."

"You stood against twelve full-blooded dryads," Sabine

reminded her with a laugh. "I'd say you're not as human as you think."

"Guess I've been elevated into badass territory," Esme said with a grin. She straightened and took a small step forward. She was still a little unsteady but rapidly finding her equilibrium.

"What about you?" Sabine asked Blossom, sending a trace of power over the pixie. "Are you hurt?"

Blossom trilled in delight. "Nope. They were happy to see me at first. It's been a long time since a pixie entered their grove. But they were more interested in Rika and how you were sworn to protect her. That's when things got weird." She cocked her head, her expression turning thoughtful. "You know, if you turned me into a dragon, you wouldn't have to keep rescuing Rika all the time. I could make everyone do whatever I tell them."

Esme snorted. "That's a scary thought."

Sabine made a noncommittal noise. The pixie would likely end up in even worse trouble running around with a dragon illusion.

"Tell me what happened here," Sabine said, stepping across the demarcation line. The dryads had crumpled to the ground in a circle around the oak tree. Most of them were dazed or unconscious, but that wouldn't last long.

"Right. Dragon talk later," Blossom said, gripping a handful of Sabine's hair. "I think something's wrong with the dryads. They mentioned corruption and said they had to protect their heart. When the guardians found out you were coming here, some of them started panicking and saying you were here to destroy them. I tried to tell them it wasn't true, but they wouldn't believe me."

Esme's eyebrow rose. "What? Why in the world would they think that?"

Blossom shrugged. "The trees carried the warning to

them. I don't know who sent the message, but I think it was someone back in Faerie. They said as long as they had another dryad to anchor the grove, you might forgive them for failing. That's when they moved part of the sacred grove to the in-between and started to fuse Rika to the tree."

Sabine shook her head in confusion. "None of this makes any sense."

Blossom whispered, "The Huntsman might not be happy you manipulated the in-between before the month was up."

"I suspect it won't be an issue," Sabine said in a low voice. They were close to the dryads, and she didn't want any careless remarks to be overheard. "I had a duty to restore the balance, even if that necessitated finding a loophole. If he claims we violated the agreement, we'll deal with it later."

"Sneaky," Blossom said with a grin. "That's why you provided the power and had Esme target the barrier. His edict didn't apply to her."

Sabine nodded and turned her attention back to the dryads. Their fear troubled her. Naturally shy creatures, they usually preferred the solitude of their forests and avoided fae politics. Their main focus was tending the plants they loved. By taking a stand against her, they'd been drawn into a game they couldn't hope to win. Sabine didn't want to destroy them, but she might not have a choice if they tried to turn the grove against her.

"What do they have wrapped around her?" Esme asked, crouching beside the giant oak tree. Rika was slumped beside it, the strange tether still tied around her waist. She'd stopped fighting against the restraint, which didn't bode well.

Sabine kneeled beside Rika, studying the unconscious seer and the strange root wrapped around her. Rika was still breathing, but her image was nearly transparent. Sabine held out her hand, allowing it to hover over the girl's body. Her life essence was fading, almost too far gone to detect. The tether was some sort of root system, and it had begun growing through Rika's midsection. Cutting her out would be impossible. Her human form was too fragile to survive the process.

"They lost one of their sisters when the wyverns attacked," Blossom said solemnly. "Rika didn't want to become a dryad, so they enthralled her with rabithyn pollen. She was trying to fight it, until she slipped out of reality a few minutes ago. Can you fix her?"

Sabine frowned and studied the root more closely, careful not to touch it or Rika. The glade might have been returned to its proper reality, but Rika's essence was still tied to the oak and trapped in the beyond. She needed to convince the dryads it was in their best interest to relinquish their claim on the human seer.

Sabine stood and leaned close to Esme. In a voice low enough not to be overheard, she murmured, "I can't release her without causing irreparable harm. I'm not sure she'll survive the attempt. For now, she's simply in an enchanted sleep. The dryads can reverse the process, but we have to convince them it's in their best interest."

A flicker of worry drifted across Esme's face, but she nodded her agreement. "I'll follow your lead."

Sabine approached one of the fallen dryads. The woman's skin was the palest of greens, marred only by the dark woody patches on her elbows and palms. Her features were as delicate as any fae, but she could never be accused as such.

Her colorful gown was made from hundreds of leaves, and it rustled softly as she rose. Leaves and vines cascaded down her back like hair, forming curls to frame her striking face. On her head and anchored by small antlers, she wore a crown of pale white flowers, a symbol of her elevated position among the dryads. A large glowing acorn hung between her breasts, the necklace swaying with her movement.

"Greetings, Your Highness," the dryad said, dropping into a graceful curtsey before Sabine. "We welcome you to our sacred grove, and ask forgiveness for any offenses we have caused."

Sabine paused, surprised by the dryad's quick apology. "What is your name?"

The dryad lifted her head, meeting Sabine's gaze briefly. "I am called Aconi, Your Highness. As always, my sisters and I live to serve the needs of the land."

Two other dryads rose to their feet and slowly approached them, their sensual movements reminiscent of an ancient fertility dance. They both held a striking resemblance to Aconi, with large mossy green eyes filled with a combination of worry and fear. Like Aconi, the newcomers' gowns were a waterfall of colorful leaves and flowers that swirled around their legs as they moved. It reminded Sabine of the endearing rainbow skirts Esme was fond of wearing.

"My eldest sisters," Aconi said softly, gesturing to the two women as they bowed before Sabine. "Clovea and Viola guard the sacred grove with me. We hold the anchors, while the rest of our sisters nurture the land."

Clovea wore a crown of clover in her hair, while Viola wore a wreath of purple flowers. They each shared similar glowing acorn necklaces. Sabine glanced at the other dryads, noting that each one wore a crown of flowers or herbs which likely represented their namesakes. While they were all lovely, each one cowered or averted their gaze from Sabine as though terrified to fall under her scrutiny.

Gentleness was called for, she decided. Until now, she'd never had the opportunity to travel to the grove. Despite their actions, these dryads were hers to care for, and she wouldn't begin her rule engendering her subjects with fear.

She'd experienced firsthand how destructive such abuses could be.

"Rise, Aconi," Sabine said, holding out her hand to Aconi and then to her sisters. At their touch, the song of the grove soared to life within Sabine. It spoke of its sorrow in losing one of their beloved sisters, their mutual love and respect for the land, and the crippling fear the dragonfire had evoked when it devoured their precious trees. The memory of the intense heat had sent shockwaves throughout the grove, and its echo rippled across the world. Although the war had occurred more than a millennium ago, the land remembered.

Guilt weighed heavily on Sabine. She would have to repay the debt she owed for her part in the destruction. But first, she needed to ease their worries.

Sabine met each of their remarkable powers with her own, surrounding them with the softer emotions of kindness, peace, and love. Her magic called out to the land, its harmony blending with hers and encompassing the dryads as the echo of their combined powers swept through the grove. For one perfect moment, she was as entwined with the land as each of the dryads. She felt the purity of their spirit and shared hers with them.

At the touch of Sabine's magic, the dryads began to weep, their amber tears streaking down their cheeks. As one, they lowered their heads in obeisance.

"You honor us, Your Highness," Aconi said, her voice filled with awe and reverence. "Though our forest weeps from its loss, our hearts rejoice at your arrival. We were misinformed of your intentions, for your magic is pure and free from the corruption permeating the land."

"That's why you moved part of the grove to the in-between?" Sabine asked, relieved the dryads hadn't sought to force her hand.

Aconi nodded. "We beg your forgiveness, Your Highness.

There is a blight upon the land. We have battled it as best as we could, but our numbers are few. We grow weaker with each passing season while the corruption strengthens. Our sisters were summoned here to protect the heart of the grove, our last line of defense. When we felt the dragons attack and your arrival, our sister returned to her forest to offer you aid. She was struck down before she could reach you."

Sabine's heart clenched. No matter their intention, they couldn't be allowed to draw upon the power of the Well. But something needed to be done to resolve their plight. If the corruption was allowed to penetrate into the heart of this place, it would spread throughout the world, infecting every part of the land touched by the sacred grove.

"My heart mourns for your loss," Sabine said quietly. "While I cannot return your lost sister to you, I ask you to accept the slain wyverns as recompense for the damage caused to the land. Allow them to nurture the forests and heal the land once more, so the cycle may once again begin anew."

Aconi lowered her head. "Your offer is gracious beyond measure. My other sisters will see the forest healed until we can appoint a new guardian to take her place."

"I heard your song," Esme said, moving to stand beside Sabine. "I hadn't realized you still protected the forests, or I might have sought you out sooner. I thought you'd all retreated from Aeslion."

Aconi regarded Esmelle with a small smile and shook her head. "Nay, little sister. A few still keep watch. We remain in hiding to preserve our dwindling numbers. We call to our kin, but our voices are softer than they once were."

Sabine gestured to Esme and said, "This is Esmelle of Northwood, known by those who love her as Esme."

Clovea took a step forward and beamed a smile at Esme.

"We rejoice at the return of one of our youngest sisters. Although, she was once known to us by another name."

"What?" Esme asked, regarding the dryad in surprise.

"Indeed. You were born in this grove, beneath the boughs of the sacred oak and gifted with the name, Camille. You were merely a day old when you were sent out into the world."

Blossom's eyes widened. "I knew it! I always thought you smelled like a flower! Wait until Barley hears about this!"

"Wait, what?" Esme interrupted, shaking her head. "Camille? The name's familiar, but I could have sworn I've only ever been called Esme."

"Esme," Clovea said the name as though it tasted odd on her tongue. "Your mother named you Camille, in honor of your red curls and the flowers that bloomed upon your birth. If you were gifted another name when you were taken to the human city, we have no knowledge of such."

With a wave of Clovea's hand, a wreath of red camellia flowers appeared on Esmelle's head.

Esme reached up, touching the wreath gingerly. "It's a crown of flowers, isn't it?"

"It becomes you," Sabine said with a smile. "Many of those with ties to the dryads return to the sacred grove to give birth. The land hides the child's magic, binding their power until they come of age. They are then taken beyond the forest boundaries to be raised by others."

Aconi bowed her head. "It is not by choice, for we would nurture all our children if we could. But they are safer out in the world than in our forests."

Esmelle lowered her hand and frowned. "Why? If your numbers are so few, why would you send them to live among humans?"

"With so few forests left, each dryad lives in constant

danger of being discovered," Sabine said quietly. "Their magic is like yours. It's nurturing and sympathetic, given more to defending the land against natural predators or healing ailments. If anyone had discovered your talents when you were young, you wouldn't have been able to protect yourself."

Esmelle stared at her in shock. "You knew all of this?"

Sabine shook her head. "No, or I would have tried to bring you here sooner. I knew you had dryad blood, but I didn't realize you'd been born in the grove. Apparently, the land masked your power a little too well."

"Some of our children were sent to live among the fae, but their ways are not ours," Clovea said, her eyes glistening again with amber tears. "While they were cared for when they were young, they did not have the defensive capabilities needed to survive adulthood. Many of our children are now raised by humans. As they grow, some hear the call of the land and return to the sacred glade to embrace their dryad heritage. Only then can the bindings harnessing their power be lifted."

Esmelle swallowed. "You're saying I could become one of you?"

Aconi nodded. "Yes, little sister. The land would rejoice at your return."

Blossom tugged on Sabine's hair and whispered, "Make her stop, Sabine. Don't let them turn Esme into a tree. She wouldn't be happy. You know she wouldn't."

Sabine reached out and grasped Esmelle's hand. "Consider carefully, Esme. Once done, it cannot be undone. A dryad's power is no small thing and cannot be contained in your mortal form. You'll be bound to this grove, your soul embraced by the land, and become both more and less than what you are now."

Aconi tilted her head in acknowledgment. "Queen

Sabin'theoria speaks truth. But there is a great need for another anchor. Will you ignore the call of the land?"

Blossom flew onto Esmelle's shoulder and said, "Don't do it, Esme. Think about Levin. Think about opening another shop. You loved helping your customers back in Akros."

Esme frowned and glanced over at Rika. "If I do this, will they release Rika?"

"No," Sabine interjected, holding up her hand to stop Esme. "If you want to do this, make sure it's right for *you*. Rika is my ward, and as such, it's my responsibility to negotiate for her release."

Aconi studied Sabine thoughtfully. "You wish us to release the young human?"

Sabine nodded. "I do."

"Nay," Clovea said, reaching for Aconi. "We need her, sister. If our Esme refuses to heed our call, we must have another to act as anchor. The young one entered our grove willingly and embraced the spirit of the oak. Her heart is pure and untouched by the corruption that plagues many humans."

Aconi clasped her sister's hand and turned back to Sabine, her eyes pleading. "Do not ask this of us, Your Highness. Without suitable anchors to sustain the life of the grove, all our forests will wither. Our magic is not strong enough to penetrate cities of dead wood and stone. If any of our sisters hear our call, they do not answer. Dozens of us once guarded this glade, but we now number three while the rest tend their forests."

Sabine looked at Aconi in surprise. "So few?"

Aconi nodded. "The three of us act as anchors, but our sisters often visit our grove to rejuvenate themselves and renew their bonds. It wasn't until the corruption entered our grove that we summoned our sisters home to protect our heart."

Sabine rubbed her temples. The Huntsman had warned her the corruption was spreading, a symptom of the world's imbalance. The Dragon Portal had to be reopened, or this blight would continue to spread like an infection.

The marks on her wrist warmed again. Lachlina wanted the grove protected at any cost. While the goddess may consider either Rika or Esme a suitable sacrifice, Sabine didn't. In times past, the dryads had either called their children home or lured lost humans to embrace the magic of the land. The forest guardians could be masters of seduction, if given the opportunity.

Sabine lifted her head to regard Aconi. "While I understand your need to guard the grove and replenish your numbers, you've attempted to claim a human under my protection. I cannot allow this to pass."

Blossom sighed. "I told you not to turn Rika into a tree. She's on a very important mission with Sabine."

"The pixie spoke truth?" Aconi asked, her face troubled. "A lesser fae speaks with your voice?"

Sabine held out her hand for Blossom to land. "Blossom is one of my most-trusted advisors. If she carries word or warning, it's with my voice."

Blossom put her hands on her hips and puffed out her chest. Her wings twitched, sending a light cloud of glittering pixie dust into the air.

Aconi and her sisters bowed low. "We have never heard of a lesser fae being elevated to such a status, but we will carry your words to the rest of the forests. The pixie and her clan shall be allowed to move through our forests unhindered."

Blossom tapped her finger against her chin. "Yeah? You know, we could help you out too. If your voices aren't loud enough to penetrate the human cities, we might be able to get close enough to spread the word. Pixies can move unseen pretty well."

A flash of hope crossed Viola's face. "Truly? The little ones are unhindered by steel and stone?"

Sabine sighed. "No, they're as hindered as any fae. But pixies are a curious and stubborn lot."

Blossom flew to Sabine's shoulder and whispered, "My brothers and sisters can help them, Sabine. I know we can! Make them free Rika, and we'll do it."

Sabine considered Blossom for a moment. It would be dangerous for them, but if she helped supplement their power, they could move through the cities relatively unharmed.

Turning back to Aconi, Sabine said, "If you agree to release Rika and sever all ties to her, Blossom and the rest of her siblings will help carry your voices to your lost children."

Aconi's eyes widened, staring at Sabine and Blossom with a mixture of hope and wonder. Her sisters mirrored Aconi's astonishment as they clasped hands.

The wind swirled around the sisters and teased their vined hair. Aconi's acorn pendant began to glow with a golden light. When she spoke, her musical voice filled with the power of the land. "From this day forward, all pixies carrying the essence of camellia flowers shall be allowed safe passage through any forests. Offerings will be left in designated places, to provide refreshment and to ease the burden of their travels."

At Aconi's gesture, Esme plucked one of the flowers from her crown and handed it to Blossom. The pixie grinned and exclaimed, "I can't wait to tell my brothers and sisters! My cousins can help too!"

Clovea stepped forward and said, "While the small, winged ones will attempt to carry our message, it does not resolve our immediate need. Without another sister to take Dahlia's place, Silverleaf Woods will fall outside of our influence. The forest will be lost to us forever."

"Silverleaf Forest is where we came from?" Esme asked.

Viola nodded. "It was named such long ago by Elis'andreia. In honor of her memory and sacrifice, we have safeguarded it as best as we could."

Sabine froze. Elis'andreia was the name of Malek's fae grandmother, who had been captured during the war. If the forest was her creation, Malek's family might be the reason it still remained while much of the land had been scorched during The Dragon War. She shook her head, unable to consider the implications at the moment.

Blossom's dress changed color to match the red of the camellia blossom she'd been given. A tiny wreath, similar to Esme's, appeared on the pixie's head. Sabine watched her adjust the wreath, mildly surprised it wasn't simply glamour. Blossom had grown exponentially in power after the underworld mishap.

The thought gave her pause.

Sabine lifted her head to regard the dryads. "I think I know how you can find another anchor sooner. Restore Rika, and we'll ensure your voices will once again soar throughout the land."

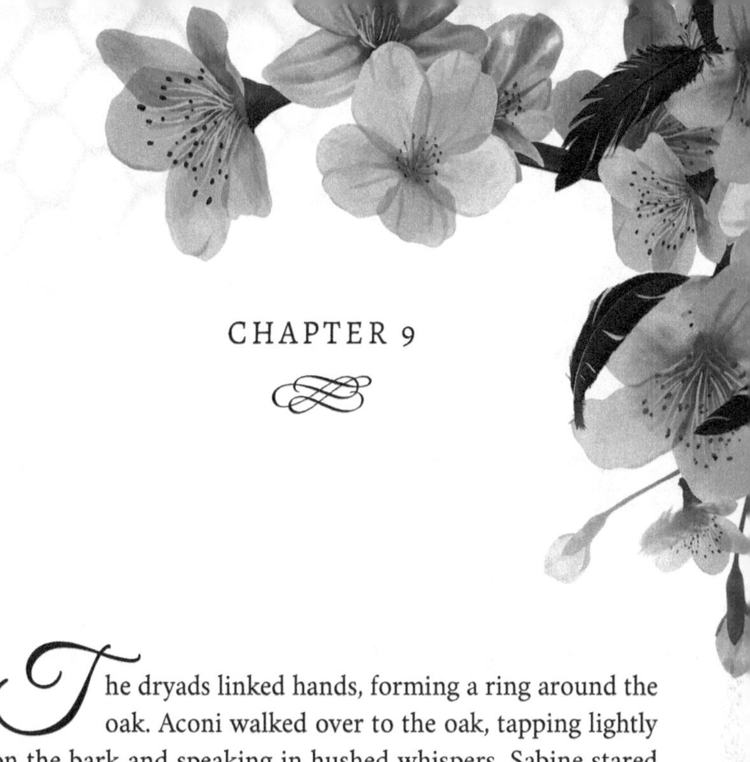

CHAPTER 9

The dryads linked hands, forming a ring around the oak. Aconi walked over to the oak, tapping lightly on the bark and speaking in hushed whispers. Sabine stared up at the tree, feeling a strange resonance every time Aconi knocked. She absently traced one of the marks of power etched into her arms. Her skin was almost vibrating as though responding to Aconi's call.

"What's she doing?" Esmelle asked quietly.

"Aconi is calling to Theoria, the spirit of the oak," Viola said, motioning for Esmelle to sit on the mossy ground beside Rika's body. "We must ask her to bless this rite, for our magic is not designed to reverse an awakening. We are simply guardians of this grove, entrusted and ordained by Theoria to nurture and protect the land in her stead."

"You sure this isn't going to hurt Rika?" Blossom asked, hovering over Rika's translucent body. "I mean, there's a tree growing right through her middle."

Viola shook her head. "Nay. With Theoria's guidance, we'll ensure the young human returns unharmed to this realm."

"Okay, good. Because there's an angry demon waiting for us who will be pretty irritated. Trust me. You don't want to make him mad."

Viola paled at Blossom's pronouncement.

Sabine shot Blossom a warning look. The last thing they needed was for the dryads to flee to their trees in safety. Linking arms with Viola, Sabine sent a reassuring wave of power over the forest guardian. "Esme is still learning much about her magic. She would benefit from your direction, Viola."

Esmelle nodded, quickly grasping the situation. "As long as you don't want me to rhyme, I'm pretty good at following instructions."

Viola seemed to collect herself.

The dryad placed her hand on Esmelle's shoulder and said, "The ties of blood bind us together, little sister. You must channel our collective power into the human child. With Queen Sabin'theoria's guidance, we will sever her ties to the Beyond. Once she's firmly in this reality, the rest of our sisters will be able to complete the task."

Esmelle held out both her hands over Rika and said, "All right. I think I'm ready."

"Stay strong, little sister," Viola said, taking her place among the ring of dryads. Aconi stepped away from the oak, the leaves of her skirt swirling around her ankles. She lifted her hands to the sky and looked up at the oak.

"And so it begins," Aconi said, her words echoing throughout the grove. "Awaken, Theoria. Hear our plea."

The dryads began to sing a wordless melody, their voices rising and falling in time with wind's gusts. The sound of the rustling leaves acted as an accompaniment to the dryads' song. As the wind strengthened, the magic of the dryads filled the air, cocooning the heart of the sacred grove with their power.

Sabine stepped forward and clasped hands with Aconi. Keeping a tight hold on her ties to Malek, Bane, and Lachlina, Sabine reached for her connection to the Well of Dreams. She felt Azran, the hellhound who safeguarded the Hall of Awakening, slip inside her thoughts. His presence was faint, the barest glimmer of awareness.

It startled her for a moment. Azran had warned that he wouldn't be able to reach her thoughts once she left the underworld. But the Veil here was already thin, weakened by the dryads' efforts to merge the grove and the in-between.

In her mind's eye, she saw the fiery hellhound race toward the Well. He lowered his head and took a long drink, the water temporarily quenching his flames and sending a surge of magic through Sabine.

"Be well, little goddess," Azran said, his mental voice touching her one last time before it slipped away.

"In all things, balance," Sabine whispered, slipping into the ancient tongue of the gods. Her skin began to glow a brilliant gold, each of her skin markings flaring with power. She harnessed the magic of the Well, using it as a conduit to illuminate the thin ribbons of power entwined around Rika like an elaborate root system.

Slowly and carefully, Sabine and the other dryads unwound each of the threads the dryads had used to tether Rika to the in-between. With each severed thread, Rika's essence was restored a little more. The dryads began to glow a soft green, their energies merging together and surrounding Rika and the ancient oak. The oak's gnarled roots retreated from Rika, relinquishing their claim on her.

"Speak to the young one, little sister," Aconi said in her musical voice. "Call her essence back to this realm. Remind her of the reasons she should return. We have little magic left to accomplish this task without your aid."

"Come back to us," Esmelle urged Rika, stroking the

seer's dark hair away from her face. "Remember who you are. Don't let the magic sweep you away. You're the Seer of Karga and destined for great things. Think of your home, of your family, of traveling with us. Think about all the wondrous adventures we've had so far and how many are yet to come. We miss you, Rika. We want you to come home."

Sabine felt Rika's struggle to surface, using Esmelle's coaxing to better unravel the tangled web keeping the young seer from being restored. The dryads worked faster, their song becoming almost frenzied as their magic faded.

"You have to come back, Rika," Blossom shouted, hovering over Rika. "Bane hasn't discovered that we switched the cooking spices yet. He'll eat me for sure if you're not there!"

Esmelle stared at Blossom for a moment before grinning. "Rika, you have to come back to us now. I want to hear all about your adventures in the underworld and all the trouble you and Blossom have been getting into."

"Switching spices was Rika's idea!" Blossom protested. "I only put sand in his boots."

Esmelle laughed and stroked Rika's hair again. "You've become part of our family, Rika. Only someone confident in their place would dare tug on a demon's horns. Please come back to us."

"We must hurry," Aconi whispered, squeezing Sabine's hand. "My sisters are fading."

Perspiration trickled down the side of Sabine's face. She was using too much magic. With the loss of their sister, the dryads were far too weak to attempt this. She wished she could call upon Malek or Bane's power to help her. But their magic was foreign and terrifying to the dryads.

"I promised to show you how to plant a garden," Esmelle said to Rika. "And how to make some of my teas. Bane doesn't like them very much, but I bet he'll drink them if you ask him."

"Umm, Esme?" Blossom asked. "I think Sabine is running low on juice."

"Almost done," Sabine said, plucking apart another thread. Rika was getting much closer. She just needed a little more strength to restore Rika's consciousness and fully merge her back into their reality.

One of the dryads cried out and crumpled to the ground, her energy spent. Her vined hair had dried out and wilted as though left in the sun too long. The loss caused Sabine and the other dryads to stagger. She called upon the recesses of her magic, using it to fill the void the dryad had left. Sabine's vision blurred, her efforts to channel the Well's power becoming clumsy and threatening to drown her.

Esmelle leaped to her feet, taking the place of the fallen dryad. She clasped Sabine's hand tightly and said, "Use my strength."

Sabine nodded, drawing upon Esmelle's power to complete the circle. The pounding in her temples eased slightly. The dryads quickly finished severing the last of the threads and then collapsed on the ground, exhausted. Sabine did the same, her palms resting on the moss and one of the large roots of the ancient oak.

The root lifted off the ground, wrapping around Sabine and cradling her. Sabine leaned into it and ran her hand across the rough bark. A sharp stab of pain lanced through her as a splinter pierced her skin.

Tired beyond measure, she allowed a drop of her blood to fall against the weathered root.

The ancient tree began to glow with a golden light, encompassing Sabine as their powers resonated in harmony. A surge of energy swept through the branches and into the canopy above. Dozens of shimmering golden leaves drifted downward like falling stars. As the dryads reached up to catch them, the energy coursed through their bodies, restoring and renewing them with the tree's ancient strength.

"Theoria greets you, Shining One," Aconi whispered, her eyes welling with amber tears. "She has been silent so long. We thought she had grown displeased with our efforts. This… this was more than we hoped. She's blessed all of us."

The other dryads began to weep, hugging one another and stroking the tree.

The golden glow continued to spread through the oak's branches. More leaves floated downward, surrounding Rika in a golden aura. The young seer opened her eyes and blinked several times. She sat up, looking around in confusion. She picked up one of the glowing leaves and stared at it with a puzzled frown.

"Sabine? Sabine!" Rika dropped the leaf and sprang to her feet. She raced over to Sabine, slamming into her with enough force to steal Sabine's breath. "Don't let the tree eat you!"

Sabine managed a laugh and disentangled herself from both Rika and the tree root. "I don't think we have to worry about such a thing."

Rika frowned, looking down at the large hole in her shirt. She touched her exposed stomach and said, "I can't believe they tried to turn me into a tree."

"You know I would never allow that to happen."

"Well, it's about time you decided to wake up," Esmelle teased.

Rika's eyes widened. "Esme! You're back!"

Sabine grinned as Rika and Esmelle hugged each other. Rika looked around and asked, "Where's Blossom? I thought she was right here."

Blossom peered at them over a large stack of golden

leaves. She waved at Rika and said, "Don't mind me. I'm… collecting mementos. Yeah. Mementos." She turned and marched over to another leaf, hefted the stem over her shoulder, and began hauling it back to the growing pile.

Rika turned back to Sabine and asked, "Do I want to know?"

Sabine sighed and shook her head. "With the amount of magic in each of those leaves, Blossom will likely be building and holding court in a leaf fort before the day is out."

Esmelle laughed. "Well, I'm just glad to see everyone is back to normal."

Aconi and Viola approached them. Rika tensed, narrowing her eyes at the dryads. Aconi lowered her gaze and said, "We owe you an apology, young one. When we felt your power, it was as though the land reached out to us through your blood. We would never force anyone to join us unless they embraced our Call."

Sabine frowned. "I suspect that may have been my influence. I swore to protect Rika, and my magic safeguards her from those who would cause her harm."

Aconi caught another golden leaf as it cascaded downward. She offered it to Rika and said, "Theoria offers you a rare gift, young one. Should you seek solace or protection, you alone may enter the Heartwood. Here, you will find a haven without any expectations in return."

Rika hesitated. "You won't try to turn me into a tree again?"

Aconi smiled and shook her head. "Nay. We understand your loyalty is to another and will not make such a mistake again."

Rika accepted the leaf and gasped as it disappeared, leaving the impression of a golden leaf on the palm of her hand. Aconi closed Rika's hand and said, "Place your palm upon a tree within any of our forests. Knock thrice, and the way will be opened to you."

Rika stared at her hand in amazement, touching the leaf design reverently.

Sabine turned to Aconi and said, "I promised to aid you in finding a replacement anchor."

Aconi's eyes filled with hope. "We would welcome any aid you are willing to offer."

"We're planning to travel to the nearby human settlement of Imenel, just outside of the Sky Cities." Sabine gestured to Blossom who had started gathering a second pile of golden leaves. "I'll offer up enough of my power to Blossom so she can spread the message throughout the city. With its proximity to one of your forests, it's likely some of your lost children are residing amongst the humans there."

Blossom's head jerked up. "More magic? Yes, please!"

Sabine arched her brow. "As long as you remember it's to be used for this task only, Blossom."

"Right," Blossom agreed, nodding eagerly. "But if there's any leftover after we find a new dryad, I'll make sure it goes to good use."

Sabine gave her a wry smile. "Of course you will."

Esmelle touched her flower crown thoughtfully. "I might not ever be ready to become one of you, but I'm able to move within cities without too much discomfort. I'd be willing to help carry your message wherever I may travel. But Sabine and I made an agreement years ago. I intend to help see her mission and purpose fulfilled. That promise must come first."

Sabine looked at Esmelle in surprise. Technically, their formal agreement only required Esmelle to help conceal Sabine's abilities. In exchange, Sabine agreed to teach her the principles of magic and its uses. Esmelle knew more about the human world than Sabine did, but Sabine had a better grasp of magic.

"Esme," Sabine began, but Esmelle shook her head.

"I've learned more from you than I ever imagined. There's still so much I want to understand, if you're willing to keep teaching me. And besides, do you really want to try to navigate a city full of dragons without me?"

Sabine smiled and squeezed Esmelle's hand. "If you could keep two demons in line back in Akros, the dragons won't stand a chance against you. Besides, there's a certain sailor who would definitely miss your presence."

"Exactly," Esmelle said with a grin.

Sabine turned back to Aconi. "Will this be a suitable arrangement until we find a more permanent solution to your problem?"

Aconi exchanged looks with her sisters and then nodded. "We agree, but we have another request of our youngest sister."

Esmelle arched her brow. "What is it?"

Aconi clasped her hands together and said, "We would ask that you return to us when you can. While you may not be ready to embrace your birthright, we would share our song with you and teach you our ways."

Esmelle stared at Aconi in surprise. "You're offering to teach me, even if I'm not willing to become one of you?"

"The forest has always been generous with its gifts, and we've learned its lessons well," Aconi said. "You are the chosen companion of a Shining One, a great boon to be granted to one of our kind. We would welcome the opportunity to teach our youngest sister all she needs to know to support her purpose and to safeguard the last of the Shining Ones with ties to the land."

Blossom landed on Sabine's shoulder and lightly tugged her hair. "You *are* rather shiny now."

Sabine glanced down and sighed at the glow that seemed

to be escaping more often. She was beginning to feel like a walking nightlight.

"I would suggest you consider their offer, Esme," Sabine said. "Aconi and the other dryads can instruct you in ways I can't. While our magics are similar, there are nuances to theirs that aren't intuitive for me."

Esmelle turned back to Aconi and said, "If you're willing, I'd be honored to learn from you. Sabine's mission takes priority, but you have my word I'll return to learn more about my heritage."

Aconi nodded. She clasped her hands together and lowered her head for a moment. A faint glow surrounded her. When she opened her hands, a small, glowing acorn pendant appeared in her palms. It was a smaller version of the one Aconi wore around her neck.

She held it out to Esmelle and said, "Simply touch the pendant and let our song flow through you. When you move throughout the land, our song will spring forth from your lips."

Esmelle picked up the necklace. "I feel it humming already."

Aconi smiled and helped fasten it around her neck. "Your lost sisters will be drawn to your song. Share with them the voice of the forest, and they will know we welcome them home. Once you are ready to return, use the song to open a path back to the grove."

Esmelle nodded, touching the pendant. "I'll remember."

Sabine lifted her gaze to stare up at the oak tree. She had the feeling there was something more Theoria wanted from her. The same root that had cradled her before lifted from the ground. Sabine touched it gently, allowing her magic to blend with the tree's power. The branches overhead rustled gently, creating a soothing lullaby. The faintest sound of music reached her ears. It was familiar somehow. She closed her eyes, trying to understand what she was hearing.

"Um, Sabine? You're glowing again."

Sabine's eyes flew open. Her skin was once again a brilliant gold. The dryads had gathered around her, humming a soft melody. It wasn't the one she'd heard, but they complemented one another. Sabine clamped down on her magic, shaking her head to clear it.

"We should go," Sabine said, staring up at the oak tree one last time. Malek and Bane were waiting for her back in the forest. They'd taken far too long as it was, especially when danger could descend again at a moment's notice.

Blossom tugged on Sabine's hair and pointed to the piles of golden leaves. "Hey, Sabine? Any chance we can bring some souvenirs with us?"

Rika grinned. "I've got it."

Blossom flew over to Rika's shoulder and began instructing her on how best to carry the leaves. Aconi approached Sabine and said, "For centuries and despite our pleas, Theoria has remained dormant within this grove. Your presence has once again awakened her."

"Do you know why?"

Aconi shook her head. "I know not where your path takes you, but Theoria would not have roused if the need wasn't dire."

Sabine frowned and absently ran her fingers over the symbols etched on her wrist. She couldn't help but wonder if Theoria had sensed her mission.

"Do you know anything about the Dragon Portal?"

Aconi tilted her head, studying Sabine carefully. "That way remains sealed. It can only be opened by those who possess the keys and the power to wield them."

A flicker of hope filled Sabine. "I'm searching for the last of the artifacts used to seal the portal. I was told to seek the answers among the dragons."

Aconi lowered her gaze. "I cannot aid you in your task, Shining One. When the aderyan fell, their floating cities were closed to us. The forests within their domain were set aflame. With the loss of their wings, the aderyan were silenced. Our seeds will no longer take root."

"Then I'll continue my search," Sabine said quietly. "I would only ask that you not disclose my purpose to any sidhe or their allies who might enter your grove."

Aconi bowed low. "As you will it, Shining One. We will keep your silence."

Esmelle and Rika approached them. In Esmelle's arms was a small twig basket filled to the brim with golden leaves.

Blossom sat in the middle of the pile, carefully smoothing out each leaf as she counted them. "Fourteen, Fifteen, Sixteen…"

Esmelle rolled her eyes and said, "Viola was kind enough to loan us a basket. I told her we'd leave it at the edge of the forest so they could retrieve it. Blossom was insistent we needed to take all her 'mementos' with us."

Blossom lifted her head and said, "I have forty-two brothers and sisters. Do you know how hard it is to find souvenirs of this magnitude for all of them?"

Aconi smiled. "The bounty of our forests shall remain open to you, little messenger. Safe travels to all of you."

Sabine said her goodbyes to Aconi and her sisters before heading down the path and away from the Great Oak. With every step she took, she felt the distance from Malek begin to lessen. She reached for him through their bond, reassured when a surge of love and protectiveness wrapped around her.

"So what's this I heard about you switching cooking

spices on Bane?" Esmelle asked, balancing the basket in the crook of her arm.

Rika's face reddened. "Ah, well. Did you know a demon's horns will glow for hours if they eat something spicy?"

Esmelle arched her brow. "You wanted his horns to glow?"

"Of course! We've been camping in the woods for weeks."

When Esmelle continued to look puzzled, Rika threw her hands up in exasperation.

"You try waking up in the middle of the night and needing to pee! I can't tell you how many rocks I've tripped over trying to navigate in the dark. Glowing horns make an excellent nightlight." She gestured at Sabine and Blossom and grumbled, "I don't have night vision like they do."

Esmelle grinned, her green eyes twinkling with laughter. "Oh, Rika. Just wait until I teach you how to make some of my teas. There's a reason they're not always palatable to non-humans."

Sabine arched her brow and then shook her head. Nope. She didn't want to know. She *really* didn't want to know.

CHAPTER 10

*S*abine stepped through the portal, landing lightly on the other side. She released Rika's hand, turning to wait for Esmelle.

Blossom tugged on Sabine's hair. "Riding with you is a lot smoother than going on my own."

Rika nodded. "Yeah. It took a lot longer when Blossom and I went through."

"The dryads test the strength of your will before granting entry," Sabine said, frowning at the tree. It shouldn't be taking Esmelle this long to cross over.

She had to be the last one to leave the grove, but only to prove her intention of remaining separate from the grove. If Esmelle was having doubts about her future, the dryads may have delayed her departure until she'd convinced them of her sincerity — one way or another.

"Did you encounter the dragon?" Bane asked from behind her.

Sabine spun around. "What? Malek followed me?"

Bane gave her a curt nod. "Shortly after your second power pull. He opened a portal somehow."

She paled. The dryads wouldn't have allowed him past their defenses. If he used their bond to break through the barrier and into the grove, Sabine would have sensed him. She'd felt him but had assumed it was simply because he was waiting outside for her.

"I haven't been able to reach Malek since he went after you," Levin said with a frown. "Where is he? Where's Esme?"

"Esme was right behind us," Rika said. "Sabine had to take us through the portal first. Esme was going to close it right after she stepped through."

"Something's wrong," Sabine said, summoning her magic to reopen the doorway. If either or both of them were lost in the in-between, she had to find them quickly. The longer they were gone, the worse their chances. She wasn't sure she even had the power to locate them once she stepped through. Maybe Blossom might have some ideas. The pixie had navigated the in-between before and was trying to teach Sabine how to create new portals.

"Sabine, stop!" Blossom shrieked. "You gave your word to the Huntsman. No more portals!"

Bane grabbed her wrist, pulling it away from the tree. "The bug is right. If you are forsworn in your oath, the Huntsman will claim his due."

Rika held out her palm with the golden leaf design. "Can I reopen it?"

Sabine shook her head. "No. You'll open a doorway to the grove. Malek never entered the sacred grove, and I felt Esme right behind us when we departed. They're in the in-between. Esme might have been pulled back to the grove, but Malek—"

Her voice trailed off. She refused to finish the thought. She had no intention of losing him. Esmelle had to find her own way out, but Malek... There had to be some loophole she could exploit, or some way to reach him without risking the Huntsman's wrath.

"A Calling," Bane said and wrapped his arm around her waist. "Call him to you, Sabine. With blood and magic, he'll be able to find you. The lizard won't be able to resist."

She glanced up at him in surprise. Despite her presence, Bane wasn't nearly as strong during the daylight hours. For him to even make the offer meant he understood the severity of the situation.

"Hurry, little one," Bane said quietly. "I won't be able to shield you for long."

Sabine closed her eyes, lowered her glamour and let her mental shields fall. Power surged through her like a breaking tide, untethered, ancient, and alive. The earth seemed to pause around her as her magic stirred, no longer caged but not yet unleashed. Air coiled around her like a living thing, rustling leaves and lifting her hair in wild strands. The sky darkened, heavy with rain, responding not to a summons but to her presence. Raindrops began to fall, soft at first, then in silvery sheets, drawn to her as naturally as breath.

Only Bane's arms around her kept her grounded, a quiet reminder that control mattered more than strength. If she let go, even for a heartbeat, her magic could consume everything she meant to protect.

Reaching across the magical bond she'd forged with Malek, she felt for the mark she'd left on his wrist months ago. She slid her dagger from its sheath. With a practiced hand, she sliced through her skin to mirror the same marks on Malek's wrist and traced the Calling symbol in blood. Pressing her bleeding wrist against the tree, she shouted in the language of Faerie, "By blood and by magic, and by my rights to both, I *call* Malek Rish'dan."

A deep vibration ran through the ground beneath her

feet. The tree in front of her began to glow, dimly at first and then building with intensity. Golden leaves began to fall around them. She heard Levin gasp, and Blossom's voice whispering excitedly to Rika.

"Thirty-five, thirty-six… just a few more leaves!"

"Come back to me, Malek," Sabine whispered, her wrist still pressed against the tree. "Heart to heart, soul to soul. Until the last of the magic fades from this world."

She lowered her wrist, her emotions raw and untethered. It was done. If Malek didn't return to her in the next few minutes, she'd appeal to the Huntsman. She just hoped the price for his aid didn't take her away from the dragon she loved.

"You should not make such an oath when the magic is high," Bane said, turning her in his arms. He caught one of her tears, studying it for a moment before pressing it to his lips.

Sabine looked up at him. "An oath is nothing more than a truth brought into the light. It's why you drink my tears, Bane. There's power in the depth of such emotion."

Bane cradled Sabine's bleeding wrist in his clawed grasp. Dark energy pulsed through his touch as he called on his demonic healing. She winced at the sharp sting that followed, feeling the wound pull tight as her skin knit itself closed.

"Guard your heart carefully, little one," Bane said quietly. "There are those who would use your fondness for the dragon simply to take advantage of the situation. We will be traveling among enemies, both yours — and his."

The tree glowed brightly for a moment, a swirling miasma of gold and green.

Esmelle stumbled out, landing hard on her backside. "Ouch! Of all the—"

"Move!" Bane shouted, pushing Sabine away from him and the tree. He grabbed Rika and leaped aside. Levin snatched Esmelle up and dashed away from the tree, just as an enormous dragon burst through the portal.

"See! This is why I need to be a dragon!" Blossom said, pointing at Malek. "He knows how to make an entrance."

Sabine ran over to Malek, running her hands along the side of his neck. She felt the slight ridges and indentations of each of his scales, as his muscles relaxed beneath her touch. Pressing her forehead against his neck, she said, *"I thought I'd lost you."*

"I'll always find you, Sabine. No matter which side of the Veil you're on. You shine with the brilliance of a thousand suns." Malek wrapped his tail around her protectively. *"Should I ask what it cost you to light my path back to you?"*

Sabine smiled. *"Nothing I wouldn't pay a thousand times over."*

Esmelle stomped over to Malek and put her hands on her hips. "Oh, I don't think so. Next time you try to shove me through a portal, I'll turn you into a toad. We'll see how well you maneuver me when I stuff you into a sack."

Sabine blinked at the furious redhead. "What?"

"Traffic jams in the in-between are ugly," Blossom said, brushing a speck of dirt from one of her prized leaves. "It happens more than you might think."

Malek lowered his head to the ground, staring at Esmelle with his large golden eyes. Esmelle crossed her arms and shook her head. "Nope. Don't even try doing the big, sad-eyed dragon thing. If it won't work with Levin, it certainly won't work with you."

She turned on her heel and stomped away. Blossom giggled and took off after her.

Bane walked over to Sabine and asked, "Are you going to tell her it was your fault for calling him back?"

Sabine shook her head. "Not a chance. I've seen firsthand how lethal her temper can be."

Malek huffed. *"Really? You're throwing me to the wolves?"*

She kissed Malek's cheek and said, "Don't dragons eat wolves?"

Malek's eyes narrowed. *"If I touch a hair on Esme's head, you'll skin me before she tosses me into that sack of hers."*

"I'll make it up to you later," Sabine teased, running her hand over Malek's brow ridge.

A blinding flash of light erupted from Malek. A moment later, he was back in his human form and she was pinned against the tree. Malek lowered his head, his lips claiming hers in a way she could only describe as possession. She threw her arms around him, her body instinctively softening against his hardness as raw need coursed through her. Their kiss turned primal, fueled by both indescribable longing and desire. She answered him with her touch, giving as much as she received, and together, they were lost—in the moment and in each other.

"In case anyone's forgotten, that wyvern is likely on his way back with reinforcements," Bane said, his tone almost bored. "I wouldn't mind killing a few more, but these two flying lizards get cranky when they have to kill their brethren."

Malek broke their kiss and muttered a curse. He cupped her face and pressed another kiss on her lips, this one impossibly gentle. "As much as I hate to stop, Bane's right. The forced shift through the portal took the last of my strength. We need to get away from here before we're spotted."

"Not to mention the witch's aversion to the forest being burned," Bane reminded them, nodding toward Esmelle.

"About that," Sabine said with a sigh. "It turns out she might not be as human as we thought. Esme was born in the grove."

Bane froze, a wicked smile curving his lips. "Are you telling me the wyvern decided to claim a dryad as his mate?"

When Sabine nodded, Bane chuckled. "Well, I'll be damned. He doesn't know yet, does he?"

Sabine turned to see Esmelle and Levin locked in a scorching embrace. "Not yet, no."

Bane's grin widened. "Excellent."

Malek took Sabine's hand in his and asked, *"Bane's about to make Levin's life hell, isn't he?"*

Sabine looked up at the dragon she loved. *"Absolutely."*

THE GROUP MOVED QUICKLY and quietly through the forest in pairs with Malek and Levin taking up the rear. Bane and Sabine were at the forefront, allowing the demon to use his senses to track any potential dangers. So far, they hadn't sensed any approaching wyverns and the skies remained clear.

Malek wanted Sabine safe within the boundaries of Imenel by nightfall. Fortunately, the witch's cabin was right on the outskirts of the town. Once he'd secured another medallion from her, they could blend in with the other humans in Imenel without arousing suspicion.

"Did you tell her?" Levin asked in a low voice.

Malek frowned, not terribly surprised by the question. Levin had been pushing for him to tell Sabine the truth about their mission since before they arrived in Razadon.

"In a manner of speaking," Malek admitted. "The Huntsman forced me into revealing my intentions before I was ready. It wasn't how I planned to tell her, but she knows most of it."

Levin stared at him and whispered, "The Huntsman? As in… The Wild Hunt?"

Malek scowled and ducked beneath a low-hanging branch. "One and the same. When he's leading the Hunt, I think he shares the same purpose that fuels the Hunt. But when he's alone, it's a different story."

"What do you mean?"

Malek hesitated. Sabine and Bane were walking together up ahead, deep in hushed conversation. Esmelle and Rika were side by side right behind them, while Esmelle pointed out some of the trees and plants they passed. Blossom kept darting into the foliage and then back to Sabine. He likely only had a few minutes before Blossom came to find out what he and Levin were discussing.

"The Huntsman saved her life back in Razadon," Malek said quietly. "I've never heard of such a thing before. It's not the first time either. Every time I turn around, it seems as though he's watching Sabine, protecting her, or leaving gifts for her. A few times, he's sent me into an enchanted sleep so he could speak privately with her. She hasn't been forthcoming about their conversations, even when I've asked."

"This isn't good, Malek."

"No kidding," Malek muttered. "He told Sabine I was hiding something from her. When she confronted me, I told her our people were dying. Taking control of the portal and allowing enough magic through might be the only way to save them. It wasn't how I wanted to have the discussion, but she knows most of it now."

Levin blew out a breath. "Malek, you need to be careful. The Huntsman is the one individual we've made it a point to avoid. He remained neutral throughout the war, but things could go badly for our people if he decides to turn against us."

"You think I don't know that?" Malek demanded and then lowered his voice when Sabine and Bane glanced their way. "I have no idea why he's so focused on her. She told me she thought it was because their magic was similar, but I'm not buying it. When I broke through the portal earlier to follow Sabine, he stopped me. Levin, I've never felt power such as his. He shrugged off my magic like it was water."

Levin sucked in a quiet breath. "Flame and fury, Malek. What are you going to do?"

"I don't know," Malek admitted grudgingly. "I was hoping either my parents or our clan would have some knowledge about him. But given this recent attack and the possibility of spies, I'm reluctant to tell anyone the truth about Sabine's identity. It will likely put her in more danger."

Levin frowned. "I see your point. It might be best not to say anything."

Malek's gaze sharpened. "Did something happen?"

"I saw her without glamour and in full power. We need to find a way to control the portal, but..." Levin's voice trailed out, and he shook his head.

"What happened?"

"Her magic isn't like any fae I've ever heard of. She's golden, Malek. There are stories from the war, and the golden magic that slaughtered our people. If anyone sees her like I did..."

Malek muttered a curse. "I know. It's getting worse. Every time she absorbs one of the artifacts, Lachlina's control over her grows. Her magic has been changing too. She has more power than she used to, and doesn't burn out the same way."

"We need to find a way to control the portal, but I'm not sure how this will end. If our people suspect she's anything other than fae or has ties to the one who trapped us here—"

Malek held up a hand to silence Levin. "*Nothing* will happen to her. I won't allow it. We put her in this position, and I'll protect her until my last breath. If I have to call in every marker and every clan loyalty tie within my power, so be it."

Levin snorted. "Aha. There's the mating instinct you've been trying to hide."

"Flap off," Malek muttered, but without much heat. "I think it would be best to allow Sabine to keep up the guise of being human with some fae ancestry. Once we know more about the situation in the Sky Cities, we can decide who to trust."

Levin nodded. "And it would probably be for the best if we don't let on about Esme being a dryad either." He rubbed his temples and muttered, "Shit. A dryad."

Malek grinned. "Your parents are going to love that."

"Shut up," Levin retorted and then groaned. "How the hell did this happen?"

Malek watched Sabine walking ahead of them and how the dappled sunlight danced upon her fair skin. She moved with such effortless grace, reminding him of the dance she'd performed for him back in Razadon. They'd shared hundreds of small intimacies over the past few months, and each one made him fall a little deeper in love with her. There were so many nuances to her personality. Her kindness, loyalty, and compassion made her just as beautiful on the inside as she was on the outside.

When he'd felt her Calling him back to her, it had never even dawned on him to resist. Her voice had been like a siren's song, luring him back to her side. And that kiss would likely have sent the forest aflame again if Bane hadn't interrupted them.

As though sensing the direction of his thoughts, Sabine glanced at him over her shoulder. The look in her eyes and the teasing curve of her lips promised a continuation of that kiss as soon as they were alone. Realizing Sabine was distracted, Bane glanced over his shoulder and gave them a look of disgust. Whatever the demon said to Sabine caused her to laugh and focus again on the path in front of them.

Malek shook his head. "No idea how it happened, but I wouldn't change a damn thing."

Levin sighed and stared at Esmelle with the same sort of longing. "Yeah. Me neither."

CHAPTER 11

"*I*'m capable of lacing my own boots," Sabine said, watching as Malek kneeled in front of her and tied her laces.

He ran his hand up her leg and slowly inched up her dress. Leaning down, he pressed a kiss against her inner thigh. She inhaled sharply as he blew against her skin with his heated breath.

"I'm well aware of what you can do," Malek said with a grin. "I'm simply reminding you of what *I* can do."

She leaned forward and nipped his lower lip. "Keep it up, and we won't make it to the witch's cabin before nightfall."

"One more reason to kill whoever sent those wyverns after us," Malek said and stood. He held out his hand and helped her to her feet. "It won't take us long to reach Idola's cabin from here."

She nodded and smoothed out her dress. At least she wouldn't have to expend more magic hiding her torn and disheveled appearance. The replacement dress she was wearing was made from a heavier material that helped ward against the slight chill in the air.

"Rika?" Sabine called over her shoulder. "Did you find something to wear?"

"Yeah," Rika said, stepping out the bushes where she'd ducked for some privacy. She stuffed her torn shirt into the traveler's pack. "I really liked that shirt. There's no way to even mend it. That tree root went right through the center."

Sabine carefully removed a leaf from Rika's dark hair. "If it's that important to you, I'll see if it can be mended through arcane means."

Rika's eyes widened. "You can do that?"

Sabine smiled. "All natural fibers come from the land. Brownies and some of the lesser fae are far more gifted than I am at such magic, but it can be done. If we offer her honey or something suitably sweet, we may even be able to convince Blossom to help."

"Or I could just take you shopping in Imenel," Malek said with a grin.

Rika's eyes lit up. "Let's go shopping."

Sabine laughed.

As they left the woods and rejoined their group, Sabine paused to take in the sight. The witch's cabin stood above them on a steep outcropping, accessible only by a single path leading out of the forest and up the mountain.

At the bottom of the mountain was the walled city of Imenel. The cabin was close enough to make trading with Imenel a viable option, but far enough away to offer sanctuary from the noise and bustle of the city.

In the distance, Sabine caught sight of the floating islands she'd only heard about in stories. Dark specks soared over them, the sight sending a frisson of fear through Sabine.

Dragons.

Blossom landed on Sabine's shoulder. "Please tell me they don't eat pixies."

"We don't eat pixies," Malek said, placing his hand against

Sabine's lower back to steady her. Or perhaps it was to prevent her from changing her mind and retreating back into the forest. She glanced over at Bane, but his expression was a stony mask as he gazed at the floating islands.

Rika's mouth dropped open. "Those are the Sky Cities? They're uh… really high up there."

"Yes," Malek said, his thumb absently stroking Sabine's back. "When we're closer, you'll see several of the greater dragons and wyverns patrolling the skies. Each clan has claimed various parts of the islands for themselves."

"Conquered," Bane clarified, the visceral description serving as a reminder of the warning he'd given Sabine while they trekked through the forest. No matter how much she might care for Malek and he for her, she was going to be surrounded by enemies. They all were.

Blossom squeaked in dismay and huddled against Sabine's neck. "Maybe we should skip this part of the trip and go visit the dryads again. I could use a few more golden leaves."

"Oh?" Esmelle asked with a small smile. "What happened to the brave adventurer who used to sneak out of my garden and stalk the demons in their den?"

Blossom poked her head out of Sabine's hair. "That's supposed to be a secret!"

"Is it now?" Esmelle asked, giving her an innocent look.

Blossom huffed and pulled Sabine's hair back in place like a curtain. Malek frowned, arching his brow in question.

But it was too late. Blossom was on a tirade.

"What happens if a dragon sneezes? Whoosh… there goes the garden. What happens if a dragon yawns and I fly right into his mouth? Crispy pixie. Nope. Nope. Nope."

"Weren't you asking me to turn you into a dragon?" Sabine asked. "The Sky Cities would be the best place to learn how to act like one."

"Malek can teach me!"

Sabine sighed and gestured for Malek to help her out.

Malek lifted Sabine's hair and said, "You know, my fae grandmother had pixies living in her garden for years. She used to sing to them while she planted. They were safe and protected in her garden."

"Yeah, but what happened to them? Did a dragon step on them? I've seen the size of your feet. I think you stepped on a dwarf back in Razadon. We're even smaller. You wouldn't even notice!"

"They likely went to find another strong source of Faerie magic," Sabine said and sent a reassuring wave of power over the pixie, infusing it with peace and love. "You don't have to worry about such things while you're with me, do you?"

Blossom was quiet for a moment. "Maybe you should give me a boost of magic again. You know, to make sure I can outfly any big-footed dragons."

Sabine smiled and sent another wave of magic over Blossom. "Better?"

Blossom trilled happily. She started to braid Sabine's hair, humming a happy tune while she worked.

"Is she okay?" Malek asked.

"Pixies have stories about the dragons, just like the fae," Sabine said. "It might help if we can collect a few more of her favorite flowers before we head into the city. We're still close enough to the forest to find some wildflowers growing near the path."

Esmelle squeezed Sabine's arm and said, "Rika and I will keep an eye out."

Sabine nodded. Hopefully, the flowers and braiding would keep Blossom calm and out of trouble.

They continued walking up the steep trail to the cabin. Though it was wide enough for four people to walk side by side, someone had installed a sturdy wooden fence along the edge to prevent accidental falls. A heavy hemp rope had been strung between the posts, serving as a secondary barrier. Sabine couldn't help but wonder why such precautions were necessary.

"How many dragon clans are there?" Rika asked, her gaze drifting back to the floating islands.

"About two dozen," Malek said, his fingers brushing against Sabine's. "Some of the smaller clans have aligned themselves with more powerful ones to coexist under a shared banner. With limited space in the Sky Cities, it's been necessary to keep the peace. Dragons don't share well."

"Your control over the entirety of the Sky Cities has made it difficult to infiltrate," Bane said, sweeping his gaze along the path and up toward the skies. "Still, nothing is infallible. I'm sure there are ways to enter and leave without being detected."

Malek made a noncommittal noise. "Idola's cabin should be over the next rise. We don't have much coin with us, but she should accept a clan marker."

"I'm interested to see how she crafts these warding medallions," Esmelle said, tucking some blue wildflowers into her knapsack. "I hadn't thought such a thing was possible for a witch. I'm wondering if I might be able to duplicate it in the future."

Malek motioned for Levin to stand guard along the path before leading Sabine and the others across a narrow bridge. Sabine stepped off the wooden planks, charmed by the cozy and inviting cabin ahead.

A small vegetable garden was neatly tended on the side of the house, with several large pots overflowing with sweet-smelling herbs. Esmelle breathed deeply as they passed, a small smile playing upon her lips. Blossom giggled and darted off Sabine's shoulder and into the garden, no doubt in search of some sweet nectar. At least the pixie was acting more like herself. She wouldn't get into *too* much trouble in a garden—at least nothing Sabine couldn't fix before they departed.

Sabine stepped onto the porch, the floorboards creaking beneath her boots. Large racks lined the wall outside the cabin, each one filled with a variety of herbs in various stages of drying. The cabin's shutters were wide open with colorful patchwork curtains dancing in the breeze. Sabine caught a faint whiff of some sort of fragrant stew simmering inside. It reminded her of the delicious meals Martha used to make back in Akros when she ran the tavern's kitchen.

A growl split the air.

Sabine turned just as a massive beast leaped through one of the shutters, aiming straight toward her. In one seamless move, Malek stepped in front of Sabine with his weapon drawn. Sabine spun away, shoving Rika and Esmelle toward the garden. "Ward yourselves!"

Esmelle slapped her hand against the ground, forming a thick barrier of plants to protect her and Rika from harm.

Bane's eyes flashed silver as he leaped toward the giant white hound. It darted out of Bane's grasp, its body morphing to slide through the demon's extended claws. Bane shouted something in the demonic language, but the hound ignored him, still trying to reach Sabine.

"Bad magic! Really bad magic!" Blossom shrieked, flying toward Sabine. "Don't let it bite you!"

"Blossom, watch out!" Sabine shouted as the hound's sharp teeth snapped at the tiny pixie.

"Stinky breath! Bad magic! Possessed dog!" Blossom zipped around the porch, shedding glittering pixie dust everywhere. The enormous dog lunged at Sabine again, but Malek blocked the attack, forcing the hound back. Whatever magic was fueling this dog wasn't natural.

"Blossom," Sabine shouted, pointing toward the cabin. "Flush out the witch."

Blossom dove through the open window and into the house. "One witch, coming right up!"

Bane slammed into the creature, knocking it against the wall. His horns glowed a brilliant silver as he shouted again in his harsh demonic language.

A woman screamed from inside the cabin. The beast howled, its white fur glowing blue and matching Bane's skin when his power was upon him.

"Idola!" a man shouted from somewhere behind the cabin. He leaped over the porch railing, a curved blade in his hands.

Malek moved to intercept him, striking out with lightning-fast reflexes. Sabine dodged out of the way.

"Release the hound, witch," Bane shouted.

A woman stumbled out of the doorway of the cabin. She was a striking woman, with dark curly hair that framed delicate facial features. Her blue dress was simple, but the color and cut had obviously been selected with care. It was her eyes, though, that drew and kept your attention.

Angry scars across the top half of her face spoke of a harsh and tormented past. Someone had blinded this woman, possibly as a child. Although the wounds had healed, the scars still remained. Magic swirled around her, her sightless eyes glowing with the same strange blue light that encompassed the huge hound.

"The hound is mine," the witch shouted and raised her hands to expel a burst of magic in Bane's direction.

Sabine's hands shot up, simultaneously reaching for the power of the land and sending it toward the woman. Thorny vines wrapped around the witch, attempting to curtail her movements. The witch withdrew a dagger from her belt and swung the blade, but every slice against the vines only multiplied the number of vines that sought to restrain her.

"Way to go, Sabine!" Blossom cheered, hovering out of harm's way.

The witch screamed in fury, spewing curses from her lips. Sabine clenched her hand into a fist, silencing the woman and holding her tightly with her magic. She wasn't willing to risk any of those curses containing power.

Malek lowered his weapon and stepped over the crumpled body of the man he'd fought. "He lives yet, Idola, but he'll die if he raises a blade against me or mine again."

"Release the hound, witch," Bane repeated with a snarl. "If you resist, I'll sever your connection myself—and neither one of you will survive it."

Sabine moved toward the woman, getting a closer look at the creature Bane had pinned against the wall. It was an enormous hound with a rough white coat and red ears. Pale blue eyes that appeared far too human stared at her with murderous intent.

With both of her protectors neutralized, the last of Idola's fight vanished. The bluish glow surrounding the animal faded, and its eyes shifted back to their natural, fiery red. The hound slumped in Bane's arms, whining from its injuries. Idola lowered her head, her dark hair masking her face and covering her sightless eyes.

Bane carefully lowered the animal to the ground and said, "He never would have attacked if the witch wasn't controlling him. He's a visionhound, one of Faerie's lost hounds, and a close cousin to the underworld hellhounds."

Blossom landed on Sabine's shoulder. "That explains the sulfur breath."

Sabine kneeled beside Bane. "How close of a cousin?"

"Close enough."

Sabine nodded and placed her hand on Bane's shoulder. She sent a strong surge of magic toward Bane. His midnight skin began to glow blue as he ran his hands over the hound, speaking softly in the demonic tongue. The hound's bones knit back together, the healing energy of Bane's magic causing him to whimper in pain.

"Will he live?"

"Yes," Bane said, running his hand over the visionhound's white coat. "He has something he wishes to show you. Touch him, and the vision will be true."

Blossom tugged on her hair. "Careful, Sabine. The goddess says the witch can still take control over him."

"Then the witch will die," Malek said, his tone cold and unyielding.

Idola lifted her head. "You have made your wishes known, Dragon Lord. Basco will not harm her at my direction."

The dog whined, staring up at Sabine with fiery eyes that reminded her so much of Azran. Sabine reached over to gently brush her fingers against his fur. He leaned into her touch, shifting his head to reach her.

Her eyes fluttered shut, and she saw for a moment a younger Idola wrapping Basco's swollen and angry paws with wet dock leaves. In the vision, Idola wasn't blind. She was a mere girl of seven or eight, yet she was fearless in the face of such a large hound. She sat beside him and shared her meager lunch, promising to return the following day to check on him.

The vision flashed to a different scene, and she saw an older man holding Idola down as another poured boiling liquid over Idola's eyes while she screamed. Basco leaped to Idola's defense, taking the hand of her tormentor. The two of them ran off together, with Basco leading a burned and blinded Idola to safety.

Sabine opened her eyes and took a shaky breath. She'd seen worse torments in Faerie's courts, but few such punishments were given to a child. It was impossible to feel anything other than outrage and sympathy for what Idola had endured.

"She wrapped your paws with dock leaves after you encountered some nettles. You rescued her in return and escaped together," Sabine said, touching one of his large paws.

The hound licked her hand in acknowledgement.

Bane's eyes silvered as he glared at the captive witch. "Regardless of whether a debt was due, he did not consent to being used as a weapon against us."

Basco whined again, a plea in his eyes as he gazed up at her.

Sabine ran her fingers through his fur, accompanying her gesture with a gentle and reassuring brush of her magic. "She may have erred, but Basco loves her. He would not have stayed with her this long otherwise. Any debt between them was fulfilled long ago. They've bonded to one another, almost as if she were fae."

Bane narrowed his eyes. "Are you suggesting we leave him with the witch?"

"If he wishes, but with one caveat," Sabine said and withdrew her knife. She pricked her finger and held it out to the visionhound. He licked it clean and whined, his entire body trembling uncontrollably for a moment.

"Uh oh! Everyone get back! Major magic coming through!" Blossom said, flying off Sabine's shoulder. Malek wrapped his arm around Sabine, hauling her up and out of the way just as Bane leaped to his feet.

Basco's skin beneath his fur began to undulate. He stood and howled, the sound eerily similar to the hellhounds. He was only slightly smaller than them, but larger than the biggest wolf she'd ever seen.

He shook himself, his white coat shifting to reveal a light

dusting of gold on the ends. He turned to face Sabine and lowered his head in fealty.

"Shit," Malek muttered, releasing Sabine and sheathing his weapon. "He's gold."

Bane sighed. "At least the witch won't be able to coerce him into doing her bidding again."

Blossom landed on Sabine's shoulder and whispered, "The goddess is laughing, Sabine. I'm not sure that's a good thing."

Sabine rubbed Basco's ears. He panted happily, gazing at her with adoration. She wasn't sure what had prompted her to make such an offering, but it was done. She could now feel Basco, almost in the same way she sensed Azran. There was a rightness to the connection, as if she'd somehow repaired damage done long ago.

"You will need to remind Idola of your purpose, Basco. What you share with her is a gift forged from love and affection. If she does not respect that, you have the freedom to choose your own path. With the blood offering you've accepted, you will always have a place in my court if you wish it. You are once again a hound of Faerie."

Basco nuzzled Sabine's hand again before trotting over to Idola. He sat in front of her and whined. Malek held out his hand, helping Sabine to her feet. He scanned her up and down, as though making sure she was truly unharmed.

Levin walked over to the unconscious man and leaned down to check on him. "You keep inviting me to the party after it's over, Malek."

"Wasn't much of a party," Malek said. "Are Esme and Rika unharmed?"

Levin nodded. "Esme's setting the garden back to rights."

Sabine released the bindings around Idola. The witch collapsed onto the ground and wrapped her arms around

Basco. He licked her face, his tail wagging with joy at being reunited. Sabine could see the magic swirling around them as Basco communicated with Idola. After a moment, Basco's eyes began to glow blue, providing Idola with the ability to see through his eyes once more. Though her gaze lingered on Bane several times, she made a point of avoiding Sabine entirely.

Basco might choose to share his vision with Idola, but she would no longer be able to rule over him. Still, the connection between them was a curious thing. Sabine had never heard of a Faerie hound bonding to a human witch—or a witch who could manipulate Faerie's magic.

Bane walked over to Idola and studied her with the same remote detachment that he might an insect. "The human male will be waking up soon. His breathing patterns have already changed. What sort of punishment do you see for the witch and her lover?"

Sabine tilted her head and studied Idola carefully. She'd heard stories about ritual blindness being performed on certain types of children, but she'd never met one who had endured it. She needed to know if her suspicions about Idola were correct before any decision could be made.

"You know who I am, don't you?" Sabine asked.

Idola pressed her lips together and didn't respond. Sabine heard footsteps approaching from behind but didn't turn away from the woman.

"I require an answer," Sabine said, infusing her voice with power. Bands of magic wrapped around Idola, tightening their grip the longer she remained silent. Idola started to fight against Sabine's magic, but Basco placed his paw on her. She stopped fighting abruptly.

"Fae," Idola whispered. "Sidhe fae wearing human glamour."

"I guess your secret's out," Blossom said. "I'm not sure your glamour's working too well. Maybe it's the pointy ears."

Rika moved to stand beside Sabine. "It's not Sabine's glamour. I recognize her magic. She's a seer, isn't she?"

Basco's glowing gaze focused on Rika. Idola gasped, her expression filled with a combination of shock and horror. "You would betray us to one of *them*?"

Rika straightened. "Us? There is no 'us.' You attacked my friends!"

Rika opened her mouth to say something else, but a sharp look from Bane had her clamping her mouth closed. Instead, she crossed her arms and glared at Idola.

"Well, that explains some things," Esmelle said, putting her hands on her hips. "I was wondering how a witch managed to craft Levin's warding medallion. If she's a seer, that definitely changes things from a magic perspective."

"It changes a lot of things," Bane said to Sabine. "Her continued existence endangers more than Faerie."

Idola released Basco and stood, her glowing eyes focused on Sabine. "I am a seer of the blood, the last of my family's line. My vision is no longer mine to command. I cannot reveal Faerie's secrets. I am no threat to your kind."

Blossom sneezed, but it sounded a lot like, "That's a load of caterpillar crap."

Bane leaned forward and said, "And humans lie very well, but not well enough to fool the Unseelie."

Idola flinched. Basco whined unhappily.

Sabine considered the woman and the hound she obviously loved. Idola had escaped her family and hidden from the fae in the last place they might look for her. Sabine had done the same thing by hiding among the humans in Akros. If she claimed Idola's life, she would be no better than her father or any of the fae who sought her death.

She refused to do that.

Bane prowled toward Idola, his eyes flashing silver. "The hound alerted you to my mistress's presence. You bound him in chains, more potent than any made of metal. You sought to destroy her—when his very existence stems from her blood!"

The last was said with a roar. Bane's brief stay in Razadon's prison had marked him. Then again, from the stony look on Malek's face, he wasn't feeling particularly forgiving either. If she didn't handle things her way and quickly, they'd take matters into their own hands.

First, she had to deal with an angry demon. Then, she'd attempt to tame a dragon.

Sabine placed her hand on Bane's arm, sending a wave of seductive magic over him. He immediately dropped his gaze to hers and blinked, his eyes reverting to their normal amber. With a low growl, he pulled her into his arms.

She leaned against his chest, breathing in his spicy scent and sending him a stronger surge of her power. He'd used too much of his magic during the battle with the wyverns and then healing the hound. Bane's arms around her relaxed, and he ran his hand over her hair.

The unconscious man began to rouse, blinking rapidly. When he eyed the curved sword Malek had kicked aside, Levin shook his head in warning and angled his blade under the man's chin. The man froze, his gaze scanning over each one of them as though assessing his chances.

"Idola?" the man asked in a gravelly voice.

"I'm unharmed, Ciro."

"For now," Malek said, holding out his hand to Sabine.

She placed her hand in his, allowing him to draw her to his side. He wrapped his arm around her and said, "You dared to attack a dragon's mate. For that reason alone, your life should be forfeit."

Idola paled. Basco whined again, sensing the seer's distress. Sabine caught the hound's gaze and made a gesture for silence. Malek had far too much control to simply execute Idola. At least, she hoped. From the anger and fierce protectiveness she was picking up through their bond, she worried Idola's attack might be what finally pushed him over the edge.

"Malek, she's human and this is her home. We're the intruders here," she reminded him silently.

Malek's arm tightened around her. *"A human does not challenge a dragon's might and walk away unscathed."*

"I wasn't aware dragons considered humans so dangerous," Sabine said mildly. *"How scary she must appear. Ooooooh."*

He narrowed his eyes on her. *"Are you teasing me?"*

She kept her expression innocent as she looked up at him. *"Are you going to protect me from the big bad humans? Shall I swoon?"*

Malek's lips twitched. *"Maybe we should wait for a larger audience. It'll do wonders for my ego."*

Sabine coughed, trying to hide her laugh. *"You really want to discuss egos, mighty Dragon Lord?"*

"You're not going to let me live that title down, are you?"

"Not a chance."

Ciro tried to stand, but Levin pressed the edge of his blade against the man's throat. A thin trail of blood trickled down his neck. Ciro froze.

"I ask your forgiveness, Dragon Lord," Idola said quietly. "I was not aware she was yours, only that an unbound fae approached."

Bane narrowed his eyes. "Unbound? Explain."

Idola flicked her gaze at Bane. "All fae are bound in iron chains and cut off from their magic."

"Iron chains?" Rika whispered in horror. Even Esmelle looked appalled.

Bane's eyes flashed to silver once again, his body practically vibrating from rage.

Malek's expression turned thunderous. For the first time, Idola looked terrified.

A sick feeling rose in Sabine. She'd seen fae captives in the underworld. Her own uncle had been one of them. That prison housed some of the most dangerous fae criminals, but not even the demons shackled their fae prisoners with iron restraints. Gods. What was she thinking walking foolishly into a den of dragons? If they ever learned who she really was, they'd never allow her to leave.

Blossom hugged her neck and whispered, "It's okay, Sabine. We can sneak away and go back to Razadon. You were happy there. They have mushrooms!"

It was a tempting thought. She liked mushrooms.

Malek captured Sabine's hand and led her away from the cabin. He marched through the vegetable garden and out the opposite side into a small meadow that lay just beyond Idola's home. A large vansheer, similar to the deer found within Faerie's forests, had been hoisted up on a rack. From the appearance of the tools neatly sitting beside the rack, Ciro had been in the middle of skinning the animal when the fight had occurred.

"Blossom," Malek said. "I need a private word with Sabine."

The pixie's eyes rounded and she took off. Sabine watched her dive under some foliage at the edge of the garden, taking on the appearance of a ladybug. It figured. Tell a pixie you need privacy, and they were more than happy to provide the *illusion* of it.

She turned around to find Malek pacing. The last time she'd seen him this furious, he'd been under the influence of magic designed to amplify emotions. Nothing of the sort was plaguing him now, but years of dealing with volatile demons had taught her the value of patience. She didn't think teasing him would help the situation.

Deciding to wait him out, she watched the ladybug fly from leaf to leaf, sneaking closer. Every time Sabine pretended to look at something else, Blossom darted to the next plant. She landed on a mushroom and lingered for a moment, wings twitching.

Maybe the pixie had a point. They'd all been happy in Razadon, especially after the threats had been neutralized—and Sabine had recovered from her encounter with cold iron.

Malek had saved her from being poisoned by an iron dart, but it had been a near thing. She shuddered, remembering how the cold had lanced through her veins like ice. It had been one of the most painful experiences of her life, second only to her magic being destroyed. It was intolerable to think of other fae being held captive in the Sky Cities and subjected to similar torments.

Malek whirled around and stalked toward her. "I will *never* allow anything of the sort to happen to you."

She met his gaze and said, "I never said otherwise."

"Dammit, Sabine," Malek said, his expression pained. "Don't you think I can feel your doubts? Your fear? I can sense it."

Sabine looked away. "We both knew this wasn't going to be easy."

Malek cupped her face and held her gaze. "I would give anything to change the past and erase the shadows from your eyes. I know it's little comfort, but there are no captive fae on the island controlled by my clan. That was something Elis'andreia insisted upon before becoming my grandfather's mate. And I swear to you—so long as I live, no fae will ever endure such torments on land controlled by the Obsidian Clan."

"And the captives on other islands?"

Malek released her and blew out a breath. "We do not

interfere with other clans. It's the only way we've maintained peace among our kind since the portal closed."

Sabine stared off into the distance, watching the forbidding dark specks circling the floating islands in the sky. "That's not peace, Malek. It's complacency."

"You want to free them," Malek surmised.

She turned back to Malek. "They're my people. What kind of ruler would I be if I left them to their fate? If I travel with you to the Sky Cities, I will do whatever is necessary to save them. I know you have your own loyalties to consider. I'm not asking for your help with this."

Malek leaned back and studied her. "Do you think for one fucking minute my loyalty to my people is less than the loyalty I have to you? Sabine, you're my mate. You're everything to me. I would burn the world before I let anything happen to you."

She blinked at him. That was the second time since they arrived that he'd referred to her as his mate. "Malek, I don't—"

He pressed his fingers against her lips. "No. I don't want to hear it. I know you don't fully understand. You will eventually. For now, just know you are beyond precious to me. I will stand by your side and protect you with my last breath. We may not always agree, but you can always depend on me. Always."

Sabine's gaze softened, and she wrapped her hand around his wrist. "I believe you, Malek Rish'dan. I've believed in you from almost the first moment we met. Even then, you were constantly in my thoughts. In my wildest dreams, I never imagined a dragon would claim my heart. But we need to discuss this mate—"

Malek leaned down and kissed her, silencing her objections. She started to resist, but he pulled her closer and deepened their kiss. To hell with it. She wound her arms around his neck, wanting and needing him like her next breath. His heated magic wrapped around her, both protective and full of need. She matched it with her own softer magic, getting lost in his power and in him. She leaned into him, needing even more. Every touch only further ignited her desire. Gods, she wanted him.

Blossom cheered. "Woo hoo! We're going to storm the Sky Cities, rescue the fae, and Sabine and Malek are going to live happily ever after!"

Malek broke their kiss and narrowed his eyes on the talking ladybug. "I think we need to revisit the definition of privacy."

"You said you needed a private word," Sabine reminded him with a smile. "Technically, she gave you that."

Blossom nodded. "I gave you several."

Malek sighed and took Sabine's hand, leading her back to the seer's cabin. "One of these days, I *will* get you alone without any interruptions."

She laughed and kissed his cheek. "Not if I get you alone first. And don't think I'm unaware you were doing your best to distract me."

"That wasn't anywhere close to my best," Malek said, glancing over at her with a smug grin. "I intend to show you my best later—when we're alone."

Sabine nearly missed a step. Well. She wasn't about to argue about *that*.

CHAPTER 12

They all crowded into Idola's cabin, except for Levin, who remained outside to keep a close eye on Ciro. Malek wanted Ciro restrained and out of the way until he reached an agreement with the seer. He didn't trust Bane not to kill Idola's lover, especially without Sabine's calming influence. And Malek wasn't ready to be separated from Sabine, not so soon after the attack.

Bane had insisted upon fully inspecting the house before Sabine entered, and now stood nearby as a forbidding sentry. His icy stare was focused on the seer seated at the kitchen table. Blossom was busy investigating all the nooks and crannies of the cabin, a glittering whirlwind that zipped around the cabin's rafters and under furniture. Malek wasn't quite sure what the pixie was searching for, but between Sabine's two unusual guards, he was relatively confident there wouldn't be any other surprises.

Malek pulled out Sabine's chair for her before taking the seat to her right. Esmelle took the chair beside Sabine, while Rika stood quietly nearby, watching Idola. The young seer kept her hand on the weapon at her side, a nervous habit she'd adopted over the past several weeks.

Malek dropped the warding medallion on Idola's table, wanting to get straight to business. "I commissioned you several years ago to create two of these medallions."

Basco rested his large head and floppy red ears on the table, sniffing at the neck piece.

Idola reached out and fingered the design etched into the medallion's metal. "I remember. This one was designed for your wyvern wingmate. The other was crafted for a greater dragon."

Malek leaned back in his chair. "That one was destroyed. I require another."

Idola lifted her glowing sightless eyes to regard him with surprise. "Destroyed? It should have been able to withstand brief exposure to dragonfire. Did it not heat properly to warn you?"

"The manner of its destruction is irrelevant," Malek said, not wanting to discuss how he'd melted the dwarven crystal back in Razadon. "How quickly can you craft a replacement medallion?"

Idola frowned, studying the medallion again. "It took several weeks last time."

Bane leaned against one of the wooden beams and crossed his arms over his chest. "The dragon didn't ask how long it previously took. He wanted to know how quickly you could craft a new one."

Idola's jaw clenched, and she didn't respond.

Malek stood, his palms flat on the table. "Do not test me, Idola. Your attack on my mate has already eliminated whatever patience I had. Your continued existence is a gift I can revoke at any time. I would suggest you make more of an effort to stay within my good graces."

A flicker of annoyance crossed Sabine's face before she

masked it. If he didn't know her as well as he did, he would have missed it.

If he could convince Sabine to openly accept she was his mate, it would offer her a great deal of protection once they were among his people. He just needed to be careful about pushing her too fast.

Esmelle leaned forward and tapped her fingernail on the medallion to draw Idola's attention. "Look, I don't know you, but I know Sabine and Malek. Sabine could easily hide Malek's identity with her magic. This medallion is simply a convenience, but it's hardly necessary. If you offer your aid, they'll be more inclined to let bygones be bygones. I suggest you take the deal."

Idola regarded Malek with skepticism. "A medallion in exchange for my life?"

Bane studied his claws. "I say we kill the bitch and move on. You can't trust anything she offers you anyway."

"I'm beginning to wonder the same thing," Malek said, debating the wisdom in negotiating with Idola. It was impossible to miss the hatred in her expression whenever her glowing gaze landed on Sabine. Despite Sabine's earlier intervention, he questioned the wisdom in allowing Idola to live.

Esmelle gave both of them a dark look. Basco whined unhappily.

Blossom landed on Sabine's shoulder and whispered something in her ear. The pixie gave Malek a salute and then took off again, this time investigating some of the containers sitting on the countertops.

Sabine placed her hand over Malek's, her soft voice slipping into his thoughts. *"Once done, some things cannot be undone. Her death may have repercussions that none of us can anticipate. You need her, Malek. She has much to offer if you can convince her to aid you."*

He looked down at Sabine, marveling at her compassion and wisdom that belied her years. She had no idea how regal her bearing, even glamoured as a human and sitting in a cabin in the woods. He wasn't sure if it was something that had always been part of her, or how the humans had missed seeing the truth of her for so long.

He lifted her hand and kissed it. *"I need you, Sabine. No other. She endangered you. That is unforgivable."*

Sabine's magic flowed over him, calming the flames of his anger. *"She currently offers no threat to us. She simply acted from a place of fear. If you reinforce those fears, it will only spread to others like seeds taking root."*

"What do you suggest?"

She looked up at him. *"One of your brethren betrayed you. If Idola can craft another warding medallion to hide your identity and help you uncover the truth, isn't that worth her life?"*

Malek lowered his head for a moment, considering the implications. Allowing Idola to live set a dangerous precedent, but he knew of no other magic user who could craft a medallion such as the one she'd forged for him. Some places in the Sky Cities were too dangerous for any fae to travel. He wouldn't risk Sabine's safety by asking her to shield him with glamour. Her magic would draw other dragons to her like a beacon.

"I will let her live, but only because you've asked it of me. If she or any other raises their hand against you again, they will die. On this, I will not negotiate. I brought you here to keep you safe, Sabine. No matter the cost."

He turned back to Idola, who was watching him silently. The hound sat beside her, his head still resting on the table.

"Very well," Malek agreed. "Your life in exchange for a warding medallion. However, time is of the essence. I wish to depart from your cabin with the medallion in hand no later than nightfall."

Idola folded her hands in her lap. "I require two other concessions before I can begin."

Malek narrowed his eyes. "What concessions?"

"The first is a piece of cold iron and some silver to infuse into the medallion," Idola said, reminding him of the same request she'd made the last time he'd commissioned the medallions.

Malek scowled. He didn't like the idea of handing over another piece of the rare and dangerous metal to her, even if it was necessary for the medallion's creation. "And the second?"

Idola's glowing gaze shifted to Rika. "The second is for you to leave the girl with me when you depart."

Rika's jaw dropped open. "What? Me? Here? With you?"

Blossom landed on the table, her hands on her hips. "Not a chance. Rika stays with us. She's ours."

"Blossom," Sabine said, holding out her hand for Blossom.

The pixie landed on her palm and said, "You can't do it, Sabine. You can't just leave her with the wicked seer of the north. It's wrong!"

Bane snarled at Blossom. "Quiet, bug. This isn't your decision."

Blossom grumbled something too low for anyone but Sabine to overhear. She hopped onto Sabine's shoulder and crossed her arms over her chest, her wings tinged with red.

Sabine regarded Idola thoughtfully. "Why do you wish Rika to remain here with you?"

Idola straightened. "She's a seer of the blood, just as I am. I will shelter the girl and ensure she does not venture into your lands. She will not be a threat to your kind."

"Will you care for her and teach her how to hide her gifts?" Sabine asked mildly.

Rika's eyes rounded, her mouth hanging open. Bane

placed his clawed hand on Rika's shoulder, and she straightened, clamping her mouth shut.

Idola hesitated, clearly sensing a trap. "I… I will not harm her. I will give her shelter and protection to the best of my abilities."

Sabine gestured to Rika. "Rika is not my captive. She will not be part of any concession or negotiation, now or ever. If she wishes to remain here with you, that is her decision. All of us will respect and abide by her choice."

Rika stepped up to the table and said, "Then I say no. Sabine saved me from the burning festival in Karga. She found a way to reverse the magic when I'd been turned into a butterfly—"

"That was an accident!" Blossom protested.

"She sat at my bedside and told me stories when I was homesick," Rika continued, not missing a beat. "She risked her life for me after a kobold pushed me off a ledge in the underworld. She stopped the dryads from turning me into a tree. Every time I get myself into trouble, Sabine is there to pull me out."

"But she's fae!" Idola sputtered.

Rika nodded. "Yes, she is. My grandmother was Seer of Karga and recognized Sabine for who she was. Her last wish was for me to escape the Fire Festival and leave with Sabine. She trusted Sabine with my life, and Sabine's proven herself a thousand times over. This is my family now, and this is where I'll stay."

Idola sat back, stunned. Malek bit back a smile.

Sabine turned to Rika and said, "You have a place with us for as long as you wish it, Rika."

Blossom grinned and flew over to Rika's shoulder. "I still think you should have kept the butterfly wings."

"Um, wings are definitely not my thing."

Esmelle smiled. "I think she pretty much said it all, Idola.

If you were hoping to protect another seer from the fae, it's not necessary. Your intentions may be honorable, but Rika is safer with Sabine than anywhere else in the world."

"My own family tried to keep me safe the only way they could," Idola said, gesturing to her scarred face. "The fae have been hunting seers for generations. They use trickery and deceit to get what they want. My aunt and older sister were stolen in the middle of the night when I was but a babe. How can you trust her?"

"Sabine would never do that," Rika said, shaking her head. "I know the type of person she is."

"You're blinded by her magic, child," Idola said and turned back to Sabine. "What do you hope to gain from this girl? Will you use her against your enemies? Or do you seek to learn the secrets of our blood?"

Sabine stood, her glamour melting away like ice on a hot summer day. Her fair skin shimmered gold with barely restrained power. "I do not owe you any explanations, seer. Rika has declined your offer, and you *will* respect her decision."

Basco growled a warning at Idola, but she ignored him. She slapped her hands on the tabletop and stood. "She only declined because you've bewitched her! The dangers she mentioned were likely a result of exposure to your kind! The fae won't rest until all of us are dead or destroyed. I've seen it! I know the truth!"

"That's enough, Idola," Malek snapped, his patience at an end.

Sabine narrowed her eyes on Idola, and the ground trembled. Dishes and herb containers toppled from their shelves, shattering into thousands of pieces.

"*You* are blinded by hate, Idola. You cling to your beliefs, even when a gift from one of Faerie's hounds allows you to see the truth. You and your kind have come to this world and attempted to claim a piece of it, but Aeslion will never hear your pleas. I would suggest you consider carefully the wisdom in making me an enemy."

Sabine stepped away from the table and walked out the door. Basco lifted his head and let out a low, mournful howl. A peal of thunder rumbled in the distance.

Bane gave Malek a sharp look and said, "Deal with this bitch, and be done with it. Or I'll do it for you."

Malek heard the door slam behind Bane, but he didn't spare him a look. Only Sabine's earlier words kept him in the room. He wouldn't kill the seer outright, but he wouldn't let this additional slight go unpunished—especially now that she knew Sabine was his.

Blossom landed on the kitchen table and pointed at Idola. "You're rude, mean, and I don't like you. Sabine is one of the best people I know, even if she doesn't have wings. She could have squished you like a bug, but she didn't because she's *nice.*"

"Blossom, I think you've said more than enough," Esmelle said, her voice sharp. "It would be best if you harvested some nectar in the garden until we're done here."

"Nope," Blossom said, crossing her arms. "I'm staying here where I can keep an eye on this one. Sabine needs some quiet time. Trust me."

Malek sent a silent message to Levin, instructing him to collect a piece of cold iron and some silver from a nearby supply cache.

"You do know Sabine just came out here in all her golden glory, right? Walked right past me and the other human."

"Shit."

"Yeah. I'll get the iron, but word is going to get out if we don't do something."

Malek turned back to Idola. The seer was watching him

warily. She knew she'd crossed a line and was waiting for him to declare her sentence.

Malek leaned down and allowed the dragon within him to reflect in his gaze. Idola gasped and sat back, losing her grip on the magic that allowed her to see through Basco's eyes.

"You will be provided with the metals necessary to complete your task. In exchange for your life, you will craft the medallion we discussed. However, you are henceforth banished from all land currently controlled by dragonkind. If you are still on our lands by dawn tomorrow, I will send a squadron of wyverns to hunt you down. Your burned body will be mounted at the entrance of Imenel as a warning to any who might challenge our will."

Idola swallowed, her breath coming in quick, shallow pants. "I-I understand, Dragon Lord. I will be gone by dawn's light. I-I thank you for my life."

Esmelle sighed and rested her head in her hands. "This just gets messier and messier. Magic is hard enough without trying to do it under such pressure. Blossom, go find something quiet to do. Rika, you can stay but only if you promise not to let Idola fill your head with nonsense about the fae."

Rika gave Esmelle a dry look. "I think we're beyond that, don't you?"

"Smart girl," Esmelle said with an approving nod. She stood and shooed Malek toward the door. "Go. Do… dragon things. Let me handle this for now."

Malek scowled but allowed her to push him out the door. Levin had already taken off for the supply cache, leaving a bound and gagged Ciro on the porch. Malek studied him for a moment, weighing the human's potential danger to Sabine. As far as he knew, Ciro was completely human without any affinity for magic.

"You overheard my edict?"

Ciro gave him a curt nod.

"Then ensure Idola is gone by dawn, or you may find yourself suffering the same fate."

Ciro's jaw hardened, but he inclined his head in understanding. Malek turned away. He'd either leave with Idola or not. Either way, Malek had more important things to consider.

As he walked toward the garden in the direction Sabine must have gone, he heard the clink of glass bottles and Esmelle asking Idola about the reagents needed to prepare the medallion.

At least he wouldn't have to waste any more time dealing with Idola. Esmelle sounded like she had things well in hand. Shaking his head at the way she'd chased him out of Idola's cabin, he couldn't help but think Levin had finally met his match in the feisty dryad.

It was about time.

SABINE LEANED AGAINST THE TREE, mentally kicking herself. After she'd stormed out of the cabin, she'd been too angry to attempt reapplying her glamour. She'd strode past a surprised Levin and Ciro, through the garden and into the meadow behind the cabin. The small forested area that lay just beyond it had called to her, but it was doing little to quell her tumultuous emotions.

Bane's footsteps were soundless behind her, but she felt his presence draw closer. He didn't say a word, but wrapped his arms around her, offering his silent strength.

She sighed and leaned against him. "It would have been better to hold my tongue."

"What are you trying to prove, Sabine?"

She gestured in the direction of the cabin. "In her eyes,

the fae are monsters. We're the boogeymen in the dark, either out to steal human children or murder them in their beds."

Bane bit out a laugh. "Have you forgotten who you're talking to?"

She turned to face him and managed a smile. "I suppose it sounds absurd to a demon. Your people have been accused of far worse."

Bane studied her thoughtfully. "Have you been pretending to be human for so long that you've forgotten who you are?"

"It feels that way at times," Sabine admitted. "I've been away from my people for so long, I scarcely remember what it's like to live among them."

He grasped her chin and tilted her head back to meet his gaze. "You are more than fae. You are the descendant of gods. You're Queen of the Unseelie, a ruler to be feared and admired. You reunited the merfolk, turned ambivalent dwarves into enthusiastic allies, thwarted the King of Demons, and walked through the Hall of Gods and drank of the Well's power."

"And I just allowed a human to cause me to lose control and forget myself," Sabine said in irritation.

Bane leaned back against a tree. "Yes, you did. Why was that?"

"I don't know! I was just so angry. This human, this mortal, dared to question *me*. For a brief moment, I wanted to strike her down for such insolence. If I had stayed, I might have."

"Why didn't you?"

"Because I didn't want to justify her fear and become that monster," Sabine said and then pressed her hand against her queasy stomach. "Gods, Bane. I don't know what's happening to me. One second I feel fine, but the next it's as though everything is jumbled in my head."

Bane captured her hand and nodded toward it. "Look at your skin, Sabine."

She lowered her gaze to see the golden glow still shimmering brightly.

Bane lifted a lock of her hair and said, "Every day, there's more gold in it. You haven't lost control of your glamour in years, but it's happening more often."

"My magic's changing," she whispered, unable to deny the truth.

"Or she's becoming stronger."

Sabine lifted her head and met his amber gaze. He might be right, but that wasn't the entirety of it. Sabine had felt something change within her ever since she drank from the Well of Dreams.

"Lachlina's part of it," Sabine admitted. "We were separate before, but her thoughts keep bleeding into mine. Half the time, I don't know where she begins and I end."

"Then you need to trust me or Bane to tell you when you've gone too far," Malek said, his boots crunching on the fallen leaves behind her.

Sabine turned and glanced in the direction of the cabin. "The seer?"

"Idola had been warned twice about provoking me. I've given her leave to craft the medallion in exchange for her life, but she's been banished. If she's still on land controlled by my kin when dawn breaks, her life is forfeit."

Bane crossed his arms over his chest. "I still would have skewered the bitch, but what can you expect from a giant flying lizard?"

"You may still get the chance," Malek said dryly.

Bane chuckled. "Your dragon's growing on me, Sabine."

She sighed and looked away. "Idola may be the only seer we ever find. I'd hoped she might be open to the possibility of teaching Rika more about her gifts. Even if she were at this point, I don't think any of us would trust her."

"Who taught the first seers their magic?" Bane asked.

Sabine frowned. "The Faerie archives may have information about them, but they were only a footnote in my education. They came to Aeslion with the first wave of humans who crossed through the portal. Beyond that, I have no idea. My people were more interested in eliminating the threat they posed to us."

"Then Rika will learn by our side," Bane said, his tone settling the matter. "Should the day come when she wishes to learn more about her birthright, we can explore the possibility. But there are other matters far more pressing."

Malek approached Sabine, his expression full of concern. "He's right, Sabine. I need you to tell me what's going on. I can't help if I don't know what's happening."

Sabine squeezed her eyes shut. He needed to know, but such an admission was humiliating. Bane and Dax had spent years introducing stressors to ensure her human glamour wouldn't falter under any circumstances. She'd been so sure of herself, and now she was losing control like an untrained child.

"When my emotions run high, the barriers between me and Lachlina blur," Sabine said, touching the marks on her wrist that were her connection to the goddess. "My magic becomes untethered, and not even my skin markings help harness my power anymore. I didn't trust myself to remain in that cabin. Despite Basco's plea for leniency, I would have struck Idola down for challenging me."

Malek frowned. "This is something new, isn't it?"

"With every artifact Sabine discovers and absorbs, Lachlina's hold on her deepens," Bane said. "There's only one portal key left. If we have any hope of extricating Sabine from her clutches, we need to act now."

Sabine pressed her hand against the rough bark of a nearby oak tree. She could almost feel Theoria with her, offering her strength. She needed to tell Malek and Bane everything—at least everything she was allowed to say.

Lachlina was quiet within her for the moment. The goddess had likely exhausted herself attempting to influence Sabine and would need to rest for a time. There was no better opportunity to tell Malek and Bane the truth.

Sabine turned to face both of them. "When we were in the underworld, the Huntsman spoke to me about the portal. He told me I'd soon be faced with a choice."

Bane stilled.

Malek raised his eyebrows. "This was while we were in the Hall of the Gods?"

Sabine nodded. "When Lachlina sealed the portal, she created an imbalance. Limited amounts of magic can flow into our world, but the gods can no longer draw upon Aeslion's power. It's created a vacuum. The Huntsman said the gods are no longer interested in sustaining our world when we aren't able to give anything back to them."

Something flickered in Bane's eyes, but he remained silent.

Sabine ran her fingers over the marks of power on her wrist that represented each of the portal keys she'd acquired. Vestior, in the guise of Huntsman, had insisted opening the portal was necessary for Aeslion's continued survival.

Lachlina, on the other hand, didn't want the portal reopened and had sacrificed everything to ensure that outcome. It wasn't that the goddess wanted Aeslion to die; Lachlina was simply convinced the only way to safeguard the memory of Theoria's sacrifice was to end the war that had decimated the world.

She lifted her head to meet Malek's concerned gaze. "The Huntsman told me the seals on the portal are fracturing and poisoning the remaining magic in our world. If it continues to stay closed, Aeslion and everyone living here will die. It *must* be reopened, but we risk being swept up in the war once again. I'm not sure what will happen to Aeslion when that day comes."

"What happens to *you* if we reopen the portal?" Malek asked, taking a step closer to her. "If Lachlina's strengthening with every artifact we locate, where does that leave you, Sabine?"

Sabine fell silent. She hadn't asked the question, in part because she didn't want to know. It was unlikely she would survive the eventuality. Both Malek and Bane had to suspect the truth too. No fae had ever been meant to control all the power contained within the artifacts. The magic had been split up and divided for a reason.

Bane shook his head in disapproval. "In battle, you must go armed with as much information as you can gather. You do yourself and the rest of us no favors by remaining ignorant."

"I know," she said quietly.

A storm was brewing behind Malek's eyes. "What else did the Huntsman tell you, Sabine?"

Something in his tone made her pause. She studied him, but his expression was guarded. She couldn't even sense his emotions through their bond. Shaking her head, she said, "There are some things I can't share."

"With me? Or with anyone?"

Sabine turned away and didn't answer. She'd already said too much. The Huntsman had placed a geas upon her, forcing her silence to prevent anyone from learning his true identity. Even if he hadn't, some secrets weren't hers to share.

Malek captured her hand. "The Huntsman spoke to me in the in-between."

Her gaze flew to him. "What?"

Bane narrowed his eyes. "When was this?"

"He stopped me before I entered the grove," Malek said before turning back to Sabine. "I asked him about your connection to Lachlina and whether he could protect you from her."

Sabine's eyes widened. "He can't."

"So I was informed," Malek said in irritation. "But he said the bond between you could be broken, but only by mutual agreement and without malice."

"Then we need to find a way to convince her she's better off without Sabine," Bane said, as though it should be a simple matter.

Sabine didn't bother to hide the exasperation in her tone. "She's locked away in a dead garden and trapped in the in-between. Nothing we offer her, short of freedom, will prompt her to release me."

"Then how do we free her?" Malek asked.

Sabine shook her head. "I don't believe we can. She betrayed the gods. They sentenced her to be locked away in a prison for eternity."

"There is another possibility," Bane said.

Malek met Bane's gaze, and a world of meaning passed between them. Sabine fell silent, suddenly uneasy.

They couldn't be thinking about killing a goddess, could they?

CHAPTER 13

Sabine waited with Bane a short distance away from the cabin while Malek completed his transaction with the seer. Nightfall was quickly approaching, and Sabine could already sense the moon beginning its ascent. The sky was turning shades of violet and dark blue, making the lights of the city look like hundreds of small stars below them.

"It's beautiful from up here," Sabine said, gazing down at Imenel's twinkling lights.

Bane grunted. "Only because we're upwind from the stench of unwashed humans and refuse."

Sabine laughed. "That's one thing I don't miss about living in Akros."

Voices caught Sabine's attention, and she turned to look up the hill. Esmelle and Rika were walking side-by-side talking together. Blossom came zipping down the hill ahead of them, sending a cascade of glittering pixie dust in her wake. Sabine held out her hand for Blossom to land.

Blossom hopped up and down, both eager and excited. "I almost saw a human get eaten by a dragon!"

Sabine glanced back at Esmelle and Rika who were both

thankfully still out of earshot. In a low voice, she whispered, "I'm not sure our friends will appreciate your enthusiasm."

Blossom considered that for a moment and then shook her head. "No. I'm pretty sure they'd be okay with it."

"Okay with what?" Esmelle asked, stopping to stand beside them.

Sabine shook her head as Blossom took a seat on her shoulder. "Don't ask."

Before Esmelle could respond, a huge emerald green wyvern with gold dusted wings landed on the roof of the cabin, causing it to bow from his substantial weight. Screams sounded from inside. The wyvern's nails pierced the roof as he raised his head, trumpeting a stream of dragonfire toward the sky. His powerful wings flapped as he lifted into the air, ripping the roof completely off and dropping the debris onto the ground.

Esmelle stopped beside her and put her hands on her hips. "Well, that was hardly necessary. It was a delightful little cabin before Levin decided to muck it up."

Rika stared wide-eyed at the cabin. "T-that's Levin?"

"Aye," Esmelle said, tapping her foot impatiently. "And I'll be having words with him about leaving his trash in the garden. If he thinks for a minute I'm going to put up with that nonsense, we'll definitely go a round or two."

Bane made a noise of approval. "The lizard knows how to make a point."

Sabine elbowed Bane. "You're not helping."

"I wasn't trying to, nor should you," Bane reminded her. "The seer would have seen you dead if she could have gotten away with it. You would do well to remember that before you indulge in any form of pity."

Blossom smacked her forehead. "Don't tell me I actually agree with a demon. Do you know how wrong that is? I need a bath. Does anyone have a bathing leaf? This is what happens when pixies go to the underworld! Sulfur lingers, people!"

Rika plucked a leaf from a nearby tree and handed it to Blossom. She grabbed it and flew straight for the small river. Sabine sighed.

A moment later, Malek emerged from the cabin and began walking down the hill toward them. Even without Levin's display, Sabine knew things hadn't gone well based on the stormy expression on Malek's face. Sabine took several steps toward him, watching the intensity in his gaze shift from silent fury to a focused determination that nearly stole her breath. She felt her body automatically respond to his unspoken need, her magic thrumming just below the surface.

Levin descended rapidly, shifting forms back to human before he touched the ground. He landed beside Malek, speaking quietly with him. Malek barely spared him a glance, his focus squarely on Sabine. Levin followed his gaze and chuckled before changing directions and making a beeline for a still angry Esmelle.

"Oh, no!" Esmelle protested, shaking her head. "Don't think you can come over here and charm me after making a mess of that sweet garden. Do you have any idea how much magic it took to—"

Levin kissed Esmelle soundly, muffling her protests. Apparently, Esmelle wasn't feeling all that confrontational anymore because she threw her arms around Levin's neck and returned his kiss. Sabine smiled. It was about time Esmelle found some happiness.

Bane eyed them with disgust. "I was hoping she would have turned him into a toad."

Rika giggled and pinched her thumb and forefinger together. "Or a very tiny lizard."

Bane rubbed his chin. "Not too small, or I'll never get enough leather for a new pair of boots."

Malek swept Sabine into his arms, surrounding her with his heated power. She ran her hands up his chest and wound them around his neck.

"It's done," Malek said, pressing his forehead against hers. "She'll be out of the area by dawn. I thought she might resist, but Levin made my point clear enough. I don't like loose ends."

"Nor do I," Bane said in irritation. "She's a continued threat as long as she draws breath. Even a human can show teeth when the situation arises."

Sabine didn't respond. Humans could be as varied as the fae, each with their own motivations and penchant for destruction. Idola might no longer be the innocent child who'd bravely soothed the hurts of a Faerie hound, but a glimmer of her must still remain. Otherwise, Basco wouldn't have remained by her side for as long as he had.

Levin put his arm around Esmelle's shoulders and said, "I'll make sure they're both gone tomorrow, Malek. I need to take care of a few things here anyway."

Esmelle cleared her throat. "One big thing. In the garden."

Levin grinned. "I'll work on my aim next time I drop a roof."

Esmelle's gaze traveled wistfully to the cabin. "It really is a pity. She's created a lovely little place for herself. I can't say I disagree with your decision though, Malek."

"I didn't like her," Rika said, brushing one of her dark braids away from her face. "She reminded me of the Kiervan back in Karga. She'd already judged all of us before we even walked through the door. I don't understand how people can be so closed-minded."

"Fear," Bane said, placing his clawed hand on Rika's shoulder. "The Kiervan believe all magic is evil and should be destroyed. Magic in itself is neither good, nor bad. You know better after having witnessed it for yourself."

Rika nodded. "My grandmother wasn't evil. She tried to help and protect people when she could. I intend to do the same."

"Then you'll honor your grandmother's memory," Esmelle said with a smile.

"I've missed you, Esme," Rika said and hugged her tightly.

Esmelle laughed and returned her hug. "Ah, but you'll need to miss me a bit longer. Malek and Levin said something about splitting up again?" She winked and whispered loudly, "I think they're worried we'll cause too much trouble if we stay together."

"We can't have that," Sabine said, watching Malek fasten the new medallion around his neck. A strange and eerie coldness passed through her. She blinked, and for a moment she could have sworn she'd seen a familiar garden. In the next instant, she was standing with her friends on the path leading toward Imenel.

Blossom tugged on her hair and whispered, "Um, are you okay? Your magic went wonky all of a sudden."

Sabine frowned and rubbed her temples. She hadn't even realized Blossom had returned. Such a lapse in awareness wasn't like her. "It's been a long day."

"I haven't missed wearing this thing," Malek said, adjusting the medallion so it touched his bare skin. A peculiar broken circular symbol had been etched into the metal. It was a twin to the one he'd worn when they'd first met. Even then, she'd sensed something different about him, as though his power was carefully hidden beneath the surface.

Blossom sniffed at him. "You don't smell as smoky anymore. Hey Sabine, come sniff him."

Sabine leaned in close, but she couldn't detect the familiar scent of burned leaves. It was strange that a seer's warding medallion could affect her senses like that. Even a fae's glamour primarily relied upon sight. She reached up to touch the metal, but Malek caught her hand and pressed a kiss against it.

"I don't trust Idola not to do anything to harm you, Sabine. It feels the same as the last one, but I won't gamble with your safety. Not for anything."

She arched her brow. "Isn't it better to know now than through an accidental touch?"

Malek blew out a breath and shook his head. "Not now. Maybe later."

She tilted her head, studying Malek. He held his entire body rigid, giving the illusion of a bowstring pulled taut. She reached for him with her thoughts, and nearly staggered from the overwhelming sense of loss. The warding medallion had somehow muted their bond. Only the faintest traces of Malek's emotions filtered through. She hadn't realized how much she'd come to rely upon such an intimacy until it was taken from her.

Gods. When had that happened? It was painful being this close to him without truly feeling him.

Malek reached for her, pulling her close while making sure she didn't accidentally brush against the medallion. Even through his struggle, he still treated her as though she were made of the rarest crystal found in the dwarven mines. She leaned into his touch, sending a soft wave of her power over him.

"Sabine," Malek said, his voice pained. "This damned thing isn't worth not being able to feel you. I hadn't realized—"

Sabine stopped him from removing the necklace and shook her head. "No, Malek. If this medallion helps you determine who sent the wyverns after you, you need to wear it. It's only temporary."

She pressed a light kiss against his lips. He pulled her close, his hand cupping her face as he deepened the kiss. Sabine's senses reeled. Even without his magic caressing her, it was as though his touch went straight through her to ignite all her desires. She whimpered against his lips, parting them to allow him to sweep inside and fully claim her mouth.

Levin chuckled. "For giving me such grief earlier, it's good to know I'm not the only one affected by certain instincts."

Esmelle elbowed him in the ribs. "Shush."

"Trust me, this doesn't happen often enough. Malek's got ironclad control. Or at least, he did."

"Sabine and Malek, sitting in a tree," Blossom sang, sprinkling pixie dust over top of them. "K-I-S-S-I-N-G—"

Rika giggled and said, "Blossom, you're going to get in so much trouble."

Sabine broke their kiss, trying to catch her breath. Malek was staring at her as though debating whether or not to steal her away. Part of her wanted him to. Gods. What in the world was happening to her? The minute Malek put his hands on her, she seemed to lose the ability to think. From the predatory look in his eyes, she wasn't sure they were even going to make it to the Sky Cities. She was tempted to create a thicket right here to give them a bit of privacy. He pulled her closer again, the heat from his hands causing her skin to pebble in awareness.

"Malek?" she asked, running her hands up his firm chest. She didn't want him to stop, but Malek had never been one for public displays of intimacy.

Bane narrowed his eyes. "Could the medallion be amplifying any of your emotions?"

Malek jerked his head up, blinking as though coming out of a fog. "What?"

Levin's brow furrowed. "Wait. Is that even possible? Idola wouldn't have dared do something like that, would she?"

Rika shook her head. "I know we can negate some magic, but I've never heard of a seer having the ability to amplify emotions. At least it wasn't one of my family's gifts."

Esme frowned. "She used her blood as a binder for the magic and infused it into cold iron before encasing it in silver."

Sabine pressed her hands against Malek's chest, surrounding him with the touch of her power. "Is Bane right? Is the medallion affecting you?"

Malek looked down at Sabine. Pure, unadulterated need filled his expression. He cupped the side of her face as though unable to resist touching her. Sabine pressed her hand against his, holding him against her and asked, "When you touch me, what do you feel?"

Malek gazed down at her with unmistakable tenderness. "Complete. I don't know if it's simply because the warding medallion is inhibiting my magic or if Idola's medallion changed something. I don't recall feeling this way when I wore the last one specifically designed for me."

"The medallion's muted our connection," she said, placing her hand over his heart. "I don't sense you as strongly as I normally do. Even when you were wearing Levin's medallion, I still felt you."

Bane yanked the medallion off Malek. "How do you feel now?"

Sabine gasped as Malek's dragon power wrapped around her. She nearly swayed from the sudden onslaught. His arms tightened around her. She leaned into him, breathing in the smell of burned leaves. Her thoughts cleared. She glanced down at the marks on her wrist, wondering if her connection to Malek was helping to keep Lachlina at bay.

"Now I'm feeling annoyed," Malek said, snatching the

warding medallion back from Bane. "I'm not under Idola's thrall."

"I don't think the goddess likes you taking off the medallion," Blossom said, hovering in midair. "She says her 'little flower is growing too fond of the smell of charred wood.'"

Sabine straightened. "If the goddess has an issue with my consorting with dragons, she's welcome to stay out of my thoughts."

"She's stronger when I'm wearing it?" Malek asked.

Sabine nodded. "I think our connection helps to suppress her."

Bane considered them for a moment. "Interesting. You may have more uses than I expected, dragon."

Sabine gestured to the medallion in his hand. "Malek, I know this is necessary. We won't have any semblance of safety until we can understand the wyvern threat and elimi-nate it. I should be able to keep Lachlina's influence under control for a while."

Malek's expression turned grim. "If any of you start to notice either myself or Sabine behaving out of character, I need you to point it out immediately. I'll give us until midday tomorrow until we abandon our search in Imenel and head to the Sky Cities."

Levin took a step toward Malek. "Are you sure that's a good idea? If it's interfering with your mating bond—"

Malek held up his hand to stop him. "Sabine's right, Levin. This needs to be done. I want you to fly back with Esme to the dock area. Anyone who witnessed you leave will expect both of you to return. The rest of us will enter the city by one of the main gates."

Levin gave him a curt nod. "Then we'll see you no later than midday tomorrow."

"Until tomorrow," Malek said, clasping Levin's shoulder.

Esmelle walked up to Sabine and hugged her. "And while he's investigating, I have a song to sing."

Sabine returned the hug and whispered, "Allow the dryad's song to flow through you, but hold part of yourself separate. The longer you're enmeshed in the power of the grove, the more difficult it will be to find your way out. I don't want to lose one of my dearest friends."

Esmelle touched the dryad acorn around her neck. "I'll remember." She paused and then added, "Be safe, Sabine. I only had a brief glimpse of Imenel, but it was enough to know you need to hide yourself well behind your human glamour."

Sabine swallowed her misgivings and nodded. "Stay well, Esme."

Levin transformed off the side of the path, turning back into a huge wyvern.

Rika scooted closer to Sabine. "He looks a lot like the ones who tried to kill us."

Esmelle laughed and hugged Rika tightly. "He wouldn't dare even sneeze in your direction, Rika. You're going to need to keep the rest of this crew focused and on task while I'm gone. Think you can handle that?"

Rika smiled. "I'll see what I can do."

"Good," Esmelle said, walking over to Levin. He lowered himself to the ground, using his wing to help Esmelle climb onto his back. She grabbed hold of two of the barbs between his shoulders. Levin's back legs tensed as he pushed off the ground. Spreading his giant leathery wings, he glided down toward the city.

Malek pressed his hand against Sabine's lower back. "One day, I intend to have you soar the skies with me. Nothing between us, except our magic."

Sabine stared at him, disconcerted by the suggestion. "You want me to ride you?"

"I thought you did that the other night in camp," Blossom whispered loudly.

Malek grinned. "Blossom's not wrong, but wings make everything better."

Blossom nodded. "That's what I've been saying!"

Rika clamped a hand over her mouth, fighting back laughter.

Sabine squeezed her eyes shut and shook her head. "Don't we need to get moving?"

Blossom eyed Bane and asked, "Um, how are we going to keep tall, dark, and demonic hidden from sight? Aren't we going to a human city?"

Sabine looked up at Bane and waggled her fingers in his direction.

He scowled and shook his head. "No glamour."

Sabine rolled her eyes and said, "Very well. Then how do you expect to walk into Imenel without issue?"

Bane reached into the traveler's pack and withdrew several hooded cloaks. Sabine accepted the twilight blue cloak he offered. She ran her hands over the velvety softness, admiring its workmanship. Intricate silver threading and crystal beadwork had been woven throughout, shimmering softly like falling water.

"Allow me," Malek said, draping the cloak over her shoulders. He carefully lifted her hair out of the way before fastening the moon-shaped clasp.

Malek stepped back and shook his head. "This isn't going to work."

"What?" she asked, glancing over to see Rika fawning over a cloak that was the color of a dark red wine. Golden thread wound upwards from the bottom in a complicated geometric pattern that reminded her of some of the artwork they'd seen back in Karga. Bane's cloak was the color of midnight, shielding the wearer from any touch of light. He flung it over his shoulders and fastened the knife-shaped clasp around his throat.

"We need to blend in," Malek said, tugging lightly on the ends of Sabine's hair. "You look a little too much like a Faerie queen, even while wearing human glamour."

Bane grunted and handed Malek a cloak. This one was the darkest shade of obsidian, but the silver threading on his reminded Sabine of the stardust appearance of his scales while he was in dragon form. The moon-shaped silver clasp was a twin to hers, a matched pair.

"I'll show you." Sabine pressed her hand against the clasp and said, *"Crescero."*

The cloak shimmered briefly, becoming nothing more than a plain and ordinary cloak any traveler might wear.

Malek arched his brow. "Will it work for all of us?"

Sabine nodded. "These cloaks were designed by Faerie for each of us to wear. They won't make us invisible, but there's a subtle obfuscation charm embedded into each one. As long as we don't draw anyone's direct attention or alert them to our presence, we should be able to move relatively unhindered through the city."

"Where's mine?" Blossom asked, flying over to the traveler's pack Bane was searching through.

The demon scowled at her. "You're a flying bug. Bugs don't wear cloaks."

Blossom's lower lip trembled and her wings turned red. "Sabine? I don't get a cloak?"

"Of course you do," she said, walking over to Bane.

He narrowed his eyes. "You aren't seriously going to make her a cloak."

"Blossom is as much a member of our traveling party as the rest of us," Sabine said, reaching into the traveling pack and digging through the contents. "Faerie likely knew Blossom's skill with glamour had increased dramatically. She might not *need* a cloak, but if she wants one, I'll see that she has one."

Sabine pulled out two of the golden leaves they'd acquired in the dryad grove. She withdrew her dagger and cut off several strands of her hair. She carefully tied the strands of hair around the leaves before crushing them in her palm. Summoning her magic, she closed her eyes and blew softly on the crushed leaves.

When she opened her hand, a tiny golden cloak shimmered in the fading sunlight.

"Ohhhhh," Blossom murmured, her eyes wide as she landed on Sabine's palm. She picked up the cloak and buried her face in it. "It's the most beautiful cloak I've ever seen! And look! It even has holes for my wings!"

"Wear it well, my courageous friend," Sabine said with a smile.

Blossom grinned and tried to put it on, but her delicate wings got caught in the material. Sabine carefully helped her tuck her wings through the holes. When it was on, Blossom spun around, modeling it for them.

"It looks great on you," Rika said with a grin.

"A great waste of magic," Bane grumbled, motioning for them to start heading down the hill.

"Magic is never wasted on those you care about," Sabine said with a smile, watching as Blossom flew down the hill in her sparkling cloak. She leaned against Bane and sent a wave of her magic over him.

"Your soft heart is going to get you in trouble one day," Bane warned.

"It's fortunate I have such valiant friends who will help pull me out of trouble then, isn't it?" she teased.

Bane merely grunted in response. But when he affectionately ran his hand over her hair, she knew he wasn't quite as unhappy with her decision as he pretended.

CHAPTER 14

The tall and forbidding iron gates of Imenel loomed ahead of them. Twin dragon statues stood as sentinels above the ramparts over the main gate. In the center, a dark blue wyvern lay sprawled on top of the wall. His wings were tucked against his body, while his large scaled head hung over the side of the wall. The wyvern would periodically open his golden serpentine eyes and scan them over the crowd before closing them again, appearing to doze in the waning sunlight.

At least thirty people, carts, and mounts were lined up at the entrance, each one being stopped by the guards before being granted entry. Sabine quickly summoned a cloud of glamour over her companions, using her magic and the surrounding foliage to hide them from sight.

Rika started to step beyond the tree line, but Bane pulled her back, keeping her within the confines of the glamoured wall Sabine had erected. Another cart and horse lumbered down the path, falling in line with the others. Bane motioned for Rika to keep her voice lowered until they had passed.

Rika stood on her toes, trying to peer ahead. "What's going on?"

"Nothing good," Sabine said quietly. "I'm masking our presence, but we can't get too close."

"They're looking for something or someone," Bane said, gesturing to some guards who were rummaging through the contents of a traveling cart. Each of the merchant's baskets and chests were opened, their contents inspected before the guards waved them through.

Malek frowned. "I don't like this. To my knowledge, they've never stopped people from entering the city or assigned guard duty to a wyvern. He's feigning sleep, but if you watch him closely, he's a little too alert and focused on the travelers."

Sabine held out her hand for Blossom to land. Sending a wave of power to reinforce the pixie's glamour, she asked, "Can you see what you can find out?"

"On it!" the pixie said, her image shimmering until she took on the appearance of a large moth. She swooped off Sabine's shoulder and down the path, headed directly for the main gate.

"Could this be related to the wyverns who attacked us earlier?" Sabine asked.

"Perhaps," Malek said, sounding less than pleased by the possibility. "I don't recognize the one at the gate. He's older than the ones who attacked us. If Levin were here, he'd probably know." He gestured to the wyvern's wings that were tucked by his side. "Most wyverns have distinctive marks that identify their clans. These markings are either on their wings, their bellies, or, more rarely, on their heads. With the way he's positioned, he's managed to hide his clan allegiance. I doubt that's a coincidence."

"What are the chances he'll recognize you in human form?" Sabine asked.

"Unlikely, but anything is possible," Malek said, glancing over at her. "He would know me immediately if I were in dragon form or if he could detect my power. If the warding medallion works correctly, it'll mask my identity—even if I'm right under his nose."

Bane leaned down and whispered, "They may not recognize Malek on sight, but the cloaks will not be enough to hide my identity or yours. I suggest we make our entry using more covert methods."

Sabine was inclined to agree, but she nodded discretely toward Rika. While she and Bane might be able to slip through any sentries, Rika's presence posed a different sort of problem. For good or ill, Rika was still human. Even if they managed to get Rika past the wyvern and over the wall, Sabine would need to hold glamour over their entire group. She wasn't sure such an expenditure of magic could withstand Rika's blossoming seer abilities.

A pale white moth flew toward them and landed on Sabine's outstretched hand. Its image shimmered, reforming as a tiny pixie.

"They're looking for spies," Blossom said, her wings fluttering in agitation. "The guards were told to check everyone who comes in to make sure they're who they say they are."

"And the wyvern on the wall?" Malek asked.

Blossom shrugged. "Incentive? The guards don't know why he's there, but the captain is yelling at them to check more thoroughly. I think he's worried they're going to be wyvern food if they don't obey."

Rika swallowed. "Yeah, that would definitely be an incentive. What should we do?"

Malek frowned. "I'm not willing to risk harm coming to any of you. We may need to abandon our plan and head directly to the Sky Cities. Hopefully, Levin and Esme will learn something."

"Um, there's an itty bitty problem with that plan," Blossom said, pinching her thumb and forefinger close together. "Sabine told the dryads I'd carry their song throughout the city. If we leave before doing that, Sabine will be forsworn and they'll turn Rika into a tree."

Malek stared at her. "What?"

Bane's eyes narrowed on her. "You negotiated with a bunch of plant women to put yourself in harm's way? Have you learned nothing over the past ten years?"

Sabine straightened and jabbed her finger in Bane's chest. "Keep your voice down, Bane'umbra Versed. I did what was necessary to ensure Rika would remain safe and unharmed, while also preserving the sacred grove."

He grabbed her finger and snarled. In a low voice, Bane demanded, "What in the underworld were you thinking? Look at where we are, Sabine. I watched hundreds, if not thousands, of your people and mine die at the hands of these dragons. Yet you insist upon waltzing into a city filled with them to appease some fucking dryads? You are their queen! You order them, and they obey. If they refuse, chop the bitches down."

Malek grabbed Bane's wrist and said, "Unhand her, or I'll do it for you."

Bane's eyes flashed to silver. "Try it. This is your doing, lizard."

"Enough!" Sabine said in a loud whisper and stepped between them. Blossom squeaked and flew under her hair. Rika took a big step back, her eyes wide as she stared at the three of them.

"Bane, you weren't there or privy to the circumstances surrounding my decision," Sabine said. "I rely upon your counsel, but I am not ruled by it. If you don't trust my judgment as your queen to act in the best interests of *all* my people, then we need to reconsider our arrangement."

She turned to Malek and continued, "I am not some wilting flower who is unable to defend herself, especially from a trusted advisor. If you put your hands on my sworn protector again and threaten him, then you and I will need to reconsider our arrangement as well."

They both stared at her.

She narrowed her eyes, feeling her magic beginning to build below the surface. *Is that understood?*

Bane's eyes reverted back to amber. He scowled at her before turning his gaze back toward the city entrance. Malek frowned and turned to study the wyvern over the gate.

"You're a fool, dragon," Bane said in a conversational tone. "If the mating instinct doesn't kill you, stupidity will."

Malek snorted. "I won't argue that, but it wasn't one of your brightest moments either. One of those plant women happen to be Esmelle." He shook his head. "I'm still getting my head around the wilting flower bit."

"That particular flower has quite a few thorns," Bane said, his still gaze focused on the guards. "Prickly when provoked."

"So I've noticed," Malek said mildly. "I've always been partial to night-blooming roses though."

Sabine threw up her hands in exasperation. "If you two are finished, we need to discuss our options."

Malek and Bane exchanged a look. It was almost as though an entire unspoken conversation was happening in front of her.

Bane glanced over at her and said, "The sun will touch the horizon in the next twenty minutes. Once it does, Malek and Rika should head to the gate. You and I will need to find our own way through that doesn't involve any additional scrutiny. The bug won't raise suspicion either way, but she's less likely to get into trouble if she remains with you."

"Not a bug," Blossom squeaked from under Sabine's hair.

"You were disguised as a giant moth a few minutes ago," Rika reminded her.

Blossom sniffed. "That's why Sabine should turn me into a dragon."

Sabine took a deep breath, desperately trying to find some patience. "I think we have enough dragons to contend with right now, Blossom."

"That's okay," Blossom agreed, patting Sabine's neck. "We can talk about it later. I need to figure out what color dragon I should be anyway. Do they have pink dragons?"

Sabine closed her eyes and counted to ten.

It didn't help.

Images of terrifying pink dragons swirled in her head.

She was going mad. That was the only explanation.

To hell with it. If Blossom really wanted to be a pink dragon, she deserved to be a pink dragon. At least once they managed to get out of this mess.

Malek took her hand, running his thumb across her palm. When she looked up at him, he lifted her hand and kissed it.

Sabine sighed. "I'm assuming no one else has any better ideas?"

When Blossom started to speak, Sabine quickly said, "Any ideas other than turning all of us into dragons so we can blend in with the crowd?"

Blossom sniffed. "They wouldn't suspect it."

Sabine looked up at Malek. "You'll keep Rika safe?"

"Even if I have to transform and fly her over the wall myself," Malek said, tucking a lock of Sabine's hair behind her ear. "I don't like the idea of separating, especially with our bond being muted. But I trust Bane to keep you safe."

Sabine placed her hand over Malek's heart. "I'm still with you, even if you can't feel me."

Malek drew her into his arms. "Once this is done, I have

no intention of wearing this damned medallion again. I won't be parted from you, Sabine. Not for anything."

Sabine arched her brow. "Be careful with your words, Malek. Such things are dangerous around a fae."

"And it's even more dangerous to try and escape a dragon," Malek said and kissed her as though she were the very air he needed to survive. She wrapped her arms around him, willingly surrendering to his silent demand. Her magic surrounded them both, filled with seductive promises and longing. His hands slid under her cape, his warmth searing her like a brand.

"For fuck's sake," Bane muttered. "I need a bucket of water."

Blossom flew out from under Sabine's hair. "I'll wait over here where it's dry."

Rika giggled. "I don't think there's a river close enough, Blossom. You're probably safe."

Sabine broke their kiss and smiled. "I think Bane's getting impatient."

"Too bad," Malek murmured, his heated hands caressing her skin as he kissed her again. "If he's taking you away from me, I'm going to take every opportunity to make sure you come back."

"Assuming you actually let her go first," Bane grumbled.

Malek sighed and released her. "Your demon protector can be a pain in the ass."

"He says the same thing about you," Blossom said, landing on Sabine's shoulder. "I figure those of us with wings need to stick together."

Malek arched his brow. "Is that so?"

Rika looked up at the darkening sky. "Wow, would you look at that? It's almost time to go, isn't it?"

"Smooth," Sabine said, winking at Rika.

Rika grinned at her. "I have my moments."

"A word, dragon," Bane said, motioning for Malek to follow him a short distance away. Bane and Malek spoke quietly to one another in hushed tones, too low for her to overhear.

Rika adjusted the collar of her cloak and asked, "What should we say if the guards question us?"

"Follow Malek's lead," Sabine said, taking Rika's hands in hers. "Can you stay calm enough to keep your magic in check?"

Rika took a deep breath and nodded. "Yes. Bane's been trying to work with me."

"Good," Sabine said, squeezing Rika's hands before releasing them. "It's better to be cautious using any magic until we know how these people view outsiders. Malek won't let anything happen to you, even if he has to remove the warding medallion. You just need to act like a normal human, the same way you did back in Karga."

"I won't let you down, Sabine," Rika promised.

Sabine smiled. "If I didn't believe in your abilities, we wouldn't be attempting this. Trust in yourself, Rika. I already do."

Rika straightened and nodded.

"Blossom, I'm going to need you to scout ahead for us. Once we're inside and Malek gives us the all clear, I'll supply you with enough magic to carry the dryad's song throughout the city."

Blossom saluted her. "You've got it!"

Her image shimmered, once again taking on the appearance of a tiny moth. She landed on Sabine's shoulder, her wings twitching slightly. Sabine sent a light wave of magic over Blossom to fuel her scouting endeavors.

Bane and Malek finished discussing whatever last-minute plans they were making and rejoined them. When Sabine gave Malek a questioning look, he cupped her face and pressed a light kiss against her lips.

"Be safe, and be careful. None of this is more important than your life, Sabine."

"Take care of my dragon," she murmured against his lips. "I have plans for him later."

"It's a promise."

Malek released her and after another long look, he turned away. Sabine watched as Malek and Rika stepped beyond the boundaries of her glamour and headed toward the ominous iron gates.

"It's time, Sabine," Bane said quietly. He raised his hood over his head, shrouding his features from view.

Sabine said a silent prayer to whatever gods might be listening to safeguard her dragon and the young seer accompanying him. She didn't like the idea of them going off on their own, but Rika would be far safer in Malek's company than hers. At least she hoped.

Turning away, she adjusted the hood of her cloak and followed Bane deeper into the forest. As they passed a tiny moth flitting from flower to flower, Sabine couldn't help but think Blossom was likely the safest of all of them.

Even if she wasn't a pink dragon.

CHAPTER 15

Sabine and Bane moved quickly through the rough terrain surrounding Imenel, abandoning all pretense of playing human. She'd almost forgotten what it was like to rely upon her magic to guide her footsteps. With a wave of her hand, branches moved out of their way, closing the path behind them as they passed. The wind whipped her cloak behind her as they dashed through the forest.

Mindful of the dangers from above, as well as those behind the city gates, Sabine kept a shield of glamour around them, hiding them from view. Through the trees, Sabine could barely make out the walls of Imenel. A large expanse of empty and fallow land seemed to surround the entire city. Sabine couldn't help but wonder whether it was the dragons or humans who had cleared the land, making it nearly impossible for a large force to infiltrate the city without being spotted.

After nearly thirty minutes, Bane halted abruptly and crouched low to the ground. Sabine immediately followed him, trying to determine what had caught his attention.

Blossom transformed back into her normal self and

flopped down on Sabine's shoulder with a whimper. "I think I have a wing cramp."

Sabine sent a wave of magic over the tired pixie, helping to revitalize her. Pixies could travel over great distances, but they usually needed to take frequent breaks.

"Why did we stop?"

"There," Bane said quietly, pointing to an area through the trees where the walls of the city were clearly visible. "Look with your magic, not your eyes."

Sabine leaned forward and relaxed her eyes, feeling more than seeing the flow of magic and energy around them. The symbol of an eye had been etched into the wall using an ancient form of magic that was similar to that of the gods. Her eyes widened in shock.

"I don't understand. How is this possible?"

"There are some in Imenel who resist the dragons, little one," Bane said quietly. "Where you find this symbol, you may trust."

He opened the pouch at his waist and withdrew two wayfarer biscuits. He handed both to her, along with a flask of water. "Eat and drink. You need to replenish your strength, and you won't be able to eat again for a while."

Sabine's brow furrowed, but she accepted the offering. She broke off a small piece and handed it to Blossom before taking a bite. The biscuit melted upon her tongue, making it tingle with the remnants of power. The wayfarer biscuits had been a gift from Faerie before they'd departed from Razadon. They had scarce few left, deciding to conserve them until they were truly necessary.

"Many of the bakers within the city use iron utensils or baking dishes," Bane said, scanning the field in front of them. "Do not eat or drink anything given to you by strangers, unless Malek or I hand it to you."

Sabine finished eating and took a long drink from the flask before handing it back to him. "Malek knows this?"

"He does now."

Sabine took a deep breath. "What else?"

"Can you change your appearance?"

"Yes, but I'm not sure how long I can hold a new form," Sabine admitted, touching the marks on her wrist. "Lachlina has been quiet for a while, but I don't trust her not to meddle in our affairs. She tolerates my normal glamour, but she may object if I deviate too much."

"She's resting," Blossom said, finishing off her piece of biscuit. "I don't think she likes you being around all these dragons. She says you may need her strength soon." Blossom cocked her head as though listening. "And she says you rely upon glamour too much. It's beneath you."

"It's kept me alive so far," Sabine muttered.

"And allowed you to move freely where a fae normally cannot," Bane said and then gestured to her hair. "Keep your ears covered and don't let the bug braid your hair."

Blossom's mouth dropped open. "But—"

Bane narrowed his eyes. "Humans do not have pixies chasing them around and braiding their hair."

Blossom crossed her arms over her chest. "Spoilsport."

Bane turned back to Sabine. "We'll stay off the main streets as much as possible to limit our visibility. I know of some people who may be able to provide Malek with the information he needs, but the cost will be dear."

Sabine nodded, quickly unraveling her braids and finger combing her hair. "What's your plan?"

Bane gestured toward the wall where the strange symbol was located. "You'll need to call the darkness to us. Once we're shrouded, head directly for the eye. Do not deviate from the path once you're on the field. As long as you keep the eye within your sight, the dragons should not be able to sense you."

Sabine's eyes widened. "It's a lodestone?"

"Of a sort," Bane said. "Within its sight, the dragons are blind. Unfortunately, this magic only shields us from their kind. The darkness you call should be enough to obscure our presence from the humans until we're across the field. Once I sense the guards and their locations, we'll clear the wall."

Sabine nodded and withdrew her knife. Bane placed his hand on the back of her neck, his heated magic swirling around her. She pricked her finger and allowed two drops of blood to fall to the ground.

"By blood, by magic, by rights of both, I call upon the memory of the gods who have abandoned this world. May the darkness fall and shadows dance freely within the night."

Dark and ominous clouds rolled in, stealing the light of the rising moon and cascading the world into darkness. The wind kicked up, whipping Sabine's hood and hair away from her face. The ground beneath her feet began to quake as rain pelted against them. Thunder boomed and lightning struck a nearby tower, catching it aflame. In the distance and beyond the wall, she could hear screams and shouting.

Sabine faltered. She'd used this type of magic in the past but never with these results. Something was wrong.

"Uh oh!" Blossom said, her glamour flickering uncontrollably. She dove under Sabine's hair, quaking against her neck. "Too much magic! Hold on tight!"

"Finish it," Bane said with a growl, his eyes and horns turning an almost iridescent silver.

Sabine pricked another finger, allowing two more drops of blood to fall. "By blood, by magic, by rights of both, I call upon the memory of the gods who have abandoned this world. May the light shine brightly within those who embrace the darkness."

The marks on her wrist burned, searing her with power as her skin markings turned a brilliant gold. Light and magic surged within her, slamming into both Bane and Blossom. Bane roared, his skin glowing with a bluish sheen while underneath, Sabine could make out the deep red color she'd only seen in the underworld. Blossom sneezed and tumbled off her shoulder with a giggle. Sabine barely managed to catch the pixie in her glowing hand.

A strange high-pitched call pierced the night. Sabine jerked her head up. Two wyverns soared over the wall and across the field in their direction.

"Run!" Bane shouted, pushing her forward.

Sabine threw glamour over them and raced toward the eye, stuffing Blossom into her pocket as she ran. One of the wyverns swooped downward, causing her to stumble. Bane grabbed her by the waist, hauling her upright.

"This ride is bumpy," a muffled pixie voice said from inside her pocket. "And full of lint."

"Vashado!" Sabine screamed in the ancient language of the gods, throwing her hands upward as the second wyvern swooped low enough to almost touch the tips of Bane's horns. A huge explosion of power burst from Sabine's fingertips, lighting up the night sky and sending the wyvern barreling away from them. She stared at her hands in shock. She'd never had power like that before.

"Keep the eye in sight and run!" Bane yelled. "Don't stop for anything!"

Sabine turned and ran for all she was worth. She didn't know if the wyverns were truly blind or just trying to flush her and Bane out. Her vision narrowed, her focus locked on the pulsing eye that seemed to beckon her closer.

"Faster, Sabine!" Blossom yelled from inside her pocket. "The goddess says more dragons are coming!"

Sabine didn't know how Lachlina knew that, but she

wasn't about to stop and question the goddess. Sabine and Bane raced over the landscape. The ground seemed to smooth out in front of them, with rocks and pebbles sliding out of their way. As they touched the wall, an ear-shattering roar cut through the night sky.

A dragon.

And it wasn't Malek.

"Hold on to me," Bane ordered, picking her up and swinging her onto his back. No sooner had she wrapped her arms and legs around him than he leaped upward, using his claws to find purchase between the stones of the city wall. Sabine kept the glamour over them, camouflaging them against the wall. Iron spokes jutted from the wall at random intervals, but Bane easily leaped over them.

Sabine peered around him to see three more wyverns and a greater dragon flying overhead. Dragonfire lit up the night sky, sending a cascade of embers falling to the ground like burning rain. The creatures soared over the barren field and surrounding forest, searching for any sign of her and Bane.

At the top of the wall, Bane leaped over the side. Two human guards were sitting atop strange wooden contraptions that had dozens of iron arrows pointed toward the field. He silently lowered her to the ground and motioned for her to keep quiet.

Keeping her footsteps light and breathing quiet, she followed Bane past the guards. Instead of climbing down the opposite side of the wall, Bane led her toward a nearby lookout tower. He bypassed the door and stepped onto a small platform on the outside of the tower, which overlooked the city. He leaned against the wall and held out his hand toward her.

Sabine took his outstretched hand, and he pulled her onto the rickety platform and into his arms. They stayed under the roof canopy for several minutes, listening to the sound of the human guards calling out warnings and the flapping of the wings flying overhead. If they moved from their current location, they risked being spotted by either the guards on the wall or the dragon and wyverns flying overhead.

In a voice barely audible, Bane murmured, "Now we wait and hope your dragon manages a suitable distraction."

Blossom flew out of Sabine's pocket.

Instead of her normal pixie form, she was a tiny pink dragon with sparkling scales. Sabine stared at her in shock. Such a form could only have been achieved from the massive power explosion Sabine had generated on the field.

"No need to wait. I'm on the job!" Blossom said and disappeared over the far side of the wall and into the city below them. Bane tensed, but Sabine pressed her hand against Bane's chest and shook her head.

If Malek ran into trouble, the pixie had proven to be well-suited for creating distractions.

May the gods help them all.

CHAPTER 16

*M*alek crept through the darkened stables, inhaling the earthy scent of hay and the musky odor of thundertusks. Rika was nearly as silent as she followed him, using the skills Bane had taught her to muffle the sound of her movements.

The stablehand had ensured his charges were resting comfortably for the night before he'd slipped into the inn at the end of the street for a quick bite to eat. It wouldn't take long until he returned, but Malek didn't think they'd need much time to accomplish their task.

Malek reached for the heavy wooden latch of the first stall door. With a soft groan, the door swung open, revealing the hulking silhouette of a thundertusk inside. The lantern light reflected in its luminous eyes, but the creature remained calm, accustomed to the presence of humans.

"They're bigger than I expected," Rika whispered.

"Merchants use them for transporting their heavy carts to various markets," Malek said, patting the thundertusk's thick, leathery skin. "Grab the lanterns for me while I open the rest of the enclosures."

A loud roar shook the barn, and the thundertusks all raised their heads in alarm. The sound was unmistakable—a greater dragon was on the hunt. Malek knew instinctively Sabine and Bane were in danger. They were out of time.

"Hurry!" Malek ordered, quickly unlatching the other seven stalls while Rika grabbed the lanterns and ran to the back of the stable. She placed the lit lanterns on the ground and unlatched the shutters barring the window before climbing out.

Malek tossed both lanterns into a nearby pile of hay, shattering the glass and spreading their oil. As the first sparks of fire caught, the thundertusks began to stomp and kick at the wooden dividers. The calm that had once filled the stable was shattered by deep, resonant alarm calls that reverberated through the walls. The vibrations of their trumpeting voices shook the ground. Smoke curled up in tendrils, filling the air with acrid bitterness.

Malek dove out the window and rolled onto the cobblestone street as the thundertusks burst free, stampeding out of their stalls. Their glowing tusks cast eerie shadows in the flickering firelight as they sought escape from the growing inferno.

At the sight of him, Rika yelled, "Fire! The thundertusks are loose! Fire in the stables!"

Others picked up her shouts, echoing her cries as the thundertusks barreled down the streets. People dove out of the way as the normally passive beasts turned frantic, knocking over carts and kiosks that lined the path. Malek grabbed Rika's hand, and they raced in the opposite direction, blending into the crowd of people attempting to escape the chaos.

Malek and Rika ran several blocks, only slowing once he was sure the stampede hadn't turned in their direction. He kept his eyes trained to the sky, trying to determine which direction the dragon had gone. Only his promise to Bane kept him from yanking off the medallion around his neck. The thought of Sabine in danger, especially from one of his own, was intolerable.

He looked back over his shoulder to see even more people had fled behind them. Fortunately, random fires weren't an unfamiliar occurrence in a city protected by dragons.

Rika tugged on his cloak and pointed toward the sky. "Look! It's a wyvern."

"And there's a dragon," Malek said, catching sight of a copper dragon soaring high above the city. At any given time, there might be four or five greater dragons near Imenel. Most of them couldn't be bothered with human proclivities, except in passing. Such matters were often delegated to the wyverns.

Malek didn't know if the Copper Clan had directed the wyverns to attack them over the forest, or if they were the ones searching for Sabine and Bane. He intended to find out.

Some of the townsfolk stopped to stare upward as the dragon passed overhead. Many of them placed their fists over their heart in obeisance. Malek had never understood the sentiment, unless they were simply grateful they weren't a dragon's preferred snack that evening.

"Do you think our distraction was enough?" Rika asked, searching the faces in the crowd.

Malek gripped the medallion at his throat, battling the need to yank it off. He could only sense the faintest trace of Sabine. At least he knew she was still alive. "If they're not at the meeting place, we might need to find another way to distract the guards. If all else fails, I'll remove the medallion and track Sabine. I won't allow anything to happen to them."

Rika nodded, but she still looked worried.

Malek led Rika through the maze of streets toward one of

the central markets. As they walked, the rich scents of spiced meats, fresh bread, and sweet pastries filled the air.

The market was a bustling hub of activity, with stalls and vendors offering a colorful array of goods. Fruits and vegetables were piled high, while other stalls showcased intricate jewelry and handcrafted wares. The sounds of haggling mingled with the clatter of carts and the distant roar of wyverns.

In the center of the market stood a large raised platform. Five huge urns had been placed at its edge, forming a pentagon. In the center, an artisan had crafted a decorative mosaic on the ground depicting one of the greater dragons in flight.

"What is that?" Rika asked, gesturing at the platform.

"A landing pad," Malek said, scanning the faces around him for anyone who might recognize him. Fortunately, he'd been gone long enough that most people wouldn't expect to see him. "When a dragon is about to land, they use their dragonfire to light the urns as a warning for the humans to clear the area."

Rika's eyes widened. "How do they do that?"

"Magic," Malek said with a grin.

They approached one of the main temples dedicated to the dragons. Rika stopped in her tracks, staring up at the gleaming polished obsidian and towering bronze doors.

Massive columns lined the front entrance, each carved with detailed reliefs depicting dragons in various poses of flight, combat, and repose. The central figure in the painted frieze above the doors was a colossal obsidian dragon, wings outstretched, with humans kneeling around it.

Rika's mouth dropped open. "Tell me that's not you."

Shit.

"It's not me."

Rika jerked her head up. "But you know who it is, don't you?"

Malek winced.

"Oh, come on," Rika begged. "You have to tell me."

Malek coughed. "My grandfather."

Rika cracked up laughing. "I knew it! I totally knew it! It looks just like you. Blossom and Sabine are going to freak out when they see this."

"Let's not tell—" Malek's voice cut off as a huge flock of pigeons screeched in alarm and rose from the eaves around the temple. He heard a high-pitched squeal before one of the banners affixed to the side of the temple ripped free.

Malek grabbed Rika and leaped back as a tiny pink dragon went whizzing by his head, still attached to the end of the banner. It flew down the street, racing under kiosks and over wagons shouting something that sounded like, "Dragon coming through! Rawr!"

Merchants shouted in alarm as their wares tumbled off counters, crashing to the ground. The commotion set off the other pigeons roosting nearby, and soon the entire market area was full of flying feathers, angry merchants, and befuddled customers.

And the tiny pink dragon was nowhere to be found.

CHAPTER 17

The moment the guards rushed past them, Sabine wrapped her arms around Bane's neck. He leaped from the platform where they'd been hiding and landed on the ground with a jarring thud. Without even taking time to catch their breath, Bane lowered her to the ground, grabbed her wrist, and led her toward one of the darkened alleys just as another guard patrol rushed by them.

Bane pressed Sabine against the wall of a nearby building, using his body to shield her from view. She pressed her hand against his back, reinforcing the shroud of glamour surrounding them. The iridescence of his horns had started to fade, but she wasn't sure if the magic within him was dissipating or if the danger had lessened.

She ran her hand up his back to touch his bare skin, the gesture a silent offering of more magic. He hesitated for a moment and then shook his head.

"Conserve your strength," Bane said quietly, still watching the main thoroughfare. "We need to wait here until things settle down a bit more. Your bug has her uses, but we're not completely out of danger yet."

Sabine leaned close to his ear and whispered, "Shall I tell her how much you value her efforts?"

Bane spun around, his eyes narrowing. "Didn't I just save your life?"

Sabine grinned and kissed his cheek. "You did, and it's one of the many things I love about you."

"The dragon is turning you soft," Bane muttered with disgust. "I should have taken you away while I had the chance."

Sabine studied him for a moment. "You mean that, don't you?"

Bane was quiet for so long, she wasn't sure he was going to respond.

"Yes, but not for the reasons you might believe," Bane said, glancing toward the alley again before turning back to her. "Sabine, you will be in a great deal more danger once you enter the Sky Cities. I do not believe Malek intends you harm, but he cannot protect you from all dragonkind."

"His step-grandmother lived for a number of years among his people."

Bane rubbed a lock of her hair between his fingers. "She was not an Unseelie queen, nor touched by the gods. Yours is no small power, little one. If you are captured or killed, what becomes of the Unseelie? Who will rule in your stead? Or will the Unseelie might that has maintained the balance for centuries become firmly under the heel of the Seelie?"

Sabine averted her gaze. These questions had given her many sleepless nights, but none of it changed her purpose. "If I can't locate the last artifact, none of this matters anyway. I told you what the Huntsman said. We're dying, Bane. All of us. The fae, the demons, the dwarves, the merfolk, the dragons, and countless others. Anyone with a drop of magic in their blood, whether they're native to this world or not, will succumb to the poison leaching into our world. I will not allow that to happen. I *must* go to the Sky Cities and retrieve the last artifact."

Bane grasped her chin, tilting her head toward him. "If the dragon had no claim on your heart, would you still do this?"

Sabine wrapped her hand around his wrist. "I would do this and more to save the lives of my people. This is my duty, and I will protect the land at all costs—even at the risk of restarting the war."

The marks on her wrist burned, scorching her from within. Unmistakable fury ripped through her as Lachlina made her displeasure known. Sabine gasped, jerking away from Bane and clamping her hand over her wrist.

With a low growl, Bane lowered his head and kissed her. This was no simple kiss, nor even a demand for magic. It was utterly consuming, as though he were surrendering something within himself. He yanked her wrists over her head, imprisoning her in his grip as he continued to plunder her mouth. At least Bane had found a way to temporarily quiet Lachlina's hold on her.

Bane became even more forceful, a silent demand that required a response. Cognizant of their surroundings, she resisted the urge to use her magic against him. Instead, she bit his lip hard, drawing blood. As the bitter, metallic taste of it touched her tongue and bound them together, his power flowed through her. It was more than just his magic, something far greater.

For a moment, it was almost as though Dax were with her. She could feel the blistering heat from a nearby lava pool and the sweat on his body as he led his captains through practice drills. He halted abruptly and lifted his horned head. She could feel his awareness of her and the soul shard that pulsed within him, connecting him to the thousands of demons under his command. She could feel all of them, as though Bane had shared their essence with her.

Heat poured into her, and with it came the knowledge of what Bane had done.

It had been millennia since a fae ruler had set aside personal gain or politics to safeguard all their people—not just the fae. Her declaration to defy Lachlina's wishes was simply the catalyst. Bane was the instrument binding the demons to Sabine in a blood oath more powerful than anything she'd known. That these proud demons who had lived lifetimes beyond hers would make such a vow humbled her beyond words.

She softened against Bane, returning his kiss and accepting the promise behind it and making one of her own. She would not squander their belief in her. No matter what happened, she would hold to her vow and do everything possible to ensure their survival.

Bane released her hands, cupped her face and kissed her forehead. She swallowed, pressing her hands against his chest, not willing to break contact with him yet. As long as she was touching him, the goddess was quiet within her.

"We will not allow the dragon to take you away from us, little one," Bane murmured, staring down at her with a combination of reverence and need. "We have waited several lifetimes for a queen such as you, and we will not give you up. If the dragons seek to keep you from us, the demons are prepared to declare war upon their kind once again."

"You expect treachery," Sabine murmured. "That's why you waited until Malek wasn't with us to do this."

Bane ran a claw lightly across her cheek. "Dax was concerned about the possibility before we left the underworld. He wanted you to understand the lengths we would go to keep you. If your dragon doesn't know, he cannot use such knowledge against us, even inadvertently."

She'd wanted an alliance with the demons, but this was so much more than that. The weight of Bane's oath fell heavily on her shoulders. If she erred, it wasn't only her life at stake. She could be sentencing thousands of demons to their deaths.

"If you are willing to put yourself at risk to save us, then we shall do the same for you," Bane said quietly, guessing the direction of her thoughts. "Never in living memory has any demon sworn such a promise to a fae ruler. The last time was when Theoria renounced the gods and led your people to safety in the underworld."

Sabine took a steadying breath. She'd essentially begun on the same path by refusing Lachlina's wishes to keep the portal closed. Overcome with emotion, Sabine wrapped her arms around him and laid her head against his chest. She listened to the steady beat of his heart as he held her in his arms.

"There you are!"

Sabine turned to see a tiny pink dragon flying toward her. She automatically held out her hand, giving Blossom a place to land.

"You're all right?" Sabine asked.

"Right as a light on a firefly's butt, but we need to talk about this illusion," the miniature dragon said. "It's good. I mean, really good. But I think fire breath would really give it some pizazz. I had to goose the pigeons with my tail, and it took me a while to figure out how to get it to work. Fire breath would have been much more efficient."

"Fire breath?" Sabine asked in disbelief. "You want to breathe fire?"

Bane sighed. "Don't encourage the bug. She's insufferable enough as it is."

"This is one of those times fire breath would come in

handy," Blossom said to Sabine. "We could barbecue the demon."

Bane narrowed his eyes on the tiny dragon. "I used to swim in lava pits. You think fire breath would trouble me?"

"Good point," Blossom said, her tail twitching behind her. She pounced on it—or rather, tried. Instead, she chased her tail in circles on Sabine's palm. "I need to talk to Malek about this tail thing. It keeps wanting to go in a different direction."

Blossom flopped over on her back, trying to catch her pink tail between her tiny dragon talons.

Bane held up a clawed finger. "Need some help? I can slice it off."

"No," Blossom said and leaped up, tucking her tail safely under her belly. "I'm good. Really good. Yep. This is me. All good with my tail."

Bane glanced toward the street. "Things are calming down. If you're done causing mischief, we should be on our way."

Blossom hopped onto Sabine's shoulder and said, "I sang the dryad's song from the top of the temple, all the way through the market square. I think I got a few nibbles. If you want to ramp up the power again, I bet I could even sing to the next town over."

"The next town over is the Sky Cities," Bane said dryly. "I doubt there are dryads hiding among the fire breathers."

"Dryads can be tricky," Blossom said, her pink tail tickling Sabine's neck. "I'll let you think about it for a while."

At Bane's signal, Sabine lifted her hood again, making sure it covered her hair and the tiny pink dragon nestled underneath. She released the glamour shrouding them while simultaneously reapplying her normal human disguise. They walked to the far end of the alley and onto a nearby cobblestone street. Merchants were busy putting their stalls back to rights, picking up scattered merchandise and broken crockery. Fortunately, no one paid her and Bane much attention.

It was her first real glimpse of Imenel, beyond what she'd seen from her elevated perch on the watchtower. Lanterns glowing with dwarven crystals lined the cobblestone streets, chasing away all but the darkest shadows. She'd forgotten this city had once been inhabited by the fae and other magical races, before the war had forced them to retreat to the southern lands. Someone had found a way to maintain the magic, or the crystals would have dimmed long before now.

The subsequent human and dragon influence were apparent, from the changes in architecture to even the wares for sale at the night market. The kiosks and tables that hadn't been overturned by Blossom's well-timed distraction were full of shimmering fabrics in bold colors and jewelry flavored with dragon motifs. Statues of dragons and wyverns lined the street with red and orange flowering plants at their bases, which served as a reminder of the flames the dragons could easily harness.

Sabine slowed to study a table full of bowls and serving dishes, each one hand-painted with images of dragons in flight. One of them reminded her of Malek and the way his obsidian scales gleamed in the firelight. She forced herself to turn away and continue walking before the merchant could address her.

"They worship them," Sabine said quietly, unnerved by the realization.

Bane made a noise of agreement. "The quickest way to destroy the belief in a god is to kill it."

Sabine wasn't sure if he was referring to the Tuatha Dé, the dragons, or both. She decided it was better not to ask, especially with Lachlina paying close attention to their progress.

Bane led her toward a large fountain. A towering statue of a dragon stood on its hind legs with its wings outstretched and mouth open in a silent roar. Water cascaded from the dragon's mouth, splashing into a wide, ornate basin below that was surrounded by smaller statues of wyverns. At its base, benches nestled among vibrant flower beds offered a pleasant respite in the cool night air.

"Ohhhh," Blossom exclaimed. "I want to be a big dragon like that."

Sabine made a strangled noise. "No."

"But—"

"No."

"Keep it up, bug, and I'll toss you into the fountain," Bane muttered. "Malek and Rika are supposed to meet us here."

Blossom sniffed. "What kind of flowers are those? I've never seen them before."

Sabine sat on one of the benches and leaned over the flowers. They were small, deep violet flowers with speckles of gold on their petals. They reminded Sabine of a starry night sky. She closed her eyes and inhaled deeply, breathing in the sweet, honey-like aroma.

"They're starpetals," Sabine said, staring at the flowers in wonder. "I've only seen them illustrated in books. Legends say the aderyan would throw the seeds from their aeries, and fae children would catch them. Wherever they were planted, the starpetals grew."

"Can I taste it?" Blossom asked, her entire body quivering in excitement.

"I don't believe dragons are overly fond of flowers," Sabine said, leaning over to smell the flowers again. "But if you wish to keep your illusion for a bit longer…"

Blossom turned into a moth and landed on a flower near the bench. Sabine smiled, watching her flit from flower to flower, sipping the nectar like a fine wine. At least it would keep her busy and out of trouble for a few minutes.

Bane sat on the bench beside her, scanning the crowd. He plucked one of the flowers and handed it to her. She smiled and twirled it in her fingers, touched by the thoughtful gesture.

"They're here," Bane said quietly, nodding toward the far side of the market where a large, raised platform stood. She lifted her head and met Malek's gaze from across the market square. Her stomach fluttered from the determined and heated look in his eye as he and Rika headed in her direction. It was almost as though he could see through all of her illusions, no matter how much magic she had at her command. She lifted the flower up and breathed in deeply, watching the dragon she loved stalk toward her.

The urns on the raised platform suddenly erupted in flames. A swift chill wrapped around Sabine and descended over the entire marketplace. She felt an ominous presence as the shadows lengthened and the air grew heavy with tension. The fountain's gentle splashing seemed distant and muffled as an enormous dragon swooped down from the sky, its emerald scales shimmering in the fire's light.

The dragon landed with a thunderous impact, its eyes gleaming with a fierce intelligence. A wave of paralyzing fear radiated from it, freezing the humans in their tracks. Sabine felt her magic begin to rise, her heart pounding as she struggled to maintain her composure. Bane leaned closer to her, his voice a low, urgent whisper. "Do not move. Pretend to be human."

Sabine nodded imperceptibly, forcing herself to remain still. She sent a silent request to Lachlina, asking the goddess not to intervene. The dragon began to shift, its massive form harnessing the urn's light until a tall, imposing man stood in its place. His noble bearing and cold, piercing gaze made

Sabine wonder if he was someone of great importance. Two wyverns landed beside him, swiftly transforming into cloaked guards and taking positions on both sides of him.

She caught a glimpse of Malek across the market, his gaze still focused on her. His hand gripped the warding medallion around his neck as though prepared to yank it off at the slightest provocation. He couldn't come to her aid without revealing his identity, and she couldn't signal to him without drawing attention. She doubted their mind-touch connection would work while he was wearing the medallion, but she had to try.

"Stay where you are," she urged silently.

The dragon-turned-noble surveyed the crowd, his gaze sweeping over the humans with suspicion. Sabine held her breath, hoping he hadn't sensed her attempt to communicate with Malek. His gaze briefly landed on her and Bane, but he paid them as much attention as any other human in the market square.

The urn's light finally extinguished, and the crowd began to move once more. They spoke in hushed, excited voices as the dragon shapeshifter descended the platform stairs with his wyvern companions. The nearby humans quickly moved out of their way, bowing deeply to them as they passed. Malek and Rika took the opportunity to move stealthily along the edge of the market, keeping to the shadows and out of sight of the newcomers.

As the dragon and guards moved through the crowd, they began questioning the merchants about the nature of the disturbance that had occurred that evening. Sabine overheard mutterings about a thundertusk stampede and a miniature pink dragon that seemed to magically appear and disappear after knocking over their tables.

Blossom landed on Sabine's shoulder and hid under her hair.

"I think it might be time to go," Blossom whispered.

"You think?" Sabine muttered, rising from the bench.

"Casually head toward the jewelry merchant on the end and inspect his wares," Bane said in a low voice. Sabine nodded, keeping her movements leisurely as she pretended to browse the merchandise on the tables they passed.

The dragon and his wyvern guards were moving much faster and it was only a matter of time before they caught up to them. Her heart hammered in her chest, even as she tried to project an outward calm.

At the jewelry merchant, she stopped for a moment and studied the display. Her eyes traced the intricate designs of the necklaces and rings, though her mind was focused entirely on the danger at hand. As she pretended to study a delicate necklace adorned with a small dragon pendant, she caught sight of Malek and Rika perusing the offerings at a nearby stall.

The jewelry merchant, a slender older man with kind eyes, smiled warmly at Sabine and gestured to his displays. "Are you looking for anything special, milady?"

Before she could respond, Bane showed the merchant a coin. The merchant froze, glancing toward the approaching dragon and wyverns only three stalls away from his booth. Sabine caught sight of a small eye tattoo behind the merchant's ear. The image wavered as though a thin coating of glamour was concealing it.

"I'm afraid I don't have what you're looking for here," the merchant said, nodding toward the alley. "If you've got the time, my daughter Fiona runs our shop while I'm at the market. It's the Starlight Smithy. You can find it a few streets over."

"Very well," Bane said, the coin disappearing into the folds of his cloak. "We'll head that direction."

The merchant nodded before turning to another

customer and greeting them with a friendly smile. Sabine and Bane turned away, heading toward the alley he had indicated.

A hand wrapped around hers, pulling her into the shadows. She tensed at first, then relaxed at the sight of Malek. He wrapped his arms around her, the warmth of his touch reassuring despite the circumstances.

"You're all right?" he asked, taking her hand as he guided them away from the busy marketplace.

Sabine nodded. "What form of magic did the dragon use to freeze the entire market?"

"Dragon fear," Bane said in disgust. "It doesn't work well on us, but it's useful for quickly identifying those who aren't human."

Rika rubbed her arms. "I felt it, but I knew I could break it if I tried. Malek told me to remain still. I'm guessing they wouldn't have believed I'm human."

Bane placed his hand on Rika's shoulder. "You did not allow your fear to control your magic. Few humans can withstand dragon fear, and even less maintain their composure while in the face of it."

Rika beamed at his praise.

Sabine looked up at Malek. "You know that dragon, don't you?"

"It's my uncle," Malek said with a frown. "I have no idea why he's here."

"The goddess says the dragon's getting closer," Blossom said from under Sabine's hair. "He's still looking for us. We need to find a place to hide."

Bane's expression darkened. "I'll have your oath of silence, dragon. Where we go next is a carefully guarded secret from your kind."

Malek's jaw tightened. "Aren't we beyond this?"

Sabine turned to Malek, placing her hand on his chest.

"This is not our secret to share, Malek. If you cannot swear, we'll meet you at dawn."

"He's getting closer," Blossom whispered, clinging to Sabine's neck. "We need to go!"

"Dammit," Malek muttered. "Fine. I swear. Whatever it takes to keep Sabine safe and find out what's going on."

Satisfied, Bane led them away from the crowded market. Sabine kept her head down and ears covered as she followed him through a maze of narrow streets and alleyways. The sounds of the market gradually faded behind them, replaced by the quieter murmur of distant conversations, the low croaks of frogs, and the chirps of crickets singing their nocturnal song.

Overhead, another wyvern swooped low and disappeared in the direction of the market. Sabine adjusted the hood of her cloak to better hide her silvery hair.

It should have been a peaceful night, but Sabine suspected it would be a long time before any of them felt safe.

At least not while dragons were on the hunt.

CHAPTER 18

The wooden sign over the Starlight Smithy creaked in the cool night breeze. Under a thin sheen of glamour, Sabine caught sight of the symbol of a glowing eye framed by delicate feathered wings. It had been etched under the stylized words of the business, invisible to all except those with the ability to manipulate glamour.

Rika stopped in her tracks, staring at the sign in confusion. "Is that glamour? Here?"

Sabine turned to her and asked quietly, "You see it?"

Rika nodded. "It's not as strong as yours. I think I could break it if I tried."

Malek studied the sign and frowned. "What do you see?"

"Nothing that concerns you," Bane said gruffly, motioning them toward the building.

When Malek narrowed his eyes, Sabine brushed her fingers against his lightly. He looked down at her, captured her hand in his and kissed her knuckles before lowering her hand. Even then, he didn't release her.

"Your demon enjoys trying my patience," he murmured.

She smiled up at him. "I've noticed you enjoy doing the same."

Malek chuckled, running his thumb across her hand as they approached the building.

The shop's exterior had been constructed from sturdy stone and dark, rich wood with silver inlays. Arched windows, etched with scenes of dragons breathing fire and in flight over villages had been created by a master craftsman. Overlaid atop the windows was another thin coating of glamour, this one depicting winged humanoids—the aderyan—set aflame and falling from the Sky Cities.

She frowned, hoping she hadn't made a mistake by bringing a dragon in their midst. While she trusted him implicitly, a small part of her worried his interests might not always align with hers.

Bane pushed open the door, motioning for them to enter. As Sabine's eyes adjusted to the warm interior, she scanned their surroundings. Shelves lined the walls, filled with intricate jewelry, finely wrought decorative metalwork, and odd little trinkets. The air was rich with the scents of polished wood, metal, and a hint of something floral. The large, arched windows cast a soft, ethereal glow across the room, illuminating the detailed scenes etched into the glass.

"Ohhhh," Blossom whispered. "Shinies!"

A young man with dark hair approached them, his brown eyes bright and curious. "Welcome to the Starlight Smithy," he greeted with a polite nod. "I'm Niall. How can I assist you this evening?"

As he spoke, Sabine's attention was drawn to a subtle shimmer behind his ear. She relaxed her eyes, glimpsing a tattoo of an eye partially hidden beneath his hair. Rika blinked several times, clearly seeing it with her seer abilities, and gave Sabine a slight nod to confirm.

Bane stepped forward, holding out an intricately engraved coin. "We're looking for Fiona."

The sight of the demon and the coin in his outstretched hand made Niall's expression shift from polite curiosity to sharp awareness. He swallowed and took the coin with shaking fingers.

"F-Follow me," Niall said, his voice dropping to a barely audible whisper. He led them through the shop and into a back room concealed behind a heavy curtain.

The air grew cooler as they descended a narrow staircase, each step echoing softly in the confined space. At the bottom, they stepped into a basement filled with several work-benches covered with tools and projects in various stages of completion. A large fireplace took up the far wall, but it was currently empty and cold.

A middle-aged woman stood at the far end, her hands busy weaving a delicate chain. Her braided hair was black as midnight and adorned with tiny bells that jingled as her fingers moved nimbly over the silver metal.

She looked up as they approached, her gaze shifting from Bane to Sabine, her eyes widening slightly in recognition.

"By the gods," she murmured, setting down her work. "A sidhe. That explains the commotion I heard earlier. Niall, hurry and close the shop."

Niall turned and raced up the stairs, taking them two at a time. Sabine narrowed her eyes and wrapped a gust of wind around Niall, halting him in his tracks. Malek tensed, his hand immediately going to the sword at his waist.

The woman held up her hands in a peaceable gesture. "You and your companions are welcome here. I simply seek to have the boy secure the shop from outsiders."

Sabine studied the woman carefully. "Yet you can see through glamour and choose to reveal my secrets without care?"

The woman pursed her lips. "You walked into *my* shop, Your Highness. It's been a long time since one of your kind bothered to get off their ass and venture out of Faerie. Given that your companions have eyes, I'd say the demon at your side is a pretty strong indicator you're not human."

Sabine stared at her. "I don't know if you're simply overly confident or impertinent."

"Perhaps a bit of both," the dark-haired woman said with a shrug.

"She's not a seer," Rika said quietly. "I don't sense that from her. She has limited magic, but the glamour on the sign outside has a similar resonance."

Fiona's eyes widened slightly, staring at Rika in surprise. "A seer? Well, that's a twist I didn't see coming."

Bane lowered the hood of his cloak and said, "She's not a seer. Are you, Fiona?"

"Bane'umbra Versed," Fiona snarled, leaping over the forge and grabbing a curved blade in one swift movement. Before Sabine could lift her hand, Bane had the woman disarmed and pinned against the wall with his forearm pressed against her neck. Malek's weapon was in hand, his body angled protectively in front of Sabine.

"Sabine, this hellion is Fiona Windrider, descendant of the aderyan Windrider Clan," Bane said. "The boy on the stairs is her nephew, Niall. Although, he was a mere babe when I last traveled here."

Fiona withdrew a knife from her belt and jabbed it against Bane's side. "I didn't think we'd meet again in this lifetime, Bane. Or I would have kept my weapons closer."

Bane bit out a laugh and released the woman, clasping her wrist in greeting. "Nor did I expect to return to this hellhole. The stench in this city makes the underworld downright fragrant."

Fiona snorted and sheathed her weapons. "You're welcome to let the door hit you on the way out."

Surprised and curious by the peculiar greeting, Sabine relaxed her magical hold on Niall.

He leaned against the banister for a moment, indecision warring on his face. "Aunt Fi?"

Fiona waved him off and said, "Put up the sign and close the shop. Box up that last order before you head back down, and see about heating the kettle for some tea."

Niall nodded and hastened up the stairway. Malek sheathed his weapon, but his hand didn't stray far from his blade. Fiona watched Malek curiously as though trying to figure him out, but she didn't say a word.

"I remember his mother," Bane said, gesturing toward the stairs where Niall had disappeared. "If he's here, I'm assuming his magic manifested?"

Fiona grabbed a nearby rag and wiped off her hands. "Around the age of two. The boy's a good lad. More sense than my sister had anyway. Haven't seen nor heard from her since Niall showed the first signs of magic. He's been learning the craft well enough."

Tossing the rag aside, Fiona asked, "Now, what brings you to my door? Considering you've brought fae royalty along, I'm assuming you have another purpose other than a simple assassination."

"We're looking for some information," Bane said. "In particular, anything you've heard about what's been occurring in the Sky Cities or with the dragons of late. We're also interested in whether you've heard any mention of the portal."

Fiona licked her lips, her gaze sharpening on Sabine. "I'm assuming you have something worthwhile to trade?"

Bane narrowed his eyes. "Do not provoke me, Fiona."

Fiona chuckled and said, "Don't get your horns in a twist. I was merely curious which one of you was bartering."

"It depends on the value of the information you offer," Sabine said, lowering the hood of her cloak and taking the opportunity to better study the basement. Her eyes kept going to the fireplace as though something wasn't quite right about it. Blossom peeked out from under Sabine's hair and flew off her shoulder to investigate the room.

Fiona stared at Blossom in shock. "Well, I'll be damned. A flutterfolk?"

"I'm a pixie," Blossom said, hovering in front of Fiona. "Your magic smells funny. Like a storm."

"A pixie," Fiona said with a grin. "We know your kind as flutterfolk, little skykin. I haven't had the privilege, but I've heard your legends since I was a girl."

"There are legends about us?" Blossom asked, her eyes wide.

"Aye," Fiona said with a grin, leaning against a table. "There's one I recall about three flutterfolk and a dragon. The first lived in a house made of wood. The dragon burned it down. The second lived in a house made of stone. The dragon knocked it over with its tail. The third flutterfolk was the trickiest of all."

"What did the pixie do?"

"We do not have time for this nonsense," Bane said with a sigh.

Rika shushed him and said, "I want to hear the rest too."

Fiona grinned and said, "Well, the third flutterfolk stole iron from the most powerful of dragons and asked the dwarves to help build a grand house. The dragon tried and tried, but he could not melt the iron. He returned day after day, using his dragonfire against the house. On the very last day, the dragon returned to find the door wide open. When the dragon snuck inside, the flutterfolk and dwarves sealed the trap shut with the dragon still inside. And there he remains to this day."

Blossom clapped her hands. "I haven't heard that one before. We'll have to tell Dagmar when we go back to Razadon, Sabine!"

"I'm sure she'd enjoy hearing it," Sabine said with a smile. She glanced over at Malek, but he didn't seem bothered by the story. He met her gaze, his eyes twinkling in amusement.

"The bug does not need more grandiose ideas," Bane muttered. "She's trouble enough on her own."

A bell jangled on the far side of the room. Fiona's eyes flew to it and then to the ceiling overhead. Bane's eyes silvered, and he made a motion for silence. After a moment, he lifted three fingers and gestured in the direction where the front door was located.

Fiona muttered a curse and led them swiftly to the fireplace. She grabbed Sabine's arm and whispered, "You and your companions will keep our silence or pay with your lives."

Bane grabbed Fiona's hand and bent it backward. "Touch her again, and I'll sever your arm from your body."

Fiona's eyes watered as she managed, "And all I have to do is shout for help and the dragon outside my shop will kill you for me."

Malek started to step between them, but Sabine shook her head in warning. Even if Fiona and her nephew possessed traces of magic, they were still more human than not.

"Release her," Sabine said quietly, unwilling to risk any lives until she knew what was going on.

Bane immediately released Fiona. The woman rubbed her wrist and glared at Bane.

"I make no oath to you, Fiona Windrider," Sabine said, careful to keep her voice low. "While I have no doubt about our ability to get my people out of here safely, I cannot guarantee the safety of you and yours if there is an altercation with the dragon outside."

"Spoken like a fae," she muttered in annoyance. "Stay close, and may the gods help me if I'm a fool for trusting you."

Fiona turned and pressed her hand against the stone hearth. A shimmer of glamour dissipated, revealing a hidden passage. The stone wall slid aside with a soft rumble, unveiling a narrow corridor bathed in the faint glow of enchantment. Sabine's breath caught at the sight, sensing the old, powerful magic woven into the hidden entrance.

As they stepped through the passage, the wall closed behind them, sealing them off from the shop above. The corridor opened into the basement of another building.

The ripe stench of too many unwashed bodies filled her nose. Almost twenty cots and bedrolls had been piled around the room, creating sparse sleeping places. Dwarven lanterns hung from the ceiling, providing the only light in the windowless basement.

Sabine's eyes widened at the sight of almost two dozen people huddled together in the room. At first glance, they appeared fae. But a closer look made her stagger to a shocked halt.

They were aderyan!

Rika's soft gasp of horror filled the space as all eyes turned to them. Most of them had their wings broken or clipped, their expressions a mix of defiance and weariness. Some had the ethereal beauty of pure-blooded aderyan, while others bore more human features, their diluted ancestry evident. Most of them wore little more than rags, and even those were nearly falling off their thin frames.

"Welcome to our refuge," Fiona said bitterly, her voice tinged with a hint of sadness. "This is where those with aderyan blood find sanctuary, away from the dragons' wrath. Once they've sufficiently recovered, we help them blend in, teach them to hide their magic, or, when possible, aid their escape to the refuge islands or beyond the western sea."

One of the aderyan, a girl of no more than a handful of years, hesitantly approached them. Her eyes were the deep azure of the sky on a clear day while her silken hair seemed to have been spun from sunshine. Her wings had already been severed and her chest bound with a heavy bandage.

"This is Lyra," Fiona said, tousling the girl's hair. "She has not spoken a word since her wings were clipped. We managed to smuggle her out after convincing the dragons she wouldn't survive without her wings."

Lyra pointed to the flower still in Sabine's hand and tilted her head curiously, exposing her pointed ears. But for an accident of fate, this child could have been fae. Sabine kneeled in front of the girl and offered the starpetal to her.

"It's a starpetal," Sabine said softly. "It was once a gift of friendship given from your people to the fae. I think it's time it was returned to you."

The young girl smiled shyly and took the flower, smelling its honeyed fragrance. She reached out and gave Sabine a hug. Touched beyond measure, Sabine returned her hug, careful to avoid touching where her wings had been severed.

Blossom sniffled. "Sabine, we have to help them. No one should have their wings taken away."

Lyra's mouth formed an 'O' shape as she stared at Blossom and her wings in wonder.

Sabine took Lyra's empty hand in hers, holding it flat for Blossom to land. "Lyra, I'd like you to meet Blossom. She's a pixie, but I believe your people call them flutterfolk. She's a very dear friend of mine."

The moment Blossom landed on Lyra's hand, Lyra's skin

began to glow softly. A few of the adults gasped and murmured quietly to each other.

Fiona shook her head and said, "Well, that's not something I was expecting. You tripped her magic. Didn't think it could happen once their wings were clipped."

Sabine looked at the scarred and battered aderyan gathering around them. Despite their obvious suffering, their resilient posture and hopeful curiosity shone through. Lachlina's anger matched Sabine's own at the needless suffering these people had endured. This never should have happened.

Sabine stood and demanded, "Did you know they still lived, Bane?"

"No," Bane said quietly. "Fiona did not share this with me. We thought they had been lost during the Dragon War."

"Our fates weren't your concern," Fiona snapped. "And if the fae cared so damn much, they would have left their precious forests long before now."

Sabine ignored Fiona and turned to Malek. "And you? Did you know about this?"

Malek stared at the men, women, and even the few children surrounding them. Sabine could see the barely restrained anger boiling under the surface. "No, and that in itself is unacceptable and inexcusable. I need answers, Sabine. Which clans were responsible for this?"

"They all had a hand in our suffering," Fiona bit out, her eyes blazing with temper. "They stole our land, our skies, and our people's wings. Each and every one of them is to blame."

Sabine placed a hand on Malek's arm, urging him not to engage further. Turning back to the aderyan, she asked, "Did you or any others send word to Faerie that your people lived?"

"We did," an aderyan man said, approaching them. His platinum hair touched his shoulders, but it was bound away from his face in a style that reminded her of the braids

Blossom often wove, emphasizing his pointed ears. Without his wings, he appeared more fae than many of the others in this room. His features had that same timeless quality, making it virtually impossible to know his age. She knew he wasn't an Elder, yet the people here seemed to defer to him.

"This is Aeron," Fiona said, gesturing to the man.

"We last attempted to send word to King Caden'ellesar of the Seelie more than a century ago. Others have sent similar messages in the past. We have no way of knowing whether our messages reached his ears."

If her father knew and had ignored their plea for aid, such an action was inexcusable. Sabine took a steadying breath, trying to gain control of the magic coursing through her. Everything within her demanded she right this wrong, no matter the cost.

"How strong are the wards on this building?"

Aeron studied her with measured curiosity. "They're old magic and quite powerful. They've kept our presence secret for centuries. The dragons should not detect any of us while we remain within their boundaries."

Sabine turned to Rika and asked, "What do you sense?"

Rika hesitated. "They're strong. I couldn't break them if I tried."

"Malek?" Sabine asked quietly.

"Do what you need to, Sabine," he said, placing his hand on her lower back. "If I need to intervene, I will."

That was all she needed to know. Trusting him at his word, she allowed her glamour to fall away. The room filled with a shimmering golden light as Sabine allowed the magic to build within her. She reached for Lachlina, bringing the goddess to the surface.

The power of creation is already within your grasp, my little golden flower. Use it to restore Aeslion's magic, as you were always destined to do. I shall guide your hand.

Her magic blended seamlessly together with Lachlina's power. Sabine's skin glowed with an intense, otherworldly light as she raised her hands, feeling the goddess's presence coalesce within her. The air around her crackled with energy, the very essence of creation swirling and gathering in her palms. Fiona and the aderyan surrounding her gasped.

Blossom flew into the air and called out, "Major magic coming through, people. Batten down the hatches, reinforce the wards, and hold on tight. It's go time!"

Rika picked up Lyra and moved away from Sabine. "Can you shield Sabine's magic, Bane?"

"Not while we're in Imenel." Bane turned to Fiona and ordered, "If you have a way of reinforcing the wards, do so now."

Fiona leaped into action, snapping commands to some of the aderyan standing nearby. Together they lifted their palms, sending their weakened magic into the wards to shield Sabine's building power.

Sabine extended her hands toward the nearest aderyan, Aeron, feeling the magic pulse and thrum with life. Threads of golden light streamed from her fingers, weaving intricate patterns in the air. These threads wrapped around Aeron's body, regrowing the fragile wing bones that had been severed. The process was slow and deliberate, each strand of light a testament to the balance and sacrifice required.

As the golden light enveloped Aeron, Sabine felt a tug deep within her soul, a call for something precious to balance the scales. She closed her eyes, reaching into the depths of her being. A soft, ethereal song filled the room, Lachlina's voice guiding her. Sabine knew what needed to be offered—a part of her own essence, a fragment of her magic tied to her very life force.

With a whispered incantation in the ancient tongue of the gods, Sabine surrendered a portion of her magic, feeling it leave her body and merge with the golden light. It was a sacrifice that would weaken her temporarily, but it was necessary to restore the balance. The light around Aeron intensified, and slowly but surely, his wings began to regrow to their full, majestic glory. Feathers as brilliant as the dawn unfurled, shimmering with an iridescent sheen.

One by one, she moved to each aderyan, repeating the process, her heart heavy with the weight of the magic and the sacrifice it demanded. As she restored their wings, Sabine could feel the goddess's approval and the renewed hope emanating from the aderyan. When the last pair of wings was fully restored and Lyra leaped into the air with a joyful cry, the golden light faded, leaving the room bathed in a gentle, serene glow. Sabine lowered her hands and sank into Malek's waiting arms.

CHAPTER 19

Malek caught Sabine before she collapsed, gently cradling her in his arms. Her glamour had once again been stripped away, exposing her secrets to the world. She was even more beautiful in his eyes, as though whatever had once held back her true magic had somehow been torn asunder. Her intricate skin markings still shimmered with the remnants of her remarkable power, yet there was a softness about her that awakened his need to protect her from anyone who might dare cause her harm.

"I never thought a fae could do what she's done," Fiona whispered, staring at Sabine in shock. "She's given them back their wings."

"She is no fae," Aeron whispered, dropping to his knees in front of Sabine. He placed his fist over his heart and lowered his head in obeisance. The others followed his lead, tears filling their eyes as they bowed before Sabine.

"Ummm... I don't think Sabine is going to like them bowing," Blossom said, landing on Malek's shoulder. Her wings twitched. "Uh oh. The goddess is really angry and arguing with someone."

"Can you hear what they're saying?"

Blossom's wings drooped. "She said it's none of our concern and banished me from her garden. I don't think she'll let me back in until Sabine wakes up or she's done arguing."

A loud thump sounded from somewhere above them. The noise echoed through the hidden sanctuary.

"The wards," Bane demanded, turning to Rika. "Have they held?"

Rika shook her head. "Barely. Some of Sabine's magic must have made it through. The dragon and his guards likely know we're down here."

"Niall," Fiona exclaimed. "I have to find him! He may not have made it to the neighbor's shop in time."

She started to rush toward the hidden entrance, but Bane wrapped his arm around her waist. She struggled against him, but he held her tightly.

"Release me, you oversized oaf! If the dragon thinks we've betrayed them—"

"Silence, woman!" Bane said with a growl. "The dragons don't give a damn about the boy. If you go out there, you'll expose everyone you've been trying to protect."

"Fiona," Aeron said sharply.

Fiona immediately stopped fighting Bane. He released her, and she pushed away from him. She kicked the nearby bed in frustration.

"Bane," Malek said, meeting the demon's silvered gaze. "Stay with Sabine. I'll handle the dragon."

Bane gave him a curt nod, carefully taking Sabine from Malek's arms. The loss of her was nearly a physical pain, made even worse by the warding medallion suppressing their bond. He yanked it off his neck. The aderyan hissed, some of their wings unfurling as Malek's dragon power filled the room. If the wards had weakened significantly, it should be enough to announce his presence to any of his people nearby.

"I am not your enemy," Malek said sharply, meeting their furious gazes. "Sabine is mine to protect. Harming you would harm her—and that will *never* happen."

Blossom flew to Malek's shoulder and put her hands on her hips. "Malek is a good dragon, and Sabine loves him. He only eats people who deserve it."

Rika slapped her hands over her face. "Blossom, you've got to stop telling people Malek is going to eat them."

"Bane threatens to eat me all the time," Blossom said with a shrug. "Come on, Malek. Let's go deal with this dragon."

The aderyan stared, their newly restored wings vibrating with emotion. He held their gaze before turning and making his way to the concealed entrance they had come through. Malek wasn't quite sure what to make of his pixie sidekick, but he suspected the aderyan were now more curious than angry at Blossom's endorsement.

"Your appearance may raise some questions," Malek warned, the hidden doorway sliding shut behind them with a whisper of magic.

Blossom cocked her head. "Good point. Gimme a second."

Her image shimmered briefly before reforming into a tiny insect with large wings.

Malek arched his brow. "A dragonfly?"

"Drat! I don't have enough magic to turn into a dragon again. We'll have to talk to Sabine about that when she wakes up. I guess this is close enough for now."

"I'm not sure whether to be offended by that remark," Malek muttered, heading up the stairs to the shop.

They emerged into the cool night air. Without the medallion to dampen his senses, he scanned the shadows until he saw what he was looking for—the dark silhouettes of his uncle and his guards.

At least Niall was safely out of sight.

He sent out a silent warning to Levin and took several steps into the street.

"Try not to die before I get there," Levin said, his mental voice sounding in Malek's head. *"Your mom threatened to cut off my tail if I let anything happen to you."*

"Gee," Malek said dryly. *"It's comforting to know how concerned you are for my well-being."*

"Hah. Your mom terrifies me, and Esme likes my tail."

"Too much information, Levin. Way too much information."

Levin's laughter echoed in Malek's head. He could feel his wingmate already in the air and headed directly for him. Now he just needed to stall… and not kill his uncle. Nothing was more dangerous than a dragon protecting his mate, especially when she was unconscious and just a short distance away.

"Uncle Emanthir," Malek called out. He allowed his power to billow outward, both to announce his presence and to help mask Sabine's lingering magic.

The dragon shapeshifter stepped out of the shadows, his gaze filled with suspicion. Emanthir's jet black hair and green eyes were the same as Malek's mother's, but that was where the similarities ended. While Nymira was often smiling or laughing when she wasn't threatening to cut off Levin's tail, Malek's uncle seemed to have a permanent scowl on his face. As the current head of the Emerald Clan, Emanthir held a prominent place on the Council. Until he knew the political climate in the Sky Cities, Malek needed to tread carefully.

Two wyvern guards flanked Emanthir, their expressions unreadable. Malek recognized one of them as Wyndon, Emanthir's trusted wingmate. The other was unfamiliar, but that wasn't altogether unsurprising. The number of wyverns far outmatched the number of dragons at any given time.

"Malek," his uncle replied, his voice a deep rumble. "I hadn't heard news of your return. Your presence here is highly suspect, especially given the whisperings of foreign magic that float upon the night air."

"I've only just arrived in the city," Malek said, crossing his arms over his chest. "I'm investigating a personal clan matter."

Emanthir's eyes sharpened on him. "Does this have anything to do with the reports of disturbances this evening?"

"The matters appear to be related," Malek said, stopping an acceptable distance away. Dragons who did not belong to the same clan often maintained enough space between them in case they needed to shift quickly. Neither Emanthir nor his guards seemed overly troubled by Malek's reluctance to approach.

"Very well," Emanthir said. "I would hear your report."

Malek arched a brow. "Come now, Uncle. Would you have me betray clan loyalty for a favored relative?"

Emanthir bit out a harsh laugh. "Favored, is it? You've been away far too long, Malek. The winds have changed since you last journeyed home."

"Then I'll have to remedy that," Malek said, refusing to rise to the bait.

The sound of wings overhead grew louder until they stopped completely. Levin shifted into his human form before his feet landed on the ground. At least Levin had the good sense to leave Esmelle somewhere safe.

"Well, I'll be damned," Levin said with a grin. "Emanthir, you old fossil flier. I didn't think you still dusted off your scales and came down to mingle with the humans. There are some cute ones in the tavern near the docks, just waiting for a randy dragon to flip up their skirts."

Emanthir narrowed his eyes. "You forget yourself, Levin."

Levin nodded good-naturedly. "So I've been told. Often."

Emanthir's lip curled as he turned back to Malek. "It diminishes your strength to keep a wingmate with the manners of a hatchling."

Malek glanced over at Levin and grinned. "So I've been told. Often."

Levin chuckled. Emanthir's jaw tightened, eyeing them with annoyance.

"I expect to hear from your father no later than tomorrow evening regarding the disturbances," Emanthir said to Malek. "I will give you until that time to make your report."

Emanthir pushed off from the ground, his form shifting smoothly into that of a great emerald dragon. The wyvern guards followed suit, their sleek bodies taking to the air in perfect unison. Malek watched them disappear into the night sky, their silhouettes merging with the darkness until they were no longer visible.

"I can't believe you called him a fossil flier," Malek murmured, shaking his head. "One of these days, you're going to push him too far."

Levin grinned. "It worked, didn't it?" But the amusement faded from his eyes as he switched to their silent form of communication. *"What's our next move?"*

"We need to find out what brought my uncle to the city," Malek said, knowing Emanthir's distaste for interacting with humans. *"Sabine, Bane, and Rika are downstairs in a nearby shop and out of sight. Now that we've been outed, I won't be able to learn anything more here. I'm going to take Sabine up to the Sky Cities and to safety before anyone else discovers her presence."*

"Understood," Levin said. *"I have a few more inquiries to make, and Esme is insistent she needs to hum the dryad's song down every damn street. We'll follow in the morning."*

"Keep her safe, or Sabine will have my head."

Levin clasped Malek's wrist in farewell and said, *"Be careful, Malek. The winds are dangerous tonight."*

Malek waited until Levin had taken to the skies and was out of sight before turning back to the shop.

"You know, it's not polite to have secret conversations when others are present," Blossom said with a sniff. "First, the goddess. Now, you. I thought us dragons had to stick together."

Malek smiled, surprised he'd forgotten about the tiny dragonfly on his shoulder. "You're good at being sneaky when it suits you."

"I know." Blossom's wings stopped fluttering for a moment. "Is your uncle going to try to hurt Sabine?"

"He won't get the chance," Malek promised, pushing open the door to the empty shop. "Once I bring her under my clan's protection and acknowledge her formally as my mate, any action taken against her will be the equivalent of a declaration of war."

Blossom transformed back into her normal pixie appearance. "Um, I'm not sure if Sabine is going to like that. I don't think Faerie queens are supposed to have dragon mates. Isn't that against the rules?"

"Don't us dragons need to stick together?" Malek asked, arching his brow. "You could always put in a good word for me."

Blossom cocked her head, considering it. "I'll think about it."

Well, that was better than nothing.

Blossom patted his neck. "You know, your uncle was talking to the wyverns while he was talking to you. Everyone keeps having secret conversations. It makes it hard to listen."

Malek paused. "How do you know he was communicating with them?"

Blossom pointed to her eyes. "I have two of them. Didn't

you know pixies can see and smell magic? I can't hear what you're saying, but I always know when you and Sabine talk to each other. You usually make her smile."

Malek headed downstairs, considering the potential implications. Blossom's ability to alert them when others might be communicating could come in handy.

Re-entering the hidden sanctuary, Malek found Bane standing over Sabine protectively, glaring at the aderyan whenever one of them got too close. The demon had placed Sabine on one of the dingy cots, her skin still softly glowing from the magic she'd expended.

Lyra, the young aderyan who hadn't spoken, kneeled on the dirty floor and peered at Sabine over the edge of the cot. Every now and then, she'd reach out and touch Sabine's hair. Oddly enough, she appeared to be the one exception to Bane's threatening glares.

Rika sat on the cot next to Sabine and the child, watching an aderyan woman argue with Bane. Apparently, it had been going on for a while.

"Try it, and you'll lose your shiny new wings," Bane said with a shrug.

A woman with hair the color of sunrise and wings that could have been plucked from the clouds stood in front of the demon. Her expression was furious and defiant as she said, "If you relinquish her to our care, we will take her to one of the islands. Others of our kind have escaped and found refuge there. She will be safe and protected, yet still be able to look upon the sky. That is far more than what you can offer her, demon."

Bane ignored the woman and studied his poisoned claws. At least his eyes weren't silvered yet.

Fiona shook her head. "Thalassa, you can't reason with a demon—especially *this* demon. Trust me, he's as stubborn as they come. He's not going to let you take her."

"But he must!" Thalassa said.

"She *is* our Aderylin," Aeron said, his words quieting Thalassa. "It is our duty to protect her while she is in Veylara, the healing slumber of the gods. We will not allow the dragon to steal her away while she is vulnerable, even should it cost us our lives. This is as it always has been."

"As you say, Aeron," Thalassa said, lowering her head.

"Sabine is not going anywhere, unless she chooses to do so," Malek declared. The aderyan turned at the sound of his voice. Instead of moving away, they formed a wall between him and the woman he loved.

Malek narrowed his eyes, his heated magic filling the room. "I would suggest you not attempt to keep Sabine from me."

"Well this should be interesting," Bane said, his tone amused. "Go ahead, dragon. Let's see how well you deal with the talking turkeys."

Thalassa huffed. "Of all the insulting—"

Blossom flew off Malek's shoulder and into the fray, her wings tinged red. "You should be ashamed of yourselves! You're giving us winged folk a bad name. If you don't let Malek through right now, you're going to start itching in all sorts of uncomfortable places."

"We will not allow him to imprison our Aderylin, little skykin," Aeron said, expanding his wings to block Malek's line of sight. "Until she regains consciousness and declares her wishes, we will watch over her."

Rika stood and pushed past Aeron's wings. "Sabine has already chosen. She gave all of you a precious gift, just like she did for me. Now you're throwing that gift in her face by questioning her choice. Do you honestly think she would have brought him here if she didn't trust Malek?"

Aeron blinked at Rika as though seeing her for the first time. "We did not fully realize the threat of the dragons until it was too late. They stole our home, our children, and even our magic. Would you have our Aderylin suffer in the same manner?"

Rika shook her head. "I'm not saying you're wrong about all dragons. I'm saying you're wrong about *this* dragon. Allow Malek to awaken her, and you'll see what I mean." She gestured to Bane. "Trust me, Bane wouldn't let him anywhere near Sabine if there was a chance he'd hurt her."

Thalassa's gaze turned suspicious. "You claim a dragon can awaken her when she is in Veylara?"

Rika nodded. "He's done it before."

Aeron looked down at Sabine with reverence. "She is young to have been gifted such power. That she traveled here at all speaks to her fierce and determined nature." He lifted his head to meet Malek's gaze. "I do not trust you, dragon. But the young seer carries Theoria's mark on her hand, and the flutterfolk sings your praises. We will let you pass, but we will not allow you to leave with her while she is in Veylara."

"Aeron," Thalassa exclaimed, her expression horrified.

Aeron gave her a sharp look. "Enough, Thalassa. We will allow this."

The aderyan slowly parted, allowing Malek a clear path to approach Sabine. Bane arched his brow, his expression far too amused. Malek shot him a dirty look, wondering what the demon was up to.

Bane chuckled and swept his hand toward Sabine. "Well, go ahead. Wake the sleeping Aderylin or whatever the hell they're calling her. Let's see what the turkeys think of your methods."

Malek barely resisted groaning. *That* was what Bane found amusing. The moment they realized he was using his dragonfire to awaken Sabine, they were going to lose their minds.

"You will wake her now?" Lyra asked, her musical voice barely above a whisper.

Thalassa gasped, pressing her hand against her mouth. The rest of the aderyan stilled at the sound of Lyra's voice.

Malek nodded at the child. "I will, but you may not want to touch her while I do it."

Lyra scooted back, tucking her wings against her back and out of harm's way. "I will watch."

Malek sat on the cot beside Sabine and gently brushed her hair away from her face. She was exhausted, far beyond her normal limits. He wished he could allow her to sleep, but it was only a matter of time before his uncle returned—or worse.

He leaned down and kissed her, summoning his dragonfire from the depths of his soul. Tempering his power with the strength of his love for her, he sent his magic across their bond, searing the path binding them together.

Sabine murmured his name on a sigh and wrapped her arms around his neck. He continued to kiss her, threading his fingers through her silky hair and tasting the very essence of her. The dragonfire pulsed within him, its warmth spreading from his core, through his lips, and into Sabine. He poured his energy into her, feeling the connection between them blaze brighter with every passing second.

Sabine's skin began to glow even more brilliantly, her intricate markings shimmering with renewed vigor. Malek could feel her energy returning, the exhaustion slowly ebbing away as his dragonfire infused her with strength. Her breathing steadied, and the tension in her body melted under his touch.

Finally, Sabine's eyes fluttered open, the deep lavender color of her irises more brilliant than ever. She gazed up at him with a mixture of love and utter trust, her lips curving into a faint smile.

"Malek," she whispered, her voice a gentle caress that sent a shiver down his spine. He rested his forehead against hers, relief washing over him as he felt the bond between them solidify and strengthen. He fully intended to burn that damn warding medallion at the first opportunity.

"Welcome back," he murmured, his voice thick with emotion. He kissed her once more, softly this time, savoring the taste of her lips. *"I can't tell you how much I want to continue kissing you, but I suspect the aderyan already want to skewer me for using my dragon wiles on you."*

"Maybe I should tell them all to go away," she teased. *"I'd like to learn more about these dragon wiles of yours."*

Malek grinned. *"Say the word, and I'll fly away with you right now. They'll never be able to catch a dragon."*

Sabine laughed. Malek stood and held out his hand, helping Sabine to her feet. He turned to face almost twenty shocked and furious aderyan. Each of them had silvered eyes and fangs. Their wings and claws were extended as though preparing to tear off his scales one by one.

Talking turkeys, indeed.

CHAPTER 20

*L*yra leaped in front of Sabine, her arms and wings extended protectively. "No! I kept watch! He did what he said."

"He used dragon magic, child," Thalassa said gently. "We do not know what harmful effects his magic may have on her. We cannot allow him to do so again."

Sabine straightened, her eyes narrowing on the aderyan woman. *"You cannot allow him?"*

"Uh oh," Blossom said, landing on Sabine's shoulder. "Now you've done it."

Thalassa paled. She immediately dropped to her knees and bowed her head. "I beg forgiveness, Aderylin. My concern for your safety caused me to speak out of turn."

The rest of them immediately followed suit, bowing their heads in silent deference. Lyra continued to stand in front of Sabine, her arms crossed.

Rika sighed. "Great. They're bowing again."

Sabine blinked and turned to Bane, hoping he might have some insight into their strange behavior. She'd never heard of an aderyan bowing to an Unseelie, no matter what magic she'd performed on their behalf.

Bane shrugged. "They've seen you use the powers of a goddess. Consider them the winged equivalent of pretentious Seelie temple priests and priestesses. They'll stay like that all day or even longer, if you let them."

"That doesn't look very comfortable," Blossom said. "What if they have to use a chamber pot or something?"

Sabine squeezed her eyes shut and counted to ten. It didn't help. They were still kneeling.

"Get up," she said in exasperation, reaching for Thalassa's hand. She pulled the shocked woman to her feet, then reached for the next aderyan. "I didn't return your wings so you could trade one overlord for another. Your magic was wrongfully taken from you. It's my *duty* to restore the balance, wherever and however I can."

Aeron gazed at her with reverence. "That is why you are our Aderylin. The balance must be maintained at all costs, and you have done so—at great personal risk to yourself."

Thalassa nodded. "That is why you have come, is it not? To restore the balance?"

Sabine looked at the aderyan, and the glimmer of fragile hope emanating from each of them. If she had known they still lived, she would have come sooner. She wanted to believe any of her people would have done the same, but the truth was she didn't know. Her people were reluctant to acknowledge what was happening in the world outside of Faerie, and much less inclined to leave its protected borders.

Shame filled her at the realization the fae had likely chosen to leave the aderyan to their fate. By writing them off as casualties of the dragons, they'd only helped reinforce fear and hatred while keeping themselves safely out of harm's way.

Malek took her hand, his voice slipping into her thoughts. *"This wasn't your fault, Sabine. What happened to them was unacceptable, but you cannot hold yourself responsible."*

"I can, and I do," she said. *"I blindly trusted my tutors and the rhetoric, confident the fae could not lie. If any of us had questioned or taken a closer look, we would have seen the truth masked behind a colorful deception. How many aderyan were lost because we chose not to ask the difficult questions?"*

"Then you should blame me as well," Malek said. *"I told you there were no fae captives on land controlled by my clan, but I knew they existed on others. After seeing the aderyan here, and how similar their appearance to the fae, I'm no longer certain those captives weren't wingless aderyan."*

Sabine looked up at him. *"We cannot allow this to continue, Malek. These people have committed no crime, except to have been born with aderyan magic."*

"I will do everything within my power to aid them," Malek promised, the strength of his vow permeating their bond. *"No one deserves this."*

Sabine nodded and squeezed his hand before addressing the aderyan again.

"The Huntsman told me to look toward the Sky Cities for one of the artifacts used to seal the portal. It must be located, or all magic in Aeslion and those dependent upon it will perish. I traveled here in search of this artifact, but I suspect the Huntsman directed me here for a secondary purpose as well. I *must* restore the balance, and right the wrong done to your people."

Many of the aderyan began to weep at her words. Sabine gestured to Malek and said, "Malek may be a dragon, but he is not your enemy. He is one of my most trusted allies and has proven himself to be honorable." She turned to meet Thalassa's gaze and said gently, "Trust is a fragile thing, especially given your history, but it begins by taking that first step. Both of us wish to help you and your people if you will allow it."

Aeron and Thalassa exchanged a look.

"Then you are truly our Aderylin," Thalassa said, clasping her hands together. "Only one such as you would attempt such a dangerous undertaking."

Aeron studied Malek. "We will think upon our Aderylin's words, but too many of our people have suffered at the hands of yours to forgive easily."

Malek nodded. "I understand."

Aeron turned back to Sabine. "We have heard rumors of an artifact such as the one you describe, but I have no knowledge of its location. It may already be in the hands of the dragons. If you intend to locate it, I will accompany you to the Sky Cities. There are some aderyan who may speak openly with me, provided they still draw breath."

"Aeron, no," Thalassa exclaimed. "You cannot return there without someone to act as your skyshield."

He lifted a hand to quiet her protests. "I will if I must, Thalassa. You will need to lead our people to safety and let the others know our Aderylin may require their aid."

Sabine frowned. "Did the ones who escaped suffer the same mistreatment?"

Aeron nodded. "All but a select few have had their wings clipped, but even those will serve you with honor."

Malek's voice slipped into her thoughts. *"I do not believe these people are strong enough to travel. I'd offer the use of my ship, but I doubt they'll accept if I make the suggestion."*

If she wasn't already in love with this dragon, his offer would have pushed her over that edge. She brushed her hand against his, sending a wave of gratitude over him. She closed her eyes, reaching for Lachlina with her thoughts. The goddess came to her easily, as though she'd been waiting for Sabine to ask for her help.

"*Yes, child. I know what you seek. Summon all your new would-be allies to you, and I will guide your magic to make them whole.*"

"*And the catch?*" Sabine asked.

"So *distrustful,*" Lachlina admonished. "*I have given you no cause to doubt me, my little golden flower. Every time you have asked for aid, I have graciously provided it. If you wish to begin balancing the scales between us, I suppose you could grant me a small favor.*"

She should have known it wouldn't be so simple.

Bracing herself, Sabine asked, "*What do you wish from me in exchange for helping to restore the aderyan's magic?*"

"*Once you have healed the aderyan and secured the last arti-fact, you will return to the dryad grove. Allow me the use of a vessel, so I might visit with my daughter once more.*"

It had to be a trap.

Even so, Sabine couldn't allow any of the aderyan to suffer when it was within her grasp to help them. Bane was going to be furious with her for agreeing, but this was too important to leave to chance. She didn't believe she could duplicate the complicated weaving Lachlina had helped her perform earlier without someone to help guide the magic.

"*Very well,*" Sabine agreed. "*I will do as you ask and provide a vessel enabling you to visit Theoria's grove for no more than a single hour.*"

"*The pact is sealed,*" Lachlina intoned, sending a sharp burst of magic through Sabine to seal their agreement.

Feeling slightly nauseated, Sabine opened her eyes.

Blossom patted her hair and said, "I think you made the right decision. Having your wings cut off is one of the most terrible things I could imagine."

"You heard that?"

Blossom nodded. "The goddess is humming and strolling through her garden. I think you made her happy."

Sabine bit back the retort that was on the tip of her tongue. There would be time enough for that later, especially once she told Malek and Bane what she'd done. In the meantime, she had to get these people to safety and help the others who were still suffering.

"There is a ship in the harbor called *Obsidian's Storm*," Sabine said, addressing the aderyan. "You may use it and its crew to retrieve your brethren. Once you return to the mainland, send a message to Aeron or Fiona. Any and all who are willing shall have their wings and magic restored."

Gasps and hopeful murmurs filled the room.

"The ship will be fully stocked and ready to depart before dawn," Malek added. "I suggest your people remain out of sight and below deck until you're past the lighthouse. The wyverns' patrol extends beyond it."

Thalassa clapped her hands. "Quickly. Pack only what you can easily carry. The seas may prove to be unforgiving."

The aderyan scrambled to gather their meager belongings, stuffing what they could into ragged knapsacks. While they packed, Bane approached Sabine and said, "I have no love for the Seelie, but this course of action may result in their slow death. It might be more practical to simply return them to their captors and save everyone the trouble."

"Of course you would say that," Fiona snapped. "These people have fought for their freedom using whatever means at their disposal. They're made of sturdier stuff than you could possibly imagine."

Malek frowned and said quietly, "I can stock the ship with food and basic supplies, but they need far more than that. Ocean travel isn't easy, and they're half-starved and dressed in rags."

"What do you suggest?" Sabine asked, gesturing to the

unsightly conditions in the basement. "They can't remain here."

"My clan has accounts with most of the vendors," Malek said. "If Fiona or someone known to the merchants can order some of the personal items they need, Levin will guarantee payment. At a minimum, they'll need fresh fruits and vegetables, cloaks to hide their wings, and some teas to help with seasickness. All the food in the world won't matter if they can't keep it down."

Fiona hesitated, a trace of suspicion in her eyes. "That's extremely generous. Most dragons hoard their treasures, yet you seem eager to part with yours."

Malek placed a hand on Sabine's lower back. "We do value our treasures. But when we claim the most priceless of them all, everything else becomes superfluous."

The aderyan stilled. Almost as one, they turned back to Malek with their eyes silvered, fangs exposed, and wings vibrating with anger. Several of them began to hiss. There was no confusing them with the fae now.

"Idiot dragon," Bane muttered. "Do you not remember what I told you about your mating instinct?"

Blossom waved her hands. "Go back to packing, people. This dragon has been tamed."

"Tamed?" Malek asked, arching a brow.

"Just go with it," Blossom whispered loudly. "Maybe try to look less… dragonish. Smile or something. But don't show them your teeth. We don't want to give them ideas."

Rika groaned and covered her face with both hands.

Sabine blew out a breath. She needed to get Malek out of there and soon. Turning to Fiona, she asked, "I trust you're able to order the supplies they'll need?"

Fiona nodded. "Aye."

"You can meet Levin, my wingmate, at the pier," Malek said. "He'll introduce your people to the crew and handle all payment arrangements. He won't reveal your identities, but the chances of your people being spotted will increase once the sun rises. You should be well underway before then."

Aeron and Thalassa were arguing about something quietly. Thalassa straightened and turned on her heel, marching toward Sabine. She kneeled with a flourish, her wings spread out dramatically behind her.

"Vespara will lead our people to the refuge islands and summon our allies," Thalassa announced. "I respectfully request permission to accompany our Aderylin to the Sky Cities."

"Two talking turkeys among a host of dragons," Bane said with a trace of amusement in his voice. "This one must be eager to have her wings severed again. Shall we take bets on how long they'll last?"

Several of the aderyan gasped. Thalassa tensed and gritted her teeth, but she didn't snap at Bane.

Knowing Bane's goading had been a test, Sabine glanced over at him. He gave her a barely perceptible nod of approval. If Thalassa could keep her temper in check, having two aderyan who could fly them quickly out of trouble might come in handy.

"I accept," Sabine said, motioning for Thalassa to stand. "However, Aeron must give his approval and both of you will stop kneeling before me. We need to keep a low profile once we depart."

"Of course, Aderylin," Thalassa said, rising to her feet.

Lyra looked up at Sabine. "I will come too."

"No, child," Thalassa said, shaking her head. "It will be far too dangerous for you to travel among the dragons. You will accompany the others on a grand ship."

Lyra shook her head. She held up the starpetal and reached for Sabine's hand. Her skin began to glow, the shimmer encompassing the flower she held. The color of the flower deepened until it was nearly the color of twilight, making the gold dust on its petals shine even more brilliantly. Sabine could have sworn Lyra had used fae magic, but such a thing should have been impossible.

Sabine kneeled in front of Lyra. "Why do you wish to come with me, Lyra?"

"I know the secret," she whispered.

Sabine smiled and tilted her head. "What secret?"

Lyra opened her hand, palm up, and looked at Sabine expectantly. Sabine placed her hand on Lyra's, but the girl shook her head and lowered her hand slightly, leaving space between them. Both Sabine's and Lyra's skin began to glow with the same golden luminescence, as though their magic was harmonizing. A shimmering golden quill appeared between their hands, suspended in the air.

Sabine stared at the image in shock. "That's the portal key, isn't it?"

Lyra nodded. "I will show you."

Thalassa paled. "I hadn't thought… She's too young to have received such a gift. It should not be possible."

Sabine lowered her hand, causing the magic to dissipate. "What do you mean?"

Aeron frowned and approached them. "It does not happen often, except once every few centuries. When an Aderylin awakens the magic in one of our young, there is a chance they will be bound together. If you seek something or have a need that must be fulfilled, the chosen aderyan will be able to guide you. We call these individuals Aetherbound."

Rika hesitated, then stepped closer. "Is this ability similar to foresight?"

Thalassa shook her head. "It is not a seer ability. This is a mystical connection that binds their magic together. It is a holy pact, one that allows the Aetherbound to reach heights not normally possible for our kind. When the gods still walked the land, many of them awakened several Aether-bound. They became their sworn guardians, their messengers, and the hands of justice."

She looked up at Bane. "Did you know about this?"

Bane's expression was guarded. "Yes."

Sabine looked into Lyra's azure eyes, full of trust and innocence. She couldn't protect her, especially not where they were heading. And she refused to use a child for a mystical ability that might help her to locate the portal artifact.

"Sabine," Malek said quietly, placing his hand on her shoulder. "We'll find it another way."

Sabine reached up and laid her hand over his. Lifting her head to meet Thalassa's gaze, she said, "If Lyra is bound to me through magic, then she may seek me out once she's grown. Children are precious and should be protected at all costs. We won't put her in danger."

Thalassa's gaze settled on their joined hands. "Her parents are still captives in our former aeries—the Sky Cities. Other than us, she is alone in this world."

Malek's hand tightened on hers.

Bane sighed and said, "Have the two adult turkeys watch the little one. She looks half-starved as it is. Sending her away on the ship will leave her nothing more than feathers and bones. We can at least fatten her up a bit."

Rika nodded. "As long as we keep her away from Blossom's magic, kobolds, and dryads, she should be fine."

"Turn someone into a butterfly once, and they never let you forget it," Blossom said with a dramatic sigh. "Besides, she needs someone who can teach her how to properly fly."

Sabine bit back a smile and looked up at Malek. "Will she be safe in your home?"

Malek hesitated. "Yes, once she's behind my wards. We'll take some precautions to keep her presence a secret."

Sabine nodded and turned back to Aeron and Thalassa. "Until such time as we're able to locate her parents or she becomes an adult, will you accept her as your charge?"

Aeron nodded, clasping his fist over his heart. "It will be done, Aderylin."

Thalassa repeated the gesture and said, "We shall be honored to protect and teach Lyra all an Aetherbound should know."

Sabine smiled at Lyra. "Will you travel with us to the Sky Cities?"

Lyra nodded and touched Sabine's hand again, sending a tingle of magic up her arm. Lyra giggled before Thalassa swept the girl into her arms, telling her it was time to pack and she could visit with the Aderylin later.

Deciding it would be best to give the aderyan some privacy while they made last-minute plans to purchase supplies, Sabine headed upstairs to the shop to wait with the rest of her companions.

Bane approached the window and scanned both the street and the sky. Rika joined him while Blossom investigated the wares on display in the shop.

Malek wrapped his arms around Sabine and asked, "Do you have enough magic to glamour all of them until they reach the ship?"

Sabine leaned against him and stared out the window. The moon was approaching its zenith and her magic was at its most powerful, but she'd done too much in a short period of time. No matter how much Malek and Bane tried to replenish her dwindling strength, they could only help her up to a point.

"It will have to be enough," Sabine said, not seeing an alternative.

"If you need me to share magic with you, just say the word," Malek said, his thumb tracing along her side. "Once we're finally home and you're safe behind my wards, you can rest as long as you wish."

Sabine shivered, hoping he hadn't just inadvertently lied to a fae.

Such things never ended well.

CHAPTER 21

"Additional magic from the dragon won't be necessary," Aeron said, approaching from the stairway. Thalassa carried Lyra in her arms while Fiona trailed behind them.

There was an awkward pause as the aderyan and dragon stared at each other.

"Find something that will keep you warm," Bane said, tossing his traveler's pack to Rika. "They'll need your cloak. Yours too, dragon."

Malek removed his cloak and handed it to Sabine, nodding toward the aderyan. His voice slipped into her thoughts. *"No matter what reassurances we offer, they have no reason to trust me. Only time will remedy that."*

Malek turned to Fiona and said, "I would suggest you avoid using your workshop to house any aderyan for the foreseeable future."

Fiona crossed her arms. "I gathered as much."

Malek looked down at Sabine. "I'll let you finish up in here while I make the necessary arrangements with Levin. My presence will deter other dragons only for so long. Spies will be moving in soon. You'll need to hurry if you want to avoid detection."

Sabine looked up at him and nodded. "We won't be long."

Malek pulled Bane aside and spoke quietly to him before leaving the shop.

Bane took Rika's cloak and handed it to Thalassa. "Cover your wings and the young one. The magic in the cloaks will help obscure your forms."

Sabine offered Malek's cloak to Aeron. He started to bow and then caught himself.

"Once we leave this shop, you must treat me as nothing more than a human with some fae ancestry," Sabine reminded him.

"It is disrespectful."

Sabine placed her hand on Aeron's arm. He stared at her hand with a combination of surprise and curiosity. Keeping her voice gentle, she said, "Our purpose is to restore the balance. There is no disrespect in honoring those efforts. We all must play our parts to ensure our people survive."

Aeron lifted his head to meet her gaze, his eyes as blue as a cloudless day. "It has been a long time since an Aderylin has shared their wisdom and their light with any of us. We shall do as you ask."

Sabine smiled and released him, motioning for him to try on the cloak. Rika pulled on a fur coat she'd received before they'd left Razadon. It had been a gift from a dwarven artisan in the hopes of impressing them with the quality of their wares.

"It's not as easy to reach my knife," Rika said with a frown, looking down at the heavy fabric.

Bane reached out and sliced a hole in the side of her coat with his claw.

Rika lifted the edge and stared through the tear. "Remind me not to make any further complaints."

Bane grunted and turned back to the aderyan. "Move in groups of no more than five to keep noise to a minimum. And for fuck's sake, no talking. Glamour works on sight alone."

"That won't be necessary," Aeron said. "We have our own methods for transporting aderyan refugees out of the city."

"How?" Sabine asked.

"Niall would have gone for a neighbor's trading cart as soon as the dragon approached the shop," Fiona said, walking over to the counter. She used a key around her neck to unlock a freestanding wooden cabinet Sabine hadn't noticed before. "They'll ride in the back of the cart. If they're stopped, we have magical defenses that will keep our people hidden."

Curious, Sabine approached the antique cabinet and ran her hand over it. The cabinet had been crafted from rich, dark wood, and polished to a gleaming finish that high-lighted the intricate carvings of celestial symbols adorning its surface. It wasn't fae or even dwarven craftsmanship, but it had the resonance of both. There was something in it similar to her own magic. Sabine had the suspicion she could have unlocked it even without a key.

"It's not a bloodlock cabinet, but it carries similar protec-tions," Sabine said, referring to the magical cabinets infused with demonic blood. "I don't believe I've ever seen anything like it before."

"It smells like old magic," Blossom said, dangling upside-down from the cabinet top.

"It's older than any living aderyan," Aeron said with a trace of pride. "It was crafted by one of the Aetherbound, using the magic of the gods to forge its protections. This is one of the few relics we were able to save when the dragons pillaged our aeries."

Fiona patted the key around her neck. "My great-great

grandmother was Aetherbound to Nyrion, Lord of the Skies. When the dragons invaded, she soaked this key in her blood and entrusted it to her daughter. It will be passed to Niall one day, now that he's come into his magic."

Blossom landed on one of the cabinet's inner shelves. "Hey! Some of these smell like pixie magic."

Fiona grinned. "Aye. The flutterfolk had a hand or two in crafting some of them."

Blossom pressed her face against a delicate crystal bottle swirling with star-like colors.

"Starfruit!" she squealed, licking the outside. "Mine! I called it!"

She climbed onto the vial and fumbled with the cork.

Sabine dove forward, catching the delicate bottle and pixie before they fell. "Do you always lick magical artifacts before reading the label?"

"Only the sparkly ones," Blossom said, staring at the swirling liquid like it was a three-tiered honey cake.

Fiona laughed. "It's starfruit essence. It supposedly enhances a flutterfolk's ability to create illusions and manipulate light."

"Starfruit?" Sabine asked, holding the bottle up to the light. The syrupy liquid cast a dazzling display of tiny rainbows and star-like patterns around the room. Blossom stared at it, completely transfixed.

Fiona's expression turned thoughtful. "If you truly intend to face the dragons, it may be of use. The flutterfolk abandoned our city years ago. If any still remain in the Sky Cities, perhaps they can help you. It's said a drop of starfruit essence will draw them to you like bees to a flower."

Judging by the way Blossom stared at it, Sabine had no doubt of its allure. She handed the bottle to Bane, who tucked it in his pack with a threatening glare aimed at the pixie.

"Not a good idea," Rika warned Blossom. "Bane's already grumpy."

Blossom cocked her head, but didn't seem the least bit cowed. It was only a matter of time before she devised a way to separate the bottle from the demon. Sabine sighed, making a mental note to hide it in a more secure location later.

Fiona pulled out a small box made of dark, polished wood. Intricate carvings of intertwined vines and flowers adorned the lid, with small inlaid gemstones that sparkled like dewdrops in the grooves of the design.

"It's locked with a blood enchantment," Fiona explained, placing the box reverently on the counter. "Only an aderyan can open it."

Aeron stepped forward, pricked his finger, and let a drop of blood fall onto one of the gemstones. It absorbed his blood, glowing briefly before the lid clicked open.

"Or we could have just stepped on it," Bane muttered. "Everything's a ritual with the damned Seelie. We'll be here all night if they don't get a move on."

Thalassa glared at him and opened her mouth to say something, but Aeron held up his hand in a gesture for her to remain silent.

"He may be insolent, but haste is necessary," Aeron said. "Dawn rapidly approaches, and our people must be well away before then."

Inside the box was a velvet pouch made of shimmering fabric that caught the light like water under moonlight.

"Ooooh," Blossom said, peering over the edge of the box. "What is it?"

"Dream dust," Aeron said, lifting it gently. "It's harvested from aderyan wings. A small amount can send someone into a deep, restful sleep, or act as a hallucinogen, making people see things differently, much like a fae's ability to glamour."

"And without wings, acquiring more dream dust must be nearly impossible," Sabine murmured, both surprised and amazed they'd been able to save as many people as they had.

"It hasn't been easy, which is why the small amount we have is considered precious," Thalassa said, adjusting a sleeping Lyra in her arms. "There are scarce few full-flighted aderyan still in the Sky Cities, and none have escaped with their wings fully intact."

Aeron handed the pouch to Fiona and said, "You will need to ensure our people reach the ship safely."

Fiona nodded. "It will be done."

Aeron turned to Sabine and said, "We are ready to depart, Aderylin. May the gods protect us all."

CHAPTER 22

The streets of Imenel were nearly deserted.

A wagon creaked as it wobbled over the cobblestones, the merchant at the helm guiding the thundertusk away from the marketplace. A few stragglers were still closing up their kiosks, packing away their wares in locked strongboxes or carting off their more valuable items on small handcarts. Fortunately, none of them were paying much attention to Sabine and her unusual companions as they made their way through the city.

A tiny moth flew toward them and landed on Sabine's shoulder.

"Problems?" she asked.

"There are three humans and a thundertusk at the landing pad," Blossom whispered loudly, her moth wings fluttering in the lamplight. "One of them is really stinky—like a troll's armpit after a summer dance-off stinky. We might want to find a different landing pad."

"No," Malek said, his gaze scanning both the sky and the streets for potential threats.

"Smells are the least of our problems," Sabine said,

glancing at Thalassa and Aeron as they walked. Their newly restored wings were folded tightly under their borrowed cloaks, hidden from view. Lyra slept quietly in Thalassa's arms, only a sliver of golden hair peeking out from the folds of the fabric.

Blossom made a gagging noise. "You're only saying that because you didn't smell it. I almost flew into a lamppost trying to get away."

"Less chatter," Bane warned as a rowdy group of drunken revelers tumbled out of a doorway and into the street. Rika's hand went to her knife, but a signal from Bane made her ease off. As the group broke into song and raucous laughter, Malek placed a hand on Sabine's back and guided her past them and the brightly lit tavern.

As soon as they were out of earshot, Sabine asked, "Anything to report besides the smell?"

"Nope. Just the giant landing platform. These dragons are really on to something. We should put pixie landing pads in the garden from now on. It would prevent a lot of broken flower stalks." Blossom yawned. "I should be getting paid overtime. Pixies are supposed to be in bed by now."

Malek's lips twitched in a smile. "There's an entire garden at my home. You can take your pick from whatever you find and install whatever landing pads you want."

Blossom's wings fluttered in excitement. "No takebacks!"

Sabine arched her brow. "You do realize you just allowed her to claim your entire garden, don't you?"

"That would be a bad thing?"

Sabine grinned. "You know what? I think you should just experience the wonder of Blossom."

Malek frowned. "Now I'm worried."

Sabine laughed softly, but her amusement faded as they rounded the corner. The landing platform Blossom had mentioned was a huge structure of marble and stone, lit by glowing blue crystal orbs that cast a soft light over the area. Several enclosed chariots were lined up beside the platform, each one a marvel of dwarven craftsmanship. Their crystalline bodies sparkled faintly, reflecting the light from the orbs.

"Oh, wow," Rika exclaimed. "We're riding in one of those?"

Malek nodded. "Wyverns regularly fly this route during the day, transporting humans to and from the Sky Cities."

Sabine frowned. "How do they transport supplies?"

"Larger containers are stored near the docks," Aeron said quietly. "Each clan arranges for their own deliveries."

Malek's gaze sharpened on the aderyan. "Not all are stored by the docks."

"No," Aeron replied. "Every dragon hides their individual hoard, even from those they claim to trust."

Blossom's eyes rounded.

Sabine sighed in resignation. Great. Blossom was going to make it her personal mission to identify and locate every dragon hoard possible—and likely relocate several pixie-sized treasures.

Pushing the thought aside, Sabine studied the chariots lined beside the platform. Whatever magic had once powered them now lay dormant. They were still beautiful, but Sabine couldn't shake the feeling that they had once been much more. Each one had been retrofitted with a thick metal bar on top, making the elegant lines of the chariots awkward and clunky.

As they approached, a familiar wave of nausea rolled through Sabine.

Iron.

It had to be.

She stopped short, unable to force herself to take a step closer. Even from this distance, she could feel the drain upon her magic. It was taking everything she had to keep her illusions intact.

Malek turned to her, his expression full of concern. "What is it?"

"Iron," Bane said in a low voice. "There's no way Sabine is stepping foot inside those chariots with an iron bar hanging over her head."

Malek muttered a curse. "I hadn't realized. We use them to carry the chariots up to the Sky Cities. Give me a moment. I'll take care of this."

Malek stepped away from the group and approached two human men polishing one of the chariots. They straightened immediately upon seeing him, their postures becoming rigid with a hint of fear. Sabine couldn't hear the words exchanged, but it was clear from Malek's gestures and the men's deferential nods that he was issuing orders.

Malek pointed to one of the chariots, then to the iron bar on top. The men exchanged quick glances before hurrying to the chariot, tools in hand. With practiced efficiency, they began dismantling the iron bar.

"At least the dragon has some uses," Bane said, watching the men work.

The thundertusk was brought forward by a third man. It snorted and stomped its feet, but a few calming words and gentle pats from its handler soon had it under control.

"I bet he'd be fun to ride if he wasn't stinky," Blossom said wistfully.

"Um, no," Rika said, shaking her head. "Just no. I've seen what those things can do when they run."

"Those foul beasts are not native to Aeslion," Aeron said in disapproval. "The humans brought them here during the first wave. With no natural predators other than the dragons, they have disrupted the balance and forced other, more gentle creatures to flee to other parts of the world."

"You don't like humans, do you?" Rika asked.

Aeron frowned. "My issue is not with humans, but with any who seek to disrupt the balance either through malice or ignorance."

The men attached ropes to the iron bar and, with the thundertusk's considerable strength, began dragging it away from the chariot. As it was hauled to a safer distance, the oppressive weight lifted from Sabine's shoulders. She'd mistakenly assumed Malek's dragonfire had given her some immunity to the alien metal.

The humans tied the ropes to the chariot again. This time, the thundertusk pulled it onto the far side of the platform.

Malek walked back toward them, his gaze focused on Sabine. "Are you ready?"

She eyed the chariot with skepticism. "You do realize it's made of crystal, right?"

Malek frowned and glanced at the chariot over his shoulder. "Yes. Why?"

Bane snorted. "Because in lizard form, you're the equivalent of a thundertusk in a pottery shop."

Malek chuckled. "I see your point. I assure you I have a bit more control."

"If you will allow me to assist, Aderylin," Aeron began. "If you are willing to combine magic with me, we can encase the crystal in a protective barrier. It should withstand even the strongest of dragon claws."

"No," Malek and Bane both said in unison.

Sabine turned to them and frowned. It was bad enough having to argue with one of them, but if both Bane and Malek were in agreement, there was no budging them. Still, she had to try.

"A moment," she said to Aeron and Thalassa before walking several steps away. Rika approached the aderyan and began asking them more questions about the balance.

Quickly weaving a protective soundproof barrier around Bane and Malek, she said, "All right. Explain."

"They are Seelie," Bane said with distaste. "They have an obligation to share any information about you and our mission with your father—the Seelie ruler. They are not your subjects, Sabine. Do not treat them as such."

Sabine turned to Malek and asked, "You object for a different reason?"

Malek nodded. "I awakened you with dragonfire. They know we're bound together. While you may have restored their wings, my people have been their enemies for generations. I am not willing to risk your safety under any circumstances. We don't know if this is somehow a trap."

Sabine frowned. This whole situation was beyond complicated.

"I'm not dismissing either of your arguments," Sabine said. "However, we should at least hear them out. Aeron and Thalassa are our best hope in locating the last portal artifact. If we're asking them to trust us, perhaps we need to take the first step."

Malek's jaw clenched. "I want to find the artifact just as much, if not more, than you do. However, you are my priority, Sabine. If they attempt to strike out at me through you, I *will* end them."

"On that, we both agree," Bane said, crossing his arms.

Blossom nodded. "The goddess says she'll smite them if they dare harm her little golden flower."

"Well then," Sabine said with a sigh. "I suppose that settles it."

Sabine allowed the soundproof barrier to dissipate. She walked over to the aderyan and asked, "What's involved in sharing magic?"

Aeron's gaze flicked to Malek and Bane before focusing again on her. "If you are able to act as a barrier between us and the dragon, we can control the air currents around him. This will allow us to provide a protective shield around the chariot and make travel easier. We can also mask our presence in the skies with a type of glamour, which should help ease the demands upon your magic."

"And the means to accomplish this task?"

"Intent and will," Aeron said. "It is only a temporary arrangement and will be severed the moment physical contact is broken. It has always been our purpose to supplement an Aderylin's magic with our own, or to safeguard them while they're in Veylara. I would be honored to fulfill that purpose once again."

Sabine arched her brow at Bane and Malek.

Bane scowled but gave her a curt nod. Malek didn't look altogether pleased by it, but he remained silent.

"Done," Sabine said, turning back to Aeron.

To his credit, Aeron didn't bow, but Sabine could tell the effort cost him.

Malek led them toward the modified crystal chariot. He opened the door, revealing plush, cushioned seating. It was more spacious than she'd realized, with enough room to comfortably seat at least ten people.

He helped Sabine inside, his touch lingering on her arm for a moment longer than necessary. She felt a rush of warmth and reassurance from the contact before he turned to assist Rika. The aderyan avoided Malek and climbed in silently after her.

Bane leaped inside, taking the seat next to Sabine and making it clear he intended to keep a close eye on the aderyan during the voyage. Blossom, on the other hand, was inspecting every inch.

She tapped on the crystal wall and said, "I think it's dead."

"The magic has been depleted," Thalassa said, adjusting Lyra in her arms. Sabine couldn't help but wonder if

Thalassa had used some of the dust coating her wings to lull the child to sleep.

"Without the crystals being recharged, most dwarven-crafted items have stopped working. The dragons and humans have bastardized much of what made Imenel and the Aeries beautiful."

Malek stepped onto the landing platform. His human form melted away in a brilliant flash of light, replaced by the majestic and powerful figure of his dragon self. His obsidian scales glinted in the moonlight, and his wings unfurled with a grace that took Sabine's breath away every time she saw it.

Thalassa's breath hitched, her arms tightening around Lyra. Aeron's face remained impassive, only the rigidity in his shoulders betraying his unease.

"It's not too late to reconsider," Bane said, gesturing to the door.

Thalassa huffed and sat back, shooting Bane a mulish glare.

"Aderylin," Aeron said quietly, shifting into the seat beside Sabine. "Will you allow me to share my magic with you?"

Sabine nodded and placed her hand in Aeron's outstretched palm. He covered her hand, his fingers cool and soft like the feathers of wings. She met his gaze, falling into the endless blue depths of his eyes. Clouds streaked across his irises, and she could have sworn she smelled the metallic scent of an approaching storm. As their hands clasped, a surge of energy flowed from Aeron to Sabine, intertwining with her own magic. The sensation was like a breath of fresh air after being submerged in water for too long.

His magic enveloped her, speaking to something within her she scarcely understood. Her skin markings began to glow in response to his magic. She had the distinct impression there was something Aeron wanted from her, but the thought vanished almost as soon as she had it. Before she could find the thread again, the chariot jolted as it lifted off the platform, breaking her concentration. She took a deep breath and refocused, feeling the combined power of their magic settling into a harmonious rhythm.

The crystal chariot ascended smoothly, guided by Malek's powerful wings. The city of Imenel quickly became a patchwork of rooftops and darkened streets beneath them.

Aeron's magic thrummed within her like a bird taking flight. As he let the breadth of his power soar, Sabine's magic flared between them, shielding the aderyan from the burning embers of dragonfire. It was a delicate dance of wings, one that could either elevate them to new heights or bring them crashing toward destruction.

Blossom perched on the edge of the chariot, watching the landscape unfold beneath them. "The other carrier was nice, but this one is even better. All we need are some honeycakes and maybe a flowerpot or two."

Rika grinned. "Enjoy it while you can, Blossom."

As they ascended higher, the Sky Cities came into view. Sabine had expected the land to be largely devoid of forests and trees. Instead, she was stunned to see a lush landscape with large wooded areas and equally wide open spaces. Snow-tipped mountain ranges silhouetted against the starry sky, and Sabine caught a glimpse of several waterfalls that cascaded into the sea below them.

Thalassa and Aeron both stared out the side of the crystal chariot, their expressions a mixture of longing and sadness. Sabine's heart ached for them, remembering what these floating islands had once been for the aderyan.

Malek's voice echoed in her mind. *"We're approaching the Sky Cities. I'll need to circle once to ensure we remain undetected. Hold tight."*

"Hold on," Sabine said, her grip tightening on Aeron's hand. She felt the subtle shifts in the air currents as Malek adjusted their flight path, weaving through the sky with practiced ease.

The chariot glided closer, giving Sabine a glimpse of towering structures with majestic columns that grew larger and more imposing with each passing moment. Rika and Blossom both pressed their faces against the crystal, watching the floating islands approach.

They finally reached the outskirts of the Sky Cities, and the chariot descended gently onto a hidden landing platform. Malek landed with a grace that belied his massive size, setting the chariot down with barely a jolt. Sabine released a breath she hadn't realized she was holding, the tension easing from her shoulders as the chariot came to a stop.

For good or ill, they had arrived—now they had to survive.

CHAPTER 23

"We're here!" Blossom exclaimed and zipped out of the chariot before Sabine could stop her.

Rika leaned out the door and whispered loudly, "Blossom, you have to keep your voice down!"

Sabine could hear Blossom repeat much quieter, "We're here!"

"It's a wonder the bug's managed to survive this long," Bane muttered.

"Allow me to be the first to welcome you to the former Aderyan Aeries," Aeron said to Sabine, accompanying his words with a featherlight trace of his magic. He lifted her hand and blew on it gently. "The skies above greet you, as do our hearts below. May the winds always guide you safely to our home."

Sabine tilted her head, oddly touched by the ritual greeting. "You honor me with your words."

Bane's eyes shifted to silver. "And they'll be his last if he doesn't unhand you."

Aeron held Bane's gaze for several heartbeats before

releasing her hand, making it clear he wasn't impressed by the demon's threat. A flash of light from Malek's transformation drew Sabine's attention.

"Wait here until we clear the area," Bane said and leaped from the chariot. He began scanning the perimeter, searching for any potential threats.

Sabine leaned against the window and breathed in the night. The air was cool and crisp, carrying the earthy scent of dirt and crushed leaves. Above them, the vast sky stretched endlessly, dotted with stars that seemed close enough to touch.

Malek approached the chariot and said, "It should be safe enough. Few people use this platform. By the time anyone realizes the chariot is here, we'll be firmly within my clan's territory."

Rika nodded and hopped out, jogging to catch up with Bane.

Sabine took Malek's hand and stepped out. The instant her feet touched the ground, a sense of wrongness filled her. It was almost as though the land was starved for the touch of magic. It reached out to her, begging for something only she could provide. She hesitated, the urge to respond to its plea nearly overwhelming.

She took several more cautious steps, her unease growing despite the wild beauty of the surroundings. They were standing in some sort of expansive open courtyard. Intricate mosaics, now partially hidden by moss and creeping vines, covered the ground. She could almost see the way this place had once been, before the dragons had claimed it for themselves.

The landing pad was nestled among ancient marble columns, their surfaces glowing softly in the moonlight. The graceful archways had been shattered, leaving behind nothing more than broken memories and dust.

The remains of a large podium stood at the center of the courtyard. Sabine reached out to touch it, then yanked her hand back, disconcerted by the strange resonance that hummed through her fingers. She rubbed them together, resisting the urge to touch the marble again. Her magic *liked* it.

"What's wrong?" Malek asked.

"There's something about this place," she said, immediately crouching and brushing aside the cool moss to reveal the mosaic stones underneath. The image of a graceful aderyan woman stood in front of a large archway, her wings spread wide as a golden glow eclipsed her from behind.

Sabine lifted her head, but the archway had been one of the ones destroyed. She studied the mosaic again, running her fingers over the inscription that had once been etched into the marble. It had mostly worn away, but she could make out a handful of words written in the ancient language of the gods.

"From Aeslion's breath, our purpose flows," Sabine read and then frowned. Time or the elements made the rest indecipherable.

"It's one of the verses from the Ethereal Song," Aeron said and approached her. Thalassa walked silently beside him, Lyra cradled in her arms. Lyra's hand still grasped the starpetal tightly, as though even in sleep she wasn't willing to relinquish Sabine's gift.

Sabine stood and brushed off her hands. "You know what this says?"

Aeron placed his fist over his heart and recited, "From Aeslion's breath, our purpose flows. We guard the balance where the true wind blows. As defenders of the realm and its Ethereal Song, to the Aderylin's will, our spirits belong."

Sabine tilted her head. "What's the Ethereal Song?"

"The Song is everything," Thalassa said in surprise. "It

guides us, shelters us, and keeps us upon the Path of the Light. Without the Song, the aderyan cease to exist."

Aeron studied Sabine curiously. "How is it you've never heard of our Song?"

Sabine frowned. "I left Faerie when I was little more than a child. I haven't had the opportunity to learn much about your people or your ways."

Aeron and Thalassa exchanged a look.

"There are three parts to our Song," Aeron explained. "The first verse is one of Eternal Vigilance. The second you just heard is our Divine Mandate." He gestured to the tile at her feet. "The third part is the Guardian's Oath. These are the tenets all aderyan strive to uphold in our quest to maintain the balance."

Thalassa shifted Lyra in her arms, her gaze settling on Malek. "Despite your efforts to destroy our shrines, we still embrace the Song in our hearts."

Malek frowned at her. "Do you hold all of us accountable for the actions of a few?"

"Yes!" Thalassa hissed. "You stand in the ruins of one of our temples, treating it as little more than a place to land. Aderyan blood was spilled here, while your people sought to silence our Song."

Sabine narrowed her eyes, her magic rising to the surface. Lachlina's thoughts bled into hers, outraged by the desecration and the loss of aderyan lives. She struggled to separate the goddess's thoughts from her own, but this place made it nearly impossible. Something was wrong.

As though sensing her turmoil, Malek turned and pulled her into his arms. His heated magic wrapped around her, insulating her from the echoes that clung to the ruins. His voice slipped into her thoughts as he urged, *"Focus on me, Sabine. Focus on my touch, my voice, and my magic."*

She leaned into him, allowing his presence to anchor her.

Taking a slow breath, she looked up into his piercing blue eyes and pressed her hands against his chest, feeling the steady rhythm of his heartbeat beneath her fingertips. Lachlina's thoughts began to fade, and Sabine slowly reined her magic back in.

"Thalassa," Aeron said quietly, his voice edged with barely controlled power. "If you cannot hold your tongue, you will leave the child with me and return to Fiona. You insult our host and our Aderylin with your careless words."

Thalassa stiffened, her grip tightening on Lyra. She lowered her head and said, "I will strive to be more mindful in the future, Aderylin."

Sabine turned in Malek's arms and inclined her head in acknowledgment. Aeron studied the way Malek held her, but his face was an unreadable mask.

Bane approached them, his gaze sweeping the area. "We're in no immediate danger, but something is off about this place. There are signs of a great battle being fought here. Echoes of the violence should still remain, but it's been wiped clean."

"The Veil is thin here," Sabine said. "Something happened that bled all the magic from the land."

Aeron considered her thoughtfully. "There are many places such as this throughout the former Aeries. It calls to you, does it not?"

Sabine nodded. "You've been here before?"

"I have only been to this island once. It is ruled by the Obsidian and Emerald clans." He glanced at Malek. "I am assuming we are closer to the Obsidian divide, if the color of your companion's scales is any indication."

"We are," Malek said and gestured to the south. "My estate is just over the hill. I thought it would be best to make a quiet entrance and then announce our presence in the morning."

Rika approached them and held out her hands. "I don't know where Blossom went. She said something about magic flowers and disappeared."

Sabine looked around but didn't see any sign of her. "Give me a moment."

She walked across the ancient mosaics, trying to sense the pixie. Blossom, unlike many other magical races, could slip past the Veil when it suited her. Although she'd been forbidden from creating any portals, there was always a chance she'd accidentally fallen through an existing one.

The possibility might account for the Huntsman's claims he couldn't venture to the Sky Cities. If the Veil was that thin in certain areas, the dragons might be able to cross the threshold if they sensed his presence. She wasn't sure what would happen if that came to pass.

"Can you call her to you?" Malek asked, walking beside her.

"Only with magic," Sabine said and reached for his hand. Silently, she added, *"I'm not sure I trust myself to attempt it right now. If I start, I may not be able to stop. I doubt even your dragon-fire would rouse me."*

Bane pulled out the bottle Sabine had given him earlier. "You could always pop the cork."

Sabine took it from him. At least it wouldn't alert the dragons or render her unconscious. She pried the cork free and inhaled the sweet and tangy, slightly citrusy fragrance.

Rika sniffed the air. "Oh wow! That smells really good."

Aeron gestured to Sabine's wrist. "If you place a drop on one of your pulse points, it will infuse with your magic and call the flutterfolk to you. Dragons and humans shouldn't be able to detect it more than a subtle perfume."

Sabine eyed the markings on her wrist representing each of the artifacts she'd absorbed. Nope. Not happening. She placed a dab of the starfruit essence on her other wrist and capped the bottle. Bane took it from her, placing it securely in the traveler's pack.

Sniffing her wrist, she asked, "How long does it—"

"STARFRUIT!" Blossom shouted, flying toward them in a glittering whirlwind.

Sabine held out her hand not a moment too soon. Blossom crashed into her palm, her face smushed against Sabine's wrist.

"If you lick me, we're going to have problems," Sabine warned as Blossom nuzzled her skin.

Blossom wrapped her arms around Sabine's wrist and said in a muffled voice, "Ivzmelzooogoood."

"What did she say?" Rika asked.

"I think she said, 'It smells so good,'" Sabine said, lifting her hand to study Blossom. "Where did you go?"

Blossom didn't reply, too busy sniffing her and giggling.

"The flutterfolk have been known to fall into a stupor after drinking heavily of starfruit essence," Aeron said with a frown. "Although, I've never heard of it affecting them quite like this. Your magic may be enhancing the effects."

Bane poured some water from his drinking flask onto his hand. He flicked it at Blossom and said, "Get up."

Blossom leaped to her feet and sputtered. "What? How? Who?"

"Next time it'll be the entire flask," Bane said, capping it before returning it to his belt. "You're supposed to be working."

"I was! Am! I mean, huh?" Blossom looked around in confusion. "Where are all the flowers? What happened?"

"That's what we'd like to know," Sabine said. "Where did you go?"

Blossom sat on Sabine's palm and frowned. "I was here, but then I wasn't. Something's not right in this place. I don't like it." She sniffed the air, eyeing Sabine's wrist again.

Malek's gaze lifted to the sky and to a pair of wyverns circling overhead. "We need to move. They've likely already seen us, but I want to be firmly in my clan's territory before they decide to approach."

Sabine nodded and lifted Blossom to her shoulder. She adjusted her hood to ensure her hair was completely covered.

Blossom sneezed and rubbed her nose. "I didn't mean to let you down, Sabine. It won't happen again. You sure do smell yummy though."

"It's all right," Sabine said quietly. "Something *isn't* right about this place. I don't believe it was your fault. We'll talk more about it later."

Malek took Sabine's hand and led her away from the platform and the crystal chariot. As they walked, the path wound through a forest of ancient trees, their gnarled branches creating a canopy that filtered the moonlight into delicate patterns on the mossy path. The air was filled with the whisper of leaves and the distant calls of unfamiliar nocturnal creatures, creating a symphony of the night that was strangely unsettling.

"Is that an owl? I think that was an owl," Blossom said, hugging Sabine's neck. "They eat pixies who stay up too late."

"So do demons," Bane reminded her.

"I won't let the owls or the demon eat you," Sabine promised.

"You are fortunate to have our Aderylin as your protector, little skykin," Thalassa said with a smile.

"I know," Blossom said, pressing her cheek against Sabine's.

At the top of the hill, Sabine caught sight of a sprawling estate. Towering columns reached for the sky, crafted from pale stone that glowed under the moon's light. She stopped short, staring at it in wonder.

"Oh, Malek," she whispered, awestruck by the sheer beauty.

It wasn't fae, or even dwarven in design, but she could see elements of both. Ornate balconies overlooked meticulously manicured gardens that sprawled out like a cultivated wilderness around the main building. Plants and small trees she'd only ever seen in Faerie graced the exterior of the structure. Many of the windows had glittering colored crystals Sabine knew would paint breathtaking images over the interior walls once the sun had passed above the horizon.

"You really live here, Malek?" Rika asked, gaping at the sight.

"I do," Malek said, taking Sabine's hand and leading her toward the estate. "The rest of my family lives on other parts of the island. My grandfather and Elisa preferred their privacy. I've found I enjoy the same."

"This was their home, wasn't it?" Sabine asked.

"Yes. I spent a great deal of time here in my youth. This place always felt more like home than anywhere else."

"I bet you have pigeon problems," Blossom said. "Look at those columns. I bet there's an infestation happening right now. I'll have to check."

"Or he's compensating for something," Bane suggested, eyeing the columns. "The whole thing is a little too Seelie for my taste."

"Dragons don't need to compensate for anything," Malek said, glancing at Sabine with a smug look.

Nope. Sabine wasn't going to touch that comment, especially since Malek was right. He didn't need his already dragon-sized ego inflated even more.

"You can inflate my ego anytime," Malek said with a chuckle.

Sabine tilted her head and pretended to study the columns. *"Hmm. They are rather large. Perhaps we should see how well you measure up. Although, I wouldn't mind—"*

Her words cut off when Malek swept her into his arms and began carrying her down the path. She threw back her head and laughed. Blossom grinned and flew over to Rika's shoulder.

"I've heard stories about dragons abducting fair maidens," Sabine teased.

"Mmhmm. Just wait until I get you back to my lair."

She leaned close and nipped at his earlobe. "Promises, promises."

At their approach, decorative urns flared to life with a sudden burst of dragonfire, casting a dramatic glow that washed over the entrance. The ornate silver double gate creaked as it swung open, revealing the sprawling estate beyond.

Sabine pressed her hand against Malek's chest. "It recognizes you."

"As it will also learn to recognize you," Malek said. "Each place a dragon calls home acts as an anchor point. This is one of mine. You are another. No matter how far a dragon travels, our anchor points call to us. We can always find them."

She traced her finger down his chest and said, "That's how you found me in the dryad grove?"

Malek nodded. "Does that bother you?"

Sabine considered it for a moment and then shook her head. The thought would have once made her uneasy, but there was a strange sort of comfort in the realization now. She suspected she could always find him as well, especially using their bond to guide her.

"Why a gate though?" Rika asked. "Can't someone just fly over it?"

"There are protections in place preventing anyone from entering the grounds from the air. The gate is a deterrent for anyone else, and the lit urns indicate I'm in residence."

"I do not recognize the magic of this estate," Aeron said. "It does not feel aderyan or like anything else in the Aeries."

"It wouldn't," Malek said. "My fae grandmother refused to live in a place that held the memories and suffering of your people. She insisted my grandfather build a new home, using virgin marble and materials untouched by the war. It took nearly a century to complete."

Aeron frowned at him. "You are not fae."

"No," Malek said, climbing the steps to the front entry doors. "My grandfather was Thadnir Rish'dan, Dragon Lord of the Obsidian Clan. His chosen mate was Elis'andreia of the Seelie."

"A fae captive," Bane said dryly.

Aeron's shocked gaze flew to Malek. "You are Malek Rish'dan, son of Darius? And you have brought our Aderylin to your home?"

Malek's jaw hardened as the front door swung shut behind them. "I am, and Sabine is mine to protect."

CHAPTER 24

*A*eron and Thalassa's eyes burned with a silver light. Bane snorted in amusement and began prowling through the rooms, likely determining the layout and best means of egress in case a quick exit was needed.

Sabine frowned at him.

The traitor.

He was leaving her to deal with this mess.

Blossom and Rika both looked back and forth between Malek and the aderyan.

"We need snacks," Blossom suggested.

Rika nodded. "Only if you can magic some up for us. I'm not going to miss this."

"Maybe there are some snacks in your pack?" Blossom asked.

"Nope. We ate them earlier when Bane got all growly and Malek got all 'Rawwwwr! I'm a dragon!'"

"Hmm. Next trip, we pack more snacks."

"Good plan," Rika agreed.

"Maybe you should put me down," Sabine suggested with a sigh.

Malek hesitated and then eased her to her feet. They were in a vast foyer with a high domed ceiling that featured elaborate frescoes depicting dragons in various poses of flight. The walls were lined with tall, arched windows, each pane holding stained crystals depicting scenes from the Silver Forests outside Faerie. The moonlight filtering through the windows cast a muted glow over the scenes.

A staircase crafted from dark wood curved gracefully from the foyer to the upper floors, its banisters adorned with silver filigree that sparkled under the soft light of crystal chandeliers. The air carried a hint of lavender and old books, a fragrance that seemed to emanate from the large library visible through an open doorway to the left. Her fingers itched to explore the tomes to see what hidden treasures lay within.

Malek rubbed a tendril of her silvery hair between his fingers. "I remember the way your eyes lit up when we were in the library back in Akros. I'm glad to see that hasn't changed."

Before Sabine could respond or even address the aderyan's threatening posturing, a scream sounded from somewhere deeper in the building. Rapid footsteps raced toward them from the west corridor. A middle-aged woman with a sleeping bonnet gone askew skidded to a halt. Her blonde hair was sticking out in all directions, and she had a wild look in her eyes.

"Lord Malek," the woman exclaimed breathlessly and clutched her chest. "A demon! There's a demon in the house! We're under attack!"

"We're not under—"

A man's shouts and a loud crash interrupted Malek's words. At the sound of Bane's roar, Sabine turned on her heel and raced after Malek. He shoved open the doors to a courtyard, revealing one of the most stunning gardens Sabine had encountered outside of Faerie.

Bane stood beside a marble fountain, glowering at a human wielding a clay pot overflowing with purple flowers. He was streaked with dark soil, and some sort of flowering plant had gotten tangled in his horns. The shattered remnants of another container lay at his feet.

The man threw the pot at Bane and shouted, "Get back, foul demon!"

The projectile missed its mark, spilling out a cascade of blossoms at Bane's feet.

"Or what? You'll flower me to death?"

"I'll—I'll—" The man grabbed a nearby shovel off the ground and shook it at Bane. "I'll thrash you!"

"Rupert!" Malek shouted, stalking toward them. "Bane is my guest."

"A guest? But Lord Malek!" Rupert leaned close and whispered loudly, "He's a demon."

Rika bit her lip, trying to stifle a giggle. When Bane picked a vine from his horn and tossed it aside as though it offended him, Rika lost the battle and howled with laughter. Clasping her arms around her waist, tears streamed down her cheeks. The pixie wasn't faring much better. Blossom was gripping Rika's hair and giggling so hard, she looked like she was about to fall off her shoulder.

Sabine bit the inside of her cheek, trying desperately not to laugh.

Bane shot an annoyed glare at them. "Very funny."

Sabine struggled to keep a straight face as she removed the flowers that had tangled around his horns. "It serves you right for leaving me to deal with that situation."

Bane grunted, glancing over her shoulder at the aderyan. "If I can't kill them, you have to deal with them. That goes for the humans too."

"We'll let Malek deal with the humans," Sabine said, using her magic to pull a thin stream of water from the fountain. She cascaded it over Bane to wash away the soil. He pulled off his shirt and scrubbed his face clean.

Malek had suitably calmed the couple, but they were both clearly wary of their new houseguests. At least the man wasn't threatening anyone with crockery or yard tools anymore.

Malek approached Sabine and put his arm around her. "Sabine, I'd like you to meet Rupert and Azalia. Rupert has overseen the estate grounds for the past twenty years. Azalia is his wife and manages the household and other staff. Should you need anything while I'm not around, they'll see to it."

"Well met, Rupert and Azalia," Sabine said, tilting her head in greeting. "From what I've seen so far of the gardens, your efforts rival those of some fae."

Azalia's eyes widened and she curtsied. "It's an honor to meet you, Lady Sabine." She smacked Rupert's chest and whispered loudly, "Show some manners!"

Rupert's cheeks reddened as he yanked off his cap. He bowed to Sabine and said, "Welcome to the Sky Cities, Lady Sabine. In truth, the garden requires very little tending. Things just like growing here."

Malek gestured to Bane. "The demon you've already met is Bane. When I'm not with Sabine, he's in charge of her protection. Until I say otherwise, this estate is on lockdown. No one is to approach Sabine without my leave or his, regardless of their clan ties or position. Bane is to be provided unrestricted access to the estate, including the grounds outside. He will be inspecting all areas of the estate and advising on any security concerns."

Azalia paled. "My Lord?"

"Certainly not in our quarters," Rupert sputtered in

horror. "Lord Malek, I beg your pardon, but no decent person would allow such a thing."

Bane narrowed his eyes. "Do you have weapons or traps laid out for my mistress?"

"Heavens no!" Azalia cried.

Rupert stiffened. "We would never harm one of Lord Malek's guests."

"Your flowerpots would suggest otherwise," Bane reminded him. "I have no interest in your bedchamber once I've completed my initial inspection."

Sabine pressed her hand against Malek's chest. *You might need to ease their fears until they're used to us. They've likely never encountered a demon.*

Malek covered her hand with his. *I'm not leaving your side tonight. The sooner they adjust to everyone being here, the better. Rupert and Azalia have been among dragonkind long enough to adapt to far more than a demon lurking about.*

"Of-Of course," Rupert said, his voice shaking slightly. "We have nothing to hide. I apologize for my earlier behavior. You caught me by surprise."

"Now that's settled," Malek said and gestured to Rika. "I'd like to introduce you to Rika, formerly of Karga. The pixie on her shoulder is Blossom."

Blossom waved and said, "I'll be inspecting all the hard-to-reach places. You know, for pigeons and stuff."

Azalia's brow furrowed. "Pigeons?"

Blossom nodded. "They're sneaky."

Malek's lips twitched. He cleared his throat and motioned to the three cloaked aderyan. "Aeron, Thalassa, and their ward, Lyra, are also honored guests who will be staying with us for some time."

"It's a full house you've brought us, Lord Malek," Azalia said. "I see the little one is already fast asleep. I'll be happy to show everyone to the rooms in the guest wing if you'd like."

"That won't be necessary," Malek said, motioning toward the northern end of the house. "Sabine will be staying with me. Everyone else can select rooms from the family suites. I think they'd all be more comfortable staying near Sabine."

Azalia's eyes widened. "Of-Of course, Lord Malek."

"We should have two more joining us tomorrow," Malek continued. "Levin will be here sometime before noon, along with a woman named Esmelle. They're handling some business in Imenel until then. They'll also likely choose one of the suites in the north wing."

Azalia's eyes softened. "Levin's mother will be pleased he's found a mate."

"I suspect so," Malek said with a grin. "I'll show everyone to the north wing so you and Rupert can get some rest. In the morning, let the cook and rest of the staff know we have houseguests. However, the family suites are off-limits to everyone except the two of you."

Sabine looked up at Malek. "Aeron, Thalassa, and Lyra will need some clothing and a few personal items. Is there a market we can visit in the morning?"

"You are kind to concern yourself with our comfort, Ader—Sabine," Aeron said. "We can make arrangements for ourselves."

Azalia glanced at the aderyan and said, "Oh, it's no trouble at all. I'm sure we have some items in storage. If there's anything specific you need, I can arrange to have it delivered from Imenel."

Aeron hesitated and then nodded. "Very well."

Malek ran his thumb over Sabine's hand and said, "Rupert and Azalia, I can't stress the importance of keeping the details of my houseguests quiet. If anyone attempts to question you, let me know immediately."

Both Rupert and Azalia nodded.

"We won't say a word, Lord Malek," Rupert promised.

"A newly mated dragon is always protective of their mate," Azalia said with a smile. "She's safe with us, Lord Malek."

Malek nodded and led Sabine toward the northern part of the garden.

Sabine looked up at him with narrowed eyes. "You told them I was your mate?"

"Idiot dragon," Bane muttered.

Malek cleared his throat and motioned toward one side of the garden. "Ah, well. If anyone gets hungry, the eastern part of the house contains the Great Hall, kitchens, and a vegetable and herb garden. The servants' wing can be reached through that part of the house." He gestured to the opposite side. "To the west is the library, armory, gallery, and music rooms. The guest wings take up the second floor of that side of the house."

"Wow," Rika murmured. "I'm going to get lost in here. It's even bigger than the embassy in Razadon."

"You're not distracting me that easily," Sabine warned.

Malek made a noncommittal noise. "All of the wings open to the central garden. If you find your way to the main fountain, you'll see a map etched in the mosaic tiles indicating each direction."

"Someone's going to be taking a bath in the fountain," Blossom sang.

"Weren't you supposed to be on my side?" Malek asked her.

Blossom grinned. "Sabine has starfruit. Find out where she's going to hide the bottle, and then we can talk."

Malek arched his brow, clearly considering it. Sabine glared at him.

He cleared his throat and gestured to the doors in front of them. "The northern wing is where my suite and the family suites are located. My private study and conservatory are located on the ground level. Although, as my mate, I suppose now they're officially yours as well."

Sabine stopped in her tracks and clapped her hands. A stream of water shot out of the fountain and poured over Malek's head.

Malek stared at her in surprise and then laughed.

Without a word, Sabine turned and entered the suite, leaving a dripping dragon behind her.

CHAPTER 25

Sabine's annoyance evaporated the moment she stepped into the northern wing.

Floating orbs of light drifted through the room, casting soft shadows across the high ceilings and marble floors. Rich, dark wood paneling with silver whorls lined the walls, while verdant moss and ivy climbed upward to create a living gardenscape that spoke to the fae magic within her.

An obsidian fireplace dominated one wall, with flames that flickered through a spectrum of colors in response to each person who entered the room. The hearth was framed by an elaborate arrangement of Faerie ferns and fire-resistant blossoms that thrived in the warmth of the fire, their colors vibrant against the polished stone.

She reached out to touch one of the red flowers, tears coming unbidden to her eyes as the small vine wrapped around her wrist, responding to her power and offering its own in return. She could feel Elis'andreia's magic in that small touch, and the love she felt for the children who may not have been born of her blood, but had been the ones of her heart.

"He tried to give part of Faerie back to her, didn't he?" Sabine asked. "Both worlds, dragon and fae, blended together."

Malek placed his hands on her shoulders, the warmth of his magic surrounding her. "Yes."

Sabine turned and looked up at him. "Were they able to bridge the gap between them?"

"As much as they could, given their circumstances," Malek said, tucking her hair behind her ear and trailing his fingers down her cheek. "They showed me the possibilities, but I never truly believed it until I met you."

"Hey look! Fae lanterns!" Blossom exclaimed, diving toward one of the floating globes. With a loud pop, the orb slurped the pixie up. The orb vibrated, slowly at first and then with alacrity as it began to spin across the room. It slammed into one of the walls and bounced straight into the ceiling.

"Blossom!" Rika shouted, diving for the lantern as it shot across the room. It smacked into the side of Bane's head and bounced aside, leaving a bluish glittering smear behind. Rika leaped over a plush sofa, scrambling after the bouncing orb. Bane caught Rika one-handed before the seer could fall and placed her upright.

"Who left the fae lanterns low on power when there's a damn pixie around?" Bane snarled, wiping away the pixie dust with his shirt.

Malek grabbed Sabine and pulled her aside as the orb rushed toward her head. It bounced against the fireplace and then upward toward the crystal chandeliers. The crystals rocked precipitously, beginning to tilt in Thalassa and Lyra's direction. Without thinking, Sabine summoned the dwarven power at her command, using it to stabilize the crystals. They began to glow with a golden light as Sabine's magic filled them. She pulled back abruptly, uncertain of the consequences of recharging them with her magic.

Blossom's panicked face pressed against the globe. "Let me out! I'm gonna be sick!"

Aeron flung his borrowed cloak aside and leaped into the air, his wings spread in all their golden glory. He dove for the orb and missed, but managed to swipe another orb with the tip of his wings. It flung the second orb into the first, and they both began vibrating with a frenzy. They spun and whirled, crashing into the other orbs.

Rika screamed and ducked, covering her head with her arms. Thalassa pressed into a corner, shielding Lyra from the flying lanterns.

Sabine quickly wove her power through the lanterns, freezing them in place. Malek's fae grandmother had been gone for so long, they'd barely had enough magic to stay afloat. She hummed softly, finding their proper resonance. As her magic harmonized with the fae lanterns, she began to sing softly, using her voice to fill them with the magic they'd desperately needed.

Blossom slid out of the orb with a pop, landing safely in Aeron's outstretched hands. Her dress was wrinkled, one of her wings was bent, and her hair stuck out in all directions. Aside from the slightly greenish cast to her features, she appeared mostly unharmed.

With the magic in the lanterns once again full, she released them back into the air. It should have been a trifling matter, but recharging the crystals and orbs had depleted most of her remaining magic. Her eyes suddenly felt heavy, and she swayed.

"What just happened?" Malek asked, wrapping his arm around her. "I've never seen the lanterns do that."

Bane shot him an annoyed look. "Pixies belong in the

garden, not in the house—especially when you're using fae lanterns."

"They latched onto Blossom's magic," Sabine said, trying to stifle a yawn. "Fae usually recharge them with excess magic. Blossom has more magic than most pixies, so they thought she was there to recharge them."

Aeron carried Blossom over to Sabine. "The little skykin does not look well."

Sabine frowned and carefully picked up Blossom. She still had a dazed look on her face. Turning to Malek, she asked, "Do you have any honey?"

"I'm sure we do, but you need to sit down before you fall," Malek said, leading Sabine over to the sofa. Aeron folded his wings and sat beside her, ignoring Bane's glare.

Malek headed for the garden, leaving the door slightly ajar behind him. Sabine blew on her wrist, sending a whisper of her magic infused with a hint of starfruit over the befuddled pixie. Blossom blinked and then fell over.

"The room keeps spinning," Blossom slurred.

"You're not supposed to try to steer the lanterns when you get stuck in one," Sabine said with a smile.

Thalassa approached Sabine and asked, "The flutterfolk will be okay?"

Sabine nodded. "Yes. A bit of sweetness will perk her right up and give her the energy to repair her wing."

Rika crouched beside her and said, "The last time I saw her like this was when she got into the honeyed mead in Razadon."

Malek returned quickly, holding a small container and dipper. Rika scooted out of his way, but Aeron didn't budge from his place at Sabine's side.

"I will assist," Aeron said, holding out his hand for the items.

Bane crossed his arms. "You'd better serve Sabine by

inspecting the upstairs with me for potential threats. Rika, you should join us and select rooms for everyone. The lizard can handle dunking the pixie in honey."

Aeron hesitated. "My place is at our Aderylin's side."

Thalassa nodded. "We do not need a room. We are content to keep watch."

Malek's eyes narrowed slightly, his power beginning to fill the room. Challenging a dragon in their den was beyond foolhardy, a fact the aderyan knew well. She didn't know what they hoped to achieve by provoking him, but Sabine wasn't about to allow it.

Sabine turned to them and said, "I am perfectly safe in Malek's care. All of us need to get some rest before tomorrow. Lyra will need both of you at full strength if you intend to teach her what it means to be Aetherbound."

Aeron bowed his head in acknowledgement of her words. He stood and held out his hand for Thalassa to join him. As the two of them ascended the stairs behind Bane and Rika, Malek offered her the open jar of honey.

"You fascinate them," Malek said, nodding toward the stairs. "It's the same way you captivated me when we first met."

Sabine glanced at him and smiled. "It went both ways."

Turning back to Blossom, Sabine dangled the honey dipper in front of the pixie's nose. Blossom sniffed and sat up, shoving her hands in the golden syrup and licking it off.

"What kind of flowers is this from?" she asked, her green pallor already changing to her normal rosy hue.

"I'm not sure," Malek said. "You can ask the cook or kitchen staff tomorrow, if you're feeling up to it."

"Can you heal yourself?" Sabine asked, handing the jar back to Malek. Too much honey would send Blossom into a drunken stupor.

Blossom nodded, her wings vibrating slightly until they

were no longer bent. She leaped into the air with a grin. "That was pretty good, but Faerie honey is even better. I'll go help Rika and Bane investigate."

"Stay out of trouble," Sabine warned, taking Malek's outstretched hand.

Blossom saluted her and zipped up the stairs, careful to keep a wide berth between her and the Faerie lanterns.

Malek placed the jar of honey on a nearby table. He scooped her into his arms and began carrying her toward a nearby set of double doors.

She laughed. "What are you doing?"

"I'm taking the fascinating fae to my lair before anyone comes back," Malek said.

She kissed his neck and said, "Then grab the honey. It's not only pixies who enjoy it."

Malek barely hesitated before he spun around, hefted her over his shoulder, and grabbed the honey.

She laughed, dangling upside down. "You *can* put me down."

"Not a chance."

At this angle, she had a rather nice view. She pinched his butt, accompanying the gesture with a heated pulse of magic.

Malek chuckled and pushed open the door. "You're playing with dragonfire, Sabine."

"You're moving too slow."

Malek kicked the door closed. She blew her hair out of her face, catching sight of thick throw rugs over a polished dark floor. Before she had a chance to see much else, Sabine was flying through the air. She landed on a soft bed, surrounded by thick blankets and plush pillows.

She blinked up at Malek. The look on his face was one full of fierce hunger and need. She pushed up on her elbows, but he shook his head.

"No," Malek said and pulled his shirt over his head. "Don't

move. The sight of you in my bed is one I've been imagining for months."

The urge to explore every inch of him was nearly overwhelming. She fisted her hands in the blankets and said, "We need to work on your imagination skills. I'm still fully clothed."

He chuckled, kicking off his boots and unlacing his pants. Her mouth went dry at the outline of his growing hardness that beckoned her. Gods, she wanted him.

Malek crawled up the bed, pinning her with his body. To hell with it. She ran her hands over his chest and downward until she brushed against the hard length of him. He grabbed her hands and yanked them over her head.

"Take off your glamour," he said, his voice husky.

Sabine nipped at his lower lip, hooking her leg over his. Her glamour faded away until there was nothing between them except a frustrating layer of clothing.

"Clothing," she murmured against his lips. "Now."

"I intend to take my time with you," he said, slowly untying the laces down the front of her dress. Sliding it off her shoulder, he kissed her exposed skin, flicking his tongue against the nape of her neck. His magic washed over her in a heated wave, sending warmth flooding through every part of her. He kissed even lower, sliding the dress down as he went. She trembled at his touch. If he didn't stop this slow assault on her senses, she was going to lose her mind.

"Malek," she warned, her magic rising in response to his heated caresses. In another minute, she was going to abandon this slow seduction he had planned.

"I intend to finish what I started earlier," he said, easing the dress from her body and casting it aside. He pulled off her boots and ran his hand up her leg, accompanying his touch with another heated pulse. His tongue trailed the path of one of her skin markings, and she gasped as he pressed another kiss against the inside of her thigh.

She reached down, needing to touch him. He chuckled and captured her hands again. Holding them over her head with one hand, he slowly trailed his fingers down another of her markings that began on her shoulder and curved down her side.

"You're mine, Sabine," he said, his heated breath blowing softly over her skin. "Admit it."

She gasped and shook her head before meeting his gaze.

"No," she said, refusing to give in. "You're mine."

He grinned, appearing entirely too pleased by her challenge.

"Malek," she whispered, arching her back as he cupped her breast. Her nipples hardened, aching for more of his touch. He lowered his head, taking one into his mouth. Sabine inhaled sharply as his power swirled over her sensitive skin, teasing her with the promise of what was to come.

Sabine pushed against his power with her own. He chuckled and loosened his grip on her wrists. It was enough. She rolled over, pushing him down until she was straddling him. Mentally reaching for the vines in the next room, she pulled on them with her magic. They shot upward through the cracks in the floor, binding his wrists tightly.

Malek's eyes blazed with passion, and a shiver raced through her. "Do you really think that'll subdue me?"

Sabine reached for the honey. "I could always summon a tree to keep you pinned."

"Trees aren't much of a challenge for a dragon," Malek said, his gaze devouring her.

She slid over him, his hardened length pressing against her core. Gods. He groaned at the contact, sending another delicious shiver through her.

Sabine opened the jar of honey and dipped her fingers

into it. She smeared a slow trail down his chest, stopping just above his length, then traced the path with her tongue. When her tongue brushed against his thick member, he jerked against her.

"Dammit, Sabine," Malek's voice said in a groan. "Unbind me, or I'll burn through your vines."

Sabine laughed and spread more honey over his shaft. Taking him into her mouth, she sucked and teased, licking him clean. She sent waves of power across his skin, igniting every nerve ending with her magic. She felt the exact moment he tore through the vined barriers.

He flipped her over, pinning her once again. The look in his eyes was nearly feral as he claimed her mouth. She ran her fingers through his hair, returning his kiss as his heated magic caressed her skin. He stroked her skin, each touch laced with his power.

Malek broke the kiss suddenly and reached for the bottle of honey. He poured it over her skin, and she gasped at the sudden warmth.

He chuckled and said, "I warned you about playing with dragonfire."

"Then make me burn," she challenged.

He kissed down her body, tracing the same path as the honey. His mouth closed over a nipple, swirling heat through her. Her breath hitched and she arched her back, wanting and needing him with a desperation that knew no limits.

He continued lower, circling her belly button with his tongue before trailing even farther down. When he finally parted her folds and teased her sensitive nub with slow, practiced strokes, she cried out as waves of pleasure surged through her.

Sabine's power rose up swiftly, unable to be contained any longer. Malek met it with his own in a fiery explosion of heat that rocked the room and sent her spiraling.

Before she could even catch her breath, Malek plunged deep inside her. The bond between them flared open and he met her wordless demand with one of his own, setting a relentless pace as he pounded into her. She gripped his shoulders, her nails scoring his skin as the magic between them continued to build. Her skin shone brightly with a golden light, casting a glow throughout the room. His magic wrapped around her, pouring into her and causing her power to flare to even greater heights.

As she cried out once more, their bodies and magic colliding in ecstasy, Malek followed her over the edge of the abyss, showing her just how far a dragon could make her fly.

CHAPTER 26

*S*unlight filtered through the crystal windows, painting the room with a warm glow. Malek ran his hand down Sabine's naked back, contentment filling him at the feel of her soft and pliant body in his arms. He'd made love to her several more times throughout the night, first in the bed and then moving to the bathing pool, taking their time and exploring each other until sleep had finally claimed them both.

Malek breathed in the scent of night-blooming flowers, feeling a stirring of desire again. If he lived a thousand lifetimes with her, it would never be enough.

"Malek!" A woman's voice sounded in his head with the force of a gong. *"If you don't wake up and lower these damn wards so I can hug my big brother, I'm going to burn your house down."*

"Not if you huff and puff," he retorted with a grin. *"Go away, Kaia. I'm trying to sleep."*

"Not anymore, you're not," she said smugly. *"Rupert and Azalia said you arrived back late last night, but you're not allowing visitors. Mum is seriously put out. Da won't change out of his*

dragon form because she's on a tirade. Last time, she singed his tail."

Damn.

He should have been clearer with his orders to Rupert and Azalia last night. He'd wanted Sabine to have a chance to get accustomed to his home before introducing her to his family. She was already resistant to being referred to as his mate. This wasn't going to end well.

"Malek?" Kaia asked. *"What's the deal? Lower the wards already."*

"No. I'll come out shortly. I have some things to handle first."

A resounding silence met him at this pronouncement.

After a full minute, Kaia shouted in his head, *"You found a mate, didn't you? By the ether, Malek! I want to meet her before you scare her off!"*

"Kaia, so help me, I'll string you up by your tail if you breathe a word to anyone. There are some... complications."

Kaia hesitated. *"Ummm..."*

"You already told Thom, didn't you?"

"He's my mate, Malek. Of course I told him."

Malek stared at the ceiling, muttering a thousand silent curses. *"Fine. I'll be out shortly. And tell Thom to keep his mouth shut."*

Malek carefully moved the blankets aside and eased his arm out from under Sabine. She opened her lavender eyes, blinking up at him sleepily. She ran her hand down his chest, her tactile exploration reminding him of everything they'd shared throughout the night. Damn his meddling family. Leaving this bed was the last thing he wanted to do.

"I didn't mean to wake you," he said, brushing her silvery hair away from her face. He kissed her softly. "It's early yet."

"Mmm," she murmured and stretched, causing the blankets to shift even more. He propped himself up on one elbow and traced his fingers along one of her skin markings that trailed down her side like ivy. Small flowers shimmered with a golden iridescence and graced the edges of the design, dipping slightly at her waist until it curved over her hip.

"Do you have any idea how beautiful you are?"

Sabine gave him a sleepy smile. "Is that why you were sneaking out of bed so early?"

Malek groaned and sat up. "No. My sister's waiting outside the gate."

Sabine froze, her expression immediately becoming guarded.

Damn it all to the underworld and back. He could literally feel her rebuilding the walls between them. He captured her hand and kissed her fingertips. "She's not coming inside. I just need to speak with her for a few minutes. You can meet her some other time, once you're more settled."

"Don't be absurd," she said, pulling her hand away. She stood, the light from the crystal windows forming a glowing nimbus around her. "You haven't seen your sister in several years. I will not stand in the way of that. If you think me so fragile a creature that I require protection from your own sister, why bother bringing me here?"

Without waiting for a response, she picked up the traveler's pack from the floor and headed for the bathing room. He stared after her, both perplexed and strangely aroused. He'd never been dismissed in his own home, nor so effectively put in his place.

He hesitated for a moment, wanting to go after her but suspecting she needed space. With a muttered curse, he walked over to a chest of drawers and yanked it open. Quickly dressing in a loose tunic and pants, his gaze drifted toward the closed door to the bathing room. Sabine had closed off their bond, sealing away her emotions from him. He took a step in her direction and then stopped.

Bane was right; the mating instinct was overruling common sense.

In some ways, having her here was making it more difficult to think clearly. Sabine had quickly become the most important person in his life. The urge to keep her safe behind his wards and away from anyone who might harm her was nearly overwhelming.

The quickest way to lose her would be to give into those instincts. She would never allow it, and he never wanted to stifle her light. But he would ensure she remained safe, no matter the cost—even if he had to enlist the aid of a demon.

Forcing himself to turn away, he headed toward the doors to find Bane.

The demon in question was lounging on the couch. He opened one eye, studied Malek for a moment and then snorted. "Idiot dragon. What did you do now?"

Malek pinched the bridge of his nose, a mild headache plaguing him. His sister's impatience was rapping against his thoughts like pebbles being cast against a window. "My family knows I've returned. My sister's currently waiting rather impatiently outside the gate."

Bane yawned and stretched. "Then go."

Malek lowered his hand. "I suggested that. Sabine wants me to bring her inside."

Bane pushed off the couch, his eyes flashing to silver. "Like I said before—you're an idiot. If anyone suspects she hesitated at the thought of meeting your family, they'll line up for the kill. She knows this, which is why it was *your* job to protect her from such things. You agreed to control access."

"My sister would *never* harm her," Malek said. "As far as the rest of my people are concerned, if Sabine will accept the fact she's my mate, my entire clan will protect her. But no matter what she decides, no dragon will dare touch her while I still have breath."

"And what do you think the fae or the rest of the Unseelie would do if she openly admits she's yours? She's our queen, you foolish lizard. If you try to steal her from us, you won't need to worry about the portal reopening. We'll eradicate your kind for good this time."

Malek's power filled the room. "Don't threaten me, demon. I agreed to your presence because of her love for you, but I will not allow you to come between us."

"Who are you trying to convince?" Bane said with a sneer. "If you weren't already doing damage control because you fucked up, you'd still be in bed with her."

"Enough," Sabine's voice sliced through their argument like a knife. Her silvery hair was piled on her head, with a few loose tendrils that curled around her face. The gossamer robe she'd hastily adorned shimmered like moonlight and cascaded to the floor like a waterfall. She was once again wearing her human glamour, but there was no confusing her with a mere mortal. An air of seductive power surrounded her, commanding and holding the attention of everyone in the room.

She turned to Malek and said, "Now that the entire household has likely heard your argument, I suggest you retrieve your sister while I finish dressing. Bane, I need a word with you in private."

Sabine turned and strode back toward the bedroom suite. Bane followed and nodded toward the upstairs before shutting the door behind him.

Malek glanced upward at the second-floor landing where Bane had indicated. Aeron and Thalassa stared down at him. Their expressions were carefully neutral, but it was obvious they'd been listening to every word. Lyra's face was pressed against the dark wooden spindles, watching him like an eaglet perched in a nest. Rika had halted halfway down the stairs. When Malek's eyes landed on her, she continued walking the rest of the way.

"Maybe not the *entire* household," Rika said with a tentative smile. "Blossom's out in the garden. She said something about eradicating evil beetles before she disappeared earlier. Azalia popped in earlier to see if we needed anything, but I told her we'd wait for you and Sabine."

Malek blew out a breath. "If you'd like to join me, I'll have Azalia introduce you to the cook and the rest of the staff. I'm sure everyone's hungry by now." He looked up at Aeron and Thalassa. "Would you care to join us?"

Aeron frowned at him. "No. We shall stay with our Aderylin."

Rika rolled her eyes. "They won't eat until after Sabine does. Bane said it's a Seelie thing."

"Fine," Malek said and headed toward the door. Pushing it open, he and Rika walked into the bright sunlight of the garden. Unless his sister had changed dramatically over the last several years, she would start testing the strength of his wards any minute.

"Did Azalia show you how the calling crystals work?" Malek asked.

Rika nodded. "She said they're dwarven made. We're supposed to put our hand on them and say her name. The crystal in her pocket will activate and let her know where she's needed."

"Good," Malek said, guiding Rika toward the east wing.

Rika stopped abruptly. "Bane is worried, but not for the reasons you might think."

"What are you talking about?"

Rika glanced around to make sure no one was nearby. "Did you notice he stayed outside your door last night?"

It was a little hard *not* to notice.

"I would never allow any harm to come to Sabine. He knows that."

"We all do, but Bane is a strategist," Rika said quietly. "He checked every inch of your estate last night, testing the perimeter wards. He even had Aeron test the sky wards. Afterward, Bane refused to take a room and slept outside your door in case you were suddenly called away. He doesn't trust the humans working here. Their loyalty is to your people, not Sabine."

Malek frowned. The demon's harsh words suddenly made a whole lot more sense. No matter what issues they'd had, Bane had always put Sabine's safety above everything else.

He blew out a breath and said, "I'll talk to Sabine about adding a secondary ward to the north wing like we did in the Hall of the Gods. If Bane still has concerns, I'll see about temporarily reassigning some of my staff to my sister's home. Now, more than ever, we need people we trust around us. I've been gone too long to know how loyalties may have shifted."

Rika nodded. "I already met Carlin, your cook. For what it's worth, I think you can trust him. He loves your kitchen too much to risk jeopardizing his position here. I'll let him and Azalia know your sister's going to be joining us and see about arranging breakfast for the aderyan."

Malek arched his brow. "You just wanted to have an excuse to tell me about Bane?"

Rika grinned. "You two may butt heads, but it's only because you're both working toward the same goal from opposite directions. Blossom and I are neutral, so it's easier to see what's going on."

Malek chuckled and nodded toward the kitchen. "Go on. I'll bring my sister to the garden courtyard. She'll want to meet you, I'm sure."

She nodded and started to turn away, but Malek stopped her.

"Your ability to see things clearly may be more than you think."

Rika's eyes widened. "You think it's another aspect of being a seer?"

"I think it takes an extraordinary individual to not only see things clearly, but also to wade between a dragon and a demon and show them the truth. I've seen you do it on more than one occasion, not just with me and Bane, but also with how you handled Dax in the underworld. We're fortunate to have met you, Rika. I hope you know that."

Her cheeks reddened. She threw her arms around him and gave him a quick hug before turning and running in the direction of the east wing.

CHAPTER 27

"And you call my dragon foolish," Sabine said quietly, laying her head against Bane's chest. She sent a strong wave of power over him, and his arms tightened around her reflexively. His strength was nearly exhausted, or he never would have lost his temper over so slight a matter.

"He is, but at least he recharges your magic well enough."

Sabine laughed and looked up at him. The weight of the fatigue she'd sensed was quickly fading thanks to her magic, but he needed to sleep. She pressed her hand against his cheek and asked, "If I ordered you to bed, would you go?"

"No."

Sabine sighed. "I figured as much."

She took his hand and pierced her finger with the tip of his claw. Holding it up to his mouth, she said, "Then drink."

Bane cradled her hand and accepted her offering. Power rushed through him, turning his horns a brilliant silver and casting a bluish light over his midnight skin. She'd always found him captivating when his magic came over him, but the true sight of him while they'd been in the underworld had nearly stolen her breath.

"You should not look upon me so, little one," he said knowingly and kissed her forehead. "The dragon is already agitated. You've shut him out, haven't you?"

"With good reason," Sabine said and headed for the bathing room where she'd scattered half a dozen elaborate gowns. A messy pile of priceless jewelry and embroidered shoes were nearby. She'd managed to find her brush and some hairpins, but the rest was beyond her. Malek had caught her off guard this morning, and she'd been at a loss on how to handle her first meeting with a dragon. She needed to appear human, but Faerie had packed clothing more suitable for a queen. The only other option was some of her traveling attire, but those were hardly acceptable.

She gestured to the clothing and said, "I know nothing of the dragon world or what's appropriate. Malek has concerns enough without me adding such trivialities to the mix."

Bane surveyed the disarray. "I may have a solution."

He turned and headed out of the room. She sat on the chaise lounge and pulled out a few more gowns from the traveler's pack. Malek had been wearing some sort of dark, decorative tunic. It was too risky to attempt glamouring a similar outfit. The last thing she needed was her magic to fail at an inopportune moment. She'd be forever known as the naked fae in the garden.

Lyra ran into the room, scrambled onto the chaise, and wrapped her arms around Sabine's waist. Sabine smiled and pulled her into her lap. Azalia had been true to her word and had found suitable clothing for the child. She was currently wearing a pale yellow dress that had been altered to fit her wings.

"I flew up to the second floor five times!" Lyra exclaimed.

Sabine grinned. "Well done! Once Malek says it's safe, we'll have to take you into the garden and let you practice outside."

Bane prowled back into the room and narrowed his eyes on Lyra. "How did she get in here?"

Lyra blinked at him and didn't answer.

"Allow us to assist, Aderylin," Thalassa said, sweeping into the room behind the demon. Aeron followed her and the two of them quickly began sorting her clothing into neat piles. They argued back and forth about colors and auras.

Bane studied Lyra suspiciously before gesturing to the arguing aderyan. "They know dragons and are Seelie enough to understand the nuances of politics. *My* solution would have been to either wear armor or go nude. Everything else is rather pointless."

Lyra looked at Sabine and asked, "You wear armor?"

Sabine smiled and shook her head. "Not usually. In this case, I think it would be better to wear what Thalassa and Aeron suggest. Don't you?"

Lyra nodded.

"The blue," Aeron insisted, gesturing to a lightweight dress adorned with silver accents. "Our Aderylin cannot risk outshining Lord Malek's aura without revealing her nature."

Thalassa nodded and picked up the gown. "A wise choice. This will complement Lord Malek's current attire. But she will need appropriate jewelry that showcases her value without diminishing his position. Something fae-wrought, I think."

Aeron took Lyra from Sabine while Thalassa thrust the garment in Sabine's direction. "You must dress quickly, Aderylin. I will arrange your hair."

"You will help me select suitable jewelry for our Aderylin," Aeron said to Lyra, showing her the costly assortment. "Listen for the resonance and match her aura after she puts on the dress."

Sabine quickly disrobed and stepped into the dress. Thalassa fastened the laces with a quick efficiency that made

Sabine wonder if she'd been some sort of lady's maid in her former life. She guided Sabine to a chair and quickly began coiling her hair in a complicated updo that showcased her pointed ears. So much for appearing human.

Lyra brought over Sabine's mother's necklace, a large blue diamond in silver filigree. It had once belonged to Lachlina and had been the key to escaping the prison in the underworld. Sabine ran her thumb over the priceless stone and met Bane's eyes. He stared at the necklace, his jaw hardening. He'd been the one who had led her to the prison on Kal'thorz's orders, a fact that obviously still bothered him. Sabine hadn't intended to wear it again so soon.

After a moment, Bane gave her a curt nod.

"You like this one?" Sabine asked Lyra.

The girl nodded. "It sings for you."

Sabine fastened the pendant around her neck.

Thalassa stepped back and studied Sabine's reflection in the mirror. "Elegant, yet not too formal for a morning at home." She snapped her fingers. "Shoes, Aeron. We must hurry. The wards out front have already been lowered."

Aeron brought over a pair of matching slippers and kneeled to place them on Sabine's feet. She stood and smoothed out the dress.

When everyone nodded their approval, she asked, "Any last-minute suggestions?"

Aeron folded his wings tightly against his back and said, "Lord Malek is next in line to take over the Obsidian Clan. His younger sister will defer to him in accordance with dragon law. In their culture, a greater dragon's mate is considered their equal. This can be both a boon and a detriment. Those who will challenge Lord Malek may also challenge you, but those who are weaker will not dare risk offending you."

Thalassa nodded. "While you are in Lord Malek's home,

you will be addressed as Lady Sabine by the household staff. Unless you publicly accept his mate claim, you are only afforded such courtesies while you are in his home. Outside of these walls, you may be challenged or even killed by a servant. Lord Malek may choose to protect you or not, but none will fault him for failing to safeguard your person once you leave his estate."

Bane crossed his arms over his chest. "If his family does not approve, they might be inclined to arrange an 'accident.' We'll take steps to ensure that never happens."

Sabine tried to bury her unease. "All right. Anything else?"

Thalassa and Aeron exchanged glances.

Thalassa lowered her gaze and said, "I would offer to act as your lady's maid while in their presence and to help guide you, but I am unable to bring myself to hide my wings yet. It has been a long time since my magic has been allowed to fly free. I ask for your forgiveness, Aderylin."

Sabine reached for Thalassa's hand and squeezed it. "There is nothing to forgive, Thalassa. The beauty of your wings deserves to be admired and embraced, not hidden away. You have already offered a great deal of knowledge. Bane and I can handle this."

Thalassa's eyes shimmered with emotion. "You share the light of your soul so easily, Aderylin. I will strive to emulate your wisdom and grace."

Aeron put his arm and wing around Thalassa. She leaned against him and added, "Your demon will not be welcome among any of the dragons, Aderylin."

"I would be honored to act as your guard when your demon is unable to attend you," Aeron said. "I do not have the same knowledge Thalassa does in dealing with dragon politics, but I retained my wings for most of my captivity. My strength is my magic, and I offer that freely to you."

Bane crossed his arms over his chest. "They will need to get used to me, one way or another."

Sabine nodded. "Bane's right. For this first meeting with Malek's family, I think Bane's presence is necessary. Once we have a better handle on the situation, your expertise and guidance will be invaluable."

"As you wish, Aderylin," Aeron said, bowing his head.

Lyra looked up at Sabine and said, "I will keep watch."

"I think that decision is best left to Aeron and Thalassa," Sabine said gently.

"Come, child," Thalassa said and took Lyra's hand. "We shall keep watch from the highest windows. Aeron will show you new magic that will allow you to watch unseen by dragon eyes."

"Like the blur?" Lyra asked.

Thalassa nodded and led her out of the room. "Yes, but you will remain in the quiet for this next lesson."

Sabine made a mental note to find out more about these lessons they were teaching Lyra. She knew very little about aderyan magic. It was quickly becoming obvious they had skills that were vastly different than most fae abilities.

With a steadying breath, Sabine headed toward the main room of the north wing and tried to wrest control of her nerves. She didn't think Bane would understand why this meeting was important to her. It wasn't just about meeting another dragon.

Whenever Malek had spoken of his sister, his eyes softened and his voice carried a hint of playful affection. The realization had been a pivotal moment for her. If dragons had the capacity for such love, then perhaps they weren't as terrible as the stories claimed.

Bane fell into step beside her and said, "The talking turkeys may have some beneficial magic at their command."

Sabine glanced over at him. "Is that a trace of respect I hear?"

Bane harrumphed. "They're still Seelie."

Sabine made a noncommittal noise, suspecting Bane would find a way to assess their magical skills at the earliest opportunity.

Bane opened the door leading to the garden, and Sabine stepped into the bright sunlight. The garden had been striking at night, but it paled in comparison to the beauty that lay before her.

Flowers of every shade bloomed vibrantly under the sun, creating a tapestry of color that stretched across the expansive grounds. Bees buzzed softly, darting among blossoms heavy with nectar, while the light breeze stirred the leaves, making the garden come alive with gentle movement.

The previously hidden details of the garden were now illuminated: delicate spider webs glistening with morning dew, the intricate patterns of petals, and the shouting of a furious pixie fighting off what sounded like a horde of rabid kobolds.

"Attack!" Blossom shrieked, darting out from under a leaf. Nearly a dozen other pixies followed her lead, shouting their war cries. They leaped into the air and waved sharpened thorns as they launched themselves into the bushes in a glittering whirlwind of pixie dust. Sabine caught sight of a few more shooting out from the foliage on the other side of the garden in some sort of coordinated assault.

Hundreds of green and gold beetles zipped out of the bushes and into the air, heading straight for Sabine and Bane. With a flick of her wrist, a vined barrier erupted from the ground in front of Sabine. The beetles smacked into it and released the pollen in the flowers. They fell to the ground, either stunned or sleeping from the mild toxin in the vines.

"Oops! Sorry, Sabine!" Blossom yelled. "Pull back, people! We've got civilians in the garden!"

"That's it," Bane said with a growl. "I'm going to eat your pixie. Maybe a few of them."

When the pinging of beetle bodies finally stopped, Sabine stepped around the barrier and put her hands on her hips. "Bane wants to know why he shouldn't be allowed to eat you. You can start by explaining why I was almost knocked down by a bunch of terrified beetles."

Blossom and her new friends hovered in the air around Sabine, each one talking excitedly and all at the same time. The air became thick with shimmering pixie dust, coating her skin and dress. A few of the more mischievous pixies giggled and started sneaking flowers into her hair.

"By the ether," a woman exclaimed. "You actually found a fae! And she's your mate?"

CHAPTER 28

*S*abine froze, noticing the newcomers standing with Malek for the first time. A stunning dark-haired woman stood beside Malek and another man. The woman's vibrant emerald green eyes shone with an intense, commanding light, yet there was something about the aura of power around her Sabine found almost playful. It reminded her of Malek and how he teased and joked around with her in their private moments.

The man, however, was a complete mystery. He wasn't quite as tall as Malek, but his short, chestnut hair and deep, almost black eyes gave him a look of quiet intensity. He stood protectively beside the woman, his gaze focused on Bane with a look that was anything but friendly.

"A demon?" the man asked, his voice dripping with disdain.

"Watch it, Thom," Malek snapped. "If you insult my guests, it will be the last mistake you make in my household."

"You can't be serious," Thom said, gesturing toward Sabine and Bane. "The fae may be able to help us, but bringing a demon to the Sky Cities is crossing the line."

Sabine straightened, her magic quickly rising to the surface as she narrowed her eyes on the man. The pixies squealed and dove for cover in the nearby bushes.

Blossom landed on Sabine's shoulder and crossed her arms. "Want me to dust him?"

Before Sabine could respond, Malek's fist shot out and slammed into Thom's face. His head whipped back, and he fell backward into the fountain with a splash.

Blossom cheered. "Way to go, Malek!"

"Whoa," the woman said, her eyes wide. Then she grinned and started laughing. "Thom, you're a damned fool. Get out of there and apologize before he kicks both of us out."

"Dammit, Malek," Thom said, rubbing his jaw.

Malek stared down at Thom, his face hard. "If you are anything less than cordial to my guests again, I'll rip your arms off and shove them down your throat. The only reason you're still alive is because of Kaia."

"Malek!" Kaia exclaimed, staring at her brother in shock.

"Sabine," Bane said quietly, nodding toward Malek.

Understanding the problem immediately, Sabine lowered her barriers and reached for Malek through their bond. His gaze immediately flew to her. The pain she felt from him was almost a physical blow.

He crossed the space between them in a matter of heartbeats and pulled her into his arms. She leaned against him, weaving a strong wave of love and reassuring power over him.

"I hadn't realized shutting you out would make things worse for you," she said silently. *"Why didn't you tell me?"*

"Most likely for the same reason you shut me out in the first place. Dammit, Sabine. This isn't how I wanted things to happen."

She smiled. *"We're not very good at this, are we?"*

He ran a hand down her back and exhaled, his body

beginning to relax. *"I think we're very good at this. It's the rest of the world that makes things more challenging."*

Sabine looked up at him and kissed him lightly. *"I don't think either one of us has ever been intimidated by a challenge. Now introduce me to your sister. I want to meet her."*

Malek eased back but didn't release her. Instead, he tucked her against his side in a protective gesture. Thom had climbed out of the fountain, but was making it a point to keep his distance from Malek.

Kaia was staring up at Thom with her hands on her hips. He eyed her warily, wincing slightly as he dripped water on the ground. He started to raise his hands, but she shook her head and jabbed him in the chest with her finger.

"She's yelling at him," Malek said, pointing to his temple.

"You can hear her?"

Malek nodded. "When Kaia gets worked up, she doesn't always remember to use private mental connections. Any dragon within the confines of my estate could hear her shouting."

A few of the pixies had begun peeking out from the bushes, but Blossom was conspicuously absent. However, a strange bumblebee seemed to be hovering a little too close to Thom. Sabine suspected he might be a little uncomfortable by the end of the day, in more ways than one.

After another minute, Kaia turned and flounced toward them.

Malek shook his head and said, "Out loud, Kaia. They can't hear you."

Kaia gave them a sheepish look and said, "I guess you missed most of that. Allow me to apologize for my mate's boorish behavior."

"Why would you take responsibility for someone else's actions?" Sabine asked.

Kaia blinked at her. "What?"

Malek grinned and said, "She's fae, Kaia. You remember how Elisa would get annoyed with us when we apologized or thanked her. It implies a debt. Since the insult was caused by Thom, he's the only one who can offer recompense."

"Crap," Kaia muttered and shook her head. "It's been so long. I've forgotten all the rules. Grandda would have sat on my tail for that."

Malek chuckled and said, "Sabine, I'd like to introduce my sister, Kaia. The dripping drake standing behind her is Thom."

"Well met, Kaia," Sabine said with a smile and gave a polite nod to Thom.

"I suppose I deserve that," Thom said and scratched his neck. "I'll just stand over here, admiring the fountain from dry land."

Malek gestured to Bane and said, "This is Bane. Yes, he's a demon, and no, you can't touch his horns." He glanced over at Bane. "She's been asking since the moment she saw you."

Kaia's shoulders drooped. "Come on. Really? I've never met a demon before."

"She can touch my horns," Bane said, taking a step forward. Sabine stared at them, unsure which one of them had surprised her more — Kaia by asking the question, or Bane for agreeing. Few Unseelie fae would have dared such a thing.

Kaia's entire face lit up. "Yes!"

"Kaia," Thom said in alarm, taking a step forward.

"You are not ruining this for me, Thom," Kaia said and approached Bane. She stood on her toes and touched the tip of his horn. "That's so cool! Do your eyes and horns really turn silver when you fight?"

"They do," Bane said.

"Will you fight me?" Kaia asked, practically bouncing in her boots. "We could have a practice session right here."

Bane appeared intrigued. Thom looked positively ill.

"I think you've tortured Thom enough," Malek said dryly. "And Bane isn't here to amuse you."

"We'll talk later," Kaia whispered loudly to Bane and winked at him.

"I apologize to both of you for my earlier rudeness," Thom said quickly, taking a tentative step forward and placing his hands on Kaia's shoulders. "As Kaia has reminded me, I would have done far worse if someone had come into my home and insulted my mate and guest in the same manner."

Kaia turned and beamed at him. "See? That wasn't all that hard." She sniffed the air. "Is Carlin cooking? Something smells divine. Are you feeding me, Malek?"

She turned and headed toward the east wing. Thom sighed and shook his head, turning to trail behind her.

Malek glanced down at Sabine. "Are you hungry?"

"I'm trying to figure out what just happened," Sabine said.

"The little dragon just gave you a lesson on how to deal with a stubborn mate," Bane said with a chuckle.

"He's not wrong," Malek admitted, sending a wave of delicious heat over her. "Although, I much prefer your way of dealing with me."

Sabine laughed and kissed his cheek. "Later. I need to get to the bottom of this pixie situation and then we can have breakfast."

At her words, Blossom transformed back into a pixie and whistled sharply. Almost three dozen pixies emerged from the bushes and foliage, their curious faces focused on Sabine.

"I guess you have questions," Blossom said, landing on Sabine's outstretched hand.

"Several. Unfortunately, I don't have a lot of time right now, so we'll have to do this quickly."

"Right," Blossom said, snapping to attention. "We'll do

introductions later. For now, this is everyone. Everyone, this is Sabine the Shiny, Malek the Dragon, and Bane the Hungry."

All the pixies ooooh'd and aaaah'd.

"These are all the pixies left in the Sky Cities," Blossom said. "They caught the scent of starfruit and your magic, and word spread like pollen. Some of them traveled all night to get here."

Malek frowned. "I haven't seen pixies in this garden since Elisa was alive."

Several of them started talking at once. Blossom fluttered her wings and shushed them. "Timing, people! They have a breakfast date, and we have a garden to clean up. You'll all get your turn."

A few more pixies began sticking flowers in Sabine's hair, taking care to avoid Bane the Hungry. None of them seemed terribly bothered by the fact Malek was a dragon.

Blossom cleared her throat and said, "Now where was I? Oh yeah… Most of the pixies live on the other floating islands. The few fae who are left in the Sky Cities don't have enough magic to sustain them. Elisa was one of the only fae who didn't wear iron chains. After she was gone, they were able to harvest some magic from her garden, but it made them sad. So they found other Faerie flowers that were planted."

"See if you can find out where the captives are located," Sabine said quietly. "In the meantime, I'll infuse them with enough magic that should keep them healthy for a while."

"Already on it!"

Sabine held out her arms. "Gather the pixies, Blossom."

Blossom nodded and motioned for the pixies to join her. They landed on Sabine's arms, shoulders, and even in her hair. Sabine summoned her magic and released a gentle wave of power over them.

The pixies took flight, zipping around the garden in a sparkling cloud, playing among the flowers and chasing the bees through trails of glittering dust.

"Messy creatures," Bane said, shaking his head.

"Have them clean up the beetles," Sabine said. "I'll meet them individually later."

"You've got it!" Blossom said with a salute.

"Hang on," Malek interrupted. "How did they get past my wards?"

Blossom grinned. "We're pixies. Wards are just… suggestions. You know, like a 'Do Not Enter' sign. Who pays attention to those?"

Sabine laughed and said, "Let's go find your sister. If there's one thing I've learned, it's that you don't want to keep a hungry dragon waiting."

Bane harrumphed. "Or a demon."

CHAPTER 29

"At least Bane and Thom didn't try to kill each other during breakfast," Malek said, threading his fingers through Sabine's hand as they entered the garden. "Rika arranged for Azalia to deliver a private meal to Aeron, Thalassa, and Lyra. She figured they'd be more comfortable staying in the north wing until our guests leave."

She smiled up at him. "*Your* guests, Malek. And one of those is a beloved sister who has obviously missed her brother."

Malek hesitated, glancing over his shoulder at Kaia and Thom as they entered the garden. Sabine placed her hand against his cheek and said, "Spend some time with her. I'm not going anywhere."

Four pixies dove toward Sabine, air dropping a flowered crown on her head. They giggled and took off for the far side of the garden, high-fiving each other along the way.

"Flowers are power, pixies!" Blossom shouted, flying after them. "Did anyone bother checking where we are in the lunar cycle before doing a flyby?"

Malek chuckled and adjusted her lopsided crown. "It becomes you, Queen Sabine."

"Very funny. Just wait until they decide we need matching crowns. Then we'll see how fearsome you look with a bunch of roses in your hair. I doubt the other dragons will cower in terror."

Malek laughed. "You have a point. I'll spend some time with Kaia while you attempt to wrangle a garden full of pixies."

Sabine sighed. "I suspect Blossom may do that all on her own, but I should probably run interference. Thom's already begun itching, and I don't want the other pixies to get ideas."

She headed toward the far side of the garden where the pixies were congregating. A few more pixies darted out of the bushes, trailing behind Sabine and leaving glittering dust in her wake. Bane and Rika had been talking a short distance away and quickly fell into step behind her.

Malek turned and waited for Kaia to catch up. She said something quietly to Thom, who nodded and headed over to the central fountain. Malek bit back a smile, watching as Thom shifted his weight and scratched at the collar of his tunic.

"One of these days, I'm going to convince Carlin to come cook for me," Kaia said as she approached. "You can't keep a gem like him all to yourself."

"I have it on good authority he's quite fond of my kitchen," Malek said with a grin. "You'll just have to visit more often. But that reminds me, any objection if I send some of my staff to your home for a few days?"

"Because of Sabine?" Kaia asked.

Malek nodded. "I've been gone too long to know if loyalties have changed. Besides, Bane makes humans nervous."

"Ah," Kaia said with a grin. "I think mum and da could use

some extra help. They're hosting the clan gala this year. You've got great timing on that front."

"Damn," Malek muttered. Now that he was back, he'd be expected to attend such an event. Exposing Sabine to a room full of dragons was the last thing he wanted to do, even if they were clan allies. Malek suspected if he tried to discourage her from attending, they'd have another incident like this morning.

He sat on a nearby bench that overlooked most of the garden. Sabine was kneeling on the ground, greeting and speaking with each of the pixies. A few of them had pulled locks of her silvery hair loose from her makeshift flowered crown and were in the process of braiding the strands. Rika sat on the ground beside her, laughing at something one of the pixies was telling them while Bane stood as a silent sentry nearby.

"I like her," Kaia said with a smile and sat beside him. "At least, I like that she makes you happy. You can't seem to take your eyes off her."

"Hmm?" Malek asked. "What was that?"

Kaia laughed. "I was telling you I like your mate. She was rather quiet and reserved at breakfast though. Is that a fae thing? Elisa was like that."

"The fae believe in balance above all else," Malek explained. "Sabine can be... cautious with her words. Once uttered, they can't be taken back. When you get to know her, she'll open up more. But I think she was a little nervous about meeting you."

"Me?" Kaia asked in surprise.

"You're the first dragon she's met other than me," Malek said. "I'd hoped to give her a bit more time before introducing her to our parents or anyone else. Now there's a damn gala to deal with."

Kaia winced. "Oof, and Thom botched things big time.

I'm sorry about that. I don't think anyone expected you to bring a demon home with you. What's the story with him anyway?"

Malek hesitated. "Let's just say Sabine and Bane have been close for a long time. He looks out for her. I'd like to think we've developed a mutual understanding of sorts, at least where Sabine is concerned."

"Mysterious," Kaia said with a grin and bumped shoulders with him. "All right. I won't keep prying. I'm just glad you're finally home. I think we were all beginning to lose hope."

Malek leaned back, watching as Sabine stood. She took Rika's hand and held it out. A butterfly landed there a moment later, fluttering its brilliant blue wings. The pixies all hovered around, clapping and cheering.

"Does she have enough magic to help us?" Kaia asked quietly, her tone far more serious than Malek had expected.

Malek studied his sister. For the first time, he noticed tiny details he'd missed—the tired lines around her eyes, the paleness of her normally golden skin, and the thinness of her frame. Realization slammed into him with the force of a dragon's tail.

"You're pregnant?"

Kaia nodded, her eyes shimmering with tears. "I can't shift, Malek. I've tried, but every part of my magic is tied to keeping this pregnancy. Without an egg to protect—"

"I know," Malek said, putting his arm around Kaia and hugging her tightly. It should have been joyous news, but all Malek felt was dread. His beloved sister had just told him he might not only lose her, but also the life of his future niece or nephew.

It was unacceptable. He wouldn't allow such an end to come to pass.

If something ever happened to Sabine, he wasn't sure he'd survive it. The thought was like a knife plunging into his heart. He met Thom's eyes across the garden, and the ragged torment on the drake's face said it all. In that moment, the two of them shared a perfect understanding.

They would do whatever was necessary to save the people they loved.

"Malek?" Sabine asked, her expression full of concern.

He hadn't realized he'd been broadcasting his emotions so loudly. He shook his head to let her know he'd explain later. She hesitated a moment and then nodded, a gentle warmth whispering softly to him through their bond.

Kaia sniffed. "I told myself I wouldn't tell you like this. Thom didn't want me to come here at all. That's why he's more protective than normal."

"I'm surprised he showed as much restraint as he did," Malek admitted. "And that he actually allowed you to touch a demon's horns. Dammit, Kaia. What were you thinking?"

Kaia laughed and wiped her eyes. "Oh, you should have heard him in my head. I didn't know he could swear so creatively. I knew it was safe, or you never would have allowed a demon past your wards and onto your estate— much less near your mate."

"It was still a risk," Malek said and blew out a breath. "How long?"

"No more than a few months," Kaia said, pressing a hand against her flat stomach. "It's early yet. Mum's been having some human, a witch, brew all sorts of nasty tonics. They taste worse than the underside of a dragon scale. But if I can shift long enough to transfer the baby into an egg, we both may survive."

Malek froze.

There had to be another human witch other than Idola. If he'd just banished his sister's last hope to save her life and that of her child, he'd send out every wyvern in the clan to hunt Idola down and bring her here. He needed to talk to his mother right away to find out for sure.

"Are the tonics helping?"

Kaia shrugged. "Who can say? They're not making things worse. When I realized you were back, I thought maybe you'd found a fae with enough magic to help us control the portal like we planned."

Malek squeezed his eyes shut. "Things are far more complicated than we expected, Kaia. We've located some of the artifacts used to seal the portal, but it doesn't appear we'll be able to control it. Sabine believes it can only be opened or closed. If it's opened again, the magic will return to Aeslion, but that also means the war will be brought here once again."

"But you don't know for sure?" Kaia asked, her hand squeezing his arm tightly. "There's still a possibility we can control it, right?"

"No, we don't know anything for sure," Malek said, knowing she needed some shred of hope. "I need to speak with our parents and tell them what I've learned. Given the circumstances, I think you and Thom may need to be there for the conversation."

Kaia nodded. "And Sabine? Is she truly willing to help us?"

Malek's eyes rested on the woman he loved. "I think Sabine will do what she can."

CHAPTER 30

"And this is Hawthorn," Blossom said, gesturing to a pixie with a wild tangle of brown hair and eyes that shimmered like dew on hawthorn leaves at dawn. He grinned at Sabine and offered a courtly bow, his delicate wings tinged with a soft rosy hue.

"Well met, Hawthorn," Sabine said with a smile.

"Word of your beauty has carried on the winds, beckoning for us to join you, Your Highness."

Blossom threw a berry at him.

He dodged out of the way and whispered loudly, "You said to compliment her!"

"You're not supposed to call her 'Your Highness,'" Blossom whispered back. "It's a secret."

"Oh." Hawthorn cleared his throat and bowed again. "Word of your beauty—"

Sabine held up her hand. "I get the general idea, and no, you can't have a sip of the starfruit essence. The compliment was lovely though."

"Are you sure?" Hawthorn asked. "I mean, maybe we need to check the starfruit essence for potency?"

Rika laughed. "I don't think there's any doubt about its potency."

"Nice try though," Blossom said, giving him a thumb's up sign. "We'll brainstorm more later. Tell her about the fae you saw."

Hawthorn saluted her and snapped to attention. "Your spymaster has indicated your interest in fae and aderyan captives. I personally know of at least one fae bound in iron who is being held in the stone estate of the daisy-colored overlords."

Sabine tilted her head. "Where?"

"Head to where the sun sets over the water and keep the tree moss in front of you. Broken wings of stone line the path."

Rika frowned. "You know what he's talking about?"

Sabine nodded. "Daisy-colored overlords indicate Gold or Topaz dragons. Malek says the clans are divided into different minerals or elemental materials, which best represent their appearance. If we head to the island where they're located and travel west and then north, we should find a path lined with broken aderyan statues."

"We need maps," Bane said from behind her.

"Malek should have some," Rika said. "His ship was full of them. He said it was a hobby of his even before he started sailing."

"We'll find out once he's finished with his sister," Sabine said and sent a light pulse of magic over Hawthorn, causing his wings to vibrate. "For your assistance."

Hawthorn bowed deeply. "It's always a pleasure to serve, Your—"

Blossom cleared her throat and hefted another berry in her palms. "Your *what?*"

Hawthorn's eyes widened. "Ah, I think I hear some nectar ripening. I should go… check."

He dove into the nearby bushes and out of Blossom's throwing range.

"Sabine," Bane said, nodding toward Malek and Kaia. They were both standing, focused on something in the southernmost part of the garden.

A rush of relief went through her as Esmelle and Levin strolled into the garden. Levin clasped wrists with Malek and then gestured to Esmelle. At the sight of the newcomers, Thom crossed the garden in a handful of steps to stand beside Kaia. Concerned about the type of greeting Esmelle might receive, Sabine started to head in their direction.

"I do not recommend approaching the drake right now," Bane warned, taking Sabine's arm. "He is already agitated by our presence. Malek is distracted and may not see the threat until it's too late."

Trusting Bane at his word, Sabine motioned for Blossom.

The pixie landed on her shoulder and asked, "Want us to run interference?"

"Lure Esme away from them," she said quietly. "But do not arouse suspicion."

Blossom saluted her and whistled sharply. She dove into the foliage with two other pixies, Hawthorn and a girl named Snowdrop. They burst out of the bushes a short distance away from Esmelle, taking on the appearance of butterflies.

Rika frowned. "You think Thom's a problem?"

Bane gave her a curt nod. "Observe his body language, little seer. What do you see?"

"Feet braced, rigid stance," Rika said, cocking her head and studying him. "He's trying to keep all of us in sight at the same time. But he's been like that since he arrived."

"Yes. Now what do you *See*?"

Rika's expression took on a faraway, almost dreamlike quality. "Oh! He's weaving bands of jagged red and purple power around Kaia. Malek's magic is able to penetrate, but he's blocking Levin and Esmelle. Kaia was tempering him earlier, but I think she's getting tired or something."

"You must use all of your senses when assessing for a potential threat," Bane said, narrowing his eyes at something a handful of steps away. "That includes those who are attempting to remain hidden."

Rika's brow furrowed. "Huh?"

Sabine shouldn't have been surprised Bane had been attempting to track Aeron, now that he knew of the aderyan's ability to move unseen. Almost as soon as they'd entered the garden, Aeron had remained a short distance from her. He'd been careful to avoid the dragons so far.

"We'll explain later," Sabine said, unwilling to divulge Aeron's presence even to the pixies.

A butterfly landed on Esmelle's shoulder. After a brief moment, she grinned and said something to Levin before heading toward them. The pixies all began talking excitedly in the bushes around them.

"A dryad!" one of them whispered.

"We've never had a dryad here!"

"We've never had a demon either!"

The bushes rustled and a stream of giggles carried through the air.

Esmelle hugged Sabine and then Rika. She started to reach for Bane, but he scowled at her. She put her hands on her hip and stared up at him. "One of these days, Bane. One of these days I'm getting a hug from you, even if I have to render you unconscious first."

"Try it, witch."

"Challenge accepted," Esmelle said, a determined glint in her eye.

The pixies all began to ooooooh in the bushes. Bane growled at them. They quieted abruptly.

Esmelle arched her brow. "I guess we have some new

friends who decided to join us? I'd wondered about the new butterflies with Blossom."

"You'll have to meet them all later when Bane the Hungry isn't around," Sabine said with a grin, then gestured to Esmelle's acorn necklace. "Any problems?"

"It worked just like they said it would," Esmelle said, touching the necklace reverently. "I could scarcely believe it, but four potential dryads heard me and came out of their homes. They embraced me like I was long-lost family. They all said something had been missing from their lives. When they heard my song, they knew Imenel was no longer the place for them."

"Oh, Esme," Sabine murmured, hugging her friend. "That's wonderful news! You've given them a purpose and anchored the grove. More of the forests can be protected now."

"It was incredible, Sabine. Levin and I walked with them to the edge of the city. A doorway opened right there and they disappeared into the grove. Part of me wanted to join them, but it's not my place right now. I think I can do much more by sharing their song with others."

Before Sabine could respond, Malek approached them and said, "I hate to do this, but I need to speak with my family on a matter of some urgency."

Sabine took a step toward him, searching his expression. "Are you all right?"

A flash of pain streaked across Malek's face. He drew Sabine into his arms, holding her tightly.

"Malek, you're worrying me."

"It's Kaia," he said, his mental voice thick with emotion. *"I swear I'll explain everything when I return, but I may have made a terrible mistake when I banished Idola from the Sky Cities."*

"Then go and do what you must," she said, knowing this was related to the despair she'd sensed from him earlier.

Malek cupped her face and kissed her. *"You are beyond precious to me, Sabine. I would burn the world to the ground before I allowed anything to harm you. I need you to believe that."*

He turned to Bane. "I'm making arrangements to have the majority of my staff temporarily relocated to my parents' estate. They're packing their things as we speak. While I'm gone, the wards around my home will remain in place to prevent anyone from entering. If you need to reach me for any reason, Levin can get word to me."

"And if we wish to leave?" Bane asked, crossing his arms over his chest.

Malek's jaw clenched. "I would prefer if Sabine and the rest of you remained within the safety of my estate while I'm gone, but I'll key the wards to allow all of you to leave should the need arise."

Bane inclined his head. "Very well, but we require maps."

"Maps?" Malek asked, his gaze turning suspicious.

"Of the Sky Cities," Sabine explained. "The pixies may have information for us, but we need to understand various landmarks to identify the locations. Their descriptions are not the same as ours."

Malek nodded. "Of course. There are maps in my office. You have absolute authority within my estate, Sabine. If you require anything, Azalia or Rupert can assist you."

She frowned at him, knowing this was related to the mate thing again. But now wasn't the time to argue about it.

Levin approached them and said, "Thom is becoming anxious. He says Kaia is getting tired and will need to rest soon. If you want her with you when you see your parents, you should go now."

A sharp stab of pain lanced through the bond she shared with Malek. Suspecting it was related to whatever news Kaia had shared, Sabine kissed him and said, "Go. We'll handle things here."

Malek nodded. "I'll be back within a few hours. Make sure they have everything they need."

"Of course," Levin said.

"Seems like we just walked into something," Esmelle said, watching Malek join his sister and her mate.

"Yes, but we'll catch up as we go," Sabine said, heading toward the north wing. "We need maps and some blank parchment from Malek's office. I need someone to show me where that is."

"It's on the lower level, adjacent to Malek's quarters," Levin said, following behind her.

Sabine sent a small pulse of magic into the air. Snowdrop, one of the new pixies, immediately came to her side. She was a little younger than Blossom with long, silvery-white hair that floated around her face like a halo of moonlight. Her lavender and sky blue dress fluttered with the pulse of her wings.

In a melodious voice, Snowdrop said, "Blossom's overseeing the removal of the humans from Malek the Dragon's estate. Can I help you?"

Sabine doubted that was all Blossom was doing, but she'd have to worry about that later. "I need you to gather all the pixies who have knowledge about the locations where aderyan and fae captives are being held."

"Of course," she agreed. "I'll see to it immediately."

Levin winced. "Sabine, please tell me you're not going to do what I think you're going to do."

"Of course she is," Esmelle said. "And we're going to help her."

Sabine reached out and squeezed her hand. "I've missed you dearly, Esme."

"Right back at you."

"At least wait until Malek returns," Levin pleaded. "He'll skin me alive if anything happens to you."

"I'll wait as long as possible for Malek to return," Sabine said, entering the north wing. "However, I intend to arm myself with as much knowledge as possible so when the time comes to act, we're ready. I will not remain idle while people are suffering."

Turning to Rika, she asked, "You've developed a friendly relationship with the cook and with Azalia?"

Rika nodded. "What do you need?"

"See if you can find some sort of refreshments or treats for the pixies. They prefer items sweetened with honey."

"No problem," Rika said, walking over to a large crystal that was situated on an end table.

"You're back," Lyra exclaimed and leaped over the second-floor balcony with her wings spread. Aeron materialized and jumped into the air, catching the young girl before she could land.

"What have I told you about flying without Thalassa or myself present?"

Lyra stared at him. "But you were here, Aeron. You caught me!"

"Whoa," Esmelle said, staring at the aderyan. "How did— Where did—What in the world did we miss? Who are you?"

"Esme and Levin, this is Aeron and Lyra," Sabine said and gestured toward the second floor. "That's Thalassa. They've agreed to help us locate the last artifact."

Aeron tilted his head in greeting. "It's always a pleasure to meet one of Theoria's beloved forest guardians. We welcome you to the former Aderyan Aeries and wish you great bounty and calm winds."

Levin stared up at Thalassa before turning to Aeron. "Okay. Not what I was expecting, but Malek said to let you know your friends boarded the ship safely last night and departed at dawn. I left instructions with Fiona about where she could reach us when they return."

Aeron bowed his head. "Fiona is a true friend."

Thalassa descended the stairs and took Lyra from Aeron's arms. "My apologies for the disruption, Aderylin. She was enthusiastic about your return."

Sabine smiled. "It's all right. I trust you all had breakfast?"

Thalassa nodded. "We did."

"I had pastries!" Lyra said with a wide smile.

Sabine touched Lyra's hand and said, "So did I. They were delicious, weren't they?"

Lyra nodded. "Can we have them again?"

"We'll ask the cook," Sabine promised and turned to Levin. "Where is Malek's office?"

Levin sighed and gestured to a wooden door with a crystal inlay above it. "Through there."

Sabine pushed open the door, breathing in the smell of parchment, polished wood, and the achingly familiar scent of burned leaves she always associated with Malek. The walls were lined with vast, detailed maps depicting various regions throughout Aeslion. She paused in front of one of the largest maps, captivated by the intricate cartographic details. Enormous mountain ranges, winding rivers, and mysterious, uncharted territories were all marked with odd symbols and notes in Malek's elegant script. She ran her fingers over the area where Faerie was marked, reading his words describing the protections he believed were in place.

"How long have you been searching for the portal, Malek?" Sabine murmured.

"It looks like a long time," Esmelle said, studying the bookshelves. "He's got all sorts of texts about magic and the history of the gods. I've never seen most of these titles."

"A great number of books on those subjects were destroyed," Levin said. "Malek has been collecting these tomes for years, hoping to find references to the portal or their artifacts. His grandfather began the search. Malek picked it up once he was gone."

Sabine turned away from the map on the wall and trailed her fingers across the large, sturdy desk that dominated the center of the room. It was made from some sort of dark, polished wood that gleamed under the Faerie lanterns overhead. Navigation tools such as astrolabes, compasses, and sextants cluttered the surface, while stacks of scrolls and books were piled nearby. Bane was busy opening the drawers and inspecting the contents.

"It looks like he just walked away from his desk one day," Sabine said, picking up one of the scrolls. It appeared to be some sort of order confirmation for trade goods that was dated more than three years past.

"That's fairly accurate," Levin said. "Until now, no one has been allowed in here when Malek wasn't present. Azalia doesn't even allow the staff to clean."

Sabine placed the scroll back where she'd found it. Although Malek had given her leave to be here, she felt like they were all intruding in his private space. "None of the maps on the walls are of the Sky Cities. Do you know where he keeps those?"

"Over here," Levin said, walking over to a cabinet on the far wall. Inside were dozens of rolled parchments. Levin pulled out two of them and walked over to an empty table. He spread the first one out, using weighted anchor stones to hold the edges flat.

"The Sky Cities are comprised of different islands," Levin said, gesturing to the map. "Each island is under the control of at least three or more allied clans. For example, we're here." He tapped his finger on one of the midsize islands. "Only members of the Obsidian, Emerald, and Amethyst Clans currently have estates on Kavi. These three clans have been allied through marriage since before the portal was sealed."

"You're referring to Malek's parents?" Sabine asked.

Levin nodded. "And grandparents. His mother, Nymira, was formerly of the Emerald clan. Her brother now acts as head of that clan, while Nymira is considered part of the Obsidian Clan. Because the ties are so close, they are considered blood allies rather than political ones. Malek's maternal grandmother belongs to the Amethyst Clan, and they claim the northernmost part of Kavi."

Sabine turned to Aeron. "Are you familiar with any of these other islands?"

Aeron tapped on one of the largest islands. "I was born on Ishu, now under the dominion of the Topaz, Garnet, Gold, and Quartz clans. I spent more than three hundred years in captivity there before I was transferred to another prison." He pointed to a smaller island not far from Imenel. "This is Havaa, current home to the Ruby, Lapis Lazuli, and Jade Clans. It was from here that I made my escape, a handful of years after I was taken to their underground prison."

Sabine lifted her head, meeting Aeron's gaze. There were no words she could offer him to ease the suffering he'd endured. Placing her hand over his, she sent a gentle wave of her magic over him to recognize his strength and mental fortitude, and also to let him know he wasn't alone.

"We will not ask you to revisit past horrors, but any information you're willing to provide may help us save your people."

He inhaled sharply, staring at her hand over his. His wing brushed against her arm tentatively. When she didn't rebuff him, his shoulders relaxed and he turned his hand, interlacing their fingers together. "I will share with you what I can, Aderylin."

Bane studied the map with a frown. "We need an overlay. Does the dragon possess such supplies?"

Levin nodded and pulled out a drawer in the bottom of the cabinet. He withdrew a sheet of parchment that was nearly transparent.

Esmelle peered over his shoulder. "How in the world did they make parchment that looks like glass? Did they use magic?"

Placing the sheet over the map of the Sky Cities, Levin said, "It's a human skill, but I believe magic would work as well. The parchment is scraped as thin as possible and then soaked in rotten egg whites. It's then stretched like a regular parchment and allowed to dry."

Bane reached for some charcoal that was in a small dish on the table. He began scratching notes, identifying the dragon clans Aeron had already identified.

"How many fae and aderyan captives are being held on Ishu? What are the weaknesses of that island?"

Aeron was quiet for a long time. "While I was captive, there were at least fifteen winged aderyan bound in iron chains on the lowest level of the prison. I rarely saw more than a handful of wingless aderyan where I was held, but I believe there may have been forty or fifty on Ishu."

Sabine looked up at him. "Does iron affect you the same way it does the fae?"

Aeron shook his head. "No. As long as we have wings, we have access to some of our magic. Iron isn't pleasant and makes it harder to use, but it won't kill us. Most aderyan have their wings severed when they're extremely young, around Lyra's age. Those who survive the process become caretakers in the prison, while a select few are chosen as servants and permitted above ground to serve in the households. Those who retain their wings are called Gyved Skykeepers."

"Your magic is what keeps the islands afloat?" Sabine asked in surprise.

Aeron nodded. "The islands are chained together and bound by magic. As long as enough of us remain on certain islands, the dragons can keep the former Aderyan Aeries in the sky."

Bane nodded, making additional notes. "We'll need to know which islands are chained together, and where. We should be able to piece together the prison locations from that information."

Levin muttered a curse. "You can't be serious about this."

Esmelle and Sabine both whirled on him. Levin quickly held up his hands and said, "Look, I'm just saying you shouldn't take action based on speculation. Aeron was held in captivity for hundreds of years, right?"

Esmelle put her hands on her hips. "What's your point, Levin?"

"He wasn't around during the war. Anything he claims about dragon clans and prison locations may not be reliable. You're talking about possibly breaking clan alliances that have stood for centuries, simply based on guesswork. I think we should find out for certain. Give us some time to make quiet inquiries."

Sabine's power rose swiftly. "I will not stand idly by while my people are suffering."

"Your people?" Levin asked, arching a brow. "Since when did the Unseelie claim the aderyan as theirs?"

Sabine flung out her hand, power exploding from her fingertips in a shocking blast. Levin slammed into the far wall, knocking over several bookshelves filled with scrolls. She held him tightly, her magic coiling around him and cutting off his air.

"Do not presume to judge the breadth of my power, wyvern. You and your kind are the interlopers here. That you have impris-

oned the fae and the aderyan is a wrong that will no longer be tolerated."

"Sabine, stop! You're killing him!" Esmelle shouted, her voice distant.

"He should not challenge our Aderylin," Aeron snapped, his wings flaring in warning. "We are honored to be claimed as hers."

"Sabine, please," Esmelle said, tears filling her eyes. "This isn't you! Bane, do something!"

At Esmelle's plea, Sabine hesitated and tried to pull back on her power. Lachlina's fury pounded at her temples, demanding she make an example of this wyvern. Her hand trembled as she fought against the goddess's hold.

"You owe me, witch," Bane snarled. He grabbed Sabine around the waist, threw her over his shoulder, and raced out of the room before anyone could object.

CHAPTER 31

alek's boots echoed on the polished marble floor of the Great Hall. The room was bathed in a warm, flickering glow from the dragonfire urns placed strategically throughout, their flames casting dancing shadows across the stone surfaces. The walls were adorned with tapestries and detailed murals depicting dragons in flight and battle, each thread and brushstroke contributing to the saga of his ancestral legacy.

As he strode through the hall, Malek acknowledged the wyverns standing guard with a curt nod. They responded instantly, snapping to attention with a crisp precision that spoke of rigorous training and respect, their fists pressed firmly against their chests above the Obsidian Clan crest on their uniforms.

Levin's voice slipped into his thoughts. *"Malek, we have a problem."*

"What's wrong? Is Sabine all right?"

"She damn near killed me!" Levin roared, the sound reverberating through Malek's head. *"Esme was practically in tears, begging her to stop. She went all golden glowy and destroyed part of*

your office. She was shouting at me in some weird language that almost sounded like ancient Greater Dragon. Her voice nearly seared my skin off. According to the aderyan, I challenged her authority."

Malek stopped short.

Kaia turned to him and asked, "Is everything all right?"

He held up his hand, asking her to wait a moment. She and Thom exchanged glances but remained silent.

"And did you?" Malek asked. *"Did you challenge her authority?"*

"What the hell does that matter?"

"Levin, answer the question. I need to know what prompted it and what stopped it."

"Fine," Levin grumbled. *"Yes. I may have poked her a bit, but in my defense, I was trying to prevent her from running off and launching a full-scale assault on one of our possible allies."*

Malek inhaled sharply. *"Tell me she didn't leave, Levin."*

"No, I suitably distracted her. She said something along the lines of the aderyan being hers to protect. I asked when the Unseelie started claiming them as theirs. That's when she tried to kill me. Bane grabbed her and ran out of your study like his ass was on fire. Aeron followed them. Esme thinks they're in your room, and Bane's talking her down. At least, we don't hear shouting or explosions anymore. You're welcome, by the way. Even Esme's mad at me."

"That's because you're a damned idiot," Malek said with a growl. *"I warned you to treat Sabine with kid gloves. Bane wouldn't have let her run into danger, unless there was no other option. She's trying to keep that so-called goddess under control. When you challenge her in such a manner or threaten those she feels the need to protect, it gives Lachlina a foothold to use Sabine's magic."*

"That's what Esme said before she threw a plant at my head." Levin was quiet for a moment. *"Malek, you can't bring her around our people. You have too many enemies who will attempt to*

provoke a reaction from her, in order to get to you. I understand Sabine doesn't know me all that well, but I'm not exaggerating when I say she nearly killed me. I've never felt power like that before."

"Don't you think I know that?" Malek squeezed his eyes shut and rubbed his temples. All of this had started when she'd begun absorbing the power from the artifacts. *"Just... stay out of her way. If Bane needs me to return, he'll get a message to you. In the meantime, see if Esme is willing to make her some calming tea or something that will help her sleep. There should be supplies in the conservatory."*

He felt Levin's quiet acknowledgement before he severed the communication thread. Malek opened his eyes and met his sister's concerned gaze. He shook his head and said, "Just some minor trouble back at the estate. I'll handle it when I return."

"Is Sabine all right?" Kaia asked.

Malek nodded. "Yes. I think Levin's ego is a bit bruised though."

Kaia laughed. "Serves him right for stirring up trouble when she has a demon looking out for her."

Malek made a noncommittal noise, unwilling to clear up the misconception. They continued through the sprawling Great Hall, stopping at a set of wooden doors that marked the entrance to his father's study. He pushed open the doors, which creaked slightly under their weight and revealed a vast, dimly lit room lined with bookshelves filled with ancient tomes and artifacts.

The air was rich with the scent of old leather, wood polish, and the faint, comforting trace of dragonfire smoke that always spoke of home. Soft, deep rugs covered the floor, muffling his footsteps as he entered, while the gentle crackle of a fire in the fireplace added a soothing undertone to the room.

Darius Rish'dan stood near the fireplace, his imposing figure silhouetted against the flickering flames. The light highlighted the silver streaks in his otherwise dark hair and the stark scar near his golden eye. Nymira Myst'ald sat in a large, ornate chair facing her husband, her dark wavy hair spilling over her shoulders. Both turned as Malek entered, their expressions transforming from intense discussion to warmth.

"Malek," Nymira said, her voice a mixture of joy and reproach, as if chiding him for his delay in greeting her. She rose swiftly, moving across the room with a grace that belied her fierceness and embraced him tightly.

"It's about time you returned to us," Darius said, his every movement resonating with the power and authority of his position, but his smile was genuine as he clapped Malek on the shoulder.

"We were beginning to wonder whether you'd received our messages," Nymira said, motioning for him to take a seat. She pressed her hand against the crystal summoning device and then sat in her chair across from him, arranging the skirt of her emerald green gown around her.

"I haven't received any messages," Malek said with a frown. "When and how were they sent?"

Kaia sat on the edge of their father's desk, swinging her legs back and forth, while Thom stood beside her. Darius narrowed his eyes on Thom, the drake's presence an obvious sore spot. Apparently, they hadn't resolved their differences while Malek had been away.

"Oh, we started sending them regularly around six weeks ago," Nymira said and then frowned at her daughter. "Wouldn't you be more comfortable on the sofa beside your brother?"

"Nope."

Malek turned to his father. "Did you use the merchants to relay the messages like we discussed?"

"Who do you take me for, boy? Of course we sent them by merchant. That was what we agreed upon." Darius glared at Thom. "Kaia, why would you bring your wingless drake into my study? He's likely to piss on my rug."

"He's housebroken, Da," Kaia retorted.

Thom snickered and leaned against the desk. "It's good to see you too, Darius."

"A chair then, Kaia," Nymira suggested. "It's unseemly to sit on the furniture."

"Aren't a chair and sofa considered furniture?"

Nymira sighed in exasperation. "Darius, do something."

Darius growled. "Since when do any of the women in this family listen to a damn thing I say?"

A knock at the door interrupted them. One of his mother's servants entered, an older woman named Tivaly who had been working at the estate for nearly as long as he could remember. She had a few more gray hairs than when he'd last seen her, but the twinkle in her brown eyes was a familiar sight. She pushed a tea tray into the room and smiled warmly at him.

"It's good to see you again, Lord Malek. Have you brought that wyvern rogue home with you?"

Malek stood and hugged the older woman. "I've missed you, Tivaly. Levin's at my estate currently, but I'm sure you'll see him soon enough. You're doing well?"

"A few aches and pains, but I've still got quite a bit of life in these old bones yet."

Nymira frowned. "No. I simply won't hear you talk about getting older. You're to go and rest until you're feeling young again. Thom, help her with the cart."

Thom rolled the cart the rest of the way into the room,

eliciting another growl from Darius as he nearly collided with the older dragon's boots.

Tivaly chuckled. "Very well, Lady Nymira. I'll take my leave." She snapped her fingers at Kaia. "And you! If you can't get off the desk and sit like a proper dragon, you have no business getting into the cookies."

Kaia eyed the tea tray. "What kind of cookies?"

"Smoked vanilla bean, your favorite."

Kaia leaped off the desk and sat next to Malek. She started to reach for the cookies, but Tivaly clucked her tongue. "Pour the tea, and be sure to serve your mother first."

"Yes, Tivaly," Kaia said demurely, her eyes focused on the covered dishes.

Malek laughed as Tivaly headed out of the room. "It's nice to see some things haven't changed."

"Shut it, big brother," Kaia said, pouring the tea into tiny cups.

"That woman is a treasure," Nymira said, lifting her steaming cup and taking a sip. "Now, where were we?"

Malek accepted the cup from his sister and said, "I didn't receive your messages. In fact, I haven't received any communication from the Sky Cities in nearly a year. My return was purely coincidental."

Nymira lowered her cup. "How is that possible?"

"I believe our network has been compromised," Malek said. "Levin departed from Razadon by ship more than a month ago and headed here, stopping at each of our designated message centers. There was nothing waiting for him. Due to circumstances outside our control, I flew the majority of the way, coming from a different direction. As I approached Imenel, I was attacked by a young squadron of wyverns."

Darius's cup shattered in his hand, spilling tea all over the rug. Nymira stood, a pillar of fury and rage.

"Which clan dared strike against us?" Nymira demanded.

"Unknown," Malek said. "There were a total of five wyverns. Four were eliminated, but one managed to escape. Levin and I both inspected the bodies, but they weren't familiar to either of us."

Darius began to pace, his long black cape swirling around his legs. "This will not stand. Someone thinks they can attack my heir and destroy our clan in one fell swoop?"

"Swooping is bad," Thom said, absently scratching at his neck.

Nymira held up her hand for silence. "There are only a handful of clans who would dare make such a move, even covertly. If our messages recalling Malek were blocked, it's clear they are attempting to curtail our efforts to control the portal. It would seem we have spies in our midst or among our closest allies."

Malek nodded. "So I assumed. That brings me to the concerns about the portal."

Nymira sat in her chair and leaned forward, her hands gripping the arms tightly. "You've located a means to control it?"

"Not exactly," Malek said. "Five artifacts were crafted to serve as portal keys. Each one contained a vast amount of power and the potential to unlock the portal.

"The first was a goblet infused with fae magic, entrusted to them after the portal was sealed. The second was a pearl gifted to the merfolk and taken to their underwater realm. The third, a crystal hammer, was left in the care of the dwarves. The fourth was a curved blade guarded by the demon king in the deepest part of the underworld."

Darius stopped pacing and looked sharply at Malek, his hands curling into fists at his sides.

Malek continued, "I believe the final artifact is some kind of feather or quill that was entrusted to the aderyan."

Thom frowned and scratched at his arm, which was beginning to turn red. "Even if we could locate some of those items, we no longer have any dragons capable of retrieving the artifact from the merfolk. The entire Aquamarine Clan was eliminated before the portal was sealed."

"He's right," Kaia said, reaching for Thom's hand. "Not to mention the number of our people who might die if we attempted to breach the underworld."

Nymira studied Malek, a small smile playing upon her lips. "No, I don't believe things are quite as dire as your brother makes them sound. You've found a way to acquire the portal keys, haven't you?"

Malek nodded. "Yes. We've managed to acquire all the artifacts except for the one gifted to the aderyan. I was told the answers I seek can be found among my own kind."

Kaia stared at him. "That's why you have Bane with you! He helped you retrieve the artifact from the demon king, didn't he?"

"Who's Bane?" Nymira asked.

"A demon," Thom volunteered. Malek shot him a dirty look. Bringing up demons around Darius Rish'dan was always a dangerous undertaking.

Darius's power filled the room as he roared, "A demon? You've brought a demon to the Sky Cities?"

"I never thought your father and I would agree on anything," Thom muttered, rubbing at his neck again.

"Shhh," Kaia whispered. "Trust me. This isn't a bonding moment. And stop scratching. What's wrong with you?"

"Darius, that's enough," Nymira said, rising to face her husband. "We agreed to send our son on this mission. If he's brought a demon here, it's because necessity demanded it. You knew we would require outside assistance to control the portal."

"Not from a demon!" Darius thundered. "It was bad

enough we agreed to allow him to recruit one of the pointed-eared tree huggers, but a demon is unacceptable!"

"Here we go," Kaia said, leaning back and nibbling on a cookie.

Malek stood. "If you are so blinded by the past and your hatred of the demons and fae, then don't expect them to come to our aid. You have the audacity to stand here and disrespect people who have survived insurmountable odds—and demand they help us? It's no wonder Elisa refused to step foot within these walls."

"Do not bring that fae bitch into this," Darius growled. "This is my home, and I'll speak how I wish!"

"Then I won't be part of it," Malek said.

"Both of you, calm down," Nymira said. "Darius, you're a scale away from shifting. If you knock the roof off this house one more time, you're sleeping outside for the next month. Malek, sit down and don't upset your sister. She needs to conserve her strength."

Malek didn't budge. He crossed his arms over his chest and glared at his father.

"SIT DOWN!" Nymira shouted, the walls trembling from her power. A thin sheen of dust drifted from the ceiling.

Both Malek and Darius immediately sat, eyeing the rafters warily. His father often had difficulty controlling his inner dragon, but his mother's tirades were legendary. She'd been known to take out an entire city block with one sweep of her tail.

Kaia offered Malek a cookie. "Trust me, cookies help."

"It's like I'm ten years old again," Malek said, taking a bite of the crisp vanilla wafer.

Kaia took a bite of her own. "See? Just keep eating. If you chew loud enough, it muffles the shouting. Just make sure you brush the ceiling dust off first."

"I want a cookie," a voice whispered near his ear. Malek

turned his head slightly and caught sight of a tiny ladybug on his shoulder. He squeezed his eyes shut, wondering why he was even surprised anymore. Bane's continued threats about eating Blossom suddenly made a lot of sense.

He discreetly pinched off a crumb and dropped it on his shoulder. Blossom hacked and coughed, spitting it out. "Blech. It tastes like smoke!"

"Did you hear something?" Kaia asked.

Malek shook his head. "Have another cookie."

Nymira picked up her teacup again, sipping daintily. "Now then. Where were we?"

"I want to know how this demon is able to stay above ground," Darius said, drumming his fingers on the arm of his chair. "Their kind have never been able to abide the surface without access to a host. If that's changed, we need to address these security concerns at once."

"Bane is an anomaly," Malek said, putting his half-eaten cookie back on the plate. Kaia quickly reached out and swiped it. He ignored her and continued, "As far as I'm aware, the demons aren't planning an invasion. The artifact that had been in their possession was given up as part of a trade. There won't be any retaliation."

"Good," Nymira said, placing her teacup on the table beside her. "You believe the only remaining key was once in possession of the aderyan?"

Malek nodded. "Yes. Have you heard any rumors about a magical quill or feather?"

"No," Darius said, making a fist and thumping it on the arm of his chair. "I suggest we focus on ensuring the demons haven't infiltrated the Sky Cities. Where is this demon now? What safeguards are in place to prevent him from learning our defenses and reporting back to our enemies?"

Nymira cleared her throat. "Have some tea, dear. Tivaly brought extra cups. She knows your temper well."

Darius scowled at her and made no move toward the pot. She shot him a warning look, and he grudgingly grabbed an empty cup. Kaia grinned and poured the steaming liquid into it. Malek couldn't help but wonder how many sets of dishes his family had gone through since he'd left.

"The demon is back at my estate," Malek said, knowing his father wouldn't abandon this line of questioning without some assurance. "I've fought side by side with him. While his goals don't always align with mine, I trust him to guard what I value most in this world."

Darius harrumphed and drummed his fingers on the armrest.

"Going back to your earlier question, I haven't heard about a magical feather, but the war resulted in a great deal of chaos and destruction. Many of the aderyan treasures were looted or destroyed," Nymira said, picking up her cup once again.

She took a delicate sip before continuing, "Most items of power—like these artifacts—are impossible to destroy, unless the magic within them is somehow removed or transferred. If you believe the key is still within the Sky Cities, another clan may be in possession of it. Whether or not they know its true value is another matter entirely."

The ladybug had crept off his shoulder and was now working her way down Malek's sleeve. He discreetly pretended to pluck at a loose thread and slid the ladybug into the palm of his hand. Leaning back, he stretched and deposited her back on his shoulder.

"Need tea," Blossom whispered and coughed. "Bad smoke taste."

"I swear I heard something," Kaia said with a frown.

"Which clans still keep aderyan captives?" Malek asked quickly, trying to distract her. "If our people don't know anything about the location of the artifact, the aderyan might."

Kaia's brow furrowed. "What are you talking about? They're gone."

Neither Nymira nor Darius responded. Nymira stared into her teacup with a frown, while Darius glared at the crackling fire.

Malek had witnessed their behavior enough to recognize the signs of his parents having a rather intense and heated private discussion.

"The aderyan aren't gone," Malek said, taking the opportunity to scoop Blossom off his shoulder and deposit her beside his teacup. "I've recently learned many have been in captivity all this time. I need to know where I can find them."

Kaia stared at their parents in shock. "Mum? Da? By the ether, is Malek telling the truth? Are the aderyan still alive?"

Nymira's gaze sharpened on Malek. "How did you come by this knowledge?"

"In my travels, I met some aderyan who managed to escape from the Sky Cities," Malek said, glancing down at his teacup. The ladybug hovered precariously on the edge, her wings fluttering wildly. "They'd heard of the artifact and suggested the remaining captives might have insight into its location."

Before he could react, Blossom fell into his tea with a small splash. He quickly picked up the cup, trying to fish her out with his fingers.

"Is something wrong with your tea?" Nymira asked.

"Uh, no," Malek said, reaching for a spoon. "I must have dropped a crumb or something."

Thom scratched at his neck. "I've heard rumors about the Topaz Clan having some sort of underground prison on Ishu."

"You never told me that," Kaia said with a frown.

Thom shrugged. "I thought they were just stories. I've only been there a handful of times. I saw a couple of fae, but never anyone with wings."

"Get another cup if a crumb bothers you so much, Malek," Nymira said with a sigh.

"Got it." Malek scooped Blossom from the cup and deposited her beside it, angling the spoon to hide her from view. "I believe most aderyan captives have their wings severed. They look much like the fae without them. I'm now wondering if the captive fae I've seen in the past were really aderyan."

"The Topaz Clan are supposedly one of our allies, but I'm now questioning the wisdom of that," Kaia said, turning toward her parents. "We should be able to just ask them."

"You will do no such thing," Darius ordered and stood. He began pacing the length of the room, his power tightly coiled and beginning to build. "I will not risk fracturing our alliances or bring our clan under scrutiny by the Council on a wild wyvern chase. If, and only if, no other option presents itself, then your mother and I will determine a course of action."

Malek arched his brow. "Since when did the Obsidian Clan begin bowing to the whims of the Council or any other clan?"

"When your grandfather decided to spit in the face of our sacrifices and claim a fae captive as a mate," Darius snarled. "When your sister took a wingless drake as hers, diluting the very magic needed to ensure the survival of my grandchild!"

"I love him!" Kaia shouted, rising to her feet. "Thom being a drake has nothing to do with the lack of magic we're facing. Dozens of dragons and wyverns over the last thirty years haven't been able to transfer their unborn into protective eggs."

"We are not having this discussion again," Nymira said,

her green eyes beginning to glow as her temper built. "Thom is part of this family and shall be treated as such. We will make some discreet inquiries at the gala to see if we can determine who is responsible for the attack on Malek and whether any of our allies know anything about this feather. However, locating the last key is only part of the problem."

Nymira turned to Malek and asked, "Have you found a fae with enough power to combine the keys? Or discovered how we can access the portal's location?"

Malek held his father's gaze. "I *have* found someone, but I will not expose her to conversations like this. She's currently back at my estate and protected by my strongest wards, a demon I trust, and all those under my command. Until I'm confident she'll be treated with the respect she's due, she won't take a single step inside this estate. And make no mistake—if that respect is not provided, we will both leave the Sky Cities permanently."

Kaia made a strangled noise. She sat and reached for another cookie. Thom rocked back on his heels and stared up at the ceiling.

Nymira's hand fluttered to her mouth. "Oh, Malek. That's why you activated the wards to prevent us from entering. Did you think we would not welcome her as part of this family?"

Thom held up three fingers and began counting down. "Three… two… one…"

"You've claimed a fucking fae as a mate?" Darius roared, the walls trembling from the force of his power. In a blinding flash of light, the roof exploded. A majestic obsidian dragon cut through the air like a knife, while ceiling plaster rained down on them.

"My cookies!" Kaia exclaimed and then burst into tears.

CHAPTER 32

"Well that went marvelously," Nymira said, putting her hands on her hips and staring up at the sky. "The humans are making a bloody fortune doing repairs for us."

A squadron of wyvern guards burst into the room, quickly assessed the situation and then moved to set up watch points on the roof and within the room.

A tiny ladybug landed on Malek's shoulder and sneezed. "I think dragons are more dramatic than pixies."

"You might be right," Malek agreed.

"Of course I'm right," Nymira said, shaking her head. "Thom, take Kaia home to get some rest. She doesn't need to be here for all this."

Kaia sniffled. "I'm fine."

"You are not fine," Nymira said and gestured to the messy room. "None of this is *fine*. Captain Fandrin, when the workers arrive to begin the repairs, I want them to first construct a large lean-to off the side of the house. Lord Darius can sleep in it until I decide to let him back in, or when the repairs are complete."

She paused, her gaze sweeping over the destruction again. "And instruct the workers to paint murals of large silver trees on each of the walls. And should the message not be clear enough, take out the fireplace and stick in a large potted plant. No. I want dozens of plants everywhere. Turn his study into a garden with a fountain of a fae pissing on his chair."

She lifted the hem of her emerald gown and stormed out of the room with her head held high.

Captain Fandrin winced and said, "Please tell me she was kidding."

Malek chuckled. "Let's start with the lean-to and go from there."

"Come on, Kaia," Thom said, taking her hand. "I'm sure Tivaly has more cookies. She always sets some aside for you."

Kaia nodded and let Thom lead her away. Malek followed them in search of his mother. He found her in the kitchens, ordering the staff to serve Lord Darius his meals outside.

"Find a thundertusk water bowl for all I care," Nymira said, waving her hands. "I've seen how large those things are. Toss in a couple of raw steaks—No. Wait. Throw in handfuls of edible leaves instead."

"Salad, Lady Nymira?" one of the cooks asked with wide eyes. "You want us to feed *salad* to a *dragon*? In a trough?"

"Yes, salad. Lots and lots of salad. Maybe a few berries. Which ones are bitter?"

"Should I tell her?" Blossom whispered.

"No."

Taking pity on his parents' staff, Malek cleared his throat and said, "Mother, perhaps you could walk with me back to my estate. I had a few other matters I wanted to discuss."

Nymira turned to him and blinked. "What? Oh. Of course, dear. I have a few more things to handle first."

Malek grinned and took his mother's arm, walking with

her toward the Great Hall. "I have a feeling Father isn't going to be returning for a while. You have plenty of time to make him miserable."

The cook mouthed a silent thank you as they passed.

"I suppose," Nymira relented with a sigh. "Oh, Malek. It pains me to know you were reluctant to tell us you'd taken a mate. Will you tell me about her?"

"Her name is Sabine," Malek said, leading his mother down the front steps. At his gesture, a wyvern guard patrol followed them at a discreet distance. "I hadn't intended to introduce her to anyone yet, but Kaia kept banging on my wards and refused to go away. I was hoping to give Sabine some time to adjust to my home before meeting my family. It took several months before she finally agreed to come here, and we can be a little overwhelming on a good day. I didn't want her running for safety before a single day had passed."

Nymira sighed. "That's understating the matter. I've had to replace that ceiling three times since you've been gone." She stopped walking and turned to face him. "You care for her deeply?"

"More than anything."

"And she cares equally for you? Even without a mate bond?"

Malek nodded. "I saved her with dragonfire after she was struck with an iron bolt. She's opened her heart to me, completely and without reservations. It may not be the same as what you share with Father, but there's a strength in the bond between us that goes beyond anything I can describe." He touched his chest. "I feel her here, like a second heartbeat. She's always with me, even when we're apart. She feels the same."

Nymira stared at him in stunned shock. "That shouldn't be possible. What you are describing is a mate bond and an anchor point, but it should only go one way. You're sure she's fae?"

Malek laughed and continued walking. "Yes, Mother. I've experienced her magic and seen her with glamour and without."

Nymira frowned. "Perhaps we're not as incompatible as I believed. Your grandfather never shared such a bond with Elisa. I suppose their beginnings had something to do with that. How did you meet your Sabine?"

"I was following up on a lead in Akros. She'd been living there for a number of years when our paths crossed. She didn't know I was a dragon at first, and I believed she only had some fae ancestry. We've had quite a few trials to overcome so far, but the past few months with her have been among the happiest of my life."

"The mate bond has never been dependent on time being a factor," Nymira said with a small smile. "It can fall into place within a matter of days, or take years to develop. Sometimes it never happens at all, despite what some may wish. I'm pleased you found someone you care so deeply about, but I fear you still have more obstacles to face—ones far greater than your father. I hope you're both prepared for that."

"I'm aware," Malek said, staring up at the Obsidian Clan wyverns patrolling overhead. "In fact, that's one of the things I wished to discuss with you. After the wyvern attack, I decided to venture into Imenel under the guise of a human. I was hoping to learn something about the clan who attacked me."

"Did you?"

"The gates were under unusually heavy guard, both human and wyvern. We decided it would be best to separate to avoid scrutiny. Sabine and Bane, the demon accompanying us, went over the wall while I escorted Sabine's human ward, Rika, through the main gate."

"You truly trust this demon with your mate's protection?"

Malek nodded. "He would give his life for hers."

"I trust your judgment," Nymira said. "However, the Council may see things differently should they learn of his presence. They've tightened all patrols around Imenel, preparing for a possible attack by enemy forces. We were told an advance scouting party would likely target the city any day. Apparently, Faerie has declared a new Unseelie queen. She's been quietly amassing armies with the intention of targeting the Sky Cities. She may have even recruited one or more of our own as spies."

Malek halted abruptly. "How exactly did the Council come by this knowledge?"

"A missive from the Seelie King with his seal affixed. He claims while he has no love for us, he would not see our ceasefire broken by Unseelie treachery."

Malek bit back a curse. "I can't go into details just yet, but the new Unseelie queen has no intention of setting her sights on the Sky Cities."

"What have you heard, Malek?"

"She *has* been forging alliances, but not with the intention of targeting us. This is simply internal Faerie politics at play."

Nymira frowned. "No one among our clan would dare question your word, but this missive was shared among all the clan leaders. Without more information or some sort of proof to take before the Council, I'm afraid your mate and the demon will be in grave danger. Even you may find yourself under some scrutiny, Malek."

"That explains Uncle Emanthir's warning."

Nymira regarded him with surprise. "What? You saw Emanthir? When?"

"When we were in Imenel," Malek admitted. "He sensed

Sabine's magic. I told him I was investigating a matter on behalf of our clan. He wants an accounting by the end of the day from Father."

"Oh, Malek," Nymira said with a sigh. "I'm afraid you won't be able to keep Sabine's presence quiet. Given this missive and Emanthir's knowledge of her, it would be best if you met this head on. I'll handle Emanthir, but you'll need to bring Sabine to the gala and introduce her as your mate. There's no other option."

"I suspected as much," Malek said, taking his mother's arm again.

"The timing of this couldn't be worse," Nymira said. "We need to be focused on controlling the portal, not on the possibility of an attack that may never come. It's still early in Kaia's pregnancy, but she'll continue to weaken as the child grows. Soon, neither one will have enough magic to sustain them."

"Kaia mentioned you had someone brewing tonics that were supposed to strengthen her magic?"

Nymira nodded. "I recalled you mentioning a powerful witch who had crafted the medallion to hide your identity. Tivaly has been acting as an intermediary, purchasing the tonics in exchange for rare herbs and gemstones. I don't know if they're helping with her magic, but Kaia seems stronger after she drinks them."

"I was hoping you'd found someone other than Idola," Malek said. "I stopped to see her on my way to Imenel. When Idola realized Sabine was fae, she tried to kill her."

Nymira's hand flew to her chest. "Malek, you didn't."

"No," Malek said. "I nearly did, but Sabine stopped me. I banished Idola from the Sky Cities instead."

"Then for that, I'm grateful to your mate," Nymira said quietly. "Malek, you have a right to vengeance for what she

attempted to do, but if Idola's tonics can help your sister..."
Her voice trailed off as though unable to continue.

"I know. With your permission, I'll arrange to have a squadron of clan wyverns track Idola down and bring her to the Sky Cities. She's to remain under guard at your estate. If Idola can keep Kaia strong for the duration of her pregnancy, then I will consider lifting the banishment and allow her to return home. However, if she raises a hand against Sabine again, she will die."

Nymira nodded. "I'll send our fastest fliers to coordinate with Levin."

Malek reached for Levin with his thoughts and said, *"You should be hearing from Captain Fandrin shortly about retrieving Idola and her partner. She's to stay under guard at my parents' estate for the time being. I'm on my way back now. Has Sabine awakened?"*

"No. Everything's been quiet, but I'm going to need to move in."

"What?"

"It was your idea to have Esme find tea ingredients in your conservatory. Now she's fallen in love with your garden and your conservatory. She claims there are plants in there she's never seen before and is refusing to come out. Since there's no hope of evicting her and keeping my scales intact, I'm putting you on notice that we're moving in. Today. Right now."

Malek bit back a grin. *"There might be some bags of potting soil you can sleep on."*

"Fuck you, Malek. Just for that, I'm telling Esme she can have her pick of whichever rooms she wants. Maybe the whole damn guest wing."

"If that's what makes her happy. Sabine will be thrilled to have Esme living so close."

"Right. You have a house full of peculiar guests. What are two more? Although, I'm beginning to think the aderyan are the oddest of all."

"In what way?"

"The little girl knew when Sabine had fallen asleep even though she wasn't in the same room. She insisted on going into your bedroom to keep watch, but Thalassa said Aeron was already watching. When Esme asked what that meant, Thalassa said one of their purposes was to watch over their Aderylin while they slept or dreamwalked. Apparently, they can see Sabine's dreams."

Malek frowned, not liking the way that sounded. *"We'll have to talk more about this later. We're approaching the estate now, and I need to speak with my mother about another matter."*

After severing the communication thread with Levin, Malek turned his attention back to his mother. Something she'd said earlier in his father's study had been bothering him.

"How much do you know about transferring power from one item to another?" Malek asked, wondering if there was a way to separate Lachlina's magic from Sabine.

"You're referring to the portal artifacts?"

Malek nodded.

"Unfortunately, very little," Nymira admitted. "The portal artifacts were created by the Tuatha Dé. Like our magic, theirs is not compatible with lesser creatures unless it is diluted, or the recipient represents an anchor point. I believe that's why the magic used to seal the portal had to be broken up and scattered among the various races."

"You're suggesting the different races act as an anchor point for each type of magic it contains?"

Nymira nodded. "I believe so. Once all the artifacts are brought together, a fae with enough magic should hopefully be able to bind them together long enough to unlock the portal. They were among the first of Aeslion's children and their magic is most similar to the Tuatha Dé. It will be a dangerous undertaking though. Even the most powerful of fae would likely only be able to combine such magic for a few moments before being overwhelmed."

Malek frowned, suspecting they were missing something. Sabine had been able to absorb the power from each artifact immediately, allowing her to draw upon it at will. Granted, there was a steep learning curve, and she still wasn't as comfortable using foreign magic as her own abilities. Other than Lachlina's influence increasing, Sabine didn't appear to be suffering any ill effects at all.

"You don't believe one person would be able to harness the power contained in multiple keys longer than a few minutes?"

Nymira stopped and turned to face him, her expression one of alarm. "What are you suggesting, Malek? Do you believe such an entity still exists on this side of the portal?"

Malek hesitated. "I believe it's within the realm of possibility."

"Then hope that's not the case, because if the Tuatha Dé have found a way to still exist on this side of the Veil—or worse, found a way to travel through it without our knowledge—then all our people are doomed."

"I don't understand," Malek said. "How could one Tuatha Dé merit our destruction?"

"Because without the portal being reopened to us, the delicate balance of this world has been sundered. We cannot exist in the same space as a Tuatha Dé without a tie to the ether. Their base of power has always been the land, and they will slowly shift the magic away from us. While they grow stronger, we shall continue to grow weaker until all hope for our people is lost."

"Opening the portal would change that?"

"Yes, but we would once again find ourselves drawn into a war without an end." Nymira sighed. "While being cut off from the ether has been painful beyond imagining, it has been a true joy watching my children grow without the threat of war hanging over their heads."

"Is there no way to make peace with the Tuatha Dé?"

Nymira laughed, but it was bitter and hollow. "No, my son. We envy humans because their memories are short, while ours last for eons. Each death has only deepened the divide. We may need one another to survive, but neither side will rest until the other is destroyed."

"You've never spoken of this before," Malek said with a frown. "What started the war in the first place?"

"A mistake," Nymira said softly. "A terrible mistake."

Malek remained silent, waiting for his mother to continue.

After a moment, she sighed and said, "The Tuatha Dé are creators. They would craft such beauty into their worlds that even the most stoic among us would weep in wonder. When those worlds became too large, or life grew unsustainable because the bloom of magic had overgrown, we descended upon the land and purged the excess from it. Then the land might thrive again, and the cycle would begin anew."

Malek nodded. "Balance and harmony."

"Yes," Nymira said, slowing as they approached his estate. "It was common practice for us to hoard some of the priceless treasures from the worlds we cleansed, as payment for maintaining the balance. Thalion was a world still in its infancy, and it promised to be richer and more full of wonders than any we had seen before. Some of our kind descended too early and discovered wealth beyond imagining. One of the greater dragons became enchanted with a daughter of Thalion and decided to claim her for himself."

Malek winced, knowing where this was going. "What happened?"

"She became enchanted with him as well and urged him to remain part of Thalion—with her. He did, but his presence disrupted the balance so dramatically, it ended her life far too soon. She did not have enough magic to sustain him, and he could not replenish hers. In his rage, he set fire to the world. When the Tuatha Dé realized what he had done, they struck down his clan and began barring us from their worlds."

"And we didn't take that well, did we?"

Nymira shook her head. "We were proud and arrogant, but the Tuatha Dé were no less so. Even worlds in need of cleansing were denied to us, and they sought to starve us of the magic we needed to survive. We began forcing our way into worlds, even ones such as Aeslion which were unripe and should not have been harvested."

"That's how our family became trapped here?"

Nymira nodded. "We answered a call from our allies. They had broken into Aeslion, but the creators of this world had defended their children well. We found armies here where none were expected. The fae lured us in with their beauty and magic, hypnotizing us into complacency. Aderyan attacked from the skies, forcing us to the ground. Hordes of demons ascended from the deepest parts of the underworld to strike as we landed. Those of us who breathed the oceans found only the wrath of the merfolk. Not even the mountains were safe from the ferocity of the dwarves."

"Why have you never told me this until now?" Malek asked, staring at the flickering glow of the wards surrounding his estate.

"Much of our past is painful to recall," Nymira said quietly. "I've never wanted you or Kaia to look upon us and feel ashamed of your legacy. I saw that in both your eyes earlier when you thought we'd ignored the plight of the aderyan captives. We've made mistakes, Malek. Far more than you can possibly fathom. While your father and I have tried to remedy them when we can, the scales will never balance completely."

She took his hands and said, "I'm proud of you, Malek. Your mate is fortunate to have found such a fierce protector who would face down his own father and clan leader in her defense. I hope you'll give me the opportunity to welcome her to our family when both of you are ready."

Malek kissed his mother's cheek. "We'll both see you at the gala tomorrow night, if not before then."

Nymira beamed a smile at him and said, "If your Sabine requires a gown, send a message to Tivaly. There's a talented new seamstress who can create wonders on short notice."

"I'll keep that in mind," Malek said, motioning for the wyvern guards. They pressed their fists over the crests on their uniforms and surrounded the Lady of the Obsidian Clan in a protective formation.

Nymira huffed and said, "Guards? Really? What do you take me for? I could toss every one of you off the island with a sneeze."

"Yes, Lady Nymira," one of the wyverns said. "Your fierceness is legendary."

"You will not assuage me with flattery, Lieutenant. I know your mother. She would be downright horrified if she knew you came to work with a rumpled uniform. I demand you take it off this instant and have one of the humans iron it, or your poor mother will be the laughing stock of the entire island. And you, Sergeant, I hear you snickering. Not terribly prudent of you, especially since just the other day, your mother told me..."

Malek grinned as she berated the wyverns all the way back down the path. No one could ever accuse his mother of being meek.

"I like her," Blossom announced, transforming back into a pixie. "If I'm going to be a dragon, I want her to teach me."

Malek chuckled. "I'm not sure the world could handle that."

He temporarily lowered the ward around his front entrance and climbed the steps, feeling the warmth flare behind him as it sealed shut.

"Why don't you check on the other pixies? I need to speak with Sabine in private."

Blossom gave him a salute and said, "Okay. I'll fill her in on all the things you forget to tell her later."

"Uh, Blossom, maybe you should—" he began, but it was too late. She'd already disappeared into the garden. He shook his head, not recalling Elisa's pixies ever causing this much trouble.

Malek headed for the north wing. The door to the conservatory was open, and he could hear Esmelle instructing Rika on the best way to harvest certain leaves. He glanced inside his office and stopped short, staring at the toppled bookcases and parchment strewn over the floor.

Levin was picking up scattered maps and glanced up as he entered. "Believe it or not, this is actually an improvement. She knocked over three bookshelves. And I don't know how your sextant ended up stuck on the chandelier."

Malek looked up to see the navigational device dangling from the delicate crystal. "It's good to know dwarven engineering is as reliable as they claim."

Levin dropped a stack of parchment on his desk. "You're not as upset as I thought you'd be."

Malek shook his head. "I need to check on Sabine. You can ask Rupert and Azalia to take care of this when they have time."

Levin scowled. "What happened to not wanting anyone in your study?"

Malek swept his gaze over what had once been his private retreat. He'd spent years collecting maps, books, scrolls, and rare navigational instruments. Now everything seemed to pale in comparison to the treasure he'd found in Sabine. "It's simply not as important anymore."

Levin blew out a breath. "Yeah. I get it. This mate stuff isn't for the faint of heart. Sabine's still in your bedroom, by the way. Everything's been quiet since we last spoke."

Malek nodded and headed for his suite, needing to hold her in his arms. He opened the door to see a similar scene as the one in his office. A cabinet had fallen on its side and clothing was strewn across the floor. Aeron was sitting in a chair near the bed with his eyes closed and hands extended. A strange band of magic flowed from his hands and hovered around Sabine, barely brushing against her skin. Aeron's eyes flew open at Malek's approach, his gaze immediately wary.

Bane was leaning against the headboard with a sleeping Sabine in his arms. He opened his eyes briefly and then closed them again, running his hand over her silvery hair. She'd lost her glamour again, and the golden glow that surrounded her pulsed softly like a heartbeat.

"Your wyvern is even more foolish than you," Bane said quietly.

"I told him the same thing," Malek said, approaching the bed. He sat beside Sabine, noticing the empty teacup sitting on the nightstand. "What happened in here? And what the hell is Aeron doing?"

"That bitch of a goddess wanted to make an example of your wyvern," Bane said with a shrug. "Sabine won the battle, but it was a near thing. Fortunately, Esme holds a soft spot with Lachlina and Sabine. It made her hesitate. The minute I brought Sabine in here, she was able to banish Lachlina's influence the rest of the way. She drank Esme's sleeping draught and asked Aeron to keep her unconscious until you returned."

"Then why is he still holding it in place?" Malek asked.

"He can see things clearer while he's connected with Sabine," Bane said, nodding toward Aeron. "Tell him what you shared with me."

"Someone or something stalks our Aderylin, even in her sleep," Aeron said with a frown. "The images are jumbled and confusing, even to her. If Lachlina is blending her thoughts with our Aderylin, some of these strange images may be hers. Our Aderylin must learn to hold herself separate, even in sleep, or it will be more difficult to remain independent when awake."

"Tell him the rest," Bane said with a scowl.

Aeron's eyes flared silver. "There is another, darker presence that actively hunts our Aderylin. The dark one uses the foulest of magic to weaken her strength and resolve. They seek to steal the warmth from her very soul. It is that one I ward against, and the one she must fight to keep from losing herself."

Malek's jaw clenched. "Go ahead and wake her. I know who's hunting her, and you all need to be aware of what's going on."

CHAPTER 33

Sabine blinked open her eyes, her thoughts sluggish and hazy. Bane's spicy scent surrounded her, layered with the equally rich smokiness she associated with Malek. Her memories began trickling back, recalling how she'd ended up in Malek's bed.

"Esme's teas should come with a warning label," she mumbled, burying her face in Bane's chest. Her skin felt overly sensitive, as though every nerve ending was on fire. Even her clothing was too restrictive, making the sensuous feel of the fabric almost seem erotic against her skin.

Bane chuckled and ran his hand over her hair, sending a shiver of awareness through her. "You agreed to drink it, little one. I would think you'd have learned your lesson by now. If you are feeling up to it, your dragon has returned with news to share."

She lifted her head to find Malek sitting on the edge of the bed beside her. Gods. He was beautiful. His golden skin practically glistened in the soft lighting, contrasting with the inky darkness of his hair and the startling blue depths of his eyes. She immediately reached for him, and he pulled her into his lap. Pressing her face against his neck, she breathed him in as his arms wrapped around her.

"I destroyed your office," she said, sliding her hand across the textured fabric of his shirt to the heated skin beneath. "And almost killed your best friend."

"The key word is 'almost,'" Malek said, his arms tightening around her. "Levin is fine. He claims he was trying to distract you from launching a full-scale rescue attempt on the aderyan while I was away."

Sabine tried to focus on his words, but it was nearly impossible when he was this close. She wound her fingers through the silkiness of his hair, luxuriating in the softness. He smelled incredible, with a sweet undercurrent below the warm, smoldering spice she'd grown to love. She kissed his neck, lightly flicking her tongue across his skin. He was more potent and intoxicating than the finest of wines.

Power began building within her, but for some reason, her skin markings didn't seem to hold her magic in check. It was almost as though something within her had become untethered. Magic spun from her hands, dancing upon his skin and teasing him with her touch.

Malek's breath caught. He captured her hands and asked, "Sabine? Are you all right?"

"Esme needs to work on her measurements." She pressed her forehead against his shoulder, trying to suppress the desire thrumming through her. "My control isn't what it should be. I can't seem to contain my magic."

"Is it Lachlina?"

"She doesn't understand my attraction to you. As long as I keep my power focused on you, she'll stay away." She gasped at the sudden heat that flooded through her body. "I can think of all sorts of ways we could keep her far, far away right now, but you're wearing too many clothes. Gods, Malek. I need you to touch me."

"What in the name of the underworld did that witch put in the tea?" Bane asked, the sound of dishes clinking together barely registering.

"Figure it out or get the hell out of the room," Malek said, not tearing his gaze from her. "I'm leaning toward the latter."

"If you will allow me," Aeron said, taking the cup from Bane. He sniffed it and frowned. "Whatever she used is not native to the Aeries. I don't recognize the scent markers. They must be from Faerie or beyond our realm."

Bane shouted, "Witch! What foul concoction have you cooked up this time?"

Allowing Malek to keep hold of her hands, Sabine shifted until she was straddling him. She leaned forward and nibbled on his earlobe.

"You realize you're torturing me, don't you?" Malek asked, continuing to hold her wrists in a firm yet gentle grip.

Softly blowing on his heated skin, she whispered, "If you release my hands, we can continue where we ended last night. Or if you want to keep trying to restrain me, I'll see if I can entice you to free me another way."

"Sabine," Malek said, his voice strained. "Are you *bargaining* with me?"

Sabine smiled against his skin and continued kissing her way down his neck. Clothing was an obstacle that would need to be remedied soon. She gasped as another wave of heat surged through her. The walls creaked and groaned as vines began snaking in the cracks and crevices toward her.

She pressed her face against his neck again, desperately trying to harness her power. All the mental training and childhood lessons failed her. It was impossible to think clearly. Focusing on the physical sensation of being pressed against Malek helped, but she was burning through a tremendous amount of power. If Malek faltered before she exhausted her magic, she might actually hurt or kill someone.

"Bargain with her if it helps her maintain some form of control," Bane ordered. "Witch! Get your ass in here now!"

"If I release her hands, her magic *will* get out of control," Malek snapped. "As will mine."

"We may have a serious problem if she's unable to contain her magic," Aeron said, eyeing the dense vines covering the window. "How thick is the glass on that window?"

"What's got your horns twisted in a knot, Bane?" Esmelle demanded. "Oh! Wow. Um, Sabine? You're glowing again. And there are plants sneaking into Malek's bedroom. Hey, wait. Isn't that eldertwist root? That's great for mental clarity. Let me collect—"

"No," Bane said with a snarl. "Fix her."

"Well, I don't know what the problem is," Esmelle said in exasperation. "You said to relax her. She looks plenty relaxed to me. Maybe *you* should drink some of the tea."

Bane growled. "What did you put in it, witch? Answer me. Now."

In the same gruff tone Bane had used, Esmelle lowered her voice and said, "I put herbs in it, demon. Herbs. From the conservatory."

Running footsteps sounded from outside and skidded to a halt.

Rika cleared her throat. "Um, there are huge plants growing up the walls outside of the north wing. Blossom and the other pixies are convinced someone planted magic beans and there might be an ogre on the loose. Thalassa and Lyra are flying up to the roof to see if the plants have reached it yet."

Rika took a breath and continued, "Azalia and Rupert are in a panic and think we need to call a squadron of wyverns to burn the plants away. Carlin, the cook, is standing guard in front of his kitchen with his sharpest knives and shouting threats at the plants if they cross his threshold. And Levin is refusing to come out from the study. He says he learned his lesson, and it's Malek's turn to deal with… things."

Aeron touched one of the vines. It immediately wrapped around his wrist, as though greeting an old friend. His wings began to glow softly. "It carries the Aderylin's magic. No one must harm the plants."

Bane scowled. "Can you send Sabine back to sleep?"

Aeron shook his head. "The Aderylin's magic is currently bound too tightly to the dragon. He will simply incinerate my efforts—and likely all of us if we attempt to separate him from his mate."

"He's right," Malek said without tearing his gaze away from Sabine. "It's not a good idea to touch her right now. My instincts are too close to the surface."

Esmelle pushed up her sleeves. "Rika, tell Levin I said to get off his ass and calm the humans down. Blossom's at least keeping the pixies busy. I'll handle things here. Malek's… well, he's got his hands full apparently. Sabine's having some control issues. And don't let anyone harm the plants."

"Got it!" Rika said and raced back out of the room.

Sabine was struggling to focus on the conversation. Her thoughts kept drifting back to Malek and the way his touch brought to mind all the wondrous things she knew he could do with those hands. The look in his eyes was both predatory and possessive, and may the gods help her, but she wanted to push him over that blissful edge and straight into ecstasy—with her.

Malek groaned. "Sabine, those thoughts are *not* helping right now."

Sabine leaned forward and kissed Malek deeply. He pulled her closer, but still refused to release her hands. She parted her mouth, and he swept in, his tongue mating with hers. She tried to reach for him, but his grip was ironclad. His magic swirled around her, making her nearly desperate to touch him. The vines began climbing up the bed like ivy, winding around the footboard until they brushed against Malek's leg and sent another wave of her magic over him.

Malek broke their kiss with a muttered curse. "I'm about thirty seconds away from kicking all of you out of this room. Tell me you have a solution because I'm not sure how much longer I want to resist her magic. She's hitting me with it through our bond too."

Bane gripped the edge of the headboard, causing it to splinter in his hand. "You are not the only one, dragon."

"Wow," Esmelle said, fanning herself. "Okay. Um, I see the problem. None of the plants in the conservatory were familiar, so I'm not sure exactly what I put in the tea. I read the plant auras like Sabine taught me. The herbs I selected promoted relaxation and... maybe I lowered her inhibitions a bit. Or a lot."

"You used unfamiliar herbs on the Queen of the Unseelie?!?" Bane said with a roar. "Every demon in the underworld is having a fucking orgy right now because of your tea!"

"I didn't see anyone else willing or able to make a sleeping draught." Esmelle grabbed the teacup and thrust it under Sabine's nose. "What herbs did I use? And what will counteract the lingering effects?"

Sabine tore her gaze away from Malek, but the effort cost her. "What?"

Esmelle stomped her foot, the acorn necklace beginning to glow. "Sabin'theoria, pay attention and honor our agreement. I followed your instructions and matched the auras with my intention. I need you to teach me."

Sabine glanced back at Malek, duty and desire warring within her. The weight of the imbalance made it impossible to ignore Esmelle's request. "If I tell you, will you go away?"

"Only to make a tea to reverse the effects."

Sabine narrowed her eyes.

Esmelle narrowed hers.

Sabine sighed and sniffed the empty teacup. "Chamomile, dreamthorn, moonpetal, and lover's lace."

Esmelle winced. "On the plus side, I think I figured out the problem."

"And on the other side?" Bane demanded.

"I don't know how to fix it except to let it run its course." Esmelle turned back to Sabine. "Is there anything that counteracts lover's lace?"

Sabine took a deep breath, clinging to their pact with every ounce of her strength. "Silvermist will minimize some of the effects if it's brewed with eldertwist root. Steep them together for no more than three minutes. The instant the tea turns silver, strain it."

"Aha," Esmelle said, walking over to one of the nearby roots. "I knew the eldertwist would come in handy. I suppose it's too much to hope you managed to grow silvermist in here."

"In the wild, it usually grows near lover's lace. They need each other to thrive, like opposing counterpoints," Sabine said, her gaze drifting back to Malek as another wave of heat flowed through her. "If it's not cultivated here, there are other ways to satiate the passion it invokes. Much more pleasurable ways."

Bane turned his silvered gaze on Esmelle. "Witch, so help me, if you ever brew another tea again without knowing the ingredients, I will thrash you."

"Go soak your head in the fountain," Esmelle said, kneeling beside one of the plants and placing her hand on it. She cocked her head for a moment and then blew her red curls out of her eyes. With a nod, she withdrew a pair of shears from her pocket.

"How long will it take the tea to run its course naturally?" Malek asked, lifting Sabine's captured hands and kissing them.

"Hours," Sabine said, leaning close to his ear. "Hours upon hours I can share with you through our bond. Every sensation, every touch, and every caress will be magnified a thousand times over."

"Out!" Malek shouted. "Everyone get the hell out."

"No," Bane said. "She cannot maintain this level of power for hours without dire consequences."

"Wasn't going to listen to him anyway," Esmelle said, pocketing the root. "You called me in here to fix it. I'm fixing it. What does silvermist look like?"

The vines had crept onto the bed. Every time they brushed against Malek's skin, she felt another wave of heat rush through their bond.

"Sabine!" Esmelle said, tapping her foot impatiently. "Silvermist. Appearance."

Sabine blinked. "Dark green leaves that look like lace. The stem has a faint purplish hue. The flowers are white, but they contain a powerful toxin. You must only gather the leaves once the edges are dusted with silver, but take care not to disturb the pollen."

Esmelle frowned. "I'll see if I can find what she's describing in the conservatory. The place is a maze. Malek, I might need you to bring Sabine in there. We can't risk misidentifying it this time."

"Guys," Rika said, poking her head back into the room. "The plants outside are still growing. Thalassa says pretty soon anyone flying overhead will be able to see them through Malek's wards. Lyra slid down one of the stalks, and now the pixies think it's a new game. That would be fine— except they're taking turns throwing berries at Levin on the way down. Blossom's keeping score. Ten points for a head shot. Fifteen if they hit his nose. He's threatening to kidnap Esme and fly away from this craziness."

"Tell Levin to put out some honey for the pixies to distract them," Esmelle said, running toward the door. "And see if Carlin can heat up more water for tea. I need it right away."

Malek kissed Sabine's hands again. "If I release you and take you to the conservatory, can you control yourself?"

"Do you really want me to?"

"Fuck no."

Sabine laughed, sending another ripple of power through the room. She tried to rein it in, but her magic refused to obey. It was like a bird taking flight for the first time and refusing to return. She pressed her face against Malek's neck again, breathing him in. If Lachlina tried to control her right now, she wouldn't be able to stop her. The heat inside her was unbearable, as though she were burning alive from within.

Malek winced. "Sabine's magic is straining the wards. We need to do this fast, but I can't release her. She's channeling so much power into me that if I let her go, the estate's defenses will fracture."

Bane scowled. "Dragon, if you are what I suspect, you have the ability to circumvent her will. If your connection is strong enough, she will not resist you."

Aeron's wings unfurled and he hissed. "You would have him turn our Aderylin into some puppet to be used and abused?"

Malek's jaw hardened. "No. It's out of the question."

"I do not suggest this lightly," Bane snapped, gesturing to the plants that were beginning to crawl up the walls and toward the ceiling. "We have only minutes before her identity is exposed. If she burns herself out, she will be defenseless and unable to withstand the ones hunting her in dreams.

The aderyan do not yet share a bond with her, except by her explicit agreement. Their magic cannot protect her now. You are simply the lesser evil, dragon."

Malek lifted Sabine's hands and kissed her fingertips. "I made Sabine a promise back in Akros. I will never use such magic upon her. What is between us is freely offered and shared. If I were to coerce or manipulate her in any way, it would fracture the trust and balance between us. That will *never* happen."

Sabine stared into Malek's eyes. The sincerity of his words and depth of his love flowed through their bond and wrapped her in a blanket of his power. In it, there was safety and security unlike anything she'd ever known. He offered her trust and balance, and that was something she needed as surely as the magic that flowed through her veins. She softened her magic to match his, allowing their combined energies to resonate in a harmonic symphony.

"*I love you, Malek Rish'dan,*" she said, embracing him through their connection. "*I trust you not to let me fall. If you lead the way, I will follow you.*"

"*Dance with me, Sabin'theoria,*" Malek urged and kissed her fingertips. "*If we fall, we fall together. From now, until the last of the magic fades from this world, I'm yours.*"

Moving as one, they kept their eyes locked and stood together. Even before Malek finished taking the first step, Sabine matched his movement. They were perfectly in sync with one another, allowing their magic and bodies to lead where their hearts had already followed. It was a dance no less intricate and masterful than what the most skilled fae dancers spent a lifetime practicing.

They moved through the north wing and into the conservatory, oblivious to everyone and everything around them—except each other.

Bound together by a love as pure as moonlight and more

powerful than the winds of a storm, the force of their combined magic swirled around them and infused their shared passion into the nearby flowers. The plants reached upward to form a graceful archway overhead with tiny bursts of white flowers that sweetened the air with their soft fragrance. The vines lowered, wrapping their clasped hands together.

Dozens of pixies flowed into the room in a stream of glittering dust. They giggled and placed matching floral crowns on Sabine and Malek's heads before hiding among the flowers overhead.

"Well, this is interesting," Esmelle said, standing in front of them and holding an athame and silver chalice. "Something you two want to tell me? Because from the looks of things, this garden just handfasted you."

CHAPTER 34

S abine stared at their bound hands. The gentle glow encompassing the vines pulsed in time with their heartbeats.

"You are my mate, my partner in this life and beyond, and that which I treasure most in this world and beyond the ether," Malek said, interlocking his fingers with Sabine's. "Your magic acknowledges it, even if the rest of you still hesitates. I love you, Sabin'theoria. I intend to spend the rest of my life proving it to you."

"Malek," she murmured, unable to deny the truth of his words. Both her magic and heart had already acknowledged him as her balance in this life and beyond.

"Kiss her!" Blossom whispered loudly from her perch overhead. The pixies all giggled, sending a sprinkling of glittering pixie dust over them.

Malek grinned at them. Leaning down, his lips brushed against Sabine's in a featherlight touch and then slowly deepened. She leaned into him and returned his kiss, still caught in the shared magical dance they'd begun. Sabine gasped as another wave of heat surged through her. Malek's hands tightened around hers, holding her steady.

Esmelle thrust the chalice in her direction and said, "Oh no. Don't start that again. Here. Drink it. Blossom confirmed the plant was silvermist and made sure the measurements were correct this time."

Sabine glanced down at the silver liquid and nodded. With their hands still bound, Malek helped her drink from the chalice. Although it had been brewed with heated water, the silvermist had cooled the liquid until it was nearly freezing. The tea coated her tongue, sending a shot of ice through her veins.

The vines around their hands retreated instantly. Sabine doubled over with a cry, dropping the empty chalice onto the ground.

Malek wrapped his arms around her, holding her tightly. "Sabine? Esme, what's wrong with her?"

Esmelle shook her head. "I—I don't know. Blossom, you said it was correct!"

"It is! It was!" Blossom exclaimed. "Look!"

The plants were already retreating to the safety and security of the land. Reaching for every trace of spare magic she'd sent outward and into the plants and soil, Sabine called it back to herself. Her skin markings flared to life, and she mentally mapped each one, locking her magic behind them. Her teeth chattered so badly, she couldn't form the words to explain. She had to focus on putting her power and the chaos she'd caused to rest.

"For the love of all things," Bane muttered in irritation and stormed out of the conservatory. He returned a moment later with a heavy blanket and draped it over Sabine's shoulders. "She's simply cold, you idiot."

Malek glared at Bane and sent a strong wave of his heated magic over Sabine.

She curled against him, seeking his warmth. "Silvermist is effective, but for obvious reasons, it's not the preferred method to counteract the effects of lover's lace."

Malek lifted Sabine in his arms and carried her back to the living area. He placed her on a plush sofa, tucked the blanket around her, and flung his hand in the direction of the fireplace. The fire roared to life, crackling with heat. After removing his flowered crown, Malek placed his hand on a crystal sitting on a side table. A knock on the door sounded a moment later, and Malek went to answer it.

Bane sat beside her and wrapped an arm around her, using his body heat to further shield her from the lingering effects. Peering up at him, she asked, "How bad?"

Bane stared up at the ceiling and scowled. "Forget Faerie wine. Now that Dax knows what lover's lace does to an Unseelie, I suspect he's going to insist I bring you back to the underworld along with a case of it."

Sabine laughed and hugged Bane tightly. "And you?"

Bane narrowed his eyes on her. "You challenge me on a good day, little one. Today, you were in rare form. If I trusted you not to get into further trouble, I'd be tempted to head inland and find a tavern for a few hours."

Sabine grinned and waggled her fingers. "I could always make you appear human temporarily. There are taverns in Imenel."

"Put those things away," Bane said, glaring at her fingers. "You're a godsforsaken menace."

Sabine grinned and kissed his cheek.

Malek brought over a small tray with a teapot, a delicate porcelain painted teacup, and a plate full of cookies. He poured the tea and handed it to her.

Bane eyed the steaming cup in Sabine's hands like a hissing serpent. "A little soon to attempt this again, isn't it?"

Esmelle threw the empty chalice at Bane's head. "I can't believe you just said that!"

Bane snatched it out of the air and stood. "Witch, I have put up with all sorts of your bizarre concoctions. Half of them, Sabine demanded I drink, likely to ensure they weren't poisoned. But this latest stunt of yours surpasses all others!"

Malek took Bane's empty seat and gestured to Sabine's cup. "It's just mint tea. Levin asked Azalia to brew it for you."

"Poison?" Esmelle sputtered at Bane. "You overgrown horned toadstool! I have never poisoned anyone!"

Sabine leaned against Malek and sniffed at the cup. All she smelled was mint. She took a hesitant sip and nodded.

Rika slid onto the couch beside Sabine. "Did I miss anything?"

"Nope," Sabine said. "They're just getting started."

Bane glared at Esme. "Dare I remind you about the time you found some mushrooms and thought they had healing properties? I spent the next four hours purging that vile brew from my system—and I grew up in the underworld eating all manner of creatures."

"They did have healing properties!" Esmelle said, crossing her arms. "I just didn't realize they were designed to purge toxins from someone's system."

"Should we intervene?" Malek asked her quietly, nodding toward Esmelle and Bane.

Sabine wrapped her hands around the cup and shook her head. "Only if she turns him into a frog."

Malek stared at her as though he wasn't sure if she was joking. She smiled and took another sip of the tea.

"Have you forgotten the time you thought you'd found a cure for hangovers?" Bane demanded.

Esmelle winced. "Okay, that one may have been an accident."

"Or the tea that was supposed to sharpen senses?"

"Hey, that one worked. There were just some unfortunate side effects."

"Witch, I could not sleep for over a week!" Bane roared.

Esmelle put her hands on her hips. "Why do you do that? Why is it always, 'Witch, do this,' or 'witch, do that'?"

"Because dryads are supposed to be shy and meek, and there is not a shy nor meek bone in your body!" Bane ended the last on a shout.

Esmelle stared at him. Finally, she sniffed and walked over to him. "It's happening."

Bane leaned back, eyeing her warily. "What?"

"A hug," Esmelle said and threw her arms around him. "Just suffer through it."

Bane stiffened and glared at Sabine. "This is your fault."

Sabine took another sip of the tea and smiled. Mmm. Minty.

Levin walked in and froze, staring at Esmelle still hugging Bane. "Do I want to know?"

Malek shook his head. "Probably not."

Esmelle grinned and released Bane. She walked over to Levin, threw her arms around his neck, and planted a loud kiss on his lips. "You're still my favorite wyvern."

Blossom landed on the back of the sofa and said, "Whatever you do, don't eat the cookies."

Sabine arched her brow. "Oh?"

Malek sighed. "She doesn't like smoked vanilla cookies, but they happen to be my sister's favorite. Carlin made these, most likely with your taste preferences in mind."

"Yum," Rika said and reached over Sabine, motioning toward the plate. "Hand them over."

Malek handed her the plate of cookies. Rika took a bite and said, "These are amazing. Blossom, you really need to try them. I think it's a honey drizzle on top."

Blossom flew over to the plate and took the small piece

Rika offered. That was all the incentive the other pixies needed. They descended en masse, hovering on the edge of the couch and pleading for cookies. Rika scrambled, trying to break up the pieces fast enough. There were too many to count, and Sabine suspected they kept moving around to make Rika lose count on equally distributing her stash.

Bane growled at them. "Who let the damn pixies into the house? Out! Now!"

They squealed and grabbed their pieces of cookie. Esmelle opened the door, and they raced into the garden, leaving a trail of cookie crumbs and pixie dust behind them. Blossom stayed behind, still munching happily on the pieces Rika handed to her.

Thalassa and Lyra had entered the north wing while Esmelle and Bane had been arguing. Aeron had been speaking quietly with Thalassa in the far corner of the room while Lyra had been stealthily sneaking away from her caretakers and toward Sabine.

Sabine crooked her finger, motioning for Lyra to join her. The little girl grinned and raced over. Sabine scooped her into her arms and sat her on the sofa with them. Rika handed her one of the few cookies she'd managed to save from the ravenous pixies.

"I didn't scare you with my magic, did I?" Sabine asked.

Lyra shook her head and took a bite of her cookie. "We got to fly up to the roof. Aeron says I need to be careful when other people are around. I'm supposed to learn how to hide my wings."

"It's a good skill to have," Sabine said softly, holding out her hand.

Lyra placed her smaller hand over hers, their skin glowing with shared magical resonance. Sabine dampened her power, masking her appearance behind a layer of human glamour. The glow faded instantly.

"Sometimes the best way to hide is by showing something else to the world. You and your magic are both rare and wonderful, Lyra. Be careful who you trust when you decide to share the gift of your true self."

Lyra cocked her head. "I trust Aeron and Thalassa."

Sabine nodded. "Those are good choices."

Thalassa approached them and said, "Aeron will teach both of us how to hide our wings later this evening. But first, we must give him some time to speak with the Aderylin while we work on your reading and writing studies. Afterward, if Aeron gives his permission, we will practice flying again."

Lyra gave Sabine a quick hug and then hopped off the sofa. She and Thalassa headed upstairs together, talking softly. Aeron watched them go before turning his attention back to Sabine.

Malek scanned the room. "Now that everyone's here and mostly back to normal, I need to speak with all of you about what I've learned."

Blossom's wings twitched. "Can I tell them?"

"No," Malek said. "Eat your cookie."

Blossom shoved another cookie crumb in her mouth and gave him a thumb's up sign.

"The Council of Dragons is made up of representatives from each of the dragon clans," Malek began. "A missive was delivered to them from the King of the Seelie and affixed with his personal seal. In it, he claims Faerie has acknowledged a new Unseelie queen. She has been forging alliances and gathering armies with the intention of turning her sights on the Sky Cities."

"He did *what*?" Esmelle demanded.

Sabine lowered her cup. "What else did my father say?"

"The King of the Seelie claims he's not interested in losing more fae lives due to Unseelie treachery. He warned of an advance scouting party and suggested betrayal may also come from within our ranks."

Bane's eyes flashed silver, and he pushed away from the wall he'd been leaning on. "He grows too bold."

Malek nodded. "We knew he likely learned of my identity when we were in Razadon. If he's had nearly two months to plan this, the wyvern attack outside of Imenel may have something to do with this missive. This could be an attempt to eliminate me and weaken Sabine's defenses."

"Since when do our people blindly believe anything the fae tell us?" Levin asked in disgust. "There is no excuse to attack one of our own without irrefutable proof. And those wyverns were too inexperienced to be running such patrols. Something about this still doesn't smell right."

"I agree we're missing something, but I can't shake the feeling they're somehow connected," Malek said.

"Sabine, you cannot allow this to stand," Bane warned. "King Cadan knows the Wild Hunt cannot pursue you within these borders, but he's determined to strike at you in any way possible. You must respond to this attack, quickly and decisively."

Esmelle crossed her arms. "And start a war between the Seelie and Unseelie? How would that benefit anyone?"

"Perhaps that's the point." Sabine stared into her cup, considering the implications. "Sending a message to the dragons was a risky and reckless move, even for my father. The Seelie and Unseelie tolerate each other, but most are united in their hatred of dragonkind."

"What are you thinking?" Malek asked.

"I'm an absent queen, and that is extraordinarily danger-ous," Sabine said, lifting her head. "I've claimed responsibility for my people, but from the moment I assumed my crown, we've been running from one disaster to another. We've forged alliances along the way, but everything we've done has been with the goal of restoring the balance and locating the portal artifacts."

She looked around the room at those she trusted most in this world. "My inner circle is extraordinarily small. It would be nearly impossible for him to plant a spy in our midst. My father has no way of keeping an eye on me or playing the typical games fae royalty have used for centuries. All he hears are rumors of remarkable feats of power."

"You're suggesting his imagination is running away with him," Malek mused.

Sabine nodded. "From the time we're children, the sidhe are trained in the intricate dance of politics. To rule, you must possess great magic, but you must also know how best to wield such a weapon. If we consider it from his point of view, I'm solidifying my power base while his grows weaker. For the first time in a millennium, an Unseelie queen has forged an alliance with the merfolk, the dwarves, and the demons. He likely sees a dagger in every shadow."

"You've secured more than alliances," Bane reminded her. "The demons have not recognized a true queen since before the portal was sealed, and the merfolk have never forged an alliance with the Unseelie in living memory."

"You've also tamed a dragon, and the Huntsman himself bowed to you before all of Razadon," Blossom said with a grin. "My brother said all of Faerie was talking about that for weeks. Well, that and the earthquake you caused in the Seelie palace."

Sabine inwardly winced at the reminder. She'd nearly forgotten about her unfortunate scrying incident.

"King Cadan's becoming desperate," Esmelle said with a frown. "That's why he sent a message to the dryads warning them about you. They were terrified you were going to strike them down."

Sabine nodded. "The dwarves showed us memory stones

of Unseelie being tormented and murdered. Each death was staged to ensure it would be witnessed by the dwarves and word would get back to my people that I failed to protect them. My father has been using my brother to further stir unrest, claiming Rhys has a right to my throne. Balkin has been doing what he can to calm tensions, but communication has been intermittent since we left Razadon. And now it appears my father is attempting to use the dragons to sow further discord among the Seelie and Unseelie."

"Regardless of his motivations, you must still make a statement," Bane warned.

"I don't disagree." Sabine shrugged off the blanket and stood. "However, there's more to consider than simply slapping at my father's hands. I will not do anything that might jeopardize freeing the aderyan or locating the portal artifact."

Bane considered her for a moment and then inclined his head. "Very well. What do you intend?"

Placing her cup on the table, Sabine said, "Blossom, I want you to send a message to your family in Faerie. We need information. Find out what's been happening in both the Seelie and Unseelie courts since we last checked in. I want reports from the pixies you've installed in the Seelie palace."

Blossom nodded and rose into the air, her wings fluttering behind her. "Do you want me to use the flowers in the conservatory to communicate?"

"Do it, but tell your brother I don't want anyone taking unnecessary risks. It's far more important their loyalty to me remains undiscovered."

"Got it!" Blossom said and flew toward the conservatory.

Sabine turned to Rika and said, "I need you to write a letter to Dagmar in Razadon. Use the cipher we developed before we left. Explain the situation and find out if she's managed to install the cave troll spies in any Seelie households. Also, see if they've received any more memory stones from Faerie. Once you're finished, let me know and I'll send it through a portal."

Malek gestured toward his study. "You can find some quills and parchment in my desk."

"No problem," Rika said and put the empty plate on the table before heading into Malek's study.

"What can Levin and I do to help?" Esmelle asked.

Sabine hesitated. No matter how much she might need information, she wasn't willing to put her friends in danger.

Malek stood and placed his hand on Sabine's back. *"You want to send her back to the dryad grove to see what they know, don't you?"*

"Not if there's a chance of them being attacked. No information is worth the risk of losing her."

Malek's gaze softened, and he touched her cheek. Turning to Levin, he said, "Captain Fandrin should be reaching out to you shortly. I'll need you to escort him and a squadron of wyverns to Idola's house. She was making some tonics for my sister, and my mother wants to secure additional supplies. If Esme wishes to travel with you, it would be an opportunity for her to check in with the dryads."

Levin frowned but glanced at Esmelle. "A full squadron of wyverns would be a deterrent from another attack. What do you say? Do you want to take a short trip?"

Realization dawned on Esmelle's face, and her eyes lit up in anticipation. She clutched the acorn pendant around her neck and said, "Absolutely! Do you think the dryads might know something about what your father's planning?"

"It's possible, but I don't want you to take any chances," Sabine said. "Levin will not be able to accompany you into the grove, but once you step inside, no one will dare harm you. Remember your magic will shape the grove to your will, so guard your thoughts carefully."

Esmelle nodded. "What do you want me to find out?"

"My father's already tried to mislead the forest guardians once. I don't want it to happen again. Now that things have settled a bit, the dryads may have other information they're willing to share with you. I'm hoping they'll give you some indication about other fae who may have crossed through their borders and when. It will also give you a chance to make sure their lost children are settling in."

Sabine thought about the oasis she'd formed in the middle of the Badlands and added, "You might want to find out what they need to cultivate and sustain a new forest. The land surrounding Atlantia will need their protection and guidance at some point now that life is returning to the area."

Esmelle gave her a brilliant smile. "You're right! I hadn't thought about that. Let's go now, Levin. I want to give the dryads the good news."

As Levin and Esmelle headed toward the door, Sabine looked up at Malek and asked, "How did the message from my father arrive? Who delivered it?"

Malek frowned. "My mother may have that information. I would suggest you consider bringing her into your confidence."

Aeron had been listening to the conversation quietly. In many ways, he reminded her of the fae and the careful mask of neutrality they often wore. She'd worn a similar one for many years. In time, she hoped he and Thalassa would allow those barriers to fall away and feel more comfortable opening up to them.

"I do not personally know the leaders of the Obsidian Clan, except by reputation. However, I would recommend caution," Aeron said, his wings tucked tightly against his back. "The more people who learn your identity, the greater your risk of exposure. Your dragon was wise to send many of the human servants away, but the magic you unleashed earlier will be discussed for some time. Rumors often fly upon the wind with the force of a hurricane."

Sabine nodded. "Malek, do you believe sharing my identity with her is more important than the risks? Not just for us, but for her too. If the rest of your people learn she's harboring the Unseelie queen, how will they react?"

"She'll keep your secrets and be a fierce ally," Malek said. "I haven't disclosed your identity to anyone in my family, so in that regard, you're safe. My sister tends to forget discretion, and I don't know her mate well enough to say otherwise. As much as I love Kaia, I'd urge caution for now. My mother won't reveal your secrets, not even to my father. On that, you have my word."

Levin nodded. "If you are going to have anyone for an ally, Lady Nymira of the Obsidian Clan is a wise choice."

Sabine turned to Bane and arched her brow. He frowned but gave her a curt nod.

"Very well," Sabine said, hoping Malek and Levin weren't simply speaking from a place of loyalty and love.

"I would suggest possibly meeting her later today," Malek said, taking Sabine's hand. "There's a clan gala scheduled for tomorrow night, and as my mate, you'll be expected to attend."

Sabine stared at him in shock.

"You idiot dragon," Bane said with a growl. "What part of keeping a low profile didn't you understand?"

CHAPTER 35

Sabine turned on her heel and walked out of the room. Malek had truly lost his mind. At some point, between leaving solid ground and arriving in the Sky Cities, he'd hit his head or become possessed by a crazed pixie.

Maybe both.

Attending a formal function hadn't even been a consideration since she'd left Faerie. Those had been stressful enough with the constant scrutiny and potential threats, but this took it a step further. There would be countless dragons in attendance, and if any fae were present, it wasn't because they were hoping to sample the wine.

She pinched the bridge of her nose, wondering again at the wisdom in coming here openly. Malek's presence offered her and her friends a modicum of protection, but it made everything else so much harder. Freeing the aderyan and fae captives was necessary, but her actions could put Malek and the family he adored at risk.

Malek's footsteps were nearly silent behind her, as if uncertain his presence was welcome. She hadn't been paying attention to where she was going and had somehow ended up back in the conservatory. A hint of moisture hung in the warm air, blending with the earthy scent of soil and sweetness of Faerie blooms, reminding her of the indoor gardens at the Winter Palace.

Unmindful of her dress and needing to touch the soil, Sabine kicked off her shoes and kneeled on the stepping stones. She reached for a new sprout that had been eclipsed by a larger plant, struggling to find enough sunlight to thrive. Using a trace of her magic to coax it toward the sun, the sleepy sapling stretched and unfurled its leaves to brush against her skin. She could feel the strength of its roots below the soil, and the sense of loss that resonated deep within the garden as the memory of the former gardener came unbidden to her mind.

"This is where Elisa departed from our world," Sabine said quietly, caressing the sapling and infusing her magic into it.

"How did you know?" Malek asked from behind her.

Sabine held out her hand for him, and he kneeled beside her. She took his hand and placed it on the soil. "Close your eyes, and open your senses. Allow yourself to feel the land through me."

Malek closed his eyes, and she reached for the essence of the land. Bridging the chasm between him and Elisa's memory, she opened herself up to the pulse of the earth. It hummed within her, the gentle rustle of the wind through the leaves and the soft sigh of the plants lapping the moisture from the soil. Beneath the layers of the land's song, she shared the soft tinkling melody of Seelie magic that had nourished the plants for centuries.

"I feel her," Malek said in wonder. "I hadn't thought to ever feel her magic again."

"This was as close to Faerie as she could touch," Sabine

said, tracing her fingers through the soil. "This garden will continue to last for centuries, nourished by the gift of her magic. I believe she wanted you to have this part of her for as long as possible."

Malek covered Sabine's hand and said, "I'm not handling things very well right now, especially where you're concerned."

Sabine turned to look at him. "Why?"

"You've made me remember things," Malek admitted. "I had always viewed Elisa through a child's eyes. She was beautiful, with laughter that could make your heart soar. Her magic was unlike anything I'd seen before. She taught me about the fae, told me stories, and shared her culture and language. I was here more often than I was at home. She seemed to look forward to my visits as much as I enjoyed them."

Sabine smiled, imagining Malek as a dark-haired child. "Most of the fae treasure children. It sounds as though your Elisa was no exception."

Malek looked around the conservatory. "She was usually in here or in the gardens. Looking back now, I don't think I realized how lonely and isolated she was. She rarely attended functions with my grandfather, and no one outside of our family was permitted entry into this estate. This was her sanctuary, but I'm beginning to wonder if it was also her prison."

Sabine touched Malek's cheek with the tips of her fingers. "Am I a prisoner?"

"Absolutely not," Malek said in surprise.

"If I told you I wanted to leave the Sky Cities right now and never return, what would you do?"

"I would go with you."

Sabine leaned forward and kissed him lightly. "And that is the difference, Malek. I don't know what the relationship was between Elisa and your grandfather, but we're not them. You've welcomed me into your home and shown me another part of yourself. One day, I hope to be able to share part of mine with you. We've created a precious balance between us, both in our magic and in our hearts. The decision to move forward together is what's important."

Malek cupped her face and searched her expression. "I don't want to take you to the gala."

"I know."

Malek's brow furrowed. "I thought you were angry with me about it."

"Oh, I'm annoyed," Sabine said, wrinkling her nose. "But I also know you well enough that you wouldn't have agreed unless it was necessary. You were reluctant to even introduce me to your sister."

Malek blew out a breath and sat on the ground beside her. He kicked out his long legs and stared up at the glass roof. "My uncle knows you were in Imenel and responsible for the magic he sensed while he was there. My mother's planning on running interference, but I need to introduce you as my mate. Once you're acknowledged as such, you'll have the same rights and protections I do. You'll be part of the Obsidian Clan, and our alliances will be yours."

Sabine caressed a pale yellow flower with a light purple dusting on its petals. "Have you considered it might not be in your clan's best interest to ally themselves with the Queen of the Unseelie?"

"Ask me if I give a damn," Malek muttered.

Sabine laughed. "I'm serious, Malek. When my father decides to strike out at me again, you'll likely be putting your family in danger. That doesn't even take into account how my decision to free the aderyan will affect you or your family."

Malek focused on her with an intensity that made her

skin prickle with awareness. "You don't seem to understand this whole mate thing. It's not optional, Sabine. You're my anchor. My family. If anyone raises a hand to you, they also raise one to me."

"I haven't agreed to be your mate, Malek," she said quietly.

"I know," Malek replied, leaning back and staring up at the glass ceiling again. "My declaration has no bearing on your acceptance. It would be different if you were a dragon, but it won't change anything between us whether or not you acknowledge my claim."

She arched her brow. "You're suggesting I have no say in the matter?"

Malek merely smiled and continued staring up at the sky. Sabine narrowed her eyes and crawled over to him. He grabbed her and rolled them, until he had her pinned to the ground. Before she could use her magic on him, he linked hands with her and kissed her.

Her annoyance fizzled as she stared up into his striking blue eyes. "You think you're clever, don't you?"

Brushing a tendril of her hair away from her face, he grinned and said, "I told you once before I could find you no matter where you were in the world."

"You did."

He rubbed his nose against hers. "Have you ever wondered how dragons navigate?"

She paused, recalling the way he'd always seemed to know the direction of the Sky Cities. He'd never consulted a map or compass while they'd flown here. "How?"

He shifted his weight off her, propping himself up on one elbow. Gently rubbing a lock of her hair with his fingers, he said, "Before the portal was closed, we soared between worlds. We had no true home, except for our clans and families. They became our anchors, these bright spots we could locate in the ether."

Sabine frowned and sat up. "You can still sense them now, even without access to the ether?"

"Only those on this side of the portal," Malek said, staring up at the sky again. "The others are lost to us. Without access to the ether, we have to live in close proximity to keep the anchor points between us strong enough. If we were to spread out to the far reaches of Aeslion, the magic would weaken and we would have difficulties finding our way home."

"That's why you became interested in navigation and ships?"

Malek nodded. "I used to visit Imenel and speak with the ship captains at length. Humans had ways of navigating the seas using maps, compasses, and even the stars to guide them. If they could learn such methods, then so could I. As it turned out, it made my ship captain persona much more believable. When the time came to send someone to locate the portal artifacts, I was a natural choice."

Sabine wrapped her arms around her knees. "You keep claiming I'm your mate and saying I'm your anchor, but is it possible you're simply sensing the bond between us? This could simply be a manifestation."

Malek chuckled. "No."

"You're that confident?"

Malek grinned. "It's the difference between hearing a beautiful song and tasting the most incredible Faerie wine. Both experiences are something to be treasured, but they rely upon entirely different senses."

"I don't understand," Sabine said with a frown.

"When I close my eyes, I can see you, Sabine," Malek said, running his thumb across her cheek. "Not your physical self, but the light that shines within you. It calls to me. I know exactly how far away you are, which direction I need to travel, and how many beats of my wings it will take to reach you. Through our bond, I can feel your emotions, your thoughts, and hear you speak to me. Together, you're with me in a way I never imagined possible."

Sabine lowered her gaze. It had been similar for her when she'd passed through the Veil or stepped through a portal with him. She'd been able to sense Malek, but she could also feel each of their companions. She wasn't sure if it was because they were tied to her or if it was a similar type of magic Malek described. Not for the first time, she wished there was someone she could ask these questions.

The skin markings on her wrist warmed gently. She pressed her hand against her dress, willing them to cool. No matter what aid Lachlina might offer, Sabine wasn't willing to open that doorway again without knowing the cost.

"If the dragon is finished apologizing, and you're done forgiving what will likely be one of his many transgressions, Aeron would like a word with you," Bane said in a bored voice. "Or if you two would rather continue rolling around in the dirt, I'll be sure to let the King of the Seelie know our illustrious queen finds his timing inconvenient."

Malek chuckled and stood, holding out his hand for Sabine. She allowed him to pull her to her feet. Brushing off her hands, she glanced down the length of the conservatory but didn't see any sign of Blossom. The pixie was likely still talking to her family and catching up with the latest Faerie gossip.

She stood on her toes and kissed Bane's cheek. "When we hear back from everyone, I'd welcome your suggestions on the best way to handle things with my father."

He opened his mouth to say something, but she quickly added, "Preferably an option that doesn't involve a demon army marching upon Faerie."

Bane sighed. "One of these days, you'll realize one of the quickest ways to achieve success is to confront it head on. Or in this case, by removing someone's head."

Sabine started toward the living area but paused when she noticed Malek standing at a small table in the corner of the conservatory. He was moving aside several small pots and gardening tools, searching for something.

"What's wrong?" she asked.

"Elisa kept several journals on this desk, detailing the plants in the garden and conservatory. It had some of her observations and even sketches she'd made. I believe one of them listed potential uses and recipes for some of them."

"That would have come in handy earlier," Bane pointed out.

Malek nodded. "I'll ask Azalia if she knows where they went. Esmelle would likely find them interesting, and it may help prevent future… mishaps. I think Elisa hoped either me or Kaia would have some interest, but we were indifferent students." He paused, considering Sabine thoughtfully. "Although, I'm now seeing a number of possibilities."

Sabine laughed and headed back into the living area. Aeron was standing in front of one of the large windows overlooking the garden, his wings tucked tightly against his back. He seemed so separate and alone in some ways. There was a closeness between him and Thalassa, but Sabine sensed he kept his distance from everyone. It reminded her of how she often felt living in Akros, observing and watching, but never truly part of things.

She slowed her steps as she approached, and he immediately turned to her. With a small smile, she held out her hands to him. Shock colored his expression for a moment before his face carefully blanked, and he took her hands. She sent a gentle trace of her power over him and said, "I felt you in my dreams earlier when Esme made the sleeping draught."

"Yes," he said, capturing her gaze in his. She could swear she saw clouds streaking across the blue of his irises. His magic flowed over her in a gentle weave, as light as air, but with an underlying strength that spoke of the potential for gales.

"I would gladly walk with you in your dreams again, Aderylin," he murmured, his voice richer and more melodic like a siren's embrace. "You already have other protectors, but none are aderyan. I asked Bane for permission to offer myself as your shield, Aderylin. Whether it is here or in Belon."

"Belon?" Sabine said, unfamiliar with the term. "You're referring to the place between wakefulness and sleep? The shadowglen of the dreamwalkers?"

"It is one and the same."

Bane approached them and said, "You may want to consider accepting such an offer, provided he is willing to swear fealty to you. The aderyan have long been masters of the shadowglen."

Surprised by Bane's endorsement and wondering what had prompted it, she turned back to Aeron. His hands were still calmly wrapped around hers, his gaze focused on her. In that instant, she had a startling realization. Aeron trusted her, absolutely and without reservation. She may have restored his wings, but such devotion was unwarranted.

She released his hands and said, "I'm honored, Aeron. But why would you offer this to me? I already intend to do everything within my power to help free and restore the aderyan people."

Aeron lowered his head and was silent for a long time. "My parents were Aetherbound. When their Chosen were expunged from the world and the portal sealed, they continued to fight their oppressors. They were among the last of the aderyan to be captured. As punishment, they were the first to have their wings severed and mounted on the prison walls."

He lifted his head and met her gaze once again. "I was born in captivity, along with my elder brother. We were bred for a single purpose—to keep the Sky Cities aloft with our magic. From an age scarcely older than Lyra, we were chained in iron and forced to channel our power for the benefit of our dragon overlords."

"Aeron," Sabine whispered, her heart aching for what he'd gone through.

"My elder brother died securing our escape. To honor his sacrifice, I have spent the last fifty years helping other aderyan flee their captors. But it wasn't until you sought sanctuary in our refuge that I realized our efforts paled in comparison to what could be accomplished with you by our side. For the first time, we had an Aderylin worthy of following. Even in Belon, where it is nearly impossible to hide your true intentions, you shine like the brightest of beacons. You give me hope for a different future."

He kneeled in front of her, his wings unfurling behind him. "You claim the Unseelie as your subjects, yet you offer to protect those who the Seelie have abandoned. I do not represent all of the aderyan people, but I do speak for myself. I would gladly follow you, Aderylin. Allow me to be the first aderyan to pledge my loyalty to you and only you. I shall act as your shield, safeguarding you from those who would do you harm in this realm and beyond. From now until the last of the magic fades from this world, I tie my future to yours in the hopes it may shine as brightly as the light burning within you."

Humbled by his words, Sabine held out her hand toward Bane. He placed one of his daggers in her hand. She nicked the skin of her palm and then offered the blade to Aeron. He repeated the gesture and placed his palm against hers.

Magic swirled around them, encasing them both in a golden glow.

"By blood and magic, and by my rights to both, I accept your honored oath," Sabine said and clasped his hand tightly. "Through shadow and light, your struggles are mine to hold. Accept this gift of my power, as our combined destinies unfold."

Her magic rose up swiftly and rushed into Aeron. His back arched as her power surged through him. His striking wings turned a rich golden hue, as though the tip of each feather had been dipped in molten gold. He lifted his once-silvered gaze and regarded Sabine with golden eyes that now matched the radiant shimmer of his wings.

"Interesting," Bane said, walking around Aeron and studying his wings and eyes.

"Whoa," Blossom said, hovering in the air near them. "I want wings like that, Sabine!"

"I thought you wanted to be a dragon?" Malek asked.

"Can I be a pink and gold dragon?"

"Aeron!" Lyra exclaimed and leaped over the balcony with her wings extended. He turned and caught her as she descended. She touched his wings reverently. "Our Aderylin shared her magic with you too."

"That she did," Aeron said gently, placing Lyra on the ground. Thalassa walked down the stairs toward them, her eyes glimmering with tears.

"Oh, Aeron," she murmured and embraced him. "Your eyes shine with the same beauty as your wings. I never thought to see such magic restored to our people again."

Aeron murmured something too low for her to overhear. Thalassa nodded and then turned to Sabine. "You have given us so much, Aderylin. I do not have Aeron's magical knowledge, but I spent a great number of years learning about our dragon overlords and their expectations. It was through these efforts that we eventually discovered some of their weaknesses and ways to smuggle our people out of the Sky Cities. It would be my honor to share my knowledge with you."

Sabine took Thalassa's hands and said, "I welcome any insight you're willing to offer, Thalassa. However, the choice on what and how much to share remains solely yours. I will not make any demands of you, and there is no debt between us."

Thalassa's eyes shimmered with emotion. "You are most gracious, Aderylin. Nothing would please me more than aiding your purpose. It's my understanding you're to attend a clan gala tomorrow evening. With your permission, I will select appropriate attire and jewelry and help prepare you for such an event. Will Rika also be attending?"

Sabine smiled and released Thalassa's hands. "Yes, she will. There should be some gowns Faerie provided in our traveler's packs. We may be able to make some modifications before tomorrow night if you think it's necessary."

Rika poked her head out of the study and grinned. "I'm going to a gala?"

"Only if you finish writing the letter to the dwarf first," Bane said, pointing toward the study. "Afterward, you're to practice your weapon drills in the garden."

"Yes!" Rika did a little dance before disappearing into the study. "No pinching armor!"

"You're still going armed!" Bane shouted.

"But I get to wear a pretty dress!" she yelled back.

Bane harrumphed. "We'll see how she feels after two hours of weapon training."

Sabine bit back a smile. Malek pressed a kiss against her temple and said, "I need to check in with Levin and speak with Azalia and Rupert about making arrangements for dinner with my mother. I'm assuming you'd prefer to eat here?"

Before Sabine could reply, Bane asked, "Will this gala be held at your parents' home?"

Malek nodded. "Yes. The lower floors are usually converted to hold the event."

"We would be remiss in not availing ourselves of this opportunity," Bane said. "Sabine and Rika should attend dinner there. If you remain with Sabine, Aeron and I will quietly assess the surroundings to ensure Sabine's safety. I would suggest the little one and her guardian remain behind."

"I'm going too," Blossom announced. "I can check all hard-to-reach secret spots."

Malek frowned and then gave him a curt nod. "I need to make some arrangements and ensure my father won't be in attendance. Do you intend to tell my mother about the aderyan?"

"That's not my decision to make," Sabine said, gesturing to Aeron and Thalassa. "We'll defer to whatever they believe is best for themselves and their people."

Aeron inclined his head. "We will consider it."

Thalassa took a step toward Sabine. "With regard to your attire for the gala, certain formalities will need to be observed. Will you be attending as Lord Malek's mate?"

"Yes," Malek said quickly.

"No," Sabine said at the same time.

Sabine glared at him. "You're not going to budge on this, are you?"

"You're my mate," Malek said firmly. "It's a dragon thing. If it serves to protect you, I'll declare it even against your wishes." He turned to Thalassa. "Azalia can show you where my formal attire is kept. She can also provide you with access to the dragon stones and appropriate companion pieces."

Thalassa frowned, glancing at Aeron for guidance. Aeron took a step backward, staring up at the ceiling as though it were suddenly fascinating. Bane looked as though he were enjoying this entirely too much.

Sabine lifted her hands in exasperation. "I don't have time to argue about this mate thing again. If it makes you happy to select or match my clothing, feel free. I need to see about sending that letter to Dagmar."

Pointing at Blossom, she added, "Blossom, come with me. I want to know what your brother said about the situation in Faerie." She motioned for Bane and Aeron to follow her. "Bane and Aeron, you'll want to hear this too. We also need to finish working on that map to free the rest of the aderyan."

Without waiting for a response, she headed into the study muttering, "A dragon possessed by a lunatic pixie. That's the only explanation."

CHAPTER 36

Sabine sat at Malek's desk and rubbed her temples, trying to ward off the dull headache plaguing her. Portal magic was challenging, and her effort lacked the finesse that would only come with practice. Blossom's teaching skills were a far cry from the structured studies she'd been tasked with as a child. At least she'd managed to send the message to Dagmar in Razadon.

Hopefully, it would be easier to retrieve the response.

Sabine closed the music box the Huntsman had gifted her. Bane picked it up and placed it back in the traveler's back. She'd thought it was simply a charming trinket at first, but the melody it played was specifically designed to help her focus on the resonance needed to connect with the magic of Faerie.

She should have known the Huntsman would have an ulterior motive in any sort of gift. Fortunately, using it only gave her a splitting headache. It didn't negate her agreement to not manipulate any doorways until the end of the month.

"Strange things are happening at the Seelie palace," Blossom said, pressing her face against a trinket box on

Malek's desk. "Barley says it's been busier than usual, with people coming and going at all times of the day. He's having trouble getting inside. They planted sleeping dahlias outside."

"Sleeping dahlias?" Sabine asked, leaning back in Malek's chair. The movement made her head throb. "That seems a little out of character for a court that's always tolerated pixies."

The box's lid clattered onto the desk, and Sabine winced at the sound. Blossom jumped inside and began rustling around, tossing out small clips and coins. Her voice was muffled as she said, "I wouldn't worry. Barley's on it. He's enlisting the help of some of my cousins and siblings."

"What of the cave troll spy?" Bane asked. "Has he been assigned a post?"

Blossom poked her head out of the box. "He lasted a day. After he accidentally knocked over Lady Verdania's china cabinet and set her curtains on fire, they banished him to one of their outlying holdings. He got bored chasing dust bunnies in an empty estate and went home."

Bane eyed her with irritation. "Then you have no new information to report?"

Blossom held up a shiny coin, admired her reflection for a moment, then tossed it aside. "King Cadan's causing trouble for Balkin. He's accusing your guardian of acting as regent without Council approval. He says they have no way of knowing if you're even still alive. He's demanding they install your brother, Rhys, as regent until you return to Faerie or are determined to be dead."

Sabine squeezed her eyes shut. She'd known it was only a matter of time before Balkin became a target. It was imperative she return to Faerie soon. If Rhys actually managed to take control of the Unseelie court, it would mean the end for her people. Sabine's father would attempt to merge the two courts under his rule, but the Unseelie wouldn't go peacefully. It would be civil war or worse.

Rika cleared her throat and said, "Hey, Blossom? Why don't we go check on the pixies in the garden? I think Sabine needs a break."

"I will escort you," Aeron said. "It is time for Lyra's flying lesson. Perhaps the flutterfolk will assist?"

Blossom flew out of the box, sending clips and coins across the desk and floor. "Oh! Sure! I'll finish looking through Malek's desk later. Did you know he has three locked cabinets in his bedroom? If we find a sharp thorn in the garden, I bet I can..."

Their voices trailed off as they headed out of the study.

Bane closed the door to the study, latching it with a quiet *snick*. Sabine opened her eyes to regard her demon protector. He was terrific at healing wounds, but she doubted he'd be able to do much for her headache.

He approached and opened the traveler's pack. Placing several wyvern scales on the desk, he asked, "What do you sense from these?"

Sabine frowned. "These are from the wyverns we killed in the forest?"

Bane gave her a curt nod.

She leaned forward and studied each of them carefully. They were all equally beautiful, like glittering gemstones.

She touched the edge of a sparkling red and black one with her fingertips. A shock of current ran through her at the contact, and she jerked back in surprise. "Did you know that would happen?"

Bane didn't respond. Instead, he pushed another scale toward her. This one was a deep orange, almost like citrine. It had flecks of red scattered within it like the flickers of a flame.

Sabine gingerly brushed her fingertips against it,

prepared for the shock, but nothing happened. It felt like nothing more than polished glass.

She lifted her head to meet Bane's gaze. "Nothing from that one. What are you thinking?"

"A suspicion," Bane said, placing another scale in front of her. This one was also familiar, appearing to be from the wyvern Sabine had nicknamed Slash.

She swallowed and touched the edge of the scale. Power slammed into her, and she quickly pulled her hand away. "I'm reacting to the ones I used death magic on."

Bane nodded. "Indeed."

Sabine frowned and eyed the scales again. "What does that mean?"

Bane leaned forward. "Do you sense the imbalance from those deaths?"

Sabine considered the question for a moment and then shook her head in surprise. "No. Nothing. I only felt the power from their sacrifice. It… energized me somehow."

Bane nodded, pushing the two scales with power toward her. He took the others and returned them to his satchel. "You need to keep these close to you. I would suggest we consider having the dwarves craft some sort of jewelry you can wear."

Sabine frowned, not wanting to touch them again. But she couldn't discount the wisdom of his words. "What are you thinking?"

"Where does your death magic come from, Sabin'theoria?"

Sabine paused, suddenly wary at the use of her full name. "From the same place all these foreign magics originated— the portal artifacts. Why are you asking me this, Bane?"

Bane's eyes flashed silver. "You know who the demons serve, daughter of Vestior. You also know some of the secrets we are sworn to keep—things that are forbidden for any outsiders to know." He moved around the desk toward her. "When you bargained and manipulated to install Dax as our king, consider who you bargained with and the reward that was offered."

Oh, gods. Sabine swallowed. Bane knew. He knew Vestior was the Huntsman.

Wait—*he knew?*

And didn't tell her or warn her?

Such information would have been helpful, especially before she'd gone for an unplanned midnight swim in the Well of Dreams. Sabine narrowed her eyes on him, wondering what other secrets he'd been keeping.

Bane pushed the wyvern scales toward her again. "Where does your death magic come from, my queen?"

She stared down at the scales again. Realization slammed into her, and she jerked her head up.

"You believe I claimed them for the Wild Hunt," Sabine whispered in shock.

Bane inclined his head. "There is no imbalance. Malek claims the magic in these scales must be gifted to be used, yet you could sense their power with a mere touch. I suspect they ride with the Hunt, and the more souls you surrender to the Hunt, the more it will respond to your command."

"This shouldn't be possible," Sabine said, trying to get her head around what he was suggesting. When she'd been near death, the Huntsman had offered her a place with him in the in-between. Her physical body had remained behind in the mortal realm while they'd spoken. "Do these wyverns still exist beyond the Veil? Is that why I don't sense any imbalance?"

"You tell me."

Sabine stared down at the scales again, wondering if it could be possible. "You don't sense anything from them? Not even through our blood bond?"

Bane's gaze sharpened on her. "I have not claimed their souls, Sabin'theoria. Even if I had ended their lives, their magic would not be mine to claim. That is the province of the Tuatha Dé. Not even the fae can wield such power."

Sabine stood abruptly. "What are you suggesting?"

"You've walked through the Hall of the Gods and drunk from the Well of Dreams," Bane said, his eyes flashing silver. "Your skin markings are no longer strong enough to mask your true identity. You shine with the brilliance of a thousand golden suns and the luminescence of the silver moon. You create portals where none existed, a magic that hasn't been duplicated in ages. You've returned the old magics and restored land that has not been touched in centuries. Even the cursed aderyan have acknowledged you as their Aderylin, their Divine Light!"

Sabine flinched. She'd thought it was nothing more than an honorary title. Her knowledge of the aderyan was sorely lacking, a fact that would likely get her into trouble if she wasn't more careful. "I cannot undo what's been done."

He grabbed her arms and demanded, "Do you not understand the danger, even now? King Cadan has suspected you are more than you appear for some time. Why else would he place the blame for your mother's murder at your feet? Why has he stalked you at every turn? You are a threat beyond imagining, Sabine. You have the potential to destroy all of Faerie and their precious hierarchy."

Sabine jerked away from him. "What would you have me do, Bane? Shall I hide under a rock somewhere? Allow Malek to keep me locked up in this fortress?"

"That dragon is so besotted with you, he'd damn his entire clan just to keep you safe." Bane sighed. "No, I don't expect you to be anything other than what you are. However, when you stand in the presence of these other dragons, you must remember few are like the one whose heart you've claimed.

"This world is not theirs. The stories of the war before the portal was sealed are not history to them. They fought in that war. They lived it. They streaked across the sky, slaughtering thousands of Unseelie and Seelie alike. And they watched their families and loved ones fall to the Tuatha Dé and to us. They will remember what it means if they witness your golden magic, and they will not care where the boundaries lie. You are a threat they *will* eliminate—and they will celebrate your death."

Sabine paled. If he'd been trying to scare her and break down her defenses, he'd succeeded. But running was no longer an option. Bane knew that.

"All right," she said quietly. "What do you suggest?"

Bane leaned against the desk and said, "Allow Dax to send an assassin to eliminate your father. It will likely not be successful, but it's a threat he will understand. A small victory will give King Cadan confidence and provide us with some breathing room."

She arched her brow. "You want me to send a demon to his or her death simply to buy us a few days of 'breathing room'?"

"Yes."

"No. I won't do it."

"Dammit, Sabine," Bane said with a growl. "Aeron claims something or someone stalks you in your dreams. It's likely your father or one of his dreamweavers. They've already gone after you in visions. If their efforts have weakened your ability to resist that bitch of a goddess, you must buy yourself some time. You endanger all of us by treating with dragons while you're not in control of your magic."

"Then find a way to help me resist him," Sabine demanded. "I've accepted Aeron's oath. If he can shield me, or even better, train me how to fight whatever stalks me, *that* is something I'm willing to do. If there's some alliance that needs to be made, or some pact I need to forge in order to buy us this necessary time to keep the goddess at bay, then so be it. However, I will not, now or ever, throw away lives simply because it's convenient."

"You cannot save everyone, little one," Bane said.

Sabine lifted her head. "No, but I intend to try."

Bane laughed, a harsh and bitter sound. He scrubbed his hands over his face. "I told Dax you wouldn't ever approve of sending assassins into Faerie. I think you're even more stubborn and willful than us."

Sabine walked over to the window that overlooked Malek's garden. Pixies darted through the bushes, playing some sort of game that involved weaving in and out of the fountain streams.

Before she and her brother had been named heirs to their respective thrones, they'd often played together in the palace gardens and surrounding woods. At least until her father had forced the end to such adventures.

"My father's always hated me," she said quietly. "When I was four or five, he tried to have me murdered for the first time. I killed the assassin, and my mother had his head sent back to my father in a box. Before the assassin reached me, he killed a brownie who had gotten in his way. She was simply in the wrong place at the wrong time."

"She was a brownie, Sabine."

Sabine stiffened. "Yes, Bane. A brownie who always had a kind word for me. A brownie who turned a blind eye when I snuck out of the palace to play in the forest. A brownie who had a family and a life before she died from an assassin's blade meant for me."

"How many times has he tried to kill you?"

Sabine shook her head. "I don't know. The next time was

a few years later. Balkin killed that one, and the one after that. They seemed to stop for a time, but I believe it was only because Balkin and my guards made more of an effort to hide their deaths from me."

"He did," Bane said gruffly. "Queen Malia had him beaten for it. She said you needed to witness Cadan's efforts if you were to defend yourself against such attacks in the future. Balkin refused, even when she banished him from your side for several months. That's when we met him for the first time. He was the emissary she'd sent to the underworld on her behalf."

"I hadn't realized that's why he'd left me." Sabine ran her index finger over the cool crystal window. "It was that summer when I asked my mother why my father hated me. She laughed and told me it was the nature of a rat to fear and loathe the lion. She claimed he had a purpose to serve. Once she no longer needed him, I could eat the rat for all she cared. She never explained further, and I never asked again."

"And what of your brother?"

"Rhys wasn't a factor as far as she was concerned," Sabine admitted, placing her palm on the window. "He was inconsequential in her eyes, much to his everlasting frustration. Rhys was allowed to come and go in the Unseelie court as he pleased, but I was banned from the Seelie court by my mother's command. She refused to let me to step foot in it unless she was with me."

Sabine turned to face him. "I know my magic is different, Bane. Even before I claimed the first artifact, I could do things no one else could. The normal Seelie and Unseelie rules of magic didn't apply to me."

"In what manner?"

Sabine gestured to the marks on her arm. "I was younger than Lyra when my mother hired Seelie Elders to help etch my skin for the first time. The Unseelie ones weren't enough.

They came to the palace in secret, and she paid them handsomely for their silence. They returned several times a year to etch my skin. My mother always closed the palace during those times, traveling to Razadon and elsewhere to discourage visitors. Once the Elders were finished, she would return and assess their work. A few months later, the process would begin again."

"Did your father's assassination attempts begin around the same time the skin etchings did?"

Sabine nodded. "Yes. The first mark I received was from an Unseelie Elder. Unfortunately, my father happened to be visiting when I dropped an acorn and accidentally grew a forest outside the palace. My mother had been delighted, but my father accused her of trickery and deceit. He claimed I shouldn't have access to both aspects of magic, since Rhys hadn't come into his powers yet. But even when he did several years later, his abilities were unremarkable for a Seelie."

Bane was quiet for a long time.

Sabine studied him and said, "You've thought of something."

"Yes. I need to leave. Tonight."

Sabine's eyes widened. "What?"

"After the dinner this evening, I will need to leave your side for several hours. Aeron will be required to accompany me." He crossed the room toward her. "You must give me your word you will remain with Malek and not sleep during the time I'm gone."

"You aren't going to tell me, are you?"

Bane's eyes flashed silver. "What happened in the Hall of the Gods, Sabine? What did Vestior tell you?"

Sabine stared up at him, the mark on her wrist beginning to warm. She pressed her fingers against it, and Bane gave her a curt nod. There were some things neither one could share. They simply had to trust each other. For whatever reason, he didn't want Lachlina to know what he was doing.

"Be careful," she said and hugged him tightly, sending a strong wave of her magic over him.

Bane ran a hand over her hair and said, "I would not leave you alone in this place if it weren't of vital importance, little one. Do not sleep, and keep that dragon of yours close."

Sabine nodded. "I know. You have my word. Just come back to me safely."

He kissed her forehead. "As you command, my queen."

CHAPTER 37

aking Malek's arm, Sabine walked up the steps to the imposing front door of his parents' estate. While Malek's home had a warm and inviting feel, there was something darker and far more ominous about this place. The building was constructed of obsidian-like stone that gleamed like the shadows of the underworld, even under the daylight. Golden accents traced the edges of the sharp, angular pillars, yet these embellishments accentuated the structure's formidable nature rather than softened it. This was a house built and designed for dragons, and it had never been more apparent that Sabine was very much out of her element.

Several wyvern guards clad in dark, austere uniforms snapped to attention as they approached, their fists pressed solemnly against their chests in salute to Malek, but their eyes were cold when they fell upon her and her companions.

To his credit, Aeron had been able to hide his wings by combining something he called the blur along with shifting the light around him. While it wasn't a true form of glamour, he appeared more fae now. At least no one would suspect him of being an aderyan.

Bane, on the other hand, didn't seem the least bit disturbed over the suspicious glares. He returned them with equal measure, but Sabine didn't miss the way some of the wyverns tightened their grip on their weapons as they passed.

At least Rika and Blossom were too busy fawning over all the small details to be overly troubled by their less than stellar welcome.

"Lord Malek," a dark-haired man greeted them. He wore a guard uniform similar to the wyverns, but there was a gold flame emblem near his collar that made Sabine wonder if he was some sort of superior. He gave a slight bow to Malek and then to her, but his smile didn't meet his eyes.

"Captain Fandrin," Malek said and gestured to Sabine. "I'd like you to meet my mate, Lady Sabine, and her ward, Lady Rika."

Blossom cleared her throat.

"And the pixie, Blossom," Malek added.

Blossom twirled in the air in her new pink and gold gown. "That's Lady Blossom, pixie extraordinaire and dragon-in-training."

"I stand corrected," Malek said dryly.

"Welcome to House Obsidian," Captain Fandrin said, giving them a curt nod. "We were not told to expect anyone other than Lady Sabine and Lady Rika."

Malek gestured to Bane and Aeron. "Bane and Aeron are two of Sabine's trusted guards. I've given them permission to inspect the premises to ensure her safety for the gala."

Captain Fandrin's eye noticeably twitched. "Lord Malek, your father—"

Malek shot him a dark look. "Are you challenging my orders, Captain Fandrin?"

"Of course not, my Lord," Captain Fandrin said quickly. "But I would be remiss in my duties if I did not express concern. Your father has made his… position clear."

"Your concern is noted. My orders stand. Lord Darius is not currently in residence, correct?"

"No, my Lord," Captain Fandrin said, clearly uncomfortable.

"Then there's no objection," Malek said firmly. "Should my father risk Lady Nymira's wrath and step foot inside, advise me at once. In the meantime, Bane and Aeron are to be given the freedom to move about unhindered."

"I shall also require freedom to move about unhindered," Blossom announced.

Rika made a noise, quickly disguising it as a cough. "Are you sure you don't want to join us for dinner, *Lady* Blossom?"

Blossom landed on Sabine's shoulder. "Well… maybe a quick snack. I need to learn more about being a dragon from Lady Nymira. Then I can help investigate."

"A wise choice," Sabine murmured.

Captain Fandrin turned to Malek and said, "Lady Nymira is currently awaiting your arrival in the parlor. Dinner will be served shortly. I'll escort Lady Sabine's guards to the areas being used for tomorrow evening's gala. However, the staff is still in the process of setting up."

"Very well," Malek said, offering Sabine his arm again.

Sabine glanced back at Bane and Aeron. They both gave her a brief nod to indicate they had the situation well in hand. At least they could draw upon her power if there was trouble, but she worried about being separated from them. Bane sometimes got a little too much pleasure out of scaring humans, and he might decide to see how far he could push some of the wyvern guards.

Malek lifted her hand and pressed a kiss to the back of it,

his mental voice brushing against her through their bond. *"No one will harm you, or anyone under our aegis, while we're in my parents' home. By declaring you my mate, our companions are also off-limits."*

"I was more concerned about your parents' staff," Sabine said, allowing Malek to lead her down a marble hallway. There were more wyvern guards here, but with the absence of the heavily-armed Bane and Aeron, their gazes were now more curious than suspicious.

Halfway down the hall, two wyvern guards opened a set of double doors. Malek led them into a small circular room with tall windows that reached from the floor to the ceiling. Through them, Sabine caught a glimpse of a pretty garden with several flowering plants. It didn't have the same effect as Malek's garden, but it was quite lovely and appeared to be expertly maintained.

A woman stood as they entered, her appearance an older and more mature version of Kaia. But the slope of her eyes, golden skin, and cheekbones reminded her of Malek. There could be no doubt. This striking woman with dark, wavy hair and sparkling green eyes was Malek's mother.

Malek stepped forward and said, "Mother, I'd like to introduce you to my mate, Sabine. Sabine, I'd like you to meet my mother, Lady Nymira."

"Well met, Lady Nymira," Sabine said, tilting her head in greeting.

Nymira beamed a smile at her and approached. "Oh, you really are fae. How extraordinary! I'd nearly forgotten, but Elisa had the same musical quality to her voice." She turned to her son and added, "Malek, you didn't tell me Sabine was absolutely stunning. I suppose I shouldn't be surprised she caught your eye."

"It was one of many reasons," Malek said with a grin and

gestured to Rika and Blossom. "This is her ward, Rika, and the pixie, Blossom."

Rika curtseyed. "It's a pleasure to meet you, Lady Nymira."

Blossom waved and said, "Hi! We would have met earlier but—Oh! Flowers!"

Blossom flew over to investigate a small bar area with a large number of glasses and bottles. A bowl of freshly cut flowers was artfully arranged as a centerpiece and had drawn the pixie's attention.

Sabine, on the other hand, was fascinated by dozens of small, dangling crystals strung along the wall of the bar area. As the sunlight streamed through the window, the crystals illuminated the bottles in a kaleidoscope of colors. It reminded her of the stained crystal windows the dwarves often crafted.

"You have a remarkable home, Lady Nymira," Sabine said, charmed by the inventive design. "Malek's spoken of you and the rest of his family with a great deal of fondness."

"Call me Nymira," she said, motioning for them to sit down. "And if I thought the fae could lie, I'd say you were pulling my tail. I think we exasperate him more than anything. It's wonderful to have him back though."

"You're only saying that because I just got here," Malek said, heading over to the bar area where Blossom was exploring. He opened a bottle of wine and began to pour. "Give it another week or two, and you'll be suggesting some far-off place for me to visit."

Sabine took a seat on the couch while Rika sat beside her. Rika kept fidgeting with her dress, picking at the intricate beading and staring at everything. Blossom had gotten bored with the flowers and was now on the opposite side of the room investigating the bookcase. After seeing the aderyan hideout in Imenel, Blossom was convinced all buildings had hidden rooms.

"Now Rika, are you part fae as well?" Nymira asked, taking a fluted glass from Malek.

Rika shook her head. "No, I'm completely human. Well, except for being a sidhe seer."

Nymira choked on her wine. "Pardon? You're a seer?"

Rika nodded. "It runs in families, but only for the women in mine. My grandmother was training me until she became sick."

Sabine reached over and squeezed Rika's hand. "She would be proud of all you've accomplished."

Malek handed a glass to Sabine and then to Rika. "Rika has become more like a younger sister. With her seer training cut short, Sabine's been trying to work with her."

Nymira lowered her glass, regarding Sabine in surprise. "You want her to learn to use her seer abilities?"

"Of course," Sabine said and took an experimental sip of the cool wine. It wasn't quite on the same level as Faerie wine, but it was very good. "Her abilities are part of her birthright. If she wishes to embrace her heritage, then I will do everything within my power to ensure she receives proper training."

"I'm surprised to hear a fae say that," Nymira said, tapping her finger against her glass. "I thought seers were a threat to your people."

"No more than my people are a threat to hers," Sabine said, watching as Blossom began swinging from the chandelier. Fortunately, Nymira hadn't noticed—yet. "I do not fear Rika or her abilities, nor does she fear me or mine. With me, she's safe to explore her gifts and the tools at her disposal. How she chooses to use her talents is her decision alone, as are the consequences."

Rika wrinkled her nose. "No pressure, right?"

Sabine laughed. "You've done well so far, and a few bumps along the way is perfectly natural. Remind me to tell you about some of my mishaps when I was learning how to control my magic."

"Deal," Rika said with a grin.

Nymira leaned forward and said, "I find myself strangely fascinated by this dynamic. What sort of lessons have you been working on?"

Rika grinned. "Sabine's been teaching me different meditation methods, and how to gain better control. I keep accidentally stripping her glamour at the worst possible times."

Sabine rolled her eyes and took another sip of her wine.

Malek chuckled and put his arm around Sabine's shoulders. *"She's not wrong."*

"I've also been doing weapon training and combat with Bane, but sometimes I think he just likes barking orders. Malek's been teaching me about navigation and map reading. Esmelle's showing me all sorts of things about plants and herbal remedies. Oh, and Blossom's been extremely helpful demonstrating the pitfalls of magic."

Blossom blew a raspberry at Rika and flew toward the bar area again. "It's not my fault magic is weird around you. Hey Malek, can I try some of whatever's in this red bottle?"

Malek put down his drink and went back over to the bar. "That one? It's not Faerie wine."

"No, but Sabine is drinking it."

Nymira took a sip from her glass and studied Sabine. "This may sound odd, but I have the strangest feeling I've seen you before. Perhaps you wore a slightly different glamour in the past?"

Sabine kept her face pleasantly neutral, but inwardly her heart was pounding. In all the paintings and images she'd seen of her mother and even of Lachlina, their appearances were remarkably similar. Unfortunately, many of the wyvern guards here had already seen her. Otherwise, she'd try to make some changes to her glamour before tomorrow night.

"It's unlikely unless you visited Akros in the last ten years," Sabine said, trying to prevent Malek from picking up on her fear. "Prior to that, I had never traveled outside of Faerie."

"No," Nymira said, shaking her head. "Malek will tell you I'm terrible with details, but I always remember a face. Perhaps it was someone else who looked a great deal like you. A mother or a sister?"

Malek sat beside Sabine again, his hand brushing against hers. "A relative is possible. Sabine's even younger than Kaia. She wasn't in the war."

Silently, he added, *"Even if she recognizes the similarities between you and your family, you're safe with me. I swear it."*

His words had their intended effect, and she relaxed slightly. She placed her hand over his, threading their fingers together.

Nymira looked down at their joined hands, her gaze softening. "You've never met any other dragons, have you?"

Sabine shook her head. "No. When I met Malek, I knew there was something unusual about him, but I never dreamed he was a dragon. I'd even wondered briefly if he might be fae, but his language skills were truly horrendous."

Malek gave a half-hearted shrug. "Elisa would have said the same, but at least it made you curious enough to get to know me."

Sabine smiled at him. "That it did."

Nymira watched them over the rim of her glass and smiled.

"Uh, Malek?" Rika asked, standing up and looking around. "Where's Blossom?"

Malek muttered a curse and leaped to his feet. Blossom was doing the backstroke in a bottle of wine while singing off-key about falling flower petals. "How the hell did she fall in there? I need a string or something to fish her out."

"She's too drunk to pull herself out," Rika said, tapping on the edge of the bottle. Blossom started singing even louder.

Rika grabbed several glasses and said, "Start pouring the wine. Then you can smack the bottom of the bottle and dump her out."

Sabine sighed and set her glass on the table. She walked over to the bottle and ran her finger along the rim. Infusing her breath with a trace of magic, she blew gently over it.

Blossom sank to the bottom and then launched upward like a rocket, shooting straight out of the bottle. Sabine caught the dripping pixie with one hand and tossed her onto a cloth napkin.

Leaning down, Sabine pointed her finger at Blossom and said, "We talked about this. No more alcohol unless you can drink responsibly. I will not have another bowling incident on my hands. Is that clear?"

"But, Sabinnnnnneeeeeee," Blossom slurred. "It was almost as gud as Faerie wine."

"No," Sabine said firmly. "No excuses. Those were prized crystals, and the dwarves were not happy you decided to have a bowling tournament with your cave troll friends. We're here at Malek's mother's invitation. I thought you wanted to make a good impression?"

Blossom nodded, her pink hair plastered against her head and dripping down her face. "I want her to teach me how to be the best dragon ever!"

Malek bit back a grin and handed Sabine a glass of water. She dipped the corner of the cloth into it and gently wiped Blossom's tiny face. "Then I suggest you get cleaned up and behave like the best dragon you can be. Do you need to change your dress? There's a garden right outside."

Blossom nodded. "My wings are sticky."

Rika picked up the glass of water and the sticky pixie. "Come on, Blossom. We can let them talk for a bit while you take a bath and pick out a new flower to turn into a dress. Why don't we go purple this time?"

Rika opened the door to the garden and stepped through, much to the surprise of the two guards standing nearby. They wandered through the small garden, looking at the different flower options.

"Did I hear her correctly?" Nymira asked, staring after them. "She wants to be a dragon?"

Malek chuckled. "Blossom has rather large ambitions for being so tiny. Her latest fixation is becoming a dragon and challenging me to a race."

"You've managed to acquire quite a household," Nymira said with a small smile. "Now, before we head to dinner, why don't you tell me what you needed to speak with me privately about?"

Malek glanced over at Sabine. "Can you ward the room?"

Quickly gathering her magic, Sabine identified several focal points and cast her power outward to surround them. A thin bubble formed, shimmering with a faint golden hue. "Our voices will not carry beyond the ward's boundary."

Nymira studied the magic carefully. "This is not any fae magic I've ever seen."

"If Sabine says it's safe to speak, you can trust her word on that," Malek said.

Nymira inclined her head. "Very well. What did you want to discuss?"

"Do you have the message the Seelie king sent to the Council?" Malek asked.

Nymira frowned. "No. It was passed around to all of us, but the original is likely with the Emerald, Gold, or Amethyst clans. They were acting as facilitators at the last Council meeting. Why?"

"Sabine is interested to learn whether King Cadan'ellesar penned the missive himself, or if someone else did so on his behalf."

Sabine placed her hand on Malek's arm. "King Cadan'ellesar has skilled magic users at his disposal who can subtly weave coercion into ink, in the same manner some fae can speak with the ability."

Malek looked at her in surprise. "You didn't tell me that."

"I didn't consider it until now," Sabine admitted with a frown. "Among the sidhe, it's not easy to use such methods of coercion. We expect such treachery between courts, and steps are usually taken to circumvent it before breaking the seals. If your people don't have regular contact with mine, they may not have a way to easily detect that type of magic."

Nymira considered her for a long time. "You seem to know a great deal about this."

"I've had some experience with these types of messages," Sabine said, recalling a rather unpleasant one from the former demon king.

"If we can get ahold of the message, could you tell if there was a spell in the ink?" Malek asked.

Sabine hesitated. "It's possible. The magic usually does not linger. The more times it's read, the weaker the hold on the recipient."

"I'll speak with Emanthir," Nymira said. "If he has the original, he can bring it with him to the gala. If such magic is at work, I'm afraid the Council may not simply take your word for it. Despite your relationship with my son, you're still fae."

Sabine nodded, having assumed as much. "I understand."

Malek straightened.

Before he could argue the point, Nymira said, "Malek, I know she's your mate. You are within your rights to defend her honor, however I am simply warning her of obstacles that *may* occur. Nothing worth having is ever easy. Wait and see if there's even a battle to be fought."

Malek's jaw clenched, but he gave her a curt nod.

"I'm assuming your new mate has shared some insight into this new Unseelie queen. Do you know beyond a doubt she's not planning to target the Sky Cities?"

"She has no such plans," Sabine said firmly, hoping Malek was right about confiding in his mother. "For the past several months since she claimed her throne, her only intention has been to restore the balance and locate the portal artifacts. She has no desire to seek war against your son's beloved family or his people."

Malek took Sabine's hand in his. "Mother, allow me to formally introduce you to Sabin'theoria, Queen of the Unseelie."

Nymira's fluted glass fell to the ground and shattered. "By the ether, you're Theoria's kin. Granddaughter to the Tuatha Dé, Lachlina and Vestior. Daughter of Queen Malia and King Cadan." Her hand flew to her mouth. "Oh, Malek. What have you done?"

"Her ties to them change nothing," Malek said.

"They change everything!" Nymira shouted. "Malek, you cannot do this. You cannot pass her off as a simple fae. No matter how much you might care for her, the others will take one look at her and know! She's wearing glamour, and I still recognized her! Look at this golden bubble around us!"

Sabine flinched. This was what Bane had warned her about.

Nymira spun away and began to pace. "I knew you looked familiar. Not even with a hundred layers of glamour can you hide those features. You look just like them. Theoria had a bit more gold in her hair and on her skin, but the eyes were the exact same. If you lost the human glamour, you could be sisters."

Sabine took a deep breath. "Lady Nymira, I did not come here to cause problems for you or your family. In fact, I argued with Malek against coming to the Sky Cities. It's one of the reasons why I refuse to acknowledge his mate claim."

Nymira halted. "You refused him?"

"I did, and I still do," Sabine said quietly. "I love your son, Lady Nymira. It is because I love him that I will do nothing to put him or the family he adores in danger. My people will not accept a dragon by my side, and your people will not accept me. I have no illusions about this, despite what my heart desires."

Malek narrowed his eyes on her. "Sabine, if you think—"

Nymira held up her hand to stop him. "Let her finish."

"Malek has told me why he was sent to find the portal artifacts," Sabine admitted. "In our travels, I've learned your people are not the only ones who have suffered from corrupted magic. All of us have been affected, from the weakest to the most powerful. I have given Malek my word I will do everything within my power to help save your people, provided it does not further destroy what is left of the precious balance in our world. Unfortunately, I do not believe it's possible to control the portal like he hoped."

Nymira squeezed her eyes shut. "Then it must be reopened."

Sabine nodded. "Yes, and we must once again embrace the ether—even if that means we also rejoin the war."

Molten fire lanced through her wrist at these words, flooding her entire body with liquid heat as Lachlina's fury erupted. Malek's gaze immediately flew to her, and he swept her into his arms.

"Breathe, Sabine. You're stronger than Lachlina. You can resist her."

She pressed her face against his chest, breathing him in. Focusing on Malek helped push Lachlina back, but it did little to quench the heat of her markings. The pain was nearly overwhelming.

Screams sounded from somewhere nearby, accompanied by the pounding of boots on the marble floor. A sharp pull on her power made her gasp. Bane and Aeron were in trouble.

Nymira turned to Malek, her face ashen. "You brought a demon into my home? Have you gone mad? Your father's ripped a hole through my ballroom!"

CHAPTER 38

"I warned you Sabine was bringing guards with her," Malek said, his arms still wrapped around her. "Why else did you think I made sure he was truly banished from the premises?"

"We'll discuss this later," Nymira said as she raced from the room, dissolving Sabine's warding as she passed through it.

"I need to get to them," Sabine said, pulling away from him. A wave of nausea rose swiftly as the fire in her wrist flared, roaring through her. She sent a mental plea to the goddess, reminding her that Bane and Aeron were under Sabine's protection.

"And what of your oath to me, my little golden flower? You have allowed my husband to lead you astray. The fire serves as a reminder of what awaits should the portal be reopened to the destruction of the dragons."

"She's determined to teach me a lesson," Sabine managed to say.

"I'd like to teach her a few of my own," Malek said, grabbing a cloth from the bar and soaking it in a pitcher of water. "We need a cold compress, or you'll pass out from the pain."

Steam rose from the fabric as he quickly wrapped it around her wrist. Sabine gritted her teeth and drew on the moisture in the air, using the merfolk's power to keep the cloth as cool as possible.

Rika burst into the room with Blossom on her shoulder, wings still dripping from her recent bath.

"The goddess is really angry," Blossom said, clutching Rika's hair and shaking out her wings. "She says the Huntsman is deceiving Sabine, and his actions are going to lead Sabine down the same path as Theoria. He's there in the garden, and they're shouting at each other and destroying everything."

"Not now," Malek said, taking Sabine's hand. "We've got to find Bane. My father's going to demolish the house if we don't stop him. The guards are all converging on the ball room."

"Stay close," Sabine said to Rika as they ran from the room. They turned down several corridors until Sabine was thoroughly lost. The only indication they were getting closer were the humans running in the opposite direction and the sound of shouting becoming louder.

Malek skidded to a halt inside an enormous two-story ballroom. Sabine nearly slammed into him, but he turned and pulled her and Rika out of the way just before a massive chunk of ceiling crashed down.

"Is that—is that Malek's dad?" Rika asked, staring up at an enormous obsidian dragon with a jagged scar slashing across one eye. He was tearing through the ballroom with claws and tail, knocking down parts of the house as he barreled toward something at the far end of the room.

The wyvern guards, still in human form, were quickly ushering the humans out. Nymira stood in the middle of the destruction, hands on her hips, glaring up at the dragon.

"I'm going to tie your tail into a knot!" Nymira shouted. "Look at this mess! Look at it! We're hosting the gala tomorrow night, and you've destroyed my ballroom!"

The dragon ignored her and kept digging with his massive claws, pulling down part of the second-floor balcony. Sabine scanned the ballroom, trying to locate Bane or Aeron.

She reached for Malek's arm and spoke silently into his thoughts. *"Aeron's using my glamour and his own abilities to shield them from view. They're safe for the moment, but I can't tell where they are."*

"My mother's attempting to keep my father distracted while the humans are evacuated," Malek said. *"I can't tell if he actually has Bane and Aeron pinned down or not."*

"Damn you, Darius," Nymira continued to shout at the dragon. "I was in the middle of getting to know our son's new mate. She's perfectly lovely, I'll have you know. She won't put up with any of his nonsense. It's a good thing too. Obsidian dragons are a right pain in the ass."

The dragon turned his golden eyes on Nymira and huffed, steam curling from his nostrils.

Nymira pointed at him. "Don't you dare take that tone with me, Darius Rish'dan. If you keep this up, you'll live in this heap of rubble by yourself. I'll go move in with Malek and Sabine."

"Oh, hell no," Malek said and turned to Sabine. "If she moves in, we're leaving. We'll go live with the dwarves. Or the demons. I don't really care which."

"I vote for mushrooms," Blossom said.

Rika leaned close and whispered, "I think I see Bane and Aeron, or at least I see your magic. They're on the second-floor balcony trying to move in our direction."

Trusting Rika's judgment, Sabine whispered, "Blossom, I need you to act as a beacon for me and mark their location."

"On it!" Blossom's image shimmered, turning into a tiny ladybug.

"What are you thinking?" Malek asked.

"They can't move easily without being detected. Get the rest of the humans out of here, and I'll create a different illusion. It should disorient your father enough to allow Bane and Aeron to escape. Warn your mother and the wyverns, so they're not caught unprepared."

Malek nodded and motioned toward a nearby wyvern guard. They immediately fanned out, locating the rest of the humans who were hiding behind furniture or too terrified to move.

"The demon is here at our son's invitation," Nymira said to the dragon, putting her hands on her hips. "I don't give a damn if you say otherwise. I will not have my family torn asunder because of old issues. He's your son, and she's his mate. If she wants to bring an entire horde of demons to the gala tomorrow, that's her right. She's now your daughter too."

Rika offered Sabine her dagger. She took it and nicked her finger, allowing a drop of her blood to fall onto the marble floor. The power from the stone and earthen ground beneath her feet roared through her, infusing her with strength.

Sabine reached for Bane and Aeron through their bonds, sending a powerful wave of magic toward them. As she did, she spread her magic through the room, calling upon both her fae ancestry and the dwarven magic at her command to embrace the stone.

Each of the giant marble pillars in the room became living silver trees, while the tiled floor transformed into rich moss and fallen leaves. The broken furniture turned into lush foliage and colorful flowers, and the ceiling took on the appearance of a canopy of trees with a smattering of starlight filtering through.

In the center of one of Faerie's oldest forests, Sabine allowed a single beam of moonlight to fall upon Nymira. Her rich green gown shimmered softly as she moved toward her mate. The dragon raised his head in alarm, blinking his golden eyes as though trying to see through the glamour.

"Darius," she chided gently. "It's simply a gift. One given to us by our son's mate. She offers you peace."

Tracking Blossom's movement, Sabine created the illusion of several glowbugs to mask the pixie's progress. When Blossom stopped moving, Sabine began weaving more complicated designs to slowly shift the landscape to mask Bane and Aeron's progress. Her wrist throbbed with pain, threatening to break her concentration. Attempting to juggle different foreign magics simultaneously was taxing her reserves.

"It's working," Malek said quietly.

Bane and Aeron leaped down from the second floor with scarcely a sound. The faint trickle of foreign magic brushed against hers, a sign Aeron had tapped into his own power to aid their descent. Darius's head whipped in Bane and Aeron's direction, but Sabine quickly darkened the shadows hiding them from view.

"She loves him," Nymira said, drawing the dragon's attention back to her. "It is a love as young and pure as the one that guided us together. She spoke simply and from the heart, leaving nothing to doubt. It is rare to find that even among our kind, but unheard of between our people and theirs. Do not destroy their moment of happiness with centuries-old vengeance."

Malek placed his hand on Sabine's shoulder, offering his strength. She could hear his voice far away and knew he was speaking with someone. It was too muffled to make out the words, nor could she hear the response. But it was surprising she could sense even that much.

Darius lowered his large head to the ground, peering at Nymira with his golden gaze.

She shook her head and said, "No. Do not give me the sad eyes. It won't work."

Bane and Aeron made their way to Sabine, touching her arm briefly to let her know they were at her side. She caught Malek's eye, and he nodded his understanding.

A moment later, Nymira placed her hand on the dragon's snout. "You hold my heart, Darius. You always have. But so help me, you will repair this rift between your children and their chosen mates, or I won't be held responsible for my actions."

Darius huffed and then nodded. He turned around, waddling away in his dragon form.

"And you will help me find a way to repair the hole in our ballroom by tomorrow evening!" Nymira yelled after him.

Darius pushed off the ground and flew upward into the air. Sabine allowed the illusion to fall away, reverting the ballroom back to its true appearance.

Blossom landed on Sabine's shoulder. "Now I definitely want to be a dragon. They can knock down walls!"

Nymira frowned at the destruction. "Maybe we should just burn it down and celebrate on its ashes. I don't see how we can possibly hold the clan gala here." She walked over to Captain Fandrin and began speaking to him, gesturing to the broken furniture with sweeping motions.

Sabine turned to Bane and Aeron. "Are you all right?"

Aeron inclined his head. "Neither one of us were harmed, Aderylin."

Bane scowled. "He spotted us through the window. It was

either retreat to the shadows or kill him. I did not think your dragon would appreciate the latter."

"No, he would not," Malek said. "Not that you would have had much success. My father's crafty."

Bane snorted.

Rika looked around the room. "Is there anything we can do to help? Lady Nymira looks really upset."

Sabine hesitated. "Malek, this was partly our fault. With your mother's permission, I would like to help make it right."

Malek frowned. "Sabine, I can feel how much your marks are hurting you."

"What happened?" Bane demanded, reaching for her bandaged wrist.

Sabine shook her head. "It's not important right now. Allow me to repay the debt our presence has caused, and then we should take our leave. I think we've overstayed our welcome."

"No, Sabine," Malek said, taking her hand, careful not to touch the makeshift bandage. "We'll leave because you need a break after this. You have not, nor could you ever, overstay your welcome. This is your home as much as it's mine, for as long as you want it." He paused. "If you do this, there will be talk. Too many here witnessed my father's destruction."

Bane's gaze swept over the room. "Even if she does nothing, there will still be talk of the illusions she created. Restoring the room may minimize the effect of these stories, provided we minimize the number of witnesses."

"If the Aderylin believes a debt is owed, then it shall be honored as my own," Aeron said. "I would aid you in this endeavor if you will permit it, Aderylin."

Sabine took a deep breath and nodded. "It must be done."

Malek lifted his head, and she could hear his voice once again sounding very far away. Nymira walked over a moment later, her gaze falling on Bane and Aeron.

Sabine gestured to them and said, "Allow me to introduce Bane and Aeron, my most trusted advisors and bloodbound protectors."

Nymira glanced over at Rika and said, "The demon is the one who likes to bark orders at you?"

Rika grinned. "Yep."

"By the ether," Nymira breathed and then laughed. "How marvelous!"

Sabine smiled. "I know we cannot undo what's been done here tonight, but I would like to offer my assistance in attempting to restore your home."

Nymira frowned. "With glamour? I'm not sure how well that would hold up, and it will be exhausting trying to maintain it tomorrow evening."

Sabine shook her head. "No, something a little more permanent."

"Clear the room," Malek said to Captain Fandrin. "Anyone who remains behind must swear to keep their silence on what occurs here tonight."

Nymira nodded her agreement.

Captain Fandrin began barking orders. The wyvern guards exchanged glances but began to depart. A couple of them remained positioned outside, keeping watch from a safe distance. Sabine would have preferred to do this completely without an audience, but there was little choice. The imbalance of what had occurred here tonight hung over her head, demanding she make it right.

Blossom rubbed her hands together. "Major magic incoming!"

Sabine slid off her shoes and walked barefoot to the center of the room, careful to avoid the piles of debris. Bane and Aeron followed her, like opposing bookends—one made of darkness and the other light. They placed their hands on her shoulders, offering up their power for this task.

The marble was cold beneath Sabine's feet, with a strength and power that called to her. She closed her eyes and summoned the dwarven power within her, allowing it to fill her body.

She reached for the toppled columns and broken beams, seeing them as jigsaw pieces in her mind's eyes. Calling upon Aeron's power, she used the wind to move them into place and then sealed them with Bane's volcanic heat. The ground beneath her feet rumbled as she coaxed the stone into its proper shape.

If there had been a place better suited for Bane and Aeron to hide, none of this would have happened. Knowing they would need such a place for the gala, Sabine visualized what she had in mind and sent her thoughts toward the nearby trees. With a gentle brush of her power, she asked them to supply their wood to bring her vision to life. They willingly obliged, offering her the raw materials. In exchange, she blessed them with growth and bounty, touching them with her magic and encouraging them to grow.

Using her fae magic to shape the offered wood, she crafted new rafters where none had previously existed. Bane and Aeron's approval reached her through their bond, and she moved on to her last task—the shattered crystal windows. Using Aeron's power, she lifted them with a pulse of wind. They swirled in the air, rejoining with other shards as though seeking out their lost companions until the window was once again whole. The realization was enough to make her reflect on one last gift she wanted to share.

"Malek," she called out, dimly aware her voice had taken on the strange quality it did when she was steeped heavily in magic.

Bane and Aeron released her and stepped back. She took Malek's hand and walked with him toward the large window.

She held the image in her mind and sent it across their bond.

Malek regarded her with surprise. *"You can do this?"*

"With your help, I believe so," Sabine said, staring up at the enormous window. *"It would be a gift from both of us, a reminder of what could be."*

Malek lifted her hand and kissed it. *"Or a reminder of what already exists between us."*

Sabine smiled at him. *"Touch the window, and allow your power to blend with mine."*

Malek pressed his hand on the crystal, and Sabine felt his heated magic surround her. She nearly faltered again as the heat from her wrist came to the forefront of her mind, but she managed to push it aside. She *would* do this.

Closing her eyes, she drew upon the powers at her command. She was no great artist, but the fae had always prided themselves on recognizing beauty. Channeling her magic in the way of the dwarves, she etched the scene that would forever be embedded in her mind. Then, drawing upon Malek's dragonfire, she sealed the image into the crystal.

She opened her eyes and stepped back.

"It's incredible," Malek said, staring up at the window.

In the middle of an ancient Faerie forest, a dark-haired woman in an emerald green dress stood beneath the moonlight. With her hand pressed against his scaled snout, she tamed a scarred obsidian dragon with words of love.

Sabine turned to Malek and smiled. "Love often is."

Malek stared up at the crystal image of his mother and father. He'd seen stunning artistry from the dwarves, but none compared to the love and magic Sabine had poured into this one. The green of his mother's gown swirled with the pulse of fae magic, making the window almost seem alive.

"By the ether," Nymira whispered, her eyes filling with tears. She reached up to touch the window and then pulled her hand away before making contact. "I have never seen such a thing in all my days. It's as though you've captured a moment in time and embedded it in crystal."

Malek wrapped his arms around Sabine, and she leaned against him. Restoring the ballroom had taken a lot out of her. He could still feel the pain in her wrist and the effort it was taking to continuously weave the merfolk's power to cool it.

Rika approached them and said, "It's even better than the ones we saw in Razadon."

Blossom hovered in front of it and pressed her tiny hands

against the crystal. "When I get my own garden, will you make me one, Sabine?"

Sabine smiled. "I'll see what I can do."

"If your father destroys this window in a fit of temper, I will not be held responsible for my actions," Nymira declared.

Malek chuckled and ran his hand down Sabine's back. "I think we're going to need to have dinner with you another time, Mother. Sabine's exhausted, and there's still quite a bit that needs to be done to get the ballroom ready before tomorrow."

"I already gathered as much," Nymira said with a knowing smile. "I sent a message to the cook to wrap your plates. They should be waiting for you by the entrance. Get some rest, and I'll see all of you at the gala."

Nymira reached for Sabine's hand and said, "I listened to what you had to say earlier, and now it's your turn. You may object and protest all you wish, but once a dragon proclaims they've found their mate, they recognize your essence and the light burning within you. It calls to him, becoming a beacon that anchors him to this reality and transcends all boundaries. You alone possess the power to guide him through the darkness, because you represent home, love, and family. That means, by extension, you are now my daughter."

Malek grinned.

Sabine stared at her in shock. "Lady Nymira, I—"

"I'm not finished," Nymira said, pinning Sabine with a hard look she'd been practicing on Malek and Kaia for years. "I feel beyond blessed to have been gifted with a daughter who has the grace and heart of a dragon, even if they consider themselves fae. The rest of your concerns are simply details. All of that can be sorted in time. Now come here and give me a hug."

Malek released Sabine, and his mother immediately

enveloped Sabine in a hug. Sabine tentatively returned the embrace, as though uncertain about the sincerity of such a gesture. He doubted Sabine realized how vulnerable and bemused she appeared in that moment. Fae stoicism would never be a match for his mother.

Nymira gestured to the crystal window and sniffed. "That is one of the most beautiful gifts I've received. I will treasure it always."

Nymira reached out and hugged Rika. "And you are a marvelous little human. I will cherish getting to know my first grandchild."

Rika gaped at her. "Wait, what?'

Nymira waved her hands at them. "Shoo. Go eat and relax. I have furniture to replace and a ballroom to make ready. I'll see you all tomorrow evening."

Malek chuckled and led a bewildered Sabine and Rika out of the room and toward the front entrance. Bane and Aeron fell into step behind them.

One of the wyvern guards stopped them at the door and held up two large baskets. "Lady Nymira instructed us to have dinner prepared for you and the rest of your companions. She suggested you might consider..." The wyvern cleared his throat. "A romantic picnic with your mate."

Malek moved aside the linen cloth and stared at the artfully packed meal and bottle of Faerie wine with a red cap. "Of course she did."

Privately, he reached out to his mother with his thoughts. *"A picnic, Mother? With Faerie wine?"*

Her laughter echoed in his mind. *"A little something we had in our wine cellar. I thought you might appreciate the irony."* She paused for a moment, her tone becoming more thoughtful. *"Perhaps it's time for all of us to consider a new way forward. We cannot change the past, but seeing the two of you together makes me wonder if there's still hope for the future. I look forward to getting to know your mate better, Malek."*

Malek covered the contents again. *"As do I."*

"Now go and enjoy yourself. The bluff is lovely this time of year. Very romantic. I've heard Faerie wine can be quite an aphrodisiac."

Malek blew out a breath. *"I'm not discussing this with you. Goodnight, Mother."*

He handed the second basket, containing another set of meals, to Aeron and debated whether staying in the Sky Cities was worth it. Maybe after they located the last artifact, he and Sabine could find a private island somewhere where no one would ever find them.

As they headed down the path toward his estate, Blossom landed on Sabine's shoulder and announced, "I'm going to be just like Lady Nymira when I grow up."

Malek made a pained noise.

"May the gods help us," Sabine murmured, shaking her head.

Rika giggled. "You have an interesting family, Malek."

"You're one of us now," Malek reminded her, climbing the steps to the front entrance of his estate. "My mother's claimed you. There's no going back."

He waved aside the warding, allowing them to pass.

"I need a private word with you," Bane said to him.

"What is it?" he asked.

Bane's gaze landed meaningfully on Sabine, but he didn't say a word.

After a moment, Sabine nodded, kissed Bane's cheek, and then repeated the gesture with Aeron. "Be safe, both of you. Malek, I'll be in the garden when you're finished."

Bane waited until Sabine was out of sight before turning back to him. "Aeron and I need to leave the Sky Cities. We'll return as soon as possible, but it's imperative you do not allow Sabine to fall asleep before Aeron returns."

"What is this about?" Malek asked.

"I need to return to the underworld. Tonight. It's a matter of some urgency."

Malek straightened. "You wouldn't leave Sabine unless she was in danger. What's going on?"

Bane was silent for a long time. "A suspicion that requires confirmation before I say more. I need to travel to the underworld to seek an audience in the Hall of the Gods."

Malek stared at him. "You're going to see the Huntsman?"

Bane gave him a curt nod. "He has the answers I require."

Malek looked at Aeron. "You're going to the underworld as well?"

Aeron inclined his head. "Bane will be unable to move swiftly enough in the allotted time without my aid. If he has not concluded his business by dawn, I will return to the Aderylin without him."

"Give me a moment," Malek said, and headed into the foyer. "Azalia? Rupert?"

Azalia appeared from the west corridor, wiping her hands on her apron. "Lord Malek! You've returned from dinner already?"

"Change of plans," Malek said, picking up one of the communication crystals from a side table. "Do you have your crystal on you?"

"Of course," she said, pulling the glowing crystal from her pocket.

Malek took it from her. "I need it for a few hours. Maybe a day. I think there's a spare in my study if you need it. Try the desk."

Azalia gaped at him. "You want me to search your *study*?"

Malek nodded. "It's probably a mess. There was an incident earlier. Bane and Aeron will be gone for a while, so don't be alarmed if they return in the middle of the night. Also, let Carlin know Rika will probably want to join Thalassa and Lyra for dinner."

"Of-of course, Lord Malek," Azalia said, staring at him as though he'd grown a second head. "I'll let Rupert and Carlin know about the change in plans."

"Great," Malek said, and returned to where Bane and Aeron were waiting.

He pressed the crystals together until they both turned blue. Handing one to Bane and the other to Aeron, he said, "Security around Imenel has been heightened. These two crystals are now linked. If Aeron needs to return without you, press the top and bottom of the crystal at the same time. His crystal will light up and guide him to your location."

Bane studied the crystal. "What's the range?"

"Levin and I tested them several years ago. We were able to receive signals between my estate and Imenel." He gestured to the basket. "Take the food with you. Carlin will prepare something for Rika, Thalassa, and Lyra."

Bane nodded and pocketed the crystal. "I do not part with Sabine's company lightly, dragon. Keep her safe."

"You have my word."

Bane and Aeron turned and headed back through the warding. His attempt at getting answers out of the Huntsman had been relatively unsuccessful. Maybe Bane would have better luck. It was strange how much he'd come to trust the demon, even extending that trust to Aeron because Bane seemed to respect him.

Uneasy at the thought of leaving Sabine alone, he entered the garden in search of her. She was sitting on the same bench where he'd spoken with his sister earlier that day. Two pixies were braiding Sabine's long hair, while another one was placing tiny flowers in the plaits. She was humming softly, and the pixies almost seemed hypnotized by the sound of her wordless song.

The sight of her settled something within him. She was watching the fountain, her fingers dancing in the air and causing the water to sputter and splash over some nearby pixies. They appeared delighted by the game, diving in between the streams and Sabine's magic.

"Malek, we found her," Levin's voice slipped into his thoughts.

Malek's attention whipped back to Levin and his urgent task. *"You found Idola?"*

"Yeah. The seer, her lover, and that gigantic golden beast of a hound. They're heading back now and should arrive in a few hours. Captain Fandrin's going to keep Idola contained in the guest wing of your parents' estate once she gets there. We told her about your conditional offer to rescind the banishment."

Malek let out a sigh of relief. *"Good. Hopefully, her tonics will continue helping Kaia. Is Esme okay?"*

"She's still with the dryads. I'll pick her up before I return. You may have some issues with Idola. I don't think she's overly pleased about this new arrangement. She agreed to make the tonics but insists she'll need additional herbs."

Malek didn't give a damn whether Idola was happy, especially after she'd tried to kill Sabine. *"Have her get a list to Tivaly. We'll deliver the necessary ingredients first thing in the morning. Make sure Fandrin knows I want each tonic tested before Kaia touches them. I don't trust Idola, but I'm hoping her desire to live peacefully within our borders outweighs her need for vengeance."*

"I'll take care of it."

"Fly safe, brother," Malek said before severing the mental connection.

Sabine turned at his approach, her eyes warming as she gazed at him. "Bane and Aeron have departed?"

Malek sat beside her and placed the food basket on the ground. "Yes. They didn't tell you why they were leaving, did they?"

"No." Sabine winced and lightly touched the makeshift bandage on her arm. "Bane doesn't often keep such things from me. I can only assume it has to do with the goddess."

Malek took her hand and carefully unwrapped the bandage around her wrist. She hissed at the pain and looked away. His anger toward Lachlina erupted into barely restrained fury at the sight of the inflamed red markings on Sabine's wrist.

He stood and dipped the cloth in the cool water of the fountain, silently cursing Lachlina to the deepest pits of the underworld. If Bane didn't find a way to sever the connection between Sabine and the goddess, Malek would reach out to the Huntsman himself. Someone had to know something.

He paused, wondering if someone already did.

Carefully dabbing at Sabine's wrist, he asked, "Where's Blossom?"

"She's checking on the beetle situation," one of the unfamiliar pixies volunteered.

"Blossom!" Malek yelled.

"What? What?" Blossom asked, zooming toward them. "Did something happen?"

Malek glanced at the pixies surrounding Sabine and asked silently, *Any chance you can distract the pixies for a few minutes? I'd like to speak with Blossom about what happened earlier without an audience.*

With a dramatic sigh, Sabine said, "This garden is beautiful, but I've barely had a chance to explore it. I'd love to know which flower is the rarest in the garden."

"I bet I can find out!" one of the pixies volunteered.

"I'll find out first!" another one called out.

Dozens of faces peered out from the foliage, talking excitedly about which flower Sabine might find the most rare.

Sabine smiled. "I'd also like to see a flower with an unusual color, one with five petals, and the sweetest-smelling flower. Can you find all of those for me?"

"Ohhhhh," all the pixies chorused before darting off in every direction.

"Not you, Blossom," Sabine said.

"Awww," Blossom grumbled, her wings drooping. "Fine, but can I play in the next scavenger hunt?"

"Yes," Sabine agreed. "Now tell us what happened earlier in the garden with Lachlina."

Blossom hopped onto the arm of the bench and looked up at them. "I've never seen her so angry. She was yelling at the Huntsman for leading you astray. The goddess said the war will end up killing you, and she refuses to lose another daughter. She blew up part of the garden."

Malek frowned. "What did the Huntsman say?"

"Nothing at first. When she tried to pull Sabine into the garden, he stopped her somehow. That only made her madder. She said the burning would continue until Sabine agreed to seal the portal permanently. The Huntsman told her it was Sabine's choice. He said if the goddess tortured Sabine into meeting her demands, she'd lose her the same way she lost Theoria. That's when the goddess blew up part of the garden."

Sabine stared at the fountain and didn't respond. The water began to bubble, as if the force of her emotions could no longer be contained.

"Uh oh," Blossom said, eyeing the bubbling water.

Malek reached over and took Sabine's hand. "Tell me what you need."

Sabine stood, her anger making her eyes even more

striking than usual. "What I need is for Lachlina to stop trying to manipulate me. I need the Huntsman to start being more forthcoming with answers. I need both of these ancient beings to stop meddling in affairs that no longer concern them."

Sabine yanked aside the cloth covering her wrist and glared at the marks. "The Huntsman does not belong to this realm. He visits, but he is not truly one with it. Lachlina is imprisoned in the in-between, clinging to the memory of a daughter who died to preserve our world. They remain a world apart from us, yet have the audacity to dictate our futures based on their wishes? No more!"

Sabine straightened, her bearing regal as her glamour began to dissolve. Storm clouds gathered overhead, echoing the fury within her. Blossom grabbed a leaf and held it over her head.

"The Unseelie denounced the gods for this very reason. If Lachlina thinks she can punish me with pain, so be it. I'll take it. I'll take everything she throws at me and more. I'll take this pain as a sacrifice and use it to fuel my magic as *I* see fit. This will serve as a badge of honor and my due as Queen of the Unseelie, and she can sit in her prison and watch."

The marks on her wrist flared gold, then faded. The makeshift bandage slipped from Sabine's hand and floated to the ground. Slowly, the storm clouds began to dissipate.

Blossom scratched her head. "Um, she laughed. She said her little golden flower has grown thorns. And then she laughed."

"What sort of game is she playing?" Malek demanded, rising to his feet. The pain he'd been sensing through their bond had vanished. He reached for Sabine's wrist, studying the marks that were once again back to normal.

Blossom held up her hands. "I'm just the messenger. She

says, 'The strongest of weapons is tempered in fire, but take care not to bend too far, or you'll break the balance.'"

"This isn't about me," Sabine said, lifting her head to meet Malek's gaze. "It's never been about me or even the portal. It's always been about them. She stopped tormenting me because I denounced both of them."

"It may not be about you for them," Malek said and drew Sabine into his arms. "But for me, for Bane, for Blossom, for Rika, and for everyone else who loves you, it's about you. We're going to figure out how to stop this, Sabine."

Sabine sighed and leaned against him. "Your mother knew Theoria by sight. I wasn't expecting that. Perhaps your people know more than I realized."

"We're even longer lived than the fae," Malek said. "It's just getting my people to talk about the past that's a little challenging."

Sabine nodded. "It's the same among my people."

"Hey, is this Faerie wine?" Blossom asked, snooping through the picnic basket.

"Faerie wine?" Sabine asked, pulling away from Malek. She reached into the basket and withdrew the bottle, staring at the red cap for a moment before meeting his eyes. "You know what this is?"

Red. Passion. Love.

Malek had been wondering how to get his hands on a bottle of that particular Faerie wine ever since he'd learned about it. Sharing a gold-capped bottle with Sabine had been one the most memorable and exhilarating experiences of his life. The thought of partaking in this type of wine was even more stimulating.

"Someone back in Akros might have mentioned it," Malek said, trying to gauge her mood.

Sabine gave him a brilliant smile and said, "Blossom, tell Rika she's welcome to the dinner in the basket. Thalassa and

Lyra have already eaten. Malek and I are going to be unavailable for the next several hours."

Malek captured her hand and said, "Only several? I have more staying power than that."

Sabine laughed and pulled him toward the north wing. "I think you're going to need to prove it."

"Challenge accepted."

CHAPTER 40

Tucked against his side, Sabine ran her fingers across Malek's bare chest in random patterns. The magic of the wine had faded, but she was reluctant to face reality yet. Once they left this bed, a host of problems awaited them—each more complicated than the last.

He captured her hand and kissed her fingertips. "You're thinking again."

Sabine tilted her head to look up at him. "Have I become that transparent to you?"

"I have an unfair advantage where you're concerned," he said with a smile. "And you fidget when you're in deep thought."

Sabine wrinkled her nose. "Maybe I was just enjoying touching you."

He gestured to his naked body. "By all means, think away."

Sabine laughed and pressed her face against his chest. "Gods, Malek. Sometimes I wonder how I managed these past ten years without you."

"Terribly," he said with mock dismay, threading his

fingers through hers. "I don't recommend attempting such a thing ever again."

She stared at their joined hands and wished things were that simple. Being with Malek was liberating in so many ways. She'd never thought a relationship could offer such a beautiful balance. Their differences challenged and frustrated her at times, yet she always felt safe and protected with him. The thought of not having him by her side hurt in ways she'd never imagined.

"Talk to me, sweetheart. At the very least, I can listen."

Her heart melted. He always seemed to know how far he could push, and how far she could go before she'd break.

"It's Lachlina," Sabine admitted. "She may have stopped her assault for now, but it won't last. She doesn't mind exposing me at inopportune moments, but if anyone dares threaten me or mine, her fury roils through me with enough force to steal my breath. Yet, when I challenge her authority, she almost seems pleased."

"Do you know what she wants?"

"Not entirely," Sabine said and frowned. "When we found the aderyan, she used my magic to return their wings. In exchange for helping me restore the other aderyan captives we find, I promised to temporarily provide her with a living vessel to visit Theoria's grove."

Malek stilled. "You did *what?*"

Sabine sat up, frustrated with the whole situation. "I'm not happy about it either. I know the power to restore the aderyan is within me, but I don't know how to wield it. She showed me what I was capable of in Imenel. It was *my* magic, Malek. Not hers. I gave up just enough control to allow her to guide me. If she can help me heal the rest of the aderyan, the bargain is worth it. This is too important to leave to chance."

Sabine stared down at her hands, wanting to explain but

unsure she had the right words. "I *need* to restore the balance, Malek. It's an ache that never quiets. Something happened when Lachlina guided my magic. I had a choice in that moment. I could walk away from the aderyan, or sacrifice the tiniest piece of myself to restore them. And when I gave up that part of me, their power became mine. Their magic was mine, but it was also so much more."

"You still feel that way?"

Sabine nodded. "Yes, but it's more a sense of knowing. If I think about Thalassa, I can feel her at the edge of my thoughts. She's distracted right now and focused on Lyra, but if I linger too long, I think she'll become aware of my presence. I can dimly feel the others who left on your ship, but they're not as strong. I get a sense of the ocean and salt, hope and fear."

Malek frowned. "And Aeron?"

Sabine hesitated. "He shields better than Thalassa does, but I believe that's a courtesy on his part. I have the impression he's waiting for me to reach out to him, almost like he's listening for me. Even now, there's an awareness of him that's hard to explain. I sense Lyra the same way. Perhaps it's because the magic between us is stronger."

Her gaze drifted to Malek's window and the moon creeping closer to the horizon. It would only be another hour or two before dawn. She could feel both Bane and Aeron tiring. Neither one had pulled on her magic yet, which meant they either didn't want her to know what they were doing, or they were trying to protect her from something.

Malek stretched out again, putting his hands behind his head. "Esme and Levin returned a few hours ago."

Sabine straightened. "Why didn't you tell me?"

He smiled lazily. "You were in the middle of doing that really creative thing with your—"

She grabbed a pillow and swatted him. He chuckled and pulled it away from her before pinning her back to the bed.

He kissed her nose and said, "They're safe and probably sound asleep by now. Esme said she'll tell you about the dryad grove in the morning, but they didn't have any new information to share."

Sabine ran her fingers lightly down the side of his face. "What happened earlier that caused you to send Levin away so abruptly? Is your sister all right?"

Malek rolled away from her and stared up at the ceiling. Sabine propped herself up on her elbow and waited. He finally met her eyes, and the pain in his gaze was enough to wound her.

She reached for him, sending a gentle caress of reassuring magic over him. "Malek, what is it?"

"Kaia's pregnant," he said, covering her hand with his. "She doesn't have enough magic to shift into dragon form and transfer the child into an egg."

Sabine frowned. "I'm not sure I understand."

"Dragons… feed on magic," Malek said carefully.

She blinked, unsure whether she'd heard him correctly. "You—*what?*"

He sighed. "It sounds worse than it is. We require magic to sustain ourselves or to perform extraordinary feats."

Sabine paused, recalling the way he'd flown with the ship and the carrier. He'd expended a tremendous amount of magic both times. He'd never asked or demanded anything from her, but she'd offered the gift of her magic to supplement his power with her own several times.

"You can't regenerate magic on your own, can you?"

"Not in the same way the fae do," Malek said. "Normally, we pull magic from the ether. Since we've been cut off, our magical supply has dwindled. We've been forced to conserve our strength, or we risk stripping it from the land. That's part of the reason we've adhered to an unspoken truce with your people and why we rarely leave the Sky Cities."

Sabine squeezed her eyes shut, understanding the ramifications of what he was saying. His people didn't belong here, and they knew it. Eventually, they would be forced to consume the remaining magic in their world or die. The Huntsman's solution was to reopen the portal and restart the war, but Lachlina was determined to see the dragon threat at an end. Was that what the goddess wanted? Did she intend to kill the dragons?

"This is why your people have been struggling to reproduce," Sabine said quietly. "A pregnancy requires a great deal of magic."

Malek nodded. "Normally, once a dragon becomes pregnant, she shifts and encases the child in a protective egg. It contains enough magic to nourish the hatchling until it's ready to emerge. If the child requires additional magic, such as in the case of a greater dragon, other family members can supplement the egg's reserves with their own."

Sabine placed her hand over Malek's heart. "And if Kaia's unable to shift?"

"The child will continue to consume Kaia's magic until she weakens and they both die."

"Oh, Malek," she murmured, her heart aching for all of them.

Malek sat up and scrubbed his face with his hands. "My mother was using Idola, the seer we met outside Imenel, to create tonics to help boost Kaia's magic. I don't know if they were working, but it's the only option we have right now. If we can't find the last artifact and control the portal, or hell, reopen it, I'm going to lose my sister and her child."

"You sent Levin and the other wyverns to retrieve Idola?"

Malek nodded. "She'll be confined to my parents' estate.

If her tonics work and help Kaia, I've agreed to reconsider her banishment."

Sabine took Malek's hand in hers. "You should tell Esme about your sister."

"What?"

"Idola was likely using traces of the land's magic contained in the plants to create these tonics. Esme has a way of sensing imbalances within people and knowing which herbs can help bring them into alignment. It's one of the reasons her teas were so popular in Akros."

Malek pinched the bridge of his nose. "Sabine, I've also seen the way her teas have gone terribly wrong. In case you've already forgotten, your plants nearly ate my house today."

"There may be a few kinks to work out," Sabine admitted. "But you can trust Esme's intentions far more than a seer you've already banished."

Malek laughed and wrapped his arms around her. "That's a fair point. I'll talk to her after the gala."

Sabine leaned against him and trailed her fingers over his chest. Whether or not her suspicions about Lachlina were true made no difference. She loved this dragon beyond all reason and would do whatever was necessary to keep him and those he cared about safe.

"If Kaia will allow me to assess her, there may be something I can do to help," Sabine said. "If pregnant dragons require additional magic, perhaps our bond will allow me to reach her through you."

He leaned back, searching her expression. "You would do that?"

Sabine pressed her hand against his cheek. "I would do that and much more for you, Malek. I can't make any promises, but I will try."

Malek's arms tightened around her. He kissed her and

murmured, "Sometimes I wonder how the miracle of you could possibly exist, and then you say or do something that makes everything before pale in comparison. I love you beyond all reason, Sabin'theoria. I would burn the world before I allowed anything to harm you."

"Malek," she whispered. "Words have power, and that's too close to an oath."

"It *is* an oath," Malek said, running his thumb across her cheek. "As long as I have breath, I will never allow any harm to come to you. You're mine to protect, now and forever. I swear it."

CHAPTER 41

alek strode through the garden and toward the south wing. After his conversation with Sabine, he was more determined than ever to locate his fae grandmother's missing journal. If Sabine was right about Esmelle's ability to help Kaia, Elisa's detailed notes might contain some additional insight into the properties of the plants in the conservatory.

It might also prevent another incident with Esmelle's "teas." He wasn't sure they could handle Sabine sampling another one of Esmelle's experiments, even if there were some intriguing side effects.

"Dragon," Bane called out.

Malek halted abruptly, somewhat surprised Bane was already awake. He waited until the demon approached before asking, "You have news?"

"Not here," Bane said and nodded toward a nearby bush. The suspicious foliage was giggling and talking in hushed whispers. Malek bit back a grin. Apparently, the Sky Cities pixies were practicing their spying skills.

Bane turned and growled at the rustling foliage. It immediately stopped moving.

Malek chuckled and entered the south wing. He headed directly for the library and motioned for Bane to close the door. "The room is soundproof. My grandfather didn't care to be disturbed when he was in here. You can speak freely."

Bane scanned the room while Malek headed for the pile of books on a nearby table. He quickly glanced through the stack, but most of them appeared to be titles related to magic or dragons. No one other than Kaia would have attempted to pilfer his library. Not even his parents would have risked it.

"Dammit, Kaia," Malek muttered, dropping one of the books back on the table. "These books aren't going to have what you need."

Instead of being interested in the bookshelves or contents of the library, Bane was more focused on potential methods of egress and tiny winged spies who might be eavesdropping. After he finished prowling through the room and finding it pixie-free, Bane turned to him.

"Is Sabine's attendance tonight required to broker an alliance with your clan?"

Malek leaned against one of the shelves and studied the demon. Despite Sabine's efforts to share her magic with Bane when he arrived back that morning, he still looked exhausted. His cheeks were sunken and his eyes dull, and he was favoring his left side as though it pained him. Something had happened to him in the underworld, but Malek didn't think Bane would be forthcoming if he asked.

"I would never have agreed to take Sabine if there was another option," Malek said with a sigh. "She must complete the ceremony and formally be declared my mate in order for my clan's protection to extend to her. The only other option is for us to leave the Sky Cities and not return, but Sabine refuses to leave without the aderyan and fae captives."

"It's my understanding your mother recognized her?"

"In a manner of speaking," Malek admitted. "My mother saw Theoria twice during the war. The first was when Theoria led the fae to safety. The second was shortly before the portal was sealed. Apparently, the resemblance between them is strong."

"Despite your intentions, Sabine will not be safe tonight," Bane said, his eyes flashing silver briefly. "Too many of your brethren will recognize her. Even should she make adjustments to her appearance, her magic is undeniable. They will recognize it."

"I do not intend to leave Sabine's side tonight. Hopefully, my presence will confuse and shield her power from being detected."

"It will not be enough, dragon."

Malek pushed away from the bookshelf. "Then give me another option. Every alternative I've considered either breaks the balance between us or puts her directly in harm's way."

"Your other option."

Bane held out his hand to reveal a tiny blue stone that pulsed faintly with a strange sort of magic. The more Malek tried to focus on it, the more his gaze slipped away.

There was something both familiar and foreign about it. He had the oddest sensation that whatever it was didn't belong on this side of the Veil.

"I understand it's customary to provide a dragon's mate with an item to wear during the ceremony," Bane said, offering him the stone. "Infuse this into the jewelry you gift her. It will temporarily mask Sabine's ambient power."

Malek took the stone and held it up to the light. It was small, more the size of a bead than an actual stone. His hand tingled where it touched, both searing hot and icy cold at the same time. "What is it?"

"A dreamstone," Bane said, his clawed hands curling into

a fist. "A piece of demonic bone bathed in the deepest lavapit and then imbued with the power of the Well of Dreams."

Malek's gaze sharpened on the demon. "You saw the Huntsman."

Bane gave him a curt nod. "The passive magic in the fragment will only last until the moon reaches its zenith. Sabine's power is growing too rapidly to be harnessed for long. If she taps into her magic for any reason, the dreamstone will burn out."

"You trust him?" Malek asked. "This won't harm her?"

Bane's jaw clenched. "He has a vested interest in Sabine. Beyond that, he was not forthcoming with his motivations except to see her survive your people."

Malek studied the dreamstone carefully. His dragonfire should negate any harmful interactions with his bond to Sabine. "Very well. I'll infuse it into the jewelry."

Bane shifted his weight slightly, an uncharacteristic move for the master assassin. Malek suspected the piece of demonic bone had been surrendered by Bane himself. He knew the demon could heal, but he didn't know if that extended to regrowing bone.

"There is one other thing," Bane said, gesturing to the dreamstone. "You'll be able to speak with Sabine using mind-touch without disrupting the magic it holds. The Huntsman also suggested Lachlina may not be privy to any of your private discussions."

Malek stilled. "She can't hear us across our bond?"

"She may be aware you are speaking, but not the subject matter," Bane said, a slow smile curving his lips. "Lachlina was a goddess of creation. She cannot cross the Veil without another's aid. Such is the domain of the darker magics, and she has never been able to abide such."

Malek clasped the dreamstone tightly in his fist. "Then

we have a way to include Sabine in our plans without Lachlina's knowledge."

Bane inclined his head. "Indeed. It would seem your presence at Sabine's side may have benefits we hadn't considered."

Malek met his gaze. "Then after the gala, we figure out how to break the connection between them once and for all—even if that means we destroy a goddess."

CHAPTER 42

"Watch the roots," Esmelle warned, kneeling in the dirt beside Rika and Lyra. "You want to clear the weeds and overgrowth without damaging the baby plants."

"There are baby plants?" Lyra asked, cocking her head. Her wings were hidden behind a mask of glamour, making her appear even more faelike.

"I'll show you," Blossom said, landing on a flower in front of Lyra.

Sabine smiled. If someone had suggested a year ago she'd witness a dryad and pixie teaching a human seer and aderyan child how to tend a garden, she wouldn't have believed them.

Her gaze drifted to the north wing of Malek's estate. It appeared calm, but appearances were deceiving. Aeron was getting some much needed rest before the gala that evening while Thalassa, Azalia, and Lady Nymira's seamstress had turned the entire north wing into the equivalent of a dress shop. Malek had taken one look at the chaos and announced he had some urgent dragon matters to address—far, far away.

The chicken.

Sabine had suffered through two hours of it. As soon as they started tossing ribbons and fabrics in Sabine's direction and demanding her opinion on the difference between twilight blue and cobalt, she'd climbed out the window with Lyra. They'd retreated to the relative safety of the garden where the only danger was being flower-bombed by pixies. She'd have to return eventually to dress, but for now, she was enjoying the brief respite.

"Aren't we supposed to use these for weeding?" Rika asked, picking up one of the garden tools Malek had provided.

"You'll have more control if you use your hands like this," Esmelle said, plunging her fingers into the soil. Lyra watched her closely and then imitated her motions, plucking out the weeds surrounding the tiny plants.

Blossom clapped. "You've got it! Now try over here with this flower. We've got some hungry bees to feed."

Rika waved the garden tool in Esmelle's direction. "You have dirt all over your nose. I won't get as dirty with the tools."

Esmelle reached over and tweaked Rika's nose, leaving a smear of dirt behind. "Oops. Too late. Might as well use your hands."

Rika laughed and wiped her nose with her sleeve. "I guess we won't be using the tools."

Movement in one of Malek's windows caught Sabine's attention. She slipped behind one of the marble columns, making sure it blocked the view from Malek's living room.

"Sabine's hiding," Rika said in a loud whisper.

"Or she's looking for pigeons," Blossom suggested.

"Maybe I'm simply admiring the architecture," Sabine said, staring up at the columns. "These columns are really… something."

"Totally hiding," Esmelle agreed.

Sabine winked at Lyra.

Lyra giggled.

Rika snorted and then broke into laughter. Esmelle grinned and resumed weeding.

Sabine smiled. Okay, she was hiding—or rather, lurking—behind a marble column to avoid two crazed humans wielding needles and thread and an aderyan who wanted to tie her up in ribbons.

Her skin tingled in awareness at Bane's approach. He moved silently behind her and wrapped his arms around her waist. She leaned against him, comforted by his presence.

Her gaze drifted upward to the winged creatures soaring overhead. It might be a common occurrence here, but it still made her heart race. It was a wonder her people had held their own against these masters of the skies for so long. If the full force of the dragons ever turned their attention to them again, she wasn't sure either side would survive.

"I was wondering when you were going to find me." Sabine ran her fingers over Bane's arm, accompanying the gesture with a strong wave of her magic. His arms tightened reflexively around her.

He nuzzled her neck and asked, "How long do you intend to remain in the Sky Cities, little one?"

"Growing impatient already?" Sabine asked, continuing to trail her fingers across his arm. She danced her power over his skin in a silent offer, urging him to heal the rest of his injuries.

When he didn't respond, she glanced up at him. He was eyeing one of the young wyverns that had flown a little close to Malek's compound. An obsidian dragon nipped lightly at the wyvern's tail, likely thwarting his efforts to glimpse the unusual visitors to the Sky Cities.

After yesterday's debacle at Malek's parents' estate, word

had definitely gotten out about her arrival. Sabine could appreciate their curiosity, but even more, she understood Bane's distrust. Any type of scrutiny was dangerous, especially with her magic being so unpredictable. Esmelle had helped enhance Malek's wards to better obscure their visibility, but no magic was infallible.

Sabine sighed. "Malek said his parents are going to make some discreet inquiries about the portal artifact at the gala tonight. If nothing comes of it, we'll proceed with our plans to rescue the aderyan. Aeron believes one of his people might have knowledge of its location."

"And after the artifact is located?"

"We still have to find the portal. Beyond that, none of us can guess what might transpire," Sabine said, turning in Bane's arms to face him. "Something's troubling you."

Bane traced one of his claws down the side of her face until he reached her chin. He tapped on it lightly and said, "You have not mentioned how you intend to deal with your family, Queen Sabin'theoria. Do you not miss Faerie?"

Ah. So that's where he was going with this. He was concerned about whether she was going to return to Faerie or stay here with Malek.

"Of course I miss it. Faerie will always be my home," Sabine said, her gaze drifting back to the sky. The dragons were magnificent to behold, but this wasn't her place. No matter how much she loved Malek, she didn't belong on this fractured floating island that had once been a haven for the aderyan.

Every day she'd been gone from Faerie had deepened the ache inside her. But this was Malek's home. These were his people. She'd seen him relax in a way he hadn't during their travels. He laughed more often, and his easy smiles always carried such warmth. If she refused to remain here, he would insist on accompanying her. But her people would never accept him either. Lady Nymira claimed these were simply details, but they felt insurmountable. The thought of losing him threatened to break her.

She shook her head, unable to voice her fears. Pressing her hands against Bane's chest, she said, "Don't ask me to make any decisions right now, Bane. It's too soon to know anything for certain."

"All the more reason to make contingency plans," Bane said, running his hand over her hair to siphon off more of her magic. "You are the ruler of the Unseelie and have been touched by the gods. Your destiny is greater than any simple fae."

Sabine frowned and absently touched the goddess marks on her arm. She still had no idea how to sever her connection to Lachlina. If the goddess decided to expose her at the gala tonight—

When she didn't respond, Bane wrapped his hand around her wrist, covering her marks and hiding them from view. "The goddess intends to use you for her own purposes. We must find a way to circumvent her power over you and soon. Once we find the last artifact, it may be too late. Malek's efforts at intervening may not be sufficient next time she takes hold."

Sabine lifted her head to meet his amber gaze. "Do you truly think me that naïve? The gods have never given any so-called gifts without expecting something in return. I know what's at risk better than anyone."

"I've already spoken with your dragon," Bane murmured. "His kind have spent millennia studying their enemies for potential weaknesses. He broached the subject briefly with his mother. He believes she may have additional insight or know how to obtain the information we need without arousing suspicion. He intends to speak with her again after the gala."

She gently placed her hand over his ribcage, where she'd sensed the weakness. "Does this have anything to do with where you disappeared to last night? Or the wound you came back with?"

"Yes."

Sabine searched his expression. The injury hadn't been life threatening, but something had clearly torn into his chest. By the time they'd returned, he'd been severely weakened. She'd given him enough magic to heal the worst of it, and he'd promptly fallen asleep outside her door.

It hadn't been a complete healing. Something was still missing. She'd hoped he would have found her when he woke, so she could try again.

Using her hand as a focus, she directed her power into him. He inhaled sharply, his eyes and horns immediately silvering. With a shuddering exhale, he accepted the gift of her magic and pulled her back into his arms.

"Stubborn," he muttered and kissed her hair.

She smiled and leaned into him again. "You don't intend to tell me anything else, do you?"

"Not while you still wear her mark on your wrist," Bane said, running his clawed hand lightly over the spot. "You must trust us to act in your best interest, little one. I do not keep such things from you lightly."

"I know," she said, meaning every word. She trusted Bane implicitly. His methods were sometimes questionable, but she also knew Malek would rein him in before letting him go too far. It was strange how much she'd come to depend on all of them, even Aeron. She'd only known him for a short amount of time, but every instinct told her he could be trusted.

When she started to pull away, Bane stopped her and said, "Sabine, you can only delay your decision for so long. The longer you wait, the less chance you have to walk away unscathed."

She looked away. "It's too late for that."

He tilted her chin back to meet her gaze. "Do you intend to parade your dragon lover in front of your people? Or will you relinquish your throne to those Seelie pretenders?"

Her heart fell into her stomach. Sabine pulled away from Bane and wrapped her arms around herself. Gods. He knew how to cut her to the quick. The time was rapidly approaching to make a decision, but she didn't know how she could choose. Millions of Unseelie were depending on her to lead and protect them. If she turned away from her people because she had fallen for a dragon, could she live with herself? How many would die at the hands of her enemies?

Rika nudged Esmelle and whispered something to her.

Lyra had been watching Sabine and Bane with silvered eyes. The young aderyan's hands were clenched in her lap. Her glamour had faded, and her wings vibrated with barely controlled emotion. Sabine quickly wrapped a small band of glamour around Lyra, hiding her wings from view.

Esmelle stopped weeding the garden and frowned. "Dammit, Bane. Sabine had finally started to relax and unwind a little. Now you've gotten the little one worked up too. What's going on?"

Sabine swallowed, a lump forming in her throat. "Bane wants to know my plans for the future."

"No!" Lyra cried, leaping to her feet. She ran to Sabine and threw her arms around her. Sabine crouched and held Lyra tightly.

Rika gaped at them. Blossom looked up from the flower she'd been sniffing, her wings twitching in agitation.

"Shhh, it's all right," Sabine murmured. "We're just talking."

"It hurts you," Lyra said, burying her face in Sabine's shoulder. "He made you think about leaving your dragon."

"Yes, but it's Bane's responsibility to speak of things that may hurt," Sabine said gently. "He helps me see the truth, even when it's difficult. I value his wisdom and his guidance."

Esmelle narrowed her eyes on Bane. "Wisdom and guidance, my dryad ass. How is Malek any of his business? Or is his new title now 'Relationship Advisor to the Queen'?"

Bane didn't respond. He simply crossed his arms over his chest and arched his brow expectantly.

Sabine's mouth twitched. She'd missed the no-nonsense witch more than she'd realized.

"Walk away from Malek?" Blossom asked, abandoning the flower beds to hover in front of Sabine. "You can't do that. You love him!"

Sabine smiled and held out her hand for Blossom to land. "I do love him. More than I ever thought possible." Her smile faded, the next words lodging in her throat. "But I don't belong here, and he doesn't belong in Faerie. I don't see how we can make a life together when our people hate and fear one another."

"But it doesn't have to be that way," Rika said, dropping the garden rake back in the bucket. "My people hate and fear demons. Once I got to know Bane, I realized they were wrong. You realized the same thing about dragons after you got to know Malek. Maybe it can be the same way between your people and his."

"You're not really going to leave Malek, are you?" Blossom asked, her wings tinged with red. "He's your balance, Sabine. You can't leave him."

Lyra nodded. "He woke you from Veylara. I watched."

Esmelle sat back on her heels and brushed the dirt off her hands. "They have a point, Sabine. Does the location where you end up matter so much? If you love him and you're determined to share a life together, then continue on as you have been."

"To what end?" Sabine asked. "At some point, our travels will cease and we'll need to live our lives."

Esmelle absently brushed back a red curl that had escaped from her hair tie. "What the hell do you think you've been doing for the past several months? You spent ten years stagnant and hiding in Akros. You didn't even have a regular bed you slept in because you were worried about putting anyone in danger. For the first time since I met you, you're finally living your life. Not just living, but thriving. Look at everything you've accomplished!"

"I have to return home at some point. Faerie needs a ruler."

"Who made up that rule?" Esmelle asked, waving off her comment. "Legends claim the fae used to roam the land, nourishing and protecting it. Faerie moved with the fae, accessible by doorways to the in-between so they could reach their seat of power at will. They didn't retreat to their cities until after the Dragon War. Maybe it's time to go back to the old ways or find a new way forward."

Sabine stared at Esmelle in surprise. She hadn't considered the old legends. Her people were tied to the land, not their cities. Could it really be so simple? Her heart thudded at the prospect.

At the Huntsman's insistence, Blossom had been teaching her about navigating the doorways to the in-between. Perhaps he'd seen this as a possibility.

She'd always wanted to explore the world beyond the boundaries of Faerie. Traveling with Malek and their friends had already enriched her life and given her a better understanding of other cultures. If she continued along this same path, she wouldn't have to give up the dragon she loved for duty's sake.

"The witch may have a point," Bane admitted grudgingly. "There would be certain… logistics to consider, but it may be possible. The dragon's allegiance to you has proven to be somewhat advantageous."

"Somewhat advantageous?" Esmelle repeated in a dry voice. "Get off it, Bane. He's good for her, and you know it."

Blossom nodded. "I think it's a great idea! I like exploring with you, Sabine. As long as there are plants, I can reach my family back in Faerie. And we can stop and see them once you learn more about using the doorways."

Lyra patted Sabine's dress. "I want to explore with you."

Hope bloomed inside her. They'd still need to figure out about the portal and how it would affect navigating the in-between, but she might not have to walk away from Malek or her people.

"I think it's something we all need to decide together when the time is right. I'll speak to Malek about it." Sabine smiled down at Lyra. "And we'll speak with Aeron and Thalassa too."

Esmelle ran her fingers over a large, rounded leaf. "I think it may be time I changed directions too. The encounter with Aconi in the grove made me realize my dryad roots are stronger than I thought. She's offered to train me, even if I never become one of them. I'd like to take her up on it."

Understanding dawned and with it, a pang of bittersweet loss. Sabine walked over to her friend and crouched in front of her. She took Esmelle's hands in her own and said, "You intend to stay here with Levin, don't you?"

Esmelle gave her a sad smile and nodded. "He's promised to help me find a suitable garden. With Imenel being such an active trading port, I'll have the ability to market my wares. Perhaps I'll even open a new shop one day."

Sabine squeezed Esmelle's hands. "Levin truly makes you happy?"

"More than I ever dreamed possible."

Sabine nodded and kissed Esmelle's cheek. "You gave me the opportunity to begin a new life in Akros. It's my turn to do the same for you. If Levin makes you happy and you want to plant roots with him, we'll make sure it happens. Pick out a suitable location, and I'll speak with Balkin about securing the funds to purchase a new shop for you."

Tears filled Esmelle's eyes. She threw her arms around Sabine's neck and hugged her tightly. She laughed and wiped away her tears, darting a look at Bane. "If I'd known back then what your threats would bring, I wouldn't have been so resistant."

Bane snorted. "As if threats worked so well the first time."

Rika frowned. "Wait. What?"

Sabine smiled and said, "Bane and Dax threatened Esme unless she agreed to help me play human. She didn't appreciate it and made it known by stringing them up in some nearby trees. After they cut themselves down, she agreed to help, but only if they gave her enough coin to open her own shop in Akros."

"Impertinent witch," Bane muttered.

Esmelle laughed. "Arrogant demon."

Sabine grinned at them. "You're both right. And since it was through our actions you lost your old shop, it's only fair we provide the means to procure a new one."

Esmelle nodded. "A debt is due."

"And a debt shall be paid," Sabine agreed.

Blossom clapped her hands. "Yay! Esme's getting another garden! Wait until I tell the other pixies. I need a special spot in your garden. I want my very own potted house when I come to visit."

"You've got it," Esmelle agreed with another laugh.

Sabine turned to Blossom and asked, "Send word to

Balkin next time you speak with your family. He can handle the financial arrangements."

Esmelle pressed her hands against her face. "Wow. This is really happening. I'm going to open another shop."

Sabine smiled at her. "I think you're going to give Idola quite a bit of competition."

Esmelle winced. "Yeah. I'm not sure how well that's going to go over. She's already not a fan of mine. Levin said she was spitting mad yesterday when they scooped her up."

"That's no fault of yours," Sabine said. "She can embrace the challenge or not. You both have different strengths and could easily provide complementary services."

"You know why she's here?" Esmelle asked.

Sabine nodded. "I wanted to speak with you about that. You have a unique talent for assessing problems and knowing how best to treat them. If you have time, I'd like to take a look in the conservatory. Malek said Elisa kept a journal documenting the healing properties of her various plants. He was going to look for it. In the meantime, I may be able to provide you with some suggestions that may help."

Esmelle stood. "You realize we're going to be accosted the moment we walk in there?"

Lyra tugged on her dress. "Want me to fly to the second floor and sneak down to unlock another window for you?"

"Don't worry, Sabine!" Blossom said with a grin. "I've got some sharp thorns perfect for picking locks."

Bane narrowed his eyes. "Do not tell me the Queen of the Unseelie snuck out a window earlier."

"Who? Me?" Sabine asked innocently, taking Lyra's hand. "I wasn't going to say anything of the sort."

"That's not a denial!" he called after her.

"Of course it's not," she said, her head held high. "Everyone knows fae don't lie."

CHAPTER 43

$\mathcal{M}$alek entered his bedroom carrying a small silver box. Sabine stood in the center of the room while Thalassa carefully threaded thin black ribbons through her hair. It had been swept upward in a crown of silver curls, accentuating the gentle slope of her pointed ears. Several pixies zipped around the room, fastening tiny blue gemstones in her hair, which shone brilliantly under the Faerie lights.

Sabine turned her head as he entered, and he staggered to a halt. She was beyond stunning. The gown was a deep blue that almost seemed to shift colors in the light, changing from cobalt to violet, and made her eyes positively striking.

Intricate silver and black threading on her gown swirled upwards from the floor, offset by sparkling diamonds. Azalia kneeled on a cushion near Sabine's feet, carefully sewing another diamond in place while his mother's seamstress made some finishing touches to the black and silver bodice. Both human women maintained a steady stream of chatter discussing fabrics and shades that would best compliment Sabine's appearance for future gowns.

Even while wearing her normal human glamour, Sabine's faelike mien had never been more apparent. With her delicate features and silvery hair, she possessed an ethereal beauty and innate sensuality that captivated him.

No dragon who saw her like this could ever doubt she was anything other than fae royalty. It was in her bearing, her mannerisms, and surrounded her with an undeniable aura of command and power.

Damn. He hated when his mother was right.

He really hoped Bane's plan worked.

"Turn a little to your left," Azalia said, placing her hands on Sabine's waist to guide her in the direction she wanted.

"No, no, no," the seamstress complained, and pulled Sabine back to where she'd been standing. "Stay where you are. I'm almost finished sewing these diamonds on. The fasteners are being stubborn."

"The bodice should have more gemstones," Azalia insisted and grabbed Sabine's wrist. "Move this way just a bit more. Norah, you can scoot over."

Despite Sabine's carefully composed expression, Malek caught the quick flash of annoyance in her eyes and knew she had nearly reached the limit of her patience with these strangers.

Malek took one look at the room and realized the problem. Elisa had once explained to him that among the fae and others native to Aeslion, touching and more intimate caresses were often accompanied by magic. He'd experienced it for himself with Sabine, both in the way she often reached for him as a way to offer comfort, or even in their shared moments of passion. It could also be used as a way to harm or even kill, a talent Bane utilized for his own purposes.

Sabine was able to mask her discomfort, but Aeron and Lyra were too tightly bound to her. Lyra sat on the ground with her arms wrapped around her knees. The young aderyan rocked back and forth, never taking her eyes off Sabine. Aeron stood nearby, his expression dark and stormy every time Azalia or the seamstress touched Sabine.

Neither one dared intervene, since the women were performing tasks with Sabine's permission. But it was taking a toll on all of them.

Well, to hell with that.

"Out," Malek said, nodding toward the door.

Thalassa and Azalia froze.

The seamstress lifted her head and frowned. "We just have a bit more—"

"Out!" he ordered, allowing his power to fill the room.

The pixies squealed, threw their sparkling gemstones into the air, and flew out the door. Azalia and the seamstress quickly gathered their supplies and exited without saying another word. When the aderyan didn't budge, Malek narrowed his eyes.

Sabine nodded at Aeron. At her silent command, he scooped Lyra into his arms and headed toward the door. Thalassa placed the black ribbons back in her basket and followed them.

Thalassa paused at the doorway, balancing her basket in her arms. She held Malek's gaze for several heartbeats before bowing her head and closing the door. He could have sworn he saw a flicker of approval in the aderyan's eyes at his timely interruption. Apparently, Lyra and Aeron weren't the only ones uncomfortable with strange humans touching their Aderylin.

Malek placed the box on the bed and pulled Sabine into his arms. Her body was rigid, as though the slightest movement threatened to shatter her carefully constructed barriers. He simply held her and waited, knowing she needed a few minutes to compose herself.

Slowly, her body began to relax in his arms and she

leaned into his touch. Her seductive magic wrapped around him, and he met hers with his own heated strength. The faint smell of night-blooming roses surrounded him, and he inhaled deeply, wanting to memorize the feel of her in his arms.

After several more heartbeats, she sighed. "Have I told you how much I dislike formal events?"

Malek ran his hand down her back. "That makes two of us."

She lifted her head. "It's one thing I don't miss about Faerie. Everyone watches and waits for you to misstep. They smile as they plot your death, and then discuss how charming the festivities are this year."

"Dragon formal events are a little different," Malek said.

She placed her hand on his chest and peered up at him. "How?"

"No one usually discusses how charming the festivities are."

Sabine laughed and pressed her head against his chest.

Malek ran his hand down her back, knowing part of her unease stemmed from Lachlina's hold over her. "Are you having second thoughts about tonight?"

She took a deep breath and said firmly, "No. Our attendance is necessary. Aeron believes other aderyan may be among the crowd tonight, posing as fae or even human servants. If we can find a way into the prisons that doesn't involve bloodshed, that may be our best option for freeing his people. Your parents are also going to make inquiries about the portal artifact. With all of us there, we may hear things that might otherwise be missed."

"The other clans likely won't talk freely around outsiders," Malek warned. "My clan has made their position clear concerning fae and aderyan captives. If there are any doubts, those will be eliminated once I introduce you as my mate."

Sabine straightened and walked over to the full-length mirror in the corner of the room. At least she wasn't arguing the point.

She smoothed out her gown, using a trace of glamour to complete the jeweled effect the seamstress had begun. "Aeron claims to have ways of recognizing the other captives even through glamour, and Rika has become surprisingly adept at blending into any situation. Between her and Blossom, I suspect they might learn more than the rest of us combined. Rika's far more resourceful and intuitive than she realizes."

"Yes, she is," Malek said and retrieved the box from the bed. The delicate silver container was etched with celestial symbols and precious gemstones. Some would consider the contents priceless beyond measure, but it paled in comparison to the woman standing before him.

Malek carried it over to Sabine and said, "Before the portal was sealed, my people traveled the ether, weaving starlight and chasing trails of magic. We often traveled alone, with nothing but the stars and darkness to guide us. When the first dragon found their mate, they realized they'd found a home. They were no longer alone among the stars, and their combined lights were brighter than a thousand suns."

He opened the box to reveal a polished obsidian scale encased in a thin silver filigree armband. Delicate silver vines wrapped around the scale, a combination of both dragon and fae heritages blended into one. At the top was the tiny dreamstone that Bane had given him.

"Malek," Sabine whispered, staring at the armband in wonder. "It's as though you've captured the night's sky."

He lifted it from the box and slid it up her arm. "When a dragon finds their mate, they offer up a piece of themselves and bathe it in dragonfire. The more brilliantly the scale glows when it touches their mate's skin, the more powerful the bond and magic between them."

The scale turned a deep red, then white, and finally became a vibrant blue that was nearly violet. In all his years, he'd only seen such a color on a mating band twice. The first was on his parents, and the second was between a couple who had faded from this world decades earlier.

"It's the same color as your aura," Sabine murmured, touching the band.

"And your family colors," Malek said, watching as the scale continued to pulse and glimmer as though all the stars in the night sky had come alive. Something eased within him at the sight of his scale against her skin.

"The color means something else to you, doesn't it?" Sabine asked softly.

"Only the most intense fires burn indigo and violet," Malek said, drawing her into his arms. He sent a heated band of his magic across her skin and brushed his lips against hers. "It means in this world and all the ones that exist beyond the Veil, there is no one who perfectly suits me other than you. I'm beyond fortunate to have found you, Sabine. I intend to prove that to you every day for the rest of our lives. I love you, Sabin'theoria."

Her eyes softened and she wound her arms around his neck. "*Ta vashein doi.* You hold my heart, Malek Rish'dan."

Every time she said the words, it was a priceless gift. He pressed his forehead against hers, both humbled and awed by the trust she placed in him. She had every reason to hate him and the rest of his people. Instead, Sabine had opened her heart completely to him. In her, Malek had found more than he'd ever dreamed was possible. He wouldn't lose her, under any circumstances.

Silently, he reached across their bond and said, *"The band has a secondary purpose as well. A dreamstone has been infused into the armband and will help shield your magic tonight. Bane says the effect will only last until midnight, and you must avoid using any active magic or it will burn through the power of the dreamstone that much faster."*

Sabine touched the armband reverently. *"A dreamstone? That's why he disappeared last night. He returned to the underworld. And you trusted him enough to incorporate the dreamstone into your gift. Malek, I can't tell you what this means to me."*

"When it comes to you, Bane and I have an understanding," Malek said and ran his hand down her arm. His scale flared brighter against her skin as Sabine responded to his touch. *"The Huntsman told him that even though Lachlina may know when we speak privately, he doesn't believe she's aware of the details of what we discuss. This may be a way to keep our plans out of her reach, but we need to be careful not to arouse her suspicion."*

Sabine looked up at him, her eyes filled with understanding. She kissed him lightly and said, "I will treasure this gift from you, Malek."

He rubbed a silver curl between his fingers and asked, "Does that mean you forgive me for dragging you to a clan gala?"

Sabine smiled up at him. "I can think of much more pleasurable ways to spend an evening with you, but if it helps save your people and mine, it's worth it."

Malek groaned. "Now I won't be able to think about anything else for the rest of the evening." He took her hand and added, "If I don't get you out of here now, we'll never make it to my parents' estate. Seeing you in this gown makes me want to see how fast I can get you out of it. I plan to find out later."

Sabine laughed as he pulled her toward the living area, the sound lightening his heart. Unfortunately, the drama had simply spilled into another room.

Rika was wearing a striking dark blue and black gown

that complemented both his and Sabine's attire. Her dark hair was arranged in similar fashion to Sabine's, but instead of gemstones, the pixies had placed tiny blue flowers reminiscent of butterfly wings.

The charming effect was shattered by the way she was glaring at Bane with her hands curled into fists. Bane, on the other hand, was towering over Rika and glowering at her with silvered eyes. Instead of the formal attire Malek had expected, Bane was wearing assassin leathers. This was not going to go over well.

"You are *not* going to tear a hole in my dress!" Rika shouted.

"Where is your blade?" Bane demanded. "How do you expect to defend yourself without a weapon at hand?"

Before Sabine could interject, Malek cleared his throat. "I already made arrangements for that."

He turned to Azalia and the seamstress who were both standing against the wall grasping one another's hands. Their faces were bloodless and terrified.

"Has Rupert returned yet?"

Azalia didn't tear her terrified gaze away from Bane.

Malek walked in front of her and waved his hand to get her attention. "Azalia? Has Rupert returned with the item I requested?"

"W-What?" she managed, blinking wide eyes at him. "I-I can go check, Lord Malek."

He nodded and gestured to the door. "Go ahead. Perhaps Norah can accompany you?"

The seamstress gathered her skirt and raced out the door, not bothering to wait for Azalia. Malek watched as she leaped over a potted plant and continued running straight through the garden.

Sabine placed her hand on his arm. "In some ways, it's reassuring to know she's more terrified of Bane than of the dragons in her midst. Perhaps I don't have as much to fear tonight as we thought."

"Bane is never going to let me live this down, is he?" Malek asked with a sigh.

Sabine smiled and shook her head. "Probably not."

Bane sat on the floor and began sharpening his blades. As soon as he finished one, he picked up the next, assessed it with a critical eye, and then slid the sharpening stone across it. Rika huffed and flopped down on the sofa, her arms crossed over her chest.

Sabine sat beside her and said, "You look lovely, Rika."

Rika smoothed the fabric of her gown. "It's the prettiest dress I've ever worn. I feel like a Faerie princess. Blossom and the other pixies even helped with my hair. I know Bane wants me on guard duty, but it's not like I can do much anyway. He's better with knives, and Malek's going to be at your side the entire time. Aeron will be watching you too."

Sabine tilted her head. "Who are you supposed to be guarding?"

Rika frowned. "You. Aren't I?"

Sabine smiled and took Rika's hand. "Did Bane say that?"

"Well, not exactly," Rika said, her brow furrowing. "But he wants me to wear a weapon."

Malek walked over to the couch. "Sabine was just telling me your ability to adapt to any situation was one of your greatest strengths. I happen to agree with her. You can move throughout a room, putting people at ease in ways none of us can."

Rika stared at Sabine. "You said that?"

Sabine nodded. "If I'm injured, Bane can heal me. With my magic, he can heal himself. Malek can recover from most injuries when he shifts between forms. But none of us can heal you, Rika. Despite your remarkable talents and seer abilities, you're still human. Any weapon you carry tonight is to guard *you*."

Rika turned to Bane. "You've been training me to protect myself? That's why you wanted me to wear a weapon tonight?"

Bane simply scowled at her and reached for the next blade. Rika leaped from the couch and ran over to the demon. She threw her arms around his neck and kissed his cheek.

Malek bit back a smile as Bane stiffened. He glared at Sabine over Rika's shoulder and snarled, "That's twice in as many days. First the witch, and now the young seer. If the pixie comes near me, I'm eating her."

Sabine simply smiled at him.

A hesitant tap on the door interrupted them. Malek opened it to find Rupert standing outside holding an elongated oak box. Azalia was behind him, peering over his shoulder from a safe distance.

"Any problems?" Malek asked, taking the box.

"No, Lord Malek," Rupert said, shaking his head. "The artisan was pleased to be of service to you and your clan. He said if you need any other adjustments to it, he'll be happy to make them."

Malek nodded. "We'll be heading out momentarily."

"Of course," Rupert said with a bow. "I'll see to all the last-minute preparations."

Malek carried the wooden box over to Rika and said, "I gave Sabine a gift earlier. This one is for you."

Rika's eyes widened. She took the box and carefully opened the hinged lid. Nestled on top of a black velvet pillow was a jeweled silver dagger, sheath, and belt.

"Ohhhh," she murmured, pulling them out of the box. "How beautiful!"

"The silver and sapphires represent your ties to Sabine,"

Malek said, gesturing to the gemstones on the belt and sheath. "The polished obsidian and black diamonds reflect your connection to me and my clan. The dagger itself was selected by Bane."

Rika fastened the belt around her waist and grinned. "You were in on it?"

Bane huffed and stood, adjusting the sheath into a natural position on Rika's side. "As if I would allow anyone else to select a dagger for you. Now draw your weapon."

Rika did as Bane instructed, her grin widening at the sight of the silver blade.

"Sheathe your blade, and repeat until it becomes instinct," Bane ordered. "It would be wiser to have an additional hidden weapon or two on your person. We'll consider that for next time."

"Maybe I can get some of those poison hairpins like Sabine has," Rika said, drawing the blade again.

Bane grunted and adjusted Rika's stance. "We'll discuss it, however you are far more likely to poison yourself rather than your assailant. For you, I would recommend maintaining your distance in a fight. Perhaps we'll speak with the dwarves about crafting a lightweight crossbow."

Rika's smile widened.

Malek chuckled and held out his hand for Sabine, assisting her to her feet.

She kissed his cheek and murmured, "It was an extremely thoughtful gift."

"She's important to all of us," Malek said, recalling Idola's accusing words. "She's become part of our family, and I intend to make sure she knows that."

Aeron walked downstairs with Thalassa and Lyra. Once again, all of their wings were carefully hidden behind some form of glamour. A wide, dark blue sash made from a similar material as Sabine's dress had been draped across Aeron's chest and tied at the waist. The dark tunic and pants he wore underneath were a slight nod toward the Obsidian Clan, but it was clear his loyalty was to Sabine by his attire alone. If Malek were meeting him for the first time, he would have sworn Aeron was fae.

Levin and Esmelle trailed behind them, caught up in some sort of argument. Esmelle was wearing a sparkling green and black dress Malek's mother had immediately offered after meeting her. The seamstress had made a few modifications and added traces of Sabine's blue and silver to make it appear as though it had been made for Esmelle.

"It's none of our business, Esme," Levin said as he descended the stairs with her.

He wore his usual formal attire, a black tunic and pants that were standard for Obsidian Clan wyverns. The only distinction was the silver and obsidian emblem on his chest marking him as one of Malek's bloodbound wingmates.

Malek wasn't sure how she'd managed it, but Thalassa had outdone herself in ensuring every protocol had been followed.

Now they just had to prevent a renegade goddess from revealing herself, a demonic assassin from attempting to kill anyone, and a pixie with a penchant for causing mischief to behave.

Malek frowned. Blossom had been conspicuously absent for several hours. That was rarely a good sign. Before he had a chance to ask Sabine about the pixie's whereabouts, Esmelle leaned over the railing and called out, "Sabine, did you know there are going to be over two hundred dragons and wyverns at this thing?"

Sabine stilled. "No."

Malek silently cursed Levin to the underworld and back.

"Sorry, brother," Levin's voice slipped into his thoughts. *"It just came up, and Esme decided Sabine needed to know."*

Sabine lifted her head and considered Malek for a long time. "Dare I ask how many herds of thundertusks your parents had to import to feed all of them?"

"Thundertusk meat is terrible. Too stringy. Besides, after a minor debacle several years ago, my mother demanded all dragons shift out of their natural forms before stepping foot inside their wards."

She arched her brow. "Minor debacle?"

Levin coughed and muttered, "Dragon poop isn't dainty. Lady Ophelia's rose garden was never the same."

Sabine blinked at him.

Malek sighed. "Don't ask. The Topaz Clan has refused to host a gala since then."

Aeron visibly tensed for a moment. Thalassa whispered something in his ear, and the aderyan gave her a curt nod. Malek's gaze sharpened on Aeron. The aderyan's expression immediately blanked, appearing once again cool and aloof.

Esmelle gestured at Sabine. "See, Levin? She didn't even glow. It's better to know now than in the middle of the ballroom." Esmelle turned back to Sabine and added, "By the way, I saw the window last night. Excellent job. Lady Nymira adores it."

Sabine tilted her head in acknowledgment of the compliment. While she appeared relatively composed on the surface, Malek could see the tightness in her shoulders. She was once again suppressing her emotions and their bond. He doubted it was intentional after what happened earlier, but her distance grated. This mating bond was going to be the death of him.

Bane slid the sharpening stone across his blade, the sound drawing Sabine's attention. Bane held her gaze for a long time, some silent communication passing between them. The demon sheathed his blade, and Sabine gave him a curt nod before turning back to Malek.

When she spoke, her voice was measured, but he knew the effort cost her. "We all understand the importance of this gathering, but we've had little time to prepare. You'll need to lead us in the steps of this particular dance, Malek. Is there anything we should know before we depart?"

Malek reached for her hand, needing to touch her. She hesitated for a moment and then lowered the barriers between them. Her magic and emotions flowed through their bond, easing the disquiet within him.

As he ran his thumb across her soft skin, Malek said, "It may be closer to three hundred, if my mother's estimations are correct. You can expect around thirty to forty greater dragons in the room. The remainder will be wyverns, drakes, and humans. My parents will be there, along with my sister and her mate, and a handful of cousins who align themselves with the Obsidian Clan. All those in attendance are clan allies, but most are such in name only."

"What do you mean?" Sabine asked, taking a step closer to him.

"The Emerald Clan are our strongest allies because we share blood ties through my mother's line," Malek explained. "She was born to the Emerald Clan, and both of our clans currently call the floating island of Kavi our home. Many of our interests align, and the relationship between the Obsidian and Emerald Clans have been mutually beneficial for centuries."

"I see," Sabine said, her expression becoming thoughtful. "And what of your clan's other allies?"

Malek hesitated. "Our next strongest allies are those of the Ruby and Amethyst clans. While my grandparents claimed kinship with both of those clans, our relationship with the Ruby Clan became strained after my grandmother, Bryona, was killed and my grandfather took Elisa as his new mate. The Ruby clan felt it was a betrayal to my grandmother's memory."

Rika frowned and glanced at Sabine. "Were they upset because Elisa was fae?"

Sabine started to pull her hand away, but Malek held it tightly. "They'll have less of an issue with Sabine and more of a problem with Bane," he said. "My grandparents, along with my father, fought at the Battle of Blainrial Forest. Bryona was killed by demons. After my grandmother's death, my father and grandfather fell into battlelust. My father's dragon, and his instincts, have never fully retreated since that day."

Malek gestured to the side of his face. "His scar and golden eye serve as a constant reminder of all that was lost that day."

Bane's eyes turned silver as he picked up another weapon. He ran the sharpening stone across the edge of the blade and said, "Thousands of demons met their demise during the Battle of Blainrial Forest. Kal'thorz was displeased. The commander of that battle was executed. He never should have lost our positioning."

Malek narrowed his eyes on Bane. "Were you there?"

"No," Bane said, studying the sharpened edge of his blade.

"Do not press him on this, Malek," Sabine said silently. *"As Kal'thorz's eldest surviving son, he holds many of the memories his father passed down to him. Some of these are not his own, but he lives them as though they were. He does not discuss the past without great cause."*

Malek stared at her in stunned astonishment. He knew the demons had some sort of link between them. He'd suspected it was similar to the mind-touch ability to communicate over vast distances. If they had a way of inheriting shared memories and even strategy, it was no wonder the demons had been so successful at thwarting them for centuries.

Sabine had just offered him information that had the potential to shift the balance of power. It was information offered freely, but he knew enough about the fae to know there was an implied debt. He glanced over at Bane, suspecting the demon had agreed to share this information in exchange for equally valuable information about tonight's festivities. That damned demon was far too clever.

Malek squeezed Sabine's hand in understanding and said, "Before my people came to Aeslion, these clan alliances didn't exist. Dragons are solitary creatures, and we traveled the ether as we saw fit. Our only loyalty was to our mates and our families. Living in close proximity has forced us to adapt and change. In many ways, we've had to suppress our true natures. Otherwise, we'd end up killing one another. While many of us have divided loyalties internally, all of us will band together if attacked from the outside."

Sabine tilted her head. "How have you adapted and changed?"

"We spend much more time in human form," Levin grumbled, tugging on his collar.

Malek nodded. "That's definitely part of it. But more, we've had to emulate some human behaviors. That's part of the reason we've allowed them to remain nearby. Where we would once simply acquire what we wanted or needed, we've made an effort to study and model our behavior after theirs. We trade with the humans now. We hire them to perform tasks that hold little interest for us. We offer them protection in exchange for certain concessions." He chuckled. "My mother enjoys pretending to be one of the great human ladies who drinks tea in the afternoons."

"Most of Lady Nymira's tea parties end with broken

dishes or fire erupting on the carpet," Levin added with a grin.

"We're still dragons," Malek said with a shrug. "No matter how much we might appear civilized to some of the humans who live here, we aren't and never will be. We're possessive, territorial, and more likely to tear out an enemy's throat if they attempt to harm someone under our protection or steal from us. Whenever the humans forget that simple fact, one of us never fails to remind them."

"You're not like that," Rika said with a frown.

"Levin and I were born on Aeslion. We've had an easier time adapting. Suppressing our instincts has been ingrained since childhood." He pressed his hand on his chest. "But all of us feel the ache as though something fundamental is missing."

Sabine placed her hand over his, her touch settling something within him. "It's the lack of connection to the ether—the imbalance in the world you feel?"

Malek nodded. "The Tuatha Dé were considered gods because none could challenge them. We were much the same. Any who challenged us were destroyed. We were the opposing balance to the Tuatha Dé, the counterpoint to their magic. They created worlds and made them flourish, while we purged the excess to maintain the balance and prepare the way for new life. As long as we're trapped here, we're unable to fulfill our purpose. If we burn too much of Aeslion's magic, there's no one left to create new life."

"You're slowly being suffocated," Esmelle said, moving closer to Levin. He put his arm around her, tucking her against his side.

"That's an apt description," Malek said. "We require both magic and ether to exist. Without the ether, we're burning through more of Aeslion's magic. Part of the reason for this clan gala is to reaffirm our loyalties to one another. If we don't make an effort to conserve our magic or find a way to access the ether, my people will cease to exist."

Sabine leaned into him, her love and concern for him echoing across their bond in an intimate caress. The dragon-scale armband flared brightly as he pulled her closer and surrounded her with his power. Ever since he'd found her, the ache he'd always felt had diminished. Sabine was like a balm for his soul, healing what had been missing from his life.

"Our reconnaissance was cut short yesterday," Bane said, bringing Malek's attention back to the matter at hand. "What areas of the estate do we need to be concerned with?"

"Most of the lower floor will be open to the guests, including the gardens. The gala typically lasts for most of the night, but we can leave after an hour or two without raising too many eyebrows. I don't intend to leave Sabine's side while we're there."

Bane gave him a curt nod.

"Levin says we'll enter separately," Esmelle said to Sabine. "You and Malek will go in first, then Rika and Aeron, as her escort. Levin and I will follow. We'll mingle for a bit before we all head to the area designated for the Obsidian Clan."

"Greater dragons and their immediate family always enter a room first," Malek explained. "In battle, our fires burn the brightest and lead the way through the darkness."

Thalassa said, "By entering the gala at Lord Malek's side, you will be acknowledging your intended place as his mate, Aderylin. Until you complete the ceremony with him, you will be in grave danger." She said the last with a hint of fear.

Aeron took her hand and whispered something quietly in her ear. The aderyan woman took a deep breath and straightened her shoulders.

Sabine nodded. "Very well. Is there anything else?"

Malek lifted her hand and kissed it. "Just follow my lead. You won't be facing anything alone."

CHAPTER 44

$\mathcal{S}$abine took Malek's arm as they approached his parents' estate. The building was ablaze with dragonfire urns and ancient Faerie lanterns. Music, voices, and laughter carried on the wind, indicating the revelry had already begun. The number of wyvern guards at the door, however, had tripled since their last visit.

Bane leaned in close and said, "This is where I leave you, little one. Stay close to your dragon. If he is pulled away for any reason, Aeron will find his way to your side. I'll be watching from above."

"May the darkness hide you well," she murmured, brushing her hand against his arm. She started to accompany her touch with an infusion of magic and then stopped, recalling Malek's warning about the dreamstone.

"He'll be all right," Malek said softly, placing his hand over hers.

She nodded but waited until Bane had disappeared into the shadows before they began climbing the stairs to the entrance. What Bane was doing was risky, but he refused to leave her unprotected with only Malek and Aeron at her side.

A tiny ladybug landed on Sabine's shoulder.

Sabine glanced at the disguised pixie and asked, "Dare I ask where you've been?"

"Nope," Blossom said. "Plausible deniability."

Rika winced. "It's always worrisome when Blossom says that."

A leathery beat of wings echoed overhead. Sabine stared up at an enormous Emerald dragon. He sliced through the air with the precision of a knife, his golden gaze fixed on their group. At least a dozen other dragons of varying colors circled the estate like sharks eyeing prey. The emerald one dove closer, feinting an attack. Sabine straightened her shoulders and stared him down, refusing to show any weakness. As long as they had the dragon's attention, he wouldn't notice Bane.

"He's showing off, isn't he?" Rika asked.

Malek narrowed his eyes on the dragon. "Indeed."

"He's so sparkly," Blossom said. "Like a dewdrop on a leaf."

"Emerald clan?" Sabine asked, noticing small differences to Malek other than the color. Malek was a larger dragon with a tail that ended in a sharpened spike, whereas the emerald dragon's tail finned at the end.

The dragon's coloring shifted as he moved over them, reminding Sabine of the hundreds of colors in a forest's treetop canopy. While Malek could camouflage himself against the night sky, the Emerald dragon would be nearly impossible to see without the sentient Silver trees to warn her people of the danger.

"My cousin, Raynor," Malek said in a dry tone.

Sabine could dimly hear Malek speaking to someone

using his mind-touch ability, but she couldn't make out the words.

"He's so pretty," Blossom said. "Hey Sabine? Maybe I can be a sparkly, green—"

"No," Sabine said quickly.

"He's not going to fly around all night, is he?" Rika asked.

Malek glanced over at her. "There's a permanent landing pad in the rear garden, and two temporary ones located just outside the estate. If Raynor is unable to find his way, I've offered to have him escorted to one."

Levin snorted. "You told him you'd shove the nearest landing pad up his ass if he didn't stop peacocking."

Esmelle laughed. "I think it's a dragon thing. I've seen you do the same thing, Levin."

Sabine arched her brow and watched the dragon. Peacocking, indeed. The green dragon turned again in midair, once more showcasing the brilliance of his emerald scales before disappearing behind the house. The steps beneath Sabine's feet trembled slightly from his landing. Sparkly or not, it was a wonder how anyone slept with the minor earthquakes dragons caused every time they landed.

Malek cleared his throat and offered his arm to her again. "Shall we?"

They continued ascending the rest of the stairs to the main entrance. At Malek's approach, the wyvern guards placed their fists over the emblem on their chests. More than a few cast curiosity-filled glances her way, while others held thinly veiled suspicion. If that was the worst scrutiny she received tonight, they might all walk away from the evening unscathed.

Rika's hand brushed against the hilt of her dagger. "You're sure Bane will be okay?"

"I've already told the clan guards he'll be on the premises

tonight," Malek said. "As long as he doesn't draw attention from any other clans, we shouldn't have a problem."

"Don't worry about Bane," Blossom said in her ladybug form from Sabine's shoulder. "The pixies and I are on the job tonight!"

Sabine stiffened and gripped Malek's arm a little tighter. "They're *all* here?"

"Yep. All thirty-two of them. We've got you covered. Half are pretending to be glowbugs and moths in the gardens while the other half are infiltrating the house as ants, bees, and ladybugs."

Sabine winced. "You do realize ants may get stepped on?"

Blossom was quiet for a moment. "That might be a problem. I'll be back."

The ladybug zipped off her shoulder and went flying down the hall, weaving over and under people's legs.

"This isn't going to end well," Rika muttered.

Malek glanced over at Sabine. "Did she say *bees*?"

"She did," Sabine said with a sigh.

"I was not aware the flutterfolk had such a propensity for mischief," Aeron said quietly.

"That's an understatement," Rika said. "Just wait until Blossom ropes you into her shenanigans. You don't realize what's happening until it's too late."

Sabine and Malek entered the main ballroom area. The destruction from yesterday was nowhere to be seen. The broken furniture and rubble had been cleared away, and the ballroom had transformed into a breathtaking masterpiece.

Dwarven-made crystal chandeliers cast their prismatic light across the marble floor. Banners and tapestries depicting each of the emblems of the dragon clans lined the walls, while dragonfire urns flared brightly with their clan colors as each person approached them.

The room buzzed with a mix of dragons and their clan

members. Each group clustered in animated conversation, their attire a dazzling array of colors and textures that reflected their elemental affinities. Humans wearing obsidian black moved throughout the room, carrying trays of glasses filled with some sort of dark beverage that swirled with smoke.

"Look, Sabine!" Rika said excitedly, pointing toward the crystal window Sabine had infused with magic. "Lady Nymira made it the focal point for the Obsidian Clan!"

Sabine stared at the window, barely disguising her shock. Each of the different clans appeared to have a designated location set aside throughout the ballroom. The Obsidian Clan's chosen location was directly beneath the window. Two of the tallest dragonfire urns below the window were already lit and almost made the image of Malek's father seem alive, reflecting in his scales and in the golden glow of his eyes.

"So much for keeping a low profile," Malek muttered. "She's likely already received dozens of inquiries wanting to know who created it. Let's get this over with."

As Sabine and Malek made their way through the throng, the air was thick with an exotic blend of aromas from banquet tables overflowing with unfamiliar dishes. Beneath it all was the rich, smoky scent she'd come to associate with dragons.

The music shifted to a livelier tune, and several couples began to glide onto the dance floor, their movements graceful and fluid like the dragons she'd seen in flight. Sabine felt the weight of many eyes upon her, their gazes as piercing as the keenest blade, measuring and assessing. She kept her expression carefully neutral, adopting the court mien she'd perfected as a child. Showing fear or weakness to a room full of predators would be a mistake.

Beneath the crystal window Sabine had infused with

elements of her magic, Lord Darius and Lady Nymira appeared to be holding court. They were surrounded by nearly a dozen people, most of them wearing the colors of the Obsidian Clan. Sabine recognized a few of the wyvern guards who had been in attendance when Malek's father had destroyed the ballroom.

"Shit," Malek muttered at the sight of a man approaching them.

He was a tall, imposing figure with dark hair and sharp green eyes who wore his power draped around him like a mantle. Many of the onlookers moved out of his way, likely due to the sheer force of his presence. Based on the emerald accents of his rich attire, Sabine guessed this was Malek's uncle—the same one who had noted their presence in Imenel.

"Malek," Emanthir said, narrowing his eyes on Sabine. "You dare bring a fae here?"

"Uncle Emanthir," Malek replied, his tone cool. "Allow me to introduce my mate, Lady Sabine. She'll be formally joining our clan this evening once we light the urns."

"Out of the question," Emanthir said with a low growl. "If she was the cause of the disturbance in Imenel, I'll see her bound in iron before the night is out."

Sabine straightened, her magic rising quickly in response to the threat. Malek released her and moved in front of Emanthir. His power punched through the room, just as Aeron stepped beside Sabine in a defensive pose. Several people gasped, and countless heads turned in their direction.

Rika turned and ran toward the Obsidian Clan's staging area. Sabine put her hand on Aeron's arm in a silent gesture to hold. Once they revealed themselves, she wasn't sure all of them would leave this room alive. In this, they would have to trust Malek to diffuse the situation.

"Make a threat against Sabine again, and I'll see your scales flayed from your body," Malek warned.

Or maybe not.

"You overstep yourself, Malek," Emanthir's voice rumbled, making the ground tremble beneath their feet.

"I haven't even begun," Malek said, his skin beginning to glow as though intending to shift. Sabine inhaled sharply and placed her hand on Malek's back. Her touch had the intended effect, and the glow dimmed.

"Malek," Nymira exclaimed with forced cheerfulness as she approached with Rika at her side. She kissed Malek's cheek and said, "I was beginning to think you'd changed your mind about attending."

"I wasn't in a hurry to stand around and wait for Kaia," Malek said, not tearing his gaze away from Emanthir.

"Sabine," Nymira said with a warm smile and embraced her. "Is that—Oh, Malek! You've given her your band. Look, Emanthir! Your nephew's claimed a mate at last."

Nymira turned to get a better look at Sabine's armband. Her gaze flew to Malek in shock. "Blue? Why, that's..."

Malek glanced at his mother but didn't step away from Emanthir.

Nymira's eyes moistened, and she hugged Sabine again. "I'm so glad he's found you, my dear. Come and meet my brute of a mate before the lighting of the urns. I've made him promise to be on his best behavior this evening."

Emanthir scowled. "Nymira, you can't condone this—"

"Manny," Nymira chided gently. "Tonight is a celebration of family and to renew our clan ties. Why don't you bring Polara and Raynor over after you light your urns? I haven't been able to spend much time with my older brother and his family lately. I've missed you terribly."

Emanthir glared at Sabine again, his expression hard. Nymira stepped closer to him and patted his cheek. The odd buzzing Sabine had been hearing became louder, and she realized she was picking up the sounds from hundreds of silent conversations. She couldn't tell what anyone was saying, but whatever the Huntsman had done to her in the Hall of the Gods allowed her to hear the faintest hum of them communicating.

A flash of annoyance crossed Emanthir's face, but he gave Nymira a curt nod before turning away. Malek wrapped his arm protectively around Sabine and pulled her close.

"Quickly, now," Nymira said in a low voice, motioning for them to follow. "We need to get you into the Obsidian Clan area. I'd hoped you would have arrived earlier to avoid such encounters."

"I doubt we would have garnered such attention if you hadn't made the blasted window such a huge focal point, Mother."

Nymira sniffed and held her head high. "It deserved nothing less. Now smile and walk faster. I'm determined to get through this evening with my window intact."

Sabine glanced at the unfriendly and suspicious faces around them. At this point, she was beginning to think the window was a lost cause.

CHAPTER 45

"*The* urn lighting ceremony usually occurs after we've had a chance to renew some of our kindship ties," Malek said, his voice slipping into Sabine's thoughts. "*However, my mother thinks it's best if we complete the ceremony as soon as possible. The missive from the Seelie King has caused some... concerns. Until you're formally declared my mate, you won't be safe from any challenges.*"

"Malek, your people will not simply accept me because you've declared I'm your mate," Sabine said silently. "*It does both of us a disservice to hold to such wishful thinking. When they learn the truth about me, they will not forgive the deception easily.*"

He lifted her hand and kissed it. "*Trust in me, Sabine. This is the best way to keep you safe, and my people will eventually understand.*"

Sabine didn't respond, knowing it was pointless to argue. For good or ill, Malek was set upon this course of action.

They entered the Obsidian Clan area with Rika and Aeron a step behind. Several tables and chairs had been arranged, and a small repast was being stocked by a man in obsidian-colored livery. Groups of people stood nearby, talking and laughing, but Sabine couldn't tell whether they were humans, wyverns, or dragons. The heavy magic in the air, combined with the ever-present smoky scent, blurred her senses.

Nymira approached a man in the middle of a discussion and kissed his cheek. When he turned, Sabine staggered to a halt.

Darius was an older and more weathered version of Malek. While Malek's blue eyes were often filled with affection and humor, there was an almost feral intensity that shone through Darius's one golden eye.

Even though Malek had warned her, the long scar that bisected his cheek wasn't simply an old injury. She could sense the residual magic of a profound darkness that still haunted him. Whatever ancient magic had caused the wound had bridged the barrier between his human and dragon forms.

His appearance to Malek was so similar that she almost reached out to him to try to soothe that ancient hurt. From the fierce hostility emanating from him, her interference wouldn't be welcome. It was disconcerting to look upon someone who bore such familiarity to Malek, yet lacked the warmth and tenderness of the man she loved.

Malek stepped in front of her, blocking her path and facing down his father. She placed her hand on Malek's back, sensing he was speaking to his father using mind-touch speech.

"Stand aside, Malek," she said silently.

"I will not have him treat you with anything less than the respect you deserve," Malek said, his voice slipping into her thoughts.

"Then do not treat me as someone who needs to be coddled," she said. *"I will earn his respect on my own merit, or not at all. Your*

insistence on the matter does more harm than good. You asked me to trust you. Now I'm asking you to do the same."

Malek finally relented and stepped aside. "Sabine, this is my father, Lord Darius. Father, this is my mate, my anchor in this life and beyond, Sabine."

Darius swept his gaze over her and scowled. "You have mettle to face me, I'll give you that. More so than the last fae who sullied our clan name. She would hide among her plants, a wilting flower amongst the flames."

"Darius," Nymira hissed. "Do not make me shift in the middle of this ballroom. If I ruin this dress because of you, I will pluck out your scales one by one."

"I grew up in the Unseelie court, Lady Nymira," Sabine said with a small smile. "Having a dragon scowl at me is barely noteworthy."

Nymira arched her brow. "Oh?"

Sabine considered Darius for a moment. If his dragon was close to the surface, she would need to appeal to that side of him. "On my fifth name day, I was gifted an enchanted bloodlet dagger from the demon king. I used it to kill the assassin my father sent for me the next day."

Sabine didn't mention the nightmares that had plagued her afterward, or the way Balkin had stayed by her side for months to ensure another assassination attempt wouldn't be forthcoming. Nor did she mention how her mother had returned the bloody dagger to the demon king, allowing him to siphon traces of her power and the assassin's magic from the weapon as payment. Kal'thorz had sent another enchanted dagger the following day, even more rare and valuable than the last.

Darius harrumphed. "A dagger from the demon king, eh? Too bad it wasn't used against him."

"Indeed," Sabine said pleasantly. "Perhaps that's why Kal'thorz never delivered such gifts in person."

Darius barked out a laugh.

"I need a drink," Nymira said, waving over one of the serving staff. She plucked two fluted glasses off their tray and immediately downed one. She placed her empty glass on the tray and turned her attention to the second.

"Have you killed many demons?" Darius asked.

Sabine inclined her head. "While I consider every life precious, I will not abide any who seek to harm me or mine. Your son and I painted the underworld with demonic blood when they raised a hand against us."

"Is that so?" Darius asked, his gaze sharpening on Malek.

Malek raised Sabine's hand and placed a kiss against it. "Sabine can be as fierce as a greater dragon when those she loves are in danger. She saved my life."

Sabine's gaze softened as she looked up at him. "As you saved mine."

"Now there's a saga to tell," Darius said and leaned forward. "How many demons did you slaughter? I warned you about those horns and poisoned blood. You didn't try to eat them, did you?"

"You know what, just leave the whole tray of drinks," Nymira called out to the woman. "I have a feeling we're going to need it."

Malek arched his brow. "Careful, Mother. We don't need a repeat of the last clan gala."

Nymira finished off her second drink and placed the empty glass on the table. "Those curtains were far too close to the dragonfire urns last time. We staggered them to prevent such an occurrence tonight. Now, no more demon talk. I simply forbid it."

Darius crossed his arms and grunted. "My mate tells me you've adopted a human seer. Was that the small human who raced in here earlier?"

Sabine gestured to Rika. "This is Rika, formerly of Karga. Her grandmother entrusted me with her safety."

Darius turned his gaze on Rika. "And do you feel safe surrounded by dragons? Or is that why you decided to run?"

"Darius," Nymira said sternly. "She's our granddaughter. You will behave, or I'll toss you in the ocean."

Rika grinned. "It's all right. If your son's anything like you, Lord Darius, you're fierce *and* honorable. I ran to get Lady Nymira because I was worried Malek might shift and break your new window." She looked down at herself. "I'm a pretty squishy human. I doubt I'm much of a threat for any dragon. I figure that means I'm pretty safe."

Darius chuckled. "I like her."

"Of course you like her," Nymira said, picking up another glass. "I can't wait to show her off. Lady Quivara is going to have her tail in a twist. She's constantly bragging about that worthless son of hers and how the Topaz Clan is among the largest of clans, even though they don't compare to our level of magic. Now I have a new fae daughter and seer granddaughter to show off." She waved at a woman wearing a bright yellow dress. "Quivara! We'll talk soon!"

Malek placed his hands on Rika's shoulders. "Mother, perhaps it would be better to—"

Nymira held up her hand. "Oh, no. You do not get to leave for several years, suddenly come home with a new mate and her charge, and not expect me to play the doting grandmother. This is my right, Malek. I will not be denied."

Sabine bit back a smile.

Malek sighed and took two fluted glasses off the tray. He handed one to Sabine and said, "Sometimes it's better to just go along with her."

Sabine eyed the drink and sniffed, catching the faint scent of fruit and wood smoke. It might appeal to a dragon, but she had no interest in drinking burned wine.

Malek took a sip from his glass and grimaced. "I hadn't realized what it was. Let me get you something else. Dragon's breath is… an acquired taste."

"I'll take that," Nymira said, confiscating Sabine's untouched drink and waving to one of the servers. "Would you be a dear and fetch some wine for Lady Sabine and Rika?"

The server nodded and headed over to a bar area. Aeron straightened, watching the server pour Sabine's wine from a bottle.

Darius's gaze fell on Aeron, and he scowled. "Another fae? Who is this?"

"His name is Aeron," Malek said, taking the glass of wine from the server and offering it to Sabine. "Given Mother's fondness for the new window, we decided to keep Bane out of sight for the evening. He's in charge of Sabine's safety when I'm not with her."

Aeron dipped his head politely in Darius's direction and remained silent. Sabine caught the faintest trace of magic whispered upon the wind, urging Darius to ignore Aeron's presence. Darius blinked and turned back to Nymira.

Interesting. She hadn't realized Aeron possessed powers of persuasion. The fae usually had to speak or sing to use such abilities. Aeron noticed her curiosity and simply smiled knowingly at her.

She took an experimental sip of the wine and nodded at Malek. The light and fruity flavor was surprisingly refreshing.

"It's good," Rika said with a smile. "Better than the ale in Razadon."

Darius scowled. "Where the hell is Kaia? She should have been here by now. It's that drake of hers causing the delay, isn't it? He knows we can't eat until we light the damn urns. Your brother's going to gobble up all the snoslek."

Nymira took a long drink. "Kaia's on her way. Some problem with the dress not fitting right. Be delicate, dear. She's having difficulties adjusting to... her condition." She looked out among the crowd. "Oh! There's Levin and his new mate. Such a charming young woman. The green becomes her."

Levin and Esmelle approached the Obsidian Clan area. Esmelle's face was already flushed, her eyes bright with excitement. Her feet kept tapping in time with the music.

Levin gestured to Esmelle and said, "Lord Darius and Lady Nymira, allow me to introduce my mate and keeper of my flame, Esmelle of Northwood."

Nymira smiled brilliantly at Esmelle and kissed her cheek. "Welcome to our clan, Esmelle. It's wonderful to know you're willing to put up with this scoundrel. And how simply perfect you and Sabine are old friends."

Darius eyed her. "And what flavor are you supposed to be? Fae? Seer?"

Esmelle curtseyed. "Dryad."

"Are you fucking kidding me?" Darius demanded, pinning Levin with his golden gaze. "What the hell are you going to do with a tree? The minute you belch fire, she's going to run screaming."

Nymira rescued another smoking glass from the tray and waved at a couple wearing red and black. "People are staring, dear. Lower your voice and think happy thoughts."

"I'm only part-dryad," Esmelle said with a laugh. "My father was human. I also dabble a bit with witchcraft. Trust me when I tell you I can handle just about anything Levin's willing to dish out. I lived with two demons and a fae for almost a decade."

"More demons?" Darius said with a growl.

"Have a drink, my love," Nymira said, handing him one of the glasses. "Oh, look. There's Kaia."

Malek sighed and said, "Finally."

Kaia flounced into the Obsidian Clan's area while Thom walked more sedately beside her. She tugged on her dress and said, "I swear, I tried this thing on a week ago. It's already snug. The seamstress had to rush over and adjust the corset a bit." She wiggled her skirt and asked, "What did you do to Norah, big brother? She was shaking so bad, I thought she was going to poke me with that needle."

"She met Bane," Malek said.

Kaia snorted. "Is that all? Mum, you've gotta find a new seamstress. If this one gets all flustered over a demon, she's never going to be able to handle Dad."

Darius scowled. "Do not compare me with those creatures."

Nymira downed the rest of her glass and placed the empty one next to the others. "At least she managed to finish the dresses before her breakdown." She clapped her hands. "We're all here. Now we just need to get through this ceremony without shifting or setting anyone on fire. Places, everyone!"

Sabine put down her glass and asked, "What's involved with this ceremony?"

Malek gestured to the four large urns at the back of the area designated for the Obsidian Clan. "As part of our tradition to renew our clan vows, each greater dragon in our clan infuses these four urns with their dragonfire. The two in the center represent my parents and remain lit during the entire gala, since they're hosting the event. The urn on the left represents my fire, and the one on the far right represents Kaia."

Sabine glanced up at him. "And the two smaller ones beside yours?"

Malek took her hand and kissed it. "I will light one for you, indicating I'm sharing the protection of my clan and my dragonfire with my mate. The other is for Rika, announcing she's also under the protection of my clan."

Rika jerked her head up. "What? You're doing that? For me?"

Nymira turned to her. "Of course, my dear. You're part of our family now. By lighting your urn, we announce it to the world."

Rika threw her arms around Malek and hugged him.

He chuckled and returned her hug. "This just formalizes something we already know in our hearts."

Rika sniffed and nodded.

Nymira and Darius approached the urns and faced one another.

"I renew my pledge to you, Nymira Myst'ald," Darius said, his gravelly voice fueled with his power. "With the fire that burns in these urns, so too does my passion and commitment to you and all we protect. I vow to stand by your side, as your shield and your partner, guarding our clan with the strength of my will and the might of my heart. Together, we will forge a future secure and prosperous, as unyielding as the stone upon which we stand."

His urn flared to life, the flames shooting up as blue and red sparks. Smoke swirled into the air and wrapped around Nymira and Darius, binding them together. The magic within his dragonfire turned the base of the urn the blackest of obsidian.

"Darius Rish'dan, my heart's companion and fiercest protector," Nymira began, the dragonfire from Darius's urn creating a halo around her. "In the light of these flames, I reaffirm my devotion to you and our sacred trust. As these urns hold fire, so does my soul hold unwavering love for you and our people. I pledge to weave our strength together, to nurture and defend our family and every soul within the Obsidian Clan. Let our combined might light the way for our clan, offering refuge and strength, as we uphold the legacy of our ancestors with honor and grace."

Her urn ignited abruptly, shooting green sparks into the air. The magic binding them together solidified for a moment before absorbing into their skin. Once the base of the urn turned dark to match its mate, Darius and Nymira turned to face their children. Kaia and Thom held hands and walked over to the urns on the opposite side.

Malek took Sabine's hand and motioned for Rika to join them.

As they approached the large urn on the left, Sabine hesitated. She wanted Malek and everything that urn represented, but she couldn't put him or his family in danger. Everything she'd seen from the dragons so far had shown her a group full of love and strong family ties. The fact they were willing to open their hearts to both her and Rika was just one more reason she shouldn't do it.

Lachlina would destroy them.

Or her people would.

Malek turned to her and cupped her face, his voice slipping into her thoughts. *"You're wrong, Sabine. We're stronger together. We always have been. Take this leap of faith with me, and I will never let you fall."*

Sabine squeezed her eyes shut. There had been a handful of moments in her life where she could clearly see the crossroads that lay before her. This was one of those times. If she walked away now, she would lose some essential part of herself—as though pieces of her soul would be ripped away.

Opening her eyes, she lifted her head to meet his gaze. No matter the consequences, she wanted a life with Malek. She would do everything possible to protect him and his family from her people and Lachlina's wrath. As long as Malek was by her side, she would take that leap and learn to fly.

He kissed her softly, almost reverently and led her to

stand in front of the urn. Taking her hand again, he said, "Sabine, you are my anchor, my heart, and my home. With this fire, I proclaim to all that you are under my protection, woven into the fabric of my life and my clan. Your safety and happiness are as vital to me as the air I breathe. I pledge to honor, cherish, and defend you with every beat of my heart. I forever bind my life to yours, Sabin'theoria, in the sight of my kin, my clan, and the ether that eternally guides us."

Malek's power slowly began to wrap around her like tendrils of smoke. Sabine inhaled sharply as her wrist began to burn. "Malek—"

"Trust in me and in your heart, Sabine," he urged silently. *"You are stronger than Lachlina."*

Sabine tried to push Lachlina back, ignoring the heat that raced through her body. It felt as though the goddess was once again trying to burn her from within.

Malek held out his hand for Rika. She stepped up next to him and placed her hand in his. "Rika, I extend this sanctuary to you. As this flame guards against the darkness, so shall I guard you, offering the shelter of my clan and the strength of my commitment. You are now part of my family, embraced by the boundless might and warmth of the Obsidian Clan."

Rika sniffed, blinking back tears.

Malek's power began to build, filling the room and wrapping around her even tighter. Sabine gasped as he reached for the burning flame of power within her and combined it with his might. Lachlina's rage pounded against her thoughts, but Malek was resolute, accepting all of it and sending it toward the urn. Malek took their hands and touched them to the urns.

All three urns erupted simultaneously, twin blue and gold flames shooting upward to touch the ceiling. The dreamstone in her armband cracked. Several people around them gasped, while frantic whispers and shocked murmurs filled the room. The urn itself turned the blackest of obsidian, but countless streaks of gold cut through the darkness like lightning.

"Together, these flames symbolize not just my love and passion but also the fierce loyalty and protection I offer. Let them burn as a testament to my vows, illuminating our path with love, honor, and steadfast commitment."

The pain in Sabine's wrist extinguished abruptly, but she could sense Lachlina's fury at what had just transpired. It would likely only be a matter of time before the goddess expressed her disapproval in another, more painful way. To make matters worse, her magic was now at risk of being exposed.

"Malek, what have you done?" she whispered and touched the armband. When she took her hand away, a light dusting of powder coated her fingertips.

Malek gently drew her into his arms. His voice slipped into her thoughts as he wrapped his heated power around her again.

"You're mine, Sabine. I have no intention of sharing you with Lachlina. If I have to bind you to me with magic to keep you safe from her, I'll do it and much more. We all will."

She leaned into his touch, allowing her softer magic to brush against his. *"That's why Bane and Aeron didn't object to this."*

"Apparently, I'm a lesser evil," Malek said, his tone amused. *"I don't believe either one was happy about it, and none of us expected it to shatter the dreamstone. But I didn't give them much of an opportunity to argue with me. I love you, Sabine. Nothing is more important to me than you."*

Sabine leaned back and brushed a tendril of his dark hair away from his face. "I never imagined a dragon could so fully claim my heart. I will always take a leap of faith with you, Malek."

"And I will always catch you," Malek promised, kissing her again.

Nymira dabbed at her eyes with a handkerchief. "That was all very moving and quite an impressive display, but you've left scorch marks on my freshly painted ceiling. Perhaps you can do something as equally creative as the window when you decide to fix it." In a low voice, she added, "And hide the gold on that damn urn before someone realizes the Obsidian Clan just welcomed a Tuatha Dé into their family."

CHAPTER 46

*S*abine quickly spun an illusion on the outside of the urn, matching the obsidian color to the others. From the thunderous look on Darius's face and even Kaia's shocked expression, they'd all noticed. It hadn't helped that Malek had used her true name.

Malek's expression darkened, and he took a step toward his family. From his rigid stance and the loud buzzing she could hear, Malek was in a heated private argument with his family.

Levin snapped his fingers at some of the other wyverns in a silent command to surround the staging area. They immediately fell into place, but the looks she was receiving were anything but friendly.

"I'm guessing this isn't going over well?" Rika asked.

Esmelle scooted closer to them and whispered, "We might want to start making our escape. Malek drew a lot of attention just now, but most of the looks are being directed at you."

"It's never wise to run from predators," Sabine said.

"Malek has his reasons for doing what he did. I will not give anyone cause to doubt we're not united in our purpose."

"Indeed," Aeron said, scanning the nearby faces. "However, a distraction wouldn't be amiss. With your permission, I can arrange for a gust of wind to knock over a table or two."

Blossom, still in the guise of a ladybug, landed on her shoulder. "Distractions are my specialty. I've got you covered in five… four… three… two…"

Screams erupted from a woman wearing a bright yellow dress. Her hair was coiled on her head like a beehive and teetered precariously as she waved her arms and kicked out with her legs. She bumped and jostled other guests, ignoring their loud objections.

She hiked her dress up almost to her hips, revealing striped hose covering spindly legs. "It's in my dress! Get it out! Get it out!"

Sabine watched in horror as the woman jerked across the dance floor and crashed into a man wearing a purple tunic. They both staggered, then toppled into the buffet table. Food and dishes flew into the air, arcing over several of the guests before landing in messy heaps on the floor.

"Not the snoslek!" Darius shouted.

Nymira grabbed the last fluted glass on the tray and downed it.

Rika covered her face with her hands. "Bees, Blossom? Really?"

Blossom cocked her head. "Thistle might be entitled to special compensation after that. I suggested she just buzz by the lady's ear, not dive down her dress. I should probably go check on her."

"No more bees," Sabine warned as the ladybug took flight.

Malek winced as the man tried to disentangle himself

from the beehive woman's legs. "This is a side of Lady Trefani I could have lived a lifetime without seeing."

Kaia gaped. "By the ether, she has little clouds embroidered on her knickers. Is that a smiling sun on her butt?"

Aeron lowered his gaze, shoulders shaking with silent laughter.

Rika grinned. "I told you, Aeron. Blossom has a way of getting everyone caught up in her shenanigans."

Malek took Sabine's hand. "Yes, but the timing was damn near perfect."

Lady Trefani was finally upright, though her hair wasn't. It drooped like a parched tulip, and her bright yellow dress was now streaked with brownish goo. The staff had righted the overturned table and were making a valiant attempt at resuscitating her dignity, starting with her dress and hair.

The man, meanwhile, had snatched several cloths from the nearby staff and was furiously wiping himself down, scowling at the woman who had collided with him.

"A change of plans is in order," Malek said quietly. "We'll need to cut the evening short. If Aeron wants to see what he can learn, he can probably slip away quietly while we make our farewells to the other clan leaders."

When Aeron hesitated, Sabine said, "This may be our only chance to get information. Do what you must. I'll stay with Malek."

"As you wish," Aeron murmured. "Should you have need of me, I will return to your side immediately."

"I'll go with your mother," Rika said. "She wanted to introduce me to people. I'll let you know if I hear anything."

Esmelle hugged Sabine. "I'll keep an eye on Rika. We'll see what we can pick up. Levin has some wyvern duties, so it'll give us a chance to blend in and listen."

Sabine nodded, watching as Aeron slipped out of the

Obsidian Clan area. He vanished into the crowd with the effortless grace of a fae.

Nymira appeared delighted at Rika's approach and quickly ushered her toward Lady Trefani and her limp hairdo. Darius followed a half-step behind, his attention more focused on the ruins of the buffet table than the conversation ahead.

Malek captured her hand, and his voice slipped into her thoughts. *"My sister knows you're no small power, but she doesn't yet understand the full impact of the gold on the urn or your true name."*

Sabine glanced up at him. *"And your father?"*

Malek's jaw hardened. *"He knows and understands. I've made my position clear to them. My mother is going to run interference. If she's unsuccessful, we'll leave the Sky Cities in the morning. Unfortunately, the wyverns in our clan were also witnesses. My mother will do what she can to ensure their silence, but word will likely spread."*

Sabine didn't reply, knowing there were no words she could offer to ease his burden. The last thing she'd wanted was for Malek to be forced into choosing between her and his family.

He turned to her and said, *"You are the woman I've chosen to spend my life with. I've sworn it with dragonfire and proclaimed it in front of my kin and clan. If they turn away from you now, they turn away from me as well."*

Sabine placed her hand against his face and sent a small wave of compassionate magic over him. *"Neither one of us lived through the war, Malek. We cannot grasp the magnitude of their losses or recall the battles they fought and survived. You used my true name. With that name comes a great number of memories."*

"You believe I need to give them time?"

Sabine placed a soft kiss against his lips. *"You gave me the time I needed to accept you were a dragon. Does your family deserve any less?"*

Malek pressed his forehead against hers. *"I hadn't planned to announce your true name in quite so dramatic a fashion. When I felt Lachlina through our bond, I realized the best chance to keep her influence weakened was to strengthen your ties to me. Anything less than your true name wouldn't have worked."*

Sabine sighed. *"I suspect her silence is only a temporary reprieve. There will be repercussions from this, both from your people and from Lachlina."*

"We'll face them together," Malek said and drew her into his arms. *"I'll give my family the time they need to adapt, but I will not subject you to the same suspicion or accusations Elisa endured, nor will I hide you away. If that means we depart the Sky Cities, so be it."*

"I see my cousin hasn't lost his talent for causing a commotion," a man's voice interrupted them.

Malek turned, wrapping an arm around Sabine's waist. "Raynor. It's been a long time."

"So it has," a dark-haired man said, approaching them with a grin and a swagger. From his piercing green eyes to the emerald accents on his attire, Sabine guessed this was Emanthir's son. The power radiating from him was similar.

"I see you finally found the landing pad," Malek said.

"Indeed," Raynor replied, his gaze locked on Sabine. "I had some… incentive. Malek, you need to introduce me to your charming companion who can scorch ceilings with barely a touch."

"Raynor Myst'ald, this is my mate, Sabine," Malek said, glancing down at her. "Raynor is my cousin and scion of the Emerald Clan."

Sabine tilted her head in greeting. "Well met, Raynor."

"A true pleasure," Raynor said, taking her hand. He lifted

it to his lips and let a wave of his heated power ripple across her skin.

Sabine narrowed her eyes, barely resisting the urge to strike out with her magic. Malek released her and moved into Raynor, wrapping his hand around his cousin's throat.

"You dare?" Malek demanded.

Raynor grinned and lifted his hands in surrender. "You can't blame me for testing the air currents, cousin. Unless you know something I don't, the fae have never recognized our mate bonds."

"Then allow me to make it clear," Sabine said, allowing the faintest trace of power to surround her. "Malek is mine. That you would so casually disregard what is obviously an important ritual speaks to your contempt not only for your cousin, but also for your heritage. Challenge our bond again, and Malek won't be the threat you'll face—I will."

Malek released him and swept Sabine into his arms. He lowered his head and kissed her deeply, wrapping her in his heated power. She curled her fingers into his shirt and breathed him in.

Raynor laughed. "Oh, I like her. Well done, cousin. Well done, indeed."

Malek broke their kiss and grinned at him. "Find your own fae. She's mine."

"Welcome to the family, Sabine," Raynor said and gave her a courtly bow. "Malek, a private word, if you will."

Malek hesitated.

Before Sabine could say anything, Kaia hooked her arm through Sabine's and said, "Go. Sabine and I need to have some girl talk."

Malek arched his brow. "That's supposed to be reassuring?"

Kaia grinned. "She'll be fine, big brother. We won't go anywhere."

Sabine nodded at him. Malek blew out a breath and walked a short distance away with Raynor.

Sabine watched a woman carry a tray of smoking drinks over to Malek and Raynor. She frowned, wondering how the dragons could even taste the fruit beneath the smoke essence.

"I have questions."

Sabine turned to Kaia and nodded. "I gathered as much."

Kaia glanced around and frowned. "I don't know how people have private conversations without speaking in their thoughts."

"I would normally use magic to shield our words, but that may raise more questions," Sabine said with a small smile. "Unfortunately, the fae don't rely on the mind-touch ability the same way your people do."

"Wait. What? You can speak using mind-touch?"

Sabine paused, debating how much to share. What she had with Malek was still precious and new. While her companions had surmised the truth, Sabine didn't think it wise for the Huntsman's gift to become public knowledge.

"Some of the beastpeople in Faerie lack the ability to speak," Sabine said, settling on a variation of the truth. "They can, however, communicate telepathically with the families whose blood created them. It's not as fluid as the natural communication among your kind. It began as a way to issue commands over great distances, but over time it evolved into something more."

Kaia glanced around again and then asked, "Who are you, Sabine? How do you know this stuff? I thought you were part human, but that's not the case, is it?"

"No," Sabine said quietly. "I was born in Faerie."

"You're something more than Elisa," Kaia said, shaking her head. "There are similarities, but there's a strength in you I never saw in her. She never would have dreamed of threatening my cousin, much less told stories about killing demons like Mum said. And that urn... I've never seen anything like that."

When Sabine didn't respond, Kaia pressed her hand against her stomach. "Malek told you, didn't he?"

Sabine nodded. "He's worried about you."

Kaia reached for her hand. "I know you have a great deal of magic, Sabine. If there's any way you can help—"

Sabine's breath caught at the enormity of the debt Kaia's words evoked. Malek whipped his gaze toward them, and Sabine could hear a furious buzzing surround them.

Kaia glanced over at Malek and paled. "I didn't mean—By the ether, I almost made a mess of this. Elisa would have gotten up and walked away, but you can't even do that with all the dragons here. They're just waiting to pounce on you once you leave our clan area."

Sabine shook her head. "Do not bargain with a fae, Kaia. Magic moves around us differently. Allow Malek to negotiate with me on your behalf. He understands, almost as well as some fae, how far he can push without incurring additional debt."

"But—"

She squeezed Kaia's hand and said, "Trust your brother. I will do what I can. My friend, Esme, is a talented herbalist and has a keen sense for bringing things into balance. If you're willing, we'd both like to spend some time with you tomorrow to see if there's something we can do."

Kaia's eyes welled with tears. She reached out and hugged Sabine tightly. "Yes. Absolutely, yes. I know I'm not supposed to thank you, but dammit, it's hard. You've given me hope. Idola keeps going through that book and tinkering with those damn tonics, but we haven't had any luck yet."

"Kaia," Thom said and rushed over to her. "What is it? Are you all right?"

Kaia wiped her eyes and nodded. "Sabine and I were just having a bit of girl talk. You don't need to worry."

Thom hesitated, his gaze suspicious.

Kaia swatted him and said, "Knock it off. She's my sister, and I won't have you scowling at her."

Sabine stared at Kaia in surprise. The ease with which Malek's family had opened their hearts to her was disconcerting. If the situation had been reversed, Malek never would have been welcomed with such warmth and affection. She wanted to believe it was genuine, but she was hesitant to trust it.

Malek must have sensed her unease, because he started walking toward her. He slid his arms around her waist and nuzzled her neck. "Is Thom bothering you? Do I need to tie his tail in a knot?"

"Great," Thom muttered. "Now they're all ganging up on me. You try being one of the only drakes in a family full of greater dragons."

"At least you're not fae," Sabine said with a smile.

"Hah! Maybe Darius won't give me quite so much crap about not having wings now that you're around."

Malek scowled. "Tail. Knot."

Kaia grinned. "Thom was being overprotective, just like a certain obsidian dragon I know. You had your eye on Sabine the whole time we were talking, just waiting to leap to her rescue."

Sabine trailed her fingers over Malek's arm. "Is that so?"

Malek kissed her neck, right behind her ear. "Maybe it's just hard to take my eyes off you in this dress."

Raynor approached and took a sip of his smoking drink. "Ah, there's my lovely cousin. I was wondering where you've been hiding."

Kaia grinned and hugged Raynor. "Hey, Ray. How's it flying?"

Raynor hooked his arm around Kaia's shoulders. "The two of you are making me look bad. My mother's going to be after me to settle down and find a mate now."

"Uh oh," Kaia murmured. "Speaking of Aunt Polara, it looks like she and Uncle Emanthir decided to crash our little party."

Raynor sighed and straightened. "Father's in rare form tonight, and Mother's in her usual foul disposition. You've been warned."

"Shit," Malek muttered, glancing in the direction Raynor had indicated. His voice slipped into Sabine's thoughts. *"We need to greet them before heading out to meet the other clan leaders. We'll say a quick hello, and then I intend to take you back home and see how quickly I can get you out of this dress."*

Sabine gave him a teasing smile. *"Shall we wager? Perhaps I'll be the one to undress you first."*

"Dragons always win," Malek said with a grin and kissed her hand.

"We'll see."

Emanthir led a tall, wiry woman with a pinched face toward them. Her lavish green gown was trimmed with hundreds of tiny yellow gemstones that sparkled under the lights. The dress seemed impossibly heavy, but she moved as if she were wearing nothing more than silk. Her dark hair was swept upward in a severe style, fastened with large emerald and topaz clips. The gemstones around her throat and wrists were so massive, even the dwarves would envy them.

"Uncle Emanthir, Aunt Polara," Kaia said with a bright smile. "Mum just went to check on Lady Trefani, and I think Dad's rescuing what's left of the snoslek. I have no idea how a bee made its way into the ballroom, much less inside Lady Trefani's dress."

"Horrid display," Polara said with disgust. "If your mother

spent less time repairing the ballroom after your father's outbursts, perhaps insects wouldn't infest her home. The Topaz Clan will likely seek recompense for such an atrocity."

Kaia straightened. "Now, wait just a minute—"

Raynor cleared his throat and asked, "Mother, can I get you a drink?"

"I suppose," Polara said, wrinkling her nose. "Make sure it's a clean glass. Those humans touch *everything*. It's terribly inconvenient having them so close."

Raynor turned and rolled his eyes at Sabine before heading toward one of the servers with a tray of smoking drinks. Sabine bit back a smile, her estimation of Malek's cousin rising dramatically.

"Uncle Emanthir, Aunt Polara," Malek said, nodding to both. "My mother will be pleased you accepted her invitation to join us. I introduced my mate to Uncle Emanthir earlier, but you didn't have a chance to meet her, Aunt Polara."

Emanthir remained as cold as before, but Polara narrowed her eyes on Sabine. She pointed at her and said, "I know you."

Sabine stilled, making an effort to keep her expression pleasant. "I don't believe I've had the pleasure."

Malek's arm tightened around her waist. "Aunt Polara, this is Lady Sabine. We just arrived in the Sky Cities yesterday."

"Your drink, Mother," Raynor said, offering a smoking glass.

She took it without so much as a glance. "No. I never forget a face. It will come to me. The hair is a little different. The features a little more... *human*." She said the last word as if it repulsed her.

Emanthir's gaze sharpened on his mate. "You recognize her? From where?"

Polara's eyes grew distant. "It was long ago. A battlefield

of smoke and ash. She called us down from the skies with her song. I remember the demons—"

A pale moth swooped down, right in front of Polara's face. Kaia reached to shoo it away and bumped Polara's arm, spilling her drink.

Polara gasped and dropped the glass. It shattered on the floor.

"Of all the…" Polara exclaimed in dismay.

"Oops," Kaia said sheepishly, reaching for a napkin. "I guess a lot of people are wandering in and out of the garden tonight. It's letting in all sorts of bugs."

Sabine reached for Malek with her thoughts. *"Malek, Blossom's interference will only help up to a point. If Polara realizes who I am—"*

"I know," Malek replied with a frown. Out loud, he said, "We'll post some additional staff near the doors to help prevent any further disruptions. If you'll excuse us, there are still a few people we need to greet."

"I would speak with you and your… mate, Malek," Emanthir said, nodding toward the empty space where Sabine had been speaking with Kaia a few moments earlier.

Raynor handed Polara another smoking beverage and said, "Why don't we move a bit farther away from the garden doors, Mother? I doubt any bugs will come near the urns."

"Did you check for smudges?" Polara asked, holding the glass up to the light. "This won't do. Find another. Humans *touched* it. They may have even put their fleshy mouths on it."

When they were out of earshot, Emanthir turned to them and eyed Sabine. "My mate seems to have recognized you. One of Polara's gifts is perfect recall, even when events have transpired hundreds of years earlier."

"She is mistaken," Sabine said.

Malek frowned. "Sabine is younger than Kaia, Uncle Emanthir. She was not in the war, and has no history with our people. Up until a few days ago, I was the only dragon she had ever met."

Emanthir studied her. "Is this true?"

Sabine inclined her head. "It is. I was unaware Malek was a dragon until he revealed himself to me."

Emanthir rubbed his chin thoughtfully. "Nymira asked me to bring the missive we received from the Seelie King. She indicated you might be able to detect spellcraft on it?"

Sabine hesitated. "As I indicated to Lady Nymira, such magic weakens each time it's read. If there is any trace still remaining, I can tell you what type of magic was infused in the ink. At the very least, I can tell you whether it was truly penned from King Cadan'ellesar's own hand."

Emanthir's gaze turned suspicious. "How?"

Sabine knew he was testing her, but she needed to be cautious. While it was one thing for Malek's mother to learn her identity, it was another for someone like Emanthir to be handed such information.

"When one of the sidhe, or Faerie royals, writes a letter, traces of their magic are infused into the ink. It was developed as a way to ascertain whether orders were truly issued by one of the monarchs. If King Cadan'ellesar penned the missive himself, traces of his magic will be in the ink, the seal, and even absorbed into the paper itself. Such things linger longer than a spell crafted with a specific intention."

"You are surprisingly well informed for someone who wasn't able to identify a dragon," Emanthir said. "How do you know this?"

"Many children, even those with mixed ancestry, are taught at a young age to recognize the touch of power from the rulers of each of Faerie's courts," Sabine said, knowing she was dancing close to the edge of the truth. "After having experienced such power, it is not a thing one easily forgets."

Emanthir made a noncommittal noise. "What do you know of this new Unseelie queen?"

"She is a new queen," Sabine said with a shrug. "I have not lived in Faerie for many years."

"Then you don't know if the rumors claiming she's amassing armies is true?"

Malek narrowed his eyes. "Is this to be an interrogation, Uncle?"

"We can either conduct this discussion here and now, or in less pleasant surroundings," Emanthir said, his tone sharp.

"Sabine has been honest with you, Uncle," Malek reminded him. "These questions and threats are out of line. She has a great deal of experience that can benefit us and has offered her knowledge freely. I will not allow her to be mistreated."

Sabine placed her hand on Malek's arm. "Lord Emanthir, I do not know what rumors you've heard. If you're asking my opinion whether the new Unseelie queen intends to target the Sky Cities with her armies, I think it's highly unlikely. But I am not a seer who can predict the future. I think the more important question is whether you intend to give her cause."

Emanthir held her gaze for a long time. Finally, he turned to Malek. Sabine could once again hear that strange buzzing noise as though they were speaking privately with one another. Malek's jaw clenched, his expression darkening as he glared at his uncle. After a moment, Emanthir simply turned and walked over to Polara.

Sabine placed her hand against Malek's face, drawing his attention toward her.

"Tell me," she said silently.

Malek's entire body was rigid, his magic building under the surface. *"He's willing to meet us upstairs later to show you the letter from King Cadan. The Topaz Clan leaders and Amethyst Clan leaders will also be in attendance.*"

"*I see.*"

"*It's not worth the risk,*" Malek said. "*The less time you spend with them, the better—especially now that the dreamstone's broken.*"

Sabine lowered her hand and trailed her fingers over the Obsidian Clan crest on Malek's tunic. Verifying the letter had actually been written by her father might have been helpful in dealing with him, but it wasn't their priority. She wasn't willing to jeopardize rescuing the captives for such leverage.

She looked up at Malek and searched his expression. "*There's something more, isn't there?*"

Malek sighed. "*My mother told him the reason we were in Imenel was because we were trying to discover who sent the wyverns to attack us. He says that doesn't explain the power he sensed or the disturbances in Imenel that night. He knows we're hiding something.*" His jaw clenched. "*Sabine, I know my uncle. He won't let this go.*"

Sabine turned to stare up at the window they had created together. It was only a matter of time before they learned her identity. When that happened, she knew Malek's claim of her as his mate wouldn't be enough to protect her. Dragons might have a strong sense of family loyalty, but they would never accept a fae as one of them.

"*I agreed to bring Esme to meet with your sister tomorrow. If I can help her shift forms, I will. After that...*" She looked up at him. "*I can't stay here, Malek. Sooner or later, they'll realize who I am. And once the captives are freed, it will be even worse for you.*"

Malek drew her into his arms and wrapped his heated power around her. "*As long as you understand you won't be going alone.*"

She nodded, unable to put her emotions into words. As

much as she loved him, she wouldn't ask him to choose between her and his family. He needed the freedom to return to them, even if she couldn't follow. But she wasn't ready to say goodbye—and doubted she ever would be.

Malek pressed a soft kiss to her lips. *"I wanted you to see the beauty and warmth in my people, Sabine. I didn't want your first experience to be like this."*

Sabine smiled up at him. *"Then for tonight, show me how a dragon dances with his mate. We'll figure out the rest later."*

CHAPTER 47

The love that shone in Malek's eyes would have been enough to melt her heart, if it hadn't already been claimed by him. He offered her his arm, and she accepted, allowing him to lead her out of the Obsidian Clan area and toward the dance floor.

Across the ballroom, Sabine caught sight of a familiar man with tightly plaited dark hair wearing the black livery she'd begun to associate with the Obsidian Clan. Despite his human appearance, he towered over them both in height and width. Their eyes met for a fraction of a second before he turned away and picked up one of the nearby drink trays.

Before she could ask Malek why he was there, a middle-aged man stepped in front of them. His power shot outward, but Malek quickly wove his own heated magic around her to insulate her from the effects.

"Guard your magic," Malek warned silently.

The warning wasn't necessary, but the fact he'd felt the need to give it made Sabine even more wary. She blinked at the stranger, almost having the impression he'd been dipped in gold. It wasn't just his hair, eyes, and skin that gleamed as if he'd rolled naked in golden powder, but he'd somehow matched the shade in his tunic and the medallion around his neck. Every inch of him was a nauseating blur of golden revelry gone bad.

Despite being nearly the same height as Malek, he angled his head in a way that made it seem as if he were looking down on both of them.

A ladybug zipped by his head. Sabine eyed the red-and-black blur and tried to keep her expression neutral. Blossom didn't seem to like him either.

"Lord Typheron," Malek said, inclining his head. "You're looking... well. I trust you and Lady Ophelia are both enjoying the evening?"

"While your mother's hospitality holds no comparison, Lady Ophelia has been called away on clan business," Typheron said, his gaze focused on Sabine. "And who is this outsider who walks so freely among us?"

Malek narrowed his eyes. "Outsider, no longer. This is my mate, Lady Sabine of the Obsidian Clan." He gestured to the golden man. "Sabine, this is Lord Typheron, leader of the Topaz Clan and one of the current triumvirs in the Triumvirate of Flame."

Sabine tilted her head in acknowledgment. "Well met, Lord Typheron."

"Sabine," Typheron said with a frown. "That is a human name, is it not?"

"So I've been told."

The ladybug zipped by Typheron's head again, causing a waft of gold dust to lift into the air. The ladybug sneezed, her image flickering into a dragonfly for a moment.

Malek began coughing. Loudly. Sabine patted his back, trying to distract Lord Typheron from the sneezing ladybug-turned-dragonfly-turned-ladybug-again.

One of the waitstaff immediately approached with a tray

of smoking drinks, but Malek waved them off. Fortunately, Typheron was too busy studying Sabine to realize Blossom was wiping her running nose in his gold-powdered hair.

"*Is she—*" Malek asked silently.

"*Yes,*" Sabine said, desperately trying to keep a straight face. "*I almost feel bad for him.*"

Malek launched into another coughing fit, but this one had the cadence of muffled laughter. Sabine gave him a dirty look.

Lord Typheron glared at him. "Is there a problem?"

"Not at all. I must have inhaled a bit of dust." Malek cleared his throat. "My mother mentioned something about a possible union between the Topaz and Gold Clans. Your son is currently courting Lady Augatha, is he not?"

Lord Typheron inclined his head, lifting his hooked nose into the air. "Linus shall perform his duty as heir to the Topaz Clan to strengthen and fortify our proud lineage. The Gold Clan is a worthy and well-respected house."

"In that case, I wish Linus and Augatha much happiness."

Lord Typheron turned to Sabine and studied her with an intensity that made her skin crawl. "I see you decided to fly in your grandfather's currents with your… chosen mate. It is not often a fae travels to the Sky Cities, and even less common for one to walk unbound among us."

Malek's anger surged through their bond. He stepped closer, placing a protective arm around her waist.

Before he could respond to Typheron's implied threat, Sabine rested her hand on Malek's chest and said, "It is not often that one of the fae finds a dragon worthy of their attention *and* respect. That both Malek and his grandfather have claimed the hearts of those who speak with the land is a testament to *their* strength and the future of their legacy. For it is only with Aeslion's grace that dragons will ever be considered anything more than parasites."

Typheron's expression darkened. "You dare threaten me?"

"I have not threatened you, Lord Typheron," Sabine said, keeping her tone cool. "If you choose to seek deeper meaning in my words, that is your prerogative. The fae do not lie. And all choices carry a cost."

Malek placed his hand over hers. "Sabine speaks on behalf of the Obsidian Clan, Lord Typheron. No dragon among us would claim a mate who lacked the strength and ferocity of a greater dragon. She stands by my side, an equal partner and beloved mate."

Typheron eyed Malek's arm around her, his lip curling in distaste. "There was another man with you earlier, was there not?"

Sabine stilled, barely managing to keep her expression neutral. The ladybug reappeared and buzzed the top of Typheron's head. He absently waved a hand at it, sending another waft of dust into the air.

"You must be talking about Levin," Malek said, pretending to misunderstand him. "He returned with me and found a mate as well. I'm sure you'll see both of them before the night is through."

"No, I'm quite confident there was another with you," Typheron insisted. "He had the look of the fae, much like your companion. However, he seems to have mysteriously disappeared. As one of the triumvirs, I would be remiss in not investigating this issue. I would have his name, Malek. Where did you meet him?"

The ladybug buzzed loudly and landed right on Typheron's nose. He yelped and jerked his head, batting at the insect.

"That bug bit me! First, my sister is accosted by a bee, and now I'm bitten by a ladybug? What are you both playing at?"

"Malek, we must do something about the doors to the garden at once," Sabine said, feigning dismay. "Your mother would be horrified to learn more insects have snuck inside. The staff should take some precautions if they're going in and out of the ballroom."

"Of course," Malek said. "Lord Typheron, you'll have to excuse us. The Obsidian Clan would be poor hosts if we didn't make an effort to correct such an oversight at once."

Without waiting for a response, Malek led Sabine toward the garden doors. Blossom landed on her shoulder, breathing heavily.

"That golden rooster with the giant hands almost got me," Blossom exclaimed. "I don't like him. He's been watching you all night. The minute he saw you leave the Obsidian Clan area, he headed your way. And dust! So much icky dust! I still have it up my nose!"

"The Gold Clan is one of the wealthiest clans," Malek said quietly. "He thinks by showing them his vast wealth in the form of dusting his skin and hair with gold powder, he'll convince Lady Augatha to accept his idiot son."

Blossom made a gagging noise. "Gross. Who wants a dusty rooster in the house? What happened to giving someone flowers? Or a garden?"

Malek arched his brow at Sabine. "Is that what you want? Flowers? A garden?"

Sabine smiled and touched the armband he'd given her. "I don't think you need any suggestions. You've been doing quite well on your own."

"A few more ideas wouldn't hurt, especially if I keep exposing you to dragons like that," Malek said, pretending to check the garden doors to make sure they were closed.

"Ooooh, present shopping! Sabine likes sparklies too."

Sabine smiled. "You and your new friends have done a wonderful job averting several potential disasters tonight."

Blossom trilled happily. "Aeron's been hiding from the yellow people all night. Well, he's actually been hiding from *all* the dragons, but especially them. I've got some of the pixies helping him run interference."

"Can you ask them to also keep an eye on Rika? She's going to be staying close to Lady Nymira, but I'd feel better if some of you were also looking out for her."

"You've got it," Blossom said. "But I think you should know this would be a lot more fun if we were all in dragon form."

With those ominous words, the ladybug took off and disappeared into the crowd.

Malek grinned. "She's not going to let it go, is she?"

Sabine sighed. "No. I suspect I'll have to turn all the pixies into miniature dragons at least once before we leave the Sky Cities."

"That reminds me of an interesting rumor I heard earlier," Malek said and trailed his fingers down her arm.

She trembled slightly from the warmth of his touch. "Oh?"

He leaned close and whispered against her ear, "Someone claimed they saw my mate sneaking out a window."

Sabine paused a beat. "Is that so?"

"Indeed," Malek said, his voice deceptively neutral as he captured one of her curls and wound it around his finger. "Then later, I heard Blossom was holding lock-picking lessons for the pixies in the garden."

"How... industrious of her."

Malek arched his brow. "Anything you want to tell me, Lady Sabine?"

Sabine glanced up at the crystal window with the image of his parents. "That window really is lovely, isn't it?"

"It is," Malek said, eyeing her suspiciously.

She sighed. "Too bad there's a design flaw."

Malek's mouth twitched. "A design flaw?"

She leaned close and whispered, "I can't sneak out of that one."

Malek threw his head back and laughed. He wrapped his arms around her and said, "I'll endeavor to have latches installed on all windows in the future."

She grinned, but her smile faded a moment later at the sight of Aeron approaching them. As he moved through the crowd, she caught the faintest trace of his magic urging people to look away from him.

Aeron stopped beside them and said quietly, "I believe I've found someone who can help us."

Malek made a gesture for silence and motioned for Aeron to follow. He took Sabine's arm and led them down a hallway off the side of the ballroom. He opened the door to a storage closet of some sort and ushered them inside.

"Lord Typheron was asking after you," Malek said.

Aeron stilled.

Sabine reached for Aeron's hand, sending a light brush of her magic over him. "We avoided his questions, but I don't think it's safe for any of us to remain here. If he recognizes you from when you were his captive, you could be in grave danger."

Aeron took a deep breath and gave her a curt nod. "Then the news I carry is even more urgent."

"What have you learned?" Malek asked.

"There is a woman willing to help us access the prison on Ishu, but she will only speak with the Aderylin. On this point, she will not waver. She fears reprisal from the dragon overlords."

Sabine turned to Malek. "Ishu is the island north of here?"

Malek nodded and crossed his arms over his chest. "Yes. The Topaz, Garnet, Gold, and Quartz Clans all claim Ishu as their home. We're allied with the Topaz and Garnet clans, but the Gold and Quartz have different interests."

"The prison is located in the Topaz Clan's territory," Aeron said, his hand tightening around Sabine's. "On rare occasion, I saw guards from the Garnet Clan in the prison. I cannot speak to the other clans."

"Tell me about this woman who wants to meet," Sabine said. "Do you know her?"

Aeron nodded. "In a manner of speaking. I recognized her from the prison where I was born. She is bound to the Topaz Clan overlords."

"Can she be trusted?" Sabine asked.

Aeron hesitated. "She is aderyan and, like me, was born into captivity. While it's unusual for my kind to be permitted outside of Ishu, I saw the iron chains binding her legs and wrists. I suspect one of the dragons may be using her to fulfill more… personal needs."

Malek narrowed his eyes. "Who?"

Fury whipped through Sabine, causing her skin to glow brightly. Malek wrapped his arms and power around her, surrounding her with his heated magic. In a low voice, Malek warned, "If Aeron is correct, they will die for this, Sabine. But revealing yourself here and now will make it more difficult to accomplish our goals."

"You don't intend to stop me?"

"No," Malek said, holding her against him. "There is no excuse, no argument that can be made, nor any plea that will change that dragon's fate. I swear to you here and now: they will not survive our wrath."

Sabine relaxed against him and nodded. "So be it."

Aeron lowered his head and kneeled before them. "I did not believe it was possible for any dragon to earn my respect, but if you are willing to extinguish one of your own in defense of a slave, you have proven yourself honorable. You are a well-suited match for our Aderylin."

Sabine reached for Aeron and said, "You don't need to kneel to either of us, Aeron. You're among friends."

Aeron stood and stared at her with a strange sort of wonderment. It reminded her of the way she felt when Malek's mother and sister had welcomed her to the family. She desperately wanted to believe it, but it was difficult to reconcile her past. Perhaps she and Aeron were more alike than she realized. They both needed to take that step and trust.

"Gwenllian has agreed to meet with you in the garden, but she cannot remain long for fear of being discovered. If you can convince her you are our Aderylin in truth, she has agreed to help us infiltrate the prison and free the captives."

Malek frowned. "Meeting like this is risky, Sabine. Many of the dragons are inside, conducting their urn ceremonies and renewing their clan ties, but some will be flying overhead or strolling through the gardens. We caused a stir earlier. Your absence will be noticed."

"Then we'll need to do this quickly."

Sabine closed her eyes and summoned her power. Drawing on her impressions of the staff attire, she reshaped her gown into an obsidian tunic and pants. Her hair darkened to a rich nutmeg, her eyes to a soft brown, and she rounded her ears to appear fully human.

Reaching for Aeron, she wove a similar glamour around him. She kept his same height and build, but concealed his wings and rich clothing. His hair and skin darkened, and she softened his facial features, rounding his ears to make him appear less fae.

Once she was confident the illusion was as realistic as possible, she pinned the glamour into place and accepted the pain of a thousand pinpricks against her skin.

She opened her eyes and turned to Malek. "Your people have never been able to see through our glamour. As long as

Aeron stays close, I can maintain his illusion. It's the best way to move through the ballroom without being detected now that Typheron's actively looking for him."

Aeron looked down at his hands and clothing. "Your ability to glamour holds no comparison to ours, Aderylin."

Malek's gaze roamed over her, and he stepped closer. "I see the illusion, but I know it's you. I would recognize you even in a room with hundreds of people."

Sabine stared at him in shock. "What?"

A self-satisfied smile crossed Malek's face. "You're my mate, Sabine. It's the light within you that calls to me. I told you before I would always recognize you. I don't care how many layers of glamour you hide behind, I'll always be able to see your truth."

She frowned at him. "Stop. Disbelieving glamour will break it, and I need to maintain this illusion."

He grinned and held up his hands in mock surrender. "Very well. When you exit this room, turn left. There's a door to the garden at the end of the hall. You'll be able to avoid most of the guests if you sneak out that way. I'll return to the ballroom but will remain near the garden doors in case you need me."

She nodded. "The pixies in the garden will alert Blossom to our location. I suspect she'll find you as soon as she realizes I'm gone."

Malek's expression turned serious. "I'll give you twenty minutes to speak with Gwenllian. If you're not back by then, I'm coming to find you. She may not trust us, but I'm not willing to risk your safety for anything, Sabine."

He turned to Aeron. "I'm trusting you with what I value most in this world. Do not let any harm come to her."

Aeron placed his fist over his heart in acknowledgement.

Malek turned back to Sabine and kissed her. She pressed

her hands against his chest, sending a soft wave of her magic over him.

He broke their kiss and his gaze roamed over her features. "You're beautiful even in your glamour, but I much prefer the reality. It should be effective though. My people won't look too closely while you're in this disguise. But once you leave this room, I won't be able to help hide your magic. Be careful, Sabine. Tonight has shown me that I trust very few of our so-called allies with your safety."

She looked up at him, knowing he was battling his instincts to keep her safe at his side. The fact he was willing and able to let her go made her love him even more.

"I'll keep your words in mind," she said.

He nodded and gave her another long look before heading toward the door. Sabine waited until he'd slipped out of the room before closing her eyes and taking a steadying breath. She gathered her magic around her and reinforced her mental shields, ensuring every part of her magic, except her glamour, was locked behind an impenetrable wall.

Aeron touched her hand. "Aderylin?"

She opened her eyes and nodded. "I'm ready."

Heading toward the door, she opened it silently and glanced out. Several people wearing the clothing that marked them as Obsidian Clan staff were in the hall, focused on their assigned tasks. Recalling Malek's instructions, she turned left and headed down the hallway with Aeron at her side.

For good or ill, they were on their own.

CHAPTER 48

Sabine and Aeron approached one of the side doors leading to the garden. A wyvern stood guard but barely spared them a glance as they stepped outside. Sabine inhaled the cool night air, letting her eyes adjust to the darkness.

She hadn't had an opportunity to explore Malek's childhood home, but the strange sense of wrongness she'd felt upon arriving in the Sky Cities echoed here. It was as if the land were starving for magic. The urge to press her hands to the soil and infuse her power into it was nearly overwhelming.

Aeron swept his gaze over the garden and whispered, "Be cautious, Aderylin. The Veil is thin here."

"I feel it," she murmured. "The land calls to me."

Aeron's hand brushed against hers, and she had the sensation of feathered wings caressing her skin. His touch steadied her, allowing her to focus on the garden rather than the call of the land.

Tiny dragonfire urns hung from hooks and illuminated their way as they walked along the path. The stone pathway curled around meticulously sculpted flower beds and shrubbery. The grounds were pretty enough, but it somehow lacked the harmony and beauty of the garden within Malek's estate.

The low murmur of voices acted as an accompaniment to the distinct sound of crickets and frogs singing the night's song. Overhead, she caught sight of several dark shapes soaring through the sky, eclipsing the light from the moon. No matter how long she lived, she would never become accustomed to the sight of dragons soaring Aeslion's skies.

At an intersection, Sabine glanced at Aeron and asked, "Which way?"

"Gwenllian said she'd be on the southern side of the garden," Aeron said quietly. "All paths eventually lead to the central fountain. We'll likely run into some of the guests along the way."

Knowing one of the quickest ways to summon a pixie was to disturb the garden, Sabine bent down and plucked two large leaves from one of the bushes. Less than a minute later, a strange glowbug danced down the pathway. It trembled at the sight of them and then zipped over to Sabine's shoulder.

"Your Highn— err, Sabine," Hawthorn whispered. "How can we be of assistance?"

"I need half a dozen berries or small flowers," Sabine said quietly.

"Right away," the glowbug said and zipped back down the pathway.

If Aeron was puzzled by her request, he didn't say a word. A minute later, a small army of large ants came marching out of the underbrush carrying ripened burrberries.

Sabine collected the berries and whispered, "Keep watch for any who might approach, Hawthorne."

"On it!"

She arranged the berries on both leaves. When she was

satisfied they were in position, she quickly wove her glamour around them, changing the berries on one leaf to a tray filled with the smoking dragon's breath drinks, while the other turned into a small sampling of hors d'oeuvres.

"Clever," Aeron said and picked up the tray with drinks. "Is it true Faerie food?"

Sabine nodded. "What they eat or drink will be sustenance in truth, provided the glamour remains unbroken. They will not be able to tell the difference."

She lifted the other tray and said to Hawthorne, "We're going to meet someone in the garden. Once we find her, we'll need privacy. Let us know if any dragons come our way."

The glowbug blinked its light in acknowledgment. The ants transformed into matching glowbugs and vanished into the foliage.

Sabine carried the tray with one hand, in the same manner she'd seen the other waitstaff hold them. Aeron did the same, emulating a human persona with an ease that made Sabine suspect he'd used the same guise while escorting the other aderyan to safety.

They turned a corner, and Sabine caught sight of several dragons wearing colorful attire that marked them as belonging to the Topaz, Amethyst, and Ruby Clans. A few tables were set up with people lounging about and chatting. Intermingled among them were several humans, carrying similar trays to the ones she and Aeron held.

Sabine and Aeron moved together, offering refreshments to the nearest group. The buzzing around them was loud, as though several silent conversations were simultaneously taking place.

"You must be beside yourself about Malek."

Sabine discreetly glanced over to see who had spoken. The dark-haired woman appeared to be around Nymira's age, but she lacked the Obsidian Clan leader's charismatic presence. Her large, poofy purple gown swallowed her frame, lending her an air of timidity.

Curious about the woman's comment, Sabine offered her tray to one of the nearby men.

An older woman in a low-cut red gown took a drink from Aeron's tray and said, "Oh, I don't blame *him*. It was undoubtedly Thadnir and his fae whore's influence that led him astray. I suspect Darius will set him to rights soon enough. My nephew has always done what's necessary to protect Bryona's memory."

"But still—"

"Enough, Yarmina," the red-gowned woman said, nodding toward Aeron and Sabine. "It is being handled. Now Edgar, tell me more about your latest art acquisition."

As the man launched into a boastful account of the painter's skill, Sabine and Aeron slipped away toward one of the side paths.

Once they were out of sight, Aeron brushed his hand against hers. "Aderylin?"

"Bryona was Malek's true grandmother, before his grandfather met Elisa," Sabine said, less troubled by the women's words and more concerned by the fact they'd discussed them so openly. "She was part of the Ruby Clan."

Aeron nodded. "I believe the woman in that group was Malek's great-aunt, and Bryona was her sister. If you study their attire, you will see small accents that play homage to their secondary birth clan."

Sabine looked at Aeron in surprise. "That's why Malek has the green edging around his emblem?"

Aeron nodded. "His mother is a Myst'ald, one of the Emerald Clan. It is why they are so closely allied. However, the Obsidian Clan emblem on Lord Darius's blazer is edged in red, a tribute to his birth mother's clan."

Sabine fell silent as they continued to walk, surprised by

the cultural nuances she hadn't yet grasped. Family ties were as important to Malek as they were to the fae, even if they acknowledged them differently. For her people, it was a matter of keeping their magic as close to the gods' power as possible. For Malek, it was about family loyalty and alliances.

They turned a corner to find a small serving station set up. Several members of the waitstaff were dropping off items or gathering trays of food and drink to deliver to other areas of the garden.

Aeron walked over to one of the women and whispered something in her ear.

Most of the others were avoiding her, which caused Sabine to take a closer look. The woman wore the golden-yellow livery Sabine had begun to associate with the Topaz Clan, but there was an aura about her that could never be mistaken as human. From the woman's soft golden hair, finely sculpted features, and pointed ears, Sabine would swear the woman was fae.

At Aeron's touch, the woman's hands trembled and she dropped the towel she'd been holding onto the table. She murmured something to another attendant, then slipped deeper into the garden.

Aeron returned to Sabine's side and gave a slight nod.

Sabine adjusted the tray in her hand and followed, keeping a discreet distance to ensure their departure appeared coincidental. She heard footsteps nearby, but the garden was laid out like a maze, full of hidden corners and privacy dividers.

Rounding another turn, they spotted Gwenllian waiting beneath an arbor, cloaked in shadow.

"Aeron has always been skilled at magic, but I do not know you," the woman said with a soft voice. "You are not aderyan."

"Gwenllian, this is our Aderylin," Aeron said quietly. "I

swear by the balance that guides us, and the wind that calls us home, she is the one we've been waiting for."

A mix of fear and hope filled Gwenllian's blue eyes. She shook her head. "You cannot lie, but our Aderylin would not bind herself to one of *them*. I saw the urn. Why would you do this? Why would you forsake us?"

Sabine stepped closer and touched the vines along the arbor, encouraging them to grow. They wove together above her, forming a leafy canopy to shield them from watchful eyes overhead. As the vines thickened, Sabine allowed her glamour to fall away.

Gwenllian gasped, her hands flying to her mouth. The iron shackles on her wrist clanked together, the dull sound echoing through the garden. She dropped to her knees and bowed her head.

"I have not forsaken you, Gwenllian," Sabine said. "The loss of your freedom and magic is an affront to the balance of this world. It cannot and will not stand."

"She restored my wings and those of many others," Aeron added. "She has given Lyra the honor of becoming Aether-bound. She has already gifted back much of the power that was stolen from us. Our newly freed brothers and sisters have gone to bring the others here, so she might restore their wings as well."

"Forgive me for doubting you, Aderylin." Tears streamed down Gwenllian's cheeks as she sobbed into her hands. The metal cuffs on her wrists clinked softly together. A wave of nausea rose in Sabine as the cold iron came too close. Her magic faltered, but she pushed it aside and reached for Gwenllian. She would not allow her to suffer a moment longer.

"No," Gwenllian whispered, pulling away. "Aderylin, no. You mustn't remove them."

"They have no right," Sabine said, her power beginning to rise. "You do not belong to anyone other than yourself."

Gwenllian kneeled before Sabine. "I do not reject your gift for myself, Shining One. I wish to aid you in freeing all my brothers and sisters. We have all suffered, but many far worse than I. Allow me to remain their captive so I might help our people reclaim our stolen magic."

Aeron touched Sabine's arm. "The iron is uncomfortable, but it will not kill her. If I were in her place, I would do the same."

Sabine closed her eyes and nodded. "I won't take your choice from you, Gwenllian."

Gwenllian rose. "Lord Typheron's moods grow worse by the day. All live in fear of him, and some of the house staff have become sympathetic to our plight. They would be willing to help distract the guards so we might enter the prison unseen."

"You can acquire the keys?" Aeron asked.

Gwenllian nodded. "I believe so. Typheron's son, Linus, has developed a personal interest in me and a few others. He is easily distracted and will not notice if his key goes missing. That's how we managed to get the last two captives out."

The faint sound of footsteps approached. Sabine quickly reapplied her human glamour. Aeron motioned for them to wait, then slipped away from the arbor in silence.

Gwenllian leaned close and whispered, "I cannot be seen with you, Aderylin. If my people are to have any chance of surviving, I must remain undetected. Once we return to Ishu, I'll need a few hours to make the arrangements. Tell Aeron to leave his mark upon the fallen temple when he's ready to initiate the diversion."

Sabine nodded and gestured toward the path opposite their entrance. "Go the back way and circle around. Aeron says all paths lead to the main fountain."

"May the winds guide you, Aderylin." Gwenllian gathered her skirt and disappeared into the shadows.

"Is there a problem?" Aeron's voice cut through the quiet.

A low reply from another man made Sabine step away from the arbor. Hawthorne hadn't warned them of a dragon approaching, and Malek wouldn't have trusted anyone but himself, Aeron, or Bane with her safety.

Aeron stepped back into view. Before Sabine could get a clear look at the stranger behind him, a warning howl split the night. Sabine whipped her head toward the sound.

A sharp pain stabbed into her neck. She slapped her hand over it, feeling the sear of metal bite into her fingers. An icy chill rushed through her bloodstream. Cold iron.

She yanked the dart free and dropped it on the ground, but it was too late. Her blood began to freeze. When she reached for her magic, it fractured under the chill. Her glamour and mental shields shattered. Her skin began to glow with brilliant gold. The iron might not kill her, but they were now exposed.

Aeron whirled on her assailant. In the center of the garden, he fought with brutal efficiency, wings flared, against a man nearly twice his size. Sabine blinked, recognizing the man as Ciro, the human who had followed the seer, Idola, into exile.

She took a step toward them and collapsed, her teeth chattering from the spreading cold. They had focused so intently on the threat of dragons, she'd forgotten there were other dangers.

A massive golden hound burst from the bushes. With a growl and a snarl, it leaped over Aeron and clamped its jaws around Ciro's neck. He barely managed a scream before a sickening crack silenced him forever. The hound gave the lifeless body a shake and let it drop.

In the distance, the faint glimmer of glowbugs flickered. At least the pixies would warn Malek about Idola's treachery.

Sabine's vision blurred. She blinked, trying to clear it. This was more than the effects of the iron. She touched her neck. Her fingers came away slick with blood and something else. The faint scent of herbs teased her senses.

"Dreamthorn," she whispered, staring at her skin that was glowing pure gold. "Dreamthorn and chaosbriar."

She searched the ground for the iron dart, but it had rolled away. It was too late anyway. She had no idea how Idola had gotten her hands on herbs that were only found in Faerie. Combined, their effects could prove disastrous if she wasn't able to get to safety.

She tried to push up from the ground, but her limbs refused to obey. Basco trotted to her side and whimpered, nudging her with his massive golden head.

Aeron limped over, his tunic stained red where Ciro had sliced his midsection. "Aderylin, we must—"

He cried out as glowing chains wrapped around him, slicing into his skin and wings. His back arched in pain, and he dropped to his knees, the barbs tearing into him.

"Seize both of them," Typheron ordered, stepping out from the bushes with several others clad in yellow and garnet.

Sabine raised her bloodied hand with effort and shouted, *"Vashado!"*

A burst of power exploded from her fingertips, flinging several of the attackers aside. Some didn't rise, but more emerged from the bushes.

"Bind her! Now!" Typheron demanded.

Basco snarled and lunged toward him. An enormous Topaz dragon slammed down, crushing the arbor and garden underfoot. With a swing of its tail, it sent Basco flying. He hit the ground with a pained yelp.

Two men rushed her and threw barbed iron chains across her body. Sabine screamed as the metal bit into her flesh. Blood pooled beneath her as she tried to reach for the land's power. The men yanked hard on the chains, dragging her sideways. Her magic and thoughts fragmented.

Typheron loomed over her. "Did you not think we'd developed ways to see through glamour? I don't know how a Tuatha Dé still walks this side of the Veil, but it will be the last mistake your kind makes."

CHAPTER 49

"*D*id you lose your charming mate already?" Raynor asked.

"Perhaps you should spend less time ogling my mate and find one of your own," Malek suggested, partly annoyed Raynor had guessed why he was agitated. Malek glanced at the garden doors, tempted to go after her.

Raynor chuckled. "If I found one like yours, I might consider it."

Silently, he added, *"The Topaz and Garnet Clans are enmeshed in something they don't want us to know about."*

Malek scanned the ballroom. He couldn't be certain, but it looked as though the number of individuals wearing the distinctive yellow and garnet had diminished over the past hour. The two clans were now congregating in small groups, almost exclusively with one another.

"The Garnets are little more than vassals to Typheron. They don't have an original thought among them. What have you heard?"

Raynor took a sip of his drink. *"The Topaz Clan has been holding secret meetings, amassing power, and attempting to forge new alliances. It's not a coincidence Typheron is attempting to woo the Gold Clan. I suspect this may be the last of our galas they attend."*

Malek frowned. *"The Topaz Clan is your mother's birth clan. They wouldn't simply cut ties."*

"They would if an 'accident' somehow eliminated both me and Father. The color of our scales is a little too green for them. So far, we've managed to avoid three such accidents in the past few weeks. Mother has been pleading with Father to start kissing Typheron's scales."

Malek snorted. *"Uncle Emanthir would rather flay them from Typheron's burnt corpse than kiss them."*

"Careful, cousin," Raynor warned. *"Word has it you might find yourself the victim of an 'accident' as well. Or was it simply a rumor that a young wyvern squadron mistakenly attacked you outside of Imenel?"*

Malek's gaze sharpened on Raynor. *"You're claiming the Topaz Clan is responsible?"*

"My father is a bastard at times, but all know he loves his sister. Our clans have always been stronger together. Only the Topaz and Amethyst Clans are powerful enough to risk making a move against us. And Grandmother Yara would tie every Amethyst tail into knots if they dared look at our clans sideways."

Kaia approached them with a teasing grin. "What are you two conspiring about over here in the corner?"

"Catching your brother up with the latest plots and intrigues," Raynor said with a wink and then his smile turned wicked. "It appears both my favorite cousins have lost their mates. Dare I ask if they ran off together?"

"Don't make me throw my drink at you," Kaia said, tapping her nail on the edge of her glass.

Malek scowled at Raynor. "You're determined not to survive the evening, aren't you?"

Raynor laughed. "Ah, Malek. See what you've been missing these past several years?"

Someone shouted from the far side of the room. Two wyverns from the Topaz and Garnet clans were arguing and shoving each other. It wasn't unusual for a gala to become unruly, but it was rare for the wyverns to be the ones who started it.

"Trouble already?" Kaia asked with a frown.

Raynor tossed back his drink. "No, little cousin. Trouble has already begun. This is simply the call to arms." He gave a faint smile. "It appears the night's going to get interesting sooner than expected."

Pain lanced through Malek's body, the shock of it causing him to double over. Suddenly, it was gone. He couldn't feel Sabine. It was as if their bond had been severed.

Kaia grabbed his arm. "Malek? What is it?"

"Malek!" Blossom screamed, her high-pitched voice shattering the crystal glass in Kaia's hand. "You have to hurry! Hawthorn said they have Sabine! She's in trouble!"

"A pixie?" Raynor asked, staring at Blossom in shock.

"Later," Malek said, shoving the garden door open. "Kaia, get Esme and Rika to safety. I need to find Sabine."

"Go! Go! I'll take care of them!"

Bane dropped to the ground, knives drawn. "Where?"

"South end of the garden," Blossom said, her wings tinged with red. "Hurry! Hurry!"

Bane took off, vanishing into the darkness.

Malek's human form disappeared in a flash of light. He launched from the ground and reached for Levin with his thoughts. *Levin! Kaia's taking Esme and Rika to safety. Sabine's in trouble. She was in the garden with Aeron, but something's wrong. I can't feel our mate bond.*

"Dammit, Malek," Levin shouted in his head. *Don't go out there without a squadron. The Topaz Clan is clearing out, and the*

Garnets drew weapons on our humans to cover their escape. Your father just shifted and blew another hole through the roof."

"*Coordinate with Fandrin and the Emerald Clan captain,*" Malek ordered. "*The Topaz Clan betrayed us. Kill the Garnet bastards and be done with it. All drakes are to defend their estates. I want every wyvern in the air now.*"

The skies were thick with dragons and wyverns circling overhead. A Topaz dragon roared in challenge and hurled dragonfire toward him. Malek narrowed his eyes and dove at the would-be attacker. Nothing would come between him and Sabine.

An Emerald dragon shot upward, slamming into the Topaz. Its claws tore into the underbelly, drawing a scream in agony.

"*Your mother always knows how to throw a party,*" Raynor said, laughter filling Malek's mind as he tangled with the Topaz dragon. "*Go find your mate. I'll play with this one. Then you can tell me how you managed to get a demon to do your bidding.*"

Leaving Raynor to deal with the attacker, Malek turned toward the southern garden. The need to find Sabine over-powered every instinct. In his thoughts, she was simply gone —her light extinguished.

Refusing to consider what it might mean, he landed beside Bane. The demon was locked in combat with two wyverns in human form. Malek lifted his massive foot and crushed them beneath his talons.

Malek inhaled sharply. The scent of Sabine's blood clung to the air. He roared in fury. Someone had dared harm her.

Battling back his rage, he drew another breath, recog-nizing the sharp metallic odor of iron. They'd planned this, likely from the moment they learned he'd brought Sabine here.

The battle overhead raged on, but Malek ignored it.

Impatient, he shifted back into human form and demanded, "Where is she?"

Bane kneeled and placed his hand on the ground. His skin began to glow blue, and his horns shimmered with silver. He moved over to another patch of earth and repeated the motion.

Blossom flew to Malek, surrounded by a swarm of pixies. They all began chattering at once.

"Quiet!" Malek shouted, then turned to the one Sabine trusted above all others. "Blossom, what do you know?"

"Hawthorn found Sabine in the garden. He was running surveillance for her. It was a human, Malek! A human hurt Sabine! Then the dragons came and threw iron chains over her and Aeron. They took them both."

"Where is Hawthorn?" Malek asked.

Bane had begun inspecting several bodies on the ground, his skin still flickering with a blue light.

"He went with them," Blossom said, her red-tinged dust drifting to the ground. "He didn't want to leave Sabine defenseless. I came to find you the second the pixies learned what was happening."

A soft whimper drew Malek's attention. A large golden hound dragged himself out from beneath the bushes and collapsed, trembling on the stone path.

"Bane," Malek called, striding toward the injured creature. "It's Basco, isn't it? The visionhound?"

"It is."

Bane kneeled beside Basco and murmured in his harsh, guttural language. His clawed hands moved over the hound's midsection. Basco whined but didn't resist the contact, his body trembling with pain.

Bane looked up. "He'll live, but he's severed ties with the seer. The bitch and her lover conspired to strip Sabine's glamour and weaken her using cold iron and herbs from your conservatory."

"There's something sharp and stinky over here!" Blossom called.

Malek walked over and picked up a thin piece of hollowed iron, shaped like a needle. His jaw clenched with fury.

He reached for his sister with his thoughts. *"Send a wyvern to the rear southern garden to collect an iron dart. Idola used it to poison Sabine. I want to know exactly what was used and how it'll affect her. Take Esme with you when you interrogate the witch. She'll know if Idola's lying."*

"That bitch! I'm going to carve out her heart. No, I'm going to shovel those nasty tonics down her throat and then carve out her heart. Wait. I'm going to—"

Ignoring her growing rant, Malek turned back to Bane. "What else?"

"The one you called Typheron either learned of the plan or took advantage of it," Bane said. "He and his followers ambushed Sabine and Aeron after she was poisoned. They were bound in iron chains and flown away by dragon."

His silver eyes blazed. "Typheron wears a medallion that allows him to see through glamour. He knew Sabine's identity the moment the dreamstone fractured."

Malek looked skyward, toward the battle raging overhead. Typheron would have taken her to Ishu, his stronghold.

"He'll die for this."

"Hold a moment, Malek," Nymira swept into the clearing, her emerald gown whispering across the ground. Her sharp gaze scanned the scene, lingering briefly on Bane before turning back to Malek.

"Captain Fandrin and Levin have mustered the garrison. The rest of the household is being moved to the crypts. Your estate is being locked down. Azalia and Rupert are securing your staff underground. I know you intend to retrieve your mate at any cost, but Typheron would have planned for such a response. His actions tonight speak of long-term planning beyond your stolen mate. You cannot take on the entirety of Typheron's forces alone."

Malek took a step toward her. "I don't give a damn about Typheron's plans. What do you know about the prison on Ishu?"

"You believe that's where they've taken Sabine?"

He gave a curt nod. "Aeron was held there for centuries. It stands to reason that's where they'd take Sabine."

Nymira stilled. "He's aderyan?"

"Sabine returned his wings to him," Malek said. "If you know anything about this prison, I suggest you share it now. Because whether or not you have intel makes little difference in my intentions. However, it will make a difference in how many of our people survive."

Bane rose, his eyes and horns still glowing silver. When he spoke, there was an odd cadence as though thousands of voices flowed through his words.

"Mistress Dragon," he said, "I offer a warning from Dax'than Versed, High King of the Underworld and Keeper of the Heartstone. Should any harm befall Queen Sabin'theoria of the Unseelie, the demons, dwarves, merfolk, and fae will stand united against your kind. We will not discriminate by clan or deed. If she falls, we *will* eradicate your kind once and for all."

Nymira stared at Bane for a long moment. "You do not need to weave threats, demon. Despite her origins, Sabine is *ours*. She is a daughter of the Obsidian Clan—*my* daughter. By raising a hand against her, they challenge all of us."

She turned back to Malek. "A frontal assault is suicide.

You'll need to coordinate with our allies and use the chaos as cover to get inside."

"You know where the prison is?"

"No," Nymira said, her expression grim. "We've sent dozens of scouts into Ishu over the years. There are only a handful of possible entrance locations. Unfortunately, we haven't been able to get close enough to confirm anything. Typheron guards his secrets well."

Blossom zipped over. "We have an inside man. As soon as he jingles a flower petal, I'll know more." She hovered in front of Nymira. "Sorry about the bees earlier. We were on distraction duty."

Nymira's lips twitched with a smile. "Pixies, an adopted seer, a dryad, a demon, and an aderyan bodyguard for your Tuatha Dé mate. Well done, Malek. Very well done. Typheron won't see this coming."

A Topaz wyvern plummeted from the sky, the ground trembling from the impact. The shouts of the Obsidian and Emerald Clans overhead became a muffled roar in Malek's head. He ignored them and focused once more on Sabine.

The place where she should be in his thoughts was little more than a faint echo of the vibrant light that shone brilliantly within her. If he could coax out that flame, he could locate her no matter what methods Typheron had used to hide her away.

Nymira stepped closer. "The entirety of the Obsidian Clan stands with you, Malek. What do you need from us?"

He met her gaze without hesitation. "A diversion."

CHAPTER 50

Sabine blinked open her eyes, her head heavy and thoughts sluggish. A faint dripping sound echoed through the cold, damp chamber. A torch burned on the far wall, providing the barest hint of illumination.

Wherever they'd taken her reminded her of the dungeons in Faerie's Winter Palace. There was a bleakness in the air, as though all hope and happiness had been stripped away.

Another wave of nausea struck her, and her vision swam. They'd chained her arms over her head, forcing her to stretch toward the ceiling.

She tried to pull against the restraints and gasped in pain. Sharp iron needles pierced her wrists. The more she pulled, the deeper they sliced her skin. From the weight around her ankles, they'd bound her feet as well. The iron didn't seem to be doing much to stifle her glowing skin, though. She couldn't use magic, but her ability to mimic a glowbug was working just fine.

"Do not fight the restraints, Aderylin," Aeron said quietly. "It is uncomfortable for aderyan skin, but I do not know how it will affect you."

"Aeron?" she asked, turning her head. Another sharp pain pierced her neck. Once she got out of here, she was going to shove a hundred tiny needles up Typheron's—

"Oh no, my dear," Typheron said, walking into the room with an unknown wyvern carrying another torch. "Go ahead and fight the restraints. Let's see how well that precious Tuatha Dé skin fares against our iron."

Sabine glared at him and didn't answer. If their mistaken belief gave her an advantage, she intended to use it. She tried reaching for Malek and Lachlina with her thoughts and nearly cried out at the shooting pain that flooded through her. It had to be the dreamthorn and chaosbriar Idola had used on her. If she could find a way to burn it out of her system, Malek's bond might give her enough iron resistance to use her magic.

"I must applaud your efforts in returning one of our aderyan to us," Typheron said, stopping to stand in front of her. "No doubt it cost you greatly to restore his magic. But I'm curious—did he tell you how he lost his wings?"

When Sabine didn't reply, Typheron motioned to Aeron. "Go ahead, Aeron. Tell her why I decided to offload you to another clan. Let her know how *worthy* you aderyan are, especially the ones who mutilated themselves just to crawl away."

Keeping as still as possible, Sabine looked toward the direction Typheron indicated. In a large outcropping, Aeron was chained in a similar fashion. His wings, however, were fully extended, and they stirred the air in the chamber gently. With every pulse, the chains around him glowed softly.

Naked hatred burned in his gaze as he stared at Typheron. "I cut off my wings rather than continue to allow your kind to use our magic." He spat in Typheron's direction. "May our Aeries fall into the sea with you in them."

"You will remain here and serve me until your last

breath," Typheron said with a sneer. "And should you cut your wings off again, I will simply use you to breed another generation of aderyan to fulfill my purposes."

He lifted his hand as though to strike Aeron.

"I don't regret restoring Aeron's wings," Sabine said quickly, trying to draw Typheron's attention away from him. "Even if he chooses to cut them off again, I still regret nothing. Aeron is the master of his own fate. I claim no debt from him."

Typheron turned and narrowed his eyes. "What sentimental foolishness." He studied Sabine. "Malek spoke the truth, didn't he? You *are* young. Younger than I expected."

Sabine didn't reply.

Typheron approached and gripped her chin. She held his gaze, maintaining the neutral court mien that had served her well for years.

He searched her face. "Fascinating. How is it you came to be here, young one? You cannot be more than a few hundred years, if that. You are far too young to have witnessed the expulsion of your kind from this world."

Aeron's chains jangled, and he roared his fury. "Do not touch her!"

Sabine remained silent.

Typheron stroked her face with his gold-dusted fingers. She tamped down her revulsion, refusing to give him the satisfaction of a response. He would lose each of those fingers, one by one.

Typheron leaned close and whispered, "The aderyan have always been devoutly protective of your kind. It was one of the ways we broke their resistance during the war. They simply cannot abide your suffering. We'll have to see how quickly we can bring the rest of my unruly aderyan to heel, won't we?"

Rapid footsteps sounded from behind them. A woman's

soft voice said, "Pardon the interruption, Lord Typheron. Captain Hetsmer requests your presence in the War Room. The Obsidian and Emerald Clans are close to regaining control of Kavi and are moving toward Ishu."

"They should not have been able to route our forces so quickly," Typheron said with a snarl. "Why would they dare risk everything for…" His voice trailed off as he turned to Sabine. "*You.* They know what you are and seek to use your magic to control the clans. There is no other reason they would amass a full-scale assault if they believed you were simply fae."

He snapped his fingers at the wyvern who had accompanied him. "Seal this section of the prison. We're moving up our timetable to excise Kavi. I want you and two dozen others standing guard outside at all times. No one enters this chamber without my leave. If the Obsidian Clan breaches the prison and attempts to take my prize, kill the Tuatha Dé. I want her blood soaking the ground before they reach this cavern. I will not allow her magic to fall into their hands."

Typheron stormed out, slamming the iron door behind him.

The wyvern glowered at the golden-haired woman who had brought the news. "Well? What are you waiting for?"

She lifted her head just enough for the firelight to illuminate her features. Gwenllian flicked her gaze toward Sabine, then quickly looked away.

"Shall I tend to the prisoner before the chamber is sealed? She cannot remain suspended in that position. The iron will poison her. Lord Typheron will be displeased if she expires prematurely."

"Hurry up," the wyvern snapped, gesturing toward Sabine. "Typheron has little patience for those who don't follow his orders."

Gwenllian hurried to Sabine, grabbed hold of a wheel

with both hands, and spun it. With a loud clanking sound, the tension on Sabine's arms eased as the shackles, affixed to a large iron bar, began to lower.

As the bar continued its descent, Sabine was forced to sit or risk the needles driving into her neck again. She sank to the hard earthen floor with a shaky breath, her muscles trembling from the sudden release. Gwenllian pulled another lever, locking the bar in place.

Gwenllian met her gaze, some unnamed emotion in her eyes. In a low whisper, she murmured, "Vigilant eyes beneath open skies—"

The wyvern backhanded Gwenllian, knocking her to the ground. "We'll see how well your precious Song serves you when your tongue's cut out."

Outraged, Sabine tried to call upon her magic. A stabbing pain erupted behind her eyes, followed by a wave of dizziness and nausea. She battled it back and lifted her head, ignoring the piercing pain at her neck.

"Touch her at your own risk, wyvern," Sabine said coldly. "And pray I do not escape these chains, for I will revisit every injury you inflict upon her a thousandfold."

Whatever the wyvern saw in Sabine's gaze made him take a step back. He hauled Gwenllian to her feet and shoved her toward the door. He started to follow but stopped abruptly. Spinning around, he scanned the room, eyes narrowing in suspicion. After a moment, he frowned and left the chamber, slamming the door behind him. Sabine heard the clank of iron bolts sliding into place, followed by the sound of his footsteps fading away.

Sabine took a deep breath. They needed to get out of here before Malek tried to launch a rescue. She tried to reach him again with her thoughts. Some essential part of her was dormant, leaving a strange void behind. Chaosbriar didn't usually last longer than an hour or two, but the effects were compounded by the dreamthorn.

Aeron's voice cut through the silence. "Child, it was dangerous for you to come here. Thalassa has the fury of a harpy when she's been crossed."

Sabine watched in horror as Lyra materialized in the center of the chamber. The aderyan girl's wings were tucked tightly against her back, trembling slightly. She lifted her head, a determined fierceness in her gaze that made her appear far older than her handful of years.

"I used the blur, Aeron. Like you taught me. Thalassa came after me, but she's not good at hiding. She's outside near the big rock."

Aeron sighed. "I should have realized… There is naught to be done about it now. You must remember that no magic is infallible. Some of our enemies can see through such gifts."

She approached Sabine with haunted eyes. "They hurt you. They used to hurt me, too."

"Oh, Lyra," Sabine said, her heart aching for what Lyra, and the others, had endured. She pulled against the restraints in frustration. Another wave of nausea rushed through her as the needles pierced her skin. "If they come back, you need to sneak past them and escape. It's too dangerous for you to remain here."

Lyra shook her head. "I won't leave you."

"Then we shall all escape together," a tiny voice announced.

Hawthorn shed his glamoured moth illusion and zipped over to the locks on Sabine's shackles. "Tricky, tricky. I wonder if there's a thorn around here. Blossom's lock-picking class should come in handy."

Sabine blinked. "Hawthorn? How did you get here?"

"I hitched a ride on the dragon," Hawthorn said cheerfully, flying over to Aeron. He cocked his head and eyed the lock on Aeron's chains. "These may be slightly more complicated than the practice ones in Malek the Dragon's office. Never fear! The day shall yet be saved!"

"Practice locks?" Sabine asked, wondering if Malek knew his desk had been pilfered.

Aeron arched his brow. "You're quite the valiant flutterfolk. However, these shackles are magically wrought and can only be opened with a key forged from the same metal."

"Oh," Hawthorn said, his wings drooping slightly. Then he perked up. "I shall retrieve the key! Where is it?"

"Right here," Lyra said, opening her hand to reveal a dull metallic key. "Gwenllian gave it to me."

"They'll execute her once they learn it's missing," Aeron said quietly.

"Not if we get to her first," Sabine said. "Can you unlock my restraints, Lyra?"

Lyra placed the key in the top lock. The shackles around Sabine's wrists fell away, and she nearly wept with relief. Her skin was blistered and raw from the iron, and she was covered in far more blood than she'd first realized.

Lyra unlocked the shackle around Sabine's neck. Sabine carefully removed it and rubbed her throat while Lyra worked on the locks around her ankles. Too much iron. Even with the shackles gone, she could feel the weakness and cold chill taking hold. Malek could burn the residual effects away, but Sabine refused to let him walk into a trap. He was vulnerable in his human form.

"I have an urgent task for you, Hawthorn," Sabine said. "One that can only be accomplished by a skilled pixie."

Hawthorn hovered in front of her face. "How may I be of assistance, Your High—er, Lady Sabine?"

"Can you sneak through the door?"

Hawthorn nodded. "I can slip underneath. There's a gap about this big." He held up his hands to demonstrate.

Lyra pulled the chains away from Sabine. She carefully climbed to her feet and staggered as another wave of nausea and vertigo hit her. Hawthorn's rapid fluttering was doing little to help her dizziness.

"Find the nearest flower or mushroom and contact Blossom," Sabine said, hoping they weren't already too late. "Tell her where we are and everything Typheron said about what will happen if they attempt a rescue. We'll need to find our own way out. I won't risk their lives or the aderyan getting caught in the crossfire."

Hawthorn saluted her. "It shall be done at once. Perhaps after it's all said and done—"

Sabine blew out a breath. "If we all get out of here alive, I'll give you a sip of the starfruit essence."

"Yes!" Hawthorn exclaimed, pumping his fist in the air. "I'll tell Blossom the news right away."

His image shimmered into a moth, and he took off, heading straight for the door. Sabine stumbled toward Aeron, feeling a bit like a dwarf after a Razadon bar crawl.

Her vision went dark around the edges. Just a few more steps. Gods. Typheron couldn't have imprisoned them in a smaller chamber?

Aeron's chains clanked as he shifted positions. "Aderylin, you must not pass out. Lyra may be able to help if the iron is interfering with your magic."

"Malek gave me some resistance to iron," Sabine said, reaching for the shackles above Aeron's head. She took the key from Lyra and slipped it into the lock. With one twist, the iron chains around his wrists clattered to the ground.

He wrapped his arms around her before she could fall. "I am not sure you are as resistant as you believe."

She blinked up at him and reached for the shackle around his neck. She'd like to see Typheron chained up in his own dungeon for a few centuries. Or better yet, maybe she'd give him to the demons to play with. Dax was always inventive with torture.

"You might be right," Sabine admitted. "The poisoned dart cut off my ties to my magic, including my connection to Malek and Bane. Until the effects of the dreamthorn and chaosbriar wear off, I won't be of much use."

"Are you strong enough to assist me in removing the bindings from my wings?"

Sabine frowned. Glowing chains looped around Aeron's beautiful, feathery wings and disappeared into the walls. The metal was different from the iron shackles they'd used on her. Every time his wings moved, they pulsed with a strange light. Something about them reminded her of the void crystals used to drain fae magic.

"I'll have to be," Sabine said, refusing to consider the alternative. "I'm assuming it's not a simple iron chain?"

"No," Aeron said, his arms still wrapped around her. "The dragons call it a skythrall conduit. The device harnesses my magic and sends it through the iron chains using an alien form of magic akin to dragonfire. It will need to be deactivated before I can remove the chains from my wings. However, you must know that any attempt to interrupt the device will cause you great suffering, Aderylin."

Sabine arched her brow. "I doubt it's any worse than what Typheron plans for me when he returns."

Aeron lowered his gaze. "There is… another option. I will require a weapon of some kind, though."

Sabine paused, suspecting this was how Aeron lost his magic the first time. "No, Aeron. There's no other option. I'll do this."

Aeron closed his eyes, and a single tear ran down his cheek. "May the skies remember your mercy, Aderylin."

"I will help," Lyra said, ducking under Aeron's wings.

Aeron released her, and Sabine slid behind him. A strange

metal contraption was fastened to his back, almost like a harness. In the center of the device was a triangular disc or lens that pulsed in time with the chains. She'd never seen anything like it, not even in the dwarven workshops she'd visited. This must be the powerhouse of the skythrall conduit.

"How does it work?" Sabine asked, searching for a way to unhook or deactivate the device. Multiple rings were attached to the lens, each spinning in a controlled whirlwind.

"Our magic keeps the Sky Cities aloft," Aeron said. "The skythrall conduit stimulates our wings and siphons our magic through the chains into the land. The dragons have connected all of the islands with similar chains made from the same metal."

"That's why Ishu is at a higher elevation than Malek's home on Kavi?"

"Yes," Aeron said. "I do not believe there are any aderyan captives on islands other than Ishu and Torvah. Those two sustain the rest."

Lyra pointed to two small chain links at the bottom of the device that moved slightly out of sync with the others. "Those sound the best with Aeron's magic—one for each of his wings."

"Pull them out simultaneously," Aeron said, glancing over his shoulder. "Once the device is deactivated, I can remove the chains from my wings. I will do what I can to shield your suffering once I'm free."

"Here we go," Sabine said and yanked hard on the two links.

Searing pain tore through her, and she dropped to her knees with a gasp. The ice from the iron in her blood warred with the blistering heat radiating from the strange metal. Malek's dragonfire had been tempered by his love for her, but this burning agony was raw in its brutality.

Lyra's wings trembled. She batted at Sabine's hands. "You have to release them!"

"She cannot," Aeron said, quickly stripping the chains from his wings. "The dragonfire will hold her until she can overcome it."

He crouched beside her and took her fisted hands in his. "Allow me to take the pain from you, Aderylin."

Sabine closed her eyes and shook her head. No. Malek had gifted her some immunity to dragonfire, and she would use it now. Battling her instinct to recoil from the heat, she let it burn through her reserves. She cried out in agony.

Oh, gods. Maybe this wasn't such a good idea.

"It is trying to feed off your magic," Aeron said, gripping her wrists.

Malek had once used his dragonfire to save her life by burning away the iron after she'd been poisoned. She used that same memory now, offering up the iron in her blood as a willing sacrifice.

The dragonfire surged, destroying the worst of the iron within her. But still, it raged.

Fire could do more than destroy—it could also cleanse.

Sabine took another deep breath and let it flow through her. This time, she offered the seer's poison. The dragonfire attacked the foreign magic, devouring the toxin Idola had crafted.

When it was finished, the metal fell from her hands, and she pitched forward.

Aeron caught her and cradled her against him. He wrapped his wings around her, engulfing her in a feathery cocoon. His power surrounded her as he reached for her hand. Lifting it to his lips, he blew gently across her blistered palm. The cool air soothed the burn, and she relaxed against him.

He lifted her other hand and repeated the gesture. When

he finished, he tucked his wings against his back. "I am not a healer, but we have learned ways to counteract some of their magic."

Lyra inspected Sabine's hands. "It doesn't hurt as much?"

"No," Sabine said with a small smile. Her magic was depleted and traces of the iron still coursed through her, but she could dimly sense Malek and Bane at the edge of her thoughts. She clamped down tightly on their connection, not wanting them to stumble into Typheron's trap without warning. Hopefully, Hawthorn would be able to get word to them about the dangers of breaching the prison.

Aeron rose to his feet and helped her stand. She frowned at the device and chains that had been used to siphon Aeron's magic.

"Aeron, if those chains carry aderyan magic to all of the Sky Cities, what will happen when all the aderyan are freed?"

"If we abandon our former Aeries, the islands will plunge into the sea."

Sabine turned to him as a suspicion dawned. "Malek told me there are no aderyan or fae captives on Kavi. What would happen if the chains connecting his home were severed?"

Aeron stilled. "The Obsidian, Emerald, and Amethyst Clans would be destroyed."

Sabine's breath caught. "That's why Typheron said he was moving up his timetable to excise Kavi." She scanned the room for something to help them escape. "If the dragons are dying from the lack of magic, Typheron must be trying to ensure the survival of his own clan. That's why he was forming new alliances by offering his son to the Gold Clan. Why else would he be targeting his former allies?"

"Your logic is sound, Aderylin," Aeron said with a frown. "It would also explain some of the rumors we've heard from others who escaped. I had suspected Typheron's allies were complicit in keeping my people shackled, but I no longer believe your dragon, or his clan, had any such knowledge."

Lyra looked up at Aeron. "Malek woke her from Veylara."

"I know, child," Aeron said, placing his hand gently on Lyra's golden hair. "He is different from others of his kind. Our Aderylin trusts him, so must we."

Lyra nodded.

Sabine glanced around the relatively empty holding cell. Other than the chains and iron barring the door, she saw no clear way out. "We need to warn Malek and his family. Do you have any ideas how we can escape?"

"Lyra is Aetherbound to you," Aeron reminded her. "She can use your magic, even when you are unable to."

Sabine's eyes widened. "Lyra? Can you do what he says?"

Lyra placed her hand on Sabine's arm and held out her palm. A small wisp of blue light formed and cut through the darkness.

Sabine smiled at her. "Then we might have a way to escape."

CHAPTER 51

Nymira led Malek and Bane into the command center, which also doubled as an armory and repository for magical artifacts.

Nymira stopped in front of a large mounted map of Aeslion. It took up the entirety of one of the walls, and markers indicated various Obsidian squadrons and their allies currently surrounding Kavi and Ishu. One of the drakes was making notes on a parchment and updating the map as he received word from the field.

"We believe the prison entrance is located on the northwest side of Ishu, likely bordering the edge of the Garnet Clan's territory," Nymira said, gesturing to a mountainous region on the map.

Malek's frown deepened. The region was massive, with too many places to hide a prison. His jaw clenched.

He pointed to several marked locations. "Are these flagged areas possible entrances or just heavy patrols?"

"Both," Nymira said. "There are unusually heavy patrols in those areas, which has made aerial surveillance nearly impossible. We suspect they may have converted ancient aderyan caverns into their prison."

Bane stepped closer. "The caverns will be reinforced with magical protections set in place by the Tuatha Dé. Your scouts wouldn't be able to locate one unless they tripped over them. It is also the most likely reason the communication crystal is not tracking Aeron."

Malek stared at the map, silent for a moment. If the Tuatha Dé created those caverns, there would be hidden entrances and exits. In the years he'd spent searching for the artifacts, he'd realized the self-proclaimed gods often left themselves a way to escape. It was the reason none of them had remained trapped on Aeslion after the portal closed. The difficulty would be in finding one of these hidden locations before Sabine was injured—or worse.

He turned sharply, gesturing toward the shelves full of weapons and gear. "Bane, take what we need to keep our presence quiet. I can fly us in covertly, but I'll need to shift forms once we land in Topaz territory."

Nymira motioned for Bane to follow her. "Come, demon. We have a few magical items that may assist your efforts in retrieving my son's mate."

"Idola's dead."

Kaia's telepathic words hit Malek with the force of a gong. He stepped away from the map to focus on his sister's voice. *"How?"*

"The hound, from all appearances," Kaia said, her irritation apparent even in his thoughts. *"We're searching her room right now. Malek, I'm sorry. I loaned Elisa's journal to her so she could create the tonics for me. If I had known what she intended—"*

Malek slammed his fist against the table in frustration. He needed answers, not more obstacles in his path. If he'd killed Idola when he first had the inclination, all of this might have been preventable.

Bane turned and narrowed his eyes at Malek. "Sabine?"

"No," Malek said, gesturing to the shelves lined with weapons and equipment. "I want to be airborne in the next few minutes."

Bane gave him a curt nod before turning back to Nymira. Malek pinched the bridge of his nose, trying to wrest control of his emotions. Sabine's absence was affecting his judgment.

"This isn't your fault, Kaia. Right now, our focus needs to be on finding Sabine. Every minute she spends with Typheron increases the number of abuses she'll suffer at his hands."

"I—By the ether, Malek. I hope you make the bastard suffer when you find him." Her mental voice wavered. *"Esme says the poison Idola used would have interrupted Sabine's magic. She believes that's why you can't feel her, and why Sabine hasn't blasted Typheron to the depths of the underworld already."*

"Can Esme fix it?"

"She's identified two of the ingredients Idola used, but there's one component she's missing. Rika thinks seer blood was used as a binding agent. We're heading to your estate now to check the conservatory. Sabine told Esme the counteragents to most herbs grow near each other."

Malek turned back to the map. The lieutenant in charge of updating it had moved several markers. From all appearances, they were close to pushing the bulk of Typheron's forces out of Kavi.

"Take an escort, along with Thom. It should be clear, but I won't risk your safety. Send word when the antidote is ready. I'll have a wyvern pick it up."

Blossom flew into the study. "I heard from Hawthorn!"

Bane closed the traveling pack and tied it at his waist. "Report."

Blossom landed on the table and crossed her arms. "I normally wouldn't answer you, but since it's for Sabine..." Her dust flared bright red, and she sniffed. "Sabine's alive, but Hawthorn says she doesn't look too good. They threw her in prison, Malek! Chained her in iron! Her magic's gone, and she's sick. Aeron's with her, but he's hurt too."

The table cracked under the force of Malek's hands. Blossom leaped into the air and flew to his shoulder, clinging to his neck like a barnacle. The urge to shift and fly straight to Ishu burned through him, barely held in check by the knowledge that doing so would only endanger Sabine further.

"We need to go," Bane said, his eyes silvered. "Now."

Malek struggled to battle back his emotions. He motioned for Bane to follow him and headed toward the rear garden.

It took a moment before Malek noticed Blossom trembling, and he recalled Sabine's warning about the pixie burning out when overly emotional.

He sent a silent message to one of the drakes telling them he needed some honey or flowers in the armory right away. If the drake was confused by the odd request, he didn't question it.

"Do you know the location of the prison entrance?" Malek asked, trying to keep his voice calm.

"Hawthorn thinks he can find it again," Blossom said. "But you can't go in! Typheron said if anyone enters the prison, the guards are under orders to kill Sabine. He thinks you want to use her magic to control the rest of the dragons."

"We need to lure them out," Bane said.

Malek nodded and studied the map. The lieutenant frowned and moved another set of markers in accordance with the silent updates he was receiving from the field.

Nymira cocked her head as though listening. "Your father says the Gold Clan will neither join our cause nor Typheron's. Their alliance with Topaz hasn't been formalized. They'll wait to see who wins, but they'll attack anyone who breaches their airspace."

"As long as they stay out of our way, I don't give a damn what they do," Malek said and pointed to several locations on the map. "If we strike these areas of Typheron's territory at once, it might be enough to draw his reinforcements out of the prison—especially if he believes it'll assure him of victory."

One of the house staff entered quietly with a small flowerpot. She glanced at Malek, and he motioned for her to place it on the table before leaving.

"There's another problem," Blossom said, landing on the edge of the flowerpot. She buried her nose in the petals for a moment before looking up. "Lyra's in the prison with Sabine and Aeron. No one's seen her yet. Hawthorn says she's sneaky."

Malek stilled. "How?"

Blossom shrugged. "The blur. I'm not sure how it works, but Aeron taught her how to do it. She got the key to Sabine's shackles, but they're still locked in a cell."

"Is Thalassa with them?" Malek asked.

Blossom shook her head. "Nope. Just Lyra. Hawthorn says Thalassa is hiding somewhere on Ishu."

"Can he find her?"

Blossom hesitated, then held up her hands. "Maybe. If she uses her magic, Hawthorn can sniff it out."

"Try to locate her. We may need her help."

"Got it," Blossom said and stuffed her entire head inside one of the large flowers. "You hoo! Hawthorn! Come in, Hawthorn!"

Bane sealed his traveler's pack. "We have what we need. Anything else can be picked off the bodies we leave in our wake."

Malek gave him a curt nod. "Blossom, I need you to send

one of the pixies to my estate. Once the antidote is ready, they'll need to guide a wyvern to our location on Ishu."

Blossom grinned. "Do you really think I'd leave *my* garden unattended with only humans keeping an eye out for beetles? Pfft. Dewey's already there on insect duty. Give me a minute to jingle a bluebell near him. He's one of Hawthorn's younger brothers."

She buried her nose in the flower again. "Dewey, stop licking that berry! You're on duty, soldier! Now pay attention..."

Nymira approached Malek, her gaze fastened on Blossom. "Fascinating creatures. They can communicate over long distances?"

"Apparently so," Malek said, turning to Bane. "Let's go."

Bane grabbed the potted plant from the table. Blossom faceplanted in the soil. She spit out a mouthful of dirt and brushed off her tongue.

"Bleck! I was in the middle of coordinating a high-level operation."

"Talk on the way, and be grateful I have more use for you than as a snack," Bane said, heading for the door with the plant tucked under his arm.

Blossom flopped onto the soil, her wings turning green. "Help! Demon armpit! Can't breathe. Need more... flowers..." She coughed. "Must. Have. Air."

Bane growled. "Gather the pixies in the garden. Now."

Blossom eyed him suspiciously. "I'm not serving my friends as a meal."

Bane opened the traveler's pack at his side and pulled out the bottle of starfruit essence. "We need a diversion, and you've been volunteered."

Blossom's eyes rounded. She reached up and jingled one of the flower stalks. The air filled with dozens of tiny faces, all staring at the bottle in Bane's clawed hand as though it contained all the magic in the universe.

Malek arched his brow. "Are you sure about this?"

"Can you think of a better diversion?"

Blossom flew into the air and pressed her hands against Malek's mouth. "I'll tell Sabine lots of good things about you once we get her back. I promise."

The chattering of the pixies filled the air as they all made similar promises.

Malek took a deep breath. "Unleash the pixies."

Bane uncapped the starfruit essence. "Drink up, bugs. We have a Faerie queen to save."

CHAPTER 52

"Aderylin, I must caution you about what you plan to attempt. Lyra may be able to wield your magic, but it will take longer for you to recover your full strength. Your bond is still too new."

"Will this harm Lyra?"

"No," Aeron said. "You were the one who awakened her magic, and unless you will it otherwise, she will be insulated from any harmful effects. I would offer my remaining strength to you."

Sabine squeezed his hand. "We may need your strength for other things, Aeron."

Lyra sat at her feet, watching them with solemn eyes. Her feathery wings lightly brushed against Sabine's skin. If there was a chance she could at least get Lyra to safety, Sabine intended to take it.

"Very well," Aeron said with a sigh. "Lyra will only be able to manipulate the magic that is inherently yours. She will not be able to draw upon Malek's power or even Bane's gifts."

"And what of the goddess marks on my skin?" Sabine asked.

Aeron looked at her strangely. "Aderylin, those marks do not give you power. Any markings from Lachlina represent nothing more than a reminder of your agreement with her, or perhaps a way for you to access your dormant magic. Even your childhood skin markings serve no purpose beyond concealing your light from the world."

She stared at him in shock. "What?"

Aeron frowned. "You did not know?"

"I..." Her voice trailed off and she stared down at herself. The marks that adorned her arms and legs had been etched into her skin since she was Lyra's age. Some of the Elders had infused certain gifts into them, but Sabine had always believed their purpose was to help harness her magic.

Yet something about Aeron's words rang true. As much as she wanted to press him further, now wasn't the time.

She shook her head and kneeled beside Lyra. "Are you willing to try this with me?"

Lyra blinked up at her. "Yes."

"All right," Sabine said gently, hoping she wasn't asking too much. She held out her hand. Lyra placed her small palm against hers, and Sabine felt the tingle and rush of their magic connect.

"Look for the light shining within me," Sabine said, recalling the way her tutors had trained her when she was younger. "Allow it to fill your mind's eye. Hold tightly to my light and match its resonance."

"How?"

Sabine began to hum, allowing her wordless song to guide Lyra. It was the same melody that played from the music box the Huntsman had gifted her. The song was one of her first memories, and for some reason, it called to her now. As Lyra joined in, the aderyan's skin began to glow with the same soft luminescence that Sabine possessed.

"There is a song in the stone," Sabine said, guiding Lyra to the cavern wall. "Listen for the pulse of the earth, and the low sound of the rock surrounding us. Feel the land through me."

Lyra cocked her head as though listening. "It rumbles."

"Place your hand upon the stone and feel the strength within it. Allow its song to guide you. We'll focus on that place and ask it to part for us."

Lyra placed her glowing palm against the wall. "It's louder now."

They moved along the wall until Lyra stopped abruptly. "Here! The pitch changed. I have to open it here."

Aeron scanned the stone. "That should be one of the interior caverns. The aeries are similar to honeycombs, with multiple independent chambers. There may be guards or other captives on the other side. I will shield you from sight as best I can."

"Allow the rock to shift and flow beneath your hand," Sabine said, placing her palm over Lyra's hand to help guide the magic. "Listen for the resonance that matches the stone's song and push against it with my power."

The wall trembled. Stone dust fell from the surface as it began to shift. A narrow crack appeared.

Lyra gasped, and the magic faltered.

Aeron glanced at the iron door. "Hurry, Aderylin. The noise will draw their attention."

"It's all right, Lyra," Sabine said, taking her other hand and placing it against the wall. "You're doing well. We need to widen the crack, as if we're opening a door. Stretch the land and mold it to the shape you envision."

Lyra's nose scrunched as she concentrated. "Trying."

The crack widened, bringing with it a waft of cool air. Voices grew louder behind the iron door. As soon as the opening was wide enough, Sabine grabbed Lyra and pulled her through. Aeron followed a half-step behind.

"Close it," Aeron said, extending his wings. "I cannot shield us from view for long."

Sabine fought through her exhaustion and placed Lyra's hands on the stone. "Find the original resonance. Close the door and seal the land."

Lyra bit her lip, her face flushed from effort. Sabine began to hum again, and the song caused Lyra's shoulders to relax slightly. Slowly, the crevice sealed.

Lyra beamed a smile at her.

"I knew you could do it," Sabine said, reaching down to hug her. But a wave of dizziness hit, and she dropped to her knees. Her strength was gone. Even keeping her eyes open was a struggle.

"Aeron!" Lyra cried out in panic.

Aeron lifted Sabine into his arms. "Stay close and stay quiet. Use the Aderylin's power sparingly. She's cannot fall into Veylara until we reach safety."

Sabine blinked, trying to stay awake. They were in another cavern of sorts, but unlike the raw stone and dirt of their cell, this one was lined with white marble streaked with veins of gold. Faerie lanterns affixed to graceful columns flared to life, casting golden light across the polished stone.

A painted mural of the dawn sky gleamed overhead. Dozens of winged aderyan soared through the air, their wings extended in a graceful dance as they watched over the hall. The light from the lanterns made their wings shimmer and shift in color as Aeron carried her through the chamber.

The air was fresher somehow, lighter, and there was a layer of magic around them that was strangely familiar. Something about it reminded her of the Hall of the Gods.

Two pathways branched off from the room, each in opposite directions. In the distance, Sabine could make out the faint sound of flowing water, though it was impossible to tell which direction it was coming from.

"What is this place?" Sabine asked quietly.

Aeron shook his head. "My parents once spoke of our temples, but I thought they'd all been destroyed. In all the years I was held captive, I only heard rumors of one my people discovered."

Shouting echoed beyond the cavern wall. Sabine's hand tightened on Aeron's tunic. The wyverns must have discovered their escape. They hadn't had time to hide their footprints, or the evidence of shifting the wall. It was only a matter of time before the guards realized where they'd gone.

Lyra looked up at them and whispered, "I know where you need to go. He told me."

Sabine glanced at Aeron, but he shook his head to indicate he wasn't sure what Lyra meant.

"I can try to walk," Sabine murmured.

Aeron shook his head. "Conserve your strength, Aderylin. Lyra is likely still drawing upon your magic to guide us."

They took the right pathway, following a gentle slope downward. Sabine's eyelids grew heavier with each step. She tried to focus on their surroundings to stay awake. More fae lanterns lined the walls, their warm glow bursting to life in response to Aeron and Lyra's footsteps.

Ancient runes, written in the language of the gods, had been etched into the stone. Sabine searched her memory, trying to recall their meaning.

"They're symbols of protection, aren't they?" Sabine asked, brushing her hand against the wall. A faint echo of voices touched her thoughts, and the runes began to glow. Her skin markings flared in response.

"Careful, Aderylin," Aeron warned, his voice low and urgent. "There are places in the Aeries that contain far older magics than those used by my people. If you awaken the protections, it may alert our enemies to our presence."

She pulled her hand away. "You think the gods left safeguards in place?"

Aeron nodded. "Some of these caverns were once gathering places. During the war, our wounded and young retreated to these mountains and the protections they offered. But after the gods departed our world, their safeguards began to fail. We could not withstand the dragon's fury, and our haven became our prison."

They entered a large circular chamber. Gold and azure mosaic tiles marked with celestial symbols lined the floor, encircling a raised platform in the center of the room. Thin, translucent curtains shimmered around it, catching the light. The columns themselves had been sculpted into aderyan forms, their marble faces turned toward the platform, silently watching in quiet reverence.

"Aeron," Sabine whispered, inexplicably drawn to the platform. He hesitated, then carried her toward the center of the room.

"It calls to you?" he asked, lowering her to her feet. Inscriptions in the ancient language of the gods had been etched on the stone. Each carved letter glowed faintly with the same golden light as the markings on her skin.

Sabine nodded and placed her hand on the cool marble. Exhaustion tugged at her, but the connection she felt when she touched the stone was rejuvenating. She closed her eyes at the remarkable sensation of peace that filled her. She kneeled beside the platform, wanting nothing more than to rest for a few minutes.

"I believe we stand before the gateway to Belon, what you call the shadowglen of the dreamwalkers and a boundary into the Veil," Aeron said quietly. "Here, you could fall into the healing slumber of Veylara, while those sworn to serve as your shield protected you from harm. One of our highest honors was to be chosen for such a duty, for only in dreams are you truly vulnerable."

Struggling to keep her eyes open, Sabine asked, "Are all of the aderyan dreamwalkers?"

Aeron nodded. "It's how we've managed to share our Song and fragments of lore over the centuries. No matter how much the dragons tried to isolate us, we could always reach one another in dreams."

The air above the platform shimmered. Sabine jerked her hand back, and the vision vanished.

No.

It couldn't be.

Tentatively, she reached out again, letting her dwindling magic flow from her hand into the stone.

A shimmering apparition appeared above her. He stepped through the portal, his form cloaked by dark robes. A skeletal hand gripped a carved walking stick topped with a weathered skull.

Crap.

Aeron and Lyra dropped to their knees immediately, wings spread in supplication. He paid them no mind, his glowing red gaze fixed on Sabine.

"Daughter," the Huntsman's rich mental voice greeted her. *"It appears you've been busy. All of Aeslion has felt the echoes of your actions here."*

She was too tired for this. She didn't have the energy to dance another round with Vestior, the Huntsman, or whatever he wanted to be called today.

"This doesn't count as manipulating a portal," Sabine said, gesturing weakly at the platform. "I had no idea that was going to happen. You indicated I'd be on my own once I entered the Sky Cities."

When he didn't respond, she frowned. "If you're upset about the incident with the dryads, that portal had been formed by them. I simply restored the balance. Technically, I haven't broken our agreement."

"Is there anything else you feel the need to defend against?"

Sabine yawned and leaned against the base of the platform. "It depends on whether you feel the need to smite me or my companions."

Vestior's robes shook in silent laughter. Whatever. At least he wasn't chasing her down with the rest of the Wild Hunt or threatening to kill her. Somewhere along the way, she'd lost her paralyzing fear of him. Or maybe she was just too tired for common sense.

He descended the platform toward her, his walking staff echoing through the chamber. *"I don't suppose you had a chance to fully read the inscription before you bled on it?"*

Oops.

Sabine tilted her head and tried to read the inscription, but the letters swam in front of her. Summoning the vestiges of her strength, she tried to focus.

It was some archaic form of the gods' language. Only a handful of the words were remotely recognizable.

"Something about sacrifice and Aeslion's breath… bridging the ether to the water of dreams?"

Vestior was quiet for a long time. Then he spoke in the ancient tongue, and his mental voice made Sabine's skin prickle.

"Upon this sacred ground, a sacrifice shall bind.

With Aeslion's breath, unto Veylara's slumber we wind.

Thus opens the gate to waters serene,

Where flows the sacred stream from the Well of Dreams."

Sabine groaned and lowered her head to the platform. Her childhood tutors would have been horrified by her ineptitude. Granted, even they would have struggled with the translation. But Sabine knew better than to combine her blood with an object of power.

She lifted her head. "How many of the chamber's protections did I weaken or remove in my ignorance? I touched the walls too."

"Any fault is ours, for not adequately preparing you," Vestior said, and held out his skeletal hand.

She eyed it like a viper, recalling the last time she'd taken it. He'd pulled her into the in-between to save her life, but it had been a challenge trying to return to her body.

"You will not depart this realm, unless you choose to."

"I wish to remain in this realm," Sabine said, and took his bony hand.

His visage shifted, his features becoming less skeletal and more faelike. His eyes turned a striking, ageless blue, that carried the weight of worlds behind them.

Vestior's icy magic swirled around her. Recognizing the touch of death, she accepted its presence without allowing herself to succumb to its allure. Her skin cooled, matching the temperature of his magic until it felt almost warm.

The rush of approval she sensed from him both surprised and pleased her. Vestior's power lifted her gently, supporting her on a cushion of air and preventing her from falling.

She needed to learn that nifty little trick.

"What do you wish of me?"

He gestured to her bloody wrist. *"You have already sacrificed enough, Sabin'theoria. Your blood and breath were enough to open the gateway. Place your hand upon the platform and call upon the magic of the Well. Then, you may replenish your strength. With your aid, I will once again fortify the protections of this chamber before your enemies breach them."*

She placed her hand on the platform, closed her eyes, and reached for the Well of Dreams.

A rush of joy filled her as Azran, the fierce hellhound from the Hall of Gods, touched her thoughts.

"Greetings, little goddess. Vestior bids me to guide your thoughts to the Well."

She smiled. *"Hello again, Azran. You've been missed."*

Azran touched his muzzle to the water, and the fountain on the far wall began to gurgle.

"We eagerly await your return to us. May the waters flow eternal for you."

Sabine opened her eyes and stared in astonishment as water sputtered from the spigot, splashing against the side of the basin.

Still holding her hand, Vestior descended the platform stairs and carried her to the fountain on a current of air.

Sabine cupped the magical water in her hands and drank deeply. The liquid soothed as it flowed down her throat, infusing her with a revitalizing surge of energy. The fatigue weighing on her limbs dissipated, replaced by a newfound strength. The glow from her skin markings intensified, casting prismatic light across the marble walls.

Vestior's gaze shifted to Aeron and Lyra. *"You have bound them to you?"*

Aeron glanced up briefly before lowering his gaze to the floor. Sabine wiped a droplet from her chin. She hadn't realized Vestior had been using his group-chat form of telepathy. That should make for an interesting conversation later.

"They're mine to protect."

"Then summon them to your side," Vestior said, guiding her hand into the basin. She hissed as the water touched the wounds on her wrist. He motioned for her to do the same with the other.

Aeron approached and bowed low. Lyra followed a half-step behind him, trying to emulate his bow.

"May we assist, Aderylin?"

She nodded, wincing as the water continued to cleanse her wounds. Aeron quickly tore several strips from his tunic and held them under the cascading water. He handed one to Lyra, who began patting the blood from her ankles. As she switched to the other foot, Aeron tied one of the wet strips around her ankle to bind it.

Sabine took one of the strips from his hands. Blood had dried on his neck where the iron shackle had pierced him. She dabbed at it gently. Aeron stilled, his eyes wide and wings quivering slightly at her touch.

As she ran the damp fabric over his skin, his wounds vanished. She trailed her fingers across his neck, but there was no trace the shackles had ever touched him.

"Aderylin, I'm not worthy of such a gift," Aeron whispered, casting a wary glance at Vestior before lowering his gaze again.

"In my eyes, you are," Sabine said, and turned her attention to his wrists. If Vestior had any objections to her use of the Well's magic, that was too bad. Aeron had been born into slavery, abandoned by the gods, and he was still willing to risk everything to save his people and her. She'd promised to protect him, and she would not be forsworn.

Vestior placed his hand on Sabine's shoulder. His silence on the matter spoke volumes. She felt him draw gently on her magic and knew he was doing something to reestablish the chamber's wards.

Lyra carefully folded her bloodied cloth into a neat triangle and slipped it into her pocket. Sabine had seen brownies and other house servants do the same, but she hadn't expected an aderyan child to follow such a practice.

Sabine turned Aeron's wrist over and wiped away the last traces of blood. His skin was whole again, the physical memory of the chains washed away. Unfortunately, it would take far longer for other wounds to heal.

She started to rinse the cloth, then hesitated, unsure what to do with it.

"*Ties of blood contain some of the strongest magic. Such tributes were once considered badges of honor,*" Vestior said, lifting his hand from her shoulder. "*I have done what I could to aid your mission and restore this chamber's protections, but I urge you not to delay your departure. The fountain will cease flowing once you leave. What occurs outside these walls is in your hands now.*"

Sabine nodded and folded the strip in the same way Lyra had. When she finished, she tucked it inside her bodice for safekeeping. She studied Lyra for a moment, a suspicion dawning on her.

Sabine looked up at Vestior, once more in his skeletal guise. "You said you'd be unable to aid me once I came to the Sky Cities. Yet you guided Lyra to this chamber, knowing I'd open the way for you to step through. Why would you take such a risk?"

Vestior was silent for a long time. Finally, he said, "*This chamber is not yet controlled by the dragons. Until they cross its threshold, it remains connected to my domain. Had they breached these walls, I would have been unable to render you aid.*"

"That's not a complete answer," Sabine said, wishing she could discern his intentions as easily as he could read hers. "You don't interact with those of this realm, except under extreme circumstances. We have a duty to restore the balance, free the aderyan, and return their magic. The last portal artifact must be found and my only lead is the one you provided—directing me here. It's not just Aeslion's people at stake, even the dragons are dying from the portal being sealed."

When he didn't respond, Sabine took a step closer to him. "I believe Typheron is plotting to drop Kavi into the ocean. If that happens, hundreds of humans and those without wings will perish. Aeslion might not claim them as her children, but their loss will echo beyond the Veil."

The Huntsman's glowing red gaze shifted to Lyra. *"You awakened the child's magic when you restored her wings."*

Curious by the quick change in subject, Sabine reached for Lyra's hand and gave it a reassuring squeeze. "Yes. Aeron says she's Aetherbound." She gestured between them. "Lyra, this is the Huntsman."

Lyra shook her head. "He's more."

"You see true, child," Vestior said. *"The aderyan honor our secrets."*

Lyra nodded solemnly. "I will keep it."

Sabine stared at him, stunned. If Lyra, Aeron, and the other aderyan could see through his Huntsman guise, that would explain why he had needed to keep his distance.

"That's part of the reason you weren't able to return here, isn't it? You couldn't free them without alerting the dragons to your presence. Yet you sent me here hoping I'd what? Blunder my way through? Use Malek as a shield?"

"Your ignorance and youth were the best chance at righting this wrong and restoring the balance," Vestior said, resting his skeletal hand atop his walking staff. *"The dragon's love for you has kept you alive. Now they fight amongst themselves, your name their banner and scorched in fire across Aeslion's skies. Those willing to embrace change now fly at your dragon's side. It is within that shift that a seed of hope might grow and provide a future for Aeslion and her people."*

Sabine straightened and took a step toward him. "Pretty words aside, I do not appreciate being manipulated or my companions used in such a manner. I've come to expect such deceit from Lachlina, but I thought you and I had a different understanding. Endanger those I love again, and it will be the last civil conversation we have."

Vestior considered her. *"If I had told you the aderyan lived, would your actions have been any different?"*

Sabine considered it for a moment, then shook her head. "No, but—"

"If I shared the depth of the dragons' hatred for those who slaughtered their kin, would you have chosen to abandon the search for the final artifact?"

Sabine narrowed her eyes. "You've made your point. Now let me be clear about mine. Even if you had provided more information, it would not have deterred me from my duty. It would have simply given me more options and ensured those under my care were better protected. At the very least, I would have had an opportunity to ask for your guidance in restoring the aderyan's magic rather than making another pact with Lachlina."

Vestior stilled. His icy magic crept across the floor and climbed the walls. The fountain began to freeze over and crack.

Aeron and Lyra dropped to the ground, bowing low.

Vestior's voice sent a shocking cold chill through her thoughts. *"What were the terms of this pact?"*

"I'm to provide her with a living vessel so she might visit her daughter in the sacred grove. In return, she'll show me how to use my power to restore the wings and magic to all the aderyan."

Icicles formed on the ceiling. Several snapped and shattered as they hit the floor. Lyra's breath hitched. She sprang up and threw her arms around Sabine's legs.

Sabine placed her hand on Lyra's golden curls and sent a calming wave of magic over her.

Vestior's freezing assault on the room halted abruptly.

"What pact has been made cannot be unmade by another," Vestior said, his voice colder than she'd ever heard it. *"Take the child outside, where it is warmer. I have done what I can to aid you in this moment. But I would offer you another piece of advice regarding your tasks."*

"I'm listening."

"A chain is only as strong as its weakest link."

Without another word, he turned and swept his cloak behind him. His staff echoed thunderously in the chamber as he ascended the stairs to the top of the platform.

He brought the staff down with a sharp clap and vanished.

Sabine lifted Lyra into her arms. Her entire body vibrated against Sabine, from her chattering teeth to her trembling wings. The thin dress she wore did little to guard against the cold.

Aeron rose and moved to her side. "I would not wish to be in Lachlina's place, Aderylin."

"She'll likely retaliate for tattling to her husband," Sabine said, rubbing Lyra's back between her wings. "With any luck, maybe it'll distract her from the whole Malek-mate-claiming thing. Either way, we need to get out of here and get warm. I don't think it's a good idea to pull on Malek's power while we're still in this chamber."

Sabine carried Lyra out of the platform room and followed Aeron down another marble hallway. More runes of protection were etched into these walls, and they began to glow as they passed.

"They are reacting to your magic," Aeron said, glancing over at her. "I am unsure what it all means, except this place has been awakened."

"Will it help us find the exit?" Sabine asked, shifting Lyra's weight slightly. Lyra wrapped her arms around Sabine's neck. She was still cold to the touch, but at least her teeth weren't chattering as violently anymore.

"The exit should be marked in a way all aderyan can identify," Aeron said, his gaze sweeping the corridor.

Ice had crept down the hallway, coating the floor and walls. Icicles dripped from the ceiling. Aeron broke off several of the larger ones that blocked their path and tossed them aside.

Sabine's shoes slid on the ice, and she had to lift her feet carefully to avoid falling.

"I can carry her for you, Aderylin."

"I've got her," Sabine said, bracing her free hand against the wall. She winced and abruptly pulled her hand away. The wall was completely frozen.

"I'm sleepy," Lyra murmured, snuggling closer.

"You'll miss all the adventure if you fall asleep now," Sabine said gently. "Think about everything you get to tell Thalassa, Rika, and Blossom when you see them next."

"Esme too," Lyra mumbled. "The plants like her."

Sabine smiled. "Yes, they do."

Aeron stopped abruptly and turned to face what appeared to be a blank wall. He ran his hands over the surface, searching for something.

"I see it!" Lyra whispered.

Sabine tilted her head. As she relaxed her vision, the faint image of an eye with wings etched into the marble appeared in front of her.

"Vigilant eyes beneath open skies," Sabine murmured. "That's what Gwenllian said to me when she lowered me to the ground."

Lyra nodded. "It's from the first verse of our Song."

Aeron extended his wings, the feathers brushing against the marble. "The exits are always hidden, protected against unwelcome eyes. Sing, child. Let the magic of this place know we are here."

Lyra opened her mouth, and began to sing in a clear voice, "Vigilant eyes beneath open skies, silent sentinels where the horizon lies."

With a solemn expression, Aeron plucked a small feather from his wings. A single drop of blood hovered at its tip.

Using it as a quill, he outlined the eye symbol in blood and magic.

His deeper voice joined Lyra's as he sang, "Ever alert to the stir of shadow's veil, in boundless realms, our watch prevails. Through whispering winds and the storm's fierce cry, with steadfast hearts, the threat we defy."

Their voices were steeped in magic, blending into a siren's song that stirred something deep within her. The wall shuddered. Lines etched themselves into the marble, outlining a narrow doorway just wide enough for them to pass through. It shifted and swung open with a blast of warm air, revealing a dense thicket of tangled vegetation clinging to the edge of a steep cliff.

Aeron glanced at them over his shoulder. "Lyra, you must walk from here. Aderylin, stay close to the wall."

Sabine lowered Lyra to the ground and peered out, her heart pounding as she took in the sheer drop. The air was crisp, and the scent of moss mixed with the briny tang of distant waters. She could hear the cries of wyverns circling somewhere above, their calls echoing against the vast openness.

She quickly wove a thick glamour over them, hiding them from view from the wyverns overhead.

"How did Malek talk me into this?" she muttered, eyeing the drop with trepidation.

"We will not let you fall, Aderylin," Aeron said, stepping into the brush. He parted the dense foliage with his wings, making a path.

Sabine followed, her dress snagging on the branches. She yanked it free, sending several of the diamonds tumbling off the edge of the island. The seamstress was going to have a fit.

"Stay close," Aeron murmured. "If we can reach Thalassa, she can fly us to a safer location."

Sabine nodded and took Lyra's outstretched hand.

Despite Lyra's flying lessons, Sabine wasn't willing to risk her taking an unplanned dive.

They moved in silence, save for the rustle of leaves and the occasional stone that tumbled into the sky below. As they edged around a narrow bend, the ground gave way slightly under Sabine's foot. Pebbles skittered into the void.

She froze, hearing the sound of wings dangerously close to them.

"Are dragons supposed to be pink?" Lyra asked in a voice barely above a whisper.

Aeron halted. "There are no—By the Song, how is this possible?"

Sabine's head snapped up. An enormous, sparkling pink dragon soared through the air, weaving over, under, and around wyverns using tactics she'd only seen during pixie tag.

"What in the world—"

Sabine's voice faltered. A second pink dragon followed suit, leaving a glittering trail of rainbow pixie dust behind it. She stared at the sky at a complete loss for words when a third made an appearance.

Instead of fire, they belched golden glitter. Their giggles and whoops of glee echoed throughout the mountains.

The other wyverns and dragons didn't seem to know what to make of these bizarre creatures that zipped in and out of their ranks with complete disregard for their battle lines.

"The flutterfolk share the skies with dragons," Aeron murmured in stunned disbelief. "I think that one just tapped a wyvern on the butt with its tail."

Sabine nodded, her thoughts racing. If Blossom and the pixies were up to their usual mayhem, Malek and Bane had to be close. She lowered her mental barriers and reached for Malek across their bond.

A wave of fierce determination and raw power reached out to her, enfolding her in a heated cocoon. She felt him focus on her, and a rush of incessant need poured through their bond. He was coming, cutting through the air and opposition alike, his single-minded focus to reach her staggering with its intensity.

"*Don't move,*" Malek said, his voice wrapping around her.

She eyed the edge of the cliff. "*I wasn't planning on it, but there isn't enough space for you to land. We're trying to find Thalassa to fly me out of here.*"

"*Jump.*"

Sabine blinked. "*I must have misheard you.*"

"*Jump, Sabine.*"

She peered over the side to the water far below them. "*How many of those smoking drinks did you have?*"

"*Not nearly enough for the heart attack your disappearance caused,*" Malek said dryly. "*Now jump, or I'll end up tearing apart the side of that cliff wall to get to you.*"

"*Stubborn dragon,*" she said with a smile, sending a wave of love through their bond before turning to Aeron. "Shield yourself from sight and take Lyra to Thalassa. Once she's safe, we need to locate Gwenllian. I'll meet up with you once I have a chance to fill Malek and Bane in."

"Aderylin?" Aeron asked, his brow furrowed.

Sabine reached for Aeron's hand and squeezed it. "It's time for us to return your people's magic, Aeron. It begins now—with their freedom."

Without another word, Sabine took a running start and leaped off the side of the cliff.

CHAPTER 53

Malek cut through the sky and dove downward, knowing the instant Sabine's feet left solid land. Her light was blinding in its intensity, her power a beacon that called to him above all others.

"You stupid lizard!" Bane shouted over the wind, his claws digging for purchase against Malek's scales. "You told her to jump?"

Malek grinned as much as a dragon could and shot forward, angling himself below Sabine. Drawing upon his magic, he reached for his mate to soften her landing.

Bane snatched her out of the air with another colorful curse about turning him into a pair of boots. Malek ignored him, the darkness in his heart lessening at the feel of his mate's touch against his scales. The demon could threaten whatever he liked as long as Sabine was safe.

Sabine's hands tightened around the spikes along his neckline, her thoughts blending with his. *Typheron is planning on dropping Kavi into the sea. You need to warn your family. The Huntsman said something about a chain only being as strong as the weakest link.*

Malek shot upward above the cloud cover, using a thin sheen of power to hide their presence against the night sky. *"The Huntsman? You're sure about this?"*

"Typheron planned this attack well in advance. My abduction was secondary. I'm not willing to risk hundreds of innocent lives on the possibility I might be wrong. Esme, Rika, and your sister are among that number. If something happens to the chains keeping Kavi in the air, they'll all be killed."

Malek reached for Raynor in his thoughts. *"Cousin, I've found Sabine. She believes some of Typheron's forces may be targeting the bridges."*

"Clever bastard," Raynor muttered. *"That explains the reports I've received about the Garnets sneaking around by way of Direh. If they've already severed Kavi's chain bridge to that island, we may have a problem."*

"Go," Malek ordered. *"See what you can find out. Once I get Sabine to safety, I'm hunting Typheron."*

Finding a draft wind to coast upon, Malek touched his sister's mind. Kaia's impatience and frustration pounded against his temples. *"Kaia, coordinate with our family and allies on Kavi. Typheron may be going after the bridges. We need to begin evacuation of all non-flighted individuals immediately."*

"Your adopted seer already warned us," she said, sounding preoccupied. *"She's been spitting out ominous foretellings about fire in the sky, chained wings, and walking skeletal figures with fingers of ice. I'm stuck in human form, listening to this craziness instead of helping you light Typheron's reptilian ass on fire. Now shoo. I have evacuations to oversee."*

Malek dropped below the cloud cover and began circling to approach Ishu from the west. Three wyverns in tight formation rose above the ridgeline, their golden eyes focused on Malek and his riders. He quickly wrapped a protective sheath of power around Sabine and Bane before bellowing a stream of flame. It shot outward in a blazing torrent designed to scatter their formation.

The lead wyvern, coated in scales that shimmered like tarnished silver, veered sharply to evade the inferno. But the other two weren't so agile; one caught the edge of the flame, the heat singeing its wings.

Sabine extended her hand and shouted, *"Vashado!"*

Power burst from her fingertips, striking the wounded wyvern. The creature's scream pierced the sky as it spiraled downward, overwhelmed by the potency of her magic.

The remaining two regrouped, but their bellow of alarm had aroused the attention of others. Three more shot across the sky, aimed in their direction. It was only a matter of time before Sabine's magic drew the attention of the rest of Typheron's forces.

"Levin, what's your location?" Malek asked, quickly rising upward. His ability to outmaneuver them was limited with the passengers on his back.

"On my way to you, but these bastards are trying to box us in," Levin said with a snarl.

The sky was suddenly awash with flashes of pink. The wyverns, poised for another assault, paused in confusion. From the shimmering pink mist emerged four pixies cloaked in gigantic dragon glamours.

The one leading the charge was a spectacle of rainbow glitter and gleeful chaos. Blossom's laughter rang out, a bell-like sound that seemed incongruous with her fearsome, albeit sparkly, dragon façade.

"RAWR!" she shouted, wiggling her pink body and causing glittering pixie dust to fly into the air. "You've been dusted by Lady Blossom, dragon extraordinaire! Let the itching commence!"

The wyverns hesitated in their assault. The pink dragons,

with exaggerated playful snarls and swipes of their oversized paws, darted through the air, weaving intricate patterns in the sky. Their antics caused disarray among the wyverns, who couldn't decide whether to attack or retreat.

Blossom swooped down and tapped one of the wyverns on the nose with her tail. He gave out a startled yelp before she zoomed away, her trail a streak of sparkling pixie dust that left the wyverns blinking their golden eyes in bewilderment.

"Tickle, tickle," another pink dragon said with a giggle, using its tail to swipe against one of the wyvern's feet. The wyvern reared back, trying to bite at the laughing pixie as it zipped away.

Another one swatted one of the wyverns on the hind quarters and shouted, "Tag! You're it!"

Taking advantage of the distraction, Malek shot upward and used his magic to cloak himself against the night sky again.

Sabine made a strangled noise in his thoughts. *"You gave starfruit essence to the pixies?"*

"It was Bane's idea," Malek said. *"Blame your demon."*

"Considering the alternative, I think I'll kiss you both once we're safe," Sabine said, accompanying her words with the brief touch of her magic.

Malek snarled at the sense of wrongness. The cold iron Typheron had used on her had left its mark. It could take years to fully expel the poisonous metal, and Sabine wasn't yet fully recovered from her last encounter from an assassin's attack.

It was one more reason Typheron needed to die.

Malek dipped below the clouds briefly and swept his gaze over the island of Ishu below him. From what he knew of the Topaz Clan leader, Typheron didn't enjoy getting his hands dirty. Unlike Malek's parents, who were leading the wyvern charge to push back the attackers, Typheron would be lurking somewhere that would offer the best protection. The elder dragon might be crafty and cunning, but he was also a coward.

Sabine's thoughts touched his mind again. *"Bane still has the communication crystal you gave him to locate Aeron. We need to land, as close to the prison as possible. We can use the chaos of the battle to free the prisoners."*

Malek debated the probability of keeping his scales intact if he suggested she sit this one out. Still, he had to try. *"What if I took you—"*

"Finish that thought and Bane might get his wish of owning a new pair of dragonscale boots." She paused. *"Malek, Gwenllian is the reason I was able to escape. If Typheron learns of her treachery, she'll die. I can't allow that to happen."*

Damn.

"I can feel the iron coursing through you, Sabine."

"Then it's a good thing I have a dragon mate who can help purge such poison with his kiss."

Well, he wasn't about to argue with that logic.

Malek turned to approach the mountainous region that housed the prison. He caught sight of several wyverns locked in an aerial battle below him. *"The communication crystal is working again?"*

"The protections within the prison must have been interfering with it," Sabine said. *"I'll glamour our appearance while you make the approach."*

As Malek began his descent, Sabine's magic flared and enveloped them, creating a blanket of darkness around their forms. He tucked his wings closer to his body, diving swiftly toward the ground before spreading them wide at the last moment to break their fall. Beneath them, the craggy mountain rose upward in an ominous tower.

"The entrance to the prison should be due east from where I jumped," Sabine directed, her voice mentally guiding him across their bond. The faint glow of torches marked the pathways like fireflies in the darkness, betraying the movements of the guards below. Malek's wings beat silently as they hovered just out of sight of the drakes and wyverns patrolling the grounds.

Navigating by the pale moonlight, Malek found a secluded spot not far from what he assumed was the prison's entrance. From the way the grass and foliage had been flattened, it was a commonly used landing area.

Bane leaped off his back and disappeared into the darkness before Malek had even touched down. Using his power to hide his transition, Malek shielded his light and transformed into human form. He twisted at the last second, his arms wrapping around Sabine and pulling her against him as they fell to the ground.

They remained still and silent for several moments, listening for any sign their arrival had been detected. Malek ran his hand down Sabine's back, the feel of her safe in his arms settling something within him. Oh, he still intended to kill Typheron. But with Sabine no longer being held captive, he could focus on more creative forms of retribution once he got his hands on the dragon.

Sabine's seductive power rushed through their bond, diverting his dark thoughts. The discordant resonance in her magic worried him. Something about cold iron must shift a fae's inner light. Most fae didn't survive one encounter with the metal, much less two.

He lowered his head and kissed her, infusing the flames of his dragonfire into his breath to burn away the darkness. Sabine whimpered against his mouth, her body softening against him. She hooked her leg over his, drawing him even closer. As he slid his hand up her thigh, he heard a crack from a twig snapping.

Malek froze, breaking their kiss immediately. Sabine's magic wrapped around them even tighter, deepening the shadows. A louder crack sounded from somewhere nearby and then a resounding thump as something heavy hit the ground.

Sabine pressed her fingertips against his lips and said silently, *"Bane is taking care of the patrolling guards. He'll let us know when it's clear."*

The faint moonlight illuminated Sabine's features enough to see what had been hidden before. Traces of dried blood and dirt streaked across her exquisite face. Her silvery hair had fallen in disarray around her shoulders, tumbling over the damp fabric of her gown which was torn and stained with blood.

Fury raged within him. He would destroy Typheron and the entire Topaz Clan for daring to lay hands on the woman he loved. He ran his fingers down her neck, over her shoulder, and down her arm, searching for any sign of injury. Bane must have already healed her wounds while they were airborne.

"How badly did he hurt you, Sabine?"

"What I experienced was trivial compared to the suffering the aderyan have endured for centuries," she said, her softer magic flowing across their bond to accompany her words. If she sought to calm his rage with her power, the only thing that would suffice would be Typheron's scaled head crushed beneath his feet.

A second and third thump sounded from somewhere nearby. Bane had better leave some guards for him to vent his frustrations.

He ran his thumb across a dark smear on her collarbone.

"The difference is you're mine to protect. I gave my word I'd help free the aderyan, but you're my priority. Allowing Idola to live was a mistake I don't intend to repeat. I will not show such mercy again."

"Idola wasn't your fault, Malek. If we're going to accomplish our goals tonight, you must separate your emotion from the task at hand."

A pained cry pierced the night and then a fourth and fifth thump followed the others.

He arched his brow. *"Like Bane?"*

Sabine sighed and didn't reply.

Malek wrapped her in his power, wishing he could deposit her safely back at his estate while he and Bane took out the Topaz Clan trash. *"You will not dissuade me from seeking vengeance in your name, Sabine. For every moment of fear or pain Typheron caused you, I intend to visit the same against him. I'll see him and the rest of his clan ground into dust for this."*

"You're a stubborn dragon."

He pressed his forehead against hers. *"And you're my treasured mate."*

"It's clear," Bane said in a low voice. "Let's move."

Malek stood and helped her to her feet. Sabine took the dagger and sheath Bane offered and cut her dress down the sides to allow for more freedom of movement.

Malek gestured at Sabine and said to Bane, "She thinks I should separate my emotion from the task at hand."

Bane snorted. "I believe I gave her that same speech about handling you, lizard. If she had listened, perhaps I wouldn't be slicing and dicing wingless drakes in the dark."

"You'd be bored senseless back in Akros."

"There is that," Bane said and pulled out the communication crystal. Blocking the light with his clawed hand, he carefully moved it in a semicircular pattern until it pulsed with a faint blue glow. Motioning for them to follow, Bane headed into the underbrush.

Sabine slid the dagger into her thigh sheath. He'd make it a point to find the wyverns who had confiscated her weapons and return each of them back to her, once he'd used them to remove the scales from their bodies.

Sabine crept through the tall grasses that grew on the side of the mountain. Her bond with Lyra, Aeron, and Thalassa thrummed like a steady heartbeat within her. Even without the communication crystal, Sabine knew they were approaching where the aderyan were hiding.

Bane lifted his fist in a gesture to hold. Sabine froze, catching sight of two reptilian creatures up ahead, their scales shimmering under the moonlight in hues of dull silver and rust. Their eyes, a piercing shade of yellow, scanned the darkness intermittently.

Though wingless and much smaller than their greater dragon or wyvern kin, the drakes obstructing their path possessed similar muscular, serpentine bodies. She'd heard the stories about how hordes of drakes had run down her people, trampling and piercing their bodies with their sharpened talons.

Malek placed his hand on her shoulder and said silently, *"I need one of them alive to question. Can you hide our presence while Bane and I make the approach?"*

"Step lightly," Sabine warned. *"My glamour won't mask any sounds or smells."*

Malek tapped Bane on the shoulder and made several gestures. Bane held his gaze for a moment and then his eyes flashed silver.

Sabine pressed her hands against the ground and spread her glamour like vined tendrils. It crept through the grasses and over the rocks to mask Malek and Bane's movements as they stalked the unaware drakes.

Malek approached the drake on the left from behind, while Bane targeted the right. With a swift, precise movement, Malek leaped over his drake's back. As he descended, he yanked back on the creature's neck spikes, flipped it over with inhuman strength, and with a flash of light, shoved his hand through its rust-colored scales to grip its heart.

The drake's yellow eyes widened in terror, its body seizing under Malek's powerful grip. Dark power surrounded Malek as he shoved more of his magic into the drake. Through their bond, Sabine caught a glimpse of the drake's alien thoughts as Malek delved into its mind.

"Where is Typheron?"

Sabine froze in stunned astonishment at the silent mental command that carried the weight of power she'd scarcely glimpsed. It had the potential to scorch her thoughts, but Malek had somehow created a barrier to protect her mind, keeping the force of his magic directed at the drake.

Apparently, Malek had been keeping secrets.

That peculiar odd buzzing sounded in her head. Malek's magic surged, a dark ripple that made the air taste of ash and storm clouds.

"What do you know of his plan?"

A softer buzzing sound replied and then the drake went limp, its mind overwhelmed and broken by Malek's forceful intrusion. Malek released his hold on the drake, dropping it on the ground.

"You were right," Malek said, stepping away from the body. "The chain bridges were Typheron's target. He's inside the prison, using the protections placed by the Tuatha Dé to hide his presence."

Bane wiped his dagger off and sheathed the blade. "Anything else?"

"No," Malek said in disgust. "The drake's mind was warded to fracture once I took hold of it. Typheron would have planned for such an eventuality when he pitted himself against my clan. He'd rather destroy those who are loyal to him than risk endangering himself."

Sabine pressed her hands on the ground and called upon the land to embrace the fallen drakes. The ground beneath them softened, falling away to absorb their essence and hide the bodies from view. They weren't native to Aeslion, but the land had accepted their deaths as its due.

Sabine stood and brushed off her hands. "We need to keep moving."

Malek turned to her and said, "I should have told you—"

She looked up at him and placed her hand over his heart. "I already know everything I need to about you, Malek. What talents or weapons you employ to accomplish your goals are simply that."

He stared at her for a moment and then muttered a curse. He drew her into his arms and buried his face against her hair. The rush of relief and overwhelming love that flowed across their bond was staggering in its intensity.

"Aeron is close," Bane said, studying the crystal in his hand. "Let's go."

Sabine followed Bane deeper into the underbrush, the twigs and branches tugging at her clothing. It was almost as though the land itself was trying to prevent her from returning to the prison.

A winged child dropped out of a tree to land in front of Sabine. She threw her arms around Sabine's legs and whispered, "You found us!"

Aeron and Thalassa lowered themselves a moment later, their movements silent as they landed upon the ground.

"Wings," Thalassa said quietly, and Lyra immediately tucked hers tightly against her back.

"What do you know?" Bane demanded.

"The prison entrance is being guarded by at least a dozen drakes," Aeron said, drawing a quick diagram in the dirt with a stick. "Thalassa says their presence has been growing heavier over the past hour, likely a result of the Aderylin's escape."

Malek lifted his gaze to the dark shapes soaring overhead. "Levin says there are an increasing number of wyverns in the skies who aren't actively engaged in the battle. He has a squadron trying to draw them off, but they aren't taking the bait. They're hunting for Sabine."

"Suggestions?" Sabine asked.

"We're at a disadvantage with a frontal assault," Bane said, his silvered gaze focusing on Aeron. "You know the prison and its weaknesses."

Aeron nodded. "There is an entrance nearby known only to a handful of aderyan. We've used this passage to smuggle our people out of the prison, but it's dangerous. The dragons and wyverns are aware it exists and patrol one of the adjacent passages. We will need to move quickly and quietly to avoid their attention."

Bane opened the traveler's pack and began distributing weapons to Aeron and Thalassa. Aeron slid a long, curved sword from its sheath and inhaled sharply. The metal shone with a pearlescent sheen and shimmered in the moonlight.

Thalassa's eyes widened. "That's an Aetherbound blade."

"Then it's all the more fitting that it returns to your hands," Malek said. "Use it well, Aeron."

Sabine glanced down at Lyra and said silently to Malek, *"With the increased patrols, it's too dangerous to try sending Lyra back to your estate. I don't want her to step foot inside that prison again, Malek. If they discover her wings—"*

Her voice trailed off, unable to finish the thought.

Malek placed his hand on her back, his touch warming her skin through the material of her torn gown. *"Will Thalassa agree to remain behind?"*

Sabine studied the aderyan woman who was equipping the weapons Bane handed her. "Thalassa, a prison is no place for a child."

Thalassa met Sabine's gaze and shook her head. "Lyra has never been a child, Aderylin. She was a captive, a slave, and a pawn to manipulate her parents. The day you awakened her magic and she became Aetherbound, she spoke. She spread her wings and cried out in joy as the Song took flight in her heart. *She is aderyan.*"

Sabine dipped her head in acknowledgment of Thalassa's words. She turned and crouched in front of Lyra. Taking the girl's hands in hers, Sabine said, "I need you to remain close to Thalassa and use every skill you've learned to keep yourself hidden. You must not reveal yourself once we're inside. Hide your wings, and keep your magic small."

Lyra straightened and nodded. "I will watch."

Sabine traced a rune of protection on Lyra's forehead. Leaning forward, she murmured the ancient words to keep the bearer safe from harm and sealed the ward with a kiss.

"It tickles," Lyra said with a delighted smile.

Sabine stood, determined to ensure Lyra and the rest of the aderyan had the freedom they deserved.

"I will guard her well, Aderylin," Thalassa promised.

"Wait for us!" a high-pitched voice called out in a loud whisper.

Sabine turned her head to see two glowbugs darting toward them. She held out her hands to allow Blossom and her companion to land.

One of the glowbugs panted heavily and flopped on her hand, its glowing green butt sputtering like a dying ember. "Do you have any idea what kind of a workout a dragon gets? Aerial somersaults are the best thing ever when you have a tail!"

"What happened to your dragon glamour?" Sabine asked as their illusion fell away to reveal Blossom and Hawthorn.

"Bane has the rest of the starfruit essence," Blossom said, sniffing the air. "What happens if he accidentally breaks the bottle? Or drops it? Someone needs to keep an eye on things to make sure nothing spills. Besides, the fun stuff always happens around you."

Sabine sighed, not entirely surprised. "Of course."

Blossom jumped up and bumped shoulders with Hawthorn. "Hawthorn's going to wait here and coordinate between the pixies in the sky, the one in my garden at Malek's house, and at Lady Nymira's house. I figure we need to keep an eye on everyone. Dragons are sneaky."

Hawthorn nodded sagely. "At the gala, I saw one of them hoarding pastries and stuffing them down her dress. Then there was one with indigestion who kept belching fire and burning the rose bushes. Another one—"

Malek made a pained noise. "I think we get the picture."

"Indeed," Sabine said, considering another way their spying could help their situation. "Select one or two pixies with exceptional hiding skills to infiltrate Typheron's estate. I'm looking for Gwenllian, Typheron, or for anyone with knowledge of the aderyan portal artifact. They can cover more ground than we can, especially with our focus being on the prison."

Malek glanced at her. "You may want to also have them check out the Garnet Clan. As Typheron's closest allies, they may know something. If there's anything to report, my sister's at my estate and handling things from the ground. Kaia can get the information to the right dragon or wyvern."

Sabine nodded. "See it done, Hawthorn."

Hawthorn saluted her. "As you will, Your High—err, Lady Sabine."

Bane snorted. "Trusting pixies with battle plans? I've heard it all now. But if they manage to pull this off, perhaps I'll consider not eating one or two."

Hawthorn grinned before transforming into a beetle and darting away. Blossom took her familiar perch on Sabine's shoulder and rubbed her hands together.

"So when do we get to the major magic part of this adventure?"

"I'd prefer keeping a low profile," she said and turned to Aeron and Thalassa. "Where is the entrance you mentioned?"

"Follow me, Aderylin," Thalassa said, ducking under a low hanging branch. She led them a short distance away toward a large outcropping that was covered with vines and ivy. Etched into the mountainside and coated with a thin sheen of glamour was a small eye symbol with wings.

Thalassa pricked her finger and traced the edge of the design. A large boulder soundlessly slid aside to reveal a dark cave that sloped downward. A waft of damp air rushed out, carrying with it the pungent scent of decay. The stench of sewage and refuse hit them forcefully as they moved into the passageway.

Blossom clamped her hands over her nose. "It smells like dragon dung in here! I feel it in my eyes, Sabine. In my eyes!"

"Quiet," Bane snapped, surveying their surroundings.

Sabine's eyes watered from the stench. This was even worse than navigating the sewers back in Akros. The dim light from her glowing markings provided the only illumination and cast eerie shadows on the rock walls. Some sort of dark viscous liquid she didn't want to examine too closely flowed in the center of the passage.

Blossom whispered, "When we get home, we're implementing a no-dragon-poop-in-the-garden rule. Lady Nymira was definitely on to something."

Sabine made a noise of agreement and followed Bane and Aeron through the narrow tunnel. Traces of broken marble lined the walls, their once radiant gleam now covered with a dark layer of soot and dirt. A pang of loss filled her at the sight, knowing the beauty that had once graced the Aeries.

As they approached an intersection, Bane held up his hand to halt their progress.

Aeron leaned close and murmured, "This path is often patrolled by the guards. Be prepared to move quickly."

Sabine nodded and carefully deepened the shadows around them. Her glamour might not work with Typheron's medallion, but it was unlikely all of the guards had such a device. At Bane's signal, they hugged the wall and moved together as one.

The pathway opened into a much wider area that was crammed with discarded remnants from the prison above. Rotted food, broken furniture, and other refuse made the passage hazardous.

"Watch your wings," Thalassa warned Lyra, stepping carefully to avoid the sharpest of the debris. Lyra lifted her wings and kept them tight against her back, her small hand gripping Thalassa's.

"Wyverns," Malek said quietly, pointing to tracks clawed into the ground. "A good number of them passed through here."

Bane touched one of the grooves on the wall and sniffed at it. "Recent. Stay alert. There are a number of life forces near us, including opposite these walls."

"Blossom," Sabine murmured, nodding toward the passage ahead of them. "Scout ahead and guide us."

"On it!" Blossom's form shimmered into a large glowbug. Her gleaming butt danced down the passage to music only Blossom could hear. Sabine couldn't risk summoning a more substantial light source this close to the dragons.

The path sloped downward at a steep angle. Sabine's formal shoes slid in the muck, and Malek caught her arm more than once to keep her steady. The sound of distant voices and clanking metal filtered down the passage toward them.

"Where does this lead?" Malek asked in a voice barely audible.

"It should take us to the lowest levels of the prison," Thalassa whispered. "The winged aderyan and other prized captives are held there."

Malek's expression turned grim. Before he could respond, a loud rumble shook the cavern. The air thickened, laced with the faint bite of sulfur.

"Get down!" Malek shouted, disappearing in a flash of light and reforming as an enormous dragon. His tremendous body barely fit in the cavern, and he twisted himself at an impossible angle. Dust rained from the ceiling, threatening to bury them beneath the mountain.

Sabine slapped her hand on the ground, reaching for her dwarven power to widen and stabilize the rock. Malek wrapped his tail around them and lifted a wing as searing heat blasted toward them.

Scorching flames seared their bond as the dragonfire pummeled against Malek's wing. Thalassa grabbed Lyra and covered her with her own wings.

"Travatha!" Sabine shouted, yanking the moisture from the air using the merfolk's power. It rose like a tidal wave in front of Malek, protecting them with a water shield and insulating them from the worst of the flames.

The dragonfire tore through her power, unraveling her defenses. She cried out and dropped to her knees, funneling more magic into maintaining the shield. Her vision swam. Threads of magic slipped through her grasp like water through cracked stone. Steam filled the passageway, obscuring everything except the dark shimmer of Malek's scales.

"We're trapped!" Blossom shrieked, diving under Sabine's hair. "They sealed the way forward. Lots of rocks. Abort! Abort! I'm too cute to die!"

Aeron crouched behind Malek's tail. "They must have sealed it after the last escape. There are prison cells behind these walls. It's the only other way out."

"We need an opening," Bane shouted to Malek.

Malek roared in fury and struck the cave walls with his claws. The stone crumbled under the onslaught, revealing a huddled mass of aderyan captives. They gasped and cried out in alarm, scuttling away from the rising heat and steam.

Sabine gritted her teeth and clenched her fist, straining to expand the water shield and protect the captives.

"Wrong way!" Blossom yelled. "The sealed wall is behind us! Use your tail!"

Malek snarled and slammed his tail into the blocked passage, shattering the rock barrier with a thunderous crack.

"That's it! Tail of doom! Ten out of ten tail strike!" Blossom cheered.

"Aeron, see to your people," Sabine ordered, unsure how long she could both hold the water shield and keep the mountain stable.

Aeron leaped over a fallen rock with Bane a half-step

behind. Thalassa grabbed Lyra and ran into the chamber. Using the key Gwenllian had given them, Thalassa made short work of the locks, while Lyra helped remove the chains binding the prisoners.

The iron door to the cell swung open. Bane drew his knives, cutting down the guards who poured through. Aeron fought at his side, his eyes flashing gold as he sliced through his opponents using the curved Aetherbound blade.

Blossom whooped from Sabine's shoulder. "Woo hoo! Take that, evil bad guys! Demon attitude coming through! Oof! See what happens when you get on an aderyan's bad side? That one's going to leave a mark."

"Go, Sabine," Malek said, his mind touching hers. *"You're using too much magic. I'll hold them off."*

"I'm not leaving you," she snapped, grabbing her knife and slicing her palm. She slammed her bleeding hand against the stone. The ground drank her blood like parched earth, and the ancient magic buried deep within it stirred.

She reached for the land's power, but what she discovered was far older. Echoes of the gods' strength surged through her, remnants of a force that once shaped worlds. She drew hard upon it, letting the echoes guide her hand and flood her soul.

The rock beneath them trembled. Her skin flared with radiant gold as the magic surged into her. A sharp wind tore through the hallway, extinguishing the dragonfire in an instant. The land roared within her, demanding vengeance for the abuse Aeslion's children had suffered.

"No more!" Sabine shouted, fully embracing the land. She stood and clapped her hands together, expelling the power in a blast and fusing the might of the dwarven and merfolk powers. The rock soared upward, layered with a protective wall of shimmering water, forming a solid barrier between Malek and the attacking wyverns.

She reached even farther, brushing against the iron bars that dug into the land like a cancer. Calling upon the power of the in-between, of the Veil that shrouded the bridge between life and death, she excised the iron with a merciless fury that sent shockwaves throughout the prison.

Sabine lifted her hands, reaching for the skies that were hidden from view. The moon had reached its zenith and shone brightly upon those who were alien to Aeslion's skies. She called the storms down, sending torrential rain and wind to blind the land's enemies. Lightning struck wings and scales alike, sending wyverns and dragons to ground.

"Sabine, wait! You're targeting our family and friends!" Malek's voice filled her thoughts.

She faltered, his sudden fear pulling her from the brink. His leathery wing enfolded her protectively. The fierce love and worry that flowed across their bond acted as an anchor, holding her steady against the power's seductive pull.

"Then show me another way," she said, reaching for him. She opened her mind, allowing him to see and sense the world through the rocks, the trees, and even the moon's light.

His thoughts blended with hers, and the trust and love between them flowed strongly through their bond, transcending all barriers. Like the dance they'd shared when bound together, this was no different. Where he led, Sabine intuitively matched his steps.

He pictured the storm moving north, and she shaped the magic in accordance with their combined wills. With a righteous fury that summoned blistering gales, she commanded the winds to flush out the wyverns attempting to ambush Malek's mother. Malek and Sabine's thoughts spun together in a different direction, whipping the winds into a tornadic frenzy and pushing aside the wyverns pinning down his cousin, Raynor.

They moved together like two parts of a whole, their

destructive focus tempered by the love that had brought them together. Working in tandem, their reach spread across Ishu, sending strong uplifts to Malek's allies while lightning and pealing thunder struck throughout the mountainside to chase away the patrols guarding the prison entrance.

Malek pulled back and said, *"You're giving too much of yourself, Sabine. Let it go."*

Sabine released the storm and staggered from the sudden loss of magic. Malek's dragon form disappeared in a flash of light. His arms wrapped around her, cradling her gently against him. He cupped the back of her head and breathed his dragonfire into her, chasing away the weariness from her thoughts.

Blossom hiccupped. "That was... really... big... magic. Ohhhh! Look! New friends! Hi friends!"

Sabine turned in Malek's arms and blinked at the sight of dozens of wingless aderyan captives. Lyra stood as sentinel in front of her and Malek, facing down the aderyan with her wings outstretched and her skin glowing a brilliant gold.

Yet it wasn't Lyra's full-flighted form that had captured and held the captives' attention. One by one, the aderyan gracefully lowered themselves to the ground and placed their fists across their hearts in a gesture of fealty.

They stared up at Sabine with eyes full of reverence and hope, and the weight of centuries of suffering slammed into her.

This would not stand.

CHAPTER 55

Sabine flung out her hand, barricading the prison cell door with a wall of stone and ice. If this mountain wasn't full of innocent people, she'd bury the wyverns and dragons where they stood.

Blossom sniffled. "Where are all their wings? Sabine, we have to get them out of here and give them back their wings!"

Sabine turned to her demon protector. "Bane, you and Thalassa need to escort them out of the prison. The mountain has been purged of any iron's touch. If any captives are still shackled, you will need to manually remove their restraints."

Bane sheathed his daggers, his eyes still silvered from the recent battle. He pulled the traveler's pack off his belt and withdrew several weapons. "Thalassa, see which of them are steady enough to wield a blade."

Thalassa nodded and took a handful of daggers from him. She moved through the group, encouraging them to stand, and speaking quietly to each of them. When she reached an aderyan woman with golden curls and stormy blue eyes, Thalassa's soft gasp echoed through the chamber.

The woman's gaze was focused solely on Lyra. Her plain shift was little more than a rag hanging limply on her too-thin frame, but it did nothing to diminish her ethereal beauty. She took a hesitant step toward Lyra, her eyes brimming with tears.

"Mama?" Lyra whispered with trembling wings. She let out a cry and ran to the woman, flinging herself into her arms. The woman sobbed and gathered Lyra close, murmuring something too low to be heard.

"Malek," Sabine whispered, and reached for him, overcome with emotions not solely her own. "That woman... I can feel her, even though her wings haven't been restored."

Malek drew her into his arms, his touch clearing her thoughts. "Is it through Lyra?"

Sabine took a shaky breath and nodded. "She... calls to me. So much pain, sorrow, fear, yet underneath there's a fragile thread of hope. And love. Tremendous love."

In a low voice, Aeron said, "Aderylin, I did not think to warn you. Most of the upper-level prisoners never learned to shield their emotions. You are responding to her Canenaid, the call of her soul. I fear you will continue to sense such a resonance until either she, or Lyra, learns to shield properly. Distance from both of them should help."

Sabine turned to him. "What of Lyra's father? Does he still live?"

Aeron frowned. "Thalassa says he is one of the oldest of the Skythralls. Lyra was meant to take his place to hold the chain when she came into her full power. If he still lives, we will find him on the lowest levels of the prison."

"Then that's where we'll head next," Malek said, running his hand down her arm.

Blossom flew into the air and over the crowd. "Listen up,

aderyan! You're being liberated! My name is Lady Blossom, official spokespixie for Sabine. She's the shiny, glowy lady with the big magic behind me. The tall, dark, sometimes scaly one next to her is Malek, but you don't need to worry. He's a good dragon and won't eat you. The grumpy demon is Bane, and you probably already know Aeron, Thalassa, and Lyra."

"Should we stop her?" Malek asked with a frown.

"I could eat her," Bane muttered.

Sabine shook her head, feeling a tug upon her magic. "No eating my pixie. Let Thalassa and Blossom focus on the aderyan. We need to make a plan and move. The barricades won't hold off the wyverns indefinitely."

"Aderylin, if you intend to descend deeper into the prison, you will need a guide."

Sabine gave Aeron a curt nod. "Your presence should give us the best chance to move quickly. While I was connected with the land, I could sense strange voids or gaps in the magic flowing throughout the mountain. Given what Malek's told me, I believe these voids have been caused by the dragons and their kin."

"Are you suggesting they're somehow feeding off the mountain's magic?" Malek asked.

"No," Sabine said with a frown. "I believe their desecration of the land and the balance is so foul that Aeslion itself is rejecting their presence. Those voids are the result."

"How many did you sense?" Bane asked.

Sabine hesitated, trying to put her impressions into words. "They were… fluid, perhaps moving. I believe there were at least three dozen areas of null space. Some were human sized, but others were in their natural form. I had thought the protections of this place would prevent them from shifting forms, but Malek didn't seem to have a problem."

Malek frowned. "Not unless you count the passage being a tight fit. If any wards had been placed by the Tuatha Dé, Typheron must have negated them long ago."

Bane turned to Aeron. "Should we anticipate the other captives being in the same condition as these?"

Aeron nodded. "The ones on this level and above us have been mutilated. They are often forced into breeding pairs or used to maintain the prison. The aderyan who still possess their wings and magic are kept on the lowest levels of the prison. Regardless of their condition, all will fight at your side until they are no longer able to stand, Aderylin."

Sabine winced as another assault on the barricades rapped against her mental shields. They were running out of time. "I don't intend to throw away any lives if I can help it. Our goal is to get as many out safely as possible. How many levels of prisoners are above us?"

"At least three or four."

"The prison entrance is clear," Malek said. "Levin and two squadrons of wyverns will keep it that way. We've managed to cut off Typheron's reinforcements for the time being. I've given them instructions to pull another squadron from the skies to start clearing the upper levels of the prison."

Sabine withdrew her dagger and pricked the tip of her finger. Offering it to Bane, she said, "I'm entrusting you and Thalassa with the aderyan, Bane. Free as many as possible, and get them out of here."

Bane lifted her finger to his lips, accepting her blood offering. His skin began to glow with a bluish sheen, and his eyes silvered. "It will be done."

"Come back to me safely," Sabine said and kissed him lightly. "We'll seek out Typheron and the other prisoners. I believe I know where he's hiding."

"You will both guard her with your lives," Bane demanded.

Aeron pressed his fist over his heart in a solemn oath.

Malek wrapped his arm around Sabine's waist and merely gave Bane a dry look.

Sabine staggered as a renewed strike on the barricade slammed into her. Dirt and small stones began to fall from the ceiling. Several of the aderyan cried out in fear.

"They're breaking through the barrier," Sabine said, wincing at the pain that pierced her temples. "I'll seal this chamber and buy you as much time as possible. Carve my symbol into the barricade to lower it when you're ready."

Blossom whistled sharply. "To your stations, aderyan! Line up against the wall and follow the grumpy demon. If you have a knife, use the pointy end on the bad guys! We'll see you on the other side!"

With a loud whoop, Blossom landed on Sabine's shoulder and grabbed her hair. Sabine, Malek, and Aeron stepped back into the tunnel. Aeron unsheathed his curved sword and gave her a silent nod. Taking a deep breath, Sabine reached for the land again and sealed the tunnel from view.

Turning toward the large barricade she'd formed to block the wyvern's dragonfire, she pressed her hands on the rock wall. Calling upon the power at her command, she sent a roiling shockwave through the tunnel to topple anything standing beyond the boundary.

"That should do it," Malek said, grabbing her hand. "Let's get out of here."

A chorus of shouts and roars thundered through the mountain. Summoning a light source in the palm of her hand, Sabine tossed it into the air to light their path. The time for stealth was gone. Now they'd have to rely on speed and sheer luck if they hoped to survive.

They turned and raced down the sloping tunnel toward the dark void poisoning the land.

CHAPTER 56

The path dipped and curved, descending into the bowels of Ishu. At each intersection they passed, Sabine tossed another lightsource into the hallway before creating another barrier. The magic wouldn't last long, but it would hopefully draw the wyverns' attention away from Bane and the others.

As they ran, Sabine brushed her fingertips against the rock wall. Many of the odd null spaces were congregating on her large barrier, except for the giant one almost directly below them.

She staggered as another concentrated burst of dragonfire attacked the barrier. Malek caught her arm, keeping her upright.

"How much farther?" Malek asked, glancing over their shoulder as they continued to run and dodge around debris. "Sabine can't keep the barrier up much longer."

"We're close," Aeron said, leaping over some broken crockery and landing with his wings extended. "The captives should be up ahead."

Blossom sniffed. "I smell fresh air."

"There," Aeron said, pointing toward a small window-sized opening in the wall up ahead. In the distance beyond it, Sabine could make out the pale light of the moon. They were rapidly approaching the end of the tunnel.

The barricade behind them fractured, and Sabine cried out as dragonfire pierced the remnants of her water shield. Malek caught her around the waist and swept her into his arms, running toward the intersection in a dash of speed.

"Move!" he shouted to Aeron as the ground rumbled and the sharp smell of sulfur filled the air.

"Faster!" Blossom shouted, grabbing Sabine's hair. "Crispy pixie is not a good look! Run faster!"

They dove into the intersection and pressed against the wall as a blast of dragonfire shot through the tunnel. Blossom squeaked and hugged Sabine's neck. Sabine lifted her hands, forming a secondary water barrier around them to shield them from the oppressive heat. The water bubbled and boiled, but it held.

"That wyvern is going to die," Malek said in a low voice.

"Can I make him itchy first?" Blossom asked, looking over her shoulder at her wings. "Whew! No scorch marks."

Sabine leaned her head against the wall. "You have my permission to make him painfully itchy in the most uncomfortable of areas."

"We need to move," Aeron said quietly, motioning for them follow. He stepped through an opening in the wall that was too narrow for a wyvern unless it was in human form. More traces of marble were on the walls and floors in this hallway, but most had been chipped away or destroyed.

The hallway was lit with oil lanterns that cast swirls of dark smoke on the walls and ceiling. Sabine wrinkled her nose at the smelly lanterns and released her lightsource.

"Drakes," Malek said, gesturing to the ground where more claw marks were etched into the broken marble and rock. "Most are smaller than their wyvern cousins. They don't usually breathe dragonfire, but many can spit acid. These worn ridges on the marble are their work."

"Belching fire, spitting acid," Blossom said, wrinkling her nose. "You guys might want to check your diets. You need more fiber."

Sabine touched a distinctive tile that still had traces of gold gilt on the edges. She had a vague recollection of being carried through this hallway when she was slipping in and out of consciousness.

Malek placed his hand on her shoulder. "This is where Typheron brought you, didn't he?"

She nodded. "I believe so."

"All of these caverns are like honeycombs," Aeron said quietly, gesturing to another opening in the wall. "The oldest and most powerful of the aderyan are kept on this level. They are rarely left unguarded. There should be a cell through here and another across from it. That's where we were chained."

Sabine gestured toward the opening and murmured, "Blossom, scout ahead."

"You've got it," Blossom whispered.

Her form shimmered and took on the appearance of a pale moth with wings the color of moonlight. As it flittered through the opening, Malek unsheathed his sword. Blossom reappeared a moment later and landed on Sabine's outstretched palm.

"We've got two uglies with scales guarding the door. I didn't get close enough to check, but I bet they have stinky acid breath."

"Good enough." Sabine lifted her hands and wrapped a thin sheen of glamour around them. Tweaking the illusion, she blended their appearance to closely match the walls.

Malek and Aeron moved forward while Sabine remained

a step behind them to hold the illusion in place. As they rounded the turn in the corridor, Sabine caught sight of the two drakes.

Their scales were murky in the dim light, and they stood as silent sentinels guarding a heavy iron door. Without hesitation, Malek surged forward, the blade in his hand catching the scant light as he closed the distance.

The left drake barely had time to register his approach before Malek's sword arced through the air and sliced through its scales. Heat flared from Malek's hand as he reached toward the drake, punching through the creature's scales to grip its heart. The drake collapsed with a gurgling thud, its body twitching as it died.

Aeron darted toward the second drake. This one reacted quicker, its snarl filling the air as it lunged forward with bared fangs. Sabine extended her hand, shouting a command that unleashed a torrent of binding light, wrapping around the drake's legs and pinning it briefly to the ground.

Blossom darted forward, her tiny body radiating an intense light that dazzled the drake, blinding it momentarily. Aeron seized the opportunity, his sword driving deep into the creature's heart. With a final heave, he twisted the blade, ensuring the drake would not rise again.

"Woo hoo," Blossom exclaimed, dancing midair. "See what happens when you mess with wings? You end up squashed! Like a bug!"

Sabine arched her brow. "The light show is new."

Blossom gave her a sheepish grin and said, "That starfruit essence has a kick."

Sabine made a noncommittal noise. Blossom's power boost in the underworld had given the pixie a much greater propensity for magic—and mischief.

Malek grabbed the iron key off the wall and unlatched the door. With a groan, it swung open to reveal a darkened interior. Sabine summoned another lightsource and stepped over the dead drakes to follow Malek inside.

Three aderyan, two men and a woman, were chained upright with their wings extended. Their bodies were scantily clad and covered with scars from centuries of abuse. Large, glowing chains pulsed softly with every beat of their wings. They lifted their heads, a combination of defiance and exhaustion etched on their faces.

Fury roiled through Sabine, her skin markings shining with barely restrained power. The ground beneath her feet began to rumble. She forced herself to pull back on her power when all she wanted was to drop the damn mountain on Typheron's head.

Malek muttered a curse. "We need to get them down. Now."

"Aeron?" the woman said, her eyes widening in shock. "Is that truly you?"

"We have not been abandoned, Efa," Aeron said, approaching her with Malek at his side. "Our Aderylin hears our Song. We fly again."

Sabine turned at the sound of heavy footsteps and the slither of scales against the walls. Another drake rushed through the doorway.

"Sabine!" Malek shouted in warning.

The creature's golden eyes focused on her, its mouth opening and dripping with acid. It reared back as though preparing to spit the foul substance in her direction.

Sabine stepped in front of the drake and lifted her hand. *"Vashado!"*

Power burst from her fingertips, searing the room with a blinding flash of light. It slammed into the creature, ripping through his scales and slicing him in half. Steam rose up from the carcass, filling the air with the smell of charred meat. She shook out her hand, the tingles of magic sending little shockwaves up her arm. That command seemed to be growing in strength every time she used it.

Blossom pinched her nose. "This is why I'm a vegetarian."

Malek approached and took her hand. He studied her fingers before meeting her gaze. "You're unhurt?"

She nodded and gestured to the aderyan. "I am, but they're not. The devices entrapping them are sealed with dragonfire."

He lifted her hand and kissed it before releasing her. "I'll take care of it, and then I'm going to tear off Typheron's scales. I'd prefer if you avoided jumping in front of any more drakes."

Sabine watched as Aeron showed Malek how to disengage the skythrall conduit. Using dragonfire, he quickly disabled it while Aeron unlocked the restraints using the iron key. They lowered Efa to the ground, and she whimpered as she pulled her dark wings tight against her back.

"By the gods' breath, that hurts," Efa muttered and squeezed her eyes shut.

Blossom sniffed. "Her poor wings. Mine hurt just looking at her."

"How long have they kept you chained this time?" Aeron asked, helping Efa sit up.

"Too long," Efa said, her voice raspy. "They're giving us fewer breaks as our numbers dwindle. There was some commotion earlier. We thought they might be doing another purge, but they brought Jac back and then ran out of here like their scales were on fire."

Aeron glanced over at Sabine. "Our magic can weaken the longer we remain underground or without adequate time to rest. Typheron regularly culls those whose magic falters."

Sabine flexed her hands, trying to control her magic. There was no excuse or claim to power that could ever justify such acts of cruelty. If her people had known the aderyan lived and chose to do nothing, they were just as culpable as the ones who closed the shackles around the aderyan's necks.

Malek's jaw clenched. "Let's get the others down."

"I'll keep an eye out for more drakes," Blossom said, changing back into her moth disguise.

Sabine walked over to a table containing a small pitcher and wooden cup. They were both empty.

"Another torment," Aeron said in disgust.

"It will be one of their last." Sabine pulled some moisture from the air and filled the cup. She brought it over to Efa and held it for the woman to drink. Efa eagerly tipped back the cup and then gagged.

"Not too fast or you'll throw it up," Aeron warned, working on the shackles of another captive while Malek disabled the device attached to his wings. Efa scowled and took several slower sips.

Sabine studied the woman while she drained the cup. Her hair was cut short and was dark as midnight, framing a face that was thin and far too pale. Her wings were the color of the sky at twilight, when the moon was just beginning the night's journey. Despite being chained and abused, there was a fierce determination about Efa that Sabine couldn't help but admire and respect.

"More?" Sabine asked.

Efa shook her head and put the cup aside. "He's right. Too much will just come back up. You were the reason for the commotion earlier, weren't you?"

"Yes."

"Good. I hope you made them pay."

Sabine smiled and took Efa's hands. "Will you allow me to share my strength with you?"

Efa nodded and winced as she sat up straighter.

In the ancient tongue of the gods, Sabine murmured

words of protection, clarity of mind, and strength. The glow from Sabine's skin encompassed Efa's, causing her wings to tremble at the rush of magic spreading through her.

Efa looked up at her with gray eyes like the sky during a storm. In her irises, Sabine could have sworn she saw lightning flash.

"By the wind's breath, you're potent," Efa said with a laugh. "Tell me you've come to kill that bastard Typheron."

Sabine picked up the empty cup and stood. "I'm here to restore the balance and purge this land of those who would imprison and harm Aeslion's children. The land itself has rejected Typheron and his allies. I intend to see justice done in her name."

"You ally with our enemies," one of the men said, his voice hoarse as though he'd spent a long time screaming. Sabine turned to him, noting many of his wounds appeared to be recent.

Aeron shook his head as they lowered the man to the ground. "No, Tristan. I believed the same, but I have seen the difference in this dragon. Malek and his clan fight for our Aderylin, even against their own."

Sabine approached Tristan and kneeled beside him. His golden hair had been shorn on one side of his head, exposing an intricate triangle tattoo with sharp angles that had been etched into the side of his neck and across his skull.

Refilling the cup with a wave of her hand, she offered it to him and said, "Trust takes time. For now, you have my word I am not here to impose my will over you, nor elicit any oaths. I simply seek to restore the balance."

Tristan eyed her warily but accepted the cup and took a long drink. He coughed and wiped the droplets with the back of his hand.

Sabine took the cup and placed it on the ground beside

her. "I'm no healer, but I can help restore your magic. Will you allow me to share my strength with you?"

Tristan nodded and placed his hands in hers. Sabine repeated the ancient words for protection and vitality, allowing her power to flow down her arms and through him.

His blue eyes widened, and he gripped her hands tightly. His wings snapped out, the white and golden feathers brilliant against the light from the oil lanterns. "Lyra. She… lives? She is Aetherbound?"

Sabine stared at him in shock. The shape of the eyes and the coloring of his wings were undeniable. "You're her father?"

Aeron stilled. "She's yours? By the Song, Tristan. I did not know Lyra was of your blood. I would have tried to get word to you."

Tristan's expression was thunderous. "Tell me what you know."

"We managed to smuggle her into Imenel almost a year ago," Aeron said, removing the neck shackle from the last prisoner. "The bastards left her for dead. It took a long time for her to recover, even with Fiona's help. She was slated to be sent to the islands on our next trip, but our Aderylin arrived before then."

Tristan's gaze whipped back to Sabine. "You can sense her?"

Sabine closed her eyes, reaching for Lyra with her thoughts. "She's with her mother, Thalassa, and one of my trusted warriors. They're freeing the prisoners on the upper levels and are approaching the surface."

"My clan is waiting to take them and the rest of the aderyan to safety," Malek said, studying the last device.

Tristan's eyes silvered, and he snarled. "Haven't your kind done enough?"

Sabine squeezed Tristan's hands, drawing his attention

back to her. "Malek has been helping to protect her since we found her in Imenel. He would no more harm her than he would me. Lyra's a remarkable child and is very much loved."

Malek's eyes warmed, and a rush of love swept through their bond.

"You've never spoken of your daughter," Efa said quietly.

"I—" Tristan's voice broke off, and he lowered his head. "I've only seen her twice. The first was when she was born. I was allowed to ease Ceridwen's birthing pains and hold my daughter for mere moments before she was taken from me."

Tristan lifted his head, his stormy blue eyes filled with a fierce anger. "The second time they brought her to me, they placed a knife against her throat as a warning. Ceridwen pleaded with me to bind Lyra's magic, rather than have her subjected to the same torments they inflicted upon the rest of us. Neither of us believed they would cut off a child's wings. After Ceridwen and I refused to couple again, Typheron led us to believe our daughter was dead."

Sabine wrapped her arms around the man as he wept. She lifted her head to meet Malek's furious gaze. He turned back to the device on the third captive and thrust his dragonfire into the lock, shattering it into pieces.

She stroked Tristan's hair and murmured, "Lyra is alive and whole. I've returned her wings. Your daughter has been learning what it means to be aderyan. Both Aeron and Thalassa have taken her under their wings, guiding and teaching her in your absence. She flies now, Tristan."

Efa kneeled beside Tristan. "Your daughter and her mother both live. That's more than many of us can claim."

Tristan lifted his head and snapped his wings against his back. "If you intend to kill Typheron, I will aid you."

"Typheron's holed up in his lair," the other captive said, rubbing his neck where the shackle had pierced his skin.

Sabine refilled the cup of water and offered it to him. He closed his eyes and downed it quickly.

Aeron frowned. "How do you know this, Jac?"

"They brought me up an hour ago," Jac said with a scowl. "Typheron enjoys taking us down there for his little amusements. You've missed a great deal of *amusement* in the years since your escape, Aeron."

Aeron flinched. It was barely noticeable, but Jac's words had obviously hit their mark.

She moved in front of Jac and said, "I saw the conditions of the aderyans' so-called refuge in Imenel. I've seen some of what your people have suffered in this prison. I've witnessed the careless disregard Typheron and others like him have for your lives. Yet when Aeron learned I intended to travel to the Sky Cities and attempt to free your people, he was the first to step forward to aid me."

Jac's jaw clenched. "He should not have come back. He surrendered his wings, yet here he stands reborn."

Efa stepped toward him. "We can argue about this later. Aeron had the courage to do what many of us have only considered. That he found his wings again only makes us stronger."

Sabine held out her hands. "I would offer you the same strength I gave the others. Will you accept a gift of magic?"

"I'd be a fool to refuse," he said, taking Sabine's hands.

Sabine whispered the ancient words of protection and fortitude that formed in her thoughts. Her magic flowed down her arms and encompassed Jac, spreading across his body and into the tips of his dusky rose wings. He swayed from the sudden rush, and his eyes shone with unshed tears.

Blossom flew into the room, her wings tinged with red. "Incoming drakes, people! Wings up and swords out!"

Aeron tossed a sword to Tristan and unsheathed the Aetherbound blade. "We're a little short on weapons."

Sabine removed the dagger strapped to her thigh and handed it to Jac. He hesitated. After a moment, his hand curled around the hilt and he gave her a curt nod.

Malek offered his knife to Efa.

The aderyan woman stared at him for a moment before her lips curved in a wicked smile. "A pretty boy dragon just gave me a weapon? Didn't think your kind parted with your hoarded treasures."

"I'd appreciate it if you avoided stabbing me with it."

Efa's eyes silvered as the knife gleamed in the lamplight. "Want to know what I'd appreciate?"

Blossom's eyes rounded. "Don't say it, don't say it…"

"Efa," Tristan said sharply, nodding at Sabine.

"That pretty boy dragon is mine," Sabine said as the first drake stepped into the room. Power shot out from her fingertips, incinerating the drake where he stood. She narrowed her eyes on Efa. "I protect those who are mine."

Malek's gaze warmed. "As do I."

Two more drakes rushed into the room, one after the other. Malek and Aeron swept forward with the other aderyan a step behind them. Their movements were a blur as they phased in and out of sight, dispatching both creatures with deadly efficiency.

Bane was going to be so disappointed he missed this.

"More are coming," Blossom said, landing on Sabine's shoulder. "What's the plan? Barbecue? Slice and dice? Magical whammy?"

Sabine placed her hand on the ground and closed her eyes, ignoring the sounds of battle in front of her. A wave of queasiness washed over her as her magic brushed against a large null space.

"Two dozen drakes or wyverns and a dozen aderyan are on this level. More are moving this way." She tilted her head, trying to understand the stone's song. "There's a greater dragon almost directly below us."

Tristan cut down one of the drakes and said, "They will not kill our people unless absolutely necessary. If they do, Ishu falls. We need to go after Typheron before his wyverns can reach him."

"We'll have to fight our way to the other end of the tunnel," Jac said, using his wings to push back away from one of the drakes. "The entrance to Typheron's lair is on the far end of this level."

Sabine swept her gaze over the aderyan. Despite her efforts to share power with them, they were malnourished and exhausted. Fighting off dozens of enemies would weaken all of them. Even with the boost the Well had given her, she likely wouldn't have enough magic to fight off the lesser dragons *and* Typheron.

Pressing one hand against the ground, she lifted the other and shoved a wave of rock upward to seal the doorway.

Malek spun toward her. "Sabine?"

"I'm making my own entrance," Sabine said and reached for the land's magic beneath her feet. The ground trembled, forming a fissure in the rock floor. With her power, she punched through the rock.

Efa and Jac gasped and scrambled backwards.

"I thought the stories and songs of the Shining Ones were exaggerated," Efa whispered, lowering the knife.

Aeron flared his wings. "They were not."

Tristan leaned down to study the narrow hole Sabine was burrowing. "She is our Aderylin. The elements and land bow to her will. If she wishes to engage the dragon directly without any other distractions, who are we to say otherwise?"

Blossom grinned. "I like him. We're keeping him, right?"

Malek placed his hand on Sabine's shoulder and said silently, *"Take what you need."*

Holding the mountain steady so it didn't fall on their heads, Sabine carefully widened the crack. She reached for Malek's power, using the heat from his dragonfire to soften the rock and make it easier to shape. The heat molded the rock like glass, smoothing the edges until it shone like Malek's obsidian scales.

Stairs. They needed stairs downward.

Tristan's shocked gaze flew toward her and Malek. "She wields dragonfire?"

Aeron placed his hand on Tristan's shoulder and said, "They are bound together. He has claimed her as his mate before his clan, and the land accepts him as hers."

Tristan's expression darkened. "This should not be possible."

"I thought the same," Aeron said. "Yet he can wake her from Veylara."

Tristan reared back, staring at Aeron in shock.

Sabine released the magic with a gasp and slumped against Malek's leg. He reached down and drew her upward and into his arms. She leaned into his strength, knowing she was dancing perilously close to the edge of exhaustion. Malek tilted her head back and kissed her. Her hands curled into his shirt as she breathed in his dragonfire and his magic.

Heat and power flooded through her. It wasn't the same as the water from the Well of Dreams, but it was the boost she'd desperately needed. She broke their kiss and pressed her forehead against his chest, breathing him in.

He ran his hand over her hair and asked silently, *"You didn't take enough. Is it Lachlina?"*

Sabine frowned and glanced down at her wrist, suddenly uneasy. She hadn't thought about the renegade goddess for the past several hours. *"Lachlina's been silent within me since the urn ceremony. I don't want to weaken you before we face Typheron."*

He pulled her closer. *"I have some fight in me yet. Besides, I have plans with my mate later tonight."*

She lifted her head to meet his gaze. *"Good. She has plans for you too."*

"It smells weird down there," Blossom said, landing on the ground and peering into the hole. "We had a rule in the garden about not flying into dark holes that smelled funny. I'm starting to think there might be something to that."

"If Typheron is down there, I need to go first," Malek said, placing his hand against her midsection and gently moving her away from the tunnel. "Even in human form, I have more resistance to dragonfire. I'll need room to shift."

She didn't like it. They were always stronger together, but Malek was right. He had the best chance of handling the initial assault, even if the thought of letting him go made her heart hurt.

"Sabine," Malek said, and tilted her head back. "I need to know you're safe."

She grabbed his shirt, pulled him down toward her, and kissed him soundly. "You can have your head start, but that's all I'm willing to give you. Take care of my dragon."

"Always," Malek said and lifted his head to meet Aeron's gaze. "Shield her as you can. Typheron will focus on her the minute he realizes she's there."

Aeron inclined his head.

Gripping his sword tightly, Malek leaped over the edge and descended into the darkness. Blossom grinned, pinched her nose, and changed into a glowbug before diving after him.

Sabine inhaled sharply.

"Blossom!" she whispered loudly, but there was no response.

The foolish pixie was going to get eaten, roasted, or end up saving the day in the most unconventional of ways.

CHAPTER 57

"We've cleared the uppermost level of the prison," Levin's voice sounded in Malek's thoughts. *"Bane escorted a group to the surface but went back inside. Idola's giant golden beast of a hound ran past our people, plowed straight into the demon and aderyan, and went into the prison with Lyra. Bane went after him."*

"Lyra's with Basco?" Malek asked in alarm.

"She leaped right on his back like he was a thontin or a thundertusk. The girl's gone, Malek. We're keeping an eye out for them, but they've disappeared."

Malek frowned and carefully climbed down the rock steps, navigating by feel alone. Bane wouldn't allow anything to happen to Lyra, but the hound's presence was worrisome. Basco must have run nonstop and through the fighting to reach Ishu so quickly.

"I'm about to engage Typheron. We believe he's beneath the lowest level of the prison. Notify Captain Fandrin. I want patrols circling Ishu's midpoint and searching for an alternate entrance. If Typheron's dug himself in, he has a plan and an exit strategy. He's not leaving Ishu alive."

"Any chance you'll wait for reinforcements?"

"They have us pinned. Wyverns and drakes on one side, and Typheron on the other. Sabine's running low on magic, and the winged aderyan we've located aren't in much better condition than the other captives."

A glowbug darted past him, the flicker of its illuminated posterior disappearing into the darkness. Malek stared after the pixie and mentally cursed. If Typheron could see through glamour, there was a possibility he could see through Blossom's illusion.

Malek hastened his steps, and landed on the rocky ground at the end of the tunnel. An enormous earthen chamber had been hollowed out. Dozens of oil lanterns lit the room, casting a glow on mounds of gold, precious jewels, priceless works of art, and other artifacts. In the center of the dragon's hoard was an enormous yellow dragon with scales that glittered like a thousand suns and cast rainbows against the walls.

Typheron.

The ancient dragon lowered its head to the ground and blinked golden eyes at Malek. *"You were not who I was expecting. I suppose I should have anticipated the folly of youth."*

"Did you think I would stand by and do nothing when you abducted my mate, chained her in iron, and imprisoned her?" Malek said the last on a roar, his power blanketing the room. The mountain trembled around him.

Typheron huffed, steam rising from his nostrils. *"It is precisely your mate who interests me, Malek. When your uncle first mentioned your clan's asinine plan to locate the portal artifacts, none of us considered the possibility a Tuatha Dé lived on this side of the Veil."*

Malek narrowed his eyes. "You will not get your claws on her again, Typheron. You betrayed us and broke our most ancient law."

"You were not expected to survive, much less succeed," Typheron said with a snarl. *"How did you come to find her, Malek? Where is the secondary portal?"*

Malek didn't respond, trying to get a better look at his surroundings. Typheron was stalling for some reason. He didn't see any sign of Blossom, but the dragon's massive bulk was blocking a large portion of the chamber. Typheron was hiding something.

"You don't know, do you? Your so-called mate hasn't confided in you, has she?" Typheron's laughter rang in his head. *"She could not have come into her magic without access to a secondary portal. The Tuatha Dé are bound to the world where they are birthed until they come into their full powers. They must pass through the ether to unlock their potential. Even then, they are malleable for quite some time."*

"Is that what you intended? To try and mold my mate into something for your own purposes?" Malek snapped, his patience at an end.

"She is the key, you fool!" Typheron snarled. *"Unless we gain access to the ether, her magic has the potential to destroy us. I have no intention of allowing her to survive and becoming the Obsidian Clan's puppet."*

Malek took a threatening step toward Typheron, preparing to transform. Typheron shifted his massive bulk, revealing iron posts and chains dangling from the walls.

All were empty except for one, where an aderyan woman had been chained. Her dark hair covered her features except for striking gold wings that were fanned out and fastened to the wall with iron spokes. She was thin, her skin almost translucent, except for her large belly, rounded with pregnancy.

The sight filled him with rage. Piles of bones and feathers lined the wall near her feet, while other sets of wings had been mounted on the nearby walls as macabre trophies. No matter what had happened during the war, there was no justification for the abuses the aderyan had suffered.

Typheron lifted one of his talons, and pulled on an iron chain. It lifted the aderyan upright until her beautiful face was awash in excruciating pain. With tears streaking down her face, she opened her mouth and began to sing.

Her voice ripped through Malek's mind. He tried to summon his power, but the melody wrapped tighter around him, sliding under his thoughts until he could scarcely recall his true form. Her song pounded against him, and he went down on one knee, trying to fight against the haunting melody shredding his psyche.

"Malek, you must not engage Typheron underground," his mother's panicked voice sounded in his head. *"He's been feeding off the aderyan's magic. He's somehow regained abilities we thought had been lost."*

"Too late," he managed to get the words out. His gaze fell on the piles of bones and feathers, and with it came the dark realization Typheron had truly been *feeding* off the aderyan. It was an abomination of the highest order. Sabine's earlier words about how the land itself had turned away suddenly made sense.

A sound from the tunnel sent a rush of panic through him.

"Sabine! Turn back!" he shouted in his head, trying to reach her through their bond. The song clamped tighter around him, fracturing his focus. He gritted his teeth and tried to reach her again, determined to warn her before it was too late.

He pushed against the song, unwilling to burn the aderyan with his dragonfire. She was an innocent. He had to overcome her song without fracturing her mind in the process.

Aeron landed on the ground with Sabine in his arms. Efa, Tristan, and Jac were a step behind them.

"*Ah, guests,*" Typheron said, his gold gaze focused on Sabine.

"You dare use her suffering against Malek?" Sabine demanded, silencing the woman's voice with a wave of her hand. "How—"

Sabine's words cut off abruptly, and she gasped in pain. Malek leaped to his feet at the sight of Sabine's own dagger embedded in her midsection. She staggered, and fell to her knees. Rage roared through him, clearing his muddled thoughts from the aderyan's song. He shifted in a blinding flash of light, his fury pounding at his temples.

He slammed his tail down, creating a barrier between Sabine and the aderyan. Aeron and Tristan whirled on Jac, their weapons rising automatically to strike him down.

Jac stumbled back, tears streaking down his face, his hands covered with Sabine's blood. "F-F-Forgive me. I had no choice." He gestured helplessly to the chained woman. "Winifred. She won't survive the birth. He promised—If I—" He choked out a sob.

"Lower your weapons," Sabine said and yanked out the silver dagger. It fell to the ground with a clatter. She pressed her hand against her stomach and leaned against him. "Our battle is with Typheron, not one another."

Typheron's laughter sounded in his head. "*How marvelous. Such drama. Even now, the young Tuatha Dé strives to save those who would strike her down. And the dragon does nothing to defend his so-called mate.*"

Malek snarled at him. "*Levin, pull another squadron from the sky and have them clear the prison. I need Bane down here now. Sabine's hurt.*"

Typheron inhaled deeply. "*Come now, Malek. Do you smell that? The blood of a Tuatha Dé holds such power. Her very essence draws you to her, calling to the hunger within you. It is her magic you desire and hunger for. With her blood, we can destroy the barriers to the portal and fly among the stars once again."*

"*You will not touch her,*" Malek snarled, lashing out with the sharpened edge of his tail. The blow struck Typheron's side and sent him crashing into piles of precious gemstones and gold, scattering them across the chamber. With a roar, Malek wrapped his power around Typheron, forcing it beneath the dragon's scales with burning ferocity and slamming him against the wall.

Dust and debris fell to the ground as the mountain around them trembled.

Typheron hissed at him. "*You'll pay for that.*"

His topaz scales became blinding, spinning rainbows on the walls and ceiling. The aderyan crumpled to the ground. Malek blinked, the shifting colors hypnotizing in their fluctuating intensity. He couldn't focus or move, trapped in the colors that surrounded him.

Typheron reared back, preparing to unleash a torrent of dragonfire. A dozen small pink dragons burst into the room from behind Typheron. With high-pitched shouts of glee and a few taunts about the puny size of Typheron's scales, the pixies wove trails of light throughout the room, masking the hypnotic effects of Typheron's power.

Malek roared and charged forward. His jaws clamped around Typheron's throat, preventing him from incinerating everyone in the room. Using the force of his body, Malek shoved Typheron against the far wall. Dust and rocks fell around them with larger boulders beginning to dislodge. One way or another, he was getting this damn dragon away from his mate.

"Hit him again, Malek!" Blossom shouted. "Tie his tail into a knot!"

The other pixies cheered.

Aeron gestured to the captive aderyan woman. "Jac, Efa, get Winifred out of those chains. Tristan, help me slow the bleeding."

Typheron fought like a dragon possessed. Malek's jaws clamped tighter around his throat, using his claws and tail to pin the older dragon. The damned bastard was strong.

The mountain shook and trembled around them. A hole in the wall began to form. A large obsidian claw dug into the crack, widening it. A familiar golden eye peered inside and narrowed at the sight of them.

"Mine," Darius said with a snarl.

"You weren't invited to this party," Malek said, swiping outward with his tail to suppress Typheron's thrashing. He needed more room to maneuver. Then he would gladly tie Typheron's tail into a knot, right before stuffing it up his ass.

"I invited myself," Darius said and clawed at the wall, enlarging the hole. *"He abducted MY new daughter. From my fucking home. You think I'm going to sit back and let you kill him without taking my pound of scales?"*

"Fine. I'll share."

Malek reared back and shoved Typheron through the hole. The dragon screamed and tried to fly, but Malek and Darius both dove after him.

"You're all mad!" Typheron shouted, his mental voice resounding in their heads. *"I am a Triumvir! The head of my clan! You would choose a Tuatha Dé over your own kind?"*

Nymira shot downward, a stunning emerald blur that streaked across the sky. Her sharpened tail whipped out lightning fast, striking against Typheron's scales and injecting lethal poison beneath them.

She raked her talons across his back and said, *"Tuatha Dé or not, she's a beloved daughter of the Obsidian Clan. And you're the bastard who cracked my new window!"*

Malek exchanged a look with his father. Moving in

tandem, they shredded Typheron's wings and flayed the scales from his body. As Typheron's lifeless body fell toward its watery grave to the ocean below, Malek watched in satisfaction as the Topaz Clan leader's reign came to its final end.

As the water splashed upward, Malek flapped his wings and soared toward Ishu and his mate.

Raynor's voice shouted in his head, *"The chains are down! The bastards have blown up the chains from Direh. We're losing Kavi!"*

CHAPTER 58

Small rocks and dirt continued to fall from the ceiling, coating Sabine's hair and skin. Jac may not have used an iron weapon on her, but it wouldn't be long before she lost consciousness. She was already light-headed.

Sabine dug her fingers into the dirt, trying to rise above the pain and stabilize the mountain with her rapidly-depleting strength. It would be much easier to mend a dragon-sized hole in the middle of a mountain if she could reach for the land's full strength. But the barrier between the land and sky was one her magic couldn't breach. At least Malek had prevented them from being burned to a crisp by evicting Typheron.

Efa ran over to them and kneeled beside her. "How bad is she?"

Tristan placed his hands on Sabine's stomach, his wings beating softly behind him. "I cannot stave off the blood loss for long. Our healers are either dead or too weak to aid her."

Aeron cradled her in his arms. "Aderylin, we must get you to the temple."

She shook her head, unwilling to break contact with the

ground. "No. The mountain will collapse if I don't hold it. Bane and Thalassa will get your people out. I just need to buy them enough time."

Aeron exchanged a look with Tristan. "If the aderyan abandon Ishu, the rest of the Aeries will fall into the sea. The wingless do not possess the magic to keep the islands afloat."

Efa straightened and glanced over her shoulder. "Jac and Winifred, we need to get upstairs and unchain the others."

Jac shook his head, his arms wrapped around the dark-haired woman. "No good, Efa. Winifred can barely walk. I won't leave her."

Efa muttered a curse. "I'm a flier, not a swimmer. I'll go save our people by myself."

Tristan reached for her hand. "No, Efa. There is another way."

Efa pressed her lips together and nodded. "So be it."

"Bane can heal Sabine and then she can fix everything," Blossom exclaimed, still in her pink dragon form. "Pixies, fan out! Find the hungry demon with the starfruit essence."

The pixies squealed and a dozen tiny pink dragons darted in all directions, some going out the side of the mountain while others flew up the tunnel and into the main part of the prison.

"Demon?" Tristan asked, his brow furrowed.

Aeron nodded. "Our Aderylin calls many to her cause, including the demons and flutterfolk."

"They could have picked a better glamour," Efa muttered.

"Blossom is often full of surprises," Sabine said, taking a shuddering breath as a wave of dizziness washed over her. She couldn't even reach for Malek with her thoughts, or it might break the tie she had with the land. If she faltered, even for a moment, the mountain would bury them and any remaining captives.

She needed to hold out just a bit longer.

Efa spread her dusk-colored wings and said, "Take back your magic, Aderylin. Use the strength you gifted me to do what you must. I will act as part of the triad."

"I offer mine as well," Tristan said and spread his wings with a flourish. "Save our people, Aderylin. If the mountain goes, so do we. It will be my honor to act as part of the triad."

Aeron's wings flared out, surrounding her with their feathery softness. "If they provide you with their strength, I will hold the tether and complete the triad."

Sabine wasn't sure what he meant, but the other aderyan seemed to understand. Their power pulsed with every beat of their wings and spread over her like a cool breeze. Their strength merged with hers, and her weakness flowed to Aeron. Through the oath he'd sworn, they were bound together and their life force shared across the ether. Should she falter or die, Aeron would join her.

This was what it meant to be Aetherbound.

She hadn't understood.

"I'll do what I can," Sabine said, pressing her hand against the ground. She closed her eyes, using her blood to strengthen her connection to the land. The song of the stone rose within her, its rumbling voice thudding within her like a second heartbeat.

Yet there was a hollow echo, where the mountain had been sundered and the protections ripped away. Pulling upward from the rock beneath them, she carefully shaped the stone until it nearly matched the resonance of the original song.

Something was missing.

Aeron opened his mouth and began to sing, his voice a melodious tenor that evoked images of the sky at dawn. She drifted upon the magic like a feather upon the wind, searching for something she couldn't explain. Efa and Tristan's voices joined Aeron's, and their combined song added a richness and depth her magic lacked. Understanding intuitively what was missing from the mountain, Sabine wove the triad's power through the stone.

The wall reformed and became whole, with an added layer that was derived solely from aderyan magic. The power itself should have been foreign to her, but she recalled the way she'd surrendered part of herself to give the aderyan back their wings. All magic came from the same place and required some sort of sacrifice.

It was born in the ether.

They had all sacrificed to make it theirs.

The aderyan understood the concept of balance far better than the fae.

Then again, they'd always been closer to the gods.

Sabine looked up into Aeron's eyes, the barriers between them stripped away and their thoughts laid bare. He loved her, not as Malek did or even Bane, but rather with a quiet reverence their people had once shown the gods. His world had been nothing but darkness before she came. She was their Aderylin, their Divine Light who could cast her grace upon his people and share the light of her soul with them, or turn away and abandon them to the darkness once more.

He needed to be important to her to ensure his people were never forgotten again. He would be anything she needed or perform any task in the hopes his people wouldn't be cast aside. Gods. Please don't let them be forgotten again.

Sabine cupped Aeron's face and kissed him softly. If she lived for eternity, she would never, or could ever, forget them.

Humbled beyond imagining and far weaker than she had been, she released the magic and collapsed in his arms. Dimly, she heard Malek's voice calling out to her in warning, but the words floated away like feathers upon the wind.

And Aeron held her and wept.

~

THE MOMENT SABINE slipped away from him, Malek shot upward with a burst of speed. She was alive, but barely. Her life force was fading by the second.

He passed by the place where he'd thrown Typheron out of the mountain and mentally cursed. Sabine had already sealed the hole, or Malek would have gone back in the way he came out. She wouldn't have wasted magic repairing it unless he'd given her no choice.

Malek rose to the top of the mountain and shouted, *"Levin, get a healer down to the lowest level now! I'm losing her!"*

"They're working as fast as they can, Malek. She barricaded part of the mountain. If we blast through, we'll collapse the tunnels. One wrong move, and we crush her instead of saving her."

Malek snarled, eyeing the mountain for possible points of entry. He needed to find Thalassa. If she could reopen the secret entrance, he could reach Sabine quickly.

"Where's Thalassa?"

"Inside the prison bringing out some of the captives. She's the only one able to keep them calm. We were moving them to Kavi, but Raynor sent out the alarm. We're evacuating the island. Dammit, Malek. What's left of the Topaz and Garnet forces are converging on the last of the Kavi chains. They're trying to take down the island, even without Typheron at the head. My mate is still over there."

Malek was half-tempted to find Typheron's corpse, reanimate him, and kill him all over again. *"Find Linus. Typheron's son is pulling the strings now. He's as much a coward as the old man and is likely hiding somewhere on Ishu. We'll get Esme out."*

From his vantage point, he spotted a large group of aderyan captives huddled together. Several wyverns were nearby standing guard but without some direction, their presence would likely cause more damage than help. In the distance toward Kavi, he caught sight of more aerial battles being fought.

His parents shot past him, cutting through the sky as they headed toward Kavi.

Malek reached for his sister with his thoughts. *"Kaia, finalize the evacuation orders and leave Kavi immediately. I want a full squadron escorting you to Ishu. Bring Esme and Rika."*

"Already done, big brother," Kaia said, exhaustion coloring her words. *"We're on our way, loaded up with supplies and healing tonics for the aderyan. Esme's using some sort of witchy illusion to keep us out of the fighting. Rika's still spitting out predictions. She says you need to get to Sabine right now. Tell her to remember the Huntsman's warning."*

Malek turned and dove downward, following the slope of the mountain toward the hidden entrance Thalassa had shown them. He could always try to blast it open.

A tiny pink dragon shot upward in front of him and he jerked upright, halting in midair.

"You're not the hungry demon!"

Malek blinked, unsure which of the pixies was addressing him. He huffed and shook his head no, annoyed by his inability to communicate.

"I need a hungry demon to heal Queen Sabine. Have you seen one? He smells like starfruit."

Aha. Blossom sent out the recruits.

Malek nodded and pointed to the ground with his tail. He dove downward, glancing over his shoulder to make sure the pixie was following him. He landed outside of the prison entrance and transformed into his human form.

Several of the nearby aderyan gasped and moved away from him.

"Show me the fastest way to get to Sabine," Malek said to

the pixie. "I'll see what I can do about healing her and getting you another sip of the starfruit essence."

"This way! Come quick! I'll show you right now!"

Malek darted after the pixie, determined to get to Sabine. At least this time, he didn't need to worry about keeping his presence a secret.

CHAPTER 59

$\mathcal{A}$ cold, wet nose nuzzled her arm.

Sabine blinked open her eyes to stare up at a large golden hound peering down at her. "Basco? What are you doing here?"

He whined unhappily.

Bane lifted his hand from her abdomen, ignoring the three glittering pink dragons flying around him. "He was bringing us to you. A few more minutes, and even my efforts at healing you would have failed."

One of the pixies sniffed at Bane. "He smells like starfruit."

"Yum! Can we try licking him?"

Bane growled. Two of the pixies dove for cover behind a fallen rock.

The third pink dragon swished her tail and said in Blossom's voice, "No licking demons! They're like poisonous frogs. Sheesh."

Bane narrowed his eyes on the hovering pink dragon. Blossom gave him a toothy dragon grin that was more than a little disturbing.

Sabine pressed her hand against her stomach, feeling the smooth skin beneath her fingertips. Bane's healing hadn't helped the exhaustion or weakness plaguing her, but at least she was alive.

Aeron helped her sit up, his soft wings brushing against her skin.

Lyra stood next to Basco, her hand buried in his thick golden fur. She tilted her head, watching Sabine with solemn eyes. Sabine sighed, unsurprised Lyra had found her way back down to the prison.

"It was risky coming down here again, Lyra. I thought you were going to remain on the surface with your mother and Thalassa."

"I had to come."

Sabine arched her brow. "Oh?"

Lyra nodded. "Basco said you needed me. I kept my magic small like you said."

Sabine frowned and studied the hound. With the bond between him and Idola severed, Basco had apparently decided Lyra needed his protection. If Lyra was truly bound to Sabine, she would need such a stalwart defender. Although, she wasn't sure how Lyra's parents would feel about the hound.

Her gaze drifted to Tristan. He stared at his daughter as though memorizing every detail. Aeron touched Sabine's arm and shook his head sadly. Sabine nodded in understanding. They needed to find a way forward and heal the rift Typheron had caused.

Lyra turned to Bane and held out a silver dagger. "Will you kill the one who hurt our Aderylin?"

Bane's lips twitched as he took the dagger. "The little one is growing on me." He held out his hand to Sabine and helped her rise to her feet. "Tell me why I shouldn't kill the talking turkey who stabbed you with your own blade."

Jac cautiously approached them, his arm and wing wrapped protectively around the pregnant woman. She lifted her head wearily, the dark circles under her eyes a stark contrast against her pale and fragile features. Despite her exhaustion, there was an aura of peace that surrounded her as she leaned into Jac's strength. He murmured something to her, his expression filled with love and tenderness.

Sabine kissed Bane's cheek. "Because love should never be punished or used to manipulate. They've been through enough. I won't put them through any more."

Bane sighed. "You forgive far too easily."

Blossom landed on Sabine's shoulder and shed her pink dragon illusion. She sniffed and said, "I love it when those of us with wings get a happily ever after. Now we just need to find the last artifact."

Lyra blinked at Sabine. "I will show you."

Tristan cleared his throat and crouched beside Lyra. "You have seen it in visions?"

Lyra turned to him, her expression puzzled. She touched his face, running her small fingers over his cheek and across his nose. Tristan froze, remaining motionless as she traced the tattoo on the side of his head. She leaned back, her lower lip trembling slightly.

"D-Daddy?"

His eyes glimmered, and he nodded.

Lyra threw her arms around him and buried her face against his neck. "I dreamed of you. You sang to me before I left."

He hugged her tightly, his wings surrounding them. "I sang to both you and your mother in Belon. Every night. Even when I thought you could no longer hear me."

Basco whined and nudged Lyra.

She sniffed and looked over at the hound. "I have to go find it."

"You're talking about the artifact?" Sabine asked.

Lyra nodded. "The dragon was hiding the treasure. Basco says I need to show you where before it's too late. The chains are breaking."

"A chain is only as strong as its weakest link."

The Huntsman's words replayed in Sabine's mind. She turned to Aeron and asked, "Were the chains that tie the islands together always part of the Aeries? Or were they created by the dragons after they claimed this land as theirs?"

"They were a creation of the dragons," Aeron said, his gaze darkening. "When our numbers and magic dwindled, the dragons forged the chains to extend our magic beyond normal boundaries. In exchange for keeping the islands afloat, they demanded a tribute from the other dragon clans."

"How many clans knew of your suffering? How many of them turned a blind eye to your plight?"

Aeron hesitated. "If you had asked me a month ago, I would have said nearly all. I no longer believe that to be true."

Efa gaped at him. "You can't be serious. You think some were ignorant of our suffering?"

Aeron turned back to Sabine and said, "Malek's surprise was genuine, Aderylin. I do not believe he could have deceived you. I heard rumors over the years that I dismissed, but now I wonder if the Topaz and Ruby Clans kept our presence quiet to further their own ambitions and wealth. The Garnet Clan knew, and their tribute amount was offset in exchange for overseeing the prisons."

"Other islands existed before the portal was sealed," Tristan said. "Their names have been lost to us, but the dragons allowed them to fall as a reminder of what would occur should they fail to offer tribute."

Efa crossed her arms over her chest. "Or maybe it was

because they'd killed too many of us to keep the other islands in the air."

Aeron frowned. "You may both be correct."

Sabine looked around the glittering hoard. "This is the result of these tributes?"

"Indeed," Aeron said quietly, surveying the riches lying among the bones of his people.

Basco whined again and pawed the ground.

Bane frowned and thrust his clawed hand in Basco's fur. His eyes flashed silver, and his skin flickered with a bluish light. "It's here. The godsforsaken artifact is in this room. Spread out and start searching."

Sabine swept her gaze over the glittering hoard of treasure. Mounds of gold and jewels were scattered throughout the chamber, along with paintings, weapons, and peculiar devices that appeared to be dwarven or aderyan crafted. Malek and Typheron had made a mess out of the cavern. It would take them days to find a single golden quill.

Lyra took Sabine's hand and pointed on the far side of the chamber. "It's over there."

She allowed Lyra to lead her across the piles of treasure while Basco remained at their side. Diamonds, rubies, and emeralds as large as Lyra's hand glinted in the torchlight. Strange statues of creatures she'd never seen and paintings depicting places that no longer existed were heaped together like rubble. The aderyan moved among the hoard, their eyes lingering on items that had likely once belonged to their people.

"Some of these might be nice as stepping stones in my new garden," Blossom said, flying off Sabine's shoulder to inspect the gemstones.

Sabine frowned at Blossom. "You're not decorating Malek's garden with priceless gems."

"Well, not the whole garden," Blossom agreed, picking up

a thumb-sized emerald. "I need to borrow Bane's traveler's bag. These are too heavy to carry home."

Bane narrowed his eyes on her. "No. Look for the damn quill."

"After we find it?"

"No."

"I'll tell you where we hid your horn sharpener."

"I knew it," Bane said with a snarl. "That's it. You're lunch."

"Hungry demon!" Blossom shrieked, darting across the cavern and out of Bane's reach. The other pixies squealed and darted away, zipping through the cavern and leaving trails of pixie dust in their wake.

Sabine sighed and pushed aside another painting blocking their way.

Lyra halted in front of a toppled pedestal. A small decorative metal box was laying beside it, the metal gleaming dully in the torchlight. Basco whined and nudged the box before looking back at Sabine.

She inhaled sharply. "Iron?"

Bane picked up the box and looked it over. "Dwarven workmanship. They don't usually work with iron. I don't see a way to open it."

Aeron approached them and asked, "May I?"

Bane handed it to him. Aeron frowned and studied the box, turning it over in his hands.

He shook his head. "There is something aderyan about it as well, but I do not see a lock or latch."

"There's glamour on it," Blossom shouted from high above them.

Sabine looked up at her. "What sort?"

Blossom landed on her outstretched hand, darting an uneasy glance in Bane's direction. "It's pixie glamour. Strong stuff. Smells funny with the iron though."

Sabine considered the box. "When we were in Imenel, Fiona told us a story about a pixie working with the dwarves to build an iron house to trap a dragon. Could that story be related to this box?"

Blossom cocked her head. "It's the right size for a house. I prefer flowerpots though."

Sabine made a noise of agreement. "In the story, the dragon couldn't open the door. He tried using his dragonfire, but the locks held. The pixie had to open it for the dragon to get inside."

Blossom's eyes widened. "You think there's a tiny dragon in there?"

"No, but I believe there is always some truth to legends," Sabine said with a smile, recalling Malek's amusement. "What better way to hide instructions for future generations than by weaving it into a charming story? Not even the dragons would find such a tale to be threatening."

Bane eyed the box. "Open the damn box, and you can place three thumb-sized gemstones in the traveler's pack."

Blossom straightened. "Four!"

"Three, and I won't eat you *today*."

"Done!" Blossom grinned and rubbed her hands together. "Okay. Lemme think." She lifted into the air and floated over the box. She whistled sharply, and the other two pixies emerged from their hiding places.

They linked hands with Blossom and flapped their wings. Glittering pixie dust streamed downward, illuminating the iron. An image of an eye with wings appeared in the metal.

"Three by three is nine. Nine gemstones! Let's go pick them out."

"I said three," Bane said with a snarl.

Blossom blinked innocently. "Who's to say it didn't take all three of us to break the glamour?"

Sabine bit back a smile. "Go ahead, Blossom. Take your friends and select your rewards."

The pixies whooped and darted downward to search the piles of treasure.

"There should be a latch here," Aeron murmured and pressed his finger against one of the sharpened spokes on the outside of the box. He traced his blood over the eye symbol until the box clicked open.

He lifted the lid to reveal a single golden quill nestled safely upon a dark velvet cushion. The aderyan formed a circle around them, watching silently as Aeron withdrew the artifact.

Lyra looked up at Tristan and whispered, "That's it! I saw true!"

Tristan ran his hand over Lyra's golden hair. "You are truly Aetherbound, little bird. In time, you will become fierce indeed."

Lyra beamed a smile at him.

Aeron lifted his head to meet Sabine's gaze. "Before you came, many of us had lost hope. Our wings and our pride had been stolen from us. We lacked the strength to fight and sought escape, forced to leave behind our brothers and sisters."

Efa placed her hand on Aeron's shoulder, her wings brushing softly against his. Aeron gave her a sad smile before turning back to Sabine.

"When we met, I recognized the light within you and knew you to be our Aderylin. For the first time in centuries, I knew what it was to hope. When you returned my wings, the Song rose within me once again. Your light touched all of us that day, and I knew I would follow you beyond the ether and back again." He cradled the quill with unmistakable reverence and held it out to her. "I offer this gift to you, on behalf of our people, so that you might continue to restore the balance. Please, Aderylin. Let my people hear our Song once again. Allow your light to embrace all of us."

Sabine blinked back the tears that threatened and took the golden quill. A cool breeze rushed through her and slowly began to build. The distant sound of drums pounded in her ears. Suddenly, the light and airy register of a flute broke through the rhythm, sending the magic soaring through her.

The goddess marks on her wrist flared to life, and Lachlina's voice echoed in her thoughts.

Daughter. Accept this gift. Embrace the truth and your destiny.

It wasn't a gift. There was always a cost to such magic. And one person's truth was often another's lie. She didn't know if accepting this power was part of her destiny. But if she refused, the fate of Aeslion and all those who lived here would be at stake.

That was something she could never abide.

She held out her hand to Bane, and he pricked the tip of her finger with his dagger. As she offered her blood as a sacrifice and a binding for the power, she repeated the oath she had first sworn months earlier.

"I claim you, by blood and magic. In tribute to the gods and the last sacrifice of the goddess Lachlina, I swear by all I am and the last of the magic of this world to uphold my family's oath in defense from those who would see this world destroyed."

The quill began to glow brighter and sharper until it was nearly blinding. Power shot through her hand where she gripped the artifact. The marks on her wrist burned, searing her skin from the force of Lachlina's anger. Each of her skin markings flared to life, burning anew as if they were fresh and newly scored. It would appear the goddess was in the mood to have her reckoning, no matter what innocent lives the delay cost.

"You disappoint me, my little golden flower," Lachlina said with a sigh. *"Can you not see that the dragons will do everything possible to destroy us? You may believe yours is different, but he cannot change his nature. Their purpose is to destroy, while ours is to create."*

"And with that, there is balance," Sabine said, wrapping her arms around herself. *"You found that same balance with Vestior once upon a time. Would you begrudge me that same gift?"*

"Yes, if it saved you from an eternity of pain."

The agony from her marks halted abruptly, but she could sense it lurking just under the surface. No matter the reprieve, it would change nothing.

"On this, we will never agree. I will not give Malek up, no matter what threats you weave or the pain you cause. When his people turned against me, he fought for me. He was willing to sacrifice everything, including his beloved family and his home, to protect me."

Lachlina fell silent for a moment. *"If given a choice between saving your dragon or saving Aeslion, which would you choose?"*

Sensing his approach, Sabine turned to see Malek dropping into the chamber from the tunnel above. Their eyes locked, and Sabine's heart pounded at the unmistakable heat and tenderness in his eyes. As he crossed the chamber toward her, everyone and everything faded away except the dragon she loved.

And in that moment, she knew beyond all doubts the answer to Lachlina's question.

"If it came down to saving Malek or saving Aeslion, there wouldn't be a choice. Malek would be at my side saving Aeslion. He has always done whatever's necessary to help me restore the balance, no matter the cost."

Malek drew her into his arms and kissed her, the heat from his dragonfire chasing away Lachlina's ire. Sabine leaned into his touch, her body molding perfectly against his. No matter how much Lachlina tried to convince her otherwise, Sabine trusted Malek above all others—especially with her heart.

"In time, you will see the truth," Lachlina said, her voice holding a touch of regret. *"Until then, accept this gift and remember your promise. Once you have healed the aderyan, you will return to the dryad grove and allow me the use of a vessel, so I might visit with my daughter once more."*

It was as though a key suddenly turned in a lock, unleashing a torrent of magic. Power slammed into her with the force of a hurricane, and she cried out from the onslaught. Her skin glowed with unspeakable brilliance, radiating with an intensity that made Typheron's scales nothing more than a shadow of a memory.

"It's the artifact," Bane called out.

"Major magic coming through, people!" Blossom shouted. "Pixies, hold on to your wings!"

Malek's arms tightened around her. "Sabine, you have to embrace the magic. Don't fight against it."

Her blood roared within her, and she felt the answering heartbeat within the land. A wind whipped through the chamber, lifting gold coins and gemstones in a cyclone around them. The torch light flickered and extinguished abruptly. Instead of casting the chamber into darkness, Sabine's radiance illuminated the circling gemstones with a shimmering brilliance that cast spinning rainbows against the walls.

All five of the elemental magics blended into one and power exploded from her fingertips. The mountain above them peeled open, like the petals of a flower greeting the dawn.

They rose into the air, the winds welcoming her with their touch. She found herself laughing at the playfulness of

Aeslion's embrace, while understanding intuitively how quickly the winds could change to suit her needs.

"Do not release her," Bane shouted.

"Wasn't planning on it," Malek retorted.

She held out her hands for Lyra and Aeron, needing to share this power with them. As the wind touched them, their skin began to glow with a shared luminescence. Lyra's smile became radiant as she spread her wings and began to sing. Aeron's voice was the next to join in, followed by the other aderyan.

Malek's arms around her remained steady, and she opened their bond fully so he could hear and embrace the melody of the land.

She lifted her hands, feeling the strength of the power within her and the imbalance of the Sky Cities below her. She needed more voices, more of the Song to right the wrong that had been done to the land.

"I never realized how much harm we'd caused in our ignorance," he murmured, his voice heavy with emotion. "My strength to yours, Sabine. Take what you need to fix the imbalance."

There was a shift in the wind, as though Malek's words had somehow changed the fabric of the universe. Sabine raised her sight upward, knowing what needed to be done. Weaving the wind around her demon and the other aderyan, Sabine lifted them upward to embrace the sky. As they rose past each prison level, Sabine reached out with her magic. She bound her magic with Malek's dragonfire to rip apart the remaining shackles that bound the aderyan in their cold prison. They stumbled out of their cells and stared up at her with wonderment and hope.

She spread her hands, enfolding the aderyan in a loving embrace of magic. And with each one she touched, she lifted them on gentle winds while their voices joined the Song.

As they crested the top of the mountain and broke free of the prison, Sabine surveyed what remained of the aderyan's homeland. She could see what had once been, the fragile beauty that had been shattered by the dragons in their ignorance. Even now, they circled like carrion birds, watching over a large group of wingless aderyan huddled together on the pathway below them. The aderyan's fear and confusion sent a discordant echo through the Song.

Ignoring the wyverns and dragons, she called the winds to change directions. Moving swiftly upon a downdraft, she landed lightly upon the ground. She stepped away from Malek and approached the wingless aderyan. Aeron and Lyra landed on opposite sides of her, followed by Tristan, Efa, Jac, and Winifred.

Thalassa rushed out from the group and kneeled before her. "Aderylin, these are the wingless who were imprisoned in the uppermost chambers of the prison."

Sabine gazed upon the many weary faces, her heart aching for what had been lost. She called to Lachlina, and the goddess answered, *"All magic requires a sacrifice."*

Sabine closed her eyes and reached within herself to find the tiny embers where her soul resided. As she cradled that precious part of herself, she used the artifact's power to whip the sparks into a blazing inferno. Tempering the magic with her love, she released it upon the wind and cast it over the wingless aderyan.

They cried out as newly formed wings burst from their backs. Some fell to their knees and wept, while others hugged one another or called out to her with tears on their beatific faces. Tristan and the other aderyan moved throughout the group, reuniting with old friends and family. Sabine watched as he embraced Ceridwen and Lyra, their family made whole for the first time.

Malek's arms wrapped around her once more while Bane

and Aeron moved to stand at her side. The pixies had abandoned their dragon illusions and were dancing around the
aderyan, admiring everyone's wings.

Despite the aderyan's newfound joy and their Song
echoing strong and true, the darkness of the imbalance still
leached upon the land like a parasite. Basco bounded toward
her, and as she gazed into his eyes, she knew what needed to
be done.

She turned to Malek and asked, "Where are the iron
chains?"

CHAPTER 60

"The chains run underground," Malek said, gesturing toward Kavi. "Each island has multiple chain towers, which connect the various islands together. Explosives were used to destroy the chain towers between Kavi and Direh less than an hour ago. If we lose the Kavi and Ishu towers, we lose Kavi."

Sabine straightened, thinking of the humans and others who would fall into the sea should that end come. Esme and Rika were still on that island, along with Malek's sister and her mate.

She closed her eyes and reached for the land again. Her blood had already spilled here, and she was tied to Ishu through that sacrifice. Sending her awareness outward, she reached for Malek's parents' estate and the garden where they'd been attacked. Her blood had spilled on Kavi as well.

"Aeron and Bane, your will to mine," Sabine said, still enmeshed with the land. Without them to keep her tethered between the sky and the underworld, she risked losing herself in the lure of Aeslion's call.

They placed their hands on her shoulders, their strength

supplementing hers. She had a moment of revelation that the powers in the artifacts made up a whole. They should never have been sundered, because fracturing them had weakened all of Aeslion's people. She only hoped she was strong enough to reunite them the way they were always meant to be.

Blending together the magic at her command, she embraced the vastness of the land's might. The ground rumbled beneath her feet, a thunderous cry that echoed across the mountains from the wounds that had been inflicted upon Aeslion. The land bled, just as she had bled. Using Malek's power as a lodestone, she tracked the path of the foreign iron buried within the ground.

Encasing the iron in Malek's dragonfire, she slowly raised her hands and expunged the toxic metal from Aeslion's grip. It lifted into the air, glinting dully beneath the moonlight. Her hands shook from the sheer effort of carrying its weight as she laid the poisonous snake upon Aeslion's breast.

She took a step toward the giant chain, the source of so much pain and corruption. No matter how much she might want to destroy it, this next part wouldn't be up to her.

"Sabine," Malek said, reaching for her hand to pull her away. "It's cold iron. These chains were never meant to be touched by fae hands."

Sabine looked up at him. "Make them burn, Malek."

"You want me to—what?"

"Break the chains with your dragonfire. End the tyranny and release the aderyan from the last of the shackles binding them."

His eyes narrowed. "I won't kill those under my protection. This isn't you, Sabine. Esme and Rika are still on Kavi. You'd cut off your own arm before you hurt either of them. If Lachlina has some sort of hold—"

"No," Sabine said, placing her hand against his chest. "I'm

asking a dragon to end the abuse and help heal the suffering his people have caused. I'm asking the dragon I love to stand for the innocent and to trust I won't let them fall. That *we* won't let them fall."

He searched her expression. "It's about balance?"

Sabine nodded and gestured to the wyverns surrounding them. "Your people began this cycle. If I end it, nothing will change. Show them, all of them, who you really are, Malek. Show them the dragon I fell in love with."

Malek cupped her face and kissed her. "The cycle ends here."

He stepped away and transformed into his dragon form in a flash of light. The aderyan moved away, gathering closer to Sabine and edging toward the tree line. Malek's dark scales shimmered in the moonlight, a formidable and lethal creature of the skies that took her breath away every time she saw him.

Yet there was no fear on her part. With everything they'd endured and every moment they'd shared, she trusted and believed in Malek in a way she never thought possible. Lachlina believed him to be the enemy, that all of his kind were little more than parasites. But the goddess hadn't seen the fierce anger in his eyes when he'd destroyed the skythrall conduits. She hadn't seen the way he'd encouraged an aderyan child to spread her wings and fly.

Several of the wyverns landed on the ground nearby, watching and waiting. Malek spread his leathery wings, their darkness eclipsing the light from the moon. The wyverns lowered their heads and backed away, deferring to Malek's unmistakable air of command.

"The lizard's full of himself, isn't he?" Bane said in a low voice.

Sabine smiled. "He has every reason to be."

Angling his body away from her and the aderyan, Malek

expelled his dragonfire in a shocking blast. Sabine lifted her hands to create a water shield to protect them and the aderyan. Despite the barrier, the heat from his fire was nearly overwhelming.

Blossom landed on Sabine's shoulder. "Go, Malek! Give it all you've got!"

The chains began to glow, the metal turning an almost iridescent white. He released another blast of dragonfire and the links flattened, shattering the chains.

"Now, Sabine!" Malek said, his voice touching her thoughts.

Sabine dropped the barrier and spun out her magic, reaching across the land from one island to the next. Aeron began to sing. The other aderyan joined him, their voices filling the air with their hope and magic.

She wove it together with her power, using her ties of blood to strengthen and raise the islands upon great gusts of wind. The islands lifted higher and higher, fueled by her will and the aderyan's song.

When the magic had stabilized, she released the power and staggered from the sudden loss. Aeron caught her before she could fall. His beautiful wings wrapped around her and he lowered his head to her shoulder.

"You have returned our magic to us, Aderylin," he murmured. "You have given our people hope when we had all but given up. Ishu and Kavi are no longer under the dragon's control. They belong to you."

"The dragons might have some objections to that," Bane said casually.

"Dragons, schmagons," Blossom hiccupped and started to giggle. "So much yummy magic."

Malek shifted back into his human form and stepped over the broken chains. At his approach, Aeron eased her into his once-hated enemy's arms. Malek eyed the magic-drunk pixie on Sabine's shoulder who was now singing out-of-tune sea shanties.

Sabine looked up at him and said, "Ishu and Kavi will remain afloat for as long as I have breath, but there are still captives on the island of Havaa. The Ruby Clan must be held accountable for their crimes."

"Bryona of the Ruby Clan was my grandmother. Their clan harbored deep resentment after my grandfather declared Elisa his mate, but there is nothing that would excuse what they've done to the aderyan or to the fae since then." Malek turned to Aeron, his blue eyes blazing with determination. "You have my word I'll see the rest of your people freed and the prison dismantled."

Aeron placed his closed fist over his heart. Thalassa moved to stand at his side and repeated the same gesture. One by one, each of the aderyan did the same.

Two emerald dragons and an obsidian dragon landed on the pathway, crushing small bushes and stones beneath their feet. The sound of a heavy cart being pulled by an enormous drake creaked along the path behind them. At the helm was Malek's sister with Esme and Rika sitting beside her.

When the cart came to a stop, Esme stood and put her hands on her hips. She surveyed the aderyan and nodded to herself. Pointing at several of the wyverns, she said, "You and you, shift forms and start unloading the cart. If you break anything, I'll turn you into frogs." She pointed to two of the aderyan. "Assess and triage. Those who are able-bodied need to help distribute the medicines. Rika, find someone to get me some water."

"Hi Rika!" Blossom waved. "Wait, let me find my wings and I'll show her where to go."

As everyone scrambled to start doing her bidding, a familiar wyvern landed on the ground near Esme, and she narrowed her eyes on him. "If you're going to stay in that form, start a fire for me. I need to start brewing some teas."

Sabine bit back a smile as Levin shifted into his human form. He wrapped his arms around Esme and lifted her into the air, kissing her soundly. Esme started to protest and then threw her arms around Levin and kissed him back.

Thom shifted forms and helped Kaia climb out of the cart. She huffed and rubbed her lower back, making her way over to Sabine and Malek.

Malek gestured to the dragons. "My mother, father, and cousin, Raynor. Uncle Emanthir and his mate are eradicating the last traces of the Topaz and Garnet Clans from Kavi. They know you're the one responsible for keeping both Ishu and Kavi in the sky."

"Typheron wasn't working alone," Bane pointed out.

"No, he wasn't," a woman's voice called out. Gwenllian walked down the path, her golden hair curling around her finely chiseled features. Her tunic was covered with blood, but judging by the decapitated head dangling from her grip, it wasn't hers.

Despite being wingless, the aderyan woman moved with lethal grace. As she approached Sabine and Malek, she tossed the bloody head on the ground in front of the other dragons. "So ends the Topaz Clan. Linus and his mother are both dead."

She lifted her head in challenge as though daring the dragons to strike her down.

Kaia grinned. "Oh, I like her. I think Raynor does too. Look at that, Malek. Our cousin has stars in his eyes."

Malek sighed. "Of course he's fascinated by the aderyan who can cut off a dragon's head."

"As am I," Bane said. "Most likely for very different reasons. I wonder what sort of blade she used to make such a clean cut."

Sabine took a step toward her and said, "Gwenllian."

The woman turned and kneeled before Sabine. "Aderylin, I ask for your forgiveness. I had no idea of their plans until they brought you into the prison. I feared they would discover the young one—"

Sabine reached down and took Gwenllian's hands, bringing her to her feet. "There is nothing to forgive. Not only did you refuse your wings in the hopes you might save more of your people, but you also gave Lyra the key and hid her presence from the guards. I owe you a debt for her life and mine."

"You honor me, Aderylin," Gwenllian whispered, her eyes shining with emotion.

Magic swirled around them, fallen leaves and dried grasses lifting into the air and surrounding them. Sabine reached for Lachlina with her thoughts, and the goddess answered.

"In addition to the Aetherbound, we once gifted certain aderyan with abilities beyond all others. Those who were willing to sacrifice themselves to protect others possessed the strongest of voices and could manipulate the Song. Such were the Dreamsingers."

Sabine's magic flowed down her arms. Gwenllian's hands tightened around hers, and her back arched. She cried out as newly formed wings burst from her back, the feathers a brilliant white that had been dipped in gold. A golden mark appeared on Gwenllian's forearm, similar to the marks that adorned Sabine's skin. This one, however, was an eye with wings—the symbol of the aderyan resistance.

"It is the mark of a Dreamsinger," Aeron said in shock. "You have been twice blessed, Gwenllian. Our Aderylin returns more of the old magic to us."

The aderyan moved in closer, their fingers lightly touching Gwenllian's wings. Tears streaked down Gwenllian's face. "I will protect my people and this land. I swear it, Aderylin."

Malek looked down at Gwenllian's arm and frowned. "I don't see anything. Is it glamoured?"

Sabine smiled. "In a manner of speaking."

Bane studied the former captives as one might examine a weapon for flaws. Esme and Rika were already moving among the aderyan, assessing and administering necessary aid to those who were injured. Levin was helping coordinate the wyvern to set up areas where the aderyan would be more comfortable while they waited for Esme and Rika's attention.

Bane crossed his arms over his chest. "In addition to the witch's foul brews, they will need suitable quarters and adequate nutrition. It will be some time before many of them are able to fly on their own."

Malek placed his hand against Sabine's back. "Typheron's hoard will go a long way to pay for whatever they need. For anything else, the Obsidian and Emerald Clans will render assistance."

Sabine shook her head and turned to face the dragons. "The aderyan will not be dependent upon any dragon clan. Ishu belongs to the aderyan. After today, the Topaz and Garnet Clans will be no more. Any other clans currently occupying Ishu will be evicted. The dragons have lost all rights to this land."

Nymira shifted forms in a swirling emerald mist. As she reformed into her human appearance, she asked, "How do you intend to enforce your rule? The Gold Clan will not abandon their roost meekly."

"It is not my rule that needs to be enforced," Sabine said, her skin glowing with power. The land trembled beneath her feet and lightning struck the nearby ground as the wind whipped her hair away from her face. "Aeslion has rejected the dragons. Your people have desecrated this land nearly beyond redemption. Should any aderyan be hurt or injured by any dragon, wyvern, drake, or upon their orders, I will drop the rest of the Sky Cities into the sea."

Nymira arched one elegant brow. "Including the island occupied by your mate's clan?"

"Her mate's clan will help enforce this rule," Malek said, lifting Sabine's hand and kissing it. "And since I intend to open my home to aderyan who have proven themselves loyal to Sabine and her cause, we will adhere to the same rules that govern the rest of the clans. If Sabine claims the aderyan as hers to protect, they are ours as well."

Nymira's lips curved upward, and she placed her hand on Darius's snout. "Yes, my love. Our son and his mate make a fierce pair and bring pride to the Obsidian Clan."

Raynor's dragon form disappeared in a swirling mist and flash of light. His gaze fell upon the head Gwenllian had thrown, a small smile playing upon his lips. "And if an aderyan decides to attack or kill one of us without provocation?"

Gwenllian stepped forward and said, "Then they are not aderyan, for only those who have abandoned the Eternal Song would betray us in such a manner. We will not seek retribution unless our Aderylin commands otherwise. It is her will we obey, and her Song we embrace."

"They deserve to see their children grow and learn to fly," Nymira said, her eyes shimmering with tears as they fell upon Lyra and then Kaia. Darius lowered his head against Nymira's slim form. "We cannot undo the past, but we can make amends and forge a new path forward. Darius and I will carry your words to the Gold Clan and ensure they depart Ishu within the day."

As the sun began to crest over the horizon, Malek turned to Sabine and said, "My father says they'll also speak with the

Ruby Clan. They'll arrange to have the prison on Havaa empty by nightfall and all the aderyan brought here."

Kaia snorted. "He did not say that."

Malek sighed. "Dammit, Kaia. I'm trying not to scare her off."

Kaia grinned. "He said he'd sit on their house and shit on it if they dickered about."

Sabine blinked. "That seems… an effective threat."

Darius huffed, steam rising from his nostrils.

Kaia laughed. "Da really likes you. Even if you do have pointy ears."

"We got the starfruit essence!" Blossom exclaimed, flying away with a traveler's pack carried between six pixies. Several more hovered nearby and began throwing berries at Bane.

Bane cursed and dove for the traveler's pack, missing it by a hair. "Give that back, bug, or I'll eat you for lunch!"

"Nope! You can't eat me for a whole day! You gave your word!"

"I can still tear off your wings," Bane shouted after her.

"Not if you can't catch us!" Blossom yelled back amidst dozens of pixie giggles.

Malek grinned and kissed Sabine. "Why don't we finish up here and then head home? I believe I still owe my new mate a dance."

Sabine wrapped her arms around Malek's neck and lifted them into the air with her magic. "I've always wanted to see how dragons dance in the skies."

He drew her closer. "I intend to spend a lifetime doing just that."

CHAPTER 61

Sabine stepped into the conservatory and breathed in the rich scent of the fragrant herbs. Most of the pixies were passed out in the garden, and they dozed lazily in the midday sun. Hopefully, they'd continue sleeping while Sabine and Esme took care of some private business.

"I've gone over Elisa's journal several times," Esme said, flipping through the pages. "There are a few herbs that can help with pregnancy, but they don't enhance magical effects. It's more of a way to strengthen the mother and child."

Sabine nodded. "I'm familiar with those. We won't discount them, but I believe Kaia will require something beyond anything available in Malek's gardens."

Esme lifted her head and frowned. "You know what she needs, don't you?"

"Go ahead and set the ward," Sabine said quietly. "Malek is going to be bringing Kaia here in a few minutes. We need to be finished before they return."

Esme put the book aside and laid out the four candles Sabine had asked for earlier. Moving from candle to candle, Esme lit the wicks and allowed a drop of her blood to fall upon the flame. Sabine carefully placed the appropriate herbal offerings in each of the four directions and whispered the words of power to activate the circle. Moving slowly along the perimeter, Esme took a bundle of sticks and caught them on fire. She weaved the smoke upward and out, reinforcing the ward surrounding the circle.

Sabine withdrew the curved blade that had been entrusted to the demons for centuries. It was one of the portal artifacts and had once contained Vestior's magic—the ability to step between worlds and traverse the boundary between life and death. Although the knife no longer held that power, it retained another valuable trait.

Before she'd left the underworld, Vestior had told her how to summon him. She hadn't intended to use this method of calling unless it was absolutely necessary, but his reaction in the aderyan temple made her wonder if he might be more receptive than she'd originally believed.

She pricked her finger on the edge of the sharpened blade and allowed one drop of her blood to fall upon the mirrored surface. In the ancient language of the gods, she said, *"I call you, by blood and magic, kin of my kin, blood of my blood."*

The candles went out and a cold wind blew through the room. Esme rubbed her arms and her teeth began to chatter. The air began to change, thinning somehow, as if a shadow of a portal opened in front of her. A hazy image of a cloaked skeletal figure appeared before Sabine.

Vestior, wearing his Huntsman guise, studied her for a long time. *"You risk a great deal by calling me here. The Veil is already thin, and you have pierced even more."*

"Steps have been taken to reinforce the Veil," Sabine said, gesturing to Esmelle. "She is one with the land, and her dryad blood holds the balance."

"Very well," Vestior said. *"I am aware of what you seek."*

"And the cost?"

"You already know the answer, Sabin'theoria."

Sabine squeezed her eyes shut and took a deep breath. "Is it possible without the binding?"

"All magic has a cost, child. This is not your payment to bear."

The weight of his words fell heavily upon her shoulders. So many lives already depended on her—it was nearly overwhelming. Pursuing this course of action might break the fragile trust between her and Malek.

Desperate for another option, she asked, "Will she have enough magic to shift forms once I reopen the portal?"

The Huntsman's glowing red gaze studied her. *"Not in time. A dragon cannot pass beyond the Veil in their human skin."*

Sabine frowned. "I don't understand."

"Once the valve is open, magic will once again flow freely into Aeslion. However, it will also depart by way of the Well. It may take centuries for your world to establish an equilibrium."

"That's assuming the war doesn't destroy all of us in the process," Sabine muttered.

Vestior paused. *"Should the day arrive when you wish to seek asylum, I would offer you sanctuary beyond the Veil."*

Sabine stared at him. "Why? Why would you offer this?"

"Your time is running out, Sabin'theoria," Vestior reminded her. *"You have gathered the last of the artifacts and with it, the way to unlock the portal. Seek the entrance to the portal with all due haste. The Well is depleting rapidly. The plight of your dragon's sister is merely a symptom of what's to come."*

Without another word, his image disappeared. Esme rubbed her arms again and stomped her feet.

Through chattering teeth, she said, "Okay, that was downright creepy. And really freaking cold. It sounded like it didn't go well."

Sabine blinked and turned to Esme. "You heard all that?"

Esme shook her head. "No. Just your side of the conversation, but I didn't understand the last half when you started talking in a weird language I've never heard. I got to see the spooky glowing red eyes and icicles forming in my hair."

Sabine frowned. She must have switched to the language of the gods without realizing it. A tingle went through her, and she whipped her head toward the conservatory doors. "Malek and Kaia just came through the wards. Let's get this over with."

Esme dropped the ward surrounding them, and they headed out of the conservatory. Aeron met them in the north wing and fell into step beside Sabine.

"Fiona sent word the aderyan refugees are on their way back. They should be arriving with a week. Gwenllian knows to expect them."

Sabine nodded. "We'll meet them at the dock. I'll restore their wings and then escort them to Ishu. The others we liberated from Havaa's prison are settling in?"

"Yes, Aderylin," Aeron said with a smile. "Many are already flying. The gentle winds you've provided have made it easier for them to strengthen their wings. Many of the wyverns and dragons are curious about us and watch along the perimeter."

Sabine stopped at the door and placed her hand on Aeron's arm. "They're not threatening your people, are they?"

Aeron smiled. "No. Although the large green dragon is often nearby when Gwenllian is weapon training with Bane. She is… annoyed by his presence. Yet she was quite taken with the set of silver daggers that were delivered anonymously yesterday."

Esme grinned. "Silver daggers could either be a gift from Bane or Raynor."

Sabine laughed. "As long as they both remember she knows how to use them." She smoothed out her dress and turned to Aeron. "Your discretion with this next conversation means a great deal. I'd like both Malek and Kaia to understand exactly what's involved, but only what you're comfortable sharing."

"Of course," Aeron said, opening the door to the garden. "I will do what I can to explain, but I do not believe the dragons have any basis for comparison."

Sabine sighed and stepped into the garden. "Nor do I."

She spotted Malek and Kaia at the far end of the garden. It had only been a few days since she'd seen Kaia, but even from this distance, her fatigue was obvious. Vestior was right; reopening the portal might save others, but it would be too late to help Malek's sister.

Esme reached over and squeezed Sabine's hand. "I'll go find Levin. Let me know if you need me for the herbal stuff."

Sabine nodded. As Esme headed toward one of the side wings, she and Aeron approached Malek and Kaia.

Kaia glanced over at the door where Esme disappeared. "Well, that can't be good."

"Kaia," Malek said, his brow furrowed in concern. "Maybe Esme's just going to get something from the kitchen."

Kaia wearily sank onto a nearby bench and put her head in her hands. "Right, and I'm a pixie. Go ahead, Sabine. Give me the bad news."

Sabine sat beside Kaia and folded her hands in her lap. "You have a choice to make. Before you decide, I need you to listen to the options and weigh them carefully. I've asked Aeron to join us because I believe he can give you some additional insight."

Kaia lifted her head. "Okay. What choices?"

"There are some herbs in the conservatory that will strengthen you and your unborn child. Esme can craft these into tonics, similar to the ones Idola made for you."

Kaia frowned. "But they weren't working, were they?"

Sabine sighed. "They are derived from herbs originally grown in Faerie. They may strengthen your physical body and even provide mental clarity, but they will not give your magic the boost it needs to shift forms. To my knowledge, we've never had any reason to cultivate such herbs in the past. They work best on those who are tied to the magic of Aeslion."

Malek studied Sabine. "What's the other option?"

Sabine absently touched the marks on her wrist. "A binding. If I sacrifice some of my magic, the essence of myself, it will provide Kaia with enough magic to shift forms and sustain her child. However, the cost is very dear."

Malek frowned. "What is the cost, Sabine?"

She took a steadying breath. "Kaia and her child will be bound to me for the remainder of my life. Upon my death, they will both weaken considerably."

Kaia stared at her. "What?"

Aeron placed his hand on Sabine's shoulder, his wings brushing gently against her skin. "I am bound to the Aderylin. She has given up part of her magic to restore my wings. I can sense her, feel her, and know her intimately. She can do the same with me. If she were to summon me, I would gladly answer. The binding does not require it, but I would feel unsettled unless I sought her out. In her presence, I am at peace and whole. When she is in danger or suffering, I feel distressed. I will never harm her because doing so would be to harm myself."

Kaia paled. "Isn't that worse than what Typheron did to you?"

Aeron's expression darkened. "No. The Aderylin does not demand. She simply exists. Her light brings peace and joy, and it is a blessing when she reaches out to one of us. She does not often do so because it confuses and distresses her."

Sabine flushed, more than a little uncomfortable. It would have been helpful if Lachlina had warned her about all of this instead of tossing her in the deep end of the lake.

Malek studied Aeron. "Can you break the binding?"

Aeron stiffened. "No, but if the Aderylin wished for it, I would try to suppress it."

Sabine reached up and placed her hand over Aeron's. She sent a wave of her magic over him, and his shoulders relaxed. Turning back to Kaia, she said, "The ties I have with the aderyan are different from the bond I share with Malek. It's impossible for me to predict the shape and direction a binding with you and your child will take, but I want you to understand all the possibilities."

Kaia looked up at Malek. "You're bound to her, too?"

Malek hesitated. "Yes, but it's not the same. We share a bond as equals. Sabine can use my power, and I can draw upon hers. I can feel her with me, hear her thoughts when they're directed at me, and know when she's hurt or in danger. She can often do the same with me."

"You don't feel any of that other stuff?"

Malek looked over at Sabine, and his gaze softened. "I do, but I believe it stems from love. Sabine loves with her entire heart, and she shares that love easily and with so many others. It's impossible not to love her in return."

Malek approached Sabine and kneeled in front of her. He took her hands in his and asked, "Would you really do this? Sacrifice part of yourself to save my sister?"

"You love her," Sabine said quietly. "When we first met, you told me about her. You showed me the kaleidoscope you'd purchased as a gift. I saw the tenderness in your eyes when you spoke of her and the trouble she would get into climbing on roofs."

Kaia sniffed. "You told her that?"

Malek nodded. "I told her about you and Thom, too."

"If it's within my power to save your sister and keep that love alive, I would do it a thousand times," Sabine said, pressing her forehead against his. "I know what your family means to you, Malek. You love them, and through you, I love them as well."

Kaia wiped away her tears. "You're going to turn me into a blubbering mess in a minute, and that's not a good look for a hormonal pregnant dragon who can't shift."

Sabine laughed.

Malek turned to Kaia and said, "The decision is yours, but I know you can trust Sabine."

Kaia nodded. "You wouldn't have fallen for her if she wasn't everything she appeared to be." She took a deep breath. "If you're willing to sacrifice part of your magic, I'll gladly pay the cost."

Sabine squeezed her eyes shut and nodded. "Very well."

Taking a steadying breath, Sabine opened her eyes. "Malek, you will have to act as a bridge between me and Kaia's child. Your presence will be more familiar than mine."

Malek held Sabine's hand and said, "All right."

Placing her other hand on Kaia's stomach, Sabine sent her awareness outward and felt the faint pulse of life hovering at the edge of her thoughts. She smiled as it slipped away, hiding as though uncertain or fearful of who or what she was.

Sabine allowed the bond between her and Malek to open fully, guiding him toward that timid spark. She coaxed the tiniest thread of dragonfire from Malek, and allowed the flames to tickle that tiny awareness.

Curiosity.

Familiar.

Malek's eyes widened. "Is that—?"

Sabine nodded. "Yes."

Reaching within herself, she sheared away a tiny ember of her magic, accepting the pain of the loss as her due. Holding tightly to Malek's hand, she wound her essence in his dragonfire, hoping the familiar taste of Malek's magic would entice Kaia's child to accept her offering.

As the power radiated from Sabine, her skin began to glow softly at first and then built in intensity. Kaia inhaled sharply, breathing in Sabine's magic like a starving man falling upon a feast.

"Place your hand over mine," Sabine said to Kaia. "It's not enough for you to accept it. Your child must embrace the magic as well."

Kaia placed her hand on Sabine's and said, "It's all right. She's our family. She won't hurt you."

Sabine leaned down and murmured in the language of the gods, *"Peace, little one. Accept this gift and grow strong. You are already loved more than you know."*

The tiny awareness reached out with its thoughts to touch Sabine's mind. Images and impressions formed in her head. Curiosity. Magic. Family. Love. It batted a playful talon in her direction and then yawned sleepily.

Sabine eased away and lifted her hand from Kaia's stomach. Kaia's eyes welled with tears.

"I felt—You—I have to go."

She stood suddenly and looked around. Malek rose, his expression concerned. "Kaia, maybe you should sit down for a minute."

"No, no," Kaia said. "I have to go. Now. Tell Thom. Oh, by the ether, forget it. I'll show him."

With a flash of light, she shifted into an obsidian dragon. Kaia was slightly smaller than Malek in her dragon form, but no less beautiful. Her scales were the darkest of obsidian with a twinkling of stardust, especially on her tail. She blinked golden eyes at them and then pushed off the ground, tearing through Malek's wards before flying west.

Malek stared after Kaia in stunned shock. "She shifted."

He turned to Sabine and pulled her to her feet. Wrapping

his arms around her, Malek buried his face in her hair. "I know I'm not supposed to thank you, but I don't give a damn. I felt the pain it caused you, and it's a debt that can never be repaid. Thank you for my sister's life, Sabine. I will never forget what you've done for them, nor will any of my family."

She leaned back and cupped his face. "There are no debts between us, Malek."

Rika approached them, holding a steaming mug. She took a sip of her drink and said, "You don't have to worry."

Malek looked over at her and frowned. "What?"

Rika grinned. "You don't have to worry about either of them. Your nephew's going to be a strong and healthy dragon. An obsidian greater dragon. Just like you and Darius."

Malek stared at her. "A greater dragon? You're sure?"

Sabine tilted her head and asked, "You've seen it then?"

Rika looked up at the sky. "Not until she was in the air. Up to that point, there were just possibilities. But once she accepted your offer and flew away, I saw both of them. They're going to be okay. The bond you two share will make sure of that."

"What do you mean?" Sabine asked.

Rika smiled over the rim of her cup. "Your bond allows you to exchange magic freely. Now that you also share a bond with Kaia and her son, you can supplement their magic with yours."

"The number of greater dragons has diminished heavily," Malek said, his arm tightening around Sabine. "We've had an increased number of wyverns and drakes when any births occurred at all. It's why my parents were so concerned about Thom being Kaia's mate. Without enough magic, the likelihood of her surviving the birth was little to none."

Sabine looked up at him. "It's also why my people haven't

had many children either. We must reopen the portal, Malek."

He nodded and drew her closer. "I'm going to be an uncle. And you're going to be an aunt."

Sabine blinked. "An aunt? To a dragon?"

Rika laughed. "Auntie Sabine."

It had a nice ring, she decided. She stared up at the sky to the wyverns and dragons flying overhead. A few of the aderyan were inspecting the collapsed ward, including Lyra and her father, Tristan. The ward falling had also roused the pixies, who were once again wearing their pink dragon glamour and zipping around the skies.

It really was all about family.

Sabine held out her arm and pulled Rika into their hug. "We're going to have to talk to Bane about incorporating some fire-dodging skills for you, Cousin Rika."

Rika swallowed. "Fire-dodging?"

Malek chuckled. "And maybe some practice jumps to avoid swift-moving tails."

Aeron nodded. "Heavier armor might be beneficial as well. Dragon talons can be piercing."

Rika blew her hair out of her face. "Very funny. You're just as bad as Bane."

Sabine laughed. "I'm sure Bane will have even more suggestions. Speaking of Bane, aren't you supposed to be training with him and the aderyan?"

Rika froze for a split second and then raced toward the north wing, shouting over her shoulder, "I'm not even here. I'm already gone. Where the heck is my sword? Blossom! If you touched any of my stuff, I'm telling Bane about the stuffed peppers!"

Sabine winced. "I suppose our young seer's abilities are still hit-or-miss."

Malek wrapped his arms around Sabine. "Yes, but she seems to do well enough when it's important."

She looked up at the dragon she loved. "I think we all do well enough when it's important."

Malek leaned down and kissed her. "Yes, we do."

She smiled and took his hand, allowing him to lead her through the garden where a dragon and a fae had dared to fall in love centuries earlier. And as Sabine gazed up at Malek, she knew without doubt the truth of the answer she'd given Lachlina.

No matter what trials they would face when the portal reopened, they would face them together—with their family.

ACKNOWLEDGMENTS

The past several years have been challenging in a lot of ways. I've always been a private person, getting lost in my head and in stories more often than not. More than ten years ago, I took a chance and published my first book, *Beneath the Fallen City*. The outpouring of love and encouragement from readers blew me away. It gave me the courage to keep sharing my stories with the world.

While working on *Shadows and Twilight*, I began experiencing serious neurological issues. Not long after the book was released, my condition plummeted. I ended up hospitalized, and after countless tests and specialists, my doctors discovered I had a build up of cerebrospinal fluid in my brain. In addition to experiencing symptoms similar to a brain tumor, I was going blind.

I fell apart.

I tried to work on *Dance of Wings* whenever possible, but I struggled to embrace Sabine's strength and resilience when my own world felt like it was unraveling. Still, I couldn't give up. Writing had helped me through some of the darkest times of my life. I had to believe it could help me again.

It did.

About a year after beginning conservative treatments, I finally began to feel like myself again. I was writing regularly and feeling better than I had in years. Unfortunately, everything crumbled again in late 2024, when I learned the medications that were helping me... were also causing my kidneys to fail.

I was forced to push back the release of *Dance of Wings* again, as I was faced with a new eventuality—brain surgery.

One of my oldest and most treasured friends, Mary, came back into my life around this time. She helped put things in perspective for me and gave me the kick in the ass I needed. So I sucked it up, put on my big girl panties, and agreed to do the surgery. (Thank you, Mare. I love you to pieces.)

So far, things have been improving every day. I'm optimistic about what this means for the future—and with my writing.

This book wouldn't have been possible without some truly amazing people.

First, I have to say a HUGE thank you to Sam for her endless patience and masterful juggling skills. You've been a lifeline, a sounding board, and a wonderful friend over the past several years. I will be forever grateful. I don't think my sanity would have survived without you. (Also, the pixies think you're awesome too. ☺)

Another huge thank you goes to Jim for the spontaneous brainstorm sessions. Most people would find it weird to get a text at midnight asking, "How many toes does a wyvern have?" But you just roll with it and toss out ideas. Thank you for always embracing my special brand of weird.

To my mom, thank you for being the ultimate cheerleader. Your willingness to listen when I babble about character arcs or the latest research rabbit hole never ceases to amaze me. Your encouragement keeps me going, more than you know.

Tracy, I don't have words for how grateful I am to have you in my life. You were one of the first people to tell me to follow my dreams—and one of the only ones willing to cross an ocean and stand beside me in Athens while I declared the Acropolis a perfect dragon landing pad. Without your support and wicked proofreading skills (even while lounging on a beach with a tropical drink in hand), I don't think I would have had the courage to let my books step into the light.

To all the Book Dragons in my Facebook reader group: you are incredible. Your love for this series kept me motivated, and your ideas helped name several of the characters and places in this book.

A special thank you to:

- Maggie M., for naming the city of Imenel. I love the creativity behind it!
- Amorette H., for coming up with the perfect name for Malek's father: Darius.
- Julie P., for suggesting Rupert and Azalia for the human caretakers in the Sky Cities. They were perfect! Your cards, decals, and words of encouragement have meant so much to me. (Some of the Blossomisms in this book were written just for you.)

And finally, to all my wonderful readers—thank you for your patience, support, and unwavering encouragement. You've made this crazy dream of mine possible, and I'm so grateful to each and every one of you.

From the bottom of my heart, thank you! 🤍

ABOUT THE AUTHOR

Jamie A. Waters is an award-winning fantasy romance author and dragon enthusiast. Weaving together magic, intrigue, and some delicious romance, she creates memorable and immersive worlds that provide the perfect escape. Her books features strong, capable heroines and their swoon-worthy heroes who will stop at nothing to save the day.

Jamie currently resides in Florida with two neurotic dogs who enjoy stealing socks. When she's not pursuing her passion of writing, she's usually trying to learn new and interesting random things (like how to pick locks or use the self-cleaning feature of the oven without setting off the fire alarm). In her downtime, she enjoys reading on her Kindle, playing computer games, painting, or acting as a referee between the dragons and fairies currently at war inside her closet.

Learn more at: jamieawaters.com.